SEEING THE ELEPHANT

One Man's Return to the Horrors of the Civil War

T. W. Harvey

Monday Creek Publishing
Ohio USA

Seeing the Elephant! One Man's Return to the Horrors of the Civil War is a work of historical fiction that is based on letters from the period 1861 – 1865 that refers to well-known historical and public figures. It also presents characters created out of the author's imagination. All conversations and many of the instances are also products of the author's imagination and are not to be thought of as real. Where well-known historical and public figures are presented, the circumstances, instances, and conversations concerning those people are entirely fictional and are only used to enhance the nature of this historical work. In all other matters, and resemblance to people living is purely coincidental.

ISBN-13: 978-0692168486
ISBN-10: 0692168486

1.Civil War – Fiction 2. United States-History-Civil War

Printed in the United States of America
www.mondaycreekpublishing.com

For my dear wife, Paula

Preface

Seeing the Elephant! One Man's Return to the Horrors of the Civil War is a true story that I have related as it was told to me. Some time ago, my wife, Paula, and I discovered 250 letters sent to families and friends at home by two soldiers serving in the Union Army during the Civil War. Based on those documents and meticulous research, I have been able to tell the story of a man named Thomas Sumption Armstrong, a young school teacher from Muskingum County in east central Ohio. He had enlisted in the United States Army in August 1861, just four months after the bombardment of Fort Sumter, on April 12 of that year, which triggered the Civil War. That, as we know, changed life in America forever.

At the outset, we need to understand that Tom Armstrong was "everyman," not a general or a politician, but a simple country lad from a small town called Norwich, Ohio, about 65 miles east of Columbus on the National Road. Today the National Road is U. S. Route 40, running parallel to Interstate 70.

My objective in writing this book is to show readers, young and older alike, the sacrifices ordinary young men and their families made, Union and Confederate alike, when those men chose to fight for the principles they held so strongly; the principles upon which the United States was founded as contained in the Declaration of Independence and the Constitution, not the least of which was the freedom of all Americans to live their lives as they saw fit as long as they did not infringe on the freedom of others, in accordance with the law.

Secondarily, an underlying purpose in writing *Seeing the Elephant* was to encourage the reader to think about what is being read, to learn of those sacrifices and the hardships the soldiers underwent, and to realize that they, both North and South, participated in the events of 1861 – 1865, that contributed significantly to the United States of the 21st Century. It is my hope that those events and the impact they had will never be forgotten.

As I read the letters, transcribed them, and worked with them for this book, I could not help but wonder how many of the people who will read it had ancestors who went to war and had experiences like the one the letters tell about Tom Armstrong. Approximately 2.75

million men fought in the Civil War with estimates of casualties about 750,000. That simply means that just over 25% of the men who fought did not come back alive. Tom Armstrong defied those odds, just being one of about two million men who survived the terrible conflict. For those who served and fought for the Union and the Confederacy, and those who did likewise in the other military conflicts in which the United States has been involved, we should all be most grateful for their courage and willingness to do so.

Tom Armstrong was just like all of the boys, from the western United States at that time, from a small town in Ohio, a farming community. They understood the importance of family, were God-fearing, with a sense of duty, honor, love of country; patriotism at its best. Westerners were roughnecks, the lands of Ohio to the Mississippi River being a bit wild and somewhat lawless. That just meant you better be able to take care of yourself. Tom Armstrong could certainly do that, from what his letters told me.

We really don't know too much about the "everyman" who fought in the Civil War which is why this book, an historical novel, is so important and insightful.

We do know there have been volumes written about generals like Ulysses S. Grant, Robert E. Lee, William Tecumseh Sherman, Joseph E. Johnston, Philip H. Sheridan; President Abraham Lincoln; battles like Gettysburg, 1st and 2nd Bull Run, Antietam, Shiloh, Atlanta, and Vicksburg. But, what we don't know is what was going on in the lives of the ordinary soldiers, the infantry, cavalry, and artillery, which is the story these pages tell.

I have tried to get inside the minds and spirits of the characters, whom you do not know like Tom Armstrong, and those you do know, like Ulysses S. Grant, to present to you what they were thinking and feeling and then what they went through as the events of 1861 – 1865 unfolded. It is as close to the history as I can make it, but certainly not as detailed research as Shelby Foote's brilliant trilogy or James McPherson's insightful *Battle Cry of Freedom*, both of which I have drawn on extensively for background for this story. Further, I have researched it in minute detail with both primary and secondary sources that provide the setting for the main themes. Additionally, Paula and I have visited all of the places that I describe, thus we know where every event occurred.

This is a story of love, faith, patriotism, persistence, and hope that is set against the American Civil War. I have written it to show the importance of these qualities, held by one man in particular, Thomas Sumption Armstrong. I am sure that they were held by many thousands of ordinary fellows who felt called into harm's way to fight for the country they loved on both sides, Union and Confederate. Perhaps they were held by your relatives as well when they marched off to see the elephant.

Now, you ask, what does that mean? "Seeing the Elephant." To be brief, it means that a soldier has seen and been involved in battle. You will see in Chapter 1 that Tom Armstrong had, indeed, seen it and, as you go along, you will find that he sees it again. I sincerely hope, dear reader, that you will find it worthwhile reading *Seeing the Elephant* as thought-provoking and educational. From the reaction I have received when I tell people about it, many, if not all, just say that it is a marvelous story. I hope you agree.   *T. W. Harvey*

Acknowledgments

My sincere thanks go out to several people and organizations without whose help and encouragement this story could not have been told. Your willingness to help, offer suggestions, provide resources, and give me your time is greatly appreciated. Since this project took over twenty years to complete, there may be some who have helped whom I have forgotten, but, for those, I thank you as well.

Bernard Derr, Rare Books Librarian, Beeghly Library, Ohio Wesleyan University, Delaware, Ohio

Barbara and Steve Harvey, Peoria, Arizona

Carol Holliger, Archivist, Beeghly Library, Ohio Wesleyan University Delaware, Ohio

Deanne Peterson, Director, Beeghly Library, Ohio Wesleyan University Delaware, Ohio

Eugene Rutigliano, Digital Initiatives Librarian, Beeghly Library, Ohio Wesleyan University Delaware, Ohio

Penny and John Scarpucci, Atlanta, Georgia

Jeff Shaara, Gettysburg, Pennsylvania

Dr. Steven S. Shay, MD, Cary, North Carolina

Dr. John David Smith, Charlotte, North Carolina

Dr. and Mrs. Richard W. Smith, Delaware, Ohio

David "Mitch" Taylor, Curator, Muskingum County Historical Society, Zanesville, Ohio

The staff of the Cary, North Carolina Community Library

The staff of the Muskingum, Ohio, Library System

The staff of the Western Reserve Historical Society, Cleveland, Ohio

William Underwood, Acquisitions Editor, Kent State University Press, Kent, Ohio

Dr. Kathryn B. Vossler, Ed D., Lynn Haven, Florida

Joan Wood, Stewart Bell, Jr. Archives Room, Handley Regional Library, Winchester, Virginia

My sincere and heartfelt thanks to all of you. Without you, this book and its story would never have been told.

Finally, I would be remiss if I did not extend special gratitude to Dr. Vossler, Dr. Shay, and Mr. Taylor who read the manuscript, offering comments and suggestions that corrected my inaccuracies and made the book more accurate from an historical perspective.

Introduction

Most people thought the Civil War would be a short-lived affair, the majority of the people of the North thinking it would be over quickly, say, in three months. The people of the South didn't quite see it that way. President Abraham Lincoln, too, thought it would be brief since, after the Confederate bombardment of Fort Sumter, on April 12, 1861, there in Charleston Harbor, he called on the governors of the Union states to raise a militia of just 75,000 men to serve their country for three months. Thousands of men congregated in Washington, D.C. to guard the United States capital. Then, the idea of taking Richmond, the Confederate capital, just over 100 miles south of Washington, to end the war, began to take shape. But, that all changed in July.

Yielding to pressure from the politicians in Washington, on July 21, 1861, General-in-Chief of the Union Army, Winfield Scott, ordered Brigadier General Irvin McDowell, leading a force of 18,000, to launch an attack on the Confederate Army of Brigadier General P.G.T. Beauregard, with an equal number of men, just north of the town of Manassas, Virginia. Now, neither McDowell or Beauregard had sufficient time to train their troops or to develop leaders so, as you might imagine, it was a most disorganized affair, this 1st Battle of Bull Run.

Manassas was only about 25 miles southwest of Washington, so many of the residents of the United States capital region put on their Sunday best, hitched their horses to their buggies, packed a picnic lunch, and went out to watch what they thought would be an easy Federal victory. It did not end as they expected. The Confederate counterattack drove the Federals from the field in a chaotic withdrawal, terrifying the citizens as well as the retreating soldiers. Both sides had serious losses, over 2,900 men killed, wounded, missing, or captured on the Union side and over 1,800 on the Confederate side. War, now, people on both sides knew, was real. It would certainly take more than three months to convince the secessionist states to come back into the Union.

Over the next six months or so, there was continued skirmishing between the two sides, mostly in Virginia and along the eastern seaboard with some fighting occurring in Missouri. In these fights, there didn't seem to be a conclusive winner, but that changed in February 1862. You see, Major General Winfield Scott, the hero of the war with Mexico fifteen years earlier, had looked at the map of the country and came up with the "Anaconda Plan." Scott saw that if one branch of the Union Army could continually pressure the Confederates down through Virginia and points further South, while another one pushed down the Mississippi River, the combined armies could squeeze the Southerners, much like the giant snake does to its prey.

Under Brigadier General Ulysses S. Grant, Union forces had started south in early 1862, and on February 6, he landed two divisions on the Tennessee River just above the Confederate Fort Henry. This garrison was in northern Tennessee, just a stone's throw south of Kentucky and east of Illinois. This is where the story of Tom Armstrong begins. You see, he and his brother, Wilbur, and three of their friends, all from around Zanesville, Ohio, about 60 miles east of the state capital of Columbus, had enlisted in the 78th Regiment of the Ohio Volunteer Infantry of the United States Army, under the command of Colonel Mortimer D. Leggett. The regiment's assignment? Go south and open the Mississippi River as part of the 3rd Brigade, 3rd Division of the Army of the Tennessee, commanded by Major General Lew Wallace.

Grant's plan in the winter and spring of 1862 was, indeed, to free up the waterways of the South, the Tennessee, Cumberland, and Mississippi Rivers for Navy gunboat support of his army for its supplies, both men and materiel. When Grant landed at Fort Henry, the plan was for him to join forces with Flag Officer Andrew Foote of the United States Navy who would attack the fort from the river, just west, as well as by Wallace's infantry from the north. Well, Foote apparently didn't need the infantry and artillery since, after lobbing shells at Fort Henry from the Tennessee River, the Confederate commandant, Brigadier General Lloyd Tilghman, decided the garrison there should hightail it east to Fort Donelson, just 12 miles away.

The Third Brigade, with the 78th O.V.I., followed Tilghman's force to Fort Donelson. As will be seen, this is what President Lincoln liked about Ulysses S. Grant. While other commanders like George McClellan did not take the initiative to bring the fight to the enemy, there was no procrastination in Grant. He would pursue the enemy every chance he got.

On February 12 - 14, Grant's infantry probed the Confederate defenses with Foote's gunboats shelling the fort. Fort Donelson's artillery repulsed the river attack, but the ground forces had surrounded the fort. The next night, the Confederates tried to break out, toward Nashville, but Grant's counterattack suppressed the Rebel attempt. The commanders of Fort Donelson, Brigadier General John Floyd and Brigadier General Gideon Pillow, managed to get away toward Nashville with a small force, leaving Brigadier General Simon Buckner to cope with Grant. Now, Buckner, a personal friend of Grant's before the war, decided that was not a good thing to do. Looking at the hopeless situation, Buckner surrendered the fort and some 12,000 men, having about 1,500 killed, wounded, and missing in the short battle. This was a critical Union victory that accomplished the objective of opening the mighty Mississippi River to Union gunboats and supply ships. Reinforcements and supplies would now flow south freely.

The 78th Ohio got to Fort Donelson late and didn't have a chance to participate, but Tom Armstrong had another problem. His brother, Wilbur, was not feeling well. Fever and chills, diarrhea, coughing and throwing up. He looked awful. You see, it had been unseasonably warm on the way down from Ohio, and some of the men had discarded their overcoats and blankets as they marched from the Tennessee River to the fort. However, winter returned with a vengeance, cold, freezing rain, for which those men who had thrown their outer wear away were not prepared. Wilbur Armstrong, also known as "Will," was among them.

Looking at his brother's condition, Tom Armstrong decided that he needed to send him to a hospital. However, the medical tents out there in the field were jammed with casualties of the battle. So, he convinced his friend, Lieutenant John W.A. Gillespie, to sign discharge papers in the hope that Wilbur could be transported to Cincinnati. With the paperwork in hand, he and other friend, Lieutenant George W. Porter, spirited Wilbur out of camp and bribed a steamship captain to take him back to Ohio. It would not happen soon enough. The sickness was too far advanced. Wilbur Armstrong died on March 22, 1862 of Lung Fever, or pneumonia, at the 4th Street Hospital in Cincinnati.

Now, you can imagine what the victories at Fort Henry and Fort Donelson meant to President Abraham Lincoln. The President had impatiently endured the inaction of Major General George McClellan in the Eastern theater. Oh, there had been some minor battles, some won, some lost, but most were considered a draw. Lincoln was adamant that the Union Army had to be more aggressive and ordered McClellan to advance on the Confederate Army of General Robert E. Lee, but that didn't happen. Lincoln's frustration continued to mount which resulted in his replacing the General with Major General Ambrose E. Burnside later in the summer of 1862. Right then, however, in February, the President was quite pleased since he sensed that Winfield Scott's Anaconda Plan might just work, saving the Union. He also wondered if he might have found a commander in Ulysses S. Grant who would press the enemy. That was just what he wanted, but didn't have.

While the skirmishing continued in the East, Grant was pushing South, down the Tennessee River, and in early April, set up camp at a place called Pittsburg Landing in southern Tennessee, just north of the Mississippi border. On the morning of April 6, Confederate General Joseph E. Johnston launched an attack on the Union force, surprising Grant's army. No one had realized that the Rebels were there. The forces of Major General William Tecumseh Sherman bore the brunt of the attack and slowly fell back toward Shiloh Church.

The 3rd Brigade, under General Lew Wallace, arrived on the field around 6:30 PM that evening, after most of the fighting was done for the day, but not out on the right flank where the 78th had been positioned. When they arrived, they were immediately engaged by Confederate infantry in some savage hand-to-hand fighting, but were able to drive the Rebels back. To make matters worse, aside from being in battle, it was cold and wet, the rain coming down in buckets. General Wallace, at about 1 o'clock in the morning of April 7, ordered the 78th O.V.I. to take up a position on the extreme right of Grant's Army. It was the end of the line, the last line of defense, if you will. The Ohioans stayed in formation and stood there all night, leaning on their rifles and listening to the screams and cries of the wounded, lying on the field out there right in front of them. It was about as miserable a night that any of the 1,000 men of the 78th ever experienced. Worse, they knew that the fighting would continue in the morning, and they would have to protect their position. If they failed, the Confederates would be able to, in effect, surround the Yankees. Thus, it was imperative that the 78th hold. Defeat at Shiloh would be disastrous for the Union Army. If that happened, the politicians and the citizenry of the North might start thinking that this armed attempt at reunification wasn't going to be the answer and that the Confederates might just win the war.

Tom Armstrong huddled in back of the line, near a stand of trees, shivering, coughing, and generally feeling just plain awful. No way he could fight. He might have contracted the same disease that Wilbur had. But, he, too, knew that the Confederates were coming again in the morning. He couldn't move, he was so sick, but if they did come, and the 78th didn't hold, he would, no doubt, be captured and sent to a Confederate prison. He surely did not want that. He would rather die.

Four and a half hours later, at 5:30 A.M., Wallace ordered the division forward, southwest, toward the forces of Confederate General Braxton Bragg. As they left their protected position near the woods, the men had to walk over dead and dying men, and the wounded screaming for help. They could not stop to assist. The grass of the field turned red with blood and was pretty slippery, but forward they went. They intended to engage Bragg's men at just about noon, but nothing happened.

The Confederate commander, Lieutenant General P.G.T. Beauregard, had a decision to make. The day before, he had lost thousands of men, either killed, wounded, missing, or captured. Further, he was running out of food and ammunition. Beauregard could stay there and fight the advancing Union brigades, or he could retreat and live to fight another day. He opted for the latter. By 5 o'clock that afternoon, the Confederate withdrawal was complete, now being camped near the town of Corinth, Mississippi. With little sleep and the energy expended in the vicious fighting, the Union soldiers were just plain tuckered out and could not/did not pursue the enemy. The Battle of Shiloh was over, the bloodiest two days of any American war, the Union Army losing just over 13,000 men of the 63,000 that had taken the field, killed, wounded, captured, or missing while the Confederates lost over 10,000 of the 40,000 that had lined up to face them.

Tom Armstrong was not well. Seeing his condition, the officers of the 78th, Colonel Mortimer D. Leggett, Captain Zachariah M. Chandler, and Lieutenant George W. Porter didn't think that he would survive. His only chance to live was to go home.

Libby Prison Richmond Va.
July 28th A.D. 1863—

Dear friend Frank:

Ere this you've been appri-sed that I'm a Prisoner of War. On my birthday I was incarcerated in these walls June 24 1863— I may stay here for years and at present it looks pretty uncertain But I hope I shall be let out soon but all is conjecture— I have very little to hope for— I'm very well— I've not heard one word from any of my friends since I came from Winchester a few days before the Battle— I have not even heard from my regiment no not one word from any one— please to write to me If you ex-pect to get an answer from here you will have to enclose in your answer to this an Envelope, stamps, & ½ sheet of paper Be Brief in your letters tell me about your home &c it is all open-ed & inspected

Miss Frank P. Porter
Thomas S. Armstrong
July 28, 1863
Libby Prison, Richmond, Va

Contents

1 The Decision

When the paddlewheel steamer, *Lexington*, rounded the bend in the Muskingum River, nearing the city of Zanesville, Ohio, Tom Armstrong knew he was close to home. It was Friday, May 16, 1862, and he had been traveling for a week, leaving Shiloh Church, Tennessee, by steamer on the Tennessee River and heading west and then north to Ohio. He had only been in Company B of the 78th Regiment of the Ohio Volunteer Infantry (O.V.I.) for five months, but he had been discharged since he had come down with the Consumption on the way from Fort Donelson, in northern Tennessee, to Shiloh in the southern part of the state, and, as the Battle of Fort Donelson raged in mid-February, he had felt the fever attack and could hardly walk. In fact, he could hardly stand up.

You see, Armstrong and his brother, Wilbur, along with their good friend, George Porter, and two other friends, Bob Hanson and John Gillespie, had enlisted in the 78th O. V. I. in November 1861, departing for points south on February 11, 1862. The Battle at Fort Henry had commenced five days earlier, resulting in a Union victory for General Ulysses S. Grant, although it was really the Navy's gunboats that had forced the surrender of the fort. The Confederate soldiers who had survived the bombardment escaped to Fort Donelson, twelve miles to the east.

Snow covered the ground, and it was extremely cold. Many of the men of the 78th had thought it would be warm in Tennessee in February, but they were wrong. After Fort Henry, Grant and his force of 18,000 blue clad Union soldiers had pressed on to Fort Do-

1

nelson, near the little town of Dover, Tennessee, and began the assault on the fort on February 12. Confederate General Simon Bolivar Buckner surrendered Fort Donelson on the evening of February 15 with General John B. Floyd and General Gideon J. Pillow, escaping with 2,000 men. The 78th had been ordered into a position of reserve, to be called in only when necessary. The Union lost 2,800 men, either killed, wounded, or missing, but Grant's force took an estimated 12,000 prisoners. While all this was going on, Tom Armstrong didn't feel at all well.

Since the 78th had left Zanesville in January, he had lost close to twenty pounds, weighing in at 148 lbs. and was quite weak. The officers of Company B had recognized his deteriorating condition in late February and had recommended that he be discharged from the Union army. On May 1, 1862, he was informed in camp at Pittsburg Landing, just east of where the horrific Battle of Shiloh had taken place three weeks earlier, that he was free to go home. None of his comrades in the 78th ever expected to see him again, fearing that the disease would take him before he made it home. And, even if he did get back to Norwich, Ohio, it was likely that he would not make it as very few people recovered from the Consumption in the early 1860s. In fact, his best friend, 1st Lieutenant George Porter and Captain Zachariah M. Chandler, both of Company B, thought he was going to die in early April. Armstrong, himself, admitted to his parents in a letter that he thought he was a "goner." He was just 26 years old.

Papers had been prepared for his discharge in late March since he was in no condition to serve or fight, but when the Battle of Shiloh erupted on April 6, everyone forgot about them. Seeing his friend's condition when the battle was over, George Porter was reminded of them and inquired of Captain Chandler. The captain did not know, so he went to see Colonel Mortimer Leggett, the commander of the 78th, who told him that General Ulysses S. Grant's staff had them. All they needed was the general's signature. Leggett telegraphed Grant's headquarters, requesting the paperwork be processed. Later that day, a courier arrived, and Tom Armstrong was going home to recuperate.

When the *Lexington* chugged closer to Zanesville, he thought to himself that the war had been going on for thirteen months now since the Confederate army had opened fire on Fort Sumter on April 12, 1861, down there in Charleston Harbor. When the 78th had been organized, most of the volunteers thought that it would be over in three months, but they soon learned that was not to be the case. After the first Battle of Bull Run, in July 1861, just a few miles from Washington, DC, people began to realize that victory over the Confederate army would not be as easy as many in the North believed.

Before he left Pittsburg Landing, Armstrong had written his brother, Jacob, that he would be arriving somewhere around the 15th of May, asking him to bring the buckboard to take him home to Norwich, some twelve miles east of Zanesville. He had recovered somewhat, the fever was gone and the coughing was relieved, but he still felt very weak. When the steamer docked at the Dillon Wharf, there at the foot of 4th Street, he saw his brother, waved, and managed to disembark, carrying everything he had been issued the previous January except the rifle. The 78th would need it. He wouldn't.

Jacob Armstrong thought his brother looked awful. The uniform that Tom had worn so proudly back in January, was now draped around his shoulders, and it appeared that his trousers were now big enough for two men. He was dirty and badly needed a bath, Jacob thought, throwing his brother's haversack into the back of the buckboard. He helped Tom up into the seat, and they started off to Norwich, hoping to get there before nightfall. For the next two hours, they talked of the war; the crops that Jacob and their father, William, had just put in; and the sheep. Jacob was very proud of the herd of merinos that he nurtured and which continued to increase in numbers each year, even though he took a bunch of them to market every fall.

When they arrived at the farm, about five miles northeast of town, Jacob helped his brother down from the wagon. Tom picked up the haversack and started toward the house. His mother, Jane, had been sweeping the large front porch and was standing there, leaning on the broom handle, saddened by the condition of her son.

"It is good to see you, Thomas. Let me help you."

"Hello, Mother. I am glad to be home. No, I've got it," as he climbed up the three stairs to the porch. "I know I don't look too good, but I am a lot better than I was a month ago "

"I am glad for that and that you can rest and get your strength back. I will not have you doing too much. Father, Jacob, the girls, and I can make do without you exerting yourself."

Just then, his sisters, Mary, aged 22, and Flavilla, better known as Fla, 17, came out on the porch and shared embraces with him. Fla picked up the haversack and took it into the house, calling out to her little brothers.

"Frank, Gus, your brother is home from the war. Come quickly."

The two boys, Frank, being ten years old, and Gus (Augustus) being six, ran to see him and had to be cautioned about jumping up on him. And, just then, Tom Armstrong heard the hoofbeats of a horse and turned to see his father riding up from the pasture where the sheep were grazing.

"How are you, son?" he inquired.

"I was telling Mother, I am much better than I was a month ago. The fever broke before I left, and the cough isn't nearly as bad. It's been hard, and I am weak, but I feel a lot stronger than I have recently."

"That's good news, T. S. Let's get you cleaned up and have some supper."

Jane, Fla, and Mary set the table and brought out supper of venison, potatoes, and vegetables from the girls' garden. William said grace, and the family ate, with Tom telling them about the Battle of Shiloh and the long journey home. He told them that his friend, George Porter, had performed admirably in the battle even though he had been shot. When everyone was done, Jacob carried the haversack upstairs, with Tom following his brother. He was tired, and it was time for bed.

He hadn't thought about it, but his mother was still mourning the death of her son, Tom's younger brother, Wilbur, in March. Will had enlisted in the 78th Ohio with Tom and their good friend, George Porter, and had contracted Lung Fever in February before the battles of Fort Henry and Fort Donelson. He had died in Cincinnati the next month, having been pirated out of Fort Donelson by Tom and

George Porter. And, now, she thought, "Tom was sick as well, and I don't want to lose him, too."

Porter and Armstrong had snuck Will away with little fanfare or notice. George Porter had gone over to the field hospital to see if one of the surgeons could attend to him, but the medical people were overwhelmed with the wounded from the Battle of Fort Donelson. He had returned to Tom's tent with the news, and the two of them decided that Will needed to get to a hospital regardless, the nearest one they knew being in Cincinnati. They needed an officer's approval, so they went to see another of their friends, John W. A. Gillespie, 1st Lieutenant in Company G, and although Tom and George were in Company B, Gillespie agreed to approve sending Will to Cincinnati for treatment.

They had dragged his litter down to the docks on the Cumberland River and had persuaded a riverboat captain to take him back to Ohio, provided they make the appropriate payment. Tom paid the man what he thought was an outrageous sum, and they loaded Will onto the boat. When he got back to his tent, Tom wrote his father, telling him about Wilbur and that he was on the *St. Louis*, headed for Cincinnati. The *St. Louis* arrived in Cincinnati on March 15, with William there to convey Will to the 4th Street Hospital. Despite being cared for, Wilbur Armstrong died on March 22, since there was no known cure for lung fever, known today as pneumonia.

Jane Armstrong was thinking about that and was very sad. Wilbur had been a fun-loving boy who was never in trouble and was the apple of her eye. But, while Tom slept, she busied herself tidying up the downstairs. She was glad that the house was large enough for all of them, with bedrooms on the second floor and living, dining, and kitchen areas on the first. When they had first moved to Ohio from Connecticut in 1835, and since rural Licking County had few settlers, for the first few years, they just lived in a small house that William had built on a piece of land that suited him. That was when it was just him, Jane, Jacob, and the baby, Thomas. William Armstrong knew early on that wasn't going to be enough for his growing family, the crops, and the sheep. So, he purchased 90 acres in northeast Franklin Township in Licking County in April of 1839. He and his friends from Ellis Methodist Chapel built a house large enough,

5

he hoped, for what he imagined his family would be in a few years. He was right.

Over the next twenty-two years, the population in Franklin Township grew, so in April 1861, he sold the property and bought a similar one just outside of Norwich, Ohio, in Muskingum County. While he had started from scratch in Franklin Township, this property was already a working farm, with much of the land cleared to provide pastures for the sheep to graze in. The flock was getting pretty large, and William and Jacob took great pride in raising the merinos, showing them at the county fair, and then selling some of them to other breeders and local butchers. Jane used the wool to make clothing for the family, and you could hear the spinning wheel at various times throughout the day. The border collies kept the coyotes away from the herd for the most part, but every now and again, one would strike with a vengeance. When the animals became a problem, Jacob, Tom, and their sisters went hunting for them, quite successfully as all of them were pretty darn good with a rifle, especially Tom with his Springfield.

The barn out in the pasture provided relief from the searing heat of a central Ohio summer, the arctic cold and snow of winter, and the terrible thunderstorms that exploded in the spring from time to time. Most of the time, though, the sheep just stayed outside. William and Jacob didn't worry too much about the flock, except in winter when they had to make sure there was enough hay out there for the sheep to eat.

While Jacob, Tom, and their father tended to the flock of sheep, it was the girls who took care of the other animals, a few chickens, horses, hogs, and cows, but for the most part, the Armstrong family farm was pretty self-sufficient. There were peach and apple orchards; blueberry and elderberry patches; corn, wheat, and oats being grown in the fields. Harvest time was certainly a busy one for the entire family, but they had been doing it for over twenty years so it was just part of the regular routine.

Every now and again, William, Jacob, or Tom would hitch Maude and Betsy to the family wagon for a visit to Newark, some nine miles to the west where they would pick up the supplies and provisions they needed at Wallace Thayne's General Store. And, in the fall, they would saddle the horses and call the dogs in order to drive a portion of the flock to market, with a stop to see their banker, Richard Peterson, president of the Newark Farmers' Bank, once the sales were complete. Now, after the move in April 1861, they lived near the village of Norwich, some twenty miles east of Franklin Township.

The summer of 1862 arrived with its heat and humidity, and the terrible thunderstorms that scared Frank and Gus half to death. Life on the farm went on as usual, with Tom recuperating and gaining his strength back. Later in the summer, when he was stronger, he would ride Aspen into Zanesville from time to time to check on the state of the war, and particularly the 78th Ohio, and to see friends. He might even ride over to Hopewell to see George Porter's parents, John and Amanda, and his sister, Francis, who was more commonly known as Frank.

A week after he had returned home, Jacob had hitched Betsy to the buckboard and the two of them had gone into town. Tom just didn't feel strong enough to sit in the saddle as Aspen would lope her way toward Zanesville and then to make the return trip. Riding in the wagon was a lot less painful, he thought. When they got there, they saw Cyrus Bradfield sitting in front of his office, reading the paper. Cyrus had been Sheriff in Zanesville for some time and had made the acquaintance of the Armstrongs when they first moved from Franklin Township.

"Hey, Jacob! Hey, Tom!" he called. "You seen this?"

"What?" Jacob Armstrong asked as he hitched the wagon to the post outside the Sheriff's Office and walked up the steps with his brother following. Bradfield showed them the paper. When they opened it, he saw…

GOVERNOR'S PROCLAMATION
Governor's Proclamation to the gallant men of Ohio

I have the astounding intelligence that the seat of our beloved national Government is threatened with invasion, and I am called upon by the Secretary of War for troops to repel and utterly overwhelm the ruthless invaders. Rally! then, loyal men of Ohio. And respond to this call as becomes those who appreciate our glorious Government. Three classes of troops will be accepted:

1st, For three years or during the war.

2nd, For a term of three months

3rd, For guard duty within the limits of the State.

All requested to report for duty at Camp Chase where the organization will take place.

The number wanted from each county has been indicated by special dispatches to the several military committees.

Everything is valueless to us if our Government be overthrown. Lay aside, then, your ordinary duties, and help bear aloft the glorious flag unfurled by your fathers.

Signed,   David Tod

Columbus, May 26, 1862   Governor of Ohio

"Goodness," said Tom Armstrong. "I wonder how many they want from here in good old Muskingum."

"Don't know. Probably a regiment or two."

"If you hear anything, let us know," Jacob said.

"Will do. Stop by the next time you are in town."

Tom would have liked to have gone from there to Hopewell to see George Porter, and, incidentally, George's sister, Francis, but he didn't think he had the strength. And, he really hadn't confided in his brother about his interest in her. So, he asked Jacob to stop at the livery stable to have Werner Schweitzer, the blacksmith, check the shoes on the horses, before heading back. They, then, stopped at Wescott's Saloon, over in Putnam, for a glass of lemonade, and to see if any of their friends had come in. The saloon was pretty empty, Tom was tired, and it was getting late so they just decided to get on home. But, seeing the Porters would have been very good.

The Porters and the Armstrongs had known each other for years, as both were sheep herders and saw each other every year at the Licking County Fair. Further, they would run into each other at the market when they were going to sell part of the flock and, from time to time, at Wallace Thayne's General Store.

8

George Porter and Tom Armstrong had become fast friends through their mutual interest in raising flocks of sheep, their expert horsemanship, and their love of the outdoors. They would exchange letters every now and again and visit each other's home during the year, going hunting for deer, pheasant, wild turkey, squirrels, rabbits, and the occasional coyote. They would go on fishing trips up at Claylick Creek, northeast of the farm in Franklin Township with Tom's brother-in-law, A. T. Hull and would stay over for a couple of days with A. T. and his wife, the former Matilda Armstrong, Tom's sister, before returning to the Armstrong farm.

It was on one of these visits to the Porter's place in the summer of 1858 that Tom Armstrong noticed that Francis (Frank) Porter was growing up. He was 23; she was 18. He thought she was very attractive and seemed to enjoy the same things he did, good books being of primary importance to both of them. Tom Armstrong asked John Porter if it would be all right if he started a correspondence with her. Frank's father saw no reason why not, so he agreed. She was flattered. Their correspondence began soon after, and on Valentine's Day, 1860, he sent a lovely message to her. That was it! She began to feel that her brother's best friend might turn out to be her best friend as well. That had been the reason she had been upset that he was going to war with the 78th in January 1862. It was bad enough that her brother was going, and now her Tom would be in harm's way as well. Now, she hadn't let on in her letters to him that she considered him "her Tom." Girls just didn't do that in 1861. It wasn't proper.

That summer of 1862, on those rides from Norwich to Zanesville and back, he had begun to think about his future, now that he was out of the army. Before the war, he had been teaching in Browneville, in Licking County, enjoying it very much, and now he started thinking it would be a good, steady thing to do once the war was over. So, he decided to enroll at the Teachers' Normal Institute in Putnam, just west of Zanesville, where he would learn how to be a high school teacher.

You see, Putnam was separated from Zanesville by the Y Bridge and the Muskingum River. Oh, and there was one more division between the two. Zanesville had been settled by folks from Virginia with Putnam's people coming from Connecticut and other New England states. The citizens of Putnam and those from Zanesville had vastly different opinions on the matter of slavery. And, for the most part, they didn't mingle well with each other.

One day, as Tom Armstrong was walking through town to the Institute from Mrs. Palmer's boarding house where he was staying, he overheard some men talking about the "cowards who wouldn't go and fight."

"Cowards?" he thought to himself. "Disgracing themselves and their families as well as their units. I was not a coward. I went. Then, I got sick, but I can't tell anyone about the pressure to run that we all feel as the bullets are flying from the enemy's infantry and grape and shot are coming from their big guns. There's great temptation to run. I wonder if those men think that's what I did."

"If this thing with Frank goes anywhere," he thought, "and I am branded a coward, she will be branded as well. So will my family and the Porters, and I can't have that. So, I won't tell her about the temptation to run and I won't tell her about the fear that I felt." That spurred his first thoughts about re-enlisting. "But, I can't tell anyone about that either. I will write to her as often as I can because she seems glad to receive my letters, and I enjoy getting letters from her."

It was the summer of 1862, while he was attending the Teachers' Normal Institute in Putnam, an area of Zanesville just west of the Muskingum River, that he had reconnected with an old friend, the Rev. Charles C. McCabe, who was now the pastor of the Putnam Methodist Church. The Armstrong children had been raised in Methodism by their parents at Ellis Chapel in Franklin Township and then at the Norwich Methodist Church. Further, Tom had attended Ohio Wesleyan University, in Delaware, Ohio, a university that had been established as an outcome of the Methodists' newly-found interest in education. The town of Delaware had wanted to have a college there, which was accomplished on March 7, 1842. Tom Armstrong enrolled there in January 1859, and found that the university was strong in its belief and support of not only the traditions of Methodism but also of liberty and patriotic unionism. It was also decidedly anti-slavery, something that he had not thought much about. In his first semester, he took classes in Latin, history, and Greek, but his favorite was algebra taught by Professor Lorenzo Dow McCabe, Charlie McCabe's uncle.

McCabe, born in October 1836, was a year younger than Tom Armstrong, who entered this world on June 25, 1835. But while Tom was teaching and tending to the farm, Charles McCabe entered Ohio Wesleyan in the fall of 1854, having decided to become a Methodist minister. He had been teaching a bit, and working in the family store, but he did not have the educational advantage that Tom Armstrong had enjoyed as a result of his significant intellectual curiosity. Armstrong read voraciously whenever books were found, went to school every day in Newark when he was younger, and enjoyed the stories he and the other children were taught in Sunday School. Armstrong was certainly ready for college when he arrived in Delaware in 1859, but McCabe certainly wasn't when he got there four and a half years earlier. McCabe did, however, find the culture of the university, grounded in Methodism and in the liberty afforded to all men by the founding fathers and the patriotism for the Union, much to his liking.

McCabe had qualities that Tom did not. He was a charismatic leader, characterized as brave to even daring, always optimistic, and with an enviable sense of humor. He made friends wherever he went, and people wanted to listen to him since he always had something interesting to say. And say it he would. He was a brilliant orator. The Reverend McCabe preached the gospel at the Methodist Church on Sundays, oftentimes at two or three services. He also led revival meetings once a week at the church, full of "Amens" and "Hallelujahs" with baptisms of those who were accepting the gospel of God. McCabe could go on for hours, encouraging the faithful to repent and turn to the Lord, and Armstrong made sure he was there to listen and learn, his own personal faith strengthening in the process. There was one more quality about Charles McCabe that he knew he would never have: a rich, baritone voice, that was always on key. Tom played a mean fiddle, but he couldn't sing a lick, so listening to the Professor sing was a real treat.

While the introverted Tom Armstrong clung to his studies, Charles McCabe lived to see people and be with them to tell them

11

of the glory of God. Religion was his reason for living, and he preached it with joy and courage wherever he went. And, the people of central Ohio loved him for it.

While McCabe pursued this exhaustive schedule of evangelism throughout central Ohio, his studies suffered, and he decided that academic environment was not what he wanted to do with his life, and so he had decided to take the pulpit of the Putnam Methodist Church. In July of that summer, 1860, he married Miss Rebecca Peters, who had just graduated from the Wesleyan Female Seminary in Cincinnati and had asked Tom Armstrong to stand with him at the altar. The Reverend and Mrs. McCabe had their first church now, and the congregation grew and grew. One of the parishioners was, of course, Tom Armstrong, who would walk over to the church from Mrs. Palmer's boarding house, planning to spend the day. He loved the services, but he also loved going to the home of the Rev. and Mrs. McCabe for supper after the evening Prayer Service was done. They had become dear friends, enjoying each other's company as they studied the Bible in great detail and talked about the events of the day as well as Tom Armstrong's experiences with the 78th.

One day, in August, as he was walking toward the Institute for the day's studies, he was trying to decide which school would be the best for him, the one in Uniontown, also known as Fultonham, which was twelve miles southwest of Zanesville, or the one in Deavertown which was ten miles southeast of Fultonham. His boots thumped on the wooden sidewalk as he walked along Main Street, now Putnam Avenue, thinking about his future. He was pretty sure that the school in Uniontown was the better of the two, mainly because it was closer to Hopewell where Frank Porter lived. He was nearing the Institute when he spotted the Rev. McCabe striding toward him, looking quite excited. Since the Putnam Methodist Church was there on East Street, now Moxahala Avenue, in the next block from the Institute, McCabe had seen Tom walk by on his way to his classes from time-to-time, calling out best wishes of the day, so he pretty much knew when he would pass by that day.

The two men shook hands, McCabe exclaimed with great joy, "Ball, Granger, and Gary came to see me yesterday. They have been authorized to organize the 122nd Regiment of the Ohio Volunteers immediately." Armstrong remembered that he had seen the proclamation from the Governor of Ohio, David Tod, in the paper when he and Jacob had gone into Zanesville a couple of months before, so he knew that more men were needed for the war effort. From what he had read in more recent editions of the *Daily Courier* and from letters from George Porter, he also knew that things were not going well militarily in the eastern theater, but with victories at Fort Henry, Fort Donelson, and Shiloh, the Union forces were doing pretty well in the west.

"William asked me if I would serve as the Chaplain of the new regiment, and it took me about five seconds to accept," McCabe began. "Oh, I have to be formally appointed by Bishop Morris, but I don't think that will be a problem. There will be a recruiting meeting at the Putnam Presbyterian Church tomorrow night at 7:00PM. Both William and Daniel will speak, and they have asked me to say a few words and to lead everyone in a couple of songs. *Rally Round the Flag* and *The Star Spangled Banner* come to mind. Anyway, I would like you to come to the meeting and to consider your duty to your country by enlisting in the 122nd. Based on what I told them about you, they have authorized me to tell you that if you do enlist, you will come in as 2nd Lieutenant, and they expressed their kindest wishes that you will accept. They also want us, you and me, to help recruit." It was Thursday, August 7, 1862.

Tom Armstrong said he would think about it, shook McCabe's hand, and continued toward the Institute. But now his thoughts were not of teaching at Uniontown and being close to Frank Porter, but rather he had a dilemma to resolve, thanks to his good friend, the Rev. Charles C. McCabe. He wanted to talk with Frank about it, but knew he didn't have time to visit her. He also thought a conversation with Jacob would be a good idea, since he was sure that his parents would be horrified at the thought of him dodging bullets and artillery fire once again. And, there were also the diseases, one of which had killed his younger brother, Wilbur. Time was a problem because he did not think he could get out to Norwich for another week, given his studies. But, he was wrong about that. He was alone with his thoughts which was all right. He had made important decisions on his own in the past about college, teaching positions, and more recently, about Francis Porter. Resolving to attend the meeting the following evening, he wanted to keep an open mind, but his patriotism and sense of duty and honor were creeping steadily back into his mind.

That day, he absently went through the lessons being taught by Principal Stoughton and the other members of the faculty at the Institute, his mind wandering as to the prospect in front of him. He had seen the elephant at Fort Donelson and Shiloh. Although he didn't actually fight, he saw first-hand what battle meant. It was horrific, period! That he understood. He hadn't known that in February, 1861, when he, Wilbur, George and the rest of the 78th Ohio Volunteer Infantry boarded the steamers for Cincinnati and the south. But, now he knew what war was, and it wasn't pretty. It meant marching for days at a time, carrying all of your possessions and rifle; eating whatever the quartermasters could provide or whatever he could scrounge off the land; sleeping in mud, as rain and sleet continued to fall, sometimes with a blanket, and sometimes not; occasionally being unprotected from the wind and the snow; and oh, yes, there was the enemy who would do anything he could to stop you. The bullets and artillery fire would fly into them, there would be their own infantry charges right into the fire, men would fall dead or wounded, those who were spared would load, ram, and fire their rifles over and over again. Bayonets would be fixed, with hand-to-hand combat commencing. There would be the screams of the wounded and dying lying on the field waiting for medical help. There would be piles of dead horses and the stench that attended them. There was the disease: typhoid, dysentery, lung fever, consumption, smallpox. There was also the boredom that sapped their energy. Not very pleasant thoughts running through his head. The elephant is real.

And, it would be worse for, this time, he would be an officer which meant gaining the trust of the men as they were getting organized at camp, teaching them *Hardee's Tactics* through drills and other lessons on how they might survive, all the while knowing full well that he and the other officers would be expected to lead them into battle. He had been a corporal in the 78th but that just meant that

14

he did what the senior officers told him to do. He could still hear the repetitive commands from Lieutenant Wiles and Lieutenant Munson when the 78th was drilling at Camp Gilbert in Zanesville, the regiment having moved there the previous December. "OK, boys, when he comes, find some protection; keep your head down, except when you fire; and aim low." Tom Armstrong would never forget that, but he always wondered about keeping his head down when he had to aim his rifle before he fired. This time, he would have to do everything he wanted them to do, and more. He wondered if he had the courage to be the first one out of the breastwork trenches, across the field, or over the wall when the Colonel yelled, "*CHARGE*!!!"

His day at the Institute concluded, he walked back toward Mrs. Palmer's boarding house. He was leaning toward going, even though he knew his family and Frank Porter would not understand. He then thought that maybe a conversation with Charlie would help. He would try to see him in the morning. The sun was still hot on that August afternoon, but he did not think about it. He had other words circulating through his brain. "Duty." "Honor." "Flag." "Mr. Lincoln's Union." "Pressure from the Others." "Cowardice." He spoke with Mrs. Palmer about his meeting with Charlie McCabe that afternoon.

"So, are you going?" she asked.

"I think so," he replied. "It is my duty as an American to fight for the Union against this rebellion. My parents won't like it, but it is something that I feel compelled to do. I may get killed, I may not. I will leave that up to God."

She looked at him with excitement in her eyes. She had come to admire this farm boy with his curiosity about learning, deep faith, and love of country.

"I am proud of you. When will you leave?"

"Thank you, and I will find out tomorrow about the details. I'll fill you in tomorrow night or Saturday morning before I head out to Norwich to talk with the family."

He headed up the stairs, off to bed, knowing exactly what he was going to do. He rose early, as he wanted to talk with Charlie McCabe. He had decided that he did not need to go to the Institute that day; there were pressing matters to take care of. He knocked on the door of the parsonage which was right next door to the church, as parsonages usually are, and when Rebecca answered, she could tell he had something on his mind. While her husband was an eternal optimist, she knew that Tom Armstrong was a realist. Charlie had told her about seeing Tom on the street and having that short exchange, so she knew instantly what he wanted to discuss.

"Charles, Tom's here. He wants to visit with you about something." The parsonage wasn't that large, but there was a sitting room to the right of the main hall. The Rev. Charles McCabe came out from a smaller room that he used for a study and ushered Tom through the double doors and lit some candles. The candlelight warmed the room. McCabe motioned for Tom to sit down in a rather comfortable chair across the room.

"What can I do for you, my friend?"

Tom Armstrong stroked his mustache, looking intently at the Reverend Charles McCabe. "Where do I sign up?"

"Whoa, that was fast," exclaimed the Rev. McCabe. "Why not tonight?" he asked. "At the war meeting? Why don't you just be the first one to stand up, move to the front of the sanctuary, and sign your name. That will be a sign to the rest that we need them to sign up, too. Colonel Ball, Major Granger, Captain Gary, and Lieutenant Black will be very pleased, as am I. We have been worried that finding 1,000 men to fill a regiment here in Muskingum County will be difficult. We still don't know how difficult it really will be, but having you on board helps very much."

Thomas S. Armstrong felt pride swell up in his breast and simply said, "Thank you, Charlie. Is there anything we need to do today?"

"Let's go find Colonel Ball."

"Don't you have to get ready for the meeting?" Tom asked.

"No, not really. I know all the songs and hymns we're going to sing, and I have been doing revivals for a long time now so I think I will be fine when it comes my turn to speak."

McCabe kissed his wife as they left for Colonel Ball's law office, telling her that Tom had wanted to be a part of the newly-formed 122nd OVI. She was happy that her husband's friend would be there with him, but saddened by the fact that they were both going to war. The Reverend hitched his horse to the buggy, and they started north

16

on Main Street, then turned left on Front Street, turning right on the 3rd Street Bridge. McCabe reined the horse in and hitched her to the post outside of Colonel Ball's office there at 9 N. 4th Street. They hopped out of the buggy and went up the steps to knock on the door.

William H. Ball, Esq. opened the door. "Reverend! Mr. Armstrong! Good morning. It is good to see you. Do I have a feeling that I know for what purpose you have come here this morning?"

"Tom here has expressed a desire to go with us, Bill," Rev. McCabe started. "As I told you, he was with the 78th, got sick, and they sent him home after Shiloh. He has seen the elephant where the new boys have not. That makes him a very valuable resource to Dan, Moses, and yourself. My understanding is that he comes in as 2nd Lieutenant. Am I correct in that?"

"Yes, Reverend, you are correct. Welcome, Mr. Armstrong. We can certainly use someone like you. You have the war experience, but I have also heard that you are an excellent horseman and a crack shot. True?"

"It depends on who said that, "Armstrong replied." I will let you judge for yourself," thinking back to the days at Porter's and Franklin Township hunting with George.

"Are you coming to the meeting tonight?"

"Yes, sir. I plan to be the first one to stand and enlist. That was Charlie's idea."

The Colonel looked at McCabe with a twinkle in his eye. "Good thinking, Reverend, or should I call you Chaplain now?"

"Whatever your pleasure, Colonel."

They talked a little more about the meeting to be held that night, and then Tom and Rev. McCabe bade Colonel Ball goodbye, saying that they would see him at the meeting. McCabe wondered, "When will you tell your parents?"

"Soon," Tom said with a finality that the Chaplain knew was the end of that conversation.

"Maybe we should have a prayer about how you will go about that."

"Maybe we should."

The Chaplain asked God for wisdom, clarity, and understanding, as Tom Armstrong would have to have some very difficult conversations. When he was finished, Armstrong said he would see him later and walked back down the wooden sidewalk toward Mrs. Palmer's. He needed to be alone to think. How in the world would he be able to tell his parents that he was going back to war? And, Frank? Charlie McCabe didn't know about her. He concluded that he would tell all of them the truth about what he was feeling, no more, no less. Was the decision irrational? Probably. Illogical? Probably. But it was his decision to make, knowing of all of their concern for his well-being. He would go home the next day but wondered how he could get to Hopewell to talk to Frank in person. That would be tough, indeed.

Later that day, as he walked near the Putnam Presbyterian Church, he could hear the band playing *Yankee Doodle* over and over again from inside the church. He saw Charlie McCabe on the front stoop and shook his hand with a firm grip. He was taller than the Chaplain, being just under six feet, and he carried his 165 pounds well. He walked into the sanctuary, placed his black felt hat on the hat rack and proceeded to take a seat in a pew about half way down, sitting on the aisle so that he could get up when the time came.

The choir belted out *Rally Round the Flag* and *The Star Spangled Banner,* everyone in attendance joining in. William Ball stood in the pulpit in front of Tom Armstrong and gave a stirring speech about the formation of the 122nd Regiment of the Ohio Volunteer Infantry. He talked about duty, honor, the Union, the flag, the Constitution, and the liberty upon which the country had been founded in 1776. There were cheers from the audience, and the band broke in with *Yankee Doodle* once again. Moses Granger fueled the fire with a rousing speech that took up where Colonel Ball had left off. *Yankee Doodle* again. Then it was Daniel Gary's turn, and the frenzy got louder as he raised his voice to encourage the men in attendance to volunteer their services. "You can do that right here, *tonight,"* he bellowed and the cheering continued. *Yankee Doodle* one more time or two.

Tom Armstrong was feeling the pull of patriotism that was gripping the room and was anxious to go forward to sign his name on the enlistment document. That would have to wait for it was Charlie McCabe's turn to speak. The Chaplain was a brilliant orator, and he touched the men with his fervent plea for them to come forward. He did not say that God would be on the side of the Union or that they would be protected and spared, but he did stress the importance of faith and prayer. He said that he would be with them, holding services every week and being there to talk with them when things got rough. He knew many of the men in attendance as he cut a pretty wide swath in Zanesville, and he concluded that "We cannot let our families, Zanesville, Ohio, or the Union down." More cheering, *Yankee Doodle* once again. And then, in his rich baritone voice, he broke into *We are Coming Father Abraham*

We are coming, Father Abraham, 300,000 more,
From Mississippi's winding stream and from New England's shore.
We leave our plows and workshops, our wives and children dear,
With hearts too full for utterance, with but a silent tear.
We dare not look behind us but steadfastly before.
We are coming, Father Abraham, 300,000 more!

Chorus: We are coming, we are coming our Union to restore,
We are coming, Father Abraham, 300,000 more!

If you look across the hilltops that meet the northern sky,
Long moving lines of rising dust your vision may descry;
And now the wind, an instant, tears the cloudy veil aside,
And floats aloft our spangled flag in glory and in pride;
And bayonets in the sunlight gleam, and bands brave music pour,
We are coming, father Abr'am, three hundred thousand more!

By the second time through, everyone was on their feet singing lustily with the Chaplain. Suddenly, he spread his arms above his head to quiet them, motioned for them to sit down and nodded at Tom Armstrong. With everyone seated and in the quiet of the church, Armstrong stood up and walked slowly to the front of the sanctuary where there was a table with an open book upon it. Major

Moses Granger, in uniform, sat behind the table. There was a slight stir among the men.

"What's your name, son?" asked Maj. Granger.

"Thomas Sumption Armstrong, sir."

"Where do you live?"

"Norwich, sir."

"What is your purpose?"

"I wish to enlist in the 122nd Regiment of the Ohio Volunteer Infantry, sir."

"Sign here, Mr. Armstrong."

With pen in hand, he placed his signature on the first line of the page marked "Soldiers of the 122nd Regiment of the Ohio Volunteer Infantry." He shook hands with Major Granger and started back to his seat. Colonel William Ball motioned for him to stay up front with them.

For a moment, there was silence in the church which suddenly turned into a deafening roar. The others knew what had just happened, the first man had enlisted in the Regiment. Now, it was their turn. A few came forward and signed their names, staying in the front of the church after they had done so.

Ball thundered, "We need you men for the preservation of the Union. We need you to come with us. We cannot let our families, Zanesville, Putnam, Ohio or the Union down," to thunderous applause. Tom wondered "if they are cheering and applauding, why don't they come up?" The only answer was that they weren't ready. They believed in the Union cause for sure. You could hear it. But, for their own reasons, they could not make an immediate commitment like Tom Armstrong and the others had done. He and Charlie, along with officers of the other companies in the regiment, would hit the road in the morning to start recruiting. *Yankee Doodle*, one last time, but he was never more sure of anything that he had ever done than he was at that moment. Well, maybe there was one other: Francis Porter. "Yes, I may die. Yes, I may not. It is in God's hands now," he thought. "I will just tell my family and Frank to pray for me."

As the meeting broke up, he said goodbye to Ball, Granger, and Gary and told McCabe that he would be by the church in the morning to talk about recruiting. He would be going home later in the day and would suggest that the Chaplain ride out to Norwich in a couple of days to start the effort there. He took his hat off the hat rack and began the walk back to Mrs. Palmer's. Candles were still burning in the kitchen and sitting room when he opened the front door.

She appeared from the kitchen, wiping her hands on her apron, just greeting him by name. She asked about the meeting, so they sat together for an hour or so as he described what had happened. When he got to the part about being the first one to enlist in the regiment, she started to weep, unsure if it was because of the danger he would face or because she was so proud of him. Maybe it was both.

They said good-night, and he went up the stairs to his room and slept soundly, comfortable in what he had just done. There was a lot to do in the morning, he thought, as his head hit the pillow. A lot to do.

He rose early the next morning as the sun streamed through the window, poured some water into the basin on the dresser, and washed his face, thinking he could take a bath when he got home. Packing all of his things into his haversack, he went downstairs and found Mrs. Palmer in the kitchen making breakfast. And, a fine breakfast it was, with fried eggs, bacon, biscuits, orange juice, and hot black coffee. They talked until he thought he better get over to the Institute to tell Principal Stoughton that he would no longer be taking instruction. He thought, "Since I am going home to Norwich, I better ride over to the Institute and then to see Charlie before heading home." He said farewell to Mrs. Palmer who wished him Godspeed.

"Take care of yourself, and come by and see me when you get home from this terrible conflict."

"I will be sure to do that, Mrs. Palmer. Thank you."

He walked out the back door to the stable where Aspen was enjoying a bagful of oats. Saddling the big gray mare, he put the Springfield rifle in its holster, secured the haversack, and started down Main Street toward the Institute where he found the Principal sitting at his desk in his office. Principal Stoughton was a big man, two or three inches taller than he was and several pounds heavier. His hair was thinning, and his eyes always sparkled behind his spectacles when Tom came into the room. They shook hands, Tom feeling the strength in his mentor's grip.

"It is always good to see you," he said, "but I noticed that you were not here yesterday."

"Yes, that's right, Principal. You see, Mr. Ball is organizing a new regiment. and I was asked by Reverend McCabe to reenlist in the OVI. You know how I feel about a man's duty to his country and the honor it is to serve, so I agreed to go back. But, this time, I am an officer, a 2nd Lieutenant. I guess that means that my time here at the Institute is concluded since I have preparations to make. We go to Camp Zanesville in a couple of weeks. Please accept my appreciation for everything you have done for me this summer."

"I am not surprised, and you are very welcome, my boy. Perhaps you can come back when this infernal war is over. I just hate to see all of the young men from Muskingum County going off to fight when we know that many of them will not return. But, it must be that way in order to save the Union. Do be safe, and trust in the Lord."

"I will, sir. Goodbye for now." Tom Armstrong turned and walked out of the Principal's office, out the front door and down the steps to where Aspen was waiting calmly at the hitching post. He walked her a block up toward Mrs. Palmer's house to the Putnam Methodist Church where he knew Charlie McCabe would be waiting. He tied the mare to the railing in front of the porch, taking hold of the rifle.

"Greetings of the day, T. S.," said the Reverend with a cheerful lilt to his voice. "It is a splendid summer day. Shall we walk while we talk?"

"Whatever pleases you, Charlie. Lead the way."

And, so, they walked out into the sunlight down Main Street toward Zanesville, talking about the ways to convince other young men to join them in the 122nd Regiment of the Ohio Volunteer Infantry. They only needed 85 more to fill out Tom's Company I, but they would need ten times that many to complete the Regiment.

"Since I am going home today, I think I will start talking to my friends in Norwich. Maybe you could come out and help me early next week. Perhaps you could bring Rebecca and stay a couple of days. I am sure Mary and Fla would love to see her."

"Let us go back to the parsonage, and I shall ask," came the reply. "While I am there we could talk about more ways to encourage others to join us."

Rebecca McCabe thought it a splendid idea. She had not seen Tom's sisters since they had attended a revival at the church, almost a year ago, so it would be good to see them again. It was settled. Tom Armstrong and Charles McCabe walked back to the church. Tom secured the haversack on Aspen, re-holstered the rifle, climbed into the saddle, took the reins, and was off.

"See you on Tuesday," he shouted. It was Saturday, August 9, 1862. As he rode, he decided to tell the family that day to get it over with. He hoped they would understand but was pretty sure they wouldn't. Where was the logic of throwing away teaching in Uniontown, being closer to Frank Porter, to go back in the army? There wasn't any except his love of country and sense of duty and honor and the fear of being called a coward.

As he approached Norwich, the sun was very hot, but, at least, it was at his back. He tipped his hat back on his head, and wiped the sweat away from his face with his bandana. "Aspen could use a drink," he thought. He turned north onto Locust Street, and then east on North Street, and finally north again on Lodge Street, leaving him about five miles to the farm. Coming up the path to the house, Duke, one of the collies, spotted him and came bounding down through the grass to meet him. He dismounted and scuffled with the playful dog, letting Aspen just graze right there.

"T. S. ," yelled Jacob, his older brother. "I thought you were in Putnam, learning to be a teacher. It is so good to see you. You look well and hearty."

"It's good to see you, too. How are Mother and Father, the girls, and the little ones?"

"Everyone is fine, brother. Just fine." Tom thought, only for awhile. Wait 'till they hear what I am going to say.

Jacob called out, "Mother, look who's here!" Jane Armstrong came out of the house and onto the wide front porch, a broad smile on her face.

She embraced him as he came up the walk to the porch and asked if he was hungry or thirsty. All he wanted was water. He put the haversack and rifle down on the porch, asking his mother to tell him all of the news.

"Jacob," he asked, "can you take care of Aspen for me? She needs water and rest after a long, dusty ride."

Gus, aged seven, and Frank, eleven, came outside to see what was going on and jumped on their big brother, knocking him down, his big hat flying off into the yard. They were wrestling when Tom heard his younger sister, Flavilla say, "We had been hoping you would come see us one of these days, and now you're here."

Tom got up, telling his little brothers they would wrestle later, and embraced Fla, as she was called, when Mary came up from the garden. Time for another embrace. Then he saw his father, William, come riding in from the pasture after a hard day's work.

"Good to see you, son. How long can you stay?"

"Not sure," replied Tom Armstrong. "At least through the week."

"Mother," said William Armstrong, "it is nearly time for supper. I'm famished, and I bet T. S. is as well."

They talked about the Civil War during supper. The family was very curious to find out what war was really like. He had told them about it upon his return in May, but he had been pretty sick then and couldn't remember what he had said. Now that he was well, he recounted the involvement of the 78th O.V.I. at Fort Donelson and Shiloh, although he had been too sick to participate in the fight.

Supper concluded with elderberry pie that Jane had baked that afternoon. Mary and Flavilla gathered up the dishware in a basket and headed for the creek that ran under the coolhouse to wash and dry what had been used.

Tom, William, and Jacob went out on the porch to talk. Jacob and William lit up cigars. The conversation about the war continued with Tom announcing he was re-enlisting, this time in the 122nd O.V.I. just as his mother came outside. She had just put Frank and Gus to bed. The look on her face told him that she had overheard what he had told his father and brother.

"So, help me out, son." said William Armstrong. "Tell me again why you are going back into the army."

"Yes, I want to know what you are thinking," said his mother. "I worried about you the last time you went. Wilbur is gone, a casualty of the war, and I miss him so. You almost died of the consumption. And, now you want to go back into the army." She had lost three little ones early in their lives, the pain of death only rekindled by Wilbur's sudden passing.

"It's different this time," Tom replied. "When Wilbur and I enlisted in the 78th, it was an exciting time. We all got caught up in it. George Porter, Gillespie, Hanson, and other friends. It seemed like it was our duty to put down the rebellion, and we didn't think it would take too long to do. We all understood why we were going to war with thousands of others. Colonel Leggett explained it very well. It was the principle of free government, Lincoln calls it the Great Experiment. The founders made sure that the United States was to have a government by and for the people which had never been done before. What that meant was that we are free to elect our leaders and to hold them accountable for their actions. Colonel Leggett said that when the southern states seceded, they violated their commitment to the Union and the Constitution. So, we had to correct that and bring them back. We knew that it was our responsibility to preserve the Union, which had been founded just seventy years ago, on the basis of human liberty, from destruction."

Mary and Fla joined them on the porch.

"So, what's different this time? Aren't you still concerned about the experiment that Leggett talked about?" asked Jacob. "And, another thing, doesn't the Sixth Commandment say 'Thou Shalt Not Kill?' How are you going to deal with that?"

Tom Armstrong felt some frustration starting to build. He loved his family and would do anything for them, but he would not budge on this. Looking straight at his big brother, he said, "If I kill, I will ask God to forgive me. My earnest hope is that He will."

25

He went on, "The last time, there was the excitement, a sense of duty and honor, the patriotism that we have committed to as a family, community, and nation," he told them. "But, I had not seen the horrors of war. Now, I have seen the elephant. I have seen men get killed, have an arm or a leg blown off, heard screams of the dying on the field as they waited for a surgeon who never came, running for cover in sheer terror and panic as the shot and grape from the artillery rained down, gunboats destroyed and their crew drowning, piles of bodies used as shields against enemy gunfire. But, the boys fight on. Before I left, George told me about the 78th at Shiloh. He said he was shot seven times, but the thickness of his coat stopped all of the Minie balls from hitting him. He said he had to sleep standing up in the rain, after the first day's fight at Shiloh, hearing the screams of the wounded who would surely die that night, knowing that the second day could even be more brutal. Yes, I understand the danger, and that's why I have to go back. This war will not be short. Yes, I may get killed or wounded, but that is the truth about war. I will leave that up to God but will be as careful as I can. I will do my duty as an officer of the 122nd Ohio Volunteers."

"What about sickness?" asked his mother. "You came close to dying. I have already lost one beloved son to sickness and the three little ones before they were five, and now you are going to risk it again."

"Yes, Mother. I am. It's my duty. Am I scared? Sure, but I am praying that faith and family will sustain me."

"So, there is nothing we can do to change your mind?" asked his father.

"No, Father, there is not. The Union is bigger than all of us, and it must be preserved. I have promised Captain Gary that I will serve in the 122nd and have been made 2nd Lieutenant of Company I. We report to Camp Zanesville on the 1st of the month. Oh, I forgot to tell you, Charlie McCabe will be our Chaplain. I have known him since my year at Ohio Wesleyan and actually attended his wedding two summers ago. He is a good friend, and I am glad he is coming with us."

Jane Armstrong began to weep, as did his sisters. He felt for them, but he knew what he had to do.

"Jacob, can you go with me to Zanesville when I have to report? I'll need you to bring all my stuff to camp, but I'm going to take Aspen. I will be coming home before we leave for the field and will leave her here. Then, can you take me back? Tell the little ones they can ride her."

"Sure," his big brother said, drawing heavily on the cigar. "I think I understand why you are doing this. I will stay here and help Father and Mother with the farm. I am sure the army will still need wool for uniforms so attending the flock will be my contribution. It ain't much, compared to you, but it's something."

William said, "C'mon, Mother, let's go inside." Together, they got up from the swing and went back into the house, the door slamming behind them. The brothers knew that their parents weren't real happy with Tom right now, as they sat there on the porch for awhile, both trying to understand what had just happened. He was thinking, "I'm glad that's over. Now, how to tell Frank."

He would try get to see her over in Hopewell, as she had asked, before going to camp, and he hoped she would understand why he was going back into the army. There was also something else he wanted to talk to her about.

2 The Journey Begins

The sun streamed through the window of the bedroom where Tom Armstrong had spent the night. He could hear the rooster out in the yard announcing that the new day had arrived. He looked at his pocket watch that was on the table by the bed and saw it was past 7 o'clock. "Slept longer than I thought," he said to himself. It was Sunday, August 10, 1862, at the family farm outside the quiet little town of Norwich, Ohio, twelve miles east of Zanesville.

Armstrong knew that his parents were unhappy with him, given the events of the previous evening, but he was resolved to go into the 122nd Regiment of the Ohio Volunteer Infantry. As he splashed water on his face, washing the sleep out of his eyes and soaking the neatly trimmed auburn beard and mustache that he sported, he was not sure that they really understood the words "duty" and "honor" like he did. This was Abe Lincoln's war, the Southern states had violated the Constitution, and he was going to help the President win it with whatever small contribution he could make.

Sunday meant one thing to the Armstrong family: church. All day with three services, prayers, and devotions. The Norwich Methodist Church was on the corner of 1st Street and Cemetery Street, right in the center of town, five miles southwest of the farm. As he went downstairs, his mother was preparing breakfast of fried bacon, cornbread, apples, blueberries, and eggs, with hot coffee. She wasn't quite ready for the family to sit at the large table in the center of the room, so Tom, seeing his father on the porch, went out the door into the sunshine. "Good morning, Father. How are you on this fine summer day?"

William Armstrong looked up from the Bible he had been reading and saw his son standing there before him. "Well, good morning, Thomas. About time you got up. The girls are out milking the cows, but should be back shortly, and I expect to see Jacob soon. He was out checking on the sheep. I'm glad you came out here since I want to talk to you about last night. Not right now as we have to leave for church by 8:30, so I can open it up for everyone. I am leading the worship today. I have been out here for a while trying to figure out what I am going to say in my sermon; you know, forty-five minutes is a long time for me to talk. With God's help, I'll be fine once I get started," he assured his son. "Perhaps there will be time between the morning and afternoon services when we can talk."

Sitting down on the swing, Tom Armstrong said, "Just let me know, Father. I would like that very much since I want you and Mother to understand why I am doing this and then to respect that decision. I know you all will worry, but it is in God's hands. Now, there's a sermon topic for you." His father chuckled and went back to his Bible just as Jane came out and rang the bell on the porch to tell Mary, Fla, and Jacob that it was time for breakfast. Mary and Flavilla had stabled their horses and were walking toward the house as Lucky came charging across the nearby field with Jacob riding tall.

Tom walked back into the house to the delight of Gus and Frank who had just come downstairs. They jumped up on him and knocked him down, just missing Jane's spinning wheel. He loved wrestling with them. They squealed with laughter as he tickled them. "They won't understand when I leave, but that is all right. Mother and Father can help with that," he thought to himself.

Jane put the breakfast on the table just as Mary and Fla came into the house, and they heard the whinny of Jacob's horse, Lucky, not far away. William Armstrong said the grace, thanking the Lord for the bounty and silently asking for the deliverance of his son from the Confederate army. As soon as they had finished eating, the girls took the dishes and cooking pots down to the creek, and Jacob went out to the stable to tack Maude and Betsy and to hitch them to the wagon. Lucky was tied to the post outside the barn by the watering trough, so Jacob was ready to go. Tom came out, went to the stable, and saddled and bridledAspen for the five-mile trip into Norwich. His sisters and brothers climbed into the bed of the wagon, Jane gave the basket with the day's meals to Flavilla, and she and William climbed up to the front seat. William took the reins, and off they went, with Jacob and Tom riding along behind.

It took them about an hour to get to the church that had been constructed some 30 years earlier. A fire destroyed the original wooden building in 1842, so the members decided to build a brick replacement on the same plot of land. Norwich Methodist Church was a small country chapel, really, as it only had the vestibule where people could hang their hats and coats and, if they had worn a sidearm, it would go in the box that was specifically designed for that purpose. There were eight wooden pews in the sanctuary, separated by an aisle that allowed people to move in and out and also served to separate the men and women as well. Men on one side. Women on the other. The pews had been cobbled together by the men of the church from the massive oak trees in the nearby woods. Nothing fancy, just a straight back with no carvings of any sort. There was room for eight parishioners in each pew, sixteen all the way across, and, as they entered, they would pick up a kneeling pillow for use when the prayers were being said. There was an altar in front with an elevated pulpit off to the right as you faced the front.

The family said their last words to each other about thirty minutes before each service, as there was to be no talking before the service which allowed the people to prepare for worship. There was also no talking after the service to allow for reflection and prayer. William Armstrong unlocked the door to the church and opened it. He figured that there would be over one hundred people there, as Norwich was home to just over three hundred, most of whom were farmers, with Methodism attracting a good portion of them.

At precisely 10:30AM, William stood at the altar and announced the singing of the opening hymn, four verses only. When the congregation sat down, he launched into an extemporaneous prayer which ended with a plea for the safety of the boys who were about to go off to war. He read from the Old and New Testament, closed the Bible, stepped up to the pulpit, and began his sermon. Tom really wasn't paying too much attention until his father got to the part about the abolition of slavery. That woke him up, for he really didn't know that William would go that public with his condemnation of it. Then, he mentioned that there would be a recruiting meeting at the church on Wednesday evening. And, like he had said on the porch earlier that morning, he really got going. Many of the people in the congregation wanted to stand and cry out "Hallelujah," but such behavior was prohibited in Methodist church services. At revivals, it was expected, but not on Sunday. When he was finished, he announced the closing hymn, sung reverently by the congregation, and closed with the apostolic benediction from 2nd Corinthians.

Silently, the Armstrongs ate some of the food that Jane had brought, sitting at a table that had been designed just for that purpose, between the church and the cemetery. The next service wasn't until 3 o'clock. Around 1:30 or so, William got up and tapped Tom on the shoulder, meaning it was time for them to talk. They walked out behind the little church and sat down on the south bank of the creek that gurgled its way west toward the Muskingum River.

"Thomas," he began, "your mother and I understand your reasoning for going back into the army. But, we are saddened, especially because we lost Wilbur last March, and we do not want to lose you as well. But, that's not our choice. I started thinking about something you said last evening about the possibility of death. You said, 'It is in God's hands.'"

"Yes, I truly believe it is. I talked with Charlie McCabe about it for a long time, and he feels the same way."

"That's what I was thinking about this morning when you came out on the porch. I had just said to myself, 'You are going to stand up in front of a hundred of your friends and neighbors and preach the Gospel, asking them to believe and trust in God. And, at the same time, you couldn't feel that same faith that your son exhibited last night.' I was unhappy with myself. It seemed quite hypocritical to me. How can I ask the people to do what I showed last night that I couldn't? Kept me up all night."

Tom Armstrong said nothing, waiting for his father to finish.

"I resolved early this morning that I will support you in any way I can and will put your fate in the Lord's hands. And, I will put my faith and trust in His will."

"Thank you, Father. Have you told Mother?"

"No, but I will later today, after the 3 o'clock service."

William got up, looked at his son with pride and affection, and started back toward the church. "You coming?"

"No, not just yet. I reckon I want to think about things for a minute or two." Tom Armstrong felt very relieved. His family would worry, he knew, as they should, so he would try to sound as positive as he could about his circumstances in every letter he sent home. And, also in the ones he would send to Francis Porter.

Some time passed. While he was idly throwing rocks and stones into the creek, he heard Jacob coming down the hill. "T. S., it's time for the next service." And, then, "how was your talk with Father?"

"Better than I expected," he responded. "It's going to be all right. Oh, are you coming to the meeting on Wednesday? I would like you and Father to be there. I will ask him," said Tom Armstrong, walking up the hill with his older brother toward the church. "I also need to tell him and Mother that Charlie and Rebecca McCabe are coming here on Tuesday. Charlie wants to do the meeting."

The rest of the day was kind of blurry for Thomas Sumption Armstrong. While he wanted to, he couldn't concentrate on what was being said at the afternoon service. He was just thinking about what he and Charlie would do on Wednesday night. "I suppose he will do what Colonel Ball did in Putnam, and I will sign them up just like Major Granger did." The service over, the family had a light supper, after which he and his sisters went for a walk. The Prayer Service wasn't until 6:30, so they had time. As they walked down 1st Street, he told them about his conversation with their father and how relieved he was. He said that he hoped they would put his fate in God's hands, too, but he also said that worrying about loved ones in danger is just human nature, repeating the words of Charles McCabe. Flavilla and Mary Armstrong loved their older brother and feared for him, but they said they would do the best they could. They shared a quick embrace and started back to the church where he found his mother waiting.

"I just spoke with your father about his resolving the dilemma he told me about last night after you went in. He is a man of great faith, and I wish I had the same. You are a lot like him, for which I am thankful, as I hope someday you will be the wonderful husband and father that he is."

Tom's mind flitted to thoughts of Frank Porter. "I hope so, Mother, and I hope you understand why I am doing this."

"Yes, I do, but I wouldn't be honest if I didn't say I am frightened for your safety and can only pray for your safe return to us. I love you, Thomas."

"That's all I can ask, Mother. I love you, too." He embraced her. He thought to himself, "I wonder if Frank will understand like this. I sure hope so."

He was sitting on the porch the following Tuesday afternoon when Rebecca and Charles McCabe arrived in their buggy from Putnam. "Whoa, Chestnut," ordered Charlie McCabe as he reined in the big, roan gelding. Armstrong went down the porch steps to greet them, took the reins from his friend, and wrapped them around the hitching rail in front of the house.

"Welcome, friends. It is good to see you. Thank you for coming out. Won't you come inside and see my mother?"

"Thank you, Tom," said Rebecca McCabe. "We are glad to be here, as I haven't seen Fla and Mary in a long time."

"You will have all day tomorrow, Beccie," said her husband, "while T. S. and I get ready for the meeting."

They went inside where Jane was puttering around the kitchen area. She wiped her hands on her apron and greeted the visitors warmly.

"We can go out to the porch with a glass of lemonade, but if you are in need, the outhouse is over yonder."

"Lemonade will be fine," said Rebecca McCabe. "Thank you, Mrs. Armstrong."

"Oh, please call me Jane. The girls, Jacob, and my husband are out in the fields somewhere, but I can ring for them," as she moved toward the bell on the porch post.

"That won't be necessary," replied Charles McCabe. "Let them do their work while we have daylight. We can have a good visit when they come in."

"Charlie," Tom said, "let me get your things and get Chestnut to the stable for the night. He's probably thirsty, and, I imagine, hungry. There's a watering trough right by the stable, and I can get him a bag of oats." He took the carpet bag into the house, and when he came back out, went to take care of the McCabes' horse. Jane Armstrong and Rebecca McCabe were chatting away, as if Charlie wasn't even there. He got up and walked slowly toward the barn.

While the end of the work day approached, Mary and Fla walked up to the house. They were very glad to see Rebecca McCabe and soon got to talking about everything that had happened since the last time they had seen each other. Rebecca and Mary were about the same age, with Fla being several years younger. They engaged in "girl talk," as Tom and Charlie called it. The two men went down the steps to greet Jacob and William as they rode up.

"Hello, Reverend," said William. "I don't believe I have had the pleasure," shaking hands with Charles McCabe. "This is my oldest son, Jacob."

"It is nice to meet you both. T. S. has told me a lot about you, including that you are a Class Leader at your church," looking at Tom's father. There were eight Class Leaders of the Methodist church spread around Norwich who convened Bible study classes every Wednesday evening.

"Yes, Charlie," Tom said. "He preached a wonderful sermon last Sunday," admitting to himself that he hadn't listened to a lot of it. "Surprised me when he addressed the slavery issue."

McCabe addressed the issue, "I think that's the main reason the Southern states seceded and why we are in this awful war. Its economy is based on it and has been for as long as people know. It's a basic part of their culture, an institution."

Supper was ready, and they all went inside. William Armstrong asked the Reverend McCabe to bless the food, which he did. The conversation centered on the war and the formation of the 122nd O. V. I. Soon, it was bedtime for Frank and Gus, and Jane took them upstairs. The others who had gone out on the porch remained there, continuing the conversation.

"Mr. Armstrong," McCabe began. "Would you do us the honor of opening the recruiting meeting tomorrow night, encouraging the young men to enlist?" William was quite surprised at the invitation, thinking to himself "I didn't want my son to go, and now I am being asked to have the sons of friends and neighbors go."

He remembered the talk he and Tom had on Sunday, and said, "Reverend, it would be my pleasure," thinking that Divine Providence was testing him already. Looking at Tom and Jacob, "Why don't I ride with Charles in the buggy tomorrow night, and you boys can follow?"

The following day, the girls saddled Maude, Betsy, and Aspen and were off to see the rest of the farm. They talked about the war and how frightened they were for Tom and Charles. Mary told Rebecca about the conversation Tom had with their father after church. Rebecca McCabe thought she had better tell her husband about it. William, Jane, and Jacob had chores to do, getting to them bright and early. That left Charles McCabe and Tom Armstrong alone to plan the meeting.

"I hope you don't have high expectations," Tom said. "There's only about three hundred people living here in Norwich Township, and I don't expect there will be more than thirty young men showing up. We could go to town today and call on people if that would help. I doubt, though that we can get to many of the farms."

"I see, well, it couldn't hurt to go, I don't suppose."

They hitched Chestnut to the buggy and were off to the little town. On the way, they talked about how the meeting would go, using the one in Putnam as the only example they had. Arriving in Norwich around 10 that morning, they split up with Tom walking down 1st Street toward North Sundale, knocking on the door of every house on the way. McCabe did the same on North Street, meeting Armstrong at the corner of North Sundale and Main. They would tackle the stores, shops, and saloons together. Their work was done around noon, so it was back to the farm for dinner, even though it was late and the others had already eaten.

As they were preparing to leave the next evening, William assured Jane that they would have something to eat when they got back from the meeting later that evening. Chestnut was waiting patiently in the stable, as McCabe had just finished feeding and watering the big gelding when Rebecca came out. "Charles, I need to talk to you."

She then told her husband about the conversation between Tom and his father the previous Sunday.

"Oh, my," he said. "I think it is good that he and I will have an hour or so to talk on the way to the meeting."

It was a hot, humid day that August 13, 1862 in central Ohio when the four men started for Norwich. Tom kept looking to the west to see if those massive thunderstorms they experienced at this time of year would strike them, but the sky looked clear for which he was grateful. He wished he could hear the conversation that was taking place in the buggy just ahead of him and his brother.

McCabe commenced the conversation, saying "Mr. Armstrong, I had a long talk with T. S. the afternoon of the meeting in Putnam. He was conflicted about going back into the Union army, especially because he had seen the elephant, war at its worst at Shiloh. He knows he will be in harm's way and that scared him, even though he has masked it well. I told him that most every man in the service feels the same way. There are exceptions, but two things help them overcome their fear. First, there is the tremendous commitment to patriotism and the individual sense of duty. It is the basis upon which this country was founded 86 years ago, and those of us in the North feel a significant pull toward preserving the Union.

"Second, and this is a little more difficult. I asked Thomas if he trusted in the Lord. In other words, did he trust God enough to put his fate in His hands? He took a moment or two and said that he did, thanks to what you and your lovely wife had taught him and the rest of your children over the years. Then, this afternoon, I was told about what you had said to him last Sunday when the two of you talked down by the creek after the service. He appreciated that very much. He doesn't want to disappoint the two of you. Yes, you will worry. That's only natural. But as I have told him, and will be telling many of the boys who are going to war with the 122nd, the cornerstone of their lives is their faith and that trust. What you felt when he said he was going back in happens in every family. So, as best you can, you must have that faith and trust as well."

William Armstrong paused to ponder what he had just heard. "Thank you, Reverend. As you know, we lost Tom's younger brother, Wilbur, last March, and we have not gotten over it yet. It has been a severe test of our faith and trust, and we have made some progress, I think. But, the thought of losing Thomas as well frightens us immensely. We will come to grips that he might not come back, and we will help each other if he does, and, if he doesn't. That is my pledge to you, sir, and to Thomas."

They rode on in silence, arriving at the Norwich Methodist Church around 6. William unlocked and opened the front door. Jacob and Tom lit candles to illumine the sanctuary. Their father stood by the door, instructing those who were coming into the church as to where to hang their hats and to put their sidearms. He didn't want anyone to get a little out of hand and shoot a hole in the ceiling when the show got going. Jacob and Tom unbuckled their gun belts and put them in the box under the hat rack. Isaac and Jeremiah Kearney, along with their cousin, Thaddeus Brennan, came up the walk. Isaac had volunteered to play the piano, with Jeremiah with his fiddle, and Thaddeus with his guitar. The music wouldn't be as good as it was a week ago in Putnam, but at least they would have a band, no matter how small it might be.

At a little before seven o'clock, the little band struck up "*Yankee Doodle*," and the show was on. William Armstrong walked up to the pulpit and began the meeting with prayer. He then told the gathering that everyone knew why they were there, talking about patriotism, duty, and honor. It was like he had heard Col. William Ball's words in Putnam. He aroused the crowd and let them know that unlike church on Sunday, they were free to speak at any time. The band played *Yankee Doodle*, with Chaplain McCabe taking the lead in the singing with his rich, baritone voice. Then it was his turn to speak.

"Volunteering in the service of others is essential to our democracy and to our form of government, and basically, to our culture. Whether it is volunteering to lead a church service, as Mr. Armstrong did this past week, or serving in local government, on the school board, in the army, or even helping your neighbor raise a barn, volunteering is essential to what the founders wanted when they wrote the Constitution. We are given the obligation and the right to elect our government officials and, in doing so, agree to be governed by them. We then have to hold them accountable while they work for us. The Declaration of Independence gives us life, liberty, and the pursuit of happiness, but there are some times when our liberty is threatened, as it is now, and we must fight for it. This, my friends, is the most serious volunteer opportunity that you will ever have in your life. But, that is exactly what we are asking you to do." The trio struck up *Yankee Doodle* once again, and McCabe led the singing.

The song concluded, McCabe said matter-of-factly, "If you are so inclined, please come forward and talk to Lieutenant Armstrong here about enlisting in the 122nd Regiment of the Ohio Volunteer Infantry."

A big, burly young man in overalls, checkered shirt, and a black vest, with blonde hair and an unkempt, long blonde beard stood up and started forward. He was well over 6 feet tall and significantly heavier than the 165 lb. Tom Armstrong. He strode purposefully down the aisle toward the altar.

"What's your name?" asked Lieutenant Tom Armstrong.

"I think you know, sir. It's Patrick Lewis Murphy, sir."

Tom Armstrong smiled. "Where do you live?"

"You know the answer to that, sir, as I go to the same church as you, this one, and was here last Sunday and heard your father's sermon. You know that I live just south of town on our farm. So, why did you ask, sir?"

There were chuckles from the congregation. "This young man," thought Tom Armstrong, smiling again and ignoring the question, "is going to be a handful. I hope we can instill some discipline in him."

"What is your purpose?"

Patrick Murphy looked at Lieutenant Tom Armstrong with a twinkle in his eye. "You know the answer to that, too, sir." More laughter. "I wish to enlist in the 122nd Regiment of the Ohio Volunteer Infantry."

"Sign here, Mr. Murphy." Patrick Lewis Murphy signed his name on the page marked "Soldiers of the 122nd Regiment of the Ohio Volunteer Infantry." And with that, there were cheers from the congregation. Murphy turned to face them, raised his hands above his head, clasped them together, and shook them back and forth as if he had won a prize fight. The crowd loved it. Three more young men came forward and signed the register. It was nearly 8 o'clock. The chaplain stood in the pulpit.

"I won't be leaving you, boys, as I have been made the Chaplain of the 122nd. So, I will be going with you. We will have services every week, and you can come talk to me any time you feel the need." And, then he began to sing…

"Mine eyes have seen the glory
Of the coming of the Lord
He is trampling out the vintage
Where the grapes of wrath are stored
He has loosed the fateful lightning
Of his terrible swift sword
His truth is marching on.

Glory, glory, hallelujah
Glory, glory, hallelujah
Glory, glory hallelujah
His truth is marching on.

I have seen him in the watch-fires
Of a hundred circling camps
They have builded him an altar
In the evening dews and damps
I have read his righteous sentence
By the dim and flaring lamps
His day is marching on.

Glory, glory, hallelujah
Glory, glory, hallelujah
Glory, glory hallelujah
His day is marching on.

I have read a fiery gospel
Writ in burnish'd rows of steel
As ye deal with my contemptors

So with you my grace shall deal
Let the hero, born of woman
Crush the serpent with his heel
Since my God is marching on.

Glory, glory, hallelujah
Glory, glory, hallelujah
Glory, glory hallelujah
Since God is marching on.

He has sounded forth the trumpet
That shall never call retreat
He is sifting out the hearts of men
Before his judgment seat
Oh, be swift, my soul
To answer him be jubilant, my feet
Our God is marching on.

Glory, glory, hallelujah
Glory, glory, hallelujah
Glory, glory hallelujah
His truth is marching on.
Our God is marching on.

In the beauty of the lilies
Christ was born across the sea
With a glory in his bosom
That transfigures you and me
And he died to make men holy,
Let us die to make men free
While God is marching on.

Glory, glory, hallelujah
Glory, glory, hallelujah
Glory, glory hallelujah
While God is marching on.

Not a sound could be heard when the Reverend Charles McCabe came to the end of the song. There was stunned silence, and you could have heard a pin drop. Tom Armstrong turned around and looked at his friend in awe.

"Will you teach us that song, Chaplain?" he asked.

"Yes, Lieutenant, you will know it well and will be singing it with fervor before we break camp and head out to serve Father Abraham."

Everyone knew what that meant. Cheers erupted, the Kearney boys and their cousin played *Yankee Doodle* as loud as they could, and the men in the little church sang the patriotic song as never before. But, it was time to head home. The sun would be setting soon. The Armstrongs and the chaplain retraced their steps from earlier that day, riding back to the farm.

"Reverend," William Armstrong began, "where did you get that hymn? It was just stirring."

"A woman by the name of Julia Ward Howe wrote it," McCabe explained. I saw it in the *Atlantic Monthly* last spring and found it to be a powerful anthem to the cause we are fighting for. And, as I thought about it, the song speaks to the faith and trust that I hope all the boys have when we are in danger."

"Can you give me the words and the music? I'd like to sing it in church the next time I am the Leader."

"Of course, Mr. Armstrong. I will be happy to."

The McCabes left for Putnam the next morning, but not before the Chaplain and Tom Armstrong had a talk about what was next.

"I will go see some of the boys who were at the meeting last night to see if they will enlist," Armstrong promised. Then, as planned. I am going to Coshocton, for we heard that there is to be a recruiting meeting on the 18th. Maybe I can get some of those boys to enlist as well. That gives me two weeks to round up as many as I can. I have orders to report to Camp Zanesville on September 1st. To keep people thinking about it here, we should have another meeting the week after next. Can you come back out?"

"I think so, maybe a week from this coming Monday, the 25th. I will let you know. In the meantime, when I get back to Putnam, I will tell the Colonel that you are following his suggestion about widening out the recruiting process. We have to find about 1,000 men for the regiment which seems like a lot right now. He told me that Daniel Gary is going to recruit in McConnelsville over in Morgan County, and Tom Black is spending some time in Cambridge, just down the road in Guernsey County. I hope that they are successful, and I pray the same for you."

The two men shook hands. "Goodbye, Charlie. See you in a week or so."

"So long, T. S. Good luck."

Rebecca was already in the buggy with the carpet bag stowed when Charles McCabe climbed aboard, took the reins, and hollered, "Home, Chestnut." And, away they went, going down the drive to the main road back to Putnam. Tom looked after them and waved. But, now, he had to get ready to go to Coshocton, twenty-nine miles northeast of Norwich. He would start early on Saturday morning, strapping his haversack to his saddle, filling his saddlebags with food, and sliding his Springfield hunting rifle into its holster by the horn of his saddle with the Colt safely in its gun belt, tightly buckled around his waist. "Never know who I might meet on this trip," he thought to himself. It would take him about 3 hours to get to Coshocton. Aspen loped along at a very easy gait.

He arrived in the town of eleven hundred residents around 10 o'clock, having passed through Adam's Mills, Conesville, and Tyndall, with Aspen at a walk through the little villages and pausing to let her have some water to drink. The Grace Methodist Church in Coshocton, built some 20 years earlier, was on 3rd Street between Locust St. and Chestnut St. He found it with no problem. He assumed that the parsonage was next door and knocked on the door. An older, rumpled, balding man with spectacles opened it and inquired of the young man's purpose.

"Hello, sir. My name is Thomas Armstrong, from Norwich, southwest of here, and I came hoping to participate in the recruiting meeting that is to take place on Monday at this church. I have been commissioned as 2nd Lieutenant of the 122nd O. V. I. and can use all the boys I can find."

The Rev. E. P. Jacobs had been the pastor at the church for fifteen years now, and everyone in Coshocton knew him. "Well, Mr. Armstrong. You are certainly welcome to attend and speak if you so wish. I will be speaking about that in church tomorrow. I also have some things to say about the war, in general. Will you be there?" Tom Armstrong said he would make every effort, but his first concern was finding a hotel for the next three nights. "I will take you to meet Mrs. Workman, just down the street. She worships with us every Sunday."

That taken care of, he could enjoy the services the next day which he found to be remarkably like the ones at the little church in Norwich. And, yes, Pastor Jacobs did have a few things to say about the war, much like he had heard from his friend, Charlie McCabe. It all came down to patriotism, honor, and duty in the service of the Union. And, it was also about slavery. As he concluded his remarks, he reminded the congregation about the meeting to be held the next night at 7 o'clock. After Evening Prayer, Tom walked back to Mrs. Workman's place, made sure that Aspen was comfortable in the stable out back, and retired for the night.

The meeting the next evening reminded him of the one in Putnam with the band playing, patriotic songs being sung, and stimulating orations being made. It was curious, he thought, that only one of the speakers was actually going into the army. He was number two, as he was asked to say a few words about the 122nd, which he did, saying that he hoped many of the men would come and join him at Camp Zanesville early the next month. He invited the young men in the audience to come forward to enlist. Five of them did. He recognized one of them, a fellow named Edwin Bristow. He'd seen Bristow at church in Putnam that summer while he was attending the Teachers' Institute. Bristow's sister, Eleanora, was a teacher in Putnam, and he must have come to visit her and her husband, Gerald Parker, from time to time.

"Mr. Bristow, it's good to see you. I hadn't noticed you when I was speaking," Tom said, greeting the young man. Bristow looked no more than 21 years old, was just about Tom's height, but bigger across the shoulders.

"Lieutenant Armstrong, it is good to see you, too, and I am here with my friends and want to help the Union."

"Thank you. I have three questions for each of you and then a favor to ask."

Tom Armstrong questioned the boys, one by one, starting with Edwin Bristow. When the registration was complete, and the patriotic music and cheers had faded, he asked the favor.

"Mr. Bristow. You know most of the boys who were here tonight. I have to get back home, so I was wondering if I could count on you and these friends to do some recruiting for the regiment."

Edwin Bristow looked at his pals and saw heads nodding in the affirmative.

"Be glad to. We can start tomorrow. By the way, when do we report?"

Armstrong looked him square in the eye and said, "First week of September at Camp Zanesville. We can use as many as you can find."

"We will go to work, Lieutenant, and we will see you, with more friends in two or three weeks' time."

"Thank you for this. It won't be a picnic, believe me, as I have seen the effects of war, and they aren't pretty. It's called 'seeing the elephant.' Shiloh was a two-day bloodbath. I know, I was there. I will tell you, there will always be the temptation to run when things turn against you, but we will train you and equip you the best we can. I have also been told that the majority of men forget their fear when the bullets start flying, for they are too busy to think about it. I just want you to know what you are getting yourselves into.

He continued, "Our chaplain, Reverend Charles McCabe, is a man of God, always preaching faith and trust in Him. Just some things for you boys to think about. Oh, one last thing. When you arrive at camp, we will tell you the provisions you may wish to take with you in a box. There will be time to tell your folks so that they may come back with it before we leave."

"We have talked with others who have returned from the war and heard the same thing. So, we think we understand. It's about time we get on home," Edwin Bristow concluded.

Tom Armstrong shook hands with all five and watched them walk out of the church into the night.

Next morning, he put the bridle and saddle on Aspen, took the provisions Mrs. Workman had given him, slid the rifle into its holster, buckled his gun belt, and was on the road back to Norwich. When he got there, he stopped at the Kearney farm, not far from the Armstrong's, and inquired of Mrs. Kearney of the whereabouts of the boys.

"Out in the field with the sheep or tending to the stable roof that keeps leaking," she replied. "Maybe they're logging. Not real sure what they are up to. My husband is out there, too."

"Which way?"

She pointed to the northwest. "I would guess out yonder, before you get to those big oak trees."

"Thank you, ma'am." He rode slowly down the path, at the end of which he turned Aspen to the left and encouraged her to run. Galloping across the fields, he could see the sheep, hoping that Isaac and Jeremiah were there. They were. Slowing Aspen to a walk, he greeted them.

"How are you boys today?" he asked.

"Right fine," answered the older, taller Isaac Kearney. Tom looked past him and saw Jeremiah walking toward him. "Goodness," he thought. "I never realized that this boy is almost as big as Patrick Murphy."

"I want to talk to you and your cousin about joining the 122nd. Have you thought about it?"

"Yes, we have been expecting you, and yes, we have talked it over with our parents. Our family doesn't like it, but they understand why it is necessary. We've decided all three of us are going to join you. We don't really understand all of this Constitution stuff, but we do have faith in Mr. Lincoln."

"All it means, Isaac, is that we Americans are free to make our own decisions and take actions as long as we don't hurt anyone. There's more to it, but that's the basic idea. I am very glad you are coming along. Can you come into town tomorrow to sign the register? I will be in the church around 10 o'clock in the morning. Make sure you bring Mr. Brennan, too."

"We will do that. Thaddeus is more excited about this than we are. We will see you then."

They shook hands, and Tom took off for home, thinking, "I have eleven now. Not many, but we still have time." When he arrived at the house, he hitched Aspen to the rail and took his saddle bags, haversack, and rifle into the house.

"There's mail for you, Thomas," said his mother. "Father was in town last Saturday after you left and brought these home for you," handing him two envelopes. One had a postmark of "Putnam" and the other marked "Hopewell." Instantly, he knew that the letters were from Charlie McCabe and Francis Porter.

Sitting down on the porch, he read the one from McCabe who had written that he could be in Norwich on Monday, the 25th, for the next recruiting meeting. He wondered, he wrote, if William could be there as well. Tom was sure that he would. Reading the second letter, he would have to think a bit harder about how to respond. Frank Porter wanted him to come to Hopewell for a visit. She said she was lonely and longed for a walk with him on the trails of the Porter farm. "This is getting interesting," he thought. "I wonder if I can get over there before I have to report. It's only twenty-five miles from here." At that point, she did not know that he was going back in.

He wrote a few lines to McCabe, asking him to be in Norwich for the meeting the following Monday at 7 o'clock. The chaplain could stay at the house once again and be back in Putnam the next day. He also asked his friend to bring the words and music to that hymn he had sung at the first recruiting meeting. *The Battle Hymn of the Republic* he called it. But, now, he had things to do to get ready, thinking that maybe he could get to Hopewell later in the following week if all went well with the preparations. The meeting would be the same as the other one, but he better ask the Kearney boys and their cousin to be there to play some patriotic songs again. Then, he thought, maybe they only know *Yankee Doodle*, smiled to himself, and unpacked his gear, putting it all away.

He realized that if he was going to Hopewell, he would have to start assembling the things he would need in camp.

"Jacob, can you build me a box for the stuff I am taking to camp? I need it by Friday, and hopefully you have time to do that. The lid needs to fit tightly and if you could hinge it, that would be terrific."

"I will see what I can do. How big?"

"Maybe 3 feet long, 2 feet wide, and 18 inches deep."

"I'll give it a shot."

Next, he had to talk to his mother about the things he would need to see if she had them or if he had to ride into Norwich to the General Store. He was lucky that he remembered what he had taken with him to camp with the 78th and what was more important, he knew what he should have taken and hadn't. The army would issue his uniform, cartridge box, rifle, percussion cap, ammunition, and some food. The rest would be up to him. Taking pencil to paper he wrote out a list: drawers, shirts, socks, vest, scissors, eating utensils, cooking pan, canteen, comb, sewing kit, pocket knife, plate, cup, Bible, books to read, writing paper, pencils, eraser, his violin and bow, and a big ham or two.

Jane Armstrong looked at the list and shook her head. "This will take some doing, Thomas. But, you will need to go see Mr. Wescott at the Emporium in Putnam, as I don't think Mr. Turner would have all of this here in Norwich." She had plenty of clothing for him; a comb, the paper, pencils, and eraser; and could put together a sewing kit. She also had plenty of ham and mutton. Tom kept the violin in its case on a shelf in the upstairs hall. The case would have to be left behind But, for the rest, he would have to take the buckboard to Zanesville. He asked Jacob if he wanted to go.

"Not until I get the box done. You want it painted?

"If you can, sure. But I would welcome your company going over there and getting the things I need.

"You taking your rifle to camp?"

"Nah, they give me one. I am fearful that the others won't know how to use the Enfield. It's different than the ones we were issued before we went to Fort Henry and Fort Donelson. And, it is quite different from my Springfield. But, I learned to fire it pretty well before we left. Aims different. Have to shoot low."

"You'll have to show me some day. For now, let me get the box done. Maybe we can go to Zanesville and Putnam on Friday or Saturday."

"That'd be good. I can stop by and see Charlie while we're there." He went back inside, tore up the first letter he had written to his friend, and wrote him another brief letter about the meeting, saying that he would stop by later in the week.

Aspen was right there, hitched near the steps to the porch, so he put his left foot in the stirrup, pulled himself up, adjusted the wide-brimmed black hat, made sure the rifle was secure, and started for town with the letter. The Colt revolver was snug in its holster in one of his saddlebags. He didn't think he would need it, this being a Tuesday afternoon, but you just never knew.

"Jacob, I will be back as soon as I can get this letter in the mail. I can help you with the box if you would like." And, then he was off, loping down the path to the main road to Norwich.

A couple hours later, Jacob heard hoofbeats coming up the path. Tom reined in Aspen, dismounted, and led her to the watering trough outside the stable. He took the bridle, saddle, the blanket, rifle holster, and saddlebags off the big mare and let her drink to her heart's content. When she was finished, he led her to her stall, gave her a bag of oats, and closed the door as he walked over to find Jacob.

"I'll finish it tomorrow," his brother said. "Then I can paint on Thursday and Friday. We can go to Putnam when I get done."

They heard the bell ring, meaning it was almost time for supper. William would be along soon, and Tom would tell the family about his adventure in Coshocton, hoping that Edwin Bristow and his friends would deliver many recruits to Camp Zanesville. After supper, he asked his father if he needed any help with the sheep or anything else, since his mother was working on the provisions, and he and Jacob weren't going to Zanesville for a couple of days.

The next morning, father and son rode out to the east pasture on the property, ready to start reinforcing the fencing. They rode quietly, until Tom said, "Father, next week, after we get everything ready for me to report, I plan to go to Hopewell to see the Porters. I haven't heard from George for awhile."

William said "Very well. Please give our regards to John and Amanda, and say hello to Miss Francis and her brothers and sisters," a wry smile crossing his face. His son hadn't said anything about Francis Porter, but her father, John, had sent him a letter the past spring, indicating that perhaps there was something going on between the two of them. It was a pleasant little secret that he had shared only with his wife.

They worked all morning, then heard the bell indicating it was time for dinner, so they rode back to the house where Jane had put out a fine spread of chicken, potatoes, some beans from the garden, and, of course, hot apple pie, with lemonade and coffee to wash it all down. That afternoon, the fence repair continued, the box was finished, and the provisions were being assembled. Mary and Fla were darning some of Tom's socks, having created a sewing kit for their big brother. They hoped they had time to teach him how to sew.

On Friday morning, Jacob put the second coat of paint on the box and proceeded to set it in the sunshine to dry. He hitched Maude to the buckboard, and the Armstrong brothers were off to Zanesville and Putnam. William had given them enough money, they hoped, and had taken a little of their own just to be sure. They talked about the war, when they needed to leave so Tom could report, and the importance of Jacob remaining strong as Tom marched into danger. Both of them were worried about their mother who still grieved over their brother, Wilbur. They talked about that, but neither one knew what to do about it, if anything could be done.

They ate some of the food that Jane had packed and entered the town just after noon, going straight to the Emporium owned by Chauncey Wescott, across the Y Bridge and turning left on Pine Street, then straight to Front Street, before turning right on Main. Wescott wasn't there. Going in the front door, he saw Judith Wescott standing behind the counter. "Howdy, Mrs. Wescott," Jacob said. "Tom, here, needs some things to make his life livable when he goes back in the army in a few days."

"Whattya need, Thomas?" Judith Wescott asked, wiping her hands on her apron. Tom gave her the list. Looking at it, she said, "Shouldn't take too long to gather this stuff up. Chauncey and I can have it ready in less than an hour if I can get him out of the bar."

Tom Armstrong remembered that Chauncey Wescott owned the saloon next door and divided his time between it and the store. Judith Wescott, for the most part, ran the store. Rumor was that Chauncey Wescott took a belt of whiskey or two during the day as he chatted with his customers. "Good for business," he would tell his wife, she looking at him in disapproval.

"Jacob, can you help Mr. and Mrs. Wescott with this while I run down to see Charlie McCabe?"

Jacob Armstrong looked at his brother. "This is your stuff, not mine," he thought to himself. "Sure, but don't tarry too long."

Tom ran down Main Street straight north, breathlessly walking up the front porch steps to Charlie and Rebecca McCabe's house. "It's tough running in these boots," he thought, wiping the sweat off his face with his bandana. He knocked on the door. Rebecca opened it and asked him in.

"Charles is in his study, Tom," she said, guiding him down the hall.

"T. S.," the reverend exclaimed. "I got your letter and will be pleased to join you on Monday evening. How did Coshocton go?"

Armstrong explained about seeing Edwin Bristow and signing him and his friends up.

"Ah, I remember him. His sister and her husband live in the next block on Woodlawn Avenue. They attend services regularly. Nice people," McCabe mused.

"How did Captain Gary and Lieutenant Black do?" Tom asked.

"I don't know for sure. I haven't seen Major Granger to get a report. We will find out in due time."

"Charlie, I have to get back to Mr. Wescott's store. Can you be at the church by 6:30 on Monday? My father will be pleased to preside as he did the last time, but he does want the words and music to *The Battle Hymn*."

McCabe smiled and said, "Without a doubt. I hope everyone sings along."

"Father will, but you know I won't since I can't carry a tune in a bushel basket," Tom laughed. "Maybe I will bring my fiddle and help our little band out."

Charles McCabe walked his friend to the front door. "I will see you on Monday."

"Thanks, Charlie. See you then," Armstrong said, shaking hands with his mentor. He turned and started to walk back to Mr. Wescott's store. It was plenty hot and humid that August afternoon in Putnam, Ohio down by the river. He just took his time. When he arrived, Chauncey Wescott and Jacob were just sitting on the bench in front of the saloon, the carton of utensils in the back of the buckboard. Mr. Wescott had been right, as it didn't take much time at all. Assuming that the paint was dry, on Saturday, they would pack the box that Tom would take with him to Camp Zanesville.

On the way back to Norwich, Tom felt compelled to tell his brother about his pending journey to Hopewell to see the Porters. "Jacob, you ever thought about getting married? You're 30 now, and I'm a little surprised that you aren't."

"Never had the time or the wish," came the reply. "Father has me so busy on the farm that it just didn't make sense to me. Why'd you ask?"

"Now, you can't tell anyone about this, but I'm kinda sweet on George's sister, Francis, and I think she's sweet on me. We've been writing back and forth for a couple of years now, and I am thinking that maybe after the war, I might want to settle down, kinda like Charlie and Rebecca. So, after everything is made ready for me to report, I'm going to Hopewell to see her before I go."

"You're going to ask her to marry you? Now?" his brother said incredulously. He reined in Maude, stopping her and just stared at his little brother.

"No, I'm not," he said emphatically. "I don't have the courage to do that just yet. I hafta be sure about it. Just calling on the Porters to see how George is doing, and then maybe a little time with her. That's all." He thought to himself, "I have the courage to see the elephant but not to mention marriage to Frank Porter." He smiled at the thought. That would change.

Jacob Armstrong wasn't sure that he believed his brother, but he let it go. They were almost home and would have to get the carton out of the buckboard and take care of Maude. They took the things they had purchased at Wescott's store into the barn where the box lay open and stowed it all.

"Jacob, is this tight against rain?"

"It should be. Why?"

"I don't want my fiddle to get wet."

"Maybe if you take some oilskin, you could wrap it so the water couldn't get at it. You'll need one anyway. You should have had some or a rubber blanket when you left with the 78th. Probably why you got sick."

His brother agreed. Oilskin and a rubber blanket would have protected him from the rain and sleet as he and the others of the 78th faced the elements both on the march and when they were in camp. "I'll just stop at Wescott's again on my way home from Hopewell to get one."

Saturday dawned hot and muggy, but that didn't prevent the Armstrong men from going out to the pasture with the collies to make sure that everything was all right with the sheep. They wanted to make sure that all was peaceful, looking for any sign of a coyote. They didn't see any, but they had their hunting rifles good and ready just in case they did. They passed the day doing odd chores, Tom and Jacob oiling some of the hinges on the doors to the stalls, with Fla and Mary taking care of the little ones as Jane finished packing the box with Tom's belongings. She had done it willingly, as she loved her son, but underneath it all, she was very sad. She wouldn't let on to anyone about it but her husband, only to him.

The next day meant three services at the Norwich Methodist Church. In the first one, the Leader, Marcus Jenkins, was carrying on about the war and the evils of slavery. Tom Armstrong was there, but in body only, his mind being someplace else: Hopewell. He and Jacob had stopped by Jenkins' place to ask him if, as the Leader of this Sunday's services, he could mention the recruiting meeting that was to be held the next evening at 7PM. And, indeed, he did, and as he was talking about it, Tom spotted Patrick Murphy, who had turned around in a pew up front, winking at him. He smiled back, but he was still thinking about what he would say to Francis Porter and how she would react.

The Armstrongs arrived home as they usually did on Sunday evenings after a full day of worship and prayer. They were tired, and, on this night, they sat on the porch and talked about all they had heard that day. Marcus Jenkins had told the congregation that God was on the side of the Union. Tom Armstrong wasn't so sure that God took sides, but since silence had to be kept at church, he could not engage the leader in a conversation. He wasn't sure where his parents stood on the matter, and thought that he had already caused enough grief for them, it would do no earthly good to bring it up. He bade them good night and wandered off to bed, not before he took out paper, pen, and ink.

Norwich, O. Aug. 24th, 1862

Dear Friend Frank

When I came home I found a letter from you. I will come as soon as I can. I am very busy now & have been since I left school. We are doing what we can to save our county from a draft in this neighborhood. In fact, nearly all of this end of the county. I have not heard from the west end. I presume you know thus that we have undertaken the 122nd O. V. I. The military committee saw fit to put me on the list of commissions. I tried to serve my country as a soldier. I don't know as she will let me off with what I have done.

All last week I was recruiting. Tonight, Rev. C. C. McCabe and I will hold a recruiting meeting in Norwich. I have got 10 or 11 men so far. We will get more tonight. I think I am well. So are all my friends. My health is good. I weigh more than ordinarily.

I will come up as soon as I can. Business has the lead now. Our country calls & what can we do but enlist.

How nobly did the old 78th form themselves last fall to oppose Rebels? I tell you I look upon those old volunteers as heroes and heroes they are. God bless them. They deserve our best feelings. Brave fellows that they are.

Let me hear from you.

Farewell.

T. S. Armstrong

The meeting would actually be on Monday, August 25, 1862, and he would get to see her over in Hopewell later in the week as she had asked. He just hoped she would understand why he was going back into the army. When she received the letter and read it, she was not happy, the tears starting to roll down her face. Her brother, George, had already seen the elephant at Shiloh and would see considerably more action in the coming days, and she was afraid for him every day, saying her prayers for his safety. Now, her Tom was going back into serious danger. She had been worried sick when she received his letters about having the consumption and almost dying. This latest one only made her outlook worse. She just hoped she would get to see him before he left. She wanted to tell him how she felt. He, of course, would have to start that conversation, since it wasn't appropriate for women to bring up things like that.

The next afternoon with Jacob and William seated in the buckboard, Tom rode behind them on Aspen, headed for the meeting. They arrived a little after 6. William opened the church as the Rev. Charles McCabe pulled up in his buggy. "Howdy, Mr. Armstrong. I have something for you," as he hopped down, hitching Chestnut to the railing in front of the church. "T. S. told me that you would like to have the words and music for *The Battle Hymn of the Republic*. I copied them for you this afternoon," he said, handing William two sheets of paper.

"Thank you, Reverend," he said. "Will you be so kind as to lead us in it again tonight?"

"Of course, Mr. Armstrong. It will be my honor, as I love the spirit and message it has for us."

The meeting went as expected. The Kearneys and their cousin were there, and, as soon as Tom saw them, he realized that his violin was resting in the box that he would take to camp. *Yankee Doodle* came forth from the little band. William spoke, then came McCabe, both with the same message as they had delivered the week before. As the chaplain came to a close, the congregation was on its feet cheering and clapping at his words. He motioned for them to quiet down. Then, in that lovely baritone voice that cast a spell on everyone present, he began...

Mine eyes have seen the glory
Of the coming of the Lord
He is trampling out the vintage
Where the grapes of wrath are stored
He has loosed the fateful lightning
Of his terrible swift sword
His truth is marching on.

Glory, glory, hallelujah
Glory, glory, hallelujah
Glory, glory hallelujah
His truth is marching on.

At William's invitation, as McCabe began each of the verses, more and more men began to sing, and they finished with...

Glory, glory, hallelujah
Glory, glory, hallelujah
Glory, glory hallelujah
While God is marching on.

Everyone was standing and singing as loudly as they could. And then, just like the previous week, cheers for the Union and the president rang out. The meeting was a success as four more young men had come forward, but the recruiters still had work to do. Tom wondered how Edwin Bristow was doing over in Coshocton, Dan Gary had done in McConnelsville, and Tom Black had done in Cambridge, as they rode back toward the farm.

But, his mind was preoccupied with thoughts of Francis Porter. "She will not be happy, but I hope I can help her understand, just like I did with Mother and Father." He was ever so sure that going to Hopewell was the right thing to do as he prepared to go to Camp Zanesville. "No doubt about it," he said to himself. "No doubt about it."

3 Hopewell

On Wednesday morning, August 27, 1862, Tom Armstrong rose at sun-up since he wanted to get an early start to the Porter farm in Hopewell. It would take him a good two and a half hours to ride over there, some twenty-five miles to the west, and he did not want to push Aspen too hard, especially in the heat and humidity of August in south central Ohio. He had told his mother that he was going when he, Jacob, William, and Charles McCabe returned from the meeting the previous Monday evening. She asked him to remember her to the Porters, sending warm wishes and regards. Now that John and Amanda Porter and their family lived over in Hopewell, the Armstrongs did not get to see them very often, perhaps by chance in Zanesville, but always at the Muskingum County fair. Jane Armstrong was pretty sure that there was more to this visit than just finding out how George was.

Per his custom, Tom Armstrong made sure that Aspen was fed and watered before he put on the bridle and saddle. He patted the big, gray mare on the side of her head and said, "Well, girl, this is going to be interesting. I have to make sure that she understands why I am going back in, but I also have to tell her that she has become very important to me." Aspen whinnied as if to tell him that she understood. And, who knows? Maybe she did. He walked with the horse back to the house and slipped the reins around the hitching post, going inside for breakfast. Jane Armstrong smiled and asked, "You about ready to go?"

"Yep," was the reply, "as soon as I have breakfast and pack everything, I'll be going. Looks like it's going to be hot, and I don't want to push Aspen in weather like this."

Mary and Fla came in, having been out in the barn milking the cows, and pretty soon William and Jacob arrived, carrying their rifles into the house.

"Coyotes out there this morning," said Jacob. "We got three or four shots at them, and I think I hit one, but those beasts run like the wind. We'll go back out there after we eat to see if they come back."

It was the usual fare of bacon, cornbread, apples, and eggs, but Jane had picked some ripe plums out in the orchard which the family really loved this time of year. Coffee for everyone except Gus and Frank. Fla poured both boys a glass of milk. Tom didn't have much to say that morning. He wanted to get going.

"Excuse me, Mother, but it's time to go. I'll be back on Friday, probably early in the afternoon." He gave her a hug, shook hands with Jacob and William, tousled the hair of his little brothers, said goodbye to his sisters, and was out the door, with his haversack and rifle. His saddlebags were already fixed to Aspen's saddle. He'd had her since she was born eight years ago, and they were pretty much inseparable. Stuffing the Colt into the haversack, he put his left foot in the stirrup and swung himself up into the saddle.

"Okay, girl, here we go," patting her on the neck and then turning her to the left to walk down the path to the road. His pocket watch said just after 8 o'clock, so he figured he would arrive at the Porter's around 10:30 or so. He reminded himself that he had to stop by Wescott's Emporium on the way home for the oilskin, "but maybe," he thought, "I ought to stop in on the way to make sure Mrs. Wescott had one." He would do just that.

Hopewell Township was at the western edge of Muskingum County, just eight miles west of Zanesville on the National Road. It was farm country with herds of cattle and flocks of sheep in addition to vast fields of corn, wheat, barley, and oats, not to mention the orchards of pears, peaches, apples, and plums. The town of Hopewell reminded Armstrong a little of Norwich with houses on Main St. and Cross St, with little side roads that enabled the citizens to access their farms. There was a store, a Methodist church, and a saloon, but that was about it. He concluded that the Porters would have to go to Zanesville or Putnam for the supplies and foodstuffs that they could not make or grow themselves.

The Porter farm was four miles directly south of the little town, just off Cross St. Tom Armstrong rode into Hopewell about 10:30 just like he had planned, and when he got to the center of town, turned Aspen to the left and headed down Cross St. It was getting hot, and he sure could have used a cold drink, but that would have to wait until he arrived at the Porter farm. He hoped he could speak with John Porter first, to explain his presence there unannounced. Francis Porter had most likely told her parents about the letter she had received the day before in which he had said he would try to see her prior to reporting for duty. So, John knew Tom Armstrong would be coming over, he just wouldn't know when. Hopefully, he would understand, have the best interests of his daughter in mind, and permit him to court her, if only through letters that they would exchange during the war.

John Porter was 53 years old at the time, and his wife, Amanda, was just 40. They had married in 1838 when she was just 16 years of age, and he was 29. Francis Pamela Porter, better known as Frank, was born in 1840, making her 22 this day, five years younger than Tom Armstrong. She was the second of the Porter children, as her brother, George, had been born a year earlier. In addition to George, Frank Porter had three brothers, John, Jr., 20; Billy, 10; and Joe, 7; and three sisters, Huldah Jane,18; Mary, 17; and Amanda,13. They had lived up in Franklin Township until John Porter thought that it was getting "too crowded" with people and had moved the family to a farm of about fifty acres in Hopewell Township in the spring of 1860. The Armstrongs moved to Norwich a year later.

William Armstrong had done in Norwich exactly what John Porter had done in Hopewell: bought a working farm that really didn't need any significant repairs. John, Sr., George, and John, Jr. had tended to the huge flock of sheep; the cows and horses; the corn, wheat, and oats; and stable and barn while Amanda and the girls took care of the orchards of apples, peaches, and plums. Also, Francis and her sisters usually milked the cows first thing in the morning. They also minded the vegetable garden. John, Jr., aged 20, known to most as "Johnny," in George's absence assumed more of the work with the sheep and helped his father in making repairs to the house and other buildings when necessary. And so, the Porters were relatively self-sufficient.

It was right around 11 o'clock when Tom Armstrong turned off Cross St. and up the long trail to the Porter farmhouse. He had been there two or three times since they moved to Hopewell, but had really gotten to know the family when they lived near each other in Franklin Township. A couple of years earlier, maybe even before he went to college, he had noticed that George's kid sister had grown up into a very attractive young woman. That was when he asked for and received her father's permission to exchange letters with her.

Tom and George were best of friends, and it was George who started Tom thinking about enlisting in the Ohio Volunteer Infantry after the hostilities broke out at Fort Sumter in April 1861. When they decided to enlist, Armstrong had prevailed in convincing George, along with Tom's brother, Wilbur, and two friends, John Gillespie and Bob Hanson, to join the 78th O. V. I. that was being formed in Zanesville, and not a regiment being formed in Newark which was much farther from Hopewell.

The two sheepdogs, Boomer and Rascal, came bounding down the trail, barking as he was riding toward the house. They must have recognized him as the two dogs didn't take kindly to strangers. He dismounted, squatted down, and rubbed their shoulders and necks, saying, "How've you boys been? It's only been a few weeks since I've seen you." Recovering and feeling stronger, he had ridden to see the Porters in mid-July. But, it had been some time before that, what with enlisting, going on active duty with the 78th, getting sick, and finally going home to recuperate. The dogs were excited and continued barking when the little boys, Billy and Joe, came to see what was going on.

"Hi, Mr. Armstrong," the older of the two, Billy, said to him. "Are you here to see Father?"

"Billy," Tom said. "Call me Tom. You, too, Joe. Well, yes, I am. Do you know where he is?"

"Sure, he's out in the pasture with the sheep. I can show you if you want."

They walked up toward the house, with Billy running to the barn to get his pony. The saddle and bridle were in place, so he was ready to go. Amanda Porter came out of the house, saw Tom, and said, "Thomas, whatever are you doing here?" She did have an inkling about what was going on based on her conversation with Francis the night before. "You were here just a short time ago. And, now, Francis tells us that you are going back to the war with a new unit." Like her husband, she really had not expected him so soon after her daughter had read the letter.

Armstrong tipped his hat and said, "Yes'm, I am going back. Duty calls, and I just didn't think I had done enough with the old 78th. I just came to pay my respects and want to learn how George is doing, since I haven't seen you or the family for awhile, and may not see you until the war is over. Billy, here, says he will take me out to find John. I would very much like to speak with him."

"Of course, Thomas. You can ride back with him in time for dinner in about an hour."

"Much obliged. I will see you in a little bit, Amanda" he said throwing himself up on Aspen and tipping his hat once again. Billy Porter and Tom Armstrong turned and headed north across the rolling field behind the barn. Tom had rehearsed his pending conversation with John Porter on the way over and was glad that he was about to get it over with.

After a few minutes, Billy shouted, "He's over there," pointing to the stream that cut through the field where some of the sheep were grazing.

"Thanks, Billy, I can take it from here," encouraging Aspen to pick up the pace.

Billy reined in the pony, stopping, then turning back toward the house. "Good," Tom thought. "Didn't need him hearing what I have to say."

He slowed down as he approached John Porter. "Hello, John, how are you on this fine August day?"

"Thomas, what a surprise. It is good to see you. You're looking well and hearty."

"I'm pretty much healed and am regaining weight and strength. But I need to visit with you about something important. As I told you last time, I started taking instruction in how to be an effective teacher at the Teachers' Institute in Putnam. But, an odd thing happened a couple of weeks ago. After our last visit, I was in Putnam, attending the Institute, when I ran into an old friend and mentor from my days at Ohio Wesleyan who told me about the formation of another regiment, the 122nd, in Zanesville. For a number of reasons, I decided to go back into the war with the 122nd OVI. I don't think Frank knew that until I wrote to her last Sunday. It happened pretty fast."

"So, she told us when she received your letter yesterday. I had a feeling we would see you before long. What did your parents say?"

Tom climbed down from the saddle and shook hands with John Porter and said, "They were not pleased, and Mother may not be yet. But, they told me they would support my decision, and Father appears to be committed to saving the Union and ending slavery. He even preached about it at church a couple of weeks ago."

He went on, "Before I rode out here to see you, I spoke with Amanda and told her that I came out to Hopewell to pay my respects to you since I haven't seen you in a few weeks and may not see you again until after the war is over." Smiling, he went on, "As you might remember, three or four years ago, you gave me your permission to write to Frank which, as you know, we have been doing. Even though it has only been through the mail, I have developed feelings for her and would like your permission again, this time to court her, even though I will be far away."

John Porter had been expecting this since Tom's last visit in July and looked at the young man, thoughtfully, and, having done some rehearsing himself, said, "There are a couple of ways I can look at this, Thomas. I am concerned that you might not come back. Some rebel somewhere might just take aim at you, fire, and that will be the end of you. Francis would be heartbroken, just like all the wives who have become widows in this terrible conflict."

"I know, John, I know, and I am prepared in the event that happens. I have put my faith and trust in the Lord. His will be done. But I think that even if I do not court her, from the tone of her letters, she will be heartbroken anyway, if I don't come back," he said realistically.

John Porter tipped his hat back on his head and wiped his brow. It was getting warm this Wednesday in late August. He looked at Tom Armstrong with a seriousness on his face. "It has gone this far?" he asked.

"Yes, I think so, but that is why I am here. I need to share with her how I feel and to hear how she feels about me. But, I think I already know."

Smiling, now, John Porter said, "Thomas, the other way that I can look at this is this. You are a fine young man whom I have known all your life. You are a man of faith like I am, have had a fine education, will make a superior teacher one of these days, and would make a suitable husband for my daughter, if she will have you, when you get back. I have seen this coming and her concern for your welfare, and I will not stand in the way if that is what you would like to do. But, you need to talk with her about this today."

"I will and thank you, John. You will not be sorry. May I stay till Friday?" They mounted up and started walking the horses back toward the house, Tom being very relieved. Now, for the harder part, talking to Francis Porter about his feelings. He wasn't very comfortable in doing that.

"Certainly, like always, we'll put you up in the loft in the barn. You know where the outhouse is."

Frank Porter came out of the house when she heard the conversation between her father and her Tom. "Well, hello. Mother told me you were here. I'm glad. Come in, wash up, and we will have dinner."

"I am glad as well. It is very good to see you."

Her brothers and sisters were already at the huge table, waiting for the dinner to be served and wondering why Tom Armstrong was there. Perhaps the girls had an idea of what was happening, but not their brothers. Amanda busied herself with the cooking, saying, "Francis, can you and Mary take these platters to the table?"

"Certainly, Mother."

Tom had washed the dust and dirt from his face and hands and sat down between Billy and Joe, like he always had done when he came to visit with their big brother, George. While the ham, yams, corn and beans, and fresh, hot bread were being passed around, Tom asked John about George. The peach pie would have to wait.

"Before I do that, Thomas, how is your mother? Last time you were here, you said that she is still grieving."

Tom Armstrong responded, "Yes, she is, and the thought of me going back in hasn't helped, I am sure." He noticed a sadness in Frank Porter's face.

John Porter continued, "Please remember us to her. Now, about George. He is serving as an aide to Col. Leggett. Aide-de-Camp," he called it.

"Goodness," Armstrong said. "He's really moving up. Started as a sergeant and now he is aide-de-camp to the Colonel?" He would most likely be a courier, carrying the Colonel's orders to the company commanders. "Dangerous work," he thought. "Out in the open, making a fine target for rebel skirmishers."

"Good for him," Tom continued. "Any word on John Gillespie and Bob Hanson? All I know is that John was promoted to 1st Lieutenant last January."

"We haven't heard much, but there was some talk about Bob having been sick and may be losing the sight in his eyes."

"Poor Bob," said Tom Armstrong. "He's such a good friend. I hope that's not true."

Dinner concluded, John, Jr. took Armstrong and Aspen to the stable to get the horse some water and a bag of oats. He asked, "Can I call you Sump? I got a letter from George, and he tells me he and some of the other boys call you that."

"Sure, Johnny. Either way." Then, they went over to the barn, and Tom climbed the ladder into the loft, pitched his haversack and saddlebags into the hay and rested the rifle against the wall, loaded and ready. "Can't be too careful, what with coyotes and such around here."

"You want to go hunting tomorrow?" Johnny Porter asked. We can look for birds in the field or on the pond. Or, we can go after deer, rabbit, and squirrel. Mother makes a really good rabbit stew, and her squirrel stew ain't bad either."

"You bet," came the response. "I have some business to attend to, but a few hours out in the fields tomorrow morning would be first rate. I need to be going home on Friday morning, so tomorrow is all I have this time."

While Tom and Johnny were planning their hunting expedition, John and Amanda Porter were having a quiet conversation out near the vegetable garden. John didn't want the children around and had asked Francis to take care of the little ones while Huldah Jane and Mary washed the dishes, pots, and pans, drawing water from the well into a large bucket, washing everything, and setting it all in the sun to dry.

"Thomas asked me before dinner if he could court Francis," John told his wife, "even though he is going back into the army. He said that apparently they have developed feelings for each other, and he is here to talk with her about that, to make sure he isn't seeing something that isn't there."

Amanda Porter had seen this coming. "Oh, my. And, what did you tell him?"

"What could I tell him? I told him it was fine with me, but that he better talk with Francis about it. Do you remember talking about this as a possibility some time ago? Well, now he has brought it out into the open. I think that she will be very pleased, but we shall see."

"My, oh, my," said Amanda Porter. "George is courting Grace, and now Thomas will be courting Francis. John, are we getting old?"

"Yes, my dear, we are. We have two grown children who are now moving on to a very important stage of their lives. Watch out, though, Johnny will be next, then Huldah, then Mary."

"Oh, John, don't rush things. Let's not go that far." He laughed and said they should get back to the house as he had work to do. Harvest time was almost here, and he had to get prepared. They walked back toward the house. Johnny and Tom came out of the barn just about the same time.

Amanda spoke privately to Tom Armstrong. "Thomas, go back over to the stable and saddle your horse. I think you and Francis are going for a ride. I will send her over there."

"John told you?"

"Yes, he did, and I am very pleased about that even though you are going back in. Can you tell us tonight how you came to that decision?"

"I will do that. I would like to talk with Frank first. Maybe the dogs would like to run with the horses."

"I'm sure they would, but you have to find them. Maybe they will just find you and Francis. She can call them."

Tom Armstrong turned and started back to the stable. He retrieved the Springfield from the loft in the barn and was in the process of getting Aspen ready for a ride when Frank Porter came into the stable.

"Now this is awkward," he thought to himself.

"I hope you don't think this is too forward of me," he stammered, "but I thought maybe you would like to go for a ride this afternoon. That is, if you don't have anything else that you need to do."

Francis Porter smiled, thinking, "So, going for a ride is why he's here? I asked him to come over in my letter, and he said he would try. Now he's here. Hmmm…He's been awful friendly recently in his letters and the last time he was here. I wonder if Mother knows something that she's not telling me. Maybe that is why she was smiling when she told me to come out here. Okay, so let's go find out." She, then, admitted to herself that she just might have a pretty good idea of what was going to happen that hot, August afternoon.

"I'd like that very much, Tom," starting to saddle her horse, Snowflake." Where should we go?"

Feeling relieved a little and more at ease, he said, "Remember where George and I used to go hunting up by those woods northeast? Let's just ride up there. You want to take the dogs?"

"Here, Boomer," she called. "Here, Rascal."

The dogs came running from behind the house and sat down right in front of her. Francis Porter was a very pretty young woman, about 5'4" tall, slender, with long brown hair. She couldn't have weighed more than 110 lbs. Her blue eyes sparkled as she looked at Tom. She put on a wide-brimmed, brown hat and grabbed her leather riding gloves. She swung herself up into the saddle, called to the dogs, and off they went.

There was little breeze on that hot afternoon in Hopewell Township as they rode along the trail out to the woods. He thought they might talk in a small grove by the creek so that they would be protected from the sun and could get some cool water to drink. As they rode along, they had talked about him going back in, and how sad she was, but she thought she understood, although he really hadn't talked to her about it.

"I will tell you why I am going," he said." It's my duty to try to save the Union in whatever meagre way I can, and I am honored to do so. I am a lieutenant this time." They talked some more but came to a clearing by the creek where Tom dismounted and helped her down from Snowflake. They sat under an oak tree with Boomer and Rascal just lying there waiting to see where they were going next. The horses grazed lazily in the open field, maybe 10 – 15 yards away. There was no need to tether them, although Tom was always concerned about coyotes and other predators. He kept the rifle close by.

"I have mentioned an old friend, Charlie McCabe, to you. I studied under him at Ohio Wesleyan. He is now a minister in the Methodist Church in Putnam, and the two of us talked seriously about this decision. He asked me if I had faith and trust in God and that His will would be done. After a moment or two, I told him that I did and would accept my fate in His name. Mother and Father didn't understand that at first, but now they do, and I hope you can share that belief." Summoning some courage, he went on, "You see, Frank, I have developed strong feelings for you and want to share what happens in my life with you as this terrible war goes on and then after it is over. I asked your father this morning if I could court you, to which he said that I could if it is all right with you. So, I am asking you the same thing."

"I have strong feelings for you, too, Tom, and I was hoping that someday you would ask Father about that. I am pleased that he wanted you to ask me, too."

He reached over, took her hand, and smiled." I will write you as often as I can, and I would like you to write to me as often as you can or whenever you get my letters."

"I am pleased to do that. So, Father and Mother both know about this?"

"Yes. Your father told her."

"So, that's why she was smiling when she sent me out to the barn. She knew all along."

"I guess so. Are you happy?"

"Yes, very happy about this, and no, about you going to war. But, for you, I will be as brave as I can, and I will pray for you every day, just like I pray for George."

Getting somewhat bolder, Tom Armstrong said, "Frank, my brother, Jacob, asked me if I was going to ask you to marry me when I came over here today."

She looked at him with gentle, questioning eyes." And..."

"And, I said that someday that might happen, but that I didn't think we were ready for that. I hope I spoke wisely."

"Yes, you did," she said, smiling at him and taking his hand in hers. "Perhaps someday."

"My other reason was that if I should be killed, I would not want you to be a widow like so many other young ladies. I am not planning on getting killed, but that is in God's hands, just as it is every day."

"Thank you, Thomas," using his full name and thinking that he was just thinking of her and not of himself. "I am grateful for that."

Walking hand in hand, they went over to the horses for the ride back to the house." When do you report," she asked.

"Monday. Jacob is coming with me to Camp Zanesville. I have a lot to do. Most of the men don't know how to behave as soldiers, and I will have to teach them. I learned all about it as the 78th was preparing to go to the fight. Drilling and learning how the army does things. You see, there's this book, written by a fellow named Hardee six or seven years ago, while he was at West Point studying to be an officer in the army, that details every possible behavior a soldier may engage in. It's two hundred pages long, and I will have about a month to teach it."

"You'll do it well," she counselled. "When do you leave camp?"

"I don't know when or where we will go. I will come see you, though, when I get a furlough before we do leave. I should know more by then."

"I am glad of that," she said, smiling at him as they rode along with Boomer and Rascal barking as they ran alongside.

Changing the subject, Armstrong said, "Johnny asked me if I would like to go hunting with him tomorrow morning. Do you want to come along?"

"No, why don't you just go with him. You can get to know him better."

"Very well, but I will miss you."

"It's only for a morning, silly."

He laughed. He'd never been called "silly" before.

It was like there was nothing wrong with the world that Wednesday afternoon, August 27, 1862, in Hopewell Township, Ohio. Armstrong thought to himself that everything had gone just as he had wanted it to. Too bad there was a war going on in Tennessee and Virginia, and goodness knows where else. Boys dying; being maimed, losing an arm or a leg; contracting deadly disease; or being captured and put in one of the awful prisons. It was the same hell for both sides." I will get there soon enough," Tom Armstrong thought to himself, saying a prayer of thanks for the events of the day. "Wow, it's almost supper time." They had talked for quite some time.

Supper was light as usual and featured some pheasant, small potatoes, lettuce, tomatoes, and carrots from the garden. There was some small talk around the table about the coming harvest and the need for putting up the corn and bailing the wheat, canning the vegetables, and making jams and jellies. There would be a lot to do. John Porter, Sr. expressed the thought that this might be the last harvest in Hopewell. He was convinced there were too many people coming out there, and he needed his space.

"Thomas, I am thinking of moving the family to Illinois. What do you think of that?"

"Gracious, that's a long way from here, John," Armstrong replied, looking at Frank." Why would you do that?"

"Too many people here in Hopewell. I want to be out in open space."

"When would you go?"

"Not sure, but I have been out there and found some farms that I could buy. If I find a buyer for this place, I may go out there again very soon." And, then, with a grin, he continued, "Too bad you couldn't come with me."

Hearing that, Amanda Porter smiled, and John, Jr. shot a glance at Francis to see what it meant. She was smiling, too. Huldah Jane, Mary, and Amanda, the younger, started to giggle. They had figured out why Tom had come to see them, but Johnny hadn't put two and two together. The younger boys, Billy and Joe had no idea what was going on.

"Yes," said John, Sr., "that's too bad, but, anyway, I think we're going to see a lot more of you when this darn war is over." The secret was out. Frank and Tom just smiled at each other. Seeing that, Johnny Porter understood.

She said, "Yes, I think you will." And, that was that.

After supper, as they sat in the great room with their coffee, Tom related the stories of his meeting with Charles McCabe; the conversation with his parents, brother, and sisters; the private conversation he had with his father; and the recruiting meeting. He told them of his abiding faith and trust in God, and that if he should be killed, or if he died of disease, or was locked up in one of those awful Rebel prisons, or if, indeed, he did come back in one piece, it was God's will being done. He asked them to pray for him, as well as for George, Bob Hanson, and John Gillespie.

The Porter family was touched by what the young man said. "Francis," Amanda began, "are you all right with Thomas going back?"

"Mother, you know that I was very sad yesterday when I received his letter about the 122nd, but as he and I talked today, I am very frightened for him, but I understand it is his duty to his country to go. I pray that he comes back to me and will have faith that he will, just like I pray that George comes back to us alive. I am glad that he didn't ask me about his going before his mind was made up. That would have made it harder for him. He still would've gone, but he would have felt that he had disappointed me. And things will be, I imagine, tough enough without that on his mind. He knows that I am saddened at the possibilities, but his faith is such that I have hope for him. In the future, though, whenever he has to make a big decision like this, he better ask me first," Francis Porter said with a laugh. Tom Armstrong nodded as if to say "Yes, dear."

"Amen to that," said John, Sr." Let's call it a night. I understand there is to be some hunting early in the morning."

"Good night, all," Tom Armstrong said as he left for the loft in the barn. It had been a long, emotional day, and suddenly, he was very tired. The next thing he heard was Johnny climbing up the ladder to the loft.

"Hey, Sump," he exclaimed, "Great day to go hunting. You ready?"

"Just woke up. Give me a minute or two," pulling on his boots, grabbing his hat, buckling the gun belt, and picking up the Springfield.

"Mother and Francis are making breakfast. It should be ready shortly."

Armstrong stopped by the pump, filled the bucket half full, and washed his face. He really needed a bath. Maybe later today while they were out on the hunt, he could jump in the pond. That would help some.

The bacon was fried just right; the fresh eggs, too; the fruit still chilled from being in the coolhouse over the creek that ran through the Porter's property; the corn bread warm; the butter just right; and the coffee hot. It was a great way to start the day. Armstrong winked at Frank Porter when the meal was over." I will see you at dinner time. That will give us a few hours to hunt. Ready to go, Johnny?"

"Yep," came the reply. They threw saddlebags onto their horses, climbed aboard, and were off. Once they got out to the northwest corner of the farm, they decided to hide in the woods, hoping to spot deer. They waited quite some time and were quite subdued when suddenly they were rewarded. They saw a large doe coming toward them, not 25 yards away. Two others followed. Tom steadied the rifle on a tree stump, took aim, and fired a shot into the front of the animal, just below the left shoulder. At the sound, the other two bounded away, getting lost in the underbrush. The doe staggered a few steps and went down. He reloaded the Springfield in case another one would show up or in case they met a wolf or two on the way back to the house.

"Good shooting, Sump, looks like you got it. Let's get it back now, so father can dress it. Don't want no vultures finding it. Oh, boy, venison." That was about as good as it got that morning. They saw some squirrels and jackrabbits, but that was it. Shots were fired at the critters, but to no avail. It was as if the wildlife knew that the two of them, with their rifles loaded, were out there after them. As they were walking through the woods back to their horses, dragging the deer behind them, Tom told Johnny Porter about the war, seeing the elephant and all. John, Jr. was impressed and wanted to go. It sounded so exciting.

"Exciting it is until you hear that first bullet whiz a foot over your head or you see a Minie ball strike a friend of yours in the face, killing him instantly. War is ugly, Johnny. Be thankful you are not going. Your father needs you right here, just as my father needs my brother, Jacob. Besides, I'm not sure your mother could handle both you and George in the army. My mother was not really thrilled when my brother, Wilbur, and I enlisted at the same time, and now he's gone."

"But, don't you get to ride a horse and shoot rebels?"

"No horse, only senior officers and couriers get them. First time you shoot another man, it sickens you, but when you are engaged with the enemy, you just keep firing."

"You scared?"

"Don't have time to be. Load and fire. Load and fire. That's all you do in battle. Ask your brother about Shiloh when he comes home on furlough. He'll have other stories by then, too. It isn't like killing a deer or a coyote or slaughtering a cow. We're talking about taking human life."

"You done that?"

"Nope, not yet. Your brother has. Told me he caught a Secesh, a Southerner, in the chest. The Minie ball tore into him, blood exploded, dead. Didn't think much about it with the fight going on. Imagine he's killed others, too. That's war, Johnny."

They threw the carcass of the deer over the Aspen's hindquarters and rode silently back to the house. Tom wondered, "Will I be able to kill another human being when the time comes?" It wasn't easy, but he put the thought aside.

The rest of the day passed by uneventfully. Frank and Tom went for another ride, this time to the southwest, over hills and through the ancient Indian burial grounds, happier than either of them had ever been.

"Good one," said John, Sr., looking down at the carcass. "The army's going to be glad they have a shot like you. You going to be a sharpshooter?"

"Don't know. You do what you're told, period. No questions. No deviations." He thought of *Hardee's Tactics* and cringed at the notion of trying to teach them to his squad or the company. Then, he laughed to himself at the thought of teaching them to that smart aleck Patrick Murphy.

Supper was had by all, and the conversation turned to the health of the Armstrong family and things in general over in Norwich. As the evening progressed, Billy and Joe were playing marbles while John, Sr., Johnny, Amanda, the junior, and Mary sang some hymns and patriotic songs. Amanda, the senior, was straightening up the house, while Tom and Frank sat in the swing on the broad front porch.

"I wish you didn't have to go tomorrow," she said wistfully.

"I wish I didn't have to either, but I must. I am just glad we had this time together, and I will come back sometime next month when I get furloughed."

"I'll be waiting."

Tom went on, "I know this is difficult for you, and I want you to know how grateful I am that you want to be a part of my life and that you will be here for me. You have become very important to me. Knowing you are here will be of great help on those lonely nights in camp."

"You know I will worry all the time you are gone, and I am glad you came here yesterday like I hoped you would." She rested her head on his shoulder.

John Porter put down his guitar and the singing was concluded with Billy victorious in marbles. The girls asked their mother if there was anything else to be done. There wasn't, and she sent the younger boys off to bed, thinking the others should retire soon, too.

"Frank, I'll be leaving right after breakfast tomorrow. Don't want to push Aspen."

"I understand. Will you write me about when you are coming back? I may go to Illinois with Father if he asks but will not if I know you will be coming here."

"Of course. May I kiss you good night?"

"I thought you would never ask."

He kissed her gently." Good night, Frank."

"Good night, Thomas." She turned to go to the door, still holding his hand. "I will see you in the morning."

"Yes, you will." Frank Porter disappeared inside the house, and Tom Armstrong ambled over to the barn. Both were decidedly happy.

He left for Norwich around 8 o'clock the next morning. It was Friday, August 29. Sleep had not been a problem. He woke about 6 o'clock, made sure that everything was packed in the haversack, picked up the saddlebags and rifle, and climbed down the ladder, taking it all to the stable where Aspen was waiting. He got her ready for the day's journey, securing the haversack, saddlebags, and rifle in their proper places, and led her to the house.

It was the normal breakfast, but the conversation was a bit muted. Most of it was about what had to be done that day, but the tone effected a sadness. The Porters were happy about the relationship Francis now had with Tom Armstrong, but they could not get over his going back in the army. He thought of saying, "Oh, don't worry about me." But then he thought that would have done more harm than good. He thanked the Porters for everything, saying he would be back within the month, he thought.

"So, long, Thomas," said John, Sr." Good luck to you."

"Thanks, John. I am grateful."

Tom Armstrong and Frank Porter walked out the door." You be careful, Thomas."

"I will."

"Send me a letter as soon as you get to camp."

"I will try."

They shared an embrace and another brief kiss, and he was off. Tears began to well up in her eyes, and she didn't care if anyone saw them. He turned in the saddle and waved. Through the tears, she waved back. And, then he was gone.

As Aspen loped along the National Road toward Zanesville, he began thinking about *Hardee's Tactics* again. There was everything from how to stand properly to how to load, ram, and shoot your rifle to how a battalion is supposed to move. "Straight ahead, Wheel, Right or Left Oblique, you name it." And, then, all of the commands for individual soldiers, squads, companies, and brigades. "Attention, Forward, on the Double Quick, Ready, Load, Ram, Aim, Fire." There were about 1,600 of them. How in the world did Hardee write it all down? More important, how would he remember all of it?

Tom Armstrong did, however, have the advantage of having been drilled on the *Tactics* at Camp Zanesville when the 78th was preparing to be deployed. That would help, but these westerners were a fiercely independent bunch, some rough and crude, and he doubted that they would take too kindly to being ordered around by a school teacher. These were farm boys, some uneducated, but darn good with their rifles and pistols. He imagined they would be pretty good in a firefight. He would know most of the boys in his Company I. Likewise, they would know him. That was the way all regiments were formed. Boys from the same towns, villages, and neighbourhoods who would stick together.

He held that advantage of being in the 78th over the other officers in the regiment, too, since he had, indeed, seen the elephant and could teach them what to expect and how to deal with it, presuming they survived. Yes, as he had told Johnny Porter, war was ugly, and the men of the 122nd OVI were going to find out how ugly it really was very soon. He doubted that any of the other officers in the 122nd had seen or experienced it. "None, I imagine," he thought to himself. "They are in for a big surprise. They can read about Fort Donelson, Shiloh, and the battles in the east in the *Daily Courier*, but that's nothing compared to being there, in the actual fight itself. The roar of the cannons, the constant musket fire, the dense smoke, the men and horses falling dead right beside you, the shrieks of the wounded. The men will have to get used to that as well."

And, then, the entire regiment would have to cope with the boredom. It was entirely possible that it could get assigned to some place just to protect a railroad, a bridge, or part of a river. If the Confederate army didn't come to try to take whatever it was they were guarding, the regiment might sit in one place for months on end. "We better have something for the men to do," he thought. "We can only drill them according to the *Tactics* so much."

There would be 100 men in each company, give or take a few, with the 122nd consisting only of boys from Muskingum County. Colonel William H. Ball would have the overall command, taking his orders, usually by telegraph (if the Rebels hadn't cut the wires), from whatever general was in charge of the theater they ended up in, whether east in Virginia or west, down in Tennessee, or someplace in between. Major Moses M. Granger would report to Ball and would relay his orders through couriers to the company commanders. There would be ten companies in the regiment, each commanded by a captain. Daniel Gary, then, would have command over Company I, with 1st Lieutenant Thomas Black and 2nd Lieutenant Thomas Armstrong reporting to him. The lieutenants would take their orders from Gary and would repeat them to the sergeants and corporals who would, in turn, give them to the privates.

His men would see him as the one giving the orders, but he could not just yell a command and expect them to do it. He would have to do exactly what he told his men to do. When battle commenced, and Col. Leggett, Maj. Granger, or Capt. Gary screamed "*Charge*," he, and the other lieutenants, would face the hazard of being the first ones over the wall, out of the trenches behind the breastworks, or across the field. He would be the first officer the enemy would see, becoming the initial target for his muskets. Indeed, the highest casualty rate in the entire Civil War would come from the ranks of the 1st and 2nd Lieutenant. It was dangerous; very, very dangerous. But, because he had been at Shiloh, he knew that going in.

Tom Armstrong had another advantage, and it was troublesome. It was related to the advantage of having experience, but was more subtle. He knew that he had to get the men to trust him and the decisions he would make. In the 78th he had seen how the officers who the men trusted behaved. That's where he learned that the men needed to see their lieutenant right out there in front of them, whether in battle or drill, simply because they would not do something that their officers would not. He would have to lead by example, even into the jaws of death.

The enlisted men might never see the colonel or the major, goodness knows a general for heaven's sake, so the only authority they would know would be the captain and the lieutenants. It would be those officers' job to take care of the men in the company, from helping them pitch their tents, finding firewood and water, getting their rations or foraging, teaching them survival skills, assigning skirmish lines, and even ordering them into battle, knowing full well that they and the men who followed them could die. "Sobering thought," he said to himself. "But, I must get the men to trust me. Maybe those I recruited probably already do, maybe not. How about the rest of them? The ones I don't know? Maybe if I show them how to use the Enfield, that would be a start. But, I will have to demonstrate courage, knowledge, bravery, and, at times, some compassion, and maybe even some humor. And, then, what do I do when the fight gets hot, and they turn and run? Guess I can't think about that now."

He reined in Aspen since they were nearing Zanesville, and there was increased traffic on the National Road. Slowing the big, gray mare to a walk, he decided to see if Charlie McCabe was around to tell him about what happened in Hopewell. He turned her south on Main Street and hitched her to the railing in front of the McCabe's house. Rebecca opened the front door.

"Tom, do come in. Charles isn't here right now. He's over at the church."

"Much obliged, Rebecca," he replied." I think I will go over there to see him."

"Very well. But, please call me Beccie and remind him that he has a meeting here at the house after dinner."

Thinking he did not want someone stealing it, he took the rifle out if its holster and walked down Main Street to the large stone church, opened the front door, and walked in. The Reverend Charles

McCabe was in his office, behind the sanctuary. The church was much larger than the one in which Tom worshipped in Norwich. He leaned the rifle against the wall outside the office.

He saw his friend reading the Bible, seated in a big chair that looked really comfortable.

"T. S.!" he exclaimed. "To what pleasure do I owe this visit?"

"Well, Charlie, I had an interesting day and a half over in Hopewell and am going home right now."

"Hopewell? Whatever for?"

"Well, you see, there's this girl, George Porter's sister, Francis. I may have mentioned her at some point."

"Oh, ho," chuckled Charles McCabe." I think I am going to like what's coming next."

"I expect so. At least I hope so. I call her Frank, and we have been exchanging letters for a couple of years, and things got a little more serious over the last few months. I only told my father and Jacob about it earlier this week. So, anyway, I spoke to her father about our relationship and asked him if I could court his oldest daughter."

McCabe's eyes widened a bit." And..."

"He was fine with the idea, as long as she was all right with it.

"Well?"

"She was, or is, and we spent some happy time together. I told her and the family about the conversation you and I had about trusting and having faith in the Lord and that it would be His will that would be done. I do hope to come back alive so that we can be married, but only time will tell, Charlie." He would be the only one in the 122nd to call him "Charlie," and only when no one else was around.

"Good for you. I am very pleased. You have a good head on your shoulders."

"She understands the risk that I am taking and is not happy about it. She also understands why I am doing this, going back into the army, the duty I see and the honor I have in serving this great country. Her family doesn't quite understand the decision, but is quite patriotic and also shares thoughts about the evils of slavery. She just makes me very happy, and I'm 27 years old. It's about time I found someone to settle down with."

"I'm glad you stopped by to tell me. Did you talk about marriage?"

"Yep. Jacob had asked me the other day if I was going to propose. I told him that I wasn't going to since I am not ready yet and that I also wanted to be fair to her. She agreed with that, if I get back alive, but the subject will come up again, for sure."

"Very sound, my friend. Will I see you on Monday?"

"Yes, Jacob will bring me. I'm glad you were here today. I thought you should know. I better get going. My regards to Beccie and feel free to tell her."

"My regards to your family. She will be delighted."

The two friends shook hands. Tom Armstrong picked up the Springfield and headed back up the street. He climbed aboard Aspen, went back down Main Street, south to Chauncey Wescott's store. Wescott was sitting on a bench in front of his saloon, next door to the store, reading the *Daily Courier.*

"Hello, Mr. Wescott."

"Hello, Tom. Good visit in Hopewell?"

"Yes, very good."

Wescott called to his wife, "Judith, dear, would you be so kind as to bring out that oilskin blanket we got for Tom Armstrong?" And then to Tom, "She has it right near the door, since you told me that you would be coming by for it this morning."

Judith Wescott came out of the store with the blanket and handed it to him. "Here you go, Tom."

"Thank you, Mrs. Wescott," tipping his hat. "I wish I had one of these when I went off with the 78th. Might not have taken sick."

Tom paid her for the blanket, strapped it on Aspen, and took off for Norwich. He would get there a little before 1 o'clock and was hoping that his mother would have some dinner for him when he got there. He also wanted to tell her about the coming courtship of Francis Porter. "She's going to start thinking about grandchildren," he mused, riding Aspen at a walk through Zanesville until he got to the outskirts of town to the east when she was free to start loping down the National Road toward the farm. He also wanted to tell his father about John Porter's thoughts on moving to Illinois.

"Basically," he thought to himself "I'm ready to go to camp as long as Mother has packed the box. I will ride Aspen to camp and stable her there. The Springfield I'll give to Jacob to take back to the farm. When I am furloughed and go to Hopewell to see Frank, I will just take the Colt. I will also go home to say farewell and can leave Aspen there. Jacob will bring me back to camp. So, I've got all day tomorrow to get ready if I need, but Sunday is out. Church all day. Can't work then. So, I better have everything done tomorrow."

A strange thought then came over him. "I'll bet that somewhere down in Alabama or Virginia, there is a young, 2nd Lieutenant, wearing a gray uniform, who believes in God, is in love with a wonderful woman, is anxious about the coming days, and will fight to the death. Just like me. Maybe, just maybe," he thought, "we and them are pretty much the same." He wondered if he would ever meet that Confederate 2nd Lieutenant.

The collies met him as he rode up the path to the house. His father and Jacob would be out in the fields, and he had no idea where his sisters were. He heard Frank and Gus playing war around the barn. Tom had tried to discourage that, but it was of no use. He thought that pretending to have guns and shooting imaginary people was not a good idea, but their father saw nothing wrong with it. After all, south central Ohio was in the western part of the United States, and gun violence was a lot more commonplace than in the genteel confines of Boston, New York, Philadelphia, Washington, DC and the rest of the eastern part of the country. It was just part of life, so even the young ones learned it very early.

He dismounted and went into the house, placing the rifle in the rack he had made for it. Jane Armstrong came to greet him with a hug, saying "I am glad you are home."

"I am glad, too. Is anything left over from dinner?"

His mother pulled out a plate of food she had made up for him, knowing that he would be arriving just about this time.

Taking a swig of lemonade, he said, "Mother, I have something to tell you," coming right to the point. "John said that he would give me permission to court George's sister, Frank. Now, she had to agree to it, and when we talked, she said it was something she had been hoping for."

"What did Amanda say?"

"She was pleased. At least that's what she said. I think she's worried for me."

Jane looked at him approvingly. "Thomas, I already had a feeling about this. Your father told me about the letter he had received from John a few months back. So, when you told us you were going to Hopewell to pay your respects to the Porters, we kind of thought there might have been another reason for the journey. We are very happy for you both. Shall we tell your brothers and sisters?"

"Yes, we better. Huldah Jane, Mary, and Amanda already know, and it would not be good for them to send a letter to my sibs about it and have it come as a surprise. They had better hear it from me."

"You can tell them this afternoon, before supper. Is marriage in the plan?" getting to the point herself.

"Yes, I think so, but not until this terrible conflict is over, presuming, of course, that I make it back here alive."

She looked at her son with sorrowful eyes, the happiness of the courtship leaving her. "I do not like to think about that, Thomas. I have enough trouble thinking about Wilbur. He was such a sweet boy. I miss him terribly."

"I do, too. He was a fine little brother, but now he is in a better place, Mother."

Hearing that brought a little comfort, but not much. Life in the West was hard, she knew. War was even harder." Bring your things in and unpack. I want to see if I need to put any of it into the box."

"Where are the girls? I want to go and tell them."

"I think they are down in the vegetable garden, picking beans and pulling carrots. At least that's what I asked them to do. We have to start putting them up."

He emptied the haversack and saddlebags, so his mother could see if she needed to pack anything while he was with his sisters. She found a shirt and a vest, telling him to go out to the barn to pack them in the box. He did as he was told, and when finished, he wandered down to the garden to see if Mary and Flavilla were, indeed, there. He found them picking the green beans and pulling carrots out of the ground, just as their mother had asked.

Sitting down by a large sycamore tree, he called out, "Mary, Fla, I have something to tell you."

His sisters wiped their hands on their aprons and went to sit down with him. They knew he had been in Hopewell but didn't know why. They'd seen letters from Hopewell but had never asked who they were from. He told them the whole story, even about the possibility of marriage one day. They were very happy for him, but both started wondering when some nice, young men like their brother would want to court them and even get married. There were some single men at the church, but not many, and neither girl saw much promise there. That was the trouble with Norwich. They would have to find someone in Zanesville. Maybe Rebecca McCabe would know some. Maybe she would ask the Armstrong sisters to come to Zanesville someday. Maybe they might write her a letter, asking if that could be arranged.

The siblings talked some more about his time in Hopewell, but he thought he better find his father to tell him about Frank and the potential for the Porters to move to Illinois. He strolled back to the house with *Hardee's Tactics* on his mind again. He remembered that the full title of the manual was *Rifle and Light Infantry Tactics – For the Exercise and Manoeuvers...* There was more to it, but that was all he could remember. He was sure that Colonel Ball would have a copy or two at Camp Zanesville. Instruction on the *Tactics* would be the first order of business when the officers reported. Maybe he could write down the orders and drills that the Colonel stressed. That would make it much easier. Thinking about it, sitting there on the porch swing, he still worried that these rough and tumble farm boys from here in central Ohio would not respect him and not take orders. There had to be something that he could do, other than teach them how the war that they would see was fought. "Maybe Father will have some ideas about that."

Jane came out and rang the bell. Supper time. Gus and Frank came in from the barn, and pretty soon Fla and Mary came in from the garden with a big basket of vegetables, the carrots and beans. They would put them up tomorrow for storage for the winter that would soon be upon them. William Armstrong and Jacob came riding in, taking their horses to the stable. Tom went out to meet them.

"How'd it go over there in Hopewell?" his father asked. Jacob was all ears.

Walking toward the house, Tom Armstrong said, "Well, when I was riding over there, I figured I better go see John first. So, when I got there, Amanda told me where I could find him. Billy took me about all the way there, but I told him that he could go on back since I saw his father in the distance."

"And..."

"I simply asked him for permission to court Frank. He had a reservation, but I think I overcame it, since he said he would be pleased to have me court her."

"Not surprised," said his father. "Not surprised at all. Been expecting something like this for awhile now."

It began to dawn on Tom Armstrong that maybe both sets of parents had an idea about him and Francis Porter, even before he really did. "Maybe they were just hoping," he thought.

"So, Frank and I went for a ride out in the country where George and I used to hunt. Oh, shot myself a deer out there yesterday morning. Anyway, when I told Frank how I felt and that I had the permission of her father to court her, she said something about hoping that would happen, some day. Well, Wednesday was the day."

"You talk about marriage?" Jacob asked, remembering their conversation in the buckboard from earlier in the week.

"Yep. I told her about what you and I talked about, and that I wasn't ready to make that commitment. I also said that I didn't want to make her a widow."

"She saw some wisdom in that, but we both know that if I survive this thing, we probably will get married someday."

His father and brother expressed their happiness that he had found someone. "Father, there is one last thing. John told me that he may be moving the family to Illinois. Don't know when, but it sounded like soon. He thinks there are too many people over there in Hopewell."

"My, my. We've lost touch since we moved here. Maybe Mother and I should go over there for a visit, especially if such a move is going to happen soon."

"Maybe so."

The next morning, Tom found his father sitting on the front porch reading his Bible. His sisters were out in the barn, milking the cows, his mother was working on breakfast, and Jacob was probably out checking on the sheep, so father and son had a little time to talk.

"Father, I need some advice."

"Oh?" That was unusual since Tom almost always had a clear view of things.

"I am concerned that the men will not respect me and my commission as an officer. Some of them are uneducated hooligans who are fiercely independent and who may not take kindly to orders given them by a school teacher. I know I have an advantage, having already seen war at its worst, and I am familiar with *Hardee's Tactics*. I had to learn them when we formed the 78th. But I am worried that might not be enough. I just have to get the men to trust me."

"Well, that could be a problem," his father said, closing the Bible. He thought for a minute or two and then offered, "What you may need is one of them to support you as an example to the others. The others will see that there is one of their own who has respect and trust in your leadership, and perhaps they will develop their own sense of it. You know any of them well? That respect and trust you? Who will do what you tell him to do? Maybe that big kid who played the piano at the meeting the other night?"

"You mean Isaac Kearney? Don't really know him that well. If I did, how would that work?"

"Will you have sergeants and corporals reporting to you, as lieutenant?"

"Yes. Why?"

"Get a man like Kearney to be a sergeant under your command. But make sure he will do what you tell him. The privates will simply follow his lead. Make it a kind of partnership. Give him some authority and responsibility. Appeal to his sense of pride."

"That's a fine thought, Father. But, if not Kearney, who?"

"How about that young man who enlisted the other night? The kid with the smart aleck answers. Goes to the church."

"You mean Patrick Murphy?"

"Yes, that's him. You know he likes to be the center of things. Just remember his shenanigans at the meeting. I didn't tell you then, but I was quite amused. Undisciplined? Maybe. But I think he might like being a sergeant."

Tom Armstrong thought for a minute or two. "Murphy was big, irreverent, smart, quick-witted, and from what he had heard, pretty good with his fists. He also had a very dry sense of humor."

"Wow, if he'd do what I ask of him, he'd be perfect."

"Father, Thomas, it's time for breakfast. And then you have chores to do," instructed Jane Armstrong.

All during breakfast, Tom Armstrong simply thought "Patrick Murphy. Perfect."

4 Camp Zanesville

Unlike the previous two Sundays when Tom Armstrong was having trouble concentrating in church, on this day, August 31, 1862, at all three services, he was quite attentive, listening and thinking about what the Leader said in his sermons, in the prayers, and in the singing. In the afternoon service, before he pronounced the apostolic benediction, the Leader, looking directly at Tom, said, "For all of you going into this infernal war, be safe, good luck, and Godspeed. Come back to us here in Norwich."

He sat in the pew after the service was over just thinking. "This is the right thing to do. I know what I am getting myself into. The other boys don't. They think it a glorious adventure, but it's not. It is what I must do, even though Mother and Father, the Porters, and Frank are unhappy, and even though I may be killed or wounded. I could get sick, and I could get thrown into prison, but it is not my will that shall be done, although I would like to think so. It is God's will, and I will have faith and trust in Him." He was comforted knowing that he was in love with Francis Porter and she with him, and that someday, God willing, they would be married and would spend the rest of their lives together. "And, perhaps, there will be grandchildren," he mused.

He stood up and walked out of the tiny church, there in Norwich, and went to be with his family, sitting at the table where his mother had laid out some food.

An hour and a half later, Flavilla asked, "Are you scared?"

"Probably will be," came the response, "but, right now, no. I will have too much to do in camp to be scared, and there will be no danger there. Depending on where we go and what we do, I will most

85

likely be afraid, but I must leave it in God's hands. Frank understands that, and I hope all of you do, too."

At the Prayer Service, he reverently asked the Lord to be with him in the coming days and to keep him safe. He prayed for Francis Porter and her family, his own family, and for the officers who would be leading the 122nd Ohio Volunteer Infantry. "Amen," he thought to himself, got up from the kneeling pillow, and started for the door, thinking about all that would have to be done when he got to camp.

"I'll think about you and pray for you, brother," said Jacob Armstrong, walking alongside.

"Thank you, Jacob. I will write you as often as I can and will direct you where your letters will reach me. For now, use Ball's Regiment, the 122nd O.V.I., Camp Zanesville. I will try to come home before we are sent out, and I want to go to Hopewell, too."

"Just take care of yourself, Sump," he replied, using Tom Armstrong's nickname.

"Best I can, big brother. But, my first worry is to get these roughnecks from here in old Muskingum to trust me and to do what I tell them."

"You'll be fine. You'll figure it out. I have every confidence in you."

"Yeah, but it won't be easy," Tom thought, "especially if I can't get Patrick Murphy to go along with me."

In the morning, he went down to the creek to bathe. He could have heated water up for the tub but didn't want to take the time. The water in the creek was cold, but he was used to it, and the sun was up so it wasn't that bad. He toweled off, put on fresh drawers, a cotton shirt, and the uniform that he came home in. The ragged, darned blue coat and the light blue trousers fit once again; he remembered how loose-fitting they were when he had come home from Shiloh in May. He put on the grey woolen socks he had worn home and the brogans that were almost bare in the sole. Wrapping up his nightclothes in the towel, it was back to the house for breakfast. It was Monday, September 1, 1862, the day that Colonel William H. Ball had asked him to report. Imagining the other boys, who had not seen the elephant, would be quite nervous on the day they were to report, Tom Armstrong was quite calm, a comfortable peace within him.

With breakfast done, it was time to go. He kissed his mother, Mary, and Flavilla goodbye and picked up Frank and Gus, giving them a big hug, saying "You take care of things while I am gone. Do what Mother and Father tell you and study your lessons."

Thomas Armstrong looked his father in the eye. There was a sadness on his face. "Take care of yourself, son."

"I will do my best, Father. Jacob will help you with the sheep, and the girls will tend to the gardens. I hope all goes well for you." The two men shook hands. "Thank you for understanding and supporting what I must do."

"You're welcome, Thomas," and with that, Tom Armstrong swung himself up onto Aspen. The Springfield was in its holster, and the Colt was buckled tightly around his waist. Normally, he didn't carry it much, but this day was different. He was going back to war. Jacob had the box already in the buckboard. Maude seemed anxious to get going. He turned and waved at his family with Aspen slowly walking behind the buckboard down the path to the main road.

The Armstrong brothers arrived at Camp Zanesville around 10:30 that September morning since they had taken their time and had stopped at Mrs. Palmer's boarding house, so Tom could say goodbye. Camp Zanesville was located about two miles northwest of Zanesville at the confluence of the Muskingum River and the Licking Creek on the farm land belonging to Charles Snyder. The Newark Road ran right through the property with Licking Creek bordering it on the south. Now, some people called the Creek a river, but it really wasn't. As they approached the Main Gate, Tom Armstrong noticed the thick stands of trees, black and white oak, mostly at the eastern corners of the camp and was surprised to see guards in front of the eight-foot wall that was designed to keep everyone in, especially the enlisted men. There was a hitching post right there by the gate.

Getting down from the buckboard, Jacob picked up the box and put it at Tom's feet. "I guess it's time."

"Yeah, I guess it is," his brother replied, handing him the prized Springfield. "Take care of this, and yourself. Write me often." They shook hands, having done the same the previous November at Camp Goddard, as the 78th O.V.I. was being formed. He would really try to get home before being sent out but wasn't sure he could. So, he thought saying goodbye right then was the right thing to do. If he couldn't get home, he thought, getting Aspen back to the farm would be a problem, but he couldn't worry about that now.

"You take care of yourself, too." And then Jacob Armstrong was gone.

Tom Armstrong looked around and thought that it was time to find William Ball, Moses Granger, and Dan Gary. He decided that he better find the Captain first, so he inquired of the guard at the main gate where Gary's headquarters were.

"Company I, huh?" came the response. "Down this street, about a mile, on the right. You'll see the colors. You can leave the box here for now."

"Thanks," Tom Armstrong said, climbed back up on Aspen, turned to the right, and took off to find the Captain. A few minutes later, he saw Dan Gary sitting outside a small building, looking at some papers. He slowed Aspen to a walk and greeted the Captain with a salute. Mounting up, Gary said he would take him to see Colonel Ball. The two men rode down the side street a few blocks, about half a mile, to the Colonel's headquarters, a small cabin across the street from what appeared to be barracks for the officers. Tents for the enlisted men.

Saluting, he said, "My compliments, Colonel. It is good to see you."

"Lieutenant Armstrong. It is good to see you, too. We have a lot to do, and I am counting on your experience to help us. Captain Gary, take the lieutenant to the Surgeon's office so we can make sure he is fit for duty and then, assuming all goes well with Dr. Houston, it will be over to the Quartermaster for your new uniform. Have you got the right amount of money? Don't know why the War Department makes officers buy their uniforms. Doesn't make much sense, but that's the rule."

"Yes, sir," Captain Daniel Gary replied with a salute.

Dr. William Houston was a tall, lanky man, with salt and pepper hair, Tom judging him to be about 50. He peered over his spectacles with a look that would frighten most men to death since they did not know what was going to happen next. Armstrong tried to hide his apprehension, but the doctor saw it and sought to calm the lieutenant by saying some nice things about his general appearance. It didn't work. The surgeon ordered Tom to turn around, tapped his upper and lower back with a small mallet, did the same thing on his chest, and examined his fingers and toes. Houston then looked at Armstrong's eyes, checked his teeth, and said "For the good of the 122nd O.V.I." very quietly to test his hearing. Throughout this ordeal, the doctor muttered to himself from time to time. He gave no clue about what he was thinking.

"Captain, a fine specimen here. You better hope you get 99 more of them." Tom Armstrong was relieved.

"Thank you, sir." Now to the Quartermaster's office to buy his uniform.

"Dan," Armstrong said, addressing the Captain informally, "why do they make us officers buy our uniforms? As the Colonel said, doesn't make much sense to me. Seems like they owe us one."

"Don't know, Tom, that's just the way it is. Rules are rules in this man's army."

Armstrong remembered that from his time in Colonel Mortimer Leggett's 78th O.V.I. "So many darn rules," he thought, "but I guess that is the way it has to be to get the men disciplined. *Hardee's Tactics*, once more."

Sergeant George McMillen was the Company Quartermaster for the 122nd and was quite ready to start outfitting the boys who would be coming in over the next couple of weeks. When Tom and Dan Gary entered, the Captain informed the Quartermaster that Tom was commissioned a 2nd Lieutenant. Hearing that, Sergeant McMillen began getting the clothing that reflected that status, first giving him his shoulder boards to identify his rank, two blue rectangles surrounded by a solid brass border. He affixed them to the dark blue wool shell jacket that Tom would wear for the duration of the war and handed him the light blue pantaloons with the dark blue piping down the leg, white suspenders, a pair of cotton drawers, a white cotton shirt, some grey woolen socks, and his kepi, a dark blue cap. He also gave Armstrong a pair of brogans, "Jeff Davis boots," they were called, as the former U.S. Secretary of War had ordered a new style of infantry footwear produced for the Army several years before. Now, of all things, Davis was the President of the Confederate States of America. The last thing McMillen gave him was a brand new Colt. Tom Armstrong strapped the new weapon tightly about his waist. His own would go in the box that Jacob had made.

Armstrong and Gary went back to the Captain's quarters, down the street from Ball's cabin, where the 2nd Lieutenant changed his clothes, discarding the old, ragged uniform he had put on that morning.

"You'll bunk here next door with Tom Black, Tom. We like to keep the officers together and near the Colonel and Major so that orders and instructions can be given clearly and quickly with no room for interpretation. The sergeants and corporals will be in the main barracks across the street. Need 'em close to the men. You got a copy of *Hardee's Tactics*?"

"No. I better get one."

"I'll find you one. I want you to be in charge of the training of the men of this Company. Before I get to that, do you know what your specific duties are?"

"No," came the response. "But, from what I recall about my time in the 78th, I am to do as you tell me without question. Right?"

The two men were sitting at a table in Gary's quarters with the door open. It was a lovely day in Zanesville, Ohio. "Tom, you have experience in war. You've seen the elephant. I haven't. So, I will lean on you to work with me on commanding this Company. If you think we should do something different than I do, talk to me. That experience is why Ball picked you, and I asked that you be part of my Company. I will explain all of this to Lieutenant Black, since he hasn't seen the big pachyderm either."

Armstrong laughed. "The big pachyderm? You mean the elephant?"

"Yeah, the elephant. As for your daily duties, I want you to make sure that all of our equipment is in working order, including the rifles. Cleanliness is important so stress that to the men; make sure

90

that we have enough wood for our fires; always try to find a site for camp near water, the cleaner the better; no problem here with Licking Creek running toward the Old Muskingum right nearby; help me with inspections of the men; take command of guard detail; make sure that they have adequate food and clothing; and work with the other lieutenants in making sure that we are as safe and secure as we can be. You will also teach *Hardee's Tactics* and drill the men constantly, every day, in them. You'll also help me with the paperwork about this Company. Basically, you are responsible for the welfare of your squad and this Company."

"My," thought Tom Armstrong, "maybe I don't have to worry as much about getting the respect of the men. He's giving me authority. My experience with the 78th seems to count a lot."

"The day begins at first light with *Reveille*. Have the men fall in and be at attention so the *Roll Call* can be made, followed by my inspection. I want this Company to be first rate."

"Yes, sir!"

"Once we are assured that everyone is present and accounted for, I will order the Stable Call where you and Tom Black will make sure that the horses were taken care of and then you will make sure the grounds around our tents are clean and tidy, if possible. Then, there will be Sick Call where those who are not well can go to see Dr. Houston, Dr. Richards, or Dr. Bryan. When all of that is done, I shall issue the call to breakfast. After we eat, you will oversee Guard Mounting and then have one of your sergeants take the day's reports and other paperwork to the adjutant and to receive orders for me from the Colonel. That's called First Sergeant Call. You have a good man or two in mind for that duty?"

"Yes, sir!" Tom Armstrong said, thinking specifically of Patrick Murphy.

"You will drill the men according to the *Tactics* during the rest of the day. No more than two hours at a time, four times a day and make sure the men get their rest. Feed them dinner around 12 noon. We shall have a dress parade around 6PM after which I will order the call for the evening meal. When that is done, give the men free time to write letters, play their instruments, engage in a friendly game of cards, anything to take their minds off what we are doing here. The evening *Roll Call* will be at 8:30 PM, and I will conduct another inspection. *Taps* will be played around 9:45PM, after which it is lights out. You understand all that?"

"I think so. I'll get used to it as we go."

"Get used to it now, lieutenant." Daniel Gary could be quite stern and brusque when he needed to be. He hoped Lieutenant Tom Armstrong could do the same. He would have to.

"Yes, sir!"

"We will also need seven to ten men from time to time to stand guard around the wall with men from the other companies of the regiment. You make sure that it is fairly done; nobody gets extra guard duty unless he makes an error in drill or commits a crime of some sort. Keep a record. By the way, if any of the men do get out of hand, there will be punishment, like guard duty. And, if we catch any of them fighting and injuring another, they will go to the stockade. Finally, if a serious crime occurs, like a killing, I will order a firing squad. We must have very strict, rigid discipline. Understood?"

"I understand."

They heard the hoofbeats of a horse slowing in front of Gary's quarters and in walked Major Moses Granger, seeing the door was open. Gary and Armstrong snapped to attention and saluted. The Major's duty was primarily to assist the Colonel in whatever needed doing. He would work with the Adjutant in making sure that all company paperwork was correct and complete, oversee the camp guard, and help Colonel Ball with Hardee's *School of the Battalion*.

Returning the salute, the Major said, "At ease, gentlemen. Nice to see you both here so soon. I had heard you were here and thought I should come over to see how things were progressing. I would have had you come to me, but I couldn't find a messenger to deliver that request. You will come to see me from now on."

"Yes, sir," replied Dan Gary. "With compliments, sir, it is good to see you as well. For the past couple of hours, I have been telling Lieutenant Armstrong about his duties. In addition to the normal demands of a 2nd lieutenant, I want him to work directly with me on the command of my Company, especially the training of the men."

"Why him?" asked Granger, apparently forgetting the details of Tom's experience with the 78th that the Rev. Charles McCabe had extolled in the Colonel's law office on Main St. three weeks previous.

Recalling McCabe's praise, Gary began, "With all due respect, Major, he's been here before. The rest of the Company hasn't. He knows what we need to do. The others don't. He's seen the elephant, that is, been in battle. The others haven't. He can shoot an Enfield. They can't. With your permission, sir, I would like him to teach them."

"It appears you're a pretty valuable fellow to this regiment, Lieutenant. I will watch you closely. Permission granted, Captain."

"Thank you, sir. Is there anything else?"

"Yes, check in with me every day after the First Sergeant Call to see if Colonel Ball needs anything out of the ordinary done that he hasn't told you."

"Yes, sir. I will do that personally, or I will send Lieutenant Armstrong."

"Very well. You may return to the business at hand."

"Thank you, sir." With that, Major Moses Granger returned their salutes, turned and walked back out into the sunshine of September 1, 1862.

"Questions, Tom?" addressing the lieutenant informally.

"Yes. First, where can I get an Enfield? I want to practice before I start training the men. Then, do I assume correctly that I can quarter my mare in the corral until we get closer to leaving for the field? Last, will it be all right if I take leave of camp a couple times before we go?"

"I will get you an Enfield later today. You can start practicing tomorrow. The Company won't be formed for another week or so. Then, put your horse in the corral and the tack in the stable. I expect you will need her. The sergeant on First Sergeant duty will certainly need one. About leave…I will see what I can do. The enlisted men have to get a pass from the Colonel or Major Granger, but I can grant you leave every now and again. Make sure that Black can fill in for you."

"Thanks, Dan. I appreciate it and will do everything that you ask as best I can."

"Just bring your bedroll and other things over, and we will get you set up in your quarters."

"Will do," and with that, Tom Armstrong left the Captain's cabin, to put Aspen in the corral after he found someone with a wagon to bring the box Jacob had built down to his quarters. "So far, so good," he thought.

The next morning, the Enfield rifle felt just right. He hadn't shot one of them since January, but this one felt perfect. The Union army had been using the weapon for some time, importing it from England where it was first produced ten years earlier. It was a single shot, muzzle loading rifle, weighing about ten pounds. It had a "flip up" sight that made aiming it a lot easier. And, besides, it had a range far greater than the old 1842 Springfield, which was really only effective at somewhere between 50 and 75 yards. The Enfield was good at ten times that distance since the barrel was rifled and caused the Minie ball to spin.

The Enfield had another advantage: a 21-inch-long socket bayonet. When fixed, that made the weapon 76 inches long or over 6 feet in length. A deadly spear and a serious club, as well as a vicious firearm. He would teach the men to fire the weapon, to swing like a club, and to use as a spear, getting more comfortable in his role as an officer.

He spent the rest of the day familiarizing himself with the layout of Camp Zanesville, inspecting the barracks and mess hall, and insuring there was plenty of room for the supply wagons. Captain Gary had said he was to care for the welfare of the enlisted men, so he had to find out what needed to be done before they all arrived. Practice with the Enfield could wait another day.

It was Wednesday, September 3rd. That morning, Tom Armstrong rode Aspen out into the woods, the rifle carefully holstered. He had 20 rounds of ammunition in his saddlebags. He knew that the .577 caliber lead Minie ball would flatten out when it hit something which made the rifle quite deadly. One direct hit could actually take a man's head off. It was responsible for the significant number of lost arms and legs blown off by its force and also contributed to the immense number of amputations the surgeons had to perform. He had seen it at Fort Donelson and Shiloh, the surgeons' clothes stained with blood and men screaming at the sound of the saw doing its work on an arm or a leg. "Yes, war is ugly," he thought.

"Time to get to work," he thought, dropping a Minie ball down the barrel, opening the sight. He took aim at a flowering bush 100 yards away and fired. The gun roared to life, and seconds later, the bush erupted into a thousand pieces, virtually disintegrating into thin air. "Dang, I'm good at this," he thought. "Need to take longer shots."

He continued to extend the distance of his shots, hitting every target he picked out." Glad I learned to use this thing in the training with the 78th," he thought to himself. He was just about done, feeling quite good about himself, when he saw a wild turkey about 300 yards away. Dropping another Minie ball down the barrel, he popped up the sight and took aim at the bird's head. He pulled the trigger, the gun roared once again, and the Minie ball tore the turkey's head clean off, leaving the lifeless body. "I'll have to take this back and give it to the cook. "Turkey dinner tomorrow," he thought, quite satisfied with his use of the weapon. "If I can do this, I might not have as much trouble as I imagined in getting the men to respect me."

Walking back to his quarters, he found Dan Gary there with a book in his hands...*Hardee's Tactics*. Written by William J. Hardee in 1855 while he was serving as an instructor at West Point, the *Tactics* detailed everything from the formation of a regiment, to how the men should stand, to the precise procedures for loading and firing a rifle, to the exact distance between the men's steps on the march or on the double quick.

"Read up on this. Drilling of the men will start two weeks from Monday. Get with your sergeants and corporals and figure out the schedule of when you'll do what. You have the rest of the week. I'll be tied up with Granger and Ball, but I'll see you at mealtime. "You can tell me how everything is going." Armstrong put the Enfield in the corner of the cabin by the desk he would use for completing company reports and began to refresh his memory of the *Tactics*.

"Murphy's gonna love this discipline," he joked to himself. "Bet he hasn't ever followed an order from anyone. Well, maybe his father, and, for sure, his mother. But that's about all." Tom Armstrong genuinely liked Patrick Murphy and hoped he could prevail upon him to help the senior officers create a crack Company. The next morning, he took pen to paper.

Camp Zanesville
Sept 4th, 1862

Dear Father, Mother, Brothers and Sisters
I am well and hearty. I have slept 3 nights in camp. I nearly froze two nights but last night I slept well. I have not caught a bit of a cold since I came in. The Capt & 1st Lieut are out recruiting. I am left in charge of the camp. I was acting Officer of the Guard while the 97th went to town for their arms. They are clothed also & will leave soon. I tell you I need my watch. Please bring it to town and leave it at Bonnet's Jewelry Store on Main St. opposite Zane House. Bring it in soon as I well want it. The boys are swell. I like it well. Can you come in and see us soon? Ken Tucker is in our Co. I feel first Rate. I will send you all the particulars soon.
Write soon. If you find any recruits send them on.
Farewell
T S Armstrong
I will tell you where to direct when I next write.

Needless to say, the Armstrong family, over there in Norwich, was pleased to receive his first letter from camp.

Tom was working on the drill plan the next morning when he heard a familiar voice outside the cabin.

"Lieutenant Armstrong, you in there?" It was Patrick Murphy.

"Mr. Murphy, I have been waiting for you and hope you are well. It is good to see you, and I have a proposition for you to consider. You been to see the surgeon yet?"

"Yep. Says I'm fit as a fiddle. Don't know what that means, but he told me to get a uniform and sign in. So, I went over to the recruiting office, and they told me I was in Company I and where I could find you."

"Where's your uniform?"

"Ain't got one."

"Come with me," Armstrong said, "we can talk along the way." It was off to see the Quartermaster. As they walked, Tom Armstrong told Patrick Murphy that he would appoint him sergeant and would like him to have a principle role in drilling the enlisted men. He also said that he would like Murphy's help in directing the Company's affairs when he was away or was working with Captain Gary, Major Granger, or Colonel Ball. No one had said anything about helping the Colonel and the Major, but based upon the remark the Colonel had made, he just had a feeling that he would have more to do.

"Why me?" asked the curious young man. "Why not one of the others?"

"Because you have an attitude I like, I know you from church, and I think the men will work for you. I really think that down the road you are officer material, but there's one big change you're gonna have to make."

"What's that?"

"The army runs on discipline, doing what your superior tells you to do, no questions asked. Can't just do whatever you please. There's a book called *Hardee's Tactics* that instructs us on what to do, how to do it, and when and where to do it. Very detailed. I was thinking about the recruiting meeting and your performance that night and concluded that I wasn't sure that you could survive this man's army as a private, just taking orders and following them. You're a smart guy, and I could use your help and suggestions. You will have more freedom working with me than you would working for a sergeant and a corporal who are not as smart as you are. That's my proposition, Mr. Murphy, take it or leave it."

Patrick Murphy stopped dead in his tracks, turned, scratched his long beard, and looked down at 2nd Lieutenant Tom Armstrong. "You want me to work with you and to offer ideas that will help you run the Company?"

"Yep."

"Do I have to drill with the other boys? I've heard about that, and it ain't much fun."

"Nope, but you have to know the drills and instructions of the *Tactics* in order to teach them."

"You gotta deal, Lieutenant."

"Good. Now, when we are in front of people, you are to call me 'Lieutenant Armstrong' or 'Sir.' When we are in private, you can call me 'Tom' or 'Sump,' short for my middle name, but make sure never to call me that in public. You got that? Oh, and by the way, trim the beard."

"Yes, sir," and the two men were off to see the Sergeant Quartermaster about a uniform, Tom wondering if the Sergeant had clothes big enough for Patrick Murphy. "I will talk with the Captain about all this. Won't be a problem. You can change your clothes in my quarters. I will show you the barracks where you will sleep and stow your gear, and then we have to talk."

"Yes, sir," came the reply.

"Sergeant McMillen, please be sure to give Sergeant Murphy, here, his stripes."

"Yes, Lieutenant Armstrong."

Armstrong and Murphy met all afternoon, with the Lieutenant laying out what Captain Gary had lectured him about in regard to his duties earlier in the week. "Gary says he will make you a sergeant in Company I and agrees that you will assist me, Patrick, also being another pair of eyes and ears. We want to know what's going on in the Company. Also, I will have you requisition a horse to deliver our reports to the Colonel and to receive instructions and orders from him." Tom Armstrong didn't tell him how to go about such a requisition because he wanted to see how Sergeant Murphy would handle something that simple with no more details. "Gotta see how resourceful and inventive he is," he thought to himself.

"Gary's going to organize the Company a week from Wednesday at 10 o'clock in the morning. We have to be ready."

"Who's the other sergeants gonna be?"

"Don't know. Lieutenant Black will have to make a couple of choices, but I am thinking of Edwin Bristow from over in Coshocton. Known him for a while. Will make him the same proposition I put in front of you. He's a good kid, about your age. Maybe the three of us work together. I'll let you know. In the meantime, start reading this." He handed *Hardee's Tactics* to Patrick Murphy. "Dang, I hope he can read."

Murphy looked at the book and opened it, flipping through the pages. "We gotta know all this?"

"Yep. It won't be easy. Now, I have meetings with the other officers tomorrow and church with Reverend McCabe on Sunday, so let's meet again bright and early Monday morning. Find a place that's quiet. Get some paper and pencils, and we'll map out the schedule we'll use until we leave this place."

"Will do, Sump," Murphy smiling as he said it.

At 9 o'clock AM on Saturday, September 6, 1862, Colonel William H. Ball and Major Moses M. Granger stood before ten Company commanders, twenty lieutenants, the three surgeons, and Chaplain Charles McCabe of the 122nd Ohio Volunteer Infantry. They had assembled in the barn that was used primarily to house Charlie Snyder's livestock. Ball welcomed the officers and had each one stand to announce his name, rank, and hometown.

"We will be the crack regiment in the Union army," he admonished, "and will be looked upon as an example of exceptional military behavior. I will not stand for exceptions from *Hardee's Tactics*, and I expect every man in this regiment to behave accordingly. There will be no drunkenness, no gambling, no visits from prostitutes, or any other deviant behavior. While we train, you will be granted leave to go home and say farewell. The major and I cannot control what you do there. But, when you are here, you will do as we order. We will listen to your suggestions, but our orders are final. Is that clear?"

"Yes, sir!" Thirty-four voices joined together in response.

"How many of you have seen the elephant? I know Lieutenant Armstrong has, but how about the rest of you?" Lieutenant Tom Armstrong and four other men stood up. "We will count on you to lead the ones who have not lived army life and the daily marching, the sleeping out-of-doors, the skirmishes and battles, and the boredom. Our rules about the regiment's behavior will stand in the field just like they stand here. You who have re-enlisted are to be the examples to the newcomers of the way officers should behave and then to model their own behavior after yours. You will also teach the *Tactics*, so read up. Is that clear?"

Armstrong and the others who were standing, replied, "Yes, sir!" He was thinking, "I have to do this as well as help Gary? There aren't enough hours in the day. My sergeants and corporals better be darn good. Tom Black, too."

Ball went on, "You Company commanders will meet with the major and me after dinner this afternoon at 1 o'clock at my headquarters. Then, you will have meetings with your lieutenants, sergeants, and corporals no later than a week from today. Lieutenants, please inform the Adjutant of when those meetings will take place. Perhaps they should all be scheduled at the same time. The Regiment should be full by the 17th. Regardless if it is or it isn't, drill will start two weeks from this coming Monday. That will give you all a chance to memorize the *Tactics* that you will be teaching the enlisted men. Am I clear?"

In unison, "Yes, sir."

Changing his tune somewhat, Ball said, "Captain McCabe, are we ready for services tomorrow?"

"Yes, sir," replied the Rev. Charles C. McCabe, "mandatory 10 o'clock service right here, and then one at 2 o'clock, also right here."

"Very well, Chaplain. We look forward to it. I might also suggest Christian education for the men as well, perhaps between services each Sunday or on Wednesday afternoon."

"I will plan on it, sir."

With that, Moses Granger shouted "Atten-TION!" The officers of the 122nd O.V.I. stood erect, backs straight, eyes focused directly ahead, and saluted. Colonel Ball and Major Granger returned the salutes.

"Dis-MISSED!"

While the meeting had been going on, Patrick Murphy had left the barracks with the *Tactics* in his haversack along with paper and pencil in case he wanted to take notes. "Getting the horse was easy," he thought. He rode down a road out through a pasture, found a brook rippling its way toward Licking Creek, and sat down under a big hickory tree to see what Hardee prescribed. The first thing he noticed was that there were three sections of the book: *School of the Soldier*, *School of the Company*, and *School of the Battalion*. In the *School of the Soldier*, there were 363 instructions; *School of the Company*, 379; and *School of the Battalion*, 974. "Good night!" he thought to himself, "there's over 1,700 instructions in this book. How will anyone learn it?"

He scanned the first few pages and found the *School of the Soldier* on Page 8, but right above that was a section on Commands.

Commands.
There are three kinds.
1. The command of caution, which is attention.
2. The preparatory command which indicates the movement which is to be executed.
3. The command of execution, such as march or halt, or, in the manual of arms, the part of the command which causes an execution.
4. The tone of the command should be animated, distinct, and of a loudness proportioned to the number of men under instruction.
5. The command of attention is pronounced at the top of the voice, dwelling on the last syllable.
6. The command of execution will be pronounced in a tone firm and brief.
7. The commands of caution and the preparatory commands are herein distinguished by italics, those of execution by CAPITALS.
8. Those preparatory commands which, from their length, are difficult to be pronounced at once, must be divided into two or three parts, with an ascending progression in the tone of command, but always in such a manner that the tone of execution may be more energetic and elevated. The divisions are indicated by a hyphen. The

parts of the commands which are placed in parentheses, are not pronounced.

Patrick Murphy was astonished at the detail. "You mean we have to follow these commands just as Hardee wrote them? I gotta see Armstrong about that." His curiosity aroused, he thought, "I wonder what's in the *School of the Soldier*. That's what he wants me to teach." So, he read on.

SCHOOL OF THE SOLDIER
General Rules and Divisions of the School of the Soldier

Each part will be divided into lessons, as follows

PART FIRST
Lesson 1   Position of the soldier without arms, Eyes right, left and front
Lesson 2   Facings
Lesson 3   Principles of the direct step in common and quick time
Lesson 4   Principles of the direct step in double quick time and the run

PART SECOND
Lesson 1   Principles of shouldered arms
Lesson 2   Manual of arms
Lesson 3   To load at four times and at will
Lesson 4   Firings, direct, oblique, by file and by rank
Lesson 5   To fire and load, kneeling and lying
Lesson 6   Bayonet exercise

PART THIRD
Lesson 1   Union of eight or twelve men for instruction in the principle of alignment
Lesson 2   The direct march, the oblique march, and different steps
Lesson 3   The march by the flank

Lesson 4 Principles of wheeling and the change of direction

Lesson 5 Long marches in double quick time, and the run, with arms and knapsacks

LESSON I – Position of the Soldier

Heels on the same line, as near each other as conformation of the man will permit.

The feet turned out equally, and forming with each other something less than a right angle,

The knees straight without stiffness;

The body erect on the hips, inclining a little forward,

The shoulders square and falling equally,

The arms hanging naturally,

The elbows near the body,

The palm of the hand turned a little to the front, the little finger behind the seam of the pantaloons,

The head erect and square to the front, without constraint;

The eyes fixed straight to the front, and striking the ground about the distance of fifteen paces.

Sergeant Patrick Murphy kept reading. The detail was incredible. "He's actually telling us how we should stand," he said to himself. "The little finger behind the seam of the pantaloons? Every time we stand in line? And, there's fourteen more of these lessons? Now, I really hafta talk with Armstrong, but I've got a feeling it won't do any good. He may be sorry he made me a sergeant. I suppose he could bust me back to being a private." Sergeant Patrick Murphy started back toward the barracks, the late summer sun streaming down on him. It was a gorgeous day in Zanesville, Ohio.

When the officers' meeting was over, Lieutenant Tom Armstrong walked out of the barn with Lieutenant Tom Black whom he had just met. The two men exchanged pleasantries and began to share their backgrounds with one another as they walked back to their quarters. "Gary wants me to develop a schedule for the enlisted men, so I'm meeting with Sergeant Murphy to do that on Monday morning," said Armstrong. "Want to join us?"

"Sure, I have a lot of catching up to do," replied Black. "What's it really like out there? I mean, when the bullets start flying and the cannons come to life?"

"I'll meet you for supper. I will tell you then. It isn't pretty, I can assure you."

"Why do they call it 'seeing the elephant?'"

"Don't know. It just means that those who have seen it have been in battle."

They were nearing their quarters when Armstrong heard a familiar voice. "T.S., glad you made it in." Charlie McCabe, in uniform and all, slowed his horse to a walk. "I need to talk with you a minute. Do you have some time?"

Remembering that his friend was a commissioned captain, Tom Armstrong said, "Yes, Captain, at your service."

"See you later, Armstrong," said Tom Black.

"Yeah, see you later. We should also talk about the meeting with the NCOs?"

"Yes. Let's try to have them all identified by Wednesday or Thursday."

"Good idea." Tom turned toward his friend and mentor, the Chaplain.

"You heard the Colonel just now talk about a Christian education program? Well, I'd like you to help with it. You're a teacher and have placed your faith and trust in God to see you through this. Maybe we can help the other men."

Armstrong stroked his beard and fiddled with the end of his mustache, looking squarely at Charles McCabe.

"I have more duty than the ordinary 2nd Lieutenant. Dan wants me to help run the Company, and you just heard the Colonel. I may not have much time to help you, but let me know what I can do."

"Will you be at the service tomorrow morning?"

"Yes."

"Well, it won't be like the Methodist one that we're used to, as I'm sure we will have Baptists, Presbyterians, and others as well. I will work on a service that will be pretty basic for all. Hopefully, that will work."

"I'm sure it will, but if you'll excuse me, I have to go. I see Sergeant Murphy approaching, and I need to visit with him."

"Very well, T.S., I'll see you in the morning."

Patrick Murphy shared his thoughts on the *Tactics*. As Armstrong listened, he was pleased that the kid thought about what he was reading. "He's smarter than I thought," he said to himself.

"I'm going to be crystal clear, Sergeant. You will memorize the fifteen lessons in the *School of the Soldier* and will be prepared to teach them starting two weeks from Monday. I will help you, but I have my own issue: The *School of the Company*. Did you look at that? Captain Gary and Colonel Ball want me to help the other lieutenants with it, so I may not be around much. That's why you are so important to this Company."

"Whattya gotta teach them?" Patrick Murphy asked, handing the book to Tom.

"Take a look."

SCHOOL OF THE COMPANY
General Rules and Division of the School of the Company

Instruction by Company will always precede that of battalion, and the object being to prepare the soldiers for the higher school, the exercises of detail by Company will be strictly adhered to, as well in respect to principles, as the order of progression herein prescribed.

There will be attached to a Company undergoing elementary instruction, a captain, a covering sergeant, and a certain number of file closers, the whole posted in the manner indicated, Title First, and according to the same Title, the officer charged with the exercise of such Company will herein be denominated the instructor.

The School of the Company will be divided into six lessons, and each lesson will comprehend five articles, as follows:

LESSON I
1. To open ranks
2. Alignment in open ranks
3. Manual of arms
4. To close ranks
5. Alignment and manual of arms in closed ranks.
LESSON II
1. To load in four times and at will.
2. To fire by Company
3. To fire by file
4. To fire by rank
5. To fire by the rear rank
LESSON III
1. To march in line of battle
2. To halt the Company marching in line of battle, and to align it
3. Oblique march in line of battle
4. To mark time, to march in double-quick time, and the back step
5. To march in retreat in line of battle

There was more; a lot more.

"That's what I have to teach the other officers of the Regiment, Patrick. Do you see why I may be tied up? There are four more lieutenants who have been acquainted with the *Tactics* before, but I doubt they ever studied these lessons, just like I haven't. The *School of the Soldier* I know pretty well, but not this one. The five of us will have to split up and work with two Company commanders apiece, one from our own Company and then one more."

Sergeant Patrick Murphy was beginning to understand the enormity and the gravity about what was going to happen at Camp Zanesville until they were sent to the field. He was grateful to Tom Armstrong for the faith that he had in him and pledged to himself that he would do as best he could to serve the lieutenant well. He was about to speak when he heard...

"Hallo, there." Five rough-looking young men were approaching Armstrong's cabin. Murphy had never seen them before, but Tom Armstrong had. It was Edwin Bristow and his four friends.

"Howdy, boys," Armstrong said with a smile. "Good to see you. Thanks for coming in. Have you been to see the Surgeon?"

"Yep. Now we gotta find uniforms," said Edwin Bristow.

"Patrick, meet Edwin Bristow. Edwin, Sergeant Patrick Murphy."

"Sergeant, huh?"

"That's right."

"Patrick, I want to speak with Edwin. Can you take the others to see the Sergeant Quartermaster?"

"Yes, sir. Come with me, fellas."

"Make sure that they find tents and get their gear stowed."

"Yes, sir."

"Edwin, come on in. I have something I want to talk to you about. You can get your uniform later today."

"Please call me Eddie, Lieutenant Armstrong," said Edwin Bristow. They went inside and sat down.

Armstrong went through the same details about the command of the Company and Regiment as he had with Patrick Murphy.

"You want me to be a sergeant, like Murphy, and train the men? And the other stuff like getting firewood and making sure they have enough rations? Why me?"

It was an easy question to answer for the Lieutenant, using the same words he had used with Murphy.

"I'm at your service, Lieutenant," was the response.

"Good, Captain Gary wants to meet with the lieutenants and Non-Coms of this Company no later than a week from today. Also, I will need you and Patrick to work with Captain Gary, Lieutenant Black, and me to identify potential sergeants and corporals since the two of you know most of the men who have enlisted. Any chance one of your friends who came in with you could serve that way?"

"Possibly, Tom."

"I do want you and Patrick to meet Thaddeus Brennan. I think he would do well as a sergeant. Sound him out and then talk to Lieutenant Black. Brennan will report to him."

"Yes, sir."

"Now, there is one other thing. In public, you are to call me 'Lieutenant Armstrong' or 'Sir." In private with me alone or with Patrick, you may call me 'Tom' or 'Sump,' short for my middle name."

"Yes, sir."

"I am meeting with Sergeant Murphy and Lieutenant Black on Monday morning to develop the training schedule for the men. I imagine the Colonel will want to use it with the other companies. I want you at that meeting, too. Murphy will tell you where it will be. In the meantime, you have two weeks to memorize the *School of the Soldier* in *Hardee's Tactics*." He gave Eddie Bristow the book. "I suggest, that since neither you nor Patrick have ever read it, that you study together and then bring questions to me. Does that seem reasonable?"

Bristow took the book and opened it, looking over the first pages, just as Murphy had done.

"Now, before you start complaining about the level of detail in the lessons as your counterpart did earlier this afternoon, I will not listen to it. Orders are orders, and it is our job to train the men in the *Tactics*. The Captain wants this company to be the best performing one in the Regiment, and that is exactly what we are going to do. Understood?"

"Yes, sir."

"And, when you are not studying or making preparations to welcome the enlisted men and get them situated, you will be out in the county recruiting. Let's go get your uniform."

About 300 of the expected 1,000 men who would make up the 122nd Ohio Volunteer Infantry had made it to Camp Zanesville during this first week of September, and all of them showed up for church in the barn. Tom Armstrong attended with Dan Gary, Tom Black, Patrick Murphy, and Eddie Bristow. The congregation really didn't need organ music, as Chaplain McCabe simply led everyone in singing familiar hymns. The Chaplain had cobbled together a make-shift service and pledged to himself that over the next week, he would have a more polished one, making a mental note that he needed to see the Colonel about it. He had to talk with him about the Christian Education program and also about holding services and

Bible Study not just at Camp Zanesville, but in the field as well. Hymnbooks would be good to have, but he doubted that Zanesville could supply 1,000 of them. There was no chance of getting an organ, but maybe he could assemble a band. As had become his custom, he ended the service that first Sunday in September 1862, with the singing of *The Battle Hymn of the Republic*, with all three hundred or so Union soldiers standing and joining in.

The Sabbath brought no work to be done, so Tom started studying the *Tactics*: The *School of the Company*. He hoped that Murphy and Bristow had begun their own work on The *School of the Soldier*. He didn't want to bother them as they were getting to know each other and would find out in the morning.

As he studied, his mind wandered to the conversation he had with Tom Black over supper the previous evening and hoped that he hadn't scared him by recounting what he saw at Fort Donelson and Shiloh. He realized that Black had enlisted for the excitement and adventure of the war, along with some patriotic feelings and intense peer pressure from the good folks in his hometown of Fultonham. Further, he didn't know what an Enfield rifle could do to a man or a horse, and he hadn't thought about artillery fire blasting trees out of the ground, the smoke that enveloped the field, the screams of the wounded, and the possibility of getting killed or wounded himself.

Armstrong was very glad that he had seen it and could prepare himself mentally for going back to it, and he would help Tom Black. He would have Charlie McCabe talk to him, too, for he knew that Black had no knowledge of what it was like to be the first one over the wall or out of the works, much less the first one to start across an open field into the fire of the enemy that was specifically aimed at him. He also resolved to go to Hopewell the following week if Captain Gary could spare him before the drilling of the men started. He realized, that Sunday afternoon, that he hadn't thought about Frank Porter at all that week, having been so busy in organizing the Company.

He jotted a quick note to Jacob, asking that his brother keep all the letters and documents that he might send home during his time away. Tom Armstrong wasn't quite sure why that was important, he just knew that it was. He sent Francis Porter a similar note asking her to keep his letters and saying he would try to get to Hopewell sometime before the 17th. Despite the long periods of time when they would not correspond or see each other, this had only been a week or so, but he missed her. "She would be proud," he thought to himself, "of how I am handling things here. Bristow and Murphy should make things a lot easier in gaining the respect of the men. The Colonel's confidence helps immensely. So, does that of Granger and Gary. Now to live up to it."

Monday, September 8, dawned with sunshine and rising temperatures. The humidity was also high like it was most of the time in the summer down by the Muskingum River and Licking Creek. He met Tom Black, Patrick Murphy, and Eddie Bristow in the mess hall at 6 o'clock that morning as previously arranged. It was time to get to work on the daily schedule for the enlisted men. He retrieved the tack for Aspen and went into the corral to get her ready for the day's work. He saddled her, attached his saddle bags, secured the Enfield, and was ready to go. The men would go out in the country, still within Camp Zanesville, not to be disturbed for most of the day.

Black had his own horse, a buckskin mare, just about the same size as Aspen. He called her "Golden" although her color was not. He was up in the saddle. Murphy and Bristow hitched a couple of horses to a wagon, loaded the provisions, including six pumpkins, some a little more orange than others, that Armstrong had asked them to find after church the day before. The two lieutenants rode in front with the sergeants following in the wagon as they walked along a road surrounded by fields of grain that would be used to feed the men and the animals.

"What the hell does he need pumpkins for?" asked Eddie Bristow.

"Beats me," came the response from Patrick Murphy, "but knowing him, there's a good reason."

"Sergeant Murphy, are we going in the right direction?"

"Yes, sir."

"How much farther?"

"Maybe half a mile."

"Why don't you and Sergeant Bristow take the lead and get us there?"

Patrick Murphy turned the wagon horses to the right toward the brook, reined them in, and stopped.

"Good place for a meeting, Sergeant."

"Thank you, sir."

All four dismounted and sat in a circle under the hickory tree. Lieutenant Tom Armstrong repeated both what Dan Gary had asked him to do and what Colonel Ball ordered. He said that it would place a burden on them, but orders were orders.

He repeated the admonition from Colonel William Ball: "There will be no drunkenness, no gambling, no visits from prostitutes, or any other deviant behavior. The Captain told me that there will be serious punishment, even death by firing squad, if any of that happens. I trust we are clear, gentlemen."

Tom Black started thinking, "Armstrong should have been the 1st Lieutenant, not me. Maybe even captain. He just knows more about this than anyone else, maybe in the whole damn Regiment. For sure in the Company."

Remembering what Dan Gary had told him about his duties, Tom Armstrong started laying out a schedule of daily activity for the men. Black, Murphy, and Bristow listened intently.

"Sergeant," he said, addressing Eddie Bristow, "will you be so kind as to write down what I am about to go over?"

"Certainly, sir," taking paper and pencil out of his haversack.

"Here's what I am thinking, gentlemen, according to what the Captain told me. *Reveille* at 5 o'clock AM, followed by the first *Roll Call*. Presuming everyone is present, we will drill the men on the *Tactics* from 6 o'clock till 7:30 which will be followed by breakfast in the mess hall. Have the men march to meals in the formation that Hardee prescribed. The surgeon's call will be at 8 o'clock, and we must be on the lookout for those who are feigning illness. *Stable Call* and *Guard Mounting* will be at 9."

"What's that, sir?" asked Bristow.

"Guard Mounting is the changing of the guard, assignment of the officer of the day and officer of the guard, Sergeant."

"I don't know what that means."

"You will. Let me go on. The second drill will be between 9:30 and 11:30, followed by dinner. Mr. Murphy, you will be responsible for the daily First Sergeant Call after you eat. Make sure you have all of the reports of the Company commanders and deliver them to Colonel Ball's staff. Pick up any instructions or orders the Colonel has for the commanders and stop by Major Granger's quarters to see if he has any instructions for them. Deliver whatever they give you quickly, and then get back to Captain Gary's quarters."

"Yes, sir."

"The third drill will be from 1 to 3 with another one from 5 to 6. We will have a dress parade at 6:30, followed by supper at 7:30. A final *Inspection* of the day and *Roll Call* will happen at 9:30. At 9:45, the bugler will play *Taps* signaling the end of the day, lights out, and quiet. How does that sound?"

"Like a lot of work," answered Tom Black. "Let me ask you, what do the men do in their free time, between drills?"

"We will see what they like to do," was the answer. "With the 78th, we had to clean the camp, collect firewood, make sure the roads were passable, and my favorite," he said sarcastically, "fill in old latrines and dig new ones. We wrote home, played cards, practiced our instruments, and in good weather, pitched horseshoes, and chose up sides and played a game of base ball, I think he called it. Then, I also saw two squads of men face each other crouching down in two lines. A man in the back held a ball and, on command, he started running with it. The men in the lines smashed into each other. The line in front of the man with the ball tried to keep the one across from it from knocking him down. Invariably, they did, and then the whole thing was repeated. Then, for some reason, the other squad got the ball. It just looked like two miniature armies colliding against one another. Darndest thing I ever saw. But, in any event, let's let them pretty much do what they want."

The four men ate their dinner of ham, cheese, apples, bread, and water, continuing to hone the timetable that Tom had laid out. They came to an agreement about 3 o'clock, and he asked Eddie Bristow to finalize it down for Captain Gary.

"Lieutenant, you and I should meet with the Captain about this."

"Yes," said Tom Black. "The sooner the better 'cuz if he agrees, it goes to the Colonel, and you heard his orders."

"Can you arrange a meeting with him tomorrow?"

There was one other matter that Armstrong had to attend to. He walked over to the wagon, took the reins, and drove off, some 200 yards down the road. Seeing a tree stump, he slowed the wagon, unloaded the pumpkins, and put one of them on the stump.

"Okay, gentlemen, target practice. I will order you to fire using Hardee." He took the Enfield out of its holster and the cartridge box out of one of his saddle bags. He dropped a Minie ball down the barrel, rammed it tight, took aim at the pumpkin, and fired. The rifle roared to life and within seconds, the pumpkin was blasted to smithereens. "Now, Lieutenant, it's your turn. The commands are Ready, Aim, Fire, Load." He rode Aspen down to the stump and put another pumpkin on it.

Returning, he gave the Enfield to Tom Black. "Never felt a gun this heavy," he said.

Armstrong barked the commands, and Black fired. Nothing happened to the pumpkin. "Move up fifty yards and try again."

Black pulled the trigger. Again, nothing. It looked like the Minie had hit a tree, about ten feet higher than the stump.

Patrick Murphy seized the weapon, announcing that he would splatter the pumpkin. Same result as Lieutenant Black. Missed it twice.

Now, it was Eddie Bristow's turn. He, too, missed it twice.

"Here, let me show you," said Tom Armstrong. He popped up the sight and said, "Fellas, you have to aim low with this. The ball will come spinning out of the barrel on a line. You don't need to shoot high." With that, he fired once again. The pumpkin on the stump disappeared.

On the way back to camp, the two sergeants were amazed at what they had just seen. They knew that the Lieutenant would expect them to be just as good with an Enfield as he was.

"We're gonna need a lot of target practice, Eddie."

"Yeah, a lot of it and soon."

Back in camp, Tom Armstrong began to study *The School of the Company*. For some reason, he was reminded of something that Francis Porter's brother, George, told him after the Battle of Shiloh.

"Sump," he had said, "when the fight started, the Johnnies came at us from across the field in formation just like Hardee instructed. I was right in the middle of our line, standing as we had been taught. They got to about 50 yards from us, the Captain yelling, 'Hold your fire' but then all hell broke loose. The fire of their rifles was horrible. Bullets whizzing over our heads; some striking our boys dead. Saw one shot right through the neck. Killed instantly. Never knew what hit him. We opened up on them, killing or wounding many as they marched toward us. Right then, everyone forgot about *Hardee's Tactics*. It was complete chaos. All we heard was the Captain screaming 'Keep firing, boys, make it low.' The Rebs just kept coming, and we started to fall back. No precise column formation for that. You just turn and go, protecting yourself as best you can."

Tom Armstrong thought for a while. "If no one uses the *Tactics* when things get hot out in the field, maybe they are just good in theory. Maybe their use is just in establishing discipline within the Regiment." He would make sure that the *Tactics* were taught and learned well throughout the 122nd , but he would never forget what George Porter had told him about the bedlam of battle. "You just turn and go. Don't wait for the Captain's orders."

5 Goodbye

It was Tuesday, September 9, 1862. As usual, Tom Armstrong and Tom Black were up at the crack of dawn. They had work to do. Black had scheduled the meeting with Captain Gary for right after dinner, about 1PM, when they would review the schedule they had worked out the previous day. That would be the only planned interruption of their day. Oh, there would be other things that had to be done, but, for the most part, their time that day would be their own, not that of Captain Daniel Gary.

Black banged on the barracks' door, hoping to wake Patrick Murphy and Eddie Bristow, but was surprised when he walked in. They weren't there. "That's a good sign, for them to be up and at 'em this early," he said to no one in particular. Back in their quarters, he found Armstrong. It was time for breakfast, so off to the Mess Hall the two lieutenants went.

"Nothing can get in the way of studying the *Tactics*, Tom," Armstrong said. "We have to be ready to teach in two weeks, and there's a mountain of material that has to be covered." As they entered the Hall, they spotted Bristow and Murphy. Tom Armstrong repeated the message to the two sergeants. "You understand?"

"Yes, sir," came the reply.

"I have to work on the *School of the Company* with those other guys who will help train the captains. I would suggest, then, that the three of you study the *School of the Soldier* together and act out the instructions so that you have mastered them. That was what we did last year in the 78th, and it seemed to work very well. You can't just read it. You have to do it, so you can show the men what to do and how to do it. Start with the Commands and move on from there. As you drill them, do not move on to the next instruction until you are satisfied that the men can execute it in front of the Captain. All right?" Armstrong didn't like telling Tom Black what to do, but he felt he had no choice.

"Yep."

"Good. Lieutenant Black and I will visit Sergeant McMillen at the Quartermaster building to see about getting ammunition and powder, so you can practice with the Enfield and then teach the men to shoot. Can we do that today, Tom? It's important because early in the drill you will have to go over the Manual of Arms."

"Sure, let's do that this morning."

"Fine. Once you have done the Manual of Arms, march the men by squad out into the field for target practice, but only when you are satisfied that your men know the Manual."

He reached into his pocket for his watch, but the pocket was empty. "Dang, I better remind Jacob to bring it," he thought to himself.

Breakfast concluded, Armstrong and Black went to visit Sergeant McMillen. "Whattya mean we don't have any powder?" Lieutenant Tom Black exploded. "We gotta have powder to teach the men how to shoot a rifle they've never seen before. No rifles, either?" The two lieutenants were incredulous. "How in the hell can we get ready for the enemy without rifles and gunpowder? Tom, we hafta see Gary about this. Maybe at our meeting today."

As they walked back to their quarters, Armstrong said, "First time I've seen your dander up, Tom. I rather enjoyed that." Tom Black just looked at him and smiled.

When they got back, there was a message for Armstrong from Captain Gary. It seems like Colonel Ball wanted the five lieutenants who had experience with the *Tactics* and who had been in battle to meet that afternoon at 3 o'clock in his headquarters. The meeting would ostensibly be to determine the company commanders each of them would teach. He found Murphy and Bristow in his quarters, sitting at the table, intently studying the *Tactics*. Murphy was reading aloud "Heels on the same line, as near each other as the conformation of the man will permit." Eddie Bristow was standing in front of him, making sure he was standing properly.

Murphy continued, "The feet turned out equally, and forming with each other something less than a right angle. Got that, Eddie?"

Bristow shifted his feet to approximate "something less than a right angle." "The knees straight, without stiffness." Murphy started to laugh. "The palm of the hand turned a little to the front, the little finger behind the seam of the pantaloons." Pretty soon, all four of the men were laughing, but *Hardee's Tactics* was no laughing matter. This was serious business. Tom Armstrong knew; however, he could not confide in any of the others about what George Porter had told him after Shiloh.

Armstrong had done the drills identified in the *School of the Company*, but he had never read them. With the 78th, he just did what he and the others in the company were told to do. He excused Bristow and Murphy, telling them to study elsewhere and asking Tom Black to go with them, and started to read.

SCHOOL OF THE COMPANY
General Rules and Division of the School of the Company

Instruction by Company will always precede that of battalion, and the object being to prepare the soldiers for the higher school, the exercises of detail by Company will be strictly adhered to, as well in respect to principles, as the order of progression herein prescribed.

There will be attached to a Company undergoing elementary instruction, a captain, a covering sergeant, and a certain number of file closers, the whole posted in the manner indicated, Title First, and according to the same Title, the officer charged with the exercise of such Company will herein be denominated the instructor.

"So, the sergeants have to assist the Captain. Didn't know that. Better tell them. We have to do both schools on the same day, the Soldier in the morning and the Company in the afternoon. I guess we did that in the 78th. And, I have two weeks to train Gary and another captain." He continued to read:

117

4 The company will always be formed in two ranks. The instructor will then cause the files to be numbered, and for this purposed will command:

In each rank – Count TWOS

5 At this command, the men count in each rank, from right to left, pronouncing in a loud and distinct voice, in the same tone, without hurry and without turning the head, one two, according to the place each one occupies. He will also cause the company to be divided into platoons and sections, taking care that the first platoon is always composed of an even number of files.

There was more of this, too. Much more.

"I think the thing to do is have the captains read these, trying to commit them to memory, and I shall add to it with my experience. It will be trial-and-error as we start, but they should get it fairly soon. Wish I knew how long we are going to be here." Armstrong continued to read, making mental notes as to what he would tell the captains.

The meeting about the schedule with Captain Daniel Gary went well, except for the part about the Enfields and the gunpowder. Gary was quite impressed with the schedule and was determined to have the Colonel approve it. He wasn't happy about the rifles and rode off to see William Ball. Lieutenant Tom Armstrong and Lieutenant Tom Black went back to their studies. At 2:30 PM, Armstrong went to the corral, retrieved the tack, and got Aspen ready to go. "So, Gary's been with the Colonel explaining our problem and that's where I'm going right now. Wonder what kind of reception I'm going to get. Wonder if all the company commanders have a copy of the *Tactics*."

When he arrived at Ball's headquarters, the Colonel wasn't there. Neither was Dan Gary. He sat down on a bench on the porch and waited for the others. Promptly at 3 o'clock, Colonel William Ball appeared, dismounting and hitching his horse to the post in front of his quarters. The others arrived shortly thereafter. Tom knew two of them, the other two he didn't. Introductions made, the Colonel simply said, "I want you boys to help the company commanders in the drill. We have ten companies, so each of you will work with two of them, your own and one more. If two of you are in the same company, one will work with your commander and the other will have two who he presently does not know. Any questions?"

"My compliments, Colonel Ball, do each of the commanders have a copy of the *Tactics*?" asked Tom Armstrong. "I started reading this morning and thought it would be most helpful if they did and could read the Instructions prior to our meeting with them."

Remembering that Armstrong was a teacher in civilian life, he asked "Is that what you did with your students, Lieutenant?"

"Yes, sir, and it worked pretty well."

"Good suggestion. I will make it happen. Now, I have to go, but you boys can talk some more and figure out who's going to work with who. We will talk about the rifles tomorrow, Lieutenant."

Four pairs of eyes stared at Tom Armstrong, wondering what that meant. Returning their looks, he said, "Apparently we don't have any Enfield rifles. That's what the Quartermaster told me. I reported that to Captain Gary who took off like a shot to see the Colonel. Don't know the result of that conversation, but I'm going to find out tomorrow. We had Enfields when I was with the 78th. They are better guns. Don't understand why we don't have them here." The meeting continued with the five men divvying up the ten companies in the regiment, with Tom Armstrong getting Company K its commander, Captain John Ross. As the session ended, they agreed to meet each week to review each one's progress on the *Tactics* in preparation for drill on the 22nd.

As planned, the meeting to go over the schedule took place the following day at 3 o'clock in the afternoon. Daniel Gary, Tom Black, and Tom Armstrong rode to Colonel Ball's headquarters together, not too concerned about the schedule but with serious misgivings about the Enfields. Gary hoped the Colonel would repeat his words about them from the previous day.

When they had reviewed the drill schedule with Ball, he removed his spectacles and looked at the three officers from Company I. "Gentlemen, this is excellent work. Exactly what I wanted."

"Thank you, sir," said Captain Daniel Gary.

Colonel William Ball continued, "I will have my staff copy it for the other commanders, and I will call a meeting for Friday morning at 7 o'clock."

"Yes, sir. Very good, sir. But, we do have the problem of the rifles. What are we supposed to do?" asked Captain Gary.

"I told you yesterday, Daniel," said Colonel Ball quite sternly, "we don't have any. We have about half a million men out here fighting this war, and the production of Enfield rifles is not even close to that. You will have to make do with the Springfields until we can get the Enfields, if we get them at all."

Gary looked at Tom Armstrong who was taken aback by the news. The 78th had them. Why couldn't the 122nd? The Colonel said that apparently the inventory was adequate the year before, but with all the new regiments being formed, there just weren't enough to go around. The supply was gone, and there was nothing he or the others could do about it.

"Sir, can you send a requisition to Governor Tod, asking for them?"

"Yes, I can try that and will keep you posted."

"Very well, sir. May we be excused?"

"Certainly, Captain. You are dismissed."

Gary, Black, and Armstrong came to Attention and saluted with Ball returning it.

"Whew, that was easier than I thought," Gary remarked, "but, damn, we have to use Springfields. That isn't good. I will continue to hound the Colonel about it and will mention it at the Captains' meeting on Friday morning. In the meantime, it seems to me that it just might be a good time for you and the Sergeants to put your noses in the *Tactics*."

"Damn," thought Tom Black. "He's said that again. Wonder why he just doesn't say 'read.'"

Gary's meeting with the lieutenants and NCOs was scheduled for Saturday. Tom Armstrong had his two sergeants, but Tom Black had work to do. He saw that Thaddeus Brennan was in camp and met with him to discuss the possibility of him becoming a sergeant which was met favorably by the young man from Norwich, over there in Union Township. He also approached Chesley Simpson about the matter and was quite pleased when Simpson agreed as well. Black went to the Quartermaster's quarters and told Sergeant McMillen to expect Brennan and Simpson and to have their three stripes, signifying their rank as sergeant, sewn on their coats. Upon his return, he went to the barracks and found them.

"This is what you are responsible for," Black said, handing them a copy of the *Tactics*. "Learn it, and learn it well, as the bulk of the drill will come from you and the corporals who report to you."

Now, all they had to do was find eight corporals from the one hundred men in Company I. Corporals were important since much of the drill on the *School of the Soldier* would fall to them. Seeing it was already Thursday, Armstrong, Black, and the sergeants had to move fast. Luckily, they knew most of the men in the company, which made the selection process much easier. It took all day Friday, but, by supper, the four sergeants had done the job. The corporals could sew their two stripes on their jackets themselves as the Quartermaster would not have time prior to the meeting with the Captain the following day.

That evening, Tom convened a meeting in the enlisted men's barracks with Black, the four sergeants, and the eight new corporals to tell them that the schedule of activity for drilling the men had been approved by the Colonel, been presented to the Captains that morning, and was ready to be implemented.

5:00 AM (6:00 in Winter)	Reveille
5:30	Roll Call and Inspection
6:00 – 7:30	Drill
7:30 – 8:00	Breakfast
8:00	Surgeons' Call
9:00	Stable Call and Guard Mounting
9:30 – 11:00	Drill
11:00 – 12:00	Free Time
12:00 PM	Dinner
1:00 – 3:00	Drill
3:00 – 5:00	Free Time
5:00 – 6:00	Drill

6:30	Dress Parade
7:30	Supper
8:00 – 9:30	Free Time
9:30	Roll Call and Inspection
9:45	Taps

Armstrong went on, repeating his orders from Colonel Ball and emphasizing them to the corporals who had not heard it before. "There is to be no deviant behavior among the men. Missing *Roll Call*; being absent from the camp; talking back to an officer, regardless of rank; theft from a fellow infantryman, desertion. You can count on serious punishment by Captain Gary, even facing a firing squad, if any of that that happens. Do you understand?"

"Yes, sir," came the reply.

Corporal Enoch Brown asked, "He'd really shoot someone?"

"Corporal, only in the case of desertion or murder, but if you could have seen the look on the Captain's face when he was telling Lieutenant Black and me about what the Colonel wanted, he was dead serious. Just make sure the men behave. That's why you have those stripes."

He also told them about his orders to help Captain Gary and Captain Ross with the *School of the Company*, basically saying that, for the time being, Tom Black was in charge of the drill on the *School of the Soldier*. Armstrong then said that he would be there whenever he could, but he did not know how much time he would have.

He went on, "Captain Gary met with the Lieutenant and me after his meeting this morning. The Colonel has changed his mind, and this directly affects you, Patrick. He sees that there would be hardship on the companies that have a man who has re-enlisted and who has to spend time working with two Captains. Having a sergeant in those companies deliver the daily reports to the Adjutant would put an unfair burden on the other Non-Coms for managing the schedule. So, we are spared that duty. It will now fall to First Sergeant Terrance Rundle. He will take the Captains' reports to Colonel Ball and Major Granger. You better get to know him since you will be working closely together, especially in the field."

"I see, sir. Thank the Colonel when you next see him. Mighty nice of him," Patrick Murphy said with that twinkle in his eye. It was clear to Tom Armstrong that the others thought Murphy was being serious, but he wasn't.

"As more men come into camp, you sergeants can have the corporals acquaint them with the geography of the camp, especially the barracks, Mess Hall, and the parade ground. Also, make sure that each one has a copy of the schedule that he can go over with his squad. And, last, study the *Tactics* with your corporals to make sure they learn it well. I want no surprises for anyone, right Lieutenant Black?"

"Absolutely none, Lieutenant Armstrong."

"The men will have ample free time between drills to do the chores that we will assign each day. We will have eight squads, so we will rotate that detail among you. Same for guard duty. For those who are not on that duty, their free time is their own, but make sure they are rested, especially as they are getting accustomed to the schedule. Provide them with paper and pencil to write to family and friends. They may have brought in books that can be passed around, kind of like a library. Card playing is fine, but watch the gambling. You can also let them have their whiskey but watch for drunkenness. Don't want to see any prostitutes walking around here, either. If any of them have instruments, they can play them. We will also have copies of the *Daily Courier* brought in so that they can keep up with the news of the day. I try to read it every day to see if there is any news about the 78th and other news about the war. Basically, let the men do whatever they want, when not on duty. As are you, they are volunteers who are used to being independent and free to do as they please. They have no idea of what they are getting themselves into."

"Now about that, this is not just some glorious adventure that we will win in the next three months. This is war, gentlemen, and there will be some of you and some of your men who will not come back. You may be killed on the field, die in the surgeon's tent of your wounds, come down with typhoid or some other disease and die in your tent, or die of starvation in one of their prisons. You ever heard of Belle Isle?"

"No, sir."

"It's a grisly place down in Virginia, middle of a river, where they take the enlisted men that they have captured. The officers taken prisoner end up at Libby Prison in Richmond. I have only heard stories, but the treatment there is horrendous with food shortages, rampant disease, rats and other vermin underfoot, lice everywhere, no heat in the winter, unsanitary conditions, and general inhumane treatment by the Rebs. I've heard tell that men who have been paroled or exchanged think that their own death would be preferable to being in those prisons."

"One last thing. The men in your squads will only do what they see you doing. You corporals will only do what you see your sergeant doing. They will only do what they see Lieutenant Black and me doing and on it goes up the chain of command, stopping with the colonels and generals. Provide for your men as best you can and let us know what you need. We have all volunteered for this, but as officers, we must take care of the men. I trust that is crystal clear."

Heads nodded up and down, nobody saying anything. "It's getting late, and we need our rest. The meeting with the Captain is at 9 o'clock. He will probably tell you much of the same thing as I have this evening, but we wanted you to hear it from us first. Feel free to ask questions, but the meeting should be over no later than 10. Let's meet for breakfast at 0-7-30."

Tom Black and Tom Armstrong walked back to their quarters. "Guess we shouldn't bring up the Enfields," Black said with a smile.

"Guess not. I'm still mad about that. Probably will be for a while. Those Springfields are useless unless you're at close range. No farther than 75 yards. Will have to drill the men with those and with no powder, but let's say we're issued Enfields when we get to wherever it is we're going, how we going to teach them? Won't have time. Sure hope the Secesh don't have 'em."

Gary's lecture the following morning was a repeat of the one Tom Armstrong had delivered the previous evening. Armstrong was really glad he had taken the time to talk to the Non-Coms. So was Tom Black.

"When we gonna get our Enfields, Captain?" asked Patrick Murphy, not knowing what Tom Armstrong had forgotten to tell him and Eddie Bristow.

Captain Daniel Gary shot a glance at Armstrong, looking like he was sure that Tom had put his sergeant up to this. But, the lieutenant simply shrugged his shoulders, concealing a laugh. "Well done, Sergeant Murphy," he thought.

"We don't have any, Sergeant. You'll have to use Springfields."

With that, it was Murphy's turn to stare at Tom Armstrong. Another shrug. "As it has been explained to me, the gun manufacturers here in the North can't make them fast enough for all of us. And, the government can't seem to buy what we need from the English. So, we are stuck with what we have. Makes it easy for you, Sergeant. You won't have to learn how to fire one. At least not now. And, you won't have to teach the men."

Murphy smiled. "Maybe I shouldn't have asked the question," he thought. "Oh, well, Armstrong can't bust me for that. I didn't know."

"Captain, do you want to start on the *School of the Company* today?"

"Yes, come to my quarters after dinner, and we will spend the afternoon getting acquainted with it."

"Very well, sir. In the meantime, I'm going over to see Captain Ross to put a schedule together of when I can work with him. We only have ten days. I am thinking that we drill the men on the Soldier in the morning and on the Company in the afternoon. How does that sound?"

"Reasonable, Lieutenant, reasonable." Dan Gary still didn't know that Patrick Murphy's question was perfectly innocent. "Let's talk about the basics of it at dinner, unless you have other plans."

"I will stop by your quarters a little before noon. Thank you, sir."

"So, what you are saying Lieutenant?" asked Dan Gary, looking up from the plate in front of him, "what you are saying is that I have to conduct the *School of the Company*. This says, right here on Page 45, that it is the responsibility of the captain, a covering sergeant, and some file closers. What are those?"

"The covering sergeant is Sergeant Rundle. He will help us with the *Tactics*. The file closers are the sergeants or corporals who are positioned behind the Company to make sure the men do what they're told and to keep things orderly," replied Tom Armstrong, taking a sip of coffee. "You train them the way you want them to behave here in camp, on the march, and in the field. What do you think about having Captain Ross come over, so we can learn this together? It would save me a lot of time."

"Good idea, Tom. Can you see him later today?"

"Already mentioned it to him this morning after our meeting. He likes the idea. All we have to do is come up with a time. If I have Sergeant Murphy and Sergeant Bristow conduct the first drill each day, you, Captain Ross, and I could meet before breakfast to plan the drills for the afternoon."

"Already mentioned it?"

"Yes, sir. I didn't think you'd mind."

"That's two good ideas in five minutes. Got any more?"

"Not just yet, sir, but the day is still young," Tom Armstrong said with a smile.

Men kept pouring into Camp Zanesville. The camp that had been fairly quiet since Tom Armstrong's arrival was suddenly very busy with the enlisted men trying to find their companies, being examined by the surgeons, and getting fitted with their uniforms. Armstrong was glad that he had delegated that duty to the sergeants and corporals since he was quite busy with Daniel Gary and John Ross. After the first three days with them, going over the initial sections of the *School of the Company*, he began to wonder why they needed him to be involved at their level. "They can read," he thought. "But, maybe they need me to interpret for them since I have done this, and they have not. 6 o'clock every morning. I dare not tell them what George told me. It will come as a shock when we engage the enemy and his big guns, and a thousand Rebels come charging across a field at us, firing their rifles and screaming that awful yell of theirs. When that happens and our line breaks, it will be chaos."

It was Thursday, September 18, 1862. Tom Armstrong, Tom Black, and Daniel Gary were just finishing breakfast when First Sergeant Terrance Rundle burst into the Mess Hall. "The Colonel wants to see all of the officers right now," he shouted. "In the barn. Get a move on."

"Sounds serious," said Gary. "I wonder what happened."

They stood at Attention as the Colonel walked to the front of the barn. "At ease, gentlemen. It has come to my attention that, yesterday morning, at daybreak, General Hooker attacked the enemy at a place called Antietam Creek, near Sharpsburg, Maryland. I am told that neither side gained an advantage in the battle, but by noon over 12,000 men were either dead, wounded, or missing. By the end of the day, that number was almost 23,000. 13,000 of McClellan's 80,000 effectives and 10,000 of General Lee's 40,000. We received a telegraph message this morning that said that General McClellan was experiencing some skirmishing, but that was about all. It looks like General Lee wanted to fight on northern soil, but from all reports, it did not continue today. There was a tremendous loss of life. This war is real, gentlemen. This war is real. Any questions?"

No hands were raised. "Commence drilling the men on Monday."

"Atten-TION," hollered Major Granger. The officers of the 122nd Ohio Volunteer Infantry jumped up, backs straight, staring straight ahead, not moving a muscle.

"Dis-MISSED."

Gary, Black, and Armstrong walked slowly back to the Captain's quarters. Thoughtfully, he said, "Must have been an awful fight. Some 20,000 casualties in one day. Never heard of that many in one day before. Sounds like it was a draw, though. I wonder if Lee has retreated back into Virginia. You better go tell your men. Don't want them reading about it in the paper tomorrow."

Tom Armstrong went to find Patrick Murphy and Eddie Bristow; Tom Black went to locate Thaddeus Brennan and Chesley Simpson. Their message was the same. "Tell your corporals and the enlisted men. We will tell you as much as we can about things like this. This isn't a picnic, fellas."

The next morning, Black and Armstrong rode into Zanesville, just to get away for a couple of hours. Armstrong stopped at Bonnet's and, sure enough, Mr. Bonnet had his pocket watch. He said to the jeweler, "Good of my brother to bring this here. Is it working right?"

"Yes, Lieutenant. It's fine."

"Thank you, sir," he said and walked out of the store. "Shoot, looks like it might rain." He thought he might get a paper, so the two men walked down to the office of the *Courier* and bought the day's edition.

"The only place there's any news is on 2 and 3," Tom Armstrong said. "Just advertisements on 1 and 4." He opened the paper and saw a column about the affair at Antietam Creek...

HEADQUARTERS, ARMY OF THE POTOMAC
Tuesday Evening, Sept. 16
Via Frederick, 18

To the Associated Press

During the afternoon, information was received at head-quarters, showing that the enemy were re-crossing the river and concentrating their forces on the ridge of hills outside the town of Sharpsburg, within 3 miles of the main body of our army.

Jackson left Harper's Ferry this morning. His troops be-ginning to arrive in the afternoon when it became evident that Lee was disposed to engage our forces in battle at this point. Gen. McClellan sent for Franklin's corps and Couch's division, who were 7 miles distant on the other side of the Elk Ridge. There were considerable artillery firing during the day on both sides, resulting in a loss to loss of 40 killed and wounded.

Hooker's troops got into action at dark. The battle lasted two hours during which time the enemy were driven a half mile, with considerable loss.

The Pennsylvania Reserves suffered much.

The night was occupied in getting the troops in their re-spective positions, while ammunition trains and ambulances were forwarded to the different commands.

Sept. 17 – this has been the most eventful day in the his-tory of the rebellion. The battle had taken place while the army of the Potomac is again victorious. It exceeds in an ex-tent any battle heretofore fought on the continent.

At daylight the battle was renewed on the centre and right, by Hooker and Sumner, who after a short contest of two hours, drove the enemy one mile.

The rebels rallied shortly with terrible loss and regained most of the ground. At this time Hooker received a shot in the ankle and was carried from the field. The command of his troops now devolved on Sumner. Richardson, commanding the division, was seriously wounded at the same time. Sumner determined to retake the lost ground; ordered his troops to advance, driving the rebels before them with great slaughter.

They not only retook the ground but drove the rebels a quarter of a mile beyond in this action. Mansfield was shot through the lungs and died soon after.

Loss here considerable. Our troops now hold both sides of the creek. To get possession of the ridge of hills on the right and left-hand sides, from which the rebels kept thundering away with artillery, was a task not easily accomplished.

Darkness now overlooked the two armies and hostilities ceased by mutual consent – The battle lasted from five in the morning until seven at night, without a moments cessation. The conduct of the troops was without exception excellent. It is impossible now to form a correct idea of the lost on either.

It is heavy on both sides. Our loss probably reaches 10,000. That of the enemy won't exceed it.

The enemy's dead nearly all fell on our hands, being thickly strewn over the field, and in many places lying in heaps.

Our wounded were immediately carried from the field.

We took 1,500 prisoners during the day. The enemy obtained but few.

The following officers are among the killed and wounded:

Hartsoff, Duryea, Sedwick, and Captain Anderson, an aid to Sumner were wounded; Major Sedgwick, Colonel McNeil and Lieut. Allen, of the Bucktails, were killed; Col. Palla, of the 2nd U.S. Sharpshooters, was wounded.

Several other prominent officers are reported killed. Of the wounded, nothing is positively known concerning them.

"My, oh my," Tom Armstrong said to Tom Black. "They fought each other for fourteen hours. Imagine the intensity. And bodies in a heap? Saw that at Shiloh. It's awful." He continued, "Since we lost that many, I bet we're going East to reinforce McClellan. There's nothing but skirmishing going on down in Tennessee. Don't need us there. George Porter's still sitting at Bolivar with the rest of the 78th. Have been since they cleaned up the battlefields at Shiloh last April and May. They will probably winter there. If we do go East, we're gonna run into General Lee. Maybe Stonewall Jackson, too. Wonder if the Johnnies are planning to invade the North again. Didn't work this time. If they do, and we're there, maybe we can stop them. That's why the drill is so important. The men have to be as disciplined as we can make them. Still mad about the Enfields."

Riding back to Camp Zanesville, they wondered how long it would be before they were shipped out. "I would guess it's soon," said Tom Black.

"I don't know. There's a long time between battles, and I would think that Lee might want to think about where he will winter his army. Wonder where we will. Fighting in the snow, ice and wind is no fun. We did it at Fort Donelson. I'll bet both sides will stay put until Spring."

Camp Zanesville was quite astir when they got back with men everywhere and horses darting to avoid them. The two lieutenants wanted to find their sergeants to discover how many men had reported in to Company I, with the drilling starting the following Monday. Armstrong found that Bristow and Murphy were in the barracks with the Corporals who had been selected. The sergeants were telling the enlisted men what to expect. There would be drill, drill, and more drill. Murphy introduced him to the men; Armstrong counted eighty-four of them, including Isaac and Jeremiah Kearney. Thaddeus Brennan and Chesley Simpson were there, too. So was Terrance Rundle.

Tom Black motioned to Armstrong and announced, "He has seen the elephant. He knows what to expect. He will tell you." Armstrong repeated what he had told the Non-Coms the week before, not sparing any detail.

As soon as he had finished, they all heard Patrick Murphy. "When the Lieutenant tells you something, you say 'Yes, sir.'" Turning to Armstrong, he said, "If it's alright with you, sir, we're gonna take them out to the Parade Ground and teach them the basics. Attention, At Ease, Dismissed, when and how to salute, how to march. Just want to get a head start on Monday morning. Lieutenant Black is coming with us."

"Very well, sergeant. You may dismiss the men. Don't forget, church tomorrow. We will expect all of you to be there."

Saturday was the day of final preparations. Black and Armstrong had one last meeting with the Non-Coms to review the schedule one more time. They explained the importance of the drill in instilling discipline in the men. Colonel Ball wanted the 122nd to be the finest regiment in the brigade, and it was up to them to make sure that Company I stood out. It would be up to the four sergeants to make that happen, reporting to Lieutenant Tom Black, in Armstrong's absence.

"*School of the Soldier* in the morning. *School of the Company* in the afternoon," he reminded them. "Captain Gary and I will see you after dinner. That's probably what he wants to talk about this afternoon. The logistics of the drill. Do not forget, he is in charge, and he will rely on you sergeants to help him. You Corporals will act as the file closers. Got it?"

"Yes, sir," came the reply in unison.

They had guessed right about Gary's agenda for the meeting. "So, what are we going to do?"

Lieutenant Tom Black took the lead and outlined exactly what was planned. Everyone knew that Tom Armstrong would only be there half of the time because he had to be with Captain Gary and Captain Ross of Company K. So, it would be up to Black, the four sergeants, and the eight corporals. Armstrong said that he would have the Captain ready for the first day's drill of the company. He just hoped that Black could handle the *School of the Soldier*. Nothing he could do about that now.

Sunday meant church, as usual. Daniel Gary, Tom Black, and Tom Armstrong walked over to the big barn around 1:45 that afternoon. Companies F, G, H, I, and K had been given the afternoon time slot since the barn wasn't big enough to handle 1,000 men at once. Armstrong had wondered why there was no "Company J," being told that "I" and "J" looked too much like, so Hardee had left out "J." "Makes sense, I guess," he thought.

As they entered the barn, they saw a couple hundred soldiers milling about, spying Murphy, Bristow, Simpson, and Brennan arranging the men by squad. "They're taking their duty very seriously, it seems," Dan Gary mentioned to the other two, who just smiled.

Chaplain Charles C. McCabe was at his oratorical best once again and led the congregation in the singing of some familiar (he hoped) hymns. He read from the Psalms, #23, in particular, and then from the Book of Acts, said the prayers, and preached for 45 minutes on what it means to be a "Christian soldier." He kept it simple. "Yes, you will kill men of the Rebel army with them trying to kill you. You shall ask the Lord for forgiveness. You cannot ask God to preserve and protect you, but you can make peace with the Lord in case the worst happens. I hope that many of you brought your Bibles to this camp. They will be helpful to you and in our Bible study groups."

Continuing, he went on, "The Commandments say 'Thou Shalt Not Kill,' but you are soldiers and that is what soldiers do. All you can do is ask for forgiveness and hope He understands. God has not taken a side in this conflict, although some preachers are convinced He has and that we are in the right. My thinking is that God is probably very sad with what has gone on at places like Antietam Creek and with what will go on wherever this war leads. But, have faith in Him, pray whenever you can, and put your trust in Him that it is His will being done."

The Chaplain closed with The Lord's Prayer and then invited everyone in the building to stand and sing *The Battle Hymn of the Republic* with him.

"You fellas go on back. I want to talk with the Chaplain," said Tom Armstrong. He didn't get to see his friend that often here in camp, and he wanted him to know the reason for that. Maybe when camp life became more regular he would, but, then again, the Chaplain would have to minister to almost a thousand men. When would he have time to visit? He also wanted to find out about the Bible study groups that McCabe was forming. The two men shook hands and talked for about fifteen minutes. Charles McCabe was glad that Tom had stopped by and that he looked well and hearty, being quite impressed with the role he would be playing in getting the men ready.

He heard the bugler at 5 o'clock the next morning. "*Reveille*," he thought. "Here we go." He lit the oil lamp on the dresser next to his bunk, Tom Black was already awake and putting on his uniform.

They could see light in the barracks and could hear Simpson and Bristow yelling instructions. "*Roll Call* and *Inspection* in thirty minutes. Be ready in formation out in front. Right here, just like we told you on Saturday. Get to the latrine if you need to but be back here in twenty minutes." Murphy and Brennan were counting the men, making sure that the number equalled the one from the previous evening taken just before the bugler sounded *Tatoo* followed by *Taps*. "The men probably don't like this, but this is a picnic compared to what will happen in the field, if my experience in the 78th is any indication." He knocked on Captain Gary's door.

"Ready, sir?"

Dan Gary looked sharp in his new uniform, complete with his Captain's bars on his shoulders. "Yes, Tom, I'm ready," and the two men left the Captain's quarters, went outside, and waited for the men to form up. The bugler sounded *Assembly,* and the men fell into line. The roll call was exact, as Murphy and Brennan knew it would be; the inspection yielded some critical remarks to some of the men by the Captain, but all in all, for the first day, it went well.

Murphy bellowed, "Atten-TION." The men came to Attention, focusing their eyes on the Captain. "Right FACE," came the command. Tom Armstrong could see that Patrick Murphy was really enjoying this. It would be Bristow's turn later in the day. "Forward MARCH." It was ragged, Armstrong commented to the Captain, but the men were moving in two files, just as they had been taught on Saturday.

"Good luck, Tom," Armstrong said. "We will see you a bit later." Tom Armstrong and Dan Gary disappeared into the Captain's quarters to study.

For the most part, the day went smoothly. It was evident that the sergeants of the 122nd O.V.I. had studied hard and learned well. Tom Black was pleased with the morning drill, and Dan Gary had performed well in the afternoon.

"Better than our first day with the 78th. It can only get better." The Non-Coms had executed the schedule very well, and, at supper, he could see that they were pretty proud of themselves. "They should be," he thought.

In the evening of September 23, 1862, Tom Armstrong saw a column in the *Courier* that contained some words that would change the United States forever, Dan Gary rushed into his quarters around 8 o'clock shaking the paper in his hands.

"Look at this," he cried. "Look at this. The President is going to free the slaves."

"What?" Armstrong said incredulously.

"Read this, Lieutenant."

He took the paper from the Captain and started to read...

The President in the outset says, "that the war will be prosecuted for the object of practically restoring the constitutional relations between the United States and the people thereof." For the last year and a half this has been the standing proclamation of our Government, and, we may add, of the people of the Northern States. They have time and again reiterated it in their State and County conventions and through the Press. The Government has executed no punishment upon the rebels; the leniency of the Government in this respect has become proverbial; so much so that it may have concluded that it was too imbecile to resent or rebuke an insult. Our people, from the farms and the workshops, the marts of commerce, and the halls of learning have rushed to the rescue; they have fought and bled, they have died to save our Government. To this and many a brave man's wife has been made a widow, many thousands of helpless children had been made orphans, many a sister mourns the loss of a devoted brother, upon whose far-off grave she is denied the small privilege of dropping a tear or planting a flower. Many a grey-haired father and mother are waiting with crushed hearts by their hearthstones over the loss of a dear son, perhaps an only son. Many more fathers, mothers, wives, brothers and sisters throughout the loyal States, read the news, flash to them on lightning's wings with fear and trembling and tearful eyes, lest it may tell them that some dear one has slept that sleep that knows no waking, upon a gray bed.

The President, then, by the authority of Congress, proclaims that after the first of January next, should any portion of the United States continue in rebellion, the people of that portion will be treated differently – "all persons held as slaves within any State, the people whereof shall then be in rebellion against the United States, shall be then and thenceforward and forever free."

Tom Black rushed into the room. "Everybody is talking about the President. Is he really going to free the slaves?"

"Sounds like it," replied Daniel Gary.

"But that will change everything in the South," said Tom Armstrong. "The whole culture, its economy, depends on slave labor. If there is no one working in the fields, there are no crops to sell, especially cotton and tobacco. That means their economy stalls. Whoa. I wonder if the President thought of that."

"Probably did," answered Gary. "But, what it means is that if there is no cotton or tobacco being sold, money will not be changing hands. I am a lawyer, not an accountant, but it seems to me that there may not be money to continue to prosecute this war. Maybe not this week, this month, or this year. But, it is certainly going to weaken the South economically."

"That's what I meant," Tom Armstrong chimed in.

Tom Black offered, "Hey, my family runs a store in Fultonham. If we don't sell stuff, we don't make any money, so we can't buy more stuff to sell. So, if nobody can sell cotton or tobacco, they won't have any money to buy things."

"That's right," answered Dan Gary. "Wow."

Tom Armstrong observed, "But, maybe this was a morality decision. Maybe he thought it was just wrong to enslave people. Wonder what the Chaplain has to say about all this. If I may, Captain, I think I will go see him tomorrow afternoon after drill."

"Very well, Tom."

A little after 3 o'clock the following afternoon, he saddled Aspen and headed for the quarters of Chaplain Charles McCabe.

"I assume you heard the news," McCabe said.

"Yes, Charlie, I heard last night. We spent quite some time trying to figure what it means to the South. What do you think the President's motives were?" Getting right to the point.

"I think the basis for the war has changed or is changing. The President has always maintained that it was being fought over the South thinking that each state had the right to secede while the North thought otherwise. They didn't, and that violated the Constitution. But, now, he's put the abolition of slavery on the table, a threat to their very way of life."

"Do you think he listened to the abolitionists?"

"I expect so. The war may be a moral issue, now."

"If it wasn't before, what changed his mind?"

"I don't know, but if you read his words carefully, they are a threat to the Southern states. I do know that the President is a student of history, especially about the Union, having read a couple of his speeches where he talked about Benjamin Franklin and his view of the United States. The President was quoted as saying that Franklin argued with people like Adams and Jefferson for a strong middle class. Probably with all of the founders. He said that Franklin wanted the United States to be different from every other country in the world because we have a strong economy based on the work of the middle class. So, Mr. Lincoln understood what Franklin was trying to do and firmly believes that everyone has the right to improve himself economically, white or black. Both. When he looks at the South, he doesn't see that. He sees an aristocracy, slaves, and poor whites. I think he was willing to go to war so that those lesser people would have the opportunity to improve their lot in life. And, it would end the aristocratic class structure."

"So, what you are saying is that morality didn't enter into the decision. Right?"

"I didn't say that. I am just reading President Lincoln's words, but I do know he talked about slavery being immoral in the past. That's why the Southern States hate him."

"So, maybe it's economic on two levels. He wants to destroy their factories, railroads, and farms. That's pretty practical. That's what we were talking about last night."

"Yes, T.S. The second level, I do believe, is more theoretical, based on Franklin's hope for the country: freedom to offer every man an opportunity to improve. But, I also know that his views on slavery as a moral issue added to this. Just reading the President's words, both in the Proclamation and in his speeches. Obviously, I don't know what else entered into this decision. It's just very complicated."

"You're no help, Charlie," Tom Armstrong said with a chuckle. "I come over here expecting some wisdom, and all I get is just reading the President's words. Thanks a lot, Charlie," he said sarcastically. "I gotta get back. See you in church."

"So, long, T.S. Yes, I will see you there."

Tom Armstrong thought long and hard about what his friend, Charles McCabe had said. "Bet he's right. Makes a lot of sense. States' rights, economics, and morality all rolled into one decision. If that's right, that has changed the Union forever."

The inevitable boredom of camp life began to set in. The men of the 122nd O.V.I. were being trained according to the schedule with no variation. It was the same thing, day after day. Oh, there were some differences like which squad had what chores to do. And, once the men learned one skill from the *Tactics*, it was on to something else. For the most part, though, it was routine. Even Tom Armstrong was getting tired of it.

"Captain," he said, "we're getting along finely with the drilling of the men. Could I possibly have leave to go home for a day? We're probably going to be mustered in soon which means we will be shipping out shortly after that, and I'd like to see Father and Mother, and my brothers and sisters."

"When do you want to go?"

"How about a week from Friday, the 3rd? That will give me time to make all the necessary preparations. Sergeant Murphy and Sergeant Bristow can report to Tom while I am away."

"I don't have to tell the Colonel, but in your case, I think I will. Have you told Captain Ross?"

"No, I wanted to clear it with you. Will do that in the morning. I also want to send the sergeants home if that's all right. I better send the folks a note that I will be coming home."

On Thursday, September 25, he saw an advertisement in the *Daily Courier* that caught his eye. He had written it.

122d REGIMENT
MORE SOLDIERS WANTED

The undersigned wish to recruit a few more soldiers for
the
122d OHIO REGIMENT
This is a good opportunity to enlist.
$100 BOUNTY
$25 of which and one month's pay is paid in advance.
The regiment is now in camp and pay commences at
once.

Apply to
D.A. GARY, Captain
THOS. S. BLACK, 1st Lieut.
THOS. S. ARMSTRONG, 2d Lieut.

Sept. 18

"Hope we get some more boys in here," Armstrong thought to himself. "Couple of companies running a little short."

On Friday, October 3, right after breakfast, Tom Armstrong saddled Aspen, holstered the Springfield, made sure the Colt was snuggly buckled around his waist, had the pass that Dan Gary had given him, and started for the Main Gate. Once through it, he let Aspen run. She hadn't been at a sustained gallop in a month. It was a lovely early autumn day, but he had no need for any extra clothing. He was fine just as he was in his uniform.

The horse sped toward Zanesville, getting there in no time. Riding into Putnam, it was bustling with people, many of whom were soldiers. He didn't have to be back in Camp until the following afternoon, so he took his time, exchanging pleasantries with shopkeepers and other folks that he knew. He was proud to see red, white, and blue bunting adorning the stores and shops all along Main Street and East Street. The Stars and Stripes fluttered in the wind on the flagpole in front of the town hall. He was in no hurry, knowing that Aspen would get him home in time for dinner, after which he could visit with his mother and sisters or go out into the field to find his father or Jacob. His little brothers would be at the schoolhouse, so he wouldn't see them until they came home.

Riding up the path to the farmhouse, the collies spotted him and came racing to meet him. "Hello, boys," he said roughhousing with them. "Let's go find Mother."

He walked Aspen up the path with the dogs playfully tagging along and heard his mother's spinning wheel from inside the house.

Opening the door, he said, "Hello, Mother. It's good to be home, at least for a short visit." He kissed her lightly on the cheek.

"Hello, Thomas, we received your note and have been expecting you. You look hale and hearty."

"I am, Mother, camp life agrees with me, but it's boring right now."

"When do you leave?"

"I don't know, but I would guess fairly soon. The scuttlebutt is that we're going East after the great loss of life at Antietam. Father and Jacob out in the field?"

"Yes, but they will be along for dinner when I ring the bell. Mary and Fla, too."

He put the Springfield in its rack, and then took Aspen to the barn, closing the door of her stall. She had been watered, and, now, she had a bag of oats. He would miss this horse of his. He just knew it.

He heard the bell ringing loudly, announcing that it was time for dinner. Flavilla and Mary were the first to arrive, each giving him a hug. Then, he heard the horses coming: his father and Jacob. They shook hands and went to clean up for the noontime meal.

As the beef, potatoes, vegetables, and fruit were being passed around, Tom Armstrong explained to his family that he would have to be leaving for camp about this time the next day, understanding that Jacob could take him back. He had mentioned that in his note, so Jacob was well prepared to take the afternoon off to take his little brother back to Camp Zanesville. The family spent the afternoon talking about life at camp and asking questions about Antietam and President Lincoln's Proclamation about slavery. Tom wanted to know about the goings on at the farm, the condition of the sheep, how the harvest was proceeding, and the news from Norwich. Time seemed to fly by, but there was no talk of the danger that he would be in. Jane Armstrong had made sure of it. "It is good to have him here, even if it's only for a day," she mused.

The next afternoon, he patted Aspen on the nose and rubbed her head between her ears. "I'll be back, girl," he promised. The horse seemed to know that he was going somewhere, and he wasn't taking her. "But, the little boys, Frank and Gus, will take care of you."

"Goodbye, Mother," kissing her on the cheek again. The same for his sisters. Tousling the heads of his little brothers, he said, "you be good and learn your lessons."

Tom Armstrong saw the same sad look in his father's eyes as he had seen a month before. "Time to go, Father," shaking him by the hand.

"The Lord be with you, son."

He climbed up to the seat of the buckboard where his brother had been waiting. Tom Armstrong was going back to the horrors of war.

When they arrived at Camp Zanesville, Tom Armstrong said, "Goodbye, Jacob. Take care of everything. I will write as often as I can and will let you know where you can direct your letters. You can also follow us in the *Courier*. Charlie McCabe's gonna write articles."

"Goodbye, Sump. You take care and keep your head down. Good luck."

The Armstrongs shook hands. Tom turned toward the Main Gate and disappeared inside. Jacob began the long, lonely, and sad ride back to the farm. "Be with him, Lord," he prayed silently.

"Lieutenant, good to have you back," said Dan Gary. "I just found out this morning that we will be mustered in on Wednesday, here in camp, by Captain Charles C. Goddard of the 17th United States Regiment of Infantry. I also was told that we're going to the Shenandoah Valley, over there in Virginia. We may get to see Bobby Lee or Stonewall Jackson."

"Dang, I hoped we would go West, like the 78th."

"As it was explained to me, it's what is called a 'pincer movement.' It's General Scott's Anaconda Plan. Grant squeezes the Johnnies in the West, and Meade squeezes them in the East. We've blockaded all of the ports of the seceding states, and Grant is under orders to take the entire Mississippi River. That cuts off the Secesh of supply from Texas and the western territories which will hurt the enemy badly. The blockades prevent any cotton or tobacco from getting out and any war materiel from getting in. We're gonna starve them, Tom."

Knowing about the pincer movement from his time with the 78th, Tom Armstrong said, "With things heating up, Dan, we need to get you home for a day, Tom Black and the sergeants, too."

"Make out a schedule today, and let me see it. I will make the orders on Monday."

At 11 o'clock on the morning of Wednesday, October 8, 1862, the men of the 122nd Ohio Volunteer Infantry assembled for dress parade. They usually did this at 6:30 in the evening, but this was a special day. It was time for the regiment to be mustered in. Standing before them was Captain Charles C. Goddard of the 17th United States Regiment of Infantry. The men had been practicing the oath they would take that morning, and, on the command of Captain Goddard, pronounced...

"I, A_____ B_____, do solemnly swear that I will bear true allegiance to the United States of America, and that I will serve them honestly and faithfully against all their enemies and opposers whatsoever, and observe and obey orders of the President of the United States, and the orders of the officers appointed over me according to the rules and articles for the government of the armies of the United States."

With that, the Captain answered, "You are now members of the 122nd Ohio Volunteer Infantry. When you enter the theater in the East or in the West, you take with you the honor, courage, and sacrifice of those who have gone before." When he had finished, a battery of artillery fired.

"Yes, sir," came the response from the 927 men, give or take a few, of the 122nd O.V.I.

At the Captain's nod, the regimental bugler sounded "Attention." The men stood in tight formation as instructed in *Hardee's Tactics.*

"Colonel, I present the men of the 122nd Ohio Volunteer Infantry," Captain Goddard announced proudly.

"Very well, Captain. Company commanders, you may dismiss your men."

Captain Daniel Gary, 1st Lieutenant Thomas Black, and 2nd Lieutenant Thomas Armstrong took their time walking back to Gary's quarters. "Boys," Gary said, "the Colonel just told all of the company commanders that we leave for the eastern theater on the 23rd. That gives us two weeks to get ready. Armstrong, you will be the company commander while Tom and I are gone the next couple of days. We will be back on Friday so that the sergeants can go home over the weekend."

"Captain, I would like to go to Hopewell to see Frank. Will that be a problem?"

"I don't think so, but let's have you do that after everyone is back from leave. Remind me."

"Thank you, Captain. How will we go to wherever we're going?"

"Good question. Let me find out. I'll ask the Major. I think he is in charge of getting us to wherever we are going. He's working with the Regimental Quartermaster 1st Lieutenant Douglas Morgan. Don't wait for them. Start getting the men ready."

"It's about time," said Tom Black. "They are bored and getting restless. They want to see some action."

"They will, Lieutenant. We're going to a town on the north end of the Shenandoah Valley called Winchester. From what I understand, it is the gateway to the Valley from the north and the gateway to Maryland and Pennsylvania from the south. There's already been a battle there with almost constant skirmishing, so I don't think the men will be disappointed. The objective is to keep the enemy in check and to protect the Baltimore and Ohio Railroad from attack."

The lieutenants briefed their sergeants and told them to have the corporals start making the necessary plans to break camp and travel. They had never done this before, so Armstrong knew they would be coming to him, especially while the sergeants were on leave. He would make up a list of the things the men would need and have the sergeants give it to the corporals the next day.

Tom Black left that afternoon for Fultonham and returned the next day around 4 o'clock. Upon his arrival, Dan Gary went to his home in Zanesville, and, like he had promised, he was back about the same time on Friday, October 10. The four sergeants took off for their homes the next day, coming through the Main Gate at various times on Sunday afternoon and finding the preparations well underway. Dog tents and clothing for the men were being procured from the Quartermaster; ammunition was being delivered; and Springfield rifles, complete with bayonets, were stacked outside the barracks. There still was time for drill which was now limited to two sessions per day, one in the morning and one in the afternoon.

On Wednesday, October 15, 1862, Colonel William H. Ball arrived for Dress Parade, tethering his horse at Daniel Gary's quarters. "What's the occasion? he asked, just before Chaplain Charles McCabe rode up.

"You'll see, Daniel." At precisely 6:30, he commanded "Attention," and the men of Company I formed up as they had been taught by the sergeants and corporals.

"Colonel Ball, Chaplain McCabe, may I present the men of Company I of the 122nd Ohio Volunteer Infantry."

"Thank you, Captain," said Colonel Ball. "Chaplain, you may proceed."

"Thank you, Colonel. At Ease," he commanded. The men assumed the position of Parade Rest. "Men of Company I," McCabe began, continuing for about ten minutes about the way the men had performed. "It is my pleasure to present your Captain, with this fine Hunt & Goodwin Foot Officers Sword," he said. presenting the sabre, duly engraved, to Captain Daniel Gary. "Captain, I have been asked to tell you that the men of Company I pooled their resources and asked me to procure this fine weapon for you."

Thanking the Chaplain, Gary accepted the sword, shook hands with him, and looked like he was about to say something. "But, Captain, I am not done," said Charles McCabe. "Where is Lieutenant Armstrong?"

"Here, sir."

"Come forward, Lieutenant. I have something for you, too."

The Chaplain presented a similar Hunt & Goodwin, duly engraved, to the Lieutenant. "Thank you, sir," Armstrong replied.

"Now, wait, we are still not finished here. Where's Sergeant Murphy?"

"Here, sir," said Patrick Murphy, moving to the front of the Company. "Captain Gary and Lieutenant Armstrong, we, the men of Company I, just wanted you to know that as hard as the last three weeks have been, we genuinely appreciate the work you have done to turn us greenhorns into soldiers of the Union army. This is our way of saying thank you."

With that, the men cheered. Gary and Armstrong just looked at each other, smiling. They turned and faced the men, saluting them. Speaking for Armstrong as well, the Captain then expressed his heartfelt thanks in a brief, but patriotic speech. The men of Company I heard the bugler's call to supper.

"Patrick, was this your idea?" Tom Armstrong asked later.

"Lieutenant Black swore me to secrecy, Sump," Patrick Murphy said with a wry smile.

The next morning, Armstrong requisitioned a horse, buckled the Colt tightly around his waist, holstered a Springfield, and rode out the Main Gate, turning west on the National Road toward Hopewell, the sword tucked tight in its scabbard. He had written Francis Porter earlier in the week that he would be coming out to see her, and this time, he felt a lot calmer and more at ease than he had that day in August. "That's two months ago, and I haven't heard from her," he thought.

He rode down Cross St. and turned up the long trail to the Porters' farmhouse. Boomer and Rascal came racing toward him, barking loudly, their tails wagging non-stop. "They are glad to see me," he thought, "I hope she is."

Amanda Porter was sweeping the floor of the large front porch as he rode up, the Sheepdogs still barking. "Thomas, it is good to see you. My, don't you look fine in your uniform!" He dismounted and hitched the horse to the post.

"Hello, Amanda, it is good to see you, too. Is Francis around?"

Amanda Porter called out, "Francis, Thomas is here to see you."

"Be right there, Mother," came a voice from inside the house. And with that, the front door opened and out stepped Frank.

"I can only stay a few hours. Have to get back to camp in time for supper. Can we ride out to that spot we went to the last time?"

"Let me get my horse. It is very good to see you."

"And you," Tom said, feeling all the more comfortable with her.

As they rode, they talked about the last couple of months in camp and the upcoming harvest at the farm, which had already begun with the corn. When they reached the woods, over in the northeast part of the Porter property, he helped her down from Snowflake and kissed her gently. She returned it. As they sat by the brook that babbled along, he began to feel some sadness. He would not see her for a long time, maybe never again, and that made him sad.

"We're shipping out next week, Frank, and I have come to say goodbye. We're going east to Winchester, Virginia, at the head of the Shenandoah Valley, to keep the enemy at bay and to protect the B & O Railroad. I don't know if we will meet the enemy, but my hunch is that we will. I just have to remember that it is God's will that is being done."

"I will pray for you, Thomas, and I will miss you. Can you write to me from there?"

145

"Yes, I will write to you as often as I can. But, you should see all the things the Colonel and Captain have me doing. I'm one of one hundred men in the Company, who has any experience in this, so I have had to teach just about everything about what to expect and what to do."

"I am proud of you and certainly understand why you are doing this. I read about the President's proclamation. Maybe the southern states will quit fighting. That will bring you back to me sooner than if they don't."

"I will write as soon as I know something." He put his arm around her and said, "Just so you know, I love you, Francis Porter," kissing her forehead.

She raised her head and looked at him, smiling, "And, I love you, too, Thomas Armstrong." She knew that he was smitten before she was.

"I would talk to you about marriage, but my future is so uncertain, that I can't. But, if I do come back, we can talk about it then."

"I'd like that," she replied as they started to ride back toward the farmhouse for dinner.

The family gathered around the large oak table. John Porter said the grace, but added a prayer for Tom's safety. The food was hot and plentiful, and the conversation turned to the movement of the regiment. "George is still in some place called Bolivar, Tennessee," said John Porter. "Figures they're going to winter there."

"Give him my finest regards and tell him about where I'm going. We will winter in the mountains of Virginia, I am told. Most likely cold and a lot of snow."

The afternoon passed with more talk of the war, the travels of the 122nd, the President's proclamation, where George was going, and the possibility that Frank would be teaching in the spring. But, then it was time to go.

Francis Porter walked down the path with Tom Armstrong, he leading the horse. When they got to Cross St., they embraced each other tightly and kissed once again. "I cannot cry. I cannot," she thought to herself.

He swung up onto the horse. "Goodbye, Frank. I will miss you and will pray that God will bring me back here some day when the war is over. Your love will be of great comfort to me as the days pass. And, be happy knowing that I love you."

"Goodbye, Thomas," I love you, too."

"Thank you for that. I must go." With that, he spurred the horse down Cross St., stopping and turning just once to wave goodbye.

"I do love you, Tom Armstrong," she thought to herself, as she waved goodbye, not knowing if she would ever see him again. The tears began to stream down her face as she turned to walk back to the farmhouse.

6 The March

A courier came racing down the main street of Camp Zanesville, reining in his lathered stallion sharply in front of the headquarters of Colonel William H. Ball. "My compliments, Colonel. I have orders for you from the Governor." He handed the colonel an envelope.

"Thank you, Captain. Sergeant Rundle, see to the Captain's needs. Make sure that his horse is watered. Is there anything else, Captain?"

"No, sir. I am told the Governor was quite insistent that you and your men make ready to be on the move soon. By your leave, sir."

"Thank you, Captain. My compliments to the Governor."

The order came down from David Tod, Governor of the State of Ohio, at 4:30PM on Friday, October 17, 1862. As Colonel William H. Ball read it, he was both excited and apprehensive. Excited because it was time to go and see the elephant, but apprehensive because of the slaughter and devastation at Antietam. "Moses," he called out to Major Moses M. Granger. "It's confirmed. We're going east, and soon, to join Milroy's division up north in the hills of Virginia. Our task is to guard the B&O railroad there in the place called Winchester. It is a crucial defense, I am told, as there are many roads that crisscross there, in addition to the railroad."

In a foreboding recollection, Colonel Ball knew from an article in the *Daily Courier* that a major battle had been fought in Winchester, Virginia near the end of May 1862. Confederate Maj. Gen. Thomas (Stonewall) Jackson had soundly defeated Union Maj. Gen. Nathaniel P. Banks in a key victory for the South. Since then, the Rebels had control of the lower Shenandoah Valley, improving its transportation and supply lines. But, Winchester itself kept changing

148

hands. First the Confederates, then the Federals, over and over again. "Must be a damn difficult place to defend," he thought.

Ball also understood that Federal Maj. Gen. George B. McClellan had hoped to recapture the Valley with Maj. Gen. Joseph Hooker's corps and that of Maj. Gen. Ambrose Burnside, but the stalemate at Antietam, with its terrible carnage, had changed that plan. With the loss of over 12,000 men, McClellan simply needed reinforcements, which prompted his telegraphic message to Governor David Tod of Ohio. Ball was not surprised by the order to Winchester, but his apprehension was increasing about what it might mean.

"The Governor wants us moving by next Friday, the 24th. Moses, I would like you and Sergeant Rundle to get the Company commanders and especially the five officers with previous experience together in the morning right after *Roll Call* and *Inspection*. I also want to have the Regimental Quartermaster, Lieutenant Morgan, here so he can coordinate our departure and travel with the Company Quartermasters. Tomorrow, we need to discuss how we do this."

The next day, Saturday, October 18, 1862, at 8 o'clock sharp, right after breakfast, Colonel Ball surveyed the room. Major Granger, Sergeant Rundle, the ten Company commanders, and the five officers who had seen the elephant were present. So was Lieutenant Douglas P. Morgan. Upon an invitation from the Colonel, Lieutenant Armstrong, one of the men who had seen combat previously, was first to speak. "From my experience and I presume that of the others who have been out there, the main thing is to do what the Quartermaster says. When the 78th was ordered south, we were told what to pack by our Company Quartermaster which we did, but then, when the weather turned unseasonably warm last February, I saw men throwing away blankets and overcoats on our march to Fort Donelson just to lighten their load. Then, they froze when the weather turned cold again. That's probably why a lot of them got sick. Some even died, like my brother, Wilbur. I'm guessing we will spend the winter in Winchester, just like we did in Kentucky, so we will need warm quarters, blankets, and clothes. We will need shovels for the snow and digging trenches and axes for chopping firewood, cutting trees for defenses, and building quarters. And, above all, we will need food and ammunition. Many of the men and the officers of the 78th just forgot the instructions from the Quartermaster, and they paid for it."

It was Regimental Quartermaster Douglas Morgan's turn to speak. "Thank you, Lieutenant, for your kind words. You are right, but what you didn't know was that we, the Regimental Quartermasters, have explicit orders about what you are to take and how you are to take it. Our Quartermaster General, Brigadier General Montgomery Meigs, has developed a logistics system by which to get you the food, ammunition, supplies, weapons, clothing, and everything else you need to you in the most efficient way. We, Regimental Quartermasters, have been trained to implement the General's process, and I will work with all of you and the Company Quartermasters to make sure it happens."

"Lieutenant Morgan, before we go on, I have a request," said William H. Ball. "You and I have talked about this before, but the men have been clamoring for a weapon called an Enfield rifle, and we don't seem to have any success in getting them. Can you exert some pressure on the Governor's Office? Apparently, these rifles will change how we make war in the future."

"Colonel, I hate to disappoint you, and with all due respect, we just can't get them. The manufacturers can't make them fast enough, and even General Meigs can't get them, even from England. But, I will try, sir, my very best."

It was Moses Granger's turn to speak. "If I may, sir, perhaps it would be best if we let the Company commanders and their staffs work with the enlisted men today on what it means to be heading to the front. We could convene again in the morning to hear what the Quartermaster would like us to do."

"Very well, Major. Is that agreeable, Lieutenant?"

"Of course, sir, I will be prepared."

That afternoon, the Regimental Quartermaster and his staff surveyed the supply building with the ten Company Quartermasters as to what they would need, with no significant shortages found. That was a good start. They would not have to contact the Supply Depot in Columbus except for smaller items. "Enfields?" Morgan thought. "No way in hell."

The meeting with the same officers and Sergeant Rundle present, came to order the next morning in Colonel Ball's office at 7 AM. He said "Gentlemen, we will break camp on Thursday. I want to discuss how that will be done, how to get to Winchester, what we take, and the pitfalls and problems we may face and need to consider."

The Colonel continued, "The first thing we need to decide is how we are going to get to Winchester." He unfolded a large map of the eastern United States and pinned it on the wall of his office. It would stay there until they left. "Winchester, Virginia, is over here," he said, pointing to it, "almost due east of here. Looks like the first part of the march will be relatively easy for us but look at those mountains in western Virginia. The Alleghenies. Haven't ever seen anything like that before, especially in old Muskingum. Major?"

Pointing at the map, Major Moses M. Granger said "Thank you, Colonel Ball. It looks to me like we can use the Muskingum to get us to Marietta by steamboat. Then, I would think the best way to Virginia is by train, Marietta to Parkersburg; Parkersburg to Clarksburg; Clarksburg to Morgantown; and then east into the mountains. "What do you think, Lieutenant?"

"You are right, sir, we will need boats and then trains. If the Colonel agrees, I will relay our request to General Meigs' office in Washington."

"Lieutenant, do you want me to contact the General?"

"No, sir, I don't think that will be necessary. Our instruction from him was to communicate directly with his office as soon as we know where we are heading. His staff is very good at providing what the regimental commanders, like yourself, need. Actually, they want to make it as easy for you as they can."

"For you boys that have gone to the front before, was that your experience?" asked Colonel William Ball.

Heads nodded in agreement, and then Tom Armstrong offered, "Yes, sir, after we boarded the steamers, we went right down the Muskingum to Marietta where we headed west on the Ohio. We passed Cincinnati and turned south on the Mississippi toward Paducah. We really had no trouble at all."

"Thank you, Lieutenant. Lieutenant Morgan, specifically, what do you think we will require?"

"Well, we'll need a couple of boats to get us to Marietta, depending on how big they are. Gotta house all thousand of us plus the others like the wagon masters, cooks, and other civilians. Supply trains for the horses, cattle, and hogs; the supply wagons; feed for the animals; the ammunition; men's boxes; food; extra clothing. Begging the Colonel's pardon and if you will excuse me, sir, I should like to send a telegraphic message to General Meigs' office about this."

"Certainly, Lieutenant," and Douglas Morgan left the room.

Upon his return, he said, "Colonel, the Quartermaster General's staff is now aware of our initial needs for river transportation. They will start working on it."

"Very well. What's next?"

"Then, we'll need rail travel from Parkersburg to northwestern Virginia. It will be on the B&O. I have been preparing for this day for some time, so I don't think it shall be too difficult to arrange the rails. Washington knows that we are to be on the move. May I be excused once again?" The Regimental Quartermaster left the room.

When he came back into William Ball's office, he said "Colonel, General Meigs' staff will take care of all of the transportation. I presume midday on Thursday?"

"Yes. Excellent work, Lieutenant Morgan."

"Thank you, sir, it is my pleasure. Now, to the details about what the men should take. We have a list prepared by the General's staff, and I will start with that. The basic necessities are overcoats; tents; blankets, woolen and rubber; haversacks for rations; 40 rounds of ammunition for each man, a huswife, and any personal things like letters from home and photographs, Bible, eating utensils, tin cup, matches, soap, razor, and maybe a comb; paper, pen, and ink; percussion caps; musket. The other stuff can remain in the boxes the men have had prepared. My staff and I will follow in the cars with the provisions that we will need for the longer term, food, weapons, clothing, ammunition, etc."

"What the hell is a huswife?" Major Moses Granger interjected.

"All of the men have them, sir. It contains needle, thread, and scissors. It's a woman thing. All the things for darning socks, patching pantaloons, resoling boots. Things like that."

There were chuckles from the junior officers. "Oh," thought the Major, "I can have Rundle do that for me."

"Will you please write the list down, Lieutenant?"

"Already taken care of, sir. My staff is working with the Company Quartermasters at this very moment to go over the list and to discuss what we can do for them and what they have to do for themselves. We just need to use common sense, Colonel. Oh, when you know where we will be stationed in Virginia, that is, the last time we will be on the rails, can you let me know so we can have the staff in Washington get us wagons for the supplies?"

"Indeed, Lieutenant. I know we're going to Winchester, and we have to be on the march next Friday. I leave the logistics to you,"

"Thank you, sir." Douglas Morgan replied. "I forgot one thing. Our instructions from the Quartermaster General say that each Company is allowed two wagons to carry the things they need for the journey. It also says that the Colonel's staff and the Major's staff can have five wagons with all of the material for the regimental headquarters. That's the standard issue. My men are telling the Company Quartermasters about that right now. Some of them might not be too happy, only having two wagons, but that is the order."

Colonel William Ball, looked his Regimental Quartermaster squarely in the eye, rubbing his thick, black beard thoughtfully. He smiled. "So, Lieutenant Morgan, we're going to take this entire camp, pack it all up, and put it all on a couple of riverboats?"

"Yes, sir. We're working with Company Quartermasters as I have told you. May I assume, sir, that I will be working directly with Sergeant Rundle to get you, the Major, and your staffs ready to go?

"You may, Lieutenant. Isn't that right, Sergeant Rundle?"

"Yes, sir. I shall look forward to working with the Quartermaster."

"Gentlemen," said Colonel William H. Ball. "Get to it. On the double." With that the meeting ended. There would be church this day, but starting in the afternoon, the 122nd Ohio Volunteer Infantry would become a beehive of activity. It would be a very busy week for Regimental Quartermaster Douglas Morgan, his staff, and the ten Company Quartermasters. They had their orders. Now it was time to execute them.

At precisely 5 o'clock on the morning of Thursday, October 23, 1862, the regimental bugler for the 122nd Ohio Volunteer Infantry blew *Reveille*. The day would start out normally, but certainly would not end that way. *Roll Call* and *Inspection* followed, as usual, at 5:30. At 6:00, instead of another day of drill, they men were ordered to make sure that they had everything, a final inspection so to speak. Breakfast was at 7:30. But instead of returning to the barracks to prepare for drill, the men marched in a column of twos to the back of the mess hall where they picked up their rations, three-days' worth. Hard bread, salt pork, fresh beef, dried apples, coffee, and salt. "That's gonna last us three days? Don't think so," complained Patrick Murphy.

At 9 o'clock, the bugler blew *Assembly*, and all ten companies fell into place, just as ordered by *Hardee's Tactics*. Atten-TION!" yelled Moses Granger. The men snapped to, staring straight ahead, not moving a muscle except to breathe. "AT EASE!"

"We have been ordered to northern Virginia to protect the B&O Railroad and to keep the enemy from making any movement toward Maryland or Pennsylvania," announced William Ball. "You have trained well during the last month, and I commend you, the officers, sergeants, and corporals for accomplishing that directive. You will now put what you have learned to good use. We have been assigned to the 2nd brigade of Major General Robert Milroy's division. I do not know him, but I am sure I will, and soon. Once we are in Confederate territory, be on the lookout for their scouts, spies, and especially their bushwhackers. They will hide in the mountains within firing range and will shoot at us on the way by. You officers, they will primarily take aim at you, so be alert at all times when we are on foot. Those of us on horseback are particularly vulnerable.

"Commanders, be in formation precisely at noon. The steamers will be at the 5th Street pier, and the men can board them then. Start loading everything else now. The wagons first, then the animals. This is to be done by noon. You are dismissed."

Wagons loaded down with subsistence and ammunition began rolling down the main street of Camp Zanesville toward the Main Gate. Company I Quartermaster Sergeant George McMillen breathed a sigh of relief. It had been a long week. Tom Armstrong wished he had had the time to go to Norwich and Hopewell to say goodbye, but that just wasn't going to happen. He watched as the wranglers and drovers assigned to drive the cattle to the steamers began yelling at the top of their lungs for the cows to start moving. A couple of them shot their pistols in the air to hasten that movement. It was slow, very slow. Most of the herd and the hogs would have to be loaded into the supply trains for the journey to northern Virginia. So, would most of the horses and mules. Watching the parade, Armstrong hoped that the Quartermaster had gotten steamers big enough for all of what they would need to get to Parkersburg. The rest would come by train.

At 11:45 AM, the bugle sounded *Assembly* once again. The men of the 122nd O.V.I. came to attention on the parade ground in the middle of Camp Zanesville. It was a beautiful autumn day in central Ohio, with the trees showing off their full color as the 122nd assembled, each man carrying over forty pounds of materiel, plus a Springfield rifle that weighed an additional nine pounds. They had trained for this and looked sharp. They were anxious to get going. Those who had heard about the slaughter at Antietam were anxious about that as well, wondering if the same thing would happen to them. Their nerves were starting to fray. At exactly noon, the bugler sounded Forward. The Company commanders shouted to their lieutenants, "RIGHT SHOULDER, SHIFT! FORWARD MARCH!" The muskets, bayonets attached and shining brightly in the sunlight, came to the right shoulder of each of the enlisted men who would board the steamers for their trip to the East. The officers, with their sabers gleaming, led their companies, with Colonel William H. Ball, astride a huge black gelding, leading the way.

The colors of the United States of America followed, being carried by a rather large Corporal from Captain John Ross's Company K. The flag, with its thirteen red and white stripes and the thirty-four white stars on the navy-blue background in the upper left-hand corner fluttered as he marched by. Soldiers who had not been ordered to the field saluted en masse as a brass band played *Rally Round the Flag* and *Yankee Doodle*. Major Moses M. Granger and his staff came next, followed by the regimental colors, a dark blue flag with a bald eagle in flight carrying a ribbon in its beak, proudly displaying "E Pluribus Unum," which translated from the Latin meant "Out of Many, One." It was the official motto of the United States and suggested that in times of difficulty, the people of America come together as one. Interestingly, in both the North and the South that had happened, ever since April 21, 1861, the day upon which Confederate P.G.T. Beauregard ordered the artillery to bomb Fort Sumter.

Each man in the regiment wore a badge of a white, six-sided star on a navy-blue background on his sleeve, identifying him as a member of the 122nd. Slowly, in accordance with *Hardee's Tactics*, and following the senior officers and their colors, the column began its way toward the Main Gate. Tom Armstrong was relieved to be on the move again, finally; said a silent prayer of thanks and deliverance, and wondered what would happen next. The column proudly marched down to the 5th Street pier to the cheers of the townspeople who had gathered to see them go. The entire Armstrong family was there, as Tom had written them. They were very proud to see Company I go by, but at the same time, quite apprehensive. Jane Armstrong, with tears in her eyes, could hardly watch. Neither could Francis Porter who had ridden in from Hopewell with her father in hopes of spying him one last time. She did see him, but he not her, tears welling up with the thought that she might never see him again.

That morning, Colonel William Ball had asked Quartermaster Lieutenant Douglas Morgan to accompany him to make sure that the loading went smoothly. It didn't. By the time Company I arrived, not one man had boarded either of the steamers, "Jonas Powell" or "T.J. Patten." Pushing their way forward, Tom Armstrong and Daniel Gary could see the Colonel arguing vehemently with a man they presumed to be the captain of one of the boats.

"If I put all this livestock and those wagons on my boats," screamed Captain Stephen Wilson, "there won't be enough room for the men. This boat can only handle 400 people."

"I don't care where you put them, sir, but we are going to Marietta on this boat and that one over there. We are going as soon as you load up," replied William Ball. "Lieutenant Morgan, Sergeant Rundle, start boarding the essential supply wagons. Get them down below. A few cows, hogs, horses, and mules next. Captain, show the Lieutenant where they should go. The rest of the wagons and live-stock will follow in the cars."

"Like hell. I will do no such thing," screamed Stephen Wilson.

Ball drew his revolver, pointed it at the captain, and said, "Listen, you son-of-a-bitch, you will show the Lieutenant, or this is the last conversation you will ever have."

Seeing that the colonel was quite serious, Captain Wilson re-lented. "Come with me." The loading began, but it had been delayed three hours. It was chaos. It just didn't look like anyone was in charge. Even if it had been done correctly, loading the two steamers would have taken much longer than Ball wanted.

"I tried to tell him. We only put what we need for the next few days on the boats," Douglas Morgan said to Sergeant Terrance Run-dle. "We will be lucky to shove off by dark."

Loading was painstakingly slow. With the wagons on board, the animals didn't seem to want to get on a boat. The men of the 122nd O.V.I. began to wish they were back at Camp Zanesville, but, alas, they were not and simply had to wait while the huge riverboats were loaded. The wranglers and drovers whistled and shouted for the herd to move, but the cows weren't interested. Finally, about 5 o'clock that afternoon, they were safely on board, albeit mighty cramped in the lowest of the steamer's four decks. The rest of the animals were loaded by about 6:00 PM. Colonel Ball and his staff followed. Then came the rest of the regiment. By 8, on Thursday, October 23, the Patten and Powell were ready to shove off for the slow trip to Mari-etta, some 70 miles south down the Muskingum River.

By 3 AM the next morning, the boats were moored at Point Har-mar on the west bank of the Muskingum at Marietta. According to the plan, the 122nd was to go by rail thirteen miles south to Parkersburg and points east. It would take five 10-car freight trains to transport the men, animals, and supplies and certainly would be faster. But, that also meant unloading the steamers and then loading the supply trains. That would take some time and was assigned to Captain John Ross and Company K to assist the Regimental Quar-termaster Lieutenant and his men.

At daybreak, the men of the 122nd O.V.I. disembarked from the Patten and Powell and marched to the railroad and boarded the trains heading for Parkersburg. "When are we gonna get some sleep, Lieutenant," Eddie Bristow lamented.

"When we get there. It's really a short trip," replied Tom Armstrong.

"Damn! There ain't enough room in here to sit down comfortably. Move over, Patrick. I need some space here."

"Move over yourself, Bristow. I'm stuck here. Brennan on one side, you on the other. Damn it!"

Tom Armstrong had chosen to ride in the freight car on the short trip and just smiled, as he sat there, back against the wall. "The boys are complaining about this. They haven't seen anything yet. Wait'll they see, and meet, the elephant," he thought to himself.

The troop trains pulled into the depot in Parkersburg, Virginia at a little past noon. The supply trains would follow. In spite of the confusion at the 5th Street pier in Zanesville, Douglas Morgan had done a masterful job. The men of the 122nd immediately set about pitching their tents and setting up Camp Union in a nice grove of trees, 1 ½ miles from the Little Kanawha River and 2 miles from the mighty Ohio. The first chore was to find wood for their campfires. Upon orders from the Colonel, Captain Daniel Gary and the other Company commanders sent details into the woods to bring back as much wood as they could. Next, he had some of the men dig a well, probably not necessary with the rivers close by, but useful for cooking and washing their clothes. Any man who wanted to take a bath could go jump in one of the rivers. The third immediate task was the digging of latrines. Gary thought, "Armstrong told me that digging new ones isn't so bad. It's filling in old ones that's not so pleasant."

Finally, about supper time, Camp Union was operational. It was time to break out the rations and eat. Hot coffee, too. The grid on the campfire held the cooking pots. Dan Gary, Tom Black, and Tom Armstrong tasted their first meal on the march. There would be many, many more, some enjoyable, some not. They heard the whistles of the supply trains and were glad that they had arrived. The conversation after supper was full of assumptions and assertions about the rest of the journey and what they would find at Winchester in northern Virginia at the head of the Shenandoah Valley. Gary reminded Black and Armstrong to be on the lookout for Confederate scouts, spies, and bushwhackers. Around 8:45 PM, the men of the 122nd O.V.I. formed for the evening *Roll Call* and *Inspection* by the company commanders. "All present and accounted for, Colonel," shouted Dan Gary.

Darkness had fallen over Camp Union. The men were exhausted from the long day of travel. Many of them did not hear *Taps* being played to signal the end of the day. The fires continued to burn and slowly petered out. It was the end of the first day on the march to Winchester.

The next day was spent surveying the surrounding countryside. It was hilly all right, but nothing compared to what they would see in a few days. Rudimentary earthworks were dug to provide some protection in case of a raid. But, for the most part, the day was pretty peaceful.

On Sunday morning, the Colonel had decided that the men needed another day away from drill for which the officers and enlisted men were quite glad. After breakfast of some dried apples, hardtack, and coffee, Tom Armstrong, enjoying a day off, knew that it was time to write home...

> Camp Union Near Parkersburg Va
> October 26 A.D. 1862
> Dear Family,
>
> I am well. Capn Gary, Lt. Black, & I are in one side of a tent. Capn Sells, Lt. Work, & Lt. Sells are in a tent of the same. I have a hand trunk; all necessary things pertaining to camp life, indeed.
>
> This day has been rainy, sleety. Last night we slept nice and warm with our guns on some straw then put our blankets over us. Black slept in the middle; he has a bad cold. He caught it on guard duty night before last.
>
> The men have no stoves, but have plenty of wood & have good fires. We have five good tents to a company. We have one tent to six 6 officers. The tents are called "Bell Tents." We have our camp in a nice grove with a

well for water but we do not use it now. We are in Wood County. They have a beautiful courthouse in this town. We think the inhabitants are mostly Secesh. That accounts for the Bush Whackers.

Well this is hard country. We are going to the mountains I think. The boys are writing many letters home today. Milroy has telegraphed Ball to come to the Big Rendezvous.

Well I will write more soon. Write to me soon. Farewell.

> Thos S Armstrong
> Care Col. W.H. Ball
> 122d Regt O.V.I.
> Parkersburg Va

Colonel William H. Ball had been informed that the 122nd Ohio Volunteer Infantry had been assigned to the 2nd Brigade of Major Robert H. Milroy's Second Division of the VIII Corps. He would report directly to Brigadier General Gustave P. Cluseret. Cluseret, in turn, would report to Milroy, the VIII Corps part of the Middle Department of the Union army, commanded by Major General Robert C. Schenck. The Colonel and his staff had taken off at dawn by train to meet with General Milroy and General Cluseret. It would take about five hours to Milroy's headquarters.

It was unusual that Sunday morning for there to be no church services, but Chaplain Charles McCabe had not had the time to organize one for the men at Camp Union, and they had not realized that they were free to worship in the churches right there in Parkersburg. Not that they would be welcome, mind you, not that they might cause a confrontation. It was better that they stayed in camp. Tom Armstrong decided to seek out the Chaplain for a visit since he had not seen his friend in quite some time. He found him in his tent near Ball's headquarters.

"Thomas, good to see you. How have you been?"

"Good, Charlie," was the reply. "Very good. The men are anxious to get to work on the enemy. Can I ask you a question?"

"Shoot."

160

"My men have heard about what happened at Antietam, the massive slaughter there. While they want to fight the Rebels, I find that there is some anxiety among them, especially those whose faith may not be as strong as others. What do I tell them? How can I help them?"

"Well, T.S. I have heard that from other officers recently and there's not much you can do. You know better than most, war is cruel. Some of your men, and perhaps yourself, will not come back to Ohio. I can talk with them. I can baptize those who wish it. But, as you and I have discussed, it is a matter of personal faith and trust that it is God's will being done, not ours. You have embraced that and are prepared. The others know of the danger."

"But, Charlie, that's the point. They don't, really. They think they do. Some of them are just here for the glory that supposedly attends a soldier. The problem is, they haven't seen the elephant. They don't know what it is like to walk over their dead comrades across a field into blazing rifle fire from people who want them just as dead as we want them. They haven't experienced what war really is. They think they have, but they haven't."

"I know. All we can do is try to tell them to turn to the Lord, especially in the worst of times."

Tom Armstrong was thinking, "You're a big help," but had too much respect for his friend to say it.

"How's Francis?"

"Don't know. Assume she's good. Haven't heard from her in a while. Rebecca?"

"Very well. Lonesome and frightened, but very well."

The two friends continued to talk about all kinds of things. It was getting on to about noon, and Armstrong figured he better get back to his tent for dinner and to see what had been going on that morning. He also wanted to find out how long they would be in Parkersburg. No one in camp could tell. They would have to wait until the colonel returned.

It wouldn't be long. The train carrying Colonel William Ball and his staff chugged into the depot around 6 o'clock on Monday evening. Immediately, Colonel Ball issued orders to "Strike Tents" the following day, Tuesday, October 28, 1862. The 122nd O.V.I. would be heading out for points east. At 6 o'clock the next morning, *Reveille* was sounded with the order to prepare to leave Parkersburg. "The adventure has really begun," Tom Armstrong said to himself.

"Where we are going?" Eddie Bristow asked.

"Northern Virginia. Pack up and get your men ready to go. Tell Murphy the same thing. Black will have to tell Simpson and Brennan."

"Yes, sir!"

The men of the 122nd O.V.I. would go by the same train, the B&O, in freight cars. This time, for the longer journey, Armstrong would join the other officers in the passenger car. Captain John Ross and Company K would follow with Douglas Morgan and his men in the supply trains.

Captain Daniel Gary rode up. "Three days' rations, men, and be quick about it." The Company Quartermaster, Sergeant George McMillen, was about to get busy again.

The column of bluecoats was ready to move out at 10 o'clock that morning, marching toward the train depot, a mile or so away.

"Damn heavy, all of this gear," complained Eddie Bristow.

"Don't even think about throwing anything away," Patrick Murphy said, reminding his comrade of Armstrong's admonishment. "Travel light, but travel smart."

The big, black locomotives were belching dark gray smoke from their stacks when the 122nd arrived at the depot. The doors to the cars slid open, and the men climbed in. When all were aboard, the doors were closed, and they could feel the train starting to pull them eastward toward Winchester.

"Damn crowded in here," said Eddie Bristow. "No room to stretch out or nothin'."

"Quit yer bitchin', Bristow. It's the same for all of us." Patrick Murphy was sitting with his back to the wall of the car, humming *The Battle Hymn*.

The train was picking up speed, maybe to twenty miles per hour, as it carried its cargo across northwestern Virginia which would not become West Virginia until mid-1863. It crossed trestles and went through tunnels, but the men didn't know it. No windows on freight cars.

Smoke from the locomotive filled the air. "Damn! Damn hard to breathe. Can't see a damn thing. Ain't we got some clean air? Armstrong never told us about this." Eddie Bristow was not happy.

"Like hell he didn't," came the response from Patrick Murphy. "He told us everything to expect. Quit bitchin'. I told you, it's the same for all of us."

A couple hours later, they could feel the train slow and then come to a stop. The doors were opened by what looked to be cavalry officers who ordered the men out and into formation. Adjusting their eyes to the sun, they climbed out and formed up. The large sign on the depot wall said CLARKSBURG. On orders from the Colonel and the Major, Daniel Gary ordered the men of Company I forward.

"Where the hell is Clarksburg?" asked Patrick Murphy.

"About 70 miles east of where we were this morning," answered Tom Armstrong. "When we get to camp, let's talk with Lieutenant Black and have you, Bristow, Simpson, and Brennan reconnoiter firewood and water. Have the men pitch tents, and we'll need latrines dug. Get a detail for that, but we need water and wood first." That would always be the priority.

The routine from Camp Zanesville would start anew in Clarksburg the next day, Wednesday, October 29. Drill would commence at 7 o'clock, followed by breakfast at 8, more drill from 9:30 to 11, with some free time for an hour before dinner. Armstrong was pleased the way that Tom Black, Eddie Bristow, Patrick Murphy, Thaddeus Brennan, and Chesley Simpson had drilled the men up to now. He was also pleased with the progress Captain Gary and Captain Ross had made. But, he still worried about the inexperience of the men, not only in battle, but simply on the march as well. He was thinking that passing through the mountains of western Virginia would be on foot. He was also thinking that, if that happened, they were not prepared for it. You see, the area around Zanesville in Muskingum County is pretty flat. He was also painfully aware that they were not ready for battle and the awful carnage it would bring. "Please let us get the Enfields," he thought to himself.

Safely in Clarksburg, Colonel William H. Ball called for a meeting of the officers of the 122nd O.V.I. Orderly Sergeant Terrance Rundle and Quartermaster Lieutenant Douglas Morgan were there, too. Major Moses Granger commanded "Atten-TION," and everyone snapped into place.

"At ease, gentlemen," said Colonel Ball. "As you were. Find a place to sit. I met with General Milroy and General Cluseret on Sunday and Monday. As you know, we have orders to go to Winchester, over the Shenandoah Mountains, in northern Virginia, at the head of the Shenandoah Valley. The B&O runs through Winchester as do several roads that serve to bring supplies to the army that holds the town. It is a vital place that is difficult to defend, but Milroy is sure that he can do it. I'm not convinced of that. It's changed hands so many times. We won't have many friends there. Most, if not all, pro-Confederacy. I don't know when we will break this camp, so we will wait here, drilling the men, until such time as I receive orders. We will go toward Cumberland, Maryland. First, northeast to Morgantown and then due east. Lieutenant Morgan and Sergeant Rundle, make sure that we have supply wagons available to us when we get there."

"Get where?" Rundle thought to himself, shaking his head. "How the hell are we gonna get wagons to someplace we don't know where? The army way, I guess. That's Morgan's problem. Probably has instructions from Washington about that, too." He just smiled.

Colonel Ball continued, "Keep drilling the men and, commanders, I will let you know our orders as soon as I have them. Any questions?"

Seeing none, Granger again commanded "Atten-TION. Dis-MISSED!"

Gary, Black, and Armstrong walked back to their tents. "When we were in the officers' meeting back in Zanesville," Armstrong related, "we figured it was about 175 miles from here to Winchester. Sure glad we're going by the cars. Doing that on the march would have taken forever and really taxed the men. Maybe while we are here we can drill them on hills so they get used to the climb and descent."

"Good idea, Tom," said Captain Daniel Gary. "Why don't the two of you map out a place where we can do that, starting tomorrow?"

"Will do, Dan."

Even with the newness of drilling on various elevations, the boredom of camp life began to set in. The 122nd had hurried to Parkersburg, expecting orders to advance to northern Virginia, and now here they were sitting in Clarksburg. And they didn't know for how long. Armstrong and Black were still quite busy planning with Dan Gary and George McMillen, but every night, before "Lights Out," Tom Armstrong would take the picture that Francis Porter had sent him and one or two of her letters out of his haversack and remind himself of how much he loved her. As he prepared for the evening's rest, he silently recited The Lord's Prayer; thanked God for his family, Frank, President Lincoln, and his deliverance each day; and ended his day with the 23rd Psalm.

The rest of the day and all day the next, the 122nd settled into camp on the hills above the railroad depot. Colonel Ball did not want the regiment too far away from the rails in case his orders from General Cluseret demanded speed. And, it just made sense to camp close to the supply trains.

Details went out into the woods to gather wood for the regiment's campfires; Elk Creek would supply the water, and latrines had been dug. The men began to settle in, hoping that the supplies and the herds of cattle, horses, mules, and hogs would arrive soon. They did, the very next day. The men of the 122nd busied themselves building fences for the animals and constructing some primitive defenses, although no one really thought the Rebels would attack them there.

Hard drill in the hills started, but Tom Armstrong had another assignment. Captain Daniel Gary had been ordered to detail a scouting party south and had asked Armstrong to lead it. Gary asked Tom Black to go along. The two lieutenants would take four enlisted men and ride south to Weston, Virginia, some thirty miles from Clarksburg and then to Sutton, another forty miles south just to see if the Confederates were up to something. They would return to camp late that night, tired and hungry, but the excursion had been a success.

"Let's go report to the Captain, Lieutenant Black," said Tom Armstrong. "You men, go back to your tents and get something to eat." The others went back to their tents for food and rest and following orders, Gary, Black, and Armstrong rode to the Colonel's tent. "My compliments, Colonel," said Captain Daniel Gary. "The scouting party just got back and can report that they saw no Rebel activity anywhere as far down as Sutton. Not sure the citizens were real happy to see them, apparently, but nobody said or did anything. I would suggest, and begging the Colonel's pardon, that this kind of scouting should be done routinely, almost every day. We have bare minimum defense here and need to know if the enemy's coming."

"Thank you, Captain. Well done. Your information is the same as that which I received from General Milroy's staff in the Valley. It doesn't look like there is much activity at all. Perhaps the Rebels are settling into their winter camps. Wouldn't surprise me."

"Me, either, sir. If there's nothing else, their horses could use a rest, as could they. A little salt pork, hardtack, and coffee will probably go a long way, too."

Ball returned their salutes. "You are dismissed."

"Thank you, sir," he said, and Daniel Gary opened the flap of the Colonel's tent. Black and Armstrong were tired, really tired, as they walked their horses back to their tent. Lieutenant Tom Armstrong thought to himself, "Drill again in the morning. Hafta get the men ready. They think they are, but they're not. God give me rest tonight," and he crawled into the tent after Tom Black and Dan Gary, trying not to wake the others.

The two lieutenants would go on reconnaissance jaunts just about every other day, leaving the drill of the men to Captains Ross and Gary, assisted by Murphy, Bristow, Brennan, and Simpson. The scouting parties would leave early in the morning and come back after dark, but the result was always the same. Nothing. No activity at all. Well, maybe not with the Rebels, but they would stumble onto something that they thought might be worthwhile.

While Black and Armstrong were busy on the road, the drill had commenced in earnest. Gary and Ross were quite pleased with the progress they saw. Armstrong and Black were glad they had been given something else to do, rather than drill the men, but now that was over. Armstrong thought he better write a letter home. It had been ten days since he had.

Clarksburg, Va.
November 6, 1862

166

Dear Bro.

My health continues good. Off for the tented field again. Just a few months before, I left with Bro Wilbur on a similar mission, but time has changed. He is gone to eternity. I am here with a lot of soldiers. All of us will not get back home.

When I am dead you can look on my countenance & say there is "Sumption," or "Sump," or "Tom." "Thomas" just as you like, but I hope I will get home again. Pray much to our Creator that my life may be spared. Tell Father & Mother to pray for me as I have great faith in their prayers.

Write again

Goodbye

Thos S Armstrong

On what would turn out to be their last scouting expedition, Black and Armstrong walked into the only hotel in Sutton, Virginia to get a cup of coffee. It was about 1 o'clock in the afternoon on Monday. November 10. The rest of the men were told to take care of the horses and to prepare them for the long ride back to camp. The two men walked into the bar and asked the barkeep for coffee. It was strong and very hot. While they were standing there, they noticed a young man sitting by himself at a table shuffling playing cards. He was in street clothes, with a sidearm buckled around his waist, big black hat on the table, rifle leaning against it. He looked about 12 years old. Looking up, he said, "Howdy, fellas."

"Afternoon," said Tom Armstrong

"You got a minute, sir?"

"The Lieutenant and I have a little time. What's your name? Where you from?"

"David Hitchcock, but you can call me 'Davy' or 'Hitch.' I'm from Tuscarawas County, Ohio, up near New Philadelphia."

"Heard of it. We're from Zanesville, east of Columbus. Two questions, Hitch. You any relation of General Ethan Hitchcock? And, what are you doing here?"

"Grandfather, sir. He's on General Sherman's staff. Tried to enlist, sir, but they wouldn't take me. I'm only 17, but I want to help. My pappy is an abolitionist, and when I told him that I wanted to help somehow, he gave me permission to go and see the war. Granddad approved, too, but not to fight."

"You know it's dangerous to be here in Virginia, don't you? Especially a Union man."

"Yes, sir, I'm pretty careful. I hide real good."

"How can you help?" Black asked, looking at the boyish young man. "Bet he doesn't even shave," he thought to himself. The kid was lean, real lean, wiry even and looked like he could run like the wind. Black guessed he was just under six feet tall; hair cropped close.

"Well, sir, I can ride real good. You see, we raise horses on our farm in Dover. Been ridin' all my life. Shoot pretty good, too" touching the butt of the pistol in his gun belt.

"Okay, Hitch. We hafta get back to camp in Clarksburg. You want to come along?"

"Sure."

On the way back to Clarksburg, Armstrong and Black started talking, outside of earshot of the four enlisted men and Hitch. "I have an idea, Tom, as to how we can use the kid."

"Okay. Shoot," said Tom Armstrong.

"What would happen if we convince the Colonel that he could be very useful, being out in the field all the time, watching for the Rebel army?"

"You mean, the kid could be a spy?" Armstrong asked.

"Yep. I need to know a little more about him like can he get himself hidden in case there's trouble and can he forage for food and not be seen. I also would want him to have a Reb uniform so he could infiltrate their camps to find out their plans. Don't know if he can talk Southern either."

"Whattya think?"

"If it keeps you and me away from that duty, I'm all for it. Let's talk to the Captain and then the Colonel."

It was dark when they got back. Tom Armstrong and Tom Black told Dan Gary about the idea. The Captain led the way to tell Colonel William Ball about it. "Sir," began Gary, "with my compliments, the boys have an idea for you. I heard that Major Granger spoke with you that we are going to need eyes in the field all the time, and I don't think you want the two of them away from camp as often as they have been the last couple of weeks."

"No, I don't. What do you have in mind?"

Lieutenant Thomas Black told the Colonel about young, David Hitchcock, saying that the kid was eager to be the eyes of the regiment. William Ball liked the idea.

"Have him report to Sergeant Rundle. I will make sure the sergeant keeps me informed."

"Yes, sir. Will do. Thank you, sir."

"Dismissed. Good night, gentlemen."

"Good night, sir."

They would tell Hitch in the morning. When they returned to their tent, they found the young man sitting by the campfire with the four enlisted men who had been on the expedition, talking about what they had seen, and they didn't want to break that up. "I hope the kid knows what he is getting himself into, but I bet he doesn't. Pretty naive, I think, but maybe that's a good thing," Armstrong thought to himself.

The next morning, Tuesday, November 11, Tom Black and Tom Armstrong introduced Hitch to Sergeant Terrance Rundle.

"I can pay you $10 a month, Hitch, but only if your information is reliable and accurate."

"Thank you, Sergeant. It will be. I'm gonna take some notes and maybe draw maps."

Based on information about the enemy's whereabouts that would be passed on to Colonel Ball from Milroy's headquarters, Rundle would tell the youngster where there might be Rebel activity, but, basically, the kid was free to go wherever he wanted. When he reported back was up to him, but Rundle told him he wanted to see him at least once a week. He found a Rebel uniform that he thought would fit and gave it to the young man who stuffed it into his saddle bag. His final words to him were "Go find Stonewall Jackson. The

Colonel has heard he is somewhere in the Shenandoah Valley. When you come back, you can find me somewhere around Winchester. Just ask around." With a week's worth of rations and a full supply of ammunition, David, "Hitch", Hitchcock disappeared down the road toward Weston.

"Wonder if I'll ever see that kid again," he said to no one in particular.

In his letters, Armstrong did not, and would never, tell Jacob, Francis Porter, or anyone about "Hitch." Tom Black was sworn to secrecy, too. The next day, Colonel William Ball called another meeting of the officers of the 122nd O.V.I. "Gentlemen," he began, "the President has made a bold move today. I have been advised by General Milroy that McClellan has been replaced by Major General Ambrose E. Burnside as the Commander of the Army of the Potomac. From what General Milroy says, Mr. Lincoln was not happy that General McClellan failed to pursue General Lee after Antietam and his general reluctance to take the fight to the enemy. I don't know this for sure, but I would be surprised if General Schenck doesn't report directly to General Burnside. Somehow, I have a feeling that our new commander-in-chief will soon know about us. Any questions?"

A couple of days later, Chaplain Charles C. McCabe felt compelled to write a letter to the Editor of the *Daily Zanesville Courier*.

> Letter from the 122d Regiment
> In Camp, near Clarksburgh
> Nov. 14, 1862
>
> Mr. Editor:
> "All is quiet," on Elk Creek. There is as yet no certain indications of a speedy forward movement of the 122d. We are quietly waiting for orders to march. But the time spent here is by no means wasted – Even to my unpracticed eyes, there is manifest improvement in the soldierly bearing of the regiment, when on Battalion drill. The question is often asked "will the army go into winter quarters soon?" Could the soldiers have their way. "Forward march would ring

along the line of the Union army from the Atlantic to the Pacific.

The supercedure of McClellan caused considerable excitement in our midst. Some pronounced for, some against it, but all hoped for the best, and are willing to leave the matter quietly with those who are immediately responsible for the safety of the Union.

We want a leader who can show us results. A leader who can concentrate on the powers of the nation to crush the rebellion at once. We want a man whose greatness needs no advocate but his own great deeds

O that General Burnside may be the man.

The friends of the 122d will be glad to learn that the health of the Regiment is still remarkably good. That as a general thing, the soldiers are happy and contented. The only complaint I hear is the scarcity of Letters. Send them by the hundred. We want to hear from you. We often think and sing in concert about those we have left behind us. A few evenings ago, while seated on a stick of wood by a camp fire, surrounded by a large crowd of my comrades, one romantic youth said, "Chaplain can you sing Anna Laura?" to be sure, and I was soon singing.

It was too dark to see the faces of the men distinctly, but as I looked up at the silent groups around me, now and then joining me in the chorus as I sang.

They started as though by chance they had left the doors to their hearts ajar, and I had read their thoughts and had seen the tablet on which was written "name they dared not speak."

Please send me the *Courier* now and then and oblige yours.   C.C. MCCABE

It was becoming evident to Chaplain Charles C. McCabe that perhaps the reality of war was setting in and that the men did not want to think about their own deaths and the hurt it would cause their families. And especially their wives, fiancées, or girlfriends. Perhaps the slaughter at Antietam contributed to that reality and now, being out in an open field, about the railroad in Clarksburg, Virginia, it was all starting to really sink in.

That same day, Friday, November 14, Colonel William H. Ball received formal orders to go to Cumberland, Maryland and to have three days' rations cooked. Yes, it was getting real all right. Tom Armstrong had one advantage. He had seen the elephant at Fort Donelson and at Shiloh. He knew what to expect, the others didn't. While it probably wouldn't happen in the winter months, it would happen in the spring. That he knew. He didn't know exactly what was going to happen, who was going to attack whom, but they hadn't been sent to northwestern Virginia just to guard a railroad. Or, had they?

The next morning, the Quartermaster, Sergeant George McMillen, brought Armstrong a present: a brand-new Enfield rifle. "Hot damn. Now we're getting somewhere," he said to the quartermaster. "Now we have weapons that can do some real damage. I will organize training for the officers who can then train the men." That would have to wait since the Regimental Quartermaster, Douglas Morgan, could only obtain the one.

The trains to take them to Cumberland, Maryland were on the siding, ready to go. The 122nd had to pack up fast. The frantic activity of breaking camp and loading the cars took the rest of the morning. At 3 o'clock that afternoon, after dinner, the first big black B&O locomotive with Colonel William H. Ball and Moses M. Granger, along with their staffs and the rest of the officers, in the first car, slowly chugged out of the Clarksburg depot on the way to Maryland. They never got there. Climbing over and through the mountains, the trains labored until whistles sounded, announcing a stop, just about 1 o'clock on the morning of Sunday, November 16, 1862.

"Wonder where we are," Tom Black said, peering into the darkness.

"Don't know. Don't think we're in Cumberland," replied Tom Armstrong.

Climbing down from the officer car, they saw the sign on the depot that said NEW CREEK.

Black exclaimed, "Where the hell is that?"

"Where we are, Tom," said Armstrong, having a little fun at his friend's expense. "Can't go anywhere till the sun comes up. I'm gonna grab some shut-eye."

With the sun making its initial appearance in the east, *Reveille* was sounded. It was time for *Roll Call*, *Inspection* by Captain Daniel Gary, and breakfast, after which the bugler sounded *Assembly* and the ten companies of the 122nd Ohio Volunteer Infantry came to formation. At 10 o'clock, the bugler sounded *Forward*, and Tom Armstrong and the rest of Co. I heard Captain Daniel Gary yell "RIGHT SHOULDER, SHIFT! FORWARD MARCH!" The regiment was on the march, heading south. An hour later, they could see a small town, maybe about the size of Norwich or Hopewell, south of which they could see tents, thousands of them.

As they walked through the little village, the sign on the Post Office also read NEW CREEK. "Now you know where you are, Tom?" asked Armstrong.

"Yeah, we're in New Creek, Virginia, three miles from the depot, but I don't know where we are." Armstrong laughed.

"Get the men situated, Mr. Black, Mr. Armstrong," was the order from Dan Gary.

Tom Black shouted, "Sergeants, you heard the Captain, get to work. Tom, we better get our tent up and things unpacked."

That didn't take very long, so the two lieutenants went out to survey the other units that were camped there as well. As they walked along the New Creek, they found the 23rd Illinois, 106th New York, 14th and 15th West Virginia, and the 7th Battery from Pennsylvania, and three cavalry units. Somewhere around 5,000 men, counting themselves. The sun was shining, and it was pleasant there in the hills of western Virginia, as Black and Armstrong walked along. When they got back to their camp, they found some of the men of Co. I, under the direction of Patrick Murphy, playing base ball.

Armstrong shook his head. "We're probably in harm's way, and the men are playing that game. Probably good, as it might take their minds off what we are doing here." He sat down, picked up a hardtack box to use as a desk, got out paper, pen, and ink and started to write...

Camp at New Creek
Nov 16th 1862

Dear Frank

I am well. I am in the "tented field" again. I enjoy it well. I think this war will be over soon. McClellan is out I believe. Fremont will soon be in. Yesterday morning we started for Cumberland, Md. but stopped here 22 miles west of Cumberland. I have rec'd one letter from home and none from you. Our folks are well at last acct.

I left home on Oct. 23. Came by steamboat to Marietta, then to Parkersburg, Va., then to Clarksburg, Va. We staid at Clarksburg from Oct 28 to Nov 15. We are looking for a raid from Stonewall Jackson upon here or Cumberland. Our Reg is in good spirits. We have a pleasant camp. I presume we will stay here some time. I should like to see your Bro George. Where is he and how is he getting along.

Col. Mulligan who surrendered at Lexington Mo. Sept 20 & commands the 23 Ills Volunteers commands this post. I suppose you think it queer that I should go in the army again. I can give no reason why unless that I felt it to be my duty. I may lose my life, but I pray God it may not be in vain. Frank, I want you to pray for me that I may be spared to get home again. Give my love to all, to your kind mother & father, to your brothers and sisters.

Mary & Fla are going to school. Well Frank goodbye.
From your friend
    T.S. Armstrong
    New Creek, Va.
    Care Col. W.H. Ball
    122 Reg O.V.I.

He hadn't heard from Francis Porter since he last saw her in August and had begun to wonder if she had forgotten all they had talked about before he left for Virginia. "Wonder if I am starting over with her," he thought. "Maybe I better presume that."

The days passed with the routine he had established back in August firmly in place. Drill, drill, and more drill. Eat and sleep. The soldier's life in the field. But, he wished that there could be one additional drill: teaching the men how to shoot an Enfield, but he still didn't have any. Just the one.

"It's going to change the way we fight," he thought to himself, examining the rifle. "You can be 200 yards away from the enemy now and still hit him. We don't have to get real close any more. We don't have to just walk across the field into that awful fire. The rifling in the barrel means greater accuracy, too, so you have to aim low. The percussion cap will give you more power, so you don't have to shoot up. Keep it low and straight. And, the Minie ball will flatten when it hits something. It's lethal. Hope Johnny doesn't have them."

It was Saturday, November 22, 1862. Snow on the ground, and a chill in the air. Tom Armstrong pulled the four sergeants together. "Boys, you're reporting to me, now. Lieutenant Black has been detailed as our new Regimental Quartermaster now that Lieutenant Morgan is no longer with us. Bushwhacker got him yesterday when he was overseeing the men loading the supply wagons. The shooter must have figured out he was in charge and thought he could get our supplies if he killed him. Don't think that worked. One of our boys from Co. K saw him fire and shot him dead, right through the chest. Lieutenant Black is now Acting Quartermaster of the 122nd, and I am acting 1st Lieutenant of our Company. You will drill the men constantly. I won't be with you much since I will be working with the Colonel, Major Granger, and Captain Gary. Any questions?"

The four sergeants looked at each other in disbelief. "A Reb actually killed Morgan?" Thaddeus Brennan asked. "I just saw him on Thursday."

"Yep, right in the chest, just below the right shoulder. Died on Dr. Houston's table. Couldn't stop the bleeding, I'm told. The boys protecting the wagon got him and took him to the doc. Too serious a wound to fix. Be on the lookout. Be alert. The Johnnies are watching us." The war was getting close to the 122nd and becoming personal.

Ten days later, on December 3, and still in New Creek, Ball, Granger, and the other Company commanders were meeting in the Colonel's tented headquarters about the change in command. Ball was reminding the others that he would report to Brigadier General Gustave Cluseret when they heard rapid hoofbeats.

"Whoa, Sally," was heard outside the tent in a fairly high-pitched voice. "Sergeant Rundle, do you know where the Colonel is?"

"Whatcha got, Hitch?"

"Two things. I gotta tell the Colonel."

"In here. Begging the Colonel's pardon, sir, Hitch here has something to tell you."

"Two things, actually. Didn't see this first one myself, but rumor is that General Burnside's army is about forty miles west of Richmond and moving east. Don't know how much truth there is in that. But, this second one, I do know. I seen it. Down near Moorefield, there's hundreds of Rebels camped there. I don't know if it's General Jackson or not. I didn't see any movement this direction, but they're there."

"I can find out about Burnside. He really doesn't matter to us, but we must do something about the ones at Moorefield. They're probably under Jackson. I'm assuming he's in command here in the Shenandoah. Captain Gary, send a detail out in the morning to go with Hitch to verify what he has just said. This is his first report, and I must make sure that we are getting the truth. I will not move the regiment out until I hear from you. I want to know if, when, and where they are moving."

At dawn, on Thursday, December 4, 1862, Tom Armstrong, Hitch, Isaac and Jeremiah Kearney, and Lieutenant Micah Williams rode hard toward Moorefield, Virginia, pulling up in the woods in the hills north of town. "See, there they are," Hitch said proudly. "Told you you could count on me."

"Looks like they're just sitting there," said Tom Armstrong, lowering his field glasses. "No movement at all. Let's watch them today, spend the night here, see what happens in the morning, and then get back to camp." He turned his horse. "I want to go back a couple of miles to that creek we just crossed. We might be able to light a fire there. Take turns keeping watch tonight, right here. If you see any

176

torches coming this way, skedaddle back to where we are so we can get out of here."

"Yes, sir."

"Lieutenant Williams, here are the field glasses. Take the first watch. The rest of you come with me."

It was an uneventful night. No movement at all by the Rebel Army. In the morning, the scouting party made sure that the camp-fire was out, dousing it with water from the nearby creek. Then it was back to New Creek.

Upon their return, Daniel Gary reported to William Ball and Moses Granger. "It was just as Hitch told us, Colonel. The detail figures are there about 1,000 of them camped near the town of Moorefield. I think we better keep an eye on them. Sergeant Rundle, can you make sure that the young man has enough supplies to last him a week or so and get him back down there with orders to get back here when the enemy moves."

"We can watch him ourselves, Captain. Orders just came down from General Cluseret that we are to go to Petersburg, a few miles southwest of where the Johnnies are camped. We are not to engage him, just keep an eye on him. It's about fifty miles due south of here, and we will have to march west and cut down through the mountains without him seeing us. I want to be on the move tomorrow morning. Sergeant Rundle, tell the company commanders that I want to see them right away. Tell Lieutenant Black to be here. You, too."

The rest of Friday, December 5, was spent in preparation for the march. This would be the "maiden march" for the 122nd since they had always traveled by steamboat or train since they left Zanesville.

The men of the 122nd struck tents at first light which was very hard to do because of the blowing and drifting snow. The men wondered why they were going in a blizzard and howling wind, but orders were orders. Colonel Ball felt some urgency to get to Petersburg and ordered the Company commanders not to spare any time. It was a difficult march through the southern Appalachians with some of the men falling back just to rest. They had never done anything like this before. At sundown, they reached Ridgeville, having travelled sixteen miles, with some thirty miles left to go.

"Sergeant Rundle, send Hitch on ahead. I want a report as soon as we get to Petersburg," ordered Colonel William H. Ball.

"Yes, sir, Colonel. Very good, sir." And off went Terrance Rundle to give Hitch his orders.

At sunup on Sunday, December 7, 1862, the men of the 122nd O.V.I. were aroused early and after a hasty breakfast, heard the order "BATTALION, LEFT FACE! – FORWARD ROUTE STEP! MARCH! The road was frozen and icy as they passed through the mountains, crossing several darn cold creeks on the way. It was another full day, and the men were stiff and sore as they trudged toward Petersburg. They made eighteen miles that day, pitching their tents and lighting their campfires. Even Tom Armstrong was tired. Sleep came very easy that night.

It was the same routine the next day, entering serious enemy country. Even with their personal anxiety, the boys of the 122nd were itching for a fight and hoped that they could surprise the Rebels at Moorefield. They passed through a valley with the snow-covered Allegheny Mountain to the west and Branch Mountain to the east. They arrived at Petersburg around noon and set up camp on a hill, north of the town. They still did not know where they were going.

Later that day, a rider came into camp, asking the sentries of the whereabouts of Colonel Ball. One of the guards took Hitch into the center of the camp where Ball, Granger, and Rundle had established the regimental headquarters.

"They're gone, sir. Couldn't find hide nor hair of them. They just disappeared."

"Whattya mean they're gone?" cried Colonel William Ball.

"They ain't there, Colonel. Not where we saw 'em earlier. Must have pulled out yesterday."

"Well, dammit, go find them and tell me where they are. What the hell do I tell Cluseret? They're gone?"

The young man spurred his horse out of camp, heading northeast to Moorefield and hoping he could track the Confederate regiment.

When Daniel Gary told Tom Armstrong the news, he thought, "Well, I guess we are stuck here for a while. As long as they aren't around, we can start drilling in the morning." And he went to find Bristow, Simpson, Murphy, and Brennan.

And so, the routine established at Camp Zanesville was in place again while Colonel Ball and Major Granger fretted about where the Rebel Army had gone. A week later, on December 13, Terrance Rundle entered the Colonel's tent. "Hitch is back, sir. He has some information for you."

"Go find Major Granger and send the kid in."

Colonel Ball and Hitch waited for Major Moses M. Granger to arrive. When he did, Hitch began, "They're in Culpeper, Colonel. A whole mess of 'em. Can't be sure that the ones we saw are there, but I didn't see anybody else. Looks like thousands of them."

Moses Granger offered, "Shoot. Culpeper is 100 miles from here and over the Blue Ridge. Maybe they are holed up for the winter there, getting ready for the advance in the spring."

"Maybe so, Major," said Ball. "Maybe so, but I want to keep an eye on their comings and goings. I bet they're watching us, too. So, Hitch, I want you to get out of camp at night so they can't spot you and come back in at night as well. Stay near Culpeper for a week and then tell me what they are doing. Be careful. Hide yourself well and write down what you see. Draw me a map if you can."

"Hitch," said Terrance Rundle, "you can bunk with me tonight."

Petersburg, Hardy County, Va.
Sun Evening, Dec. 14th 1862

Dear Frank

Recd your letter this week or last rather dated Dec 1st and was glad to hear from you. We are all well except Capn Gary who has a sore ankle from marching. We started from New Creek the 6th and marched here making 46 miles in 2 ½ days. We arrived here on Monday at noon. I stood the march very well. I am hearty and well as I can be & weigh 159 lbs. So, you see the Army agrees with me. I eat corn fritters, fresh beef & hard crackers most of the time.

I take soldiering well. We are east of the Allegheny mountains. Gen. Milroy commands this Division.

Certainly, I expected one from you to the question "Do you expect one from me?" Have you forgotten former days? Am I a stranger that you distrust me so? I too would like to see Bro George. How would you like to see me? Wouldn't you love to see me too? Well I am coming out to see you as soon as Burnside whales the Rebels & peace is declared or I will send for you for I know you dare not refuse. What say you to that?

I like Meda, but I don't think George will ever marry her. I think she would like to be married awful bad. Frank, wouldn't you like to be married "awful bad" too. Please answer by return of mail. Well pardon me for talking so foolish. I shall send you my photograph as soon as I get it from home. I am grateful to you for your promise to pray for me.

I gave your respects to Capn Gary. Well, write to me. Send my best respects to your Father & Mother. How is Huldah and Johnny? My love to all. Write soon. Direct your letter to New Creek or this place, care of Col. W.H. Ball, 122 Regt O.V.I.

From your friend,

Thos S. Armstrong

Good night to you. Pleasant dreams. We don't know when we will go from here, we are lying here drilling, etc.

"There, I said it," he thought to himself. "Wouldn't you like to be married 'awful bad' too. Suppose I could have said that differently. Oh, well, I wonder how she will react and what she will say?" He heard *Tatoo* and then *Taps*. The campfire was almost out as he crawled into the tent, his own anxieties building. They weren't just about the war and the worries of his men. His own worries concerned Francis Porter.

7 Winchester

"Just where the hell are we going? We're s'posed to be going to Winchester," Eddie Bristow complained. "And just what the hell are we s'posed to be doing? Ain't no Rebs down here. Ain't seen any, anyway." Bristow wasn't speaking only for himself. His thoughts were echoed by many members of the 122nd Ohio Volunteer Infantry, Tom Armstrong among them.

Armstrong responded, "We told the Colonel that there weren't any Johnnies as far south as Sutton. Hitch found them over at Moorefield. They aren't there anymore. Now, they've gone east to Culpeper. Winchester's north of here, and we were ordered south to Petersburg. Wonder why. We didn't do anything there. Doesn't make any sense."

It was Monday, December 22, 1862, and the 122nd was on the march from Petersburg at 9 o'clock that morning, traveling up by the South Branch of the Potomac River toward Moorefield. It was cold that December morning. Eddie Bristow was right. Something just didn't add up. They had been ordered to leave their knapsacks behind for the sake of speed. But why? What was the hurry? They covered the eleven miles, passing through Moorefield about 2:00 PM, finding it to be a nice little town tucked in a valley with mountains on the right and on the left. These boys from Muskingum County, Ohio, had never seen mountains this high and were not real pleased at the prospect of climbing over them. But, climb they did, northeast over Branch Mountain, where the air was thin and the blue sky gorgeous, toward Romney. Nine hours after they left Petersburg, they camped after covering twenty-one miles. Nobody had any idea where they were going or why they were going there. However, they had seen Major General Robert H. Milroy and his staff ride by that morning, so it was reasonable to assume they were just following him. But where? Winchester? That's what Colonel Ball had said. Awful roundabout way to get there. Armstrong wrote to Francis Porter…

December 23d – We slept cool last night, as it was a cold night. About 8 o'clock we were on our way "left in front." The men were somewhat used up from yesterday's march. Not so much struggling to-day. The country still mountainous with cliffs and rocks abounding, making the scenery grand. Toward evening, we came to the part called "Hanging Rock." Here were on each side of the huge road jagged cliffs projecting far out and some being hundreds of feet high. Every eye of our regiment seemed to be riveted on these rocks for it was said that probably there might be bushwhackers up there. We encamped on Lost Rocks, 22 miles east of Moorefield. Soon came in four cavalrymen three of whom had been wounded in these rocks by bushwhackers firing down on them. Two of them were wounded severely. Dr. Houston dressed their wounds. They were carrying dispatches for Gen. Cluseret. The occurrence produced quite an excitement in camp and aroused the ire of the whole regiment. It is said that this Lost River runs underground awhile, then emerges and is called Cacapon River. We traveled twelve miles.

"Tom, get up," whispered Captain Daniel Gary. "We're moving out. Not all of us, just us, Company K, and B. Granger's got orders to get going." It was Christmas Eve, 1862.

Armstrong looked at his watch. In the light of the fire, he could see that it was 3 o'clock. "Where we going, Dan?"

"Don't know. Just make sure the boys are up, packed, and ready to go in an hour. Get moving. I gotta wake Black and get him going."

The advance started at 4 AM. It appeared to Tom Armstrong and Tom Black that they were, indeed, going northeast, toward Winchester. There were the three companies on the move that morning, but Gary had told them that the rest of the 122nd would be coming along shortly, including the supply wagons. That didn't make any sense, either.

"Wonder why they didn't come with us?" It was a silent march. All you could hear was the thumping of boots. A Colonel rode by. Black and Armstrong didn't recognize him. He stopped and looked at Dan Gary and said: "If you see any suspicious looking people on the mountains, put them to sleep." It was starting to get real. Tom Black and Tom Armstrong told the sergeants to make sure the men had their rifles loaded.

The sun rose, and the march continued until Major Moses Granger ordered a halt for rest and breakfast. For some reason, there were to be no fires that December morning, so breakfast consisted of hardtack and a few dried peaches. When the march resumed around 8 AM, the North Mountain range appeared in the distance. Snow everywhere. The three companies made their way through the foothills and reached Wardensville around 10 o'clock.

"Major, map says we're about half way between Moorefield and Winchester," said Sergeant Terrance Rundle.

"We will wait here for the others." No one knew why they had left early.

When the other companies of the 122nd arrived, the entire regiment formed just south of the little town and pitched their tents in a nice grove that was protected from the wind by the hills, both east and west. The routine was the same. The men were becoming accustomed to it. Firewood, water, and latrines in that order of importance. They had only gone seven miles. The footing had been that bad. Still, no one knew why they were there. Armstrong wondered, "Why didn't we go straight to Winchester from New Creek?"

While the three companies were moving northeast from Petersburg, the other companies of Brigadier General Gustave P. Cluseret's brigade were marching directly toward Winchester from the west. They would arrive later that day. Thus, the people of the town would have to get used to Union occupation again. They wouldn't like it.

"Sergeant Rundle, we got a problem." It was December 25, 1862, Christmas Day.

"What is it, Hitch? How the hell did you find us?"

183

"That's my job, sergeant. You know when we went on the scout last week?"

"Yeah."

"Well, we went south and west as far as Sutton. But, we didn't go east. That's where the Rebs are. I told you there's a mess of 'em in Culpeper. We saw that. But, when we were out there, what we didn't see was them in Staunton. Friend of mine saw them there last week. A whole cavalry brigade. Looks like thousands of them. My friend says a fella name General Grumble Jones is in command. He says there's another bunch of cavalry up in the Cacapon Valley. North of here and west of Winchester."

"Who is this 'friend,' and how does he know so much?"

"Fella came over from Scotland some twenty years ago with his folks. He's about 25. Lives in these mountains like he did back there. Aberdeenshire, I think. Hunts and traps throughout here. Lives in a cabin over near Lost City. Name's James Lindsay. He's watched the Johnnies come and go and has followed them. Met him in a saloon over in Strasburg. I walked in wearin' that Reb uniform you gave me. Sat down at his table with a beer; he had whiskey. Nobody gave me a thought. They thought I was James's kid brother. Rebs were in there, too, drinkin' and cussin' and dancin' with the women, sayin' how they was gonna whip the Yankees again if they ever came into the Valley. Heard 'em say some fella named Imboden, or somethin' like that, had a cavalry unit up at the head of the Cacapon. James don't like 'em. Don't know why. He just don't."

"Holy, crap! Hitch, when did you learn this? When can we talk to Lindsay? We gotta talk to the Colonel and the Major. A fine damn Christmas present. Holeee crap!"

"Saw James just yesterday in Strasburg. Told him I would tell the Colonel and asked him to stay put."

"Come with me," demanded Terrance Rundle. Holeee crap!"

"Colonel, sir. We know they're southeast of here at Culpeper. Now, we understand they're southwest of us at Staunton and northwest of us in the Cacapon Valley. Hitch has a friend who has seen 'em." Sergeant Terrance Rundle continued to repeat what young Davy Hitchcock had told him, with the youngster filling in the blanks when Rundle needed help.

"You sure about this?"

"Yessir, Colonel. I haven't let you down yet. You want me to go with a scout party south toward Staunton?"

"Not necessary. We'll find them."

"Colonel," said Moses Granger. "I will organize the scout right away. But, we better send one north as well. A smaller one. Hitch, go back to Strasburg. See what this Lindsay fellow has uncovered."

"I agree, Major. Sergeant Rundle, get Captain Gary over here on the double. Hitchcock, does the enemy know we are here?"

"Can't say, sir. I wanna go talk to James to see what he's found out. Supposed to meet him there tomorrow. You should see the knife he carries. Blade must be a foot long. Carries a nasty lookin' shotgun, too. Nobody's going to mess with him. He's big, too. Don't look like much of a scout, but I bet he'd make a good one. Can disappear right into thin air. Walkin' long right beside him, and next thing, he's gone. Vanished. No trace. I think I'm getting pretty good at this. Nobody better than him."

"Stay here, young man. I want you here while I tell Captain Gary."

Colonel William Ball and Major Moses Granger repeated the story as Gary listened intently. "Did we get it right, Hitchcock?"

"Pretty much, sir. They're there. In Staunton. It will be good to send a scouting party to see 'em. Gotta stay hidden though. Picket lines about two miles out. But, some trained eyes spying on them for a couple or three days would tell you a lot. Can I get going?"

"Yes. Sergeant Rundle, make sure that the young man has a warm overcoat, better than the one he has on now. Get him a woolen blanket and anything else he might need. It's going to be cold out there."

"Certainly, Colonel. You want to stay here tonight, Hitch?"

"Naw, I gotta get back. James's expecting me. He's got a room at the saloon. It ain't so bad. The ride's a might tough. I wanna get back before dark."

"Good luck and good hunting," said Colonel Ball.

"Thank you, sir," and young Davy Hitchcock was gone.

"Captain," said Ball, "send that scout party that you used the last time. Tell them to go south toward Staunton. I'll have Captain Hering of Company B send one north. You have a week, Captain."

"Yes, sir. May I go tell Lieutenant Armstrong to prepare? He'll need a little time to get everything he's going to need."

"Very well, Captain. Keep me informed."

"They're southwest of here?" Tom Armstrong was incredulous. "How'd we miss them?"

"Not a worry now, Tom. Just get with Black and get what you and the men will need. It's going to be cold. We'll probably be up north, around Winchester, most likely when you get back."

Colonel William H. Ball, Major Moses M. Granger, and 1st Sergeant Terrance Rundle looked at the map of Virginia. "So, Johnny is southeast of here in Culpeper, northwest of here in the Cacapon Valley, and southwest of here near Staunton," Ball concluded. "Looks like we're surrounded except for an escape route to the northeast towards Harper's Ferry. I wonder if Cluseret knows this. The damn Frenchman. He doesn't know anything about what we're fighting for or any of our tactics for the fight itself. He just doesn't understand. Dammit, we're surrounded except to the northeast. Damn! This isn't good."

On the day after Christmas, 1862, Lieutenant Tom Armstrong, Lieutenant Micah Williams, Isaac and Jeremiah Kearney, and Patrick Murphy rode south along the eastern ridge of Massanutten Mountain, staying in the woods as much as possible. If James Lindsay was right, there was a brigade of Rebels camped near Staunton, but this was going to take some time. The mountain made the travel slow, and the weather didn't help.

At the same time, Lieutenant Cyrus Scott and Lieutenant DeWitt Blondin of Company B were heading northwest with five enlisted men toward the Cacapon Valley where Lindsay had told Hitch that a regiment of Confederate cavalry was camped. Their mission would be finished much sooner since the terrain was less onerous and the distance was much shorter. They returned on December 28th, confirming that, yes, indeed, a regiment of Rebel cavalry was camped in the valley. "Didn't look like they were moving, though," Scott reported. "Better keep an eye on 'em."

Brigadier General Gustave P. Cluseret had entered Winchester on Christmas eve with half of his brigade of infantry, artillery, and cavalry. The people of the town were not happy, especially on that day. They were tired of military occupations. Disrupted their way of life. They, too, were westerners who were isolated from Washington, DC and Richmond, the capital of the Confederacy, by the Blue Ridge. They really had little interest in the politics that led eleven Southern states to secede or in what secession meant for them. But they did understand the value their town had to both sides: transportation of men and supplies.

Christmas morning gave the General his first look at the Shenandoah Valley with the Allegheny Mountains to the west and the Blue Ridge Mountains to the east. The town lay on the Valley Pike which ran down the Shenandoah some 200 miles and was half way between Strasburg and Martinsburg, going northeast. Five other roads met at Winchester: the Romney road; the Pughtown Pike; the Berryville Pike; the Millwood Pike; and the Front Royal Pike, which led to Front Royal and then to Culpeper, northwest to southeast. Railroads also ran in and out of Winchester. "No wonder this place is so damn important," thought Cluseret. "A lot of trade comes through here. Supplies for whoever holds it."

Indeed, Winchester was a commercial center. Martinsburg was to the north, Berryville to the east, Millwood to the southeast, Romney to the west, and Pughtown to the northwest that would lead to Berkeley Springs and eventually to Hancock, Maryland. The town was only forty miles south of the Maryland border and just fifty miles south of Pennsylvania. It seemed like all commerce of northern Virginia went through Winchester on its way to some market somewhere.

Sitting astride his golden stallion he called "Tonnerre" (Thunder, in English), he lowered his field glasses and thought, "Merde (Shit, in English) it's going to be difficult to defend this place. It's the low ground. There's mountains all around. If the Rebs come through them, they'll have the high ground, and we'll be in trouble. Look at all the ridges. The Rebs know about them and how to use them to advantage. This isn't good. I better tell Milroy when he gets here. Merde," said the Frenchman.

There were 4,400 people living in Winchester at the time, and it was a pretty little village, sitting there at the northern head of the Shenandoah. The men of Cluseret's brigade were surprised to see

187

all of the brick stores, neat and tidy with their signage. The houses were big and elegant; saloons sat on the street corners; three or four hotels could be seen; so, could some stately churches. There were sidewalks for the pedestrians, and gas lights made it possible for them to walk about in the evening. Right in the center of the town was the courthouse, in the Greek Revival tradition, that could be seen from miles around. All of this was about to change.

Unlike their neighbors in eastern Virginia who had come to the new world from England, the people of Winchester who had come to the Shenandoah were Germans, Scots, and Irish. They were Lutheran, Methodist, and Presbyterian, with hardly any Episcopalians, Catholics, or Jews. They were just interested in the agricultural opportunities that the Shenandoah Valley afforded them.

Yes, this was farm country, and the people enjoyed doing the labor themselves. They didn't need slaves like their neighbors on the east side of the Blue Ridge. They would rather till their own fields, sow their seeds, tend to their own crops, and have the family help with the harvest. The railroads enabled them to ship the harvest east and north to Harper's Ferry some 30 miles away on the Winchester & Potomac Railroad. The W&P connected to the Baltimore & Ohio there, so the farmers had access to all points east and west.

As isolated as they thought they were, their town was of immense interest to both the Union and Confederacy. It was the roads. And, they had a sharp realization of the value of their location on May 25, 1862, when the retreating troops of Union Major General Nathaniel Banks came racing through the streets of Winchester, trying to get away from the advancing cavalry of Confederate Brigadier General Turner Ashby. The Federals sped up the Valley Pike toward Martinsburg, with Banks and his staff managing to get across the Potomac to safety. What was left of his division was following. This 1st battle at Winchester was a thundering success for the commander of the Confederate forces, Major General Thomas (Stonewall) Jackson, who not only returned Winchester to Confederate hands but also took some 1,500 Federals prisoner. He became a beloved local hero and set up his headquarters there. The people of the town could see him, every Sunday, seated in the front row of the First Presbyterian Church. "A pious warrior," they called him. Jackson was revered as the best commanding officer that the Confederate States of America had.

The people of Winchester now knew what effect the war would have on them. Until it was over, the Federals and the Confederates would spar over the town just to control the supply lines. So far, on this incursion by General Cluseret, they had pretty much been left alone by the Union intruders, and under orders from the General, they had been treated nicely. Unfortunately for them, that was not Major Robert H. Milroy's style. Nor that of some of his commanders. So, an adversarial tension began to grow, amplified by what they read in the *Winchester Star* on Friday, January 2, 1863. It was the last four paragraphs that got their attention:

And by virtue of the power, and for the purpose aforesaid, I do order and declare that all persons held as slaves within said designated States, and parts of States, are, and henceforward shall be free; and that the Executive government of the United States, including the military and naval authorities thereof, will recognize and maintain the freedom of said persons.

And I hereby enjoin upon the people so declared to be free to abstain from all violence, unless in necessary self-defense; and I recommend to them that, in all cases when allowed, they labor faithfully for reasonable wages.

And I further declare and make known, that such persons of suitable condition, will be received into the armed service of the United States to garrison forts, positions, stations, and other places, and to man vessels of all sorts in said service.

And upon this act, sincerely believed to be an act of justice, warranted by the Constitution, upon military necessity, I invoke the considerate judgment of mankind, and the gracious favor of Almighty God.

In witness whereof, I have hereunto set my hand and caused the seal of the United States to be affixed.

Done at the City of Washington, this first day of January, in the year of our Lord one thousand eight hundred and sixty-three, and of the Independence of the

United States of America the eighty-seventh.

Now, in and of itself, the *Proclamation of Emancipation* didn't mean much to them since they didn't have any slaves. But, there was one important point that maybe some people had missed. Since the eleven states that had seceded had not come back into the Union, the war would go on. President Lincoln would prosecute it to make them return since he firmly believed that secession was unconstitutional. The states of the Confederacy saw it differently. They passionately believed in states' rights, in the tradition of Thomas Jefferson and had an opposing view of the Constitution, especially the 10th Amendment:

> The powers not delegated to the United States by the Constitution, nor prohibited by it to the States, are reserved to the States respectively, or to the people.

Thus, they believed they had every right to secede. Their elected officials in Richmond did not see anything in the Constitution about restricting the right of states to secede, for whatever reason they might. Their reason just happened to be the institution of slavery in their way of life. The people of Virginia and the other states believed that the 10th Amendment covered their Constitutional rights to break away. In a nutshell, they believed that President Abraham Lincoln was wrong. In a vote on May 23, 1861, the people of Virginia had approved secession by a 4 to 1 margin. Even those in Winchester were part of the majority. Their pro-Confederate sentiment was strong. And, the way they were treated by General Milroy only made it stronger.

The day before, January 1, 1863, Brigadier General Robert H. Milroy and the VIII Corps had entered the town, sitting there at the head of the Shenandoah Valley. Milroy was an ardent abolitionist who fervently supported the Emancipation Proclamation and detested the states that had seceded. With the people of Winchester believing in states' rights and being able to forge their own destiny in the Jeffersonian tradition, there was an immediate tension between them and the General. Brigadier General Cluseret had arrived with 3,000 men earlier in the week. The rest of his brigade, including Company I of the 122nd and those of Colonel Andrew T. McReynolds and Colonel William J. Ely, marched through the town at the dawn of the new year, 1863. There would be more.

Milroy went right to work at establishing his authority over the people of Winchester. Basically, it was martial law. He perceived, correctly, that the population was decidedly pro-Confederate, but he did not realize how fiercely independent these people were. One of the first things he did was require each citizen to sign an oath of loyalty to the United States. That really angered the townsfolk, and the majority of them would not sign. Milroy responded by prohibiting those who would not sign from buying groceries and other necessities, including firewood. Now, with wood fires the only source of heat in the home in the dead of winter, having no wood and no food made life unbearable for the people of Winchester, but that was Milroy's strategy. Freeze them or starve them. And, with most of the men from Winchester serving in the Confederate army, he was taking his anger out simply on women and children. He certainly wasn't making any friends. In fact, he was making the people of Winchester very angry. But, there was little they could do about it.

As Milroy tightened his grip throughout the winter of 62 – 63, stores closed; the people who could get away, did, albeit with few of their precious belongings; houses were ransacked with desks, dressers, beds, and anything else made out of wood used to warm the soldiers camped on the hills overlooking the town from the west. That's where the 122nd was. Milroy also had members of his staff spy on the people and, without the benefit of a trial, would expel suspected loyalists to the Confederate cause to points south with their only possessions being the clothes on their backs. All of the buildings in the town were being used as hospitals, schools closed, and generally, life as the people of Winchester had enjoyed in happier times, came to a halt. That's exactly what Major General Robert H. Milroy wanted, and that's what he got. A "tyrant" is what he proudly called himself, apparently enjoying it. His behavior and actions infuriated Brig. Gen. Gustave P. Cluseret. But, Cluseret had his own problems with the officers who reported to him.

In the late afternoon of New Year's Day, while the Union brigades were streaming through the streets of Winchester, Lieutenant Tom Armstrong and his scout party came into the town from the west. Nobody really noticed them. But, they were pretty darn important, what with the information they had. He asked the sentries where the 122nd was, rode up Bowers Hill and found Captain Daniel Gary warming himself in front of a roaring campfire. The 122nd had arrived around noon.

"Dan, they're there. In Staunton. We saw them. Has to be four or five regiments. We watched them for a couple of days. Nothing happening. Probably nothing will happen until Spring and the snow thaws. Now, the question is, why are they there? Where are they going? If they hook up with that bunch over in Culpeper and come north, we could have a real problem."

"Damn! So, that's what Ball was talking about last week. He showed me a map of Virginia. We're almost surrounded. Our only escape out of here would be northeast to Harper's Ferry. We have the low ground. Johnny would have the high ground when he comes over the hills. Damn. This isn't good. I'm going to see the Colonel and the Major. Come with me and have your men, rest up, warm themselves, and get some food."

"So, Captain, the scouts confirm what the kid saw?" William Ball scowled, stroking his neat black beard.

"Yes, sir. Probably 4,000 or 5,000 of them camped near Staunton, right Lieutenant?"

Tom Armstrong nodded, "Yes, sir."

Gary asked, "You heard back from Hering about Cacapon?"

"Yes, Captain. They are there, too. Hering told me the other day it's cavalry. Imboden's regiment. Probably a thousand of them. Got a barn or two built for the horses. They won't move now because of the weather, but when they do, we just might get busy. I better tell the General."

When he returned from the Colonel's office, Armstrong found that Eddie Bristow and Chesley Simpson had pitched his tent and had a fine fire blazing in front of it. He sat down and tried to warm his half-frozen fingers and toes. "Where are the others?" he asked.

Chesley Simpson briefed him. "The Captain told us to get a detail out in the woods, not just for firewood but also to fell trees that we can sharpen for our works. We found water in Abram's Creek back over there as soon as we got here, so that's taken care of. Thaddeus is out with the men felling trees. Eddie lost the coin flip and has latrine duty. They'll be back for supper."

"Good, I want to talk with all of you. It's going to get interesting. Not sure when, but it's going to get interesting." A cup of hot coffee was just what he needed.

Colonel William H. Ball had decided that he better see Brigadier General Gustave Cluseret right away. On his way to see him, Ball thought to himself, "I can hardly understand the man. Sometimes, he lapses into French, and I have no idea what he's saying. I have to make him speak English." That didn't go so well.

"Bonjour, Colonel Ball."

"My compliments, General. I need to speak with you about what my men have seen and what I make of it."

Ball told the General about the position of the Confederate Army, relating the danger that he foresaw down the road.

"Mon Dieu, Colonel! Mon Dieu!"

"May I suggest, sir, and with the General's pardon, that we go talk to General Milroy about this. I think he should know."

"He will not listen, Colonel Ball," he said in halting English. "He is as arrogant a man as I have ever known. He does not trust his commanders, especially me. I am first and foremost a fighter, a warrior, but he does not let me near the action. Even though I believe you to be telling me the truth, if Milroy doesn't see it himself, he doesn't believe it. He thinks of himself and no one else."

"It's our duty, sir. We must tell him, even if he disregards what we say."

"Very well. We can try. I will send a messenger to arrange a time when we can see him. I will have the messenger come to your quarters to inform you."

"Thank you, General."

"Au revoir, Colonel."

Colonel William Ball did not know it, but General Henry Halleck, the General-in-Chief of the Union Army, had ordered Major

General Robert C. Schenck, Milroy's superior, to adopt a defensive position in the Shenandoah Valley. Milroy would have none of it. Cluseret himself had suggested an attack on Staunton in November, 1862, only to have that request rejected by Schenck. The Union Army was in the Shenandoah to protect the roads and the railroad, that's all. General Milroy had other ideas. Dig stout defenses in Winchester and raid the Confederates every chance he could get.

The meeting with Milroy and Cluseret would take place at 2 o'clock in the afternoon on Saturday, January 3, 1863.

"Colonel, it is good to see you again. What is this information that is so important? General Cluseret, please have a seat."

"Merci, mon General."

"Before you start, Colonel, would you excuse us. I have some information of my own to share with the General."

"Yes, sir." William Ball exited the commanding general's office.

When he was asked to return, he saw Cluseret's face was white. Trying to hide it, the Frenchman looked like he was in shock. It seems that nine officers had written to General Milroy complaining about the Brigadier General, asking for his dismissal. Milroy had confronted him about it to very strenuous denials. He knew that Cluseret really did not understand Union soldiers or their ways of waging war and needed to be replaced.

If that weren't enough, Cluseret had angered Milroy personally, complaining that he didn't come into the Union Army to fight for Negroes, making the General aware of his dissatisfaction. Then, he thought that the General's harsh treatment of the women and children of Winchester was wrong and told him so. In fact, from the time he and his men occupied the town until General Robert Milroy arrived, Cluseret had been quite accommodating to the inhabitants, while being quite rigid and strict with his soldiers. His policy had been "Be nice to the people, and they will be nice to us."

When Milroy arrived a few days later, he had reversed that policy and ordered that it be the other way around: harsh treatment for the civilians and more lenient for the soldiers. General Cluseret was not happy. It turns out that Milroy had had enough of him and had asked him for his resignation while Colonel William Ball was in the ante-room outside of the General's office. A week later, on January 9, Brigadier General Gustave P. Cluseret would formally resign.

"Colonel, you may proceed," said Maj. Gen. Robert H. Milroy.

Colonel William H. Ball was well prepared and took the General through the intelligence that had been gained by Tom Armstrong and Cyrus Scott. Milroy listened politely and calmly said, "Thank you, Colonel, but I have doubts that the Rebels will do anything. If they do, it will only be cavalry, and we'll be ready for that."

"Begging the General's pardon, sir, it's not now that I am worried about. It's when the ice and snow melt, the trees turn green, and the birds fill the air with song. This place is very difficult to hold, seems to change hands once a month. It is critical to the enemy's supply line. And, we are on the low ground, and the Rebels will have the high ground if they so choose."

"Relax, Colonel, we will have earthwork fortifications that no one can penetrate."

"Perhaps so, General, but what happens if they bring the big guns? Can the fortifications take artillery fire?"

"We will have our own artillery, Colonel," said General Robert H. Milroy, becoming tired of the conversation. Brig. Gen. Gustave Cluseret was oblivious to the whole thing, being consumed by his own thoughts.

Seeing that Cluseret had been right that Milroy wouldn't listen, the Colonel concluded, "If I might suggest, sir, perhaps it would be wise to have the cavalry out there just looking around. Maybe Galligher's men?"

"Colonel, that's enough for one day! We are in no danger, but I might have Colonel Galligher and his 13th Pennsylvania or Colonel McReynolds and his 1st New York get active. We do need to know if and when the enemy is coming. I knew that before you came in. Good day, Colonel."

As Colonel William Ball rode back to his tented headquarters, he thought, "Damn, Cluseret was right. The General is one arrogant son-of-a-bitch, and he sure as hell won't listen. That may be a problem one day."

"How'd it go, Bill?" asked Major Moses M. Granger.

"Not well. But, something happened between Milroy and Cluseret. Not sure what it was, but Cluseret was obviously upset about something. Oh, well. We have no orders, so we are on our own. Have the commanders start drilling the men tomorrow."

"I think Gary's already doing that with Company I. Will get all of them together to map out the daily regimen for the troops. Are you going to send out scouting parties?"

"I want to hear from young Hitchcock. If the Rebs know we're here, which I presume they do, we should keep an eye on them, and, quite frankly, I'm not sure that the General is concerned at all. He just wants works built and believes that will be enough to withstand any attack, even with the artillery. We better keep an eye open. When's the kid coming back in?"

"Don't know, for sure, Bill. He went back to Strasburg yesterday. Don't expect him for a while. Sure would like to meet this Lindsay fellow. A real man of the mountains."

"Maybe we will, Moses. But, I kind of doubt it. He's a loner and probably wants to keep it that way. Did you make sure that Hitch has some money?"

"Yes. Gave him Confederate bills and coins."

"Good thinking. Let me know when he comes back."

Orders came to Colonel Ball a week later. There was to be a meeting of all of the regimental commanders reporting to Brigadier General Gustave Cluseret at Major General Robert Milroy's headquarters. It was January 10, 1863.

"Gentlemen," the General began. "This is Brigadier General Washington Elliott. From now on, you will report to him. He was at Wilson's Creek in Missouri when the war broke out; commanded a brigade at Corinth, at the time of Shiloh; and was involved at 2nd Bull Run. He's obviously qualified to take command."

The commanders all thought, "What happened to Cluseret?", but nobody said anything. Ball thought, "Who the hell is this guy?"

"Any questions?" Milroy asked.

Seeing that there weren't going to be any, Elliott began, "I will personally inspect your regiments this week. All of the infantry regiments: Ohio 110, 116, 122, and 123 in that order. I will get to you, Captain Carlin, and your artillery after that, and then the 1st New

York and the 13th Pennsylvania cavalry units. Understood? I will have my aide-de-camp tell you when I will conduct the inspections."

It was snowing hard when the meeting broke up and Colonel William Ball rode back to the 122nd camp. He called the officers together and told them the news about Cluseret and that the new commander, Brigadier General Elliott would be conducting an inspection soon. He wanted the 122nd to stand out as a model of excellence.

No one in the 122nd had contemplated what it would be like to winter in Winchester, Virginia. It was cold and dark with several feet of snow piled up. The men spent time clearing paths between the rows of tents, searching out firewood to keep themselves warm and to cook their food, and waiting for temperatures to rise. The boredom of Camp Zanesville seemed lively compared to this. And, General Robert Milroy wanted fortifications constructed that would protect all of them from a Confederate attack. That would have to wait until Spring.

"Why the hell did we come here?" complained Eddie Bristow. "We coulda stayed in Zanesville where we could get warm and go home every now and again. Ain't no secesh gonna try to bust up that railroad in weather like this. Dammit, it's cold. Pass the whiskey, Simpson." Moonshine, it was called. Bristow took a long pull of it. All he could say was "Wow!"

"Makes no sense to me, either," said Chesley Simpson. "All we do is sit around here, playing cards, and then we drill, then we eat, then we sleep. Coulda done that in Zanesville."

"Quit bellyachin,' boys," Tom Armstrong replied. "We're here, and we're staying here until Elliott tells us otherwise. Be thankful he hasn't sent us back out there to reconnoiter. Anyone seen Hitch?"

"Not for a week or so," said Thaddeus Brennan. "Heard he sneaks in at night and leaves before sunup. Doesn't want anyone to know where he is except the Colonel and Major Granger. Wonder what he's found? You 'bout done with that bottle, Bristow? Pass it over."

Lieutenant Tom Armstrong had his hands full. Tom Black was still the Interim Regimental Quartermaster, so Armstrong had the four sergeants reporting to him. He had to make sure the paths were clear and that the trees were being cut and sharpened for the abatis to be built when Spring came. His days were very full, but he still had time to write to Francis Porter, every now and again.

January 23, 1863
122nd OVI
Winchester, Va

I am well and enjoy myself finely in camp. This is the valley of Virginia and a beautiful valley it is too. I will "be a good boy." I hope God will make me truly good, pardon all my sins. For I may be cut off before very long. My heart is in this struggle for our good government. I believe the policy of the government is good.

Give Huldah my love. "You have my best wishes. Re-member I am the same today, etc., lest I will cherish your name as one I love. Don't forget me?" So you say. I say the same to you. Well we are lying here still & will stay in this place until spring. Write me word of how the 78 fares in the battle just coming off at Vicksburg. We get the news here the Baltimore papers & *Zanesville Courier* etc. Do you get the *Courier*? Well I must close. Give my love to all.

Write soon from your friend
T.S. Armstrong
Winchester Va.

Reading the letter she had sent him, he had been mighty relieved. He needn't have worried that she had forgotten about him. She was teaching school in Wapella, some five miles north of the Porter farm in Clinton, Illinois to which the family had moved in November. That was taking up quite a bit of her time. Plus, she didn't know where he was, so how could she write him a letter? Only when she had received his last one did she know and immediately took pen to paper. Armstrong read the lines again. "You have my best wishes. Remember I am the same today, etc., lest I shall cherish your name as one I love. Don't forget me?" He thought to himself, "Whew, shouldn't have doubted her. God forgive me."

David Hitchcock had been in and out of camp several times, each time leaving James Lindsay in Strasburg. They would meet at different places, usually in a noisy saloon where they could talk. Occasionally, they would ride out into the country. On this day, February 11, 1863, Hitch walked through the door under the sign that said SALOON right there on North Massanutten Street. The mountain man, James Lindsay, was seated at a table over in the corner, the big rifle standing by his chair. He had a glass and a bottle of whiskey in front of him and was flipping cards. His big fur hat lay on the table.

"Afternoon, James," said Davy Hitchcock. How's things?"

"They think I'm Secesh. You, too. No need for you to wear the uniform if you don't want to. Had a few whiskeys with 'em last night. Got 'em pretty drunk. Couldn't shut 'em up, they was braggin' so much. They know the Yanks are here, and they know they are up north there, 'bout twenty miles from here. This General Jones fella, well, he's a bad guy. Served under J.E.B. Stuart at 1st Bull Run. Then they gave him the 1st Virginia cavalry. Caused all sorts of hell with that outfit. Johnnies say he's gonna pester the Yanks. The other fella, Imbatten or somethin,' he was at Bull Run, too. Commanded cavalry, too. Don't know what that means. He's gonna bother the Yanks, too. Both part of Stonewall Jackson's command. They said Jackson's gonna come after 'em. He beat 'em last May, they said, and he'll beat 'em agin. You wanna whiskey?"

"Naw, just beer." The conversation lasted for an hour or so.

"You goin' back tonight, laddie?"

"Yeah. I gotta tell the Colonel to be expecting some trouble. Maybe not now in winter." Davy Hitchcock found a scrap of paper and began to draw a map of where the Confederate troops were." If they all move on Winchester at the same time, the only way out is northeast, toward Harper's Ferry. Whattya think?"

"Damn. They're in a mess of trouble. What happens if some Reb outfit comes at them from Richmond and closes that gap?"

"Be a devil of a time. Problem is, the Colonel told me, ol' Milroy don't listen. Ball tells him what I report. Milroy dismisses it."

"Why you doin' it?"

"My way of helpin,' I guess. As long as it helps Ball."

"I'll see ya. Meet me here next Wednesday."

David Hitchcock dutifully reported what he had learned to Colonel Ball, Major Granger, and Orderly Sergeant Rundle. Ball received the same response from General Robert H. Milroy. Don't worry, Colonel. They're not coming."

"Yet," the Colonel thought to himself.

By this time, Milroy's command was growing as more and more men and equipment kept coming into Winchester. By mid-February, there were two batteries, both with ten-pound Parrott guns and twenty-four-pound howitzers; six infantry regiments; three cavalry regiments; and approximately 5,300 men, over and above the 1,400 he had stationed in Romney.

Tom Armstrong was fascinated by the big, sleek Parrott guns, having never seen one, and wandered up the hill one day with Cyrus Scott to learn more about them. When he and Scott approached the battery of Captain John Carlin, known as the "Wheeling Battery," they saw the Parrotts, six of them, distinguishable by their slim, straight barrels. Armstrong saw what he assumed was the crew responsible for firing them sitting around a blazing campfire. It was still pretty cold, and the heat of the fire was welcome.

"What can I do for you, Lieutenant?" said one of them.

"I'm curious and want to find out about these guns. Name's Tom Armstrong, by the way. 122nd from Zanesville, Ohio. Taught school up there. This here's Lieutenant Cyrus Scott, B Company, 122nd. From around Zanesville, too."

"Caleb Edwards, from Wheeling, Virginia. Blacksmith before I got into this. Whattya want to know?" Caleb Edwards was a big man, broad across the shoulders, carrot-colored beard, and long red hair that fell out of his cap.

"How far do they shoot? And, what do they shoot? We're worried that when spring comes the Rebels will get active, and it would be nice to know that we, in the infantry, have some support when we hafta defend this place."

"Share your concern, boys. Heard some things. Don't know if they're true."

"We have our scouts out. We'll tell ya everything we know," said Cyrus Scott.

"Thanks. Let me tell you about this gun, and then you can tell me what you know."

"Fair deal. Rank?"

"Lieutenant, just like you. Now, these babies fire a 10-pound shell and have a range of about 2,000 yards. Takes about ten seconds to get it that far. Barrel's about six feet long, and it's rifled, makes the shell spin, so we don't have to shoot high. We can aim straight at 'em. Damn thing weighs half a ton and takes eight of us to handle each one. We got about fifty gunners here, but with everyone else, there are about a hundred of us in the entire battery."

"2,000 yards. Shoot, that's over a mile. Damn. That oughta keep 'em away." Armstrong was thinking that these gunners had rifled cannon, and he couldn't get the rifled Enfields. "Isn't right," he thought to himself.

"Damn loud, too. Coffee?"

"Yeah. That'd be good. Let us tell you what we know, and apparently what Milroy doesn't want to hear."

Lieutenants Armstrong, Scott, and Edwards talked for a couple hours before the two infantrymen had to head back to the 122nd.

"Caleb, it was nice to meet you. Thanks for the information. We'll come up here whenever we get more."

"Yer welcome. Anytime, anytime."

As February lapsed into March, not much changed for the garrison except the weather. It had been in the 40's the last two weeks of the month and now was warming into the 50's. Captain Daniel Gary had received orders from Colonel William H. Ball, presumably from Brigadier General Washington Elliott and Major General Robert Milroy, that it was time to build up the fortifications that would protect them in case the Confederate army came their way. They were fortunate not to have to start from scratch. Both the Union and the Confederate armies had occupied Winchester during the previous year and had constructed earthworks around the circumference of the town.

Milroy's order was to make them impregnable. The ground had softened to where shovels could be used, and the work began. Cheat Summit Fort had been constructed by Confederate forces in July, 1861, and abandoned by Union forces in October, 1862. It stood on

Cheat Summit, the highest hill in Winchester, between the Pugh-town Pike and the Romney Pike, northwest of the town. If there was a fight, Milroy's forces would have some of the high ground but only there. The Fort was square and was laid out over some thirty-four acres and was big enough to hold just over 2,000 soldiers. Carlin would move his Parrotts and howitzers there, and there were rifle pits along its entire perimeter. An ammunition magazine was in the center of the fort that was covered with dirt, several feet thick to protect it from enemy artillery fire. Lord help the men if it ever exploded.

Deep ditches, perhaps ten feet wide and a tall fence surrounded the earthworks to prevent attackers from gaining access. Abatis, sharpened felled trees aimed outward in an "X" configuration, protected the ditches as well. General Robert H. Milroy thought the Union soldiers, being protected by the thick walls of the works, would have an easy time of it if the enemy tried to get over the abatis and the ditch. Of course, that would depend on how many attackers there would be.

Fort Milroy, as Cheat Summit Fort was now called, was northwest of Winchester. From there, it could probably withstand an attack from General John Imboden's Confederate cavalry from up there in the Cacapon, but the question became, what about an infantry attack from the south? No need to answer that question since General Robert H. Milroy and many of his commanders did not believe that there would be an assault by the Confederate infantry and artillery, only some skirmishing with the cavalry. Colonel William H. Ball did not share that view. He had had a bad feeling about this since early January and Davy Hitchcock's first report. Nothing had happened in the interim to make him feel any differently.

Star Fort was north of Fort Milroy, on the other side of the Pughtown Pike. Built much the same, it could hold 1,500 soldiers, in its star configuration. Parrotts and howitzers sat on the parapets, and rifle pits were set up along its perimeter, just like Fort Milroy. West Fort wasn't as strong as Fort Milroy or Star, a little northwest of Fort Milroy, just south of the Pughtown Pike. It had not been finished, so work was underway, but even with that, it would be more vulnerable being out in the open at the base of Little North Mountain. Three cannons were placed on the walls and parapets, and rifle pits were dug. Also known as the West Lunette or Battery #5, West Fort could hold about 400-500 soldiers if the need arose. Battery #6 with its three guns was just north of West Fort. Battery #7 was across the Pughtown Pike with its eight cannon, and Battery #8, with only one gun faced Apple Pie Ridge to the northeast.

Basically, then, Winchester's defenses were mainly west and north of town. Confederate General John Imboden knew this. His cavalry had been scouting Winchester and the Yankee movements since they had arrived and had telegraphed General Stonewall Jackson about the various defensive positions. General Jackson had dutifully reported the same to the Commander of the Army of Northern Virginia, General Robert E. Lee. Thus, the Confederate high command knew what Milroy had. Milroy, on the other hand, did not know, or refused to know, what the Rebels had. Trouble in the making, perhaps.

Moses Granger had ordered Captain Daniel Gary and the other company commanders in the 122nd O.V.I. to rotate picket duty to the various companies under their command. So, each company would be on picket one day, every week and a half. As March came to an end and April was upon them, on Monday, April 6, 1863, the task was assigned to Company I. With Lieutenant Thomas Black still the Interim Regimental Quartermaster, the assignment fell to Lieutenant Thomas S. Armstrong. He would take Sergeants Patrick Murphy and Eddie Bristow and ten other enlisted men out of camp and up the Pughtown Road to see if General John Imboden was up to something. The previous week, the Confederate cavalry had come damn near the picket line set by Company B with shots exchanged. One Rebel was wounded. Company B lost Corporal Richard Davis, shot in the left cheek by a cavalry trooper. Reports were that he never had a chance because the rest of his mates were slow to reload their rifles and return the fire. They brought his body back and buried him outside of Fort Milroy.

"Finally, they're here!" Armstrong thought. He was very glad that a shipment of Enfield rifles had been brought to him by Lieutenant Tom Black who knew how much his friend wanted the more sophisticated weapons. He had trained Bristow and Murphy at Camp

Zanesville and thought he could use the time on picket to give the others some practice as well. When they arrived at the Fahnestock farm out between West Fort and Battery #6 about five miles northwest of town, they stopped and took up a position just south of the Pughtown Pike. He had made sure that each man had about thirty rounds of ammunition. Minie balls they were called. He would start them off at one hundred yards, just seeing if the men could hit a tree. Bristow and Murphy would teach five of the others, no more than ten practice shots in case the enemy came by, and the target practice became real.

At around 1 o'clock in the afternoon of April 6, the Enfields roared to life. Armstrong himself took the first shot and blew a branch off a tree some two hundred yards away. The advantage of the Enfield was its rifled barrel which increased the gun's accuracy by having the bullet spin. That allowed it to maintain its line of fire. The pop-up sight helped to identify the specific target and thus to aim at it. And, its range was four or five times that of a Springfield, giving anyone who had an Enfield a distinct edge.

"You don't hold it like a Springfield," Eddie Bristow said to his group of five. "You don't aim it like one neither." Bristow was working with his group while Murphy's was keeping their eyes peeled northwest up the Pughtown Road. Each one of his men fired at a tree some hundred yards away and were amazed at the power and accuracy of the weapon. Being westerners from out there in Ohio, they were certainly used to firing a musket, but this was different.

"Damn," Private Arthur Johnson said. "That's some gun, Sergeant." The practice firing continued, but, suddenly, it was real.

"Cavalry coming hard down the road. Must have heard the firing," screamed Patrick Murphy, from his lookout on a boulder above the rest.

"Take cover, men, here they come," yelled Thomas Armstrong, diving behind the stump of a tree. "And, Milroy told Ball they won't attack." There looked to be about twenty of them. Armstrong loaded the Enfield, steadied it on the stump, and fired. The lead Confederate trooper flew from the saddle and landed face down in the dirt. Bullets whizzed over the heads of the Company I picket line. The next thing he knew, Armstrong was covered with blood. Arthur Johnson had taken a direct hit, his left arm blown clear off, blood gushing out of his body, all over the Lieutenant.

He wiped Johnson's blood out of his eyes, aimed the Enfield again. Patrick Murphy had jumped down and was firing at will. Didn't seem to care that he was out in the open with no defense. "I'll kill you, you son-of-a-bitch." Riders approached. As Armstrong fired at the pack of troopers, trying to give Murphy some cover, the sergeant swung the Enfield and caught one of them square in the stomach. He toppled from his horse. The horse kept going, then fell, dead from Armstrong's shot. Patrick Murphy picked the man up and began beating the man senseless with his own hands.

"You bastard," he hollered and hit him again, right under the jaw. The man dropped to the ground. Murphy hoped he was dead. The twinkle in his eye gone...for good!

Bristow screamed, "Don't kill him, Patrick. Take him prisoner. He might tell us something." The Rebel was unconscious, and the firing continued, slowing just a bit. Bristow took aim and fired. Another Rebel went down. "Keep firing, boys." Not being used to the Enfields, the men were not very successful in hitting their attackers, but they did make a lot of noise and whistled some Minies around them.

A Confederate bullet ripped into Bristow's pantaloon, just above his right knee. "Dammit," he exclaimed. "Hurts like hell." Luckily for him, it was just a flesh wound, he thought, as he looked at the torn trousers. He turned, drew his pistol. and fired at the man who had just shot him. This time, the Rebel was aiming at Tom Armstrong. Hit him in the chest. Dead in the saddle and fell to the ground. "Serves you right, you dumb son-of-a-bitch."

"Good shooting, Eddie," yelled Tom Armstrong.

The Confederate raiders turned and started back up the Pughtown Pike. The smoke was starting to clear.

Eddie Bristow picked up Arthur Johnson's lifeless body and draped it over his saddle. He would have retrieved the Private's arm, but there were no traces of it. Even with the wound, Bristow said to Armstrong "I'll walk back with Private Johnson. He was a good man. Damn. At least he didn't know what hit him. Damn."

Putting the unconscious Rebel whom he had beaten across the pommel of his saddle, Patrick Murphy and the rest of the Company I picket, turned and headed back to camp.

"Those bastards. At least we got three of 'em."

"They probably say the same thing about us, Patrick," Tom Armstrong counseled. "Probably say the same thing." They rode slowly back to Fort Milroy.

"Boys, get cleaned up. I have to report to Captain Gary about what happened. Imagine he's gonna want to see the Colonel and the Major."

"Thank you, Captain. Good work, Lieutenant. Dammit. That's two in the last two weeks," said Colonel William Ball. "The enemy is getting bold. Wonder what's next. I better tell Milroy, but I doubt he will listen. You are dismissed."

Winchester Frederick Co. Va.
April 15th, Wednesday 1863

Dearest,

I imagine I see you and Huldah streaking across the prairie putting out fire. "I want to see you so bad." Well, Frank, I wish the war was over, then you could have that chance. I am longing for the time when you and I will be together. I rather think I will come & see you when I come to Ills. I am sorry you are living in prospect of a lonesome summer. I hope you will have a good time seeing Meda this fall.

Frank, I am afraid that this war will not be over soon. Wasn't this discouraging news that came from Charleston? About 5 of our gunboats being disabled. I am afraid the Vicksburg affair will be a failure. Well don't be discouraged. Our armies are all right. Grant, Burnside, Rosecrans, Hooker, Hunter, & Banks, are around them, enclosing them in as with a wall of fire. Secretary Chase has the finances in good condition, and we will have to fight through it manfully.

Well, Frank, don't forget your friend. T.S.A.

"Writing letters to her removes the boredom and rekindles my hope of survival, but it sure makes me want to see her, and I can't," he thought to himself. "Wonder if I ever will."

"Whattya mean they ain't there?" asked James Lindsay. It was nearing the end of April, and the two spies were hearing rumblings about Confederate troop movements. They had split up, promising to meet up in Front Royal, Lindsay had gone back up north through the Cacapon Valley while Davy Hitchcock had gone south to check on the Confederate army at Culpeper.

"James, they're gone, again, but I found 'em. They're about 35 miles east of Culpeper in a town called Falmouth, right near Fredericksburg. But what's even more interesting is that I found the Union army, too. On my way down there, I went through Front Royal, and I saw them crossing the Rappahannock, heading south. So I followed them down the river, and then I said to myself, wonder where this goes? Well, it flows all the way to Fredericksburg some seventy miles south of here. So when I got there, who do you think I saw?"

"The whole damn Confederate army?"

"Yep, and it looked to me like the Yankees were coming south to get acquainted. There was thousands of them."

"We better go see what's going on."

"Yep. I tracked them on my way back here. They're coming, James, I know they're coming."

The mountain man stroked his long reddish beard. "Let's go!" It was May 3, 1863. As they approached Fredericksburg, hiding in the dense underbrush, they could hear the cannon fire, but it was west of where they were. A place called Chancellorsville. Turning, the noise got louder and louder. All of a sudden, they could see it. Two massive armies had smashed into each other. Cannons roaring; the continuous clatter of musket fire; hand-to-hand combat with fists, swords, and bayonets; and men bleeding and dying, everywhere on the field.

James Lindsay and Davy Hitchcock wanted to see more, so they camped in the woods, with a small fire, and spent the night. In the morning, they could see the massive number of dead lying in the field, but there did not seem to be any further action until late in the day when another battle erupted. It was really time for them to go, but they wanted to see more. The next day, May 4, they could see the blue coated Yankees start to leave the field.

"Never thought I'd see that," said Davy Hitchcock. "Let's get back to Front Royal. I gotta go to Winchester to tell the Colonel."

Lindsay and Hitchcock stayed off the main road back to Front Royal. When they arrived, James Lindsay said, "Go on, lad, but be careful. You know they're all around here. Come back as soon as you can. I got a bad feeling about this."

When he got back to Winchester, he found some changes had been made. Colonel William H. Ball had been promoted to Interim Brigade Commander with Lieutenant Colonel Moses M. Granger now commanding the 122nd Ohio Volunteer Infantry, also on an interim basis. Additionally, Lieutenant Thomas Black had returned to Company I, being replaced as Interim Regimental Quartermaster by Lieutenant Andrew P. Stults.

"I know, Hitch," said Lieutenant Colonel Moses Granger. "Read about it in the *Baltimore American* this morning. Thousands of men dead, wounded, or missing. Rumor is that Stonewall Jackson was wounded. Lee routed Hooker, with about half the troop strength. Don't know how he managed that. Wonder where he's going next."

"Colonel, we think something is gonna happen and soon. Lindsay wants me back in Front Royal as soon as I am free to go."

"Get going, son. Keep your eyes and ears open. I want to know what is going on." David Hitchcock rode hard the twenty-five miles back to Front Royal.

"They're coming, kid. Too many cavalry up this far north for them not to be coming. Let's see who else is."

General Robert H. Milroy had sent his scouts out as well. They reported that the Confederate cavalry was gathering in Culpeper. But, the General was sure that his defenses could not be broken. He disagreed with Major General Henry Halleck whose staff had told him that the forts and batteries were too far apart in November. They were quite vulnerable, indeed. Each fort and each battery would be, essentially, on its own. Halleck relayed that information to Major General Robert C. Schenck who disregarded it. Like Milroy, he could not fathom an infantry attack. Maybe cavalry, but Milroy had told him that the forts could stand that. That's why Schenck sent him to increase the Federal military presence in Winchester in the first place, even though many officers in the high command believed that Winchester had limited military value. Commercial value, yes. Military value, no. Neither Schenck nor Milroy believed it. The original idea had been for Milroy to hold it as long as he could and then to get out. That just wasn't going to happen.

Lieutenant Colonel Moses M. Granger called an officers' meeting on Wednesday, May 20, 1863, the purpose of which was to find out what they all knew and to brief them on the intelligence reports he had received from Hitch and other scouts.

"The enemy is getting active," he told them. "Wouldn't be surprised if we don't see some action soon. I just talked with Colonel Keifer of the 110th who told me that he had warned General Milroy the other day that it was time to get out of here. I have told the General the same thing, and you all know that Colonel Ball did, too. Just make sure that your men are prepared in case we are surprised and get back to me with any information your scouts might pass along. Hitch and the mountain man think the Rebs are coming. They're out there watching with orders to get back here if they see any serious movement. Be on your toes, men."

Armstrong was relieved to receive a letter from Francis Porter that very day, May 20, 1863. Three days later, he wrote her back, concluding with:

I received your letter May 20, dated the 10th. My love to you. Has your feelings for me undergone any change? Do you love me better than any other man on earth, my dear wife. Let me hear from you soon. From your old friend.
T.S.

What he had hoped for and prayed about was coming true. In her last letter, she had professed her love for him and wanted nothing more than to be married to him. All he had to do was survive. That was not an easy task for any soldier, Union and Confederate. As May, 1863, came to an end, rumors continued to swirl through Winchester that Confederate General Robert E. Lee and his army were coming. No one knew what that meant; the men of Milroy's division were uneasy to say the least. Anxious, yes. Scared, you bet.

"Here he comes, James." Davy Hitchcock and James Lindsay had gotten back to Fredericksburg and were watching the Confederate army. "Must be tens of thousands of 'em. Wonder where they're going." It was June 4, 1863.

"Let's shadow them for a couple of days. We can learn a lot."

"Yeah, I gotta be sure about this or Granger might have me shot. Don't think I'd like that."

The big mountain man laughed. "We'll be sure, Davy. Count on that. Good night! Look at 'em all. They're going north. I'd bet my last bottle of 'shine on that. Let's follow for another couple of days, just to be sure. Maybe we could talk to one of 'em when they get to Sperryville or Chester Gap."

"Yeah. They won't suspect you. You talk like 'em. Take 'em some 'shine. They'll talk." And talk they did. When the column stopped just south of Sperryville, James Lindsay was riding north on Woodward Road. He was stopped by Rebel pickets and asked about his business. He replied he was a trapper, and he had to pick up some supplies in the town. They said it was okay for him to pass, but noticed the bottle sticking out of his coat.

"Whatcha got there, friend?"

"Oh, just some 'shine I made. Wanna taste?"

"You bet." The sentry took a large swig of the clear liquid.

"Wheweee. Damn that's good." He handed the bottle to the man standing next to him.

"Have another, boys. Where y'all headed?"

"Pennsylvania. That's Bobby Lee up there, leading the way. Some place called Winchester."

"Pennsylvania? Why there?"

"He's tired of fightin' in Virginia, and we sure can forage up there."

"Good luck, fellas. Keep the bottle and tear into them Yankees. Can't stand the sons-of-bitches," and James Lindsay rode slowly toward the town of Sperryville.

"Much obliged for the hooch, stranger."

"I gotta get back and tell the kid," Lindsay thought.

James Lindsay and Davy Hitchcock looked at a map. They now saw that the Confederate army had rapidly marched 79 miles from Fredericksburg to Front Royal and were now only 27 miles south of Winchester.

"He wouldn't be bringin' that train with supplies and all that artillery if he wasn't fixin' to stay," Davy Hitchcock said.

"Yeah, he's bringin' everything. Somethin' big's gonna happen, and your friends are in the way in that town."

"Damn! The damn Rebs are going right up the Valley. That's where Milroy is. Good Lord! I gotta warn them."

It was June 8, 1863, and Major General Robert Schenck had sent his aide, Lieutenant Colonel Donn Piatt to survey Winchester. Schenck had authorized Piatt to pursue one of two options. Tell Milroy to stay or tell him to leave and get to Harper's Ferry. One or the other. After looking at the fortifications, he came to the conclusion that everything was fine with what Milroy had constructed and telegraphed Schenck that the General could take care of anything the Confederates would throw at him.

"They're coming here? The whole damn army? With Lee in command?" screamed Lieutenant Colonel Moses Granger at Davy Hitchcock.

"Yes, sir. That's what the Reb told James just yesterday. I got here as fast as I could."

Granger called for his horse and was soon on his way to see Major General Robert H. Milroy, hoping that he would listen. The commander didn't. Granger knew this was big trouble.

Halleck continued to pressure Schenck who finally relented and ordered Milroy to withdraw to Harper's Ferry on June 10. Milroy ignored the order. Two days later, he wired Milroy again and repeated the order from June 10 that he leave Winchester immediately. That same day, Union scouts found a large Confederate force of artillery, cavalry, and infantry on the Front Royal Road, twelve miles west of Winchester.

The same day, he telegraphed Schenck that he could handle anything the Rebels had for him. Schenck was furious and wired back that Milroy was to leave, pending further instructions. That evening, he wired Milroy again, this time ordering him out of Winchester.

The General never received it. All of the telegraph wires had been cut. Major General Robert H. Milroy and his garrison of 6,900 men were all that stood between General Robert E. Lee and his Army of Northern Virginia on its way to Pennsylvania. Lieutenant Colonel Moses M. Granger didn't like the thought of it.

8 Cornered, Then Routed

Brigadier General Washington Lafayette Elliott stared at Major General Robert Milroy, shaking his head, absolutely astonished. The General still wouldn't listen even in the face of some pretty persuasive evidence. It was June 12, 1863, 7 o'clock in the evening. Elliott had hoped for a different outcome, but, based on his prior experience, he didn't think it would happen. He would try anyway.

"Begging the General's pardon, and at the risk of speaking out of line, we know they are here. Granger's scouts followed them up here from Chancellorsville. On the way, the Rebs told them they were going to Pennsylvania, with General Lee in command. McReynolds' 1st New York cavalry unit saw them come through the Chester Gap, some thirty miles south of here, on Wednesday, and, yesterday, Galligher's 13th Pennsylvania and Pierce's 12th Pennsylvania cavalry found them at Cedarville, less than twelve miles west. I am told they told you that. Heard an exchange of rifle fire this morning. There must be 80,000 of them, and what do we have, 7,000? General, we don't stand a chance. We must get out of here before they get here. We can take the Martinsburg Pike northeast and join up with the garrison at Harper's Ferry. But, we must go. Now!"

"General, I have orders to occupy this place, and that is what I intend to do," replied Milroy, "and, yes, you are out of line. Our works are stout enough, even if the enemy brings his artillery. But, I don't think he will do that. He doesn't want this place. I suggest you return to your brigade, General."

"But, General Milroy, Stonewall Jackson wanted this place. Made his headquarters here. Why won't Lee want it? Dick Ewell is with him, leading Jackson's old command. This place is valuable to them. It's the roads and the railroad. They need it for their supplies. And, add to that, sir, we are vastly outnumbered."

"Lee's still in Fredericksburg. We all know that. Even if he was coming north, he wouldn't come through here. This conversation is concluded, General. I don't know why I ever gave you command. You are dismissed!"

As Elliott rode back to his headquarters, he thought, "What the hell is wrong with him? Why doesn't he believe the intelligence reports? Lee's here, not in Fredericksburg. We're going to get killed just because he is too proud and too stubborn to admit he's wrong. Trouble is Keifer, Granger, and the other commanders all know that Johnny is here. Rumors flying all around. The men all know it, too. A fine mess we got ourselves into just because Milroy won't listen, much less go. Makes no damn sense. Makes no damn sense at all."

The cavalry of Andrew McReynolds, James Galligher, and Lewis Pierce knew. Hitch and James Lindsay knew. A full-fledged invasion force was on its way up the Valley Pike and the Front Royal Pike heading straight toward Pennsylvania with Winchester in the way. Galligher and Pierce had told Elliott personally that it wasn't just cavalry; there were infantry and artillery, too. Supply wagons as far as the eye could see. This was huge. Nobody knew exactly where the Confederate Army was going in Pennsylvania. But, it seemed like every member of the Union garrison at Winchester knew they were in the way of the Rebel march, except Major General Robert H. Milroy.

"Davy," James Lindsay said quietly, sitting in the saloon in Strasburg. "Our work is done here. I'm going back up into the hills and suggest you hightail it outta here. Nuthin' more you can do."

"Hate to say it, James, but I think you're right. I'll tell Granger that I've done my part. Thank him for that opportunity and then skedaddle north back home. Don't want to be there when the Johnnies start shooting."

The big man and the kid walked out of the saloon and shook hands. James Lindsay turned his horse west and started down the Strasburg Pike, disappearing into the dense woods. David, "Hitch," Hitchcock knew he better move fast and rode hard, past the sentries, to the camp of the 122nd Ohio Volunteer Infantry on Bower's Hill in Winchester. He would never see James Lindsay again.

He delivered his message to Lieutenant Colonel Moses M. Granger; had supper with Dan Gary, Tom Black, and Tom Armstrong; and bunked in Sergeant Terrance Rundle's tent. He got up early the next morning since he figured that he had better go northeast just after sunrise, out on the Martinsburg Pike toward Harper's Ferry and then into Maryland. "That's what they all should be doing, but they ain't." It was Saturday, June 13, 1863. He heard the big guns being fired behind him as he rode north. "Damn, it's starting." He had seen Moses Granger, Dan Gary, Tom Black, and Tom Armstrong for the last time. He didn't need to be in harm's way anymore. He'd had enough close calls.

"Colonel Granger," yelled Lieutenant Cyrus Scott, "just saw 'em coming on the Front Royal Road. Looks like a whole damn division, comin' right at us. Cavalry, infantry, and big, damn guns. They'll be here before you know it."

"Sergeant Rundle, get the commanders here on the double. Looks like we're in for some trouble." He could hear the fire southwest of town. The big guns of Confederate Lieutenant General Richard S. Ewell had opened fire on Fort Milroy. The artillery in the Fort returned the favor. The 2nd Battle of Winchester was on.

When the company commanders were assembled, he instructed, "Gentlemen, we are ordered to take position on the Valley Pike, just south of town. We will be on the left side of Carlin's battery with the 12th West Virginia on the right. Get moving."

"Bugler, sound *Assembly*," Granger ordered.

The men of the 122nd Ohio Volunteer Infantry marched off Bower's Hill over the Milltown Heights into earthworks the Confederates had left after the 1st Battle of Winchester a year earlier. Lieutenant Colonel Moses Granger in the lead, his sword held high, tightly above his head, pointing the way. The company commanders, with their swords raised, led their men. The regimental colors accompanied the Colonel, carried by a man from Captain John Ross' Company K. Dangerous business, carrying the regimental colors, but he was proud to do it. They marched in a column of two south off Bower's Hill, through Winchester, and stopped at the south end of Flint Ridge, their backs facing the Valley Pike, looking west. Scouts had said that the Confederates would be coming from there.

The men of the 122nd O.V.I. were about to see the elephant for real. Even though Tom Armstrong had been through this before, his throat was dry, his hands were trembling slightly, and the cold feeling in his chest would not go away. He had to pee…and did.

Armstrong knew better than most all of them what was coming, and fear started to overcome his thinking. "Black and I will be the first targets. Dan, too. Got to get him off that horse. It's in God's hands now." Dread was taking over. He could hear men whimpering, praying, cussing, vomiting. The consequence of what was to come would be severe. It was 1 o'clock in the afternoon. Then, he calmed himself, thinking "This is why I am here. This is what I told Frank and the family I must do. I know what this is. I've seen the elephant, and now I will see it again. May God be with me and all of us." He recalled his conversation with the Reverend Charles McCabe the previous August in making the decision to go back in. "Wonder where Charlie is. Sure hope he is all right."

Moses Granger found Captain John Carlin of the First West Virginia Light Artillery and Colonel John Klunk, the commander of the 12th West Virginia. Brigadier General Washington Elliott had ordered Klunk to form a skirmish line a mile out from the base of Bower's Hill on Flint Ridge, to be supported by Carlin's Parrotts and howitzers, with the 122nd on the left. As he was walking back to the regiment, he heard Carlin's big guns roar. They were firing east, not west. "Maybe Elliott's wrong. They're coming at us, not at Klunk."

In addition to the cannon fire, bullets whizzed over their heads. The smoke from Carlin's guns made it difficult to see and breathe. Granger had no idea where the bullets were coming from. "Anybody see them?"

Sergeant Terrance Rundle cried out, "Sharpshooters at about a hundred yards, hiding in those trees." He saw a flash of fire, then another, and another. The fear and dread left him. "Dear, Lord, be with us this day," he prayed, silently. The regimental color bearer went down, clutching his left leg. He would lose it to Dr. Houston's saw later that afternoon. The colors reappeared, being carried by another man from John Ross' Company K.

One of Carlin's cannoneers screamed as a bullet tore into his groin. He went down, blood spurting from his torso. He was dead. The Parrotts and howitzers continued their bombardment. Another Rebel shot found its mark. Knocked Carlin's man beside the Parrott backward, replaced by a soldier who looked a lot like Caleb Edwards. Still no orders for the 122nd. "I could've gotten a couple of 'em; saw 'em and could've fired at 'em," Terrance Rundle said to himself. "We're here to fight, so let's get at it."

An hour later, Carlin's guns fell silent. Lowering his field glasses, Tom Armstrong couldn't see the attackers and wondered if they had retired. Just then, one of General Elliott's staff officers came up. "The General's compliments, Colonel Granger. He wishes you to leave this place and move toward the Fort. You may also be needed to support Colonel Ely on the north side of town."

"Thank you, Captain. Please thank the General. We will be on the move shortly. But what about Klunk's boys? Are we just to leave them?" asked Moses Granger.

"I cannot answer that, sir. The General met with General Milroy a short while ago, came back, and told me to tell you what he would like you to do. That's all I know, sir. Wasn't privy to the conversation with General Milroy."

"I hate to leave Klunk like that, but orders are orders."

"Yes, sir. I must be off."

"Thank you, Captain. My compliments to the General. Sergeant Rundle, see how we might comply with the General's orders."

Rundle was back in a hurry.

"Can't go anywhere, sir. There's Rebel infantry flanking us on the right. Engaged with Colonel Ely's Pennsylvania boys over there. Got plenty for us, too, it looks like, if they choose to fight with us.

"Damn, now what are we supposed to do?"

"No orders about that. Doesn't seem like Milroy can make up his mind. Maybe things are happening too fast for him. That's a problem," Granger thought to himself.

Carlin's guns came to life once again, this time to the west. Klunk's West Virginians were under pressure and were pulling back toward the 122nd.

"Maybe Klunk needs us. Sergeant Rundle, go find out."

The canister and grape from Carlin's guns screamed across the sky toward the Rebel assault. Then, it was Klunk's men, rising up and firing a murderous volley into the advancing Confederates. Granger could see several of them fall, their weapons being picked up by the next line that was just walking over the dead and wounded. The fight continued for about half an hour. Several men of the 12th West Virginia went down, but Colonel John Klunk didn't seem to need the help of the 122nd. Carlin's guns were apparently enough. Around 4 o'clock, the Rebels retired, and the guns fell silent again. But, not for long. Minutes later, their artillery opened up and began shelling the earthworks there on Flint Ridge. Now, the 122nd Ohio Volunteer Infantry was in trouble. Colonel Moses Granger ordered the 122nd to head for Old Milltown where there would be protection from the old mills and other buildings up there that were vacant. They could dig in there, but, first, they'd have to run about half a mile up the hill through open territory. And, run they did.

No time for orders or Hardee's formations. "C'mon, boys," Armstrong shouted as he ran, cannon fire ringing above them. "Keep coming. Patrick, bring up the rear. Get any stragglers. Eddie, get up there as fast as you can. Find us good, safe ground." For a moment, Patrick Murphy and Eddie Bristow forgot the terror that had gripped them when they had watched and listened to the 12th West Virginia battle with the attackers. However, terror, fright, and panic would return and be frequent visitors.

It took about fifteen minutes, but, by 4:30, the men of Company I and Company K were tucked in behind the vacant mills. Safe, for now. The men huddled together with soft voices talking about the horror they had just seen. "They just walked over them. The wounded begging for help, but nobody did anything," one said softly. There was nothing else that could be done. No stretcher bearer would go to the field, unless there was a flag of truce, to retrieve any of the wounded. That would be suicide. So, whatever their wounds, they would be left to die.

Tom Armstrong could see that John Klunk's 12th West Virginia wasn't done. The firefight continued back and forth. First, the Confederates advanced to the spot where Klunk had placed the skirmish line. The West Virginians raised up again and fired a volley into them, forcing them back. The 12th pursued on foot chasing the Rebels back across Abram's Creek, and, in the process, captured three of them. Under questioning, they said they were from Louisiana, part of Ewell's command. Colonel John Klunk didn't realize it, but he had captured some very valuable information. He sent a courier to report to General Elliott about what he had been told. Elliott, upon hearing it, sent his own staff officer to see Major General Robert H. Milroy.

"Are you sure, Captain?"

"Yes, sir. Said they were part of Ewell's Corps. Said that Lee and about 60,000 men were heading North. Said that Ewell had told the General that he could take care of Winchester by himself, just with his division of 15,000. Looks like that's happening, General. General Elliott thinks we're pretty close to being surrounded. Ewell's already got the roads south of here. Southeast, too. Artillery from the west, attacking Klunk and Granger."

It was at that moment when Robert H. Milroy started to realize that it really was Major General Robert E. Lee and the Army of Northern Virginia coming toward him. He also had some thought, a bit too late, that maybe his commanders might have been right.

Lieutenant Thomas S. Armstrong, sitting by the mill race up there on the Milltown Heights, was in deep discussion with Captain Daniel Gary and Lieutenant Thomas Black. Armstrong spoke thoughtfully. "We're in trouble. They've got us surrounded. They've got superior numbers. We've only three days' rations, and I'm wondering about the ammunition. And, we have a commander who just won't listen. The men are scared and don't know what will happen tomorrow. Quite frankly, neither do I, but I got a feeling we're going to meet those Southern boys, one way or another."

Dan Gary just nodded, absorbed in his own thoughts. He hadn't seen the elephant before. Neither had Tom Black. But, from what little they saw that day, they now knew what it meant and what the new day might bring. They didn't like the prospect.

A little later that evening Brigadier General Washington Elliott, Colonel J. Warren Keifer, and Lieutenant Colonel Moses M. Granger were chewing on some dried beef and trying to get the maggots off the hardtack and out of the coffee pot. "They're just swimming in there, General, you scoop' em out with a spoon," said Keifer.

"No laughing matter, Colonel."

"Seriously, sir, we are in a fix here. But, there are ways out. Bet the Rebs will close the gap to Harper's Ferry. Also, bet we could get out of here going northwest on the Pughtown and maybe straight north on the back roads. Could be the Apple Pie Ridge Road is open. There are some smaller roads running north. Those would be open, too. Surely, the General has to understand that we hafta go, tonight."

"I'll speak with him, Warren, but even if he realizes the mess we're in, if he doesn't have orders, he won't go."

"General," said Robert H. Milroy, "we can last for twenty-four hours until the reinforcements arrive. Then, we will drive Dick Ewell back to Fredericksburg." But, that wasn't going to happen, what with Lee's Army of Northern Virginia marching north on its way to Pennsylvania. There was no way any reinforcements could get through 60,000 Confederate infantrymen, the artillery, and the wagon train. Lee's Army would be very glad to see a regiment of Union soldiers coming their way. It would make short work of the Yankees. Milroy didn't realize that.

He ordered the brigade commanders, Elliott, Ely, and McReynolds, to pull their men into the forts. And so they did, concentrating on the ground in the center of the triangle of Fort Milroy, Star Fort, and West Fort. Carlin's battery and the other artillery units tried to get to the walls of each to rain canister and grape down on the advancing Rebel army. But, just like that, the Confederates stopped coming. In fact, they had retired. The men of the 122nd could see their campfires in the distance. Looked like it was time for their supper. The fighting could wait.

Around 9 o'clock, that Saturday evening, a violent thunderstorm struck the Lower Shenandoah Valley with torrential rains pounding Winchester. Thunder rolled over the town with a tremendous roar, many times louder than the cannon fire of earlier that day. Lightning flashed through the sky, lighting it up for miles around. The men of Milroy's command were tired and hungry, and were now soaked to the skin while they waited anxiously for the fight that would come in the morning. Sleep would come at a premium, if at all. The screams of the wounded and dying only made matters worse. It was a scene that they would remember for the rest of their lives, no matter how short or how long that would be.

"Colonel Granger," said the Regimental Quartermaster Andrew Stults, "the wagons are packed. Mainly food and ammunition. Don't have enough space for much more. Got plow horses hitched up, so they're ready to go." It was 2 o'clock in the morning of Sunday, June 14, 1863.

"Very well, Sergeant. I will tell General Elliott. Sergeant Rundle, arouse the company commanders. Tell them to be ready to go as soon as I get back."

Lieutenant Thomas Armstrong could not believe what Captain Daniel Gary was telling them. "We're packed and ready to go. Heading north on the Pughtown as soon as Granger gets back. Have your men carry only their weapons. We're to stymie the left flank of the enemy. Don't want them coming in from the northwest. We may even be scouting for an escape route." Optimism replaced pessimism.

The dread in the minds of the 122nd Ohio Volunteer Infantry vanished. "We're gonna bust out of here," Patrick Murphy said to Eddie Bristow. "Probly hafta fight our way. Heard there wasn't much resistance out there. Better'n bein' here. We gotta get the men ready to go."

Colonel Moses Granger sat ashen-faced. "But, with all due respect, General, you told me to get the regiment ready to go out past West Fort on the Pughtown Pike and flank the enemy. You said those were Milroy's orders."

"He changed his mind, Colonel. Nobody's goin' nowhere tonight," said Washington Elliott.

Granger responded, "Beginning to think that nobody in the high command knows what the hell's going on or what the hell we should do. Do this; no, don't do that; do this. I'm confused. Bet the others are, too."

He thought to himself, "Who in the hell is in charge around here? Milroy or Elliott? Don't we have a chain of command?" Lieutenant Colonel Moses Granger's head was spinning. "Elliott tells us we're to flank the enemy. Milroy tells us we're not. I don't get it."

Tom Armstrong and the rest of the 122nd were devastated. "We're not going?" Armstrong asked. The fear swept over him just as the excitement of escape had a few hours earlier. He didn't use profane language, often, but he shook his head and simply said "DAMN." The way he figured it, if they went out northwest and the Johnnies concentrated on Winchester, they might forget about the 122nd. If the Rebels did, indeed, do that, the 122nd could take off north. But, now, that wasn't going to happen.

All hope was gone. "The General changed his mind," said Dan Gary. "Got orders to back up Klunk again when the sun comes up. Carlin's moved his guns out there, too."

As ordered by Milroy to back up Klunk again, the disheartened 122nd marched southwest shortly after dawn toward the Valley Pike. The men knew that Johnny was there, just waiting for them with his superior numbers of men and guns. The 123rd had gone out earlier and was engaging the enemy in the woods just east of Bower's Hill. Tom Armstrong now guessed that they were, in fact, surrounded and realized that the Confederate Army would continue to squeeze them until they gave up. Unless they could fight their way out. "Don't think that will happen," he said to himself, losing hope a little more rapidly.

It was strangely quiet out there that Sunday morning. Sitting in the mud, Armstrong said, "We should have gone Friday night, boys." Eddie Bristow and Patrick Murphy nodded in agreement. "The Martinsburg Pike was open. Weren't any Rebels out there. We could've gotten to Harper's Ferry."

"Saw some boys doin' jus' that," replied Eddie Bristow. "Looked like they just skedaddled when the firing started, the damn cowards."

"Rations getting low, Sump," added Patrick Murphy. "We got enough ammunition, I think. The men are talking about why we are still here. They're wondering. They know the mess we're in, and they also know that they will have to fight at some point today. They don't like their prospects. Get killed, worse yet, get wounded and just lie there. Maybe get taken prisoner. What's the name of that place?"

"For enlisted men like you? Belle Isle, in Richmond. South of here."

"You tol' us about it," said Patrick Murphy. "Awful place. Could starve to death, die of disease, be shot in the back trying to escape. Heard there was cannibalism, too. Men eating other men. Don't want to go there, damn. Where do officers go?"

"Libby. Old tobacco warehouse in Richmond. Ugly from what I've heard," replied Tom Armstrong. "That wouldn't be good. Maybe we'd get exchanged for some of theirs."

The conversation was interrupted by the deafening booming of cannon, close by. The day had turned hot and sunny, with stifling humidity. As Armstrong and the two sergeants turned to see what was going on, they watched the Confederates moving on the town. "They already have West Fort, both infantry and artillery" someone screamed with obvious terror in his voice. In response, the guns of Lieutenant Peter Leary's Baltimore Light Artillery had opened fire on West Fort, hoping to knock the Rebel gunners back up the Romney Road. It looked like they were having success when the order came down for the 122nd to move to the base of Bower's Hill.

It was just after noon on Sunday, June 14, 1863. The 122nd, accompanying Colonel John Klunk's 12th West Virginia, found the enemy protected by woods and a stone wall. Leary's guns continued to blast away, and now Captain John Carlin's Battery D opened up as well. Smoke hung in the air. The firing of the cannon made it impossible to hear. But, Lieutenant Colonel Moses M. Granger had orders. Take Bower's Hill.

"Bugler, sound To Arms."

"Judas Priest, here we go," yelled Tom Armstrong. "Men, fix bayonets. We're going up that hill, and we have to drive them off." He drew his sword. This was the moment he had thought about the previous summer. He would have to lead his men up the hill, a perfect target for the Rebels. Gary and Black would do the same. Two more perfect targets.

Captain Dan Gary screamed "CHARGE, ON THE DOUBLE QUICK," pointing the sword at the top of Bower's Hill, and launched into a run. Tom Armstrong ran beside, sword held high with his right hand, Colt in his left. The men of Company I cheered as they followed the Captain up the hill. "Don't stop, keep coming." Armstrong was focused on the crest of the hill, his knees and feet moving automatically. They ran across the muddy, open ground, into a hail of enemy fire, not pausing to return it. There was no place to take cover. Tom Armstrong could hear the screams of the men. "I'm hit, bad. They done killed me, those bastards." Armstrong kept running. He'd never killed a man with his sword, or his pistol, for that matter, but that was about to change as they approached the stone wall. Over he went, following Dan Gary and plunged the weapon into the gut of the first Rebel he saw. He never gave it a thought, until later. Pulling the weapon out, the man collapsing, he wiped the blood on his pants and searched for his next victim. The Colt was ready to go.

He saw a man make a run at Captain Daniel Gary. Armstrong didn't have much time to aim. Didn't need to. He fired, and the man went down, clutching his left leg. Dan Gary looked at him and smiled. The scene was duplicated all over Bower's Hill, with the Rebels retreating down the western slope. The 122nd now had the high ground, the cries of the wounded filling the air. "Damn, we whipped 'em," Armstrong heard Patrick Murphy say.

"Yeah, but they'll be back." As he said it, he heard that awful Rebel yell. "Here they come, boys. Let 'em have it." The Enfield rifles sprang to life and offered a treacherous volley down the hill into the charging Confederate infantry. They kept coming and coming. The men of the 122nd were starting to waver. They'd been fighting for an hour in that heat and humidity, made more miserable by the smoke. The back line broke and started down the east side of Bower's Hill. "Dammit, hold your position," but that fell on deaf ears. The regiment fell back, but Colonel Moses Granger wasn't about to take that.

Astride the big grey mare, he commanded, "We must regroup. We're gonna take that damn hill, and we're gonna hold it. Now, let's go."

The mass of blue started back up the hill, cheering wildly as they ran past and over their wounded comrades. Thoughts of fear disappearing in the excitement of the moment. More men were falling, but the surge continued, sweat pouring from their faces.

"Gotta go over that wall again," Armstrong thought to himself, suddenly at peace with what was going on around him. He fired again, hitting the enemy in the shoulder, knocking him to the ground.

"Sump," yelled Patrick Murphy, "Eddie's down. Took a bayonet in the gut. Blood everywhere. He's gone. He mumbled something, telling me to tell you he's sorry he's let you down."

Thomas S. Armstrong felt instant pain, but he had to go on. "We'll get him when the fighting stops." He dodged another bayonet assault, suddenly enraged by what the Rebels had done to his friend. Raising the sword, he smashed into the man's head, splitting it in two, brains and blood all over. "Serves you right for killing my friend," he said, feeling no remorse. He saw the Rebels backing down the hill again. It was nearly 1 o'clock that hot Sunday afternoon.

Dan Gary commanded, "Hunker down and get cover where you can. They'll be back." It was going to be a long day.

"Patrick, get two or three men and take Eddie back to the Fort. Bury him there, by the front gate, and then get back up here. Who should take his place?"

"Will do, Sump, and I don't know." Patrick Murphy turned, planted the bayonet of his Enfield in the ground, and trudged off to do this awful work.

It was quiet now. Lieutenant Thomas Armstrong sat down in the shelter of the stone wall. "May God forgive me for what I have done today. And forgive me for what I will do later this day. It's not over." As he looked up, he saw a flock of buzzards circling overhead, getting ready, he thought, to pick over the remains of the men who had died, and were dying, on the field. He'd seen those scavengers before, at Shiloh, and knew that they would wait until the men left before landing and attacking their prey.

A courier from General Washington Elliott arrived around 2:30 PM, telling Lieutenant Colonel Moses Granger to send two companies into Winchester to engage the enemy while it was moving on Fort Milroy. Granger dispatched riders to find Captain Daniel Gary of Company I and Captain John Ross of Company K to detach from their positions on Bower's Hill and to go north into the town.

When the companies of Dan Gary and John Ross reached the bottom of the hill, bullets started flying again. Lieutenant Tom Armstrong looked around and realized that Patrick Murphy had not returned and was, most likely isolated. He hoped that the sergeant and his detail could figure out a way to get back to Bower's Hill to rejoin the regiment, but, at that point, Murphy would have no idea where Company I had gone. Armstrong wondered if he would ever see his friend again. "Can't worry about that now," he thought to himself, crouched down behind the corner of a deserted saloon on Braddock Street in front of the rifle pits the Confederates had dug during the night. The riflemen were there to cover the infantry advance on Fort Milroy.

The fighting was hot, bullets thumping into the walls of the buildings that hid the Federals. They were outnumbered and out-positioned, but they had to try to stop the advance on Fort Milroy. The problem was, as companies of the Rebels moved north through the town, they were covered by rifle fire from the pits which kept Co. I and Co. K pinned down in various buildings, unable to do much about the advance. Armstrong saw one of the 122nd rise up to take a shot, but was immediately cut down by a Confederate sharpshooter's fire from a window across the street. "Dang, they've got 'em in some of the buildings, too. Somehow, we hafta outflank 'em."

Captains Gary and Ross ordered the men to fall back to Washington and Stewart Streets and then to go north toward Fort Milroy to try to intercept the advancing Confederates. They ran up toward Clifford and Cork Streets, hiding as best they could to shield their surprise volleys. They found an abandoned hotel on the north side of Washington Street.

Gary ordered, "Go find a room with a window facing the street. Open the window and aim at the buildings across the street. Barrel no more than six inches out the window. When you see a puff of smoke or fire, fire your weapon at it, then duck down. They may be doing the same thing to us."

Tom Armstrong said to the corporals, now that Eddie Bristow was dead and Patrick Murphy, who knows where he was, "Do as the Captain said and show your men how to do this. Watch." He opened a window slightly and put the barrel of the Enfield slightly outside. There was a puff of smoke, and he fired. He saw glass break in a window across the street and immediately slumped down, hiding from any incoming volley. "Got it?"

From behind some fences, Captain John Ross and Co. K fired three volleys into the Rebel infantry, slowing the advance. The companies of the 122nd had some good protection in the vacant buildings and fences, and although they were outmanned, they were able to hold their positions, firing at the oncoming attackers. What was amazing to Tom Armstrong was that, although the men knew it was most likely a lost cause, they kept fighting with spirit and determination. "Perhaps because they know it might be their last," he thought.

Lieutenant Colonel Moses Granger continued to hold Bower's Hill, with some difficulty, raining down as much fire as they could muster. Carlin's cannons bellowed loudly, throwing ball after ball into the Rebel works. It was hurting the enemy, but would not be enough. He saw Rebel reinforcements approaching on the run. "Fresh legs and fresh eyes. My men haven't eaten all day. Damn. This is some fix."

"Tom," Daniel Gary said, "go find out what Granger wants us to do. Ask him about Ross, too."

"Yes, sir." Tom Armstrong bounded west down Washington Street, heading for where he thought the rest of the 122nd was holed up and dodging bullets as he ran. "Keep shootin' high, fellas." He thought about the boys across the street who were trying to kill him. "Dang, that was close." A bullet ripped into the horse trough just to his right, spraying water onto the sidewalk in front of him. "Gotta go faster. Tough to hit a moving target."

The action on Braddock Street and Louden Street slowed. It almost looked to Captain Daniel Gary that the Confederates had withdrawn. "Lieutenant Black, take some men and reconnoiter the area. Be watchful." Indeed, the Rebel advance had slackened on the way toward Fort Milroy.

Tom Armstrong was running back up Washington Street and didn't see anyone. Moses Granger had told him two things. First, it looked like the Rebels were pulling back to Camp Hill to make ready for a full-frontal assault on Fort Milroy. And, second, Elliott wanted the 122nd to stay put in support of John Klunk's 12th West Virginia with the 123rd in reserve. "We're supposed to go back, Dan, on the left flank of those West Virginia boys. I'm ordered to tell Captain Ross, too." He was off again.

"Gentlemen," Lieutenant Colonel Moses M. Granger began, addressing the other eight company commanders, "Our orders are to attack the Rebels down there by those trees. Us and the 12th West Virginia, followed by Colonel Wilson's 123rd. Make ready."

The men of the 122nd were poised to charge down the hill toward the enemy they could hardly see when all of a sudden, they were under attack by artillery from the west. Huge shells exploding on Bower's Hill, and then Rebel skirmishers started up the hill.

"We're damn near out of ammunition, Colonel," yelled Captain Daniel Gary. "This ain't good."

"Captain, withdraw toward Fort Milroy. I will send couriers to tell the others."

He didn't have to. As soon as the other company commanders saw Company I hightailing down the backside of the hill to the northeast, they followed en masse. The 123rd followed leaving John Klunk and the 12th West Virginia to fend for themselves. It was just about 5 o'clock in the afternoon of Sunday, June 14, 1863 when Tom Armstrong felt the relief of being in the main fort. He thought to himself, "Klunk's gotta be the unluckiest commander in this man's army. We keep leaving him alone out there. Bet he's not happy with all the indecision."

"Where you been, Lieutenant?" It was Patrick Murphy, safe and sound. The twinkle in his eye was back. Tom Armstrong shot a look of disgust at Murphy, but then was forced to smile.

"Just having a little target practice in town, Patrick."

They heard the thunder of cannon fire, this time from the west, again. Confederate artillery was now bombarding Star Fort and Fort Milroy with incredible accuracy, not only on Fort Milroy, but also into the town of Winchester itself. Death was flying all around, killing both men and animals. Carcasses of horses were strewn in the street alongside the men who had been killed and wounded, mortally, by the flying shrapnel.

Men were crowding into whatever safe space they could find in Fort Milroy, their faces white as snow in terror. It was one thing to be able to see the attacker since you could defend yourself or become the attacker yourself. But not to see him and the destruction he brought was quite another thing. Fear gripped all of Fort Milroy that Sunday evening. The air full of smoke and the continuous thunder of the Confederate guns. Armstrong, Murphy, and several of the men huddled in the northwest corner of the fort, hoping beyond hope, that a blast of grape and canister would not find them. The men of the command of Major General Robert H. Milroy were trapped with no place to go. If they stayed, they would surely be taken prisoner. If they tried to cut their way out, they might escape, might be killed, might be wounded, or might be taken prisoner. It had already been a long day. Time for food, water, and rest.

Tom Armstrong had been awake for 36 hours. He hadn't eaten all day. His canteen was dry. He'd lost a good friend in Eddie Bristow. He might have lost more, he didn't know and wouldn't until *Roll Call* in the morning, if there was one. And, he was in Fort Milroy, with 2,000 men, maybe more, all mighty scared of what the new day would bring, and searching for any kind of cover from the might of the Confederate guns.

He finished eating some hardtack, dried beef, some moldy bread, and some dried apples, washing it all down with some brown water that Patrick Murphy had found. He needed sleep, desperately, lying there in the trench in the northwest corner of the fort. He unbuckled the scabbard at his belt and laid it beside him. The Colt would stay right where it was, on his hip. As he closed his eyes, he prayed. "Dear God, thank you for letting me survive this day and forgive me for what I have done. You know that I have placed my complete faith and trust in you and, while it is being tested, it is still there. Please welcome Eddie and the others into your eternal kingdom and heal the wounded if that be your will. Be with me tomorrow since I know the fight will be there then, and deliver me, if you so choose. Comfort Mother, Father, and the rest of the family. Comfort Francis and her family. Let me pray in your name, Lord. Amen." Sleep came quickly. It was about 8 o'clock on June 14, 1863. The sun was almost down, and the artillery fire had ceased.

General Washington Elliott received a message from General Robert Milroy that a counsel of war of the brigade commanders was to convene in an hour at 9 o'clock. He hurried to call his regimental commanders to get their opinions about what they thought was their best option. The meeting took place at a corner of Fort Milroy with Elliott, Lieutenant Colonel Moses M. Granger of the 122nd Ohio, Colonel J. Warren Keifer of the 110th Ohio, Lieutenant Colonel Thomas Wildes of the 116th Ohio, Colonel John Schall of the 87th Pennsylvania, Colonel Lewis Pierce of the 12th Pennsylvania Cavalry, Colonel James Galligher of the 13th Pennsylvania Cavalry, and Captain James Carlin of the 1st West Virginia Light Artillery. Colonel William H. Ball was there, too, having just been returned to the command of the 122nd O.V.I that day.

Warren Keifer spoke first. "Gentlemen, with my compliments, the only thing we can do is fight our way out of here. We're running out of ammunition and food and have little access to water. It looks like Dick Ewell has 50 or 100 large guns trained on us. The men are tired, and I, for one, do not want to spend any time in Libby Prison. So, we should go tonight, north on the back roads over Apple Pie Ridge toward Martinsburg. We can't go on any of the main roads since Johnny will be there. Ewell's a smart man and an excellent commanding officer. He knows the fix we're in. He knows the options we have. He also knows that we are soldiers, and soldiers fight. They do not give up easily. He knows, then, that we will not surrender. We will fight our way out if we have to. We also know he has Jubal Early out there in the west guarding the Romney Pike and south on the Valley Pike. Only one I don't know about is the Pughtown Pike, but I would guess he has cavalry out there, too. Then, I'd bet my last dollar that he has sent ol' "Allegheny" Johnson to the east to guard the Berryville Pike and north to block the Martinsburg Pike. The only way out, as I see it, is to go northwest between the two of them under the cover of darkness, no wagons, no artillery, sorry Captain Carlin. As quiet as we can be and hope and pray we can squeeze between them."

"Makes a helluva lot of sense to me," said Washington Elliott. "Lewis, Jim, what do you think? Can your cavalry cover us under darkness?"

"It won't be easy, General, but under the circumstances, sir, we will cover you."

"Moses? Colonel Ball?

"The problem, as I see it, General," said William Ball, "is that it makes so much damn sense, but Milroy doesn't listen. He will order an evacuation of some sort, and we will have to fight our way out. I like Warren's suggestion and will lead the way, if that meets the General's wishes."

"Colonel Wildes?"

"I agree. Better to run right now than to fight. We don't have the men or the firepower. Let's just leave under the cloud of night."

"Colonel Schall?"

"Yes, I agree."

"Good, thank you, gentlemen. I will so advise General Milroy. How soon can we be ready to go?"

General Washington Elliott's subordinates looked at one another, shook their heads. Warren Keifer responded, "Midnight, fellas?"

There was agreement. General Robert Milroy's command would head northwest on the backroads about midnight with the 122nd in the lead, covered by the cavalry of Lewis Pierce and James Galligher, if, and it was a big if, Elliott could convince the commander to approve it. Brigadier General Washington Elliott was off to find Major General Robert Milroy. Colonel William Ely and Colonel Andrew McReynolds were already there, talking with the commanding officer.

"Good evening, General," he started. "My compliments and apology for being a little late. I was meeting with my commanders to gauge their opinions of what we might do. Evening, Colonel Ely. Evening, Colonel McReynolds."

"Evening, General Elliott."

"And, what conclusions did you draw?" asked Robert Milroy.

With thoughts of his last meeting with Milroy running through his head, he described the plan. "Well, sir, considering we're running out of food, water, and ammunition, and that we are seriously outmanned and outgunned, we should move out tonight. It looks like Jubal Early has command of the west and the south, especially with the guns he has placed on the high ground. He's got the Valley and Romney Pikes covered, and maybe the Pughtown. Ed Johnson has most likely gone east and north. He probably has the Berryville and Martinsburg Pikes blocked. That leaves us one opening, presuming we are going to leave this place. North, by the back roads over the Apple Pie Ridge. Now, it won't be easy going tonight, but my brigade has volunteered to go out first, with the 122nd Ohio in the lead, covered by cavalry. The commanders are in full agreement that this makes the most sense."

Colonel William Ely and Colonel Andrew McReynolds looked thoughtfully at Washington Elliott, nodding ever so slightly, but offering no verbal support. Elliott was now standing there alone. Major General Robert H. Milroy finally realized the predicament he was in. He ran his left hand through his hair, contemplating what Washington Elliott had just told him.

"Don't think we can take the men out over those back roads. Too many of us. And, with the horses. No, that won't work."

"Begging the General's pardon," Elliott protested, "if we don't do it that way, where are we going to go? And, with the main roads blocked? Do you really want to fight in the dark? Would we even have enough ammunition?"

"General Elliott, I have heard this kind of talk from you and some of your commanders before, and I am tired of it. I want to go to Harper's Ferry tonight, by the Martinsburg Pike, and that's what we're going to do. I want to join the garrison there."

"But, General," Elliott went on, not giving a damn about the inherent political risk. "Understanding Johnson is out there waiting for us, and when we get into a fight that we know we can't win, we are just sacrificing our men for nothing. Why would we do that?"

McReynolds and Ely did not know what to expect next. Elliott getting demoted for insubordination? "General, it seems to me that you are not listening. You, and you other two, will spike your cannon now, and we will take nothing from here except our weapons and ammunition. Abandon everything else. We will go to Harper's Ferry tonight. Get ready to move out at 1 o'clock. General Elliott, your brigade will lead the way. Am I clear?"

Risking nothing, Washington Elliott said, "I don't believe this. It makes no sense. We have a better alternative, and you won't even consider it, just like that? What you want us to do is exactly what General Ewell wants us to do. Old Allegheny Johnson is out there waiting for us, and I wager he has some artillery out there, too. They're lickin' their chops, General. They're going to destroy your command in one night. If that's what you want, so be it!"

"That's enough, General, we are going to Harper's Ferry!"

General Washington Elliott had had it. He flipped a haphazard salute at General Robert Milroy and stormed away, furious, again, with the general's inability to listen to people who might just have a better idea than the one he had. He probably should have expected that. He thought to himself, "Now, I will sacrifice the 122nd, the 110th, and maybe the 87th and 116th since there WILL be a fight tonight. GODDAMMIT!"

The regimental commanders were waiting for him. The meeting with General Milroy had only lasted half an hour. General Washington Elliott told his commanders about the meeting.

"No, Jim," he said to Colonel James Galligher, "we can't just go out the back door on our own, although I would like to. I would be court martialed, and so would you. You would have that stain on your record forever. When the fight starts out there, I will engage the 110th and 122nd with the rest of you bolting like hell north on the Martinsburg Pike. If Bill and Warren can hold them off, you have a decent chance to escape, depending on how much trouble we encounter. It will be wild out there."

"General," replied Colonel James Galligher, "Keifer and Ball will need the protection that Lewis and I can provide. We will go with you, right, Lewis?"

"Yes, Jim."

"Captain Carlin, commence spiking your guns! The rest of you, get as much ammunition as your men can carry. Get with the mess officers to take as much hardtack as you can. The men can take their haversacks and rifles. That's it. We leave this place at 1 o'clock. Lewis, lead the way, the 110th will follow, then the 122nd. The 116th will go next. Colonel Schall, you will be the trailer. Be on the look-out for enemy cavalry and warn us if they engage. You will be supported by Jim Galligher. Warren, take command of the first wave. I must stay back with Wildes, Schall, and Galligher. We will go as we can. Dismissed."

It was close to midnight, the sky black with only a faint light of the moon. "Tom, let's go," said Captain Daniel Gary. We're leaving in an hour or so. Get up and get the men ready. Haversack and rifle, that's all. Get as much ammunition and food as they can take. Form up behind the 110th. Keifer's gonna lead us out. Pierce's cavalry will go first to reconnoiter, then Keifer, then us, then at some time Wildes, Schall, and Galligher. Don't know when they will be coming. Destroy all the equipment, but absolute silence. Johnny's not too far away."

"Yes, Dan. Will do."

"Tom, I don't like this," said Dan Gary. "If there's trouble, which I am sure there will be, we're gonna be in it again. 110th will be first, we'll be right beside. God knows what they have out there. Wish we could've scouted this. Dammit. Get the boys ready."

Tom Armstrong felt a coldness in his chest and fear in his head. His hands were sweating. He knew that this was IT. His fate and that of Milroy's entire command would be decided this day. He got down on his knees and prayed again for deliverance, asking God to be with him.

"Patrick, with Eddie gone, I will have to rely solely on you tonight. It's likely to be rough going. Take charge of the corporals. Tell them to have the men pack around 80 rounds of ammunition and as much hardtack as they can carry. If there is anything left over, have them dump it in the latrines. We're leaving this place for good."

"Shoulda done it yesterday or the day before. Maybe even a week ago."

"Yeah, I know. But this is where we are, and we gotta go, tonight.
"OK, let me get 'em ready."

Tom Armstrong was ever so thankful that Patrick Murphy had been with him. "Protect Patrick, too, Lord," he prayed.

Around half past one, Daniel Gary whispered. "Colonel Ball is back. He's gonna lead us out. Granger's right beside him. They're riding together with the colors. Out the main gate, boys, head northeast. Try to find the Martinsburg Pike. If we should happen to get separated, you're on your own, go north toward Martinsburg. We'll regroup there. Good luck."

The Colonel's staff went out into the night, silently, followed by Moses Granger's people. Captain Joseph Peach led Company A of the 122nd OVI out of Fort Milroy, and the escape was on. Colonel Warren Keifer's 110th, from over near Piqua, Ohio, had gone out first and was well on its way. The path was overgrown, but the boots of the escaping Federals had tamped it down, making the march a little easier. Colonel Lewis Pierce had to find the most cover and the most efficient way to get past the Confederate pickets. Everyone hoped they were asleep, but the men of Robert Milroy's command could see their campfires a short way south.

The men of the 122nd were out. It was about 1:45 AM on Monday, June 15, 1863. Each man followed the man in front of him, silently, matching each footstep, anxiously fearing that hideous Rebel yell that they were sure would come. Everyone worried that, even though they were walking as quietly as they could, the Rebels might just hear them and know that the evacuation of Winchester was underway.

The regiment trudged on, north, towards Martinsburg. It was tough going over the underbrush in the middle of the night, but they had no choice. Tom Armstrong had detailed Patrick Murphy to bring up the rear of Company I to corral any straggler or any of the men who decided that they had had enough and just wanted to go home. Putting one foot in front of the other, trying not to stumble or to make any noise, finally, they reached the Martinsburg Pike. The 122nd O.V.I. moved on for an hour or so when they heard rifle fire out ahead of them. It was a little past 3 o'clock in the morning.

A courier came by nursing his horse carefully in the dark. "Pierce has been attacked by cavalry and artillery as he was crossing that railroad bridge up yonder. I have orders from General Elliott. Follow the 110th up ahead. Keifer's taking it east, off the road. Get out of sight." William Ball screamed the orders to the ten companies of the 122nd.

The next thing they knew, they were under an artillery attack from the woods back across the Martinsburg Pike. The men of the 122nd could see another battery up on a little rise, not 100 feet from Milburn Road, fire belching from the Confederate cannons. Balls whistled over their heads, slamming into the ground behind them. If this was the engagement that Gary had talked about a few hours earlier, they hoped the 87th and 116th, along with Galligher's cavalry were moving cross country to the northeast in escape. But, they also knew that if this was, indeed, IT, they and the 110th would have to hold their position.

Tom Armstrong loaded his Enfield rifle just in case there was more to it than just an artillery barrage. "Men, just like in Winchester yesterday, when you see fire from a rifle, shoot at it." He was standing beside Captain Daniel Gary when the Captain went down.

"Son-of-a-Bitch!" A bullet had torn into his leg, which was bleeding badly. Gary was screaming in pain, and Armstrong knew the Captain would die if he didn't stop the bleeding. So, he took off his neckerchief and shoved it in the hole the bullet had created. Just then, Daniel Gary passed out. Tom Armstrong thought he was dead.

Lieutenant Thomas Black screamed, "Brennan, Simpson, get the Captain to cover. Get him to Dr. Houston and get back here as fast as you can." Thaddeus Brennan and Chesley Simpson picked up the wounded captain and made haste for the rear. They were back twenty minutes later.

"We gotta find Granger and Ball," Black thought. "Tom," he said to Lieutenant Thomas Armstrong, "with Dan down, we gotta tell the Colonel. Why don't you stay here? "You're better at this than I am. I will find them. Simpson and Brennan, you report to Lieutenant Armstrong while I am gone." Tom Black took off to the front of the column with the sad news about the Captain of Company I.

"Gary's down?" asked Colonel William Ball.

"Yes, sir. Took a ball in the right leg. Armstrong patched him up, and we got him to Dr. Houston."

"You are in command, now, Captain Black. Take charge of Company I."

A courier arrived from Colonel J. Warren Keifer. "Colonel Ball, Colonel Keifer has asked General Elliott if he could mount a charge into those woods where he thinks there are infantry and onto that little ridge where the big guns are. He would like you to sit on his right flank."

"Thank you, Lieutenant. Sergeant Rundle, alert the company commanders that we may be asked to rush the enemy as you just heard. Captain Black, get back to your company and prepare to charge." He thought, "I still don't know whose orders to follow."

"Yes, sir, thank you, sir." Tom Black headed back west to find Tom Armstrong to tell him the news.

"Tom," Tom Black blurted out, "for some damn reason, Ball just promoted me to Captain. Sorry, I should have let you tell him about Gary. You would be Captain now."

"Tom," responded Armstrong, "we have more important things to worry about right now. I will help you any way I can." They heard a large commotion out in front of them.

"Keifer's crossed the road into the enemy. We gotta follow." The ground was relatively flat. Artillery fire lighting the way. Colonel Warren Keifer's 110 Ohio had charged the woods where he thought the Confederate infantry was, smashing into his left side. Smoke enveloped the battlefield. The big guns on the hill raged with fury. Rifle fire was now heard.

"We're moving, Tom," said Tom Black. "Looks like we're going right into the woods. Tell the men to fix bayonets."

At this position in the rear of the action, Colonel William H. Ball screamed at a new courier, this one from General Milroy. "Who the hell is in charge around here? We get orders from Keifer and Elliott to sit on the enemy's right flank, and now Milroy says we should charge his left. We haven't heard anything from Elliott or Keifer about this. Whose damn order do we follow, Captain?"

"Just doin' what I'm told, sir. General Milroy wants you to drive the enemy back. Where's Colonel Keifer?"

"How the hell should I know? His company was moving to the northeast. We've lost him."

"You're on your own, then, Colonel."

"Moses, we're ordered into those woods. I think the enemy has big guns in there, too. I know the infantry is in there. Tell the commanders to advance."

The 122nd O.V.I. found some cover in a gully and fired a volley into the woods to see what kind of response they would get. Immediately, that volley was returned with intense rifle and artillery fire. Shrapnel flying everywhere. Bullets smashing into the ground in front of them. The cries of the wounded punctuating the air. Now it was Keifer's turn to issue orders. A courier had told Colonel Ball that Colonel Keifer wished him to charge into the fight. When the orders reached Company I, Armstrong drew the blade at his side, checked to see that the Colt was loaded, and left the Enfield in the gully when Captain Tom Black hollered "CHARGE. ON THE DOUBLE QUICK!"

Out of the gully, they came on a run, cheering wildly, forgetting the peril. When they got to the edge of the woods, they could see the enemy, formed up quickly, and fired a tremendous volley into him. The first line of Rebels went down in a heap. The rest of them retreated swiftly toward the road, followed by the cheering Union soldiers. They stopped still in the cover of the trees, with the Rebels hiding behind the big guns on the ridge. Tom Armstrong saw an artillery shell explode behind them. He looked back across the road. It was John Carlin's 1st West Virginia. Carlin hadn't spiked his guns and General Milroy had ordered. "Now, maybe we have a chance," Armstrong thought to himself. But, at that moment, the Confederate artillery opened fire on Carlin. Armstrong couldn't see what happened, but the fire was returned.

He was hiding behind a big ash tree on the edge of the woods. He heard bullets hitting it. A limb was severed and almost knocked him down. "Damn, this is getting too close. Patrick, stay tight."

He heard Tom Black again, "CHARGE, ON THE DOUBLE QUICK." Out from behind their cover, the men of the 122nd ran up toward the Milburn Road and the Confederate position. They got really close, maybe to within twenty-five yards, staring down the barrel of the Rebel howitzers. A volley of rifle fire greeted them. Armstrong and Murphy knelt, using the body of a horse that had been killed, for cover. Murphy aimed the Enfield and fired. He saw the man with the ramrod fall. "Can't use that gun now. Nobody to load it," he said.

Rifle fire was aimed in their direction. They ducked behind the horse, hearing the bullets tear into the dead animal's flesh. The fight along the line was fierce. Then, it stopped. Curious, Armstrong peeked out from behind the horse and saw the Confederate artillery retiring. The infantry, too.

"CHARGE," was the command. The men of the 122nd were now rejoined by the 110th. Both regiments took off after the Rebel guns and infantry. In hindsight, they should have run the other way, north toward Martinsburg. The next hour was as frightening a time as could be had. The artillery had stopped, turned, and unleashed an awful volley right into the 110th. That didn't stop the attack. The Yankees surged forward cheering and firing at anything that moved. Men were going down right and left as the Rebels unleashed a deadly barrage of fire on them.

Armstrong felt the bottom of his cartridge box. No more bullets for the Colt. All he had left was for an Enfield. He crawled under intense fire to get position, using a dead comrade's body as cover, found his rifle, took ammo out of the cartridge box, loaded, and aimed the big gun at a Confederate officer standing by his cannon. He fired again. The shot blew the man into the air and dropped him dead. He heard the whiz of bullets and felt something tear the sleeve of his jacket. He felt his arm. "No damage," he thought.

"Patrick, stay low. Tell the boys to be careful with their ammo. I don't want to run out. I've got probably 15 rounds for the Enfield. Whattya got?"

"About the same, Lieutenant."

"Send one of your boys back to get more. We're gonna need it. Just stick by me."

"Yes, sir. Boys, shoot only when you have a clear shot. Nothin' else. Corporal Brown, fetch us some more ammo. Get goin.'"

Tom Armstrong and his men were pinned down and were running out of ammunition. They were also running out of hope. Corporal Enoch Brown wasn't gone long. He crawled over beside Lieutenant Tom Armstrong and Sergeant Patrick Murphy. "That son-of-a-bitch. Just heard Keifer's been told it's every man for himself. Straight from Milroy as he was going northeast. That son-of-a-bitch. Sergeant, we're on our own. Dammit."

Patrick Murphy looked at Tom Armstrong and said, "Now what, Lieutenant? Any chance we could make a run for it?"

"It's over, Patrick. We're done for."

The Confederate artillery continued to pound away. The Union forces were starting to lose their nerve. Keifer ordered what was left of the 110th and 122nd to the north. Very few paid any attention. They were exhausted and were starting to walk out into the big field just west of the Milburn Road. They had no more ammunition, the dead and wounded littering the field, the latter screaming for help. There wasn't any. The surgeons in the rear had more work to do than they had ever seen. Later in the day, details would be sent out to bury the dead and to save the wounded who had any chance of survival.

All of a sudden, a cheer erupted from the Confederate force. They had seen a white flag waving near the woods. It's over, boys," Armstrong heard one of the gunners yell. "White flag is up. You Yanks are done!"

Armstrong looked back over the Milburn Road. It was true. Men in blue stacking their arms and sitting down, tired, hungry, and beaten. Apparently, Brigade Commander Colonel William G. Ely had waved the white flag, coming out of the woods west of where the 123rd Ohio was.

Tom Armstrong, Patrick Murphy, and what was left of Company I of the 122nd Ohio Volunteer Infantry rose from their protection and slowly walked across the road toward the exhausted, dirty, defeated Union force of Major General Robert H. Milroy, carrying only their Enfields. Stack 'em here, sir," a dirty, hatless Confederate sergeant said. Armstrong looked at the ragged uniform. He noticed that the soldier wasn't wearing any shoes.

"Your sword and pistol, sir," he demanded. "You are my prisoners."

"I will only surrender my sword to an officer, Sergeant. Go find one."

"What's the problem, Sergeant?"

"Captain, this man won't give me his sword."

"Lieutenant, I am Captain Benjamin Browner of General Johnson's division. I understand your request. That is our way, too. Will you please give me your sword?"

Tom Armstrong slowly and sadly unbuckled the scabbard at his side that contained the weapon the men had given him and presented it to his captor. This was the most embarrassing and humiliating action any officer on either side could take. Armstrong, though, took it like a man.

"All of you will come with me," said Ben Browner.

Certainly, Captain." And, the men of Company I followed Captain Browner to the middle of the field that had had barriers quickly constructed to fence them in.

"Sump," said Patrick Murphy, "where the hell are Black, Simpson, and Brennan? They ain't here."

Lieutenant Thomas Armstrong looked around and was mystified. Captain Tom Black and the two sergeants were gone. "Wonder how that happened?" He didn't know it, but Colonel William H. Ball had called Thaddeus Brennan aside as he and Chesley Simpson delivered the wounded Dan Gary to the rear of the Company and told him to get Tom Black out of the fight. He told them that he, Granger, and as many of the company commanders as possible were going to escape. Upon their return to the front, Brennan relayed Ball's message. In the midst of the fight, the Captain and the two sergeants took off for the rear, escaped the Rebels, and, now, they were on the way to Harper's Ferry. So was Colonel J. Warren Keifer and his staff. Brigadier Washington Elliott, too. The words rang in Tom Armstrong's head: "Every man for himself."

"Over here, gentlemen. Sergeant, get these men some food and water. Lieutenant, I will be back in a few minutes." It would be their last meal for quite some time.

Tom Armstrong thought, "The Lord has delivered me this day. I know not where I am going, but I fear it is that awful place in Richmond: Libby Prison. Patrick will end up at Belle Isle. I may never see him again."

Confederate Captain Benjamin Browner returned. He looked straight at Patrick Murphy. "Sergeant, you will go with Sergeant O'Malley here to where we are holding the enlisted men as prisoners."

"Yes, sir." Turning to Lieutenant Tom Armstrong, Murphy said, "Lieutenant, it has been my honor and pleasure to serve with you, sir." The twinkle gone again. "I hope that someday we will be reunited at home in Ohio."

"No, Patrick, it has been my honor and pleasure." He felt tears welling up in his eyes. "Good luck and may the Good Lord protect you. Perhaps you can get exchanged."

"You, too, Sump."

They shook hands, knowing that, if they survived, they would be friends for life. Sergeant Thaddeus O'Malley walked with Sergeant Patrick Murphy down Milburn Road. Murphy didn't look back.

It was 7 o'clock on the morning of June 15, 1863. The 2nd Battle of Winchester was over. A humiliating defeat for Major General Robert H. Milroy. It could have been avoided altogether, if he had only listened.

9 To Richmond

Confederate Brigadier General Wallace B. Brown was seated at his desk in his headquarters in what used to be known as Fort Milroy when a guard brought two Union soldiers to see him. "Don't look like they were in the fight," he thought to himself. "Look too soft to be anything but staff." Addressing the guard, he inquired, "Why have you brought them to me, Lieutenant? They belong with the other prisoners."

"My compliments, General, and begging your pardon, they have a request, sir."

Not really wanting to be disturbed, Wallace Brown put down his pen, took off his spectacles, and looked at the two Federal officers.

"All right. What do you want?"

"Sir, my name is Charles C. McCabe. I am a minister in the Methodist Church and am the chaplain of the 122nd Ohio Volunteer Infantry. This is Dr. William M. Houston, our regimental surgeon. We would like your permission to return to the field to help as many of the wounded, both ours and yours, as we can. We could have escaped with Colonel Ball and General Milroy, but we decided that the men lying there in the field needed us. When we have ministered to their wounds, we would then request safe passage to Harper's Ferry."

General Wallace Brown studied the two men, pondering their request thoughtfully. "That's quite honorable of you, sir. Most men wouldn't do such a thing. You have my permission. Lieutenant, arrange a detail to assist these men and accompany them back to the field."

"Thank you, General. The wounded will appreciate your kindness," said McCabe. They followed the Lieutenant out of Brown's office through the fort that would house most of the officers and enlisted men who had been captured that morning.

"Lieutenant," said Dr. William Houston, "could we ask some of our men here to help us, too, with a pledge that they not try to escape?" The Confederate soldiers had started escorting their prisoners into the fort a couple of hours earlier.

"Yes, sir, I don't see why not." The young Lieutenant spoke to the guard at the gate, telling him to count off twenty prisoners, who would supplement the Rebel detail that he would oversee.

It was brutal work that hot, humid day in mid-June. Men screaming for help from the doctor and deliverance from God from the chaplain. Men dying where they had fallen. Smoke from the massive cannon still hanging in the air. McCabe deferred to Dr. William Houston as to which of the wounded had a chance to survive. They would then be transported by litter to the makeshift hospital in the Market Street Methodist Church. There would be only emergency treatment on the field. Those who could walk were helped back to Winchester by the Confederate soldiers and Union prisoners to have the surgeons attend to them. The work was completed by 5 o'clock that afternoon. Sadly, they left the field there just west of the Milburn Road, strewn with lifeless bodies. McCabe and Houston returned to the office of Brigadier General Wallace Brown.

After they had reported on the day's work, Brown said to them. "General Early wants to see you. I told him about your ministry to the wounded, and he wants to talk with you. I will take you to his headquarters."

"Probably wants to thank us," the Reverend Charles McCabe thought to himself.

Not quite. Major General Jubal A. Early, with the nickname "Bad Old Man," was walking toward his office with three members of his staff when Brigadier General Wallace Brown approached with Dr. William Houston and the Reverend Charles McCabe. Early dismissed his staff and exchanged introductions with the two Union officers. "General Brown," Jubal Early began, "I will see these gentlemen alone in my office. You may tend to the more pressing matters that concern you."

"As you wish, sir. Good day." Wallace Brown saluted and turned away, back toward his office.

"Now, gentlemen," he began, "General Brown told me about your work, tending to the needs of the wounded. That was very good of you. The General tells me you are a preacher, Reverend McCabe."

"Yes, General, I am. Methodist. And, now that our work here is done, we would ask your permission to pass through to Harper's Ferry."

"Let me tell you something, Reverend. From what I know about the North, it seems to me that men like you ministers have done more to cause the trouble we are now having between us than any other group of people. We did not want this war. You, and men like you, raised the issue of slavery in your churches which, if you had left it alone, we would be at peace. But we are not. And, for your part in causing the trouble by preaching emancipation and stirring up people in the North against our institution of slavery, you and the good Doctor are going to Libby Prison in Richmond with the other captured officers. We will let the commandant there deal with you." He opened the office door and said to an aide who was standing guard, "Lieutenant, please escort these gentlemen to Fort Jackson. Good day, gentlemen."

Charles McCabe was shocked and said, "With the General's permission, I will go to Libby Prison, but Dr. Houston didn't stir anyone up. Please let him go to Harper's Ferry." The request fell on deaf ears.

While all of this was going on, the Confederates continued to herd over 3,000 captured Federals back to Winchester where they would be confined to the three main forts that Major General Robert H. Milroy thought would keep his soldiers safe. Fort Milroy was now known as Fort Jackson in honor of General Stonewall Jackson, with Star Fort and West Fort retaining their names.

The captured Union officers were the first to enter Fort Jackson. The enlisted men would follow. Brigadier General Wallace Brown's staff manned the Main Gate. Just under 150 Union officers, including Lieutenant Tom Armstrong of the 122nd O.V.I.; Lieutenant Caleb Edwards of Carlin's 1st West Virginia Battery; Colonel John

Klunk of the 12th West Virginia; Colonel William Wilson of the 123rd O.V.I.; Colonel William Ely, one of Milroy's brigade commanders; and those from the 18th Connecticut, 5th Maryland, and 87th Pennsylvania. Two thousand captured enlisted men, including Sergeant Patrick Murphy, came through the Main Gate shortly thereafter. The other 1,000 enlisted men were split up between Star Fort and West Fort.

It was just after noon on Monday, June 15, 1863. All Tom Armstrong wanted to do was sleep, but there was no shelter from the sun and its searing heat, nothing to lie down on, and bodies everywhere. Sleep would have to wait as the captured Union soldiers stood in line to be frisked by the Confederate guards to make sure they hadn't brought any weapons in. In the process, however, the guards extended the search of the prisoners to include anything they wanted: watches and money being the primary targets. They did, however, allow the prisoners to retrieve their haversacks, if they could remember where they had left them the night before and if they were still there.

To make matters worse, there was no food, and the Union captives had been up most of the night. Further, they had fought extremely hard that morning and were exhausted. And now, thanks to Major General Robert H. Milroy, they were incarcerated in what used to be their primary defense. But, now it was called Fort Jackson, and they were headed south to Richmond and life in prison.

With the sun beating down, Tom Armstrong decided to see if he could find some drinkable water instead of that brown stuff Patrick Murphy had brought him the day before. As he was walking through Fort Jackson, that Monday afternoon, he heard a familiar voice. "Lieutenant Armstrong, is that you?"

Armstrong turned toward the voice and exclaimed, "Caleb Edwards? They got you, too?"

"Yeah, we were bombing them pretty good, but the ammunition started to run low. Next thing I know, I see Ely coming out of the woods waving a white flag. Not that we had much left, mind you, but we coulda continued shelling the bastards a while longer. You know what Carlin told me? He was going to see Colonel Ball when Milroy rode by shouting that we were on our own. As he galloped to the northeast with his staff, the son-of-a-bitch was leaving us here to cover his escape. Every man for himself. Damn fine leadership, if you ask me," with a touch of sarcasm. "Fine way to run a damn army."

"Heard that Carlin saw him leaving," said Tom Armstrong. "Kinda fits Milroy's character. We had a devil of a time, apparently, trying to get him to go Friday and Saturday. He just wouldn't listen to his brigade commanders. Elliott tried, gave him all the facts and an escape plan for all of us, but Milroy wouldn't listen. Wonder if he'll get court martialed."

"He should," responded Caleb Edwards. "Just leaving us here with no food, no ammo, and 10,000 screaming Rebels. Was told that Elliott and Colonel Keifer got away, too. Your Colonel?"

"Yeah, Elliott wanted the brigade commanders to get out. Colonel Ball ordered the Company commanders out, too. Left me as highest-ranking officer in Co. I. Wonder what that'll mean to Johnny. Carlin gone, too?"

"Yeah, he's gone, Tom. Rebs got most of us, some got away. Got the guns, too. Glad we didn't spike them when Milroy ordered the Captain to do that. Had a whale of a time this morning firing them. Didn't have time to spike them when the surrender came. So, now, the Rebs have the Parrotts and howitzers to turn on us. Dammit."

"They must have captured half of the garrison this morning. I bet Ewell's happy. Early and Johnson, too. Wait'll Ewell tells Lee about this. His confidence is going to soar. Wonder where they're going."

"Don't rightly know. Pennsylvania is all we heard," said Caleb Edwards.

"Ball said something to Granger, I'm told, that General Meade is on the march to meet him. That'll be interesting. Could be epic. 75,000 Rebels and Meade's Corps colliding. Whew."

Edwards wiped his face with his sleeve. "Damn it's hot. Any shelter in here?"

"Nope. Gotta wait for the sun to go down. This trip to Richmond isn't gonna be much fun. Wonder how we'll go."

"Probly find out soon enough."

"What you boys talkin' about?" said a lanky Confederate officer, his uniform dirty and stained with blood. "Ben Johnson, 54th North Carolina."

Tom Armstrong and Caleb Edwards introduced themselves. "Nuthin' much," said Edwards. "Just how we got into this mess." He judged Johnson to be about 6' 2" tall, probably 175 pounds, blond hair under his hat. Pistol in the holster on his right hip. Big knife sheathed on his left leg. Gloves stuck through the epaulets of his uniform.

"Yeah," said Lieutenant Benjamin Johnson, "we were wonderin' why y'all didn't skedaddle out of here when you had the chance. Road to Harper's Ferry was wide open 'till last night when Johnson's brigade came out."

"Well, damn," said Caleb Edwards. "We coulda come out yesterday, even. You might have chased us, but we woulda had a head start."

"All I know, Lieutenant, is that we woulda done just that. Woulda tried to force you into the back of Lee's Corps. Sure, he woulda loved to see that. Y'all would've ended up prisoners anyway."

"Our commander, General Elliott, had a way that you might not have known that we were gone. Coulda gone north over the Apple Pie Ridge. You boys weren't up there, as far as we knew. Coulda gone out one company at a time. You never would have known until now. Instead, you got a whole mess of tired, hungry, and thirsty Yankees."

"Hey, I'm beginning to like y'all. I think I'll be with you on the way to Richmond. Will try to get y'all whatever you need."

"You boys got any water? Clean water, that is, none of that muddy stuff," asked Caleb Edwards.

"Think so. Come with me."

And so, the three lieutenants, two Yankees and one Rebel sauntered across Fort Jackson to find something to drink.

Armstrong remembered wondering if the Confederates had the same thoughts, fears, and emotions about going to war as he did. "Guess I've got a way to find out, now," he thought to himself.

Lieutenant Benjamin Johnson led the two Yankees to the hastily arranged Officers' Mess where they did, indeed, get a cup of cool, fairly clear water. Officers and men of both sides were milling around; some just sitting, talking, presumably about the day's events; and some trying to get some shuteye. Johnson allowed that he was from a little town in northwest North Carolina called Millers Creek. Said that the 54th came from all the little towns and villages out there.

"Only a couple hundred live in the Creek. But we gotta store, a church, and a saloon. School's in the center of town. My momma teaches there. Town's up on the Blue Ridge in Wilkes County. We gotta farm just west of there. Pappy's gotta big still out in the barn. Uses the corn. Makes white lightning'. Darn fine stuff. Sells it all over the county. Y'all ever had any?"

"Can't say as I have," said Tom Armstrong. "Not sure I want to."

"You got any?" asked Caleb Edwards, eager for the chance to take a swig.

"Nah. Mebbe I can find some for y'all on the way to Richmond."

"Might take my mind off our troubles," Edwards thought to himself. "What great luck. We got a friend who makes 'shine."

"What y'all do before the war?"

The conversation lasted until the sun went down and torches were lit throughout the Fort. Armstrong and Edwards told Johnson about their lives prior to the war. The Rebel Lieutenant seemed genuinely interested, asking some good questions about life in the North. "Sure is different than how we live down here. Y'all have all those big cities. Boston, New York, Washington, Philadelphia. All we got is 'Lanta, Richmond, Nawlens, and, right in North Carolina, Raleigh. But, they ain't anywhere near what y'all got."

"I suppose not," said Tom Armstrong, thinking to himself, "He's a lot like me in some ways. Though, I can't see Father out in the barn making moonshine with a still." He smiled at the thought. But, then he heard something familiar.

Mine eyes have seen the glory
Of the coming of the Lord
He is trampling out the vintage
Where the grapes of wrath are stored
He has loosed the fateful lightning

Of his terrible swift sword
His truth is marching on.

Glory, glory, hallelujah
Glory, glory, hallelujah
Glory, glory hallelujah
His truth is marching on.

"Why, that's Charlie McCabe," he said. "Our Regimental Chaplain and a good friend of mine. He must have gotten himself captured. Didn't think you guys did that to Chaplains."

"Usually not," said Lieutenant Ben Johnson. "He musta made somebody mad."

When the Reverend Charles C. McCabe finished *The Battle Hymn of the Republic,* he launched into *We are Coming Father Abraham*, then *My Country 'Tis of Thee*. The voices of the captured Union soldiers became louder and louder until it seemed like the whole fort was in song with the Chaplain of the 122nd Ohio Volunteer Infantry in the lead.

"Fellas," he said to Edwards and Johnson, "I want to go see him. Where're you gonna spend the night?"

"Right here, I guess. OK with you, Ben?"

"Sure, why not?"

Tom Armstrong headed in the direction of the loudest singing and saw Charles C. McCabe standing on a hardtack box, waving his hands as if he was directing a choir. Well, actually he was. When he finished the last stanza of *The Star-Spangled Banner*, he noticed Armstrong standing to the side under a burning torch, climbed down, and went to see his friend. The two of them shook hands.

"Thomas, it is good to see you," said the Chaplain. "I was worried that you were killed or wounded. I mean, I wish we weren't here, but at least we're alive."

"For now," Armstrong said. "Heard Libby Prison is a nasty, awful place."

"Stick with me, T.S. The Good Lord will see us through."

The conversation lasted well into the evening and concentrated mostly on the behavior of Major General Robert H. Milroy. Charles

McCabe said that he didn't understand it either. Colonel William H. Ball had told him all about it, and McCabe was actually quite astonished.

"He went to the Baptist church in town oftentimes, just like you went to Market Street Methodist. The only times I conversed with him, I really enjoyed his company and his tales about his life in Indiana before the war. A lot of the men liked him and thought he was a fine commanding officer."

"Huh?" was all Tom Armstrong could muster. And, then, "I didn't know him at all, only what Ball, Granger, and Gary told me. Doesn't sound like the same man. By the way, you did know that Dan is in a hospital bed in the Clark Street Methodist Church. Almost had his leg blown off."

"So, I heard, from Dr. Houston. You know that William is coming with us."

"Didn't know that. Why?"

"Apparently, we upset General Early while we were asking for our release. He blamed me for the war and inciting the spirit of emancipation in the North. Hopefully, we can get exchanged soon."

The two friends said, "Good Night" and shook hands, promising to find each other in the morning. Tom Armstrong moseyed back to the Officers' Mess where he found Caleb Edwards and Benjamin Johnson talking, just like he had left them. He hadn't realized how hungry he was, but a solution to that problem would have to wait until morning. You see, General Richard Ewell had planned the attack on the Union forces at Winchester, but he had not developed a strategy for dealing with prisoners-of-war, including providing food, water, and rest. And, it is doubtful that he knew that over 3,000 Yankees would be captured, so even if he did have a strategy, it couldn't have dealt with the situation that was presented to him that day in June, 1863.

Armstrong lay down outside the Officers' Mess. He said his prayers, thanking God for sparing him from death or being wounded, asking to be forgiven for what he had done that morning, and asking for strength and courage in the face of what would happen over the next day, weeks, and possibly months. It didn't take long for sleep to overcome him. Caleb Edwards was snoring lightly next to him, but that didn't matter. He was exhausted.

Reveille came early on Tuesday, June 16, 1863. The Union officers who had been taken prisoner marched, under guard of a company of the 54th North Carolina, out of Fort Jackson to the southeast toward Winchester. When they entered the town, they were herded down Boscawen Street toward the magnificent courthouse that stood on the corner at Kent Street. The front lawn was surrounded by an iron fence which made for a good barrier to keep the prisoners inside. Armed guards stood at the four corners of the makeshift stockade and in the middle of each side.

The people of Winchester jeered at them, taunting with all sorts of epithets, some of which the soldiers had never heard before. Bands were playing, the people were singing *Dixie*, and it looked like one big celebration there in the center of town. One by one, members of the 54th North Carolina, General Jubal Early's men, took the officers into the courthouse where they were interrogated as to their name, rank, regiment, hometown and state, and their commanding officer. Lieutenant Thomas Armstrong and Lieutenant Caleb Edwards were processed with the others and answered the Confederates' questions with short responses, just answering their queries with as few words as possible. When they were finished, they came out into the hot sunshine and saw other officers digging latrines outside of the fence. They learned they would have to have permission from the guards to use one. But, they were still very hungry and thirsty.

While Colonel William G. Ely was being questioned, he told the interrogating officer that there was food and clothing in one of the warehouses down Boscawen Street. The officer, in turn, reported that to Captain Augustus Martin of Company G of the 54th North Carolina, who dispatched a detail to go get all of it. The men came back to the courthouse with boxes of hardtack, dried meats and fruit, and potatoes. Another squad came back with buckets of clear water they had taken out of Abram's Creek. Captain Martin made sure that all 144 of the Federal officers were fed and had plenty of water.

Tom Armstrong, taking a bite of dried pork, said, "You know, Caleb, this is pretty darn good," feeling better than he had in a couple of days. "When we get done here, I want to find Chaplain McCabe. He wants to travel with us and will need our help. Don't think he's ready for a walk to Staunton."

"That where we're going? I thought it was Richmond."

"I learned from the Chaplain last night that we will march to Staunton and then take a train to Richmond. It's over 200 miles from here, I think, southeast. No railroad between here and Staunton, so we gotta walk."

"Damn! How far is Staunton?"

"Reckon it's about 100 miles south of here. Don't know when we're starting out, but it's gonna be hot. Hope they know where to find water on the way."

"Tom," said Caleb Edwards, "you think we could escape while we're going there? I mean at night; how would they know?"

"Never thought of that, Caleb. Keep the thought, and when we get going, we can see if it would be possible. I'm game if you are. But I wouldn't take Charlie McCabe. He'd slow us down. So, we can't tell him if that's what we decide to do."

"Gotcha."

Armstrong and Edwards spotted the Chaplain sitting on the courthouse steps. It was starting to get really hot, and the celebration of the townsfolk was starting to get on their nerves. "Wish that band would shut the hell up," groused Caleb Edwards. "Wish I had some of Johnson's 'shine."

"Captain McCabe, this is Lieutenant Caleb Edwards of Carlin's 1st West Virginia Battery," said Tom Armstrong.

"Pleasure, Captain. Seen you at the Methodist Church a few times since we been here. I'm Baptist from over in Wheeling, but I liked those Methodist services, especially the preaching and the singing."

Edwards and Armstrong had made it a habit to come down from Bower's Hill on Sunday mornings to the Market Street Methodist Church at the corner of Cameron and Cork Streets, just a block away from their current predicament.

The Reverend Charles McCabe said, "Nice to meet you Lieutenant. I may have seen the two of you up there in the balcony from time to time. Can I call you Caleb?"

"Sure, Reverend. You can call me whatever you want."

The conversation returned to the escape of Major General Robert H. Milroy, his staff, General Washington Elliott, and Colonel Andrew McReynolds.

"Reverend," said Caleb Edwards, "did they just leave us high and dry? Saving their own skin and sacrificing us? How about Colonel Ball and Lieutenant Colonel Granger and the company commanders?"

"Caleb, I can't speak for General Milroy, but I do know that he issued orders to the brigade commanders to head for Harper's Ferry. Ely didn't make it out as you know, the other two went as ordered. I also know that General Elliott told his Regimental commanders to leave with as many of their company commanders as they could. Ball, then, issued like orders. They hope to reform the Regiment at Harper's Ferry. Dr. Houston and I were supposed to go to, but as I told Tom last night, we wanted to minister to, and save, as many of the wounded as we could. We did that, and now we're both here. Goodness knows what will befall us in the coming days."

"So, you think their leaving the field and hightailing it to Harpers Ferry was a good thing to do?" asked Caleb Edwards.

"I think the General realized he had made a serious mistake and knew, when he saw the events of this morning, that the day would be costly. But, I think he also knew that this army needs leadership if we are to be victorious and wanted to get his commanders out of harm's way, unfortunately sacrificing you and the others in the process. Command forces men to make very serious decisions, and in war, Caleb, sometimes those decisions send men to their deaths. Some will also be wounded or captured. That is war, and you have seen the worst of it today. And, it will be most unpleasant at Libby Prison, I can assure you."

"Yeah, I've seen the elephant all right," said Edwards. "It was horrible to see, and, as I think about it, our big guns were doing the same thing to them as Early's were doing to us. We know we caused a lot of casualties; we just don't know how many and didn't have to look 'em in the eye when we did. Tom, here, and his boys had a bad couple of days."

"Yes, he did, Caleb, but he knew what he was getting into. He'd been here before."

"Doesn't make any difference, Caleb," said Tom Armstrong, addressing the Chaplain. "I killed men today with my rifle and sword. Busted one man's head wide open. I wounded them with my pistol. At the time, my job was to fight, regardless of the circumstances, and fight I did. It was exciting until I saw the white flag. Now, what I did is starting to sink in."

"Thomas," said Charles McCabe. "Caleb has a good point. It takes two to make a fight. They were trying to kill you as well. It's terrible to look into the enemy's eyes knowing that one of you may end up dead, but that's war. You knew this when we met in my office last August. You also had placed your faith and trust in God. Have you spoken with Him about what happened here today?"

"Yes, Charlie, I just don't feel good about what happened here over the last three or four days or about what I did."

"Thomas, the Lord has listened to you in the past, as you know. He will again. Say your prayers and ask forgiveness."

"I will, Charlie, I will."

"You will remember this for the rest of your life, but the hurt and sadness you feel right now will slowly disappear. You can count on it."

"Thanks, Charlie. I hope so. We gonna go to Richmond together?"

"I'd like that, T.S."

So, it was settled. The two lieutenants would accompany the Chaplain of the 122nd O.V.I. on their way to prison in Richmond. The rest of the day was spent talking about home, wondering what was going on there, how the family was, and listening to rumors about the treatment they would receive at the notorious Libby Prison, "Rat Hell," someone called it.

Their Confederate captors were trying to figure out how they would get over 3,000 men to prison. Colonel Kenneth Murchison would lead the 54th North Carolina. Colonel Francis Board would command the 58th Virginia. They would guard the prisoners all the way to Richmond, but they would also provide for them. While the Federal officers were resting in their fenced-in quarters, the Confederates were packing supply wagons and making sure of the route that would take them nearest to water on a direct path to Staunton. From there, they would head east on the Virginia Central Railroad, so all of those arrangements had to be made.

Sitting with his back against the first step into the courthouse, Tom Armstrong saw Lieutenant Benjamin Johnson approaching. He asked, "You boys need anything, like shoes, socks, cap? We found some new uniforms over yonder in that warehouse. Thought y'all might need somethin'."

"Nah, Ben. I think we are all right. Thanks, though."

"You play cards, Tom?"

"Not very well. What do you have in mind?"

"Any game that will pass the time. Poker, whist, euchre. Name it."

"Can't play poker since we Methodists don't gamble. Got a place to play?"

"How 'bout we play right here. You play euchre?"

"Nah, don't play cards at home. Only in Camp and not very often."

"Caleb," Ben Johnson said to Caleb Edwards, "up for a little euchre this afternoon?"

"Sure. I'll help ol' Tom here learn the game."

Looking at him, Caleb Edwards said, "Yer in the army, Thomas, my boy, you gotta learn sometime." And the game was on.

"Maybe God doesn't care if I play cards," Tom Armstrong thought to himself. "Bet He's got better things to do."

"Let me see if Lieutenant Jim Martin wants to get in," said Ben Johnson.

Several lively games of euchre consumed the rest of the afternoon. It was time for supper, and the Federal officers ate well. They lit some campfires, under the close scrutiny of their guards, sat around, and Charles McCabe led them in song. That relieved some of the fear, dread, and sadness that many of them felt, but those emotions would return quite frequently.

Ben Johnson was enjoying the songfest as well since he knew many of the ones that were being sung. He even sang along at times.

"Ben," Tom Armstrong asked, "what happens if one or two of our boys try to escape on the journey to Richmond?"

"Lieutenant Benjamin Johnson patted the holster strapped to his right hip. "Easy, Tom. We'd just have to shoot 'em."

"What happens if one gets away but gets recaptured?"

"Probly hang 'im. Jus' find a good tree."

The journey would take the Federal prisoners straight down the Valley Pike to Staunton. They would pass through Strasburg, Woodstock, New Market, and Harrisonburg and eventually end up in Staunton. It would be hot and dusty. Many of the men, not being used to marching day after day, having spent six months in Winchester, would have a hard time of it. It would be especially difficult for the officers like Colonel William Ely who hadn't marched at all, riding his trusty horse while his men walked. It would prove to be unpleasant and painful, marching under guard to prison.

As the sun began to set, Colonel Kenneth Murchison ordered the prisoners into formation for *Roll Call*. The prisoners lined up, alphabetically by state and then numerically by regiment number. Then, Captain Augustus Martin conducted the *Roll Call*. "All present and accounted for, Colonel." This would be a frequent occurrence over the next several days.

Tom Armstrong told Caleb Edwards what Ben Johnson had said about trying to escape. "So, we have a choice. Do we risk getting shot or hanged? Or, do we live in Rat Hell for who knows how long? May die there of starvation or disease. May get shot for no reason."

"Ain't very good choices, Tom."

"Nope, let's just see what happens on the march."

They slept well, there by the courthouse steps, the bugler interrupting their sleep as dawn broke. *Roll Call* again, and then, there was food and water. They started thinking that if captivity was like this, maybe it wouldn't be so bad and sure as hell would be better than being shot on the battlefield. They would soon be bitterly disappointed. It was Wednesday. June 17, 1863.

The order came down from General Jubal Early that the prisoner march would commence the following day as soon as the supply wagons were loaded and ready to go. That meant that this day would be one of rest for the Federal prisoners. Armstrong, Edwards, and McCabe pored over a map of Virginia that Ben Johnson had gotten them and were pleased that they would not be heading up into the hills of western Virginia like Massanutten Mountain. The Confederate lieutenant had also slipped Caleb Edwards a bottle.

There would be hills to negotiate, but for the most part, it was a straight shot south. The day would be spent sleeping, eating, playing cards, and making sure they had the right accoutrements for such a journey. Socks and shoes were of the utmost importance. So was a hat or cap. They could carry some provisions in their haversacks, but nothing else. They could also fill their canteens with water.

They were told that they would line up like they did for *Roll Call*. Caleb Edwards and Tom Armstrong would be split up, but, after a day on the march, when the Confederates saw men dropping back, general confusion in the ranks, and a lack of discipline, they would give up on that idea. Now, the plan was for Caleb Edwards to walk on the Chaplain's right with Tom Armstrong on his left.

"Fellas," said Lieutenant Benjamin Johnson, "We leave tomorrow. There's only four hundred of us now left in the 54th. I'm told by Colonel Murchison that the 3,000 enlisted men from the three forts will be transported and guarded by most of the 54th North Carolina and all of Board's 58th Virginia. Then he told me that my company, Company G, will guard y'all. So, y'all will have to put up with me for the next week. We'll make sure that y'all don't get into any trouble."

"Glad you're coming with us, Ben," said Tom Armstrong. Shaking hands with Johnson he said, "Not looking forward to the trip or what lies ahead. Just heard that General Meade's Corps is on his way to meet General Lee. Sounds like something big is gonna happen."

"Yeah, heard the same thing. Wish we were goin' there instead of watching y'all. Jus' like sittin' with young 'uns. But, orders is orders. Colonel Murchison is commanding on the way to Richmond. He ain't real happy about this duty either, puttin' up with a mess of Yankee officers."

Colonel Kenneth M. Murchison of the 54th North Carolina called the captured Union officers together. Colonel William G. Ely, commander of Major General Robert H. Milroy's 2nd Brigade, was the ranking officer of the Federals and issued the order to form up. Colonel Murchison thanked Colonel Ely and proceeded to tell the men what was going to happen on the way to Richmond. He said that they would have some freedom, as opposed to the restricted behavior imposed on the enlisted men, as long as there was no trouble from them. There would be guards, of course, since he had orders to deliver them to Libby Prison, but he added that he wanted the journey to be as comfortable as possible, given the circumstance. It would not be a forced march but rather an orderly procession with frequent stops for rest and water. He said he understood the hardship that they have endured, but that he had his orders which he hoped all of the captured officers could respect. If, however, there was insubordination or other deviant behavior, he would order a forced march or some other punishment. Colonel William Ely thanked the Colonel for his kindness and issued a strong warning to the Yankee captives.

"You men will behave as prescribed in the *Tactics*. You will not deviate from our way of doing things. You will not try to escape. You will do what Colonel Murchison and his officers order you to do when they tell you to do it. The enlisted men will not have the freedom you will so appreciate the Captain's gift. Am I clear, gentlemen?"

"Yes, sir," came the unified response.

Tom Armstrong looked at Caleb Edwards and said, "Do you really think Ely was serious about escaping? If we can get away, what's he gonna do? If we don't get away, it will be very painful." They went to see the Chaplain.

The Reverend Charles C. McCabe had stuffed some of his books into his haversack. He thought they might be useful in killing time in prison. He had developed quite a library in his office at the Regimental headquarters in Winchester. He had even held some classes in math and philosophy for the men to relieve their boredom. He couldn't get enough copies for all of them, so he lectured and then had question and answer sessions to stimulate discussion. As they talked, the Chaplain suggested that Armstrong and Edwards might want to read a little this Wednesday afternoon. He also suggested that he might resume the classes when they were confined at Libby Prison. Tom Armstrong found *Robinson Crusoe* and commenced to turn the pages. Caleb Edwards saw a book on the Mexican War and thought he might learn something. The bugle call for supper was heard. More reading after the meal. Then, it was lights out, and the men bound for prison in Richmond extinguished their campfires and went to sleep.

"Gentlemen," Colonel Ely announced, "we leave as soon as the supply wagons are ready. Colonel Murchison estimates that will be sometime this morning." He looked at the western sky. "Thunderstorms comin'. Just what we don't need," he said to himself.

With Colonel Kenneth Murchison in the lead, color bearers right behind, the procession moved out of Winchester at just about noon on Thursday, June 18, 1863. Bands were playing Confederate songs; the citizens and soldiers were singing along. Taunts and jeers were flung at the Union officers as they walked out of the courthouse yard toward the Valley Pike. The officers of the 54th North Carolina rode along behind Colonel Murchison at the start but would be detailed to the back once the march commenced in earnest.

The men of the Union army didn't know it, but, at about the same time, the main gate at Fort Jackson swung open, and Colonel Francis Board, commander of the 58th Virginia, started another procession toward Richmond to the insults and catcalls of the residents. Approximately 2,000 Federal prisoners, enlisted men, in line of march by state and regiment number, walked slowly out into the sunlight, guarded by the men of the 58th Virginia. They had been kept inside the walls of the Fort for three days with little to eat and brown water. They would follow along behind the officers.

The following day, Captain L.R. Paschall and the remainder of the 54th North Carolina led the 1,000 enlisted men who had been captured out of Star Fort and West Fort to the savage epithets being thrown at them by the citizens. They would join the prisoners of Colonel Murchison and Colonel Board when they arrived in Richmond.

When they reached the Valley Pike, the captured Federals were glad to find that it was made of stone, flat, but with a small crown. Even so, it would still be dusty. The Pike was about thirty feet wide, so the soldiers could walk in groups of two or three fairly comfortably. Better yet, the Pike was wide enough for the supply wagons to pass through. But, you had to watch your step, especially if your shoes were worn or you didn't have any. Horses had been through there, leaving piles of manure.

Farmers along the way came out to see the parade of Yankee soldiers. One of them called out, "Hey, y'all don't look any different than our boys. Uniform's different, and they got guns and you don't, but that's about all that's different." Some of them brought water, some of the women even brought food. Darn good thing because when the thunderstorm struck, there wouldn't be dinner that day. And strike the thunderstorm did. Five miles out of Winchester, everyone heard it roll down off the mountains to the west. Lightning flashed in the sky. They were out in open territory, just plain out of luck. No place to hide. No shelter, even for the Confederate guards. It lasted about forty-five minutes. Everyone was wet clear through. "Don't need a bath now," thought Tom Armstrong. For the first time, though, he noticed that the Reverend Charles C. McCabe exhibited fright.

They kept on going, passing through Newtown/Stephensburg around 5 o'clock. Two miles on the southern side of the town, they heard the order to halt. The people of this town weren't any kinder to the Union soldiers than the people of Winchester had been. Looked like the town was starting to decline a bit. Lawns and flower beds weren't being kept up, and some of the stores on Main Street, the Valley Pike, were vacant. "Bet this once was a nice little village," Caleb Edwards said to Tom Armstrong.

"Bet so. No railroad, though. Hard to get produce to market. Probly have to take it to Winchester."

"Probly."

Rain resumed. The prisoners were ordered into a field by a big lake, west of the Pike, and were told that was where they were going to spend the night. In the mud with no rations, no shelter and only hardtack to eat.

"Hadn't rained, coulda gone for a swim," remarked Armstrong.

"At least taken a bath." Charles McCabe looked a little more relaxed, even as the rain dripped off his hat.

"How you boys gettin' along?" asked Lieutenant Benjamin Johnson.

"Not bad, I guess, for being a prisoner-of-war," Tom Armstrong replied.

"Maybe I can speak to the Colonel to see if he can get you exchanged. Wouldn't hurt.

"Thanks, Ben. Much obliged. Let me know what he says."

The rain slowed about 7 o'clock, with some wood gotten from a supply wagon, fires were lit for warmth, light, and to dry their soggy clothing. Armstrong, Edwards, and McCabe wished they had some pork and potatoes. They were permitted to make a pot of coffee, nice and hot, to warm the insides. The three men nestled into some brush, under a tree. McCabe started to sing. Soon, there were 144 Union voices singing *The Battle Hymn of the Republic*. Colonel William Ely didn't think this would be considered deviant behavior, but he sought out Colonel Kenneth Murchison just in case.

The procession had made ten miles that first day. Only eighty-five more to Staunton.

"You bearin' up, Chaplain?" asked Caleb Edwards.

"Not used to this, I'm afraid," came the response from Charles McCabe. "I may have to slow down and leave you. Maybe I can talk to Colonel Ely about riding in a wagon."

"Good idea. We got a long way to go. It's gonna be difficult. There's a climb comin'. Come see us whenever we stop for the night."

They slept, not well, with pangs of hunger interrupting their slumber. Friday, June 19, dawned thick with humidity, and it was hot which would make the march even more difficult. The Union officers and their captors broke camp at 7 A.M., walking south down the Valley Pike. They saw Three Top Mountain to the south and east, and turning, there was Little North Mountain on the north and west.

"Hope we're not going over those," Tom Armstrong thought to himself.

262

They trudged on, but some of the older officers started to fall back. They just weren't used to it, but they didn't know that Colonel Kenneth Murchison had orders to be in Staunton no later than the next Tuesday, the 23rd. And, they also didn't know that the good Colonel followed his orders to a tee. If he had to be in Staunton next Tuesday, by God, that's what he would do.

Colonel Kenneth Murchison and Company G of the 54th North Carolina led the Union officers through Strasburg just after noon. "So, this is where Hitch and Lindsay met," Armstrong thought. "Wonder which saloon it was. Nice town." It was. There were churches on some of the street corners, people shopping in the stores, and men walking in and out of the three saloons there on Main Street. Armstrong noticed two very well-kept hotels, and there was a school, he had seen, on the northern edge of the town, with another on the main street. The column was given rest in a grove along the North Fork of the Shenandoah River. They could fill their canteens there. For some reason, Armstrong thought, "I wonder how Patrick is doing. Better than most, I imagine." Then, it was time to go.

They continued on and finally came to another town, Woodstock it was called. The men noticed that the fields were barren, all of the crops taken to feed the competing armies, but it looked a lot like Newtown/Stephensburg, in an advancing state of decline. You see, war has an impact on the population as a whole, not just on soldiers. They set up camp south of the town, near a small lake, when it started to rain again, but on this day, they spied a couple of barns close by. Colonel William Ely asked permission for the men to use them as shelter. Colonel Murchison allowed as how that would be just fine. Twenty miles this day. Sixty-five left to go.

Two squads of half a dozen riders each left the column just after *Roll Call* on Saturday, June 20, 1863. Lieutenant Ben Johnson was leading one of them. Seems like there were a couple of missing men during *Roll Call*. Colonel Murchison ordered the column to get moving so off marched the 142 captured officers of Milroy's command at Winchester. The terrain started to rise, making the trek more strenuous, especially for staff officers like Charles C. McCabe. In fact, the night before, he had asked Colonel William Ely if he could ride in a wagon, a request that was granted. There was the Chaplain riding in the back of a supply wagon at the end of the line.

"Wonder where those two went," Caleb Edwards asked. "If they get caught, they're in for a heap of trouble."

"Let's see what happens," said Tom Armstrong. "If they aren't, we can presume they got away which might increase our chances."

They passed through Willow Grove, just four miles south of Strasburg. The town was almost deserted. Two miles later, they were in Edinburg. Unlike Willow Grove, this village looked like it was surviving, but the fields around it looked barren just like outside Woodstock. Foraging, therefore, was not an option. The captured officers would have to rely on their captors for food. They hoped there was enough.

They walked down Main Street right through the center of the town, passed a couple of churches, some stores, and a school. And, of course, they were getting yelled at and cursed by the locals. That was getting tiresome, but the Yankees always responded with humor, trying to get the citizens to lighten up. It didn't work. A couple hours later, the procession came to a halt at Bowman's Crossing by the North Fork of the Shenandoah River. It was time to eat and rest. The day was heating up, and there was no shade. Thank goodness, there was water to wash down the hardtack and dried fruit.

They passed some mills on the banks of the river as they trudged further south into Dixie, the big wheels of the mills turning with the current of the river. Nearing Mount Jackson, seven miles south of Edinburg, the officers heard riders coming in. One of the search parties had returned with two men bound with ropes, being dragged along by two horsemen, stumbling as they went.

"Uh, oh," said Tom Armstrong. "This isn't going to be pretty."

He heard one of the members of the search party say, "Caught 'em running through a field up there by Woodstock in broad daylight. Shoulda hid during daylight and run in the dark. Dumb ass, Yankees."

The column halted and was ordered into formation. The two officers were made to sit on empty hardtack boxes in front of them, hands and feet bound with rope.

Armstrong heard the Colonel order, "Dig the graves." A detail of six men got shovels out of one of the supply wagons and began digging behind the officers. "Chaplain, do you want to pray with them?"

"Yes, Colonel," said Charles McCabe. He approached the two men, one of whom was whimpering like a baby. The other looked just plain angry. Both men knew what was going to happen that Saturday afternoon in June. So did everybody else. It took about an hour for the gravediggers' work to be done. Orders were given to the men of the 54th North Carolina.

"Count off, by fives! Lieutenant Martin, prepare the weapons." Tom Armstrong heard the Rebels count off. "ONE, TWO, THREE, FOUR, FIVE."

The Colonel continued, "Those of you who are Number Three step forward. Eight members of the Regiment stepped forward. You may choose your weapon."

Unbeknownst to them, seven of the weapons had live ammunition. One did not, containing a blank cartridge. "Gentlemen, one of these guns does not carry live ammunition. So, you do not know which one of you is holding it. Each of you may assume that it is yours. So, when the order to fire is given, you may assume that you have not killed either of these men."

Chaplain Charles McCabe finished saying The Lord's Prayer and listening to the supplications of the two men. Blindfolds were tied around their heads. They were ordered to stand.

"Proceed, Lieutenant."

"Don't shoot me," cried one of the blindfolded soldiers. "I don't want to die!"

"READY!" The firing squad stood at attention. "AIM!" Rifles were lifted into place, the two Union officers trembling visibly. "FIRE!"

Fire erupted from the Rebel rifles as the rest of the captured Federals looked on in horror. The bullets from the guns drove the bodies of the men who had tried to escape backwards into the graves that had just been dug.

"Finish your work," came the order. The gravediggers began piling dirt on the lifeless bodies.

Turning toward the Union officers, Colonel Kenneth Murchison began, "I told you, and your Colonel told you, not to try anything. These men did not listen, and now they have paid the price. You, too, will pay a price. There will be no rations tonight. I will not tolerate disobedience. You can be sure of that." He wheeled away, mounted his horse, and rode on. It didn't take long for the graves to be filled and for the march to begin again. They arrived in New Market at 7 o'clock. Twenty miles again. Forty-five to Staunton.

Tom Armstrong muttered to Caleb Edwards, "I guess we know now what they will do if we don't get away. And, the farther down this road we go, the less likely it is that we'll succeed." They'd found a stable that would serve as shelter for the night.

"That answers that question. We're going to jail, Tom," came the reply. "I will never forget what happened back there. I don't care how long I live."

"Colonel got what he wanted. Won't be any more escapes now. Never seen anything like that. They didn't waste any time. Whew!"

The Federal officers had a hard time falling asleep that night given the events of the day. Two of their friends were now lying in shallow graves along the Valley Pike somewhere in central Virginia. Colonel William Ely stared at the ceiling of the stable. "I will have to tell their families. What the hell do I say?" he thought to himself. "These boys mean business." William Ely never wrote or sent the letters.

The march was a little more than half way to Staunton, and Ely did not want any more incidents like the one that happened that day.

After *Roll Call* the next morning, he asked Colonel Murchison if he could address his men in private. "Gentlemen, I trust there will be no more foolish escapades like the one that happened yesterday. I realize that we are going to prison. But, if anyone tries that again and gets caught, which will most likely happen, you will be shot by a firing squad just like we saw done yesterday. And, I guarantee you, the punishment on the rest of us will be severe, more than just not having rations. I'm not sure what it will be, but I have heard of instances where one of us will be singled out, how I don't know, and that unlucky man will be shot or hanged as well. Do not do anything so foolish as to try to get away. You don't know the roads, and they do. Am I clear?"

"Yes, sir," came the response.

"Ben," asked Caleb Edwards. "Was that really necessary, what happened yesterday? Tom and I thought you might have been jokin' a little about shootin' or hangin' an escaped prisoner."

"Wasn't joking a'tall. Told y'all what would happen. Better believe what the Colonel says. Oh, yeah, I spoke to the Colonel about y'all being exchanged. Not his decision, he told me. Y'all hafta take it up with the commandant of the prison."

"Drat. Thought as much."

The journey continued on, ending at Harrisonburg around 3 o'clock in the afternoon of Sunday, June 21, 1863. The Union officers were corralled into a fenced-off area around the courthouse which was a perfect stockade. Chaplain Charles C. McCabe told Colonel William Ely that he would conduct a worship service for the men at 5 o'clock and invited any of their captors to participate as well if they so choose. It would be nothing special, but McCabe knew that the next time he could arrange a service would be inside the walls of Libby Prison. He led the men in song, recited some scriptures from memory, and then preached a sermon of hope, asking God's grace for all of them.

The march was beginning to take its toll on the Union officers. They had been walking for four days and were tired, sore, and sick. But, they had to go on. Colonel Murchison had his orders. The train would be waiting for them in Staunton on Wednesday morning. The depot was still thirty miles away. Some of the men wondered if they would make it. Some were helped by the healthy ones. Some just dropped to the side of the road. Some even wondered if death, itself, was better than what they were going through and would go through once they got to Richmond. Neither Tom Armstrong or Caleb Edwards was feeling very well, both physically and mentally. They both knew they would need God's help to survive whatever was going to happen next, if that was, indeed, His will. Fifteen miles this day. Thirty left to Staunton.

Roll Call on Monday morning, June 22, 1863, went off without a hitch. The column moved out at 7 o'clock, passing through Bridgewater around 10, having made seven miles. It was a nice little town with houses and stores kept up very well. This was a mill town on the North River and looked like it was quite prosperous. As the Yankees walked by, they heard the hate being spewed by the residents, and, by now, they just chose to ignore it. The men plodded on, shuffling their feet in the heat and dust of the road. It was a struggle to breathe. But, they reached Verona around 4:30 in the afternoon. They covered twenty miles and now were only ten miles from Staunton.

They were taken to an open field, just west of the Middle River. Tom Armstrong decided he needed a bath to wash off the dust and grime, explained that to one of the guards, walked over to the river, and jumped in, clothes and all. It was still plenty hot so his clothes would be dry by suppertime.

The Chaplain once again led them in the singing of patriotic songs, but Charles McCabe could tell that the reality of what was going to happen was really starting to sink in. The laughter wasn't there. The gusto with which the songs had been sung earlier in the journey was lacking. He just hoped that the men were not giving up hope. That was basically all they had left. Things were going to get very real in the next couple of days.

The march started bright and early on Tuesday, June 23, 1863 and reached Staunton about half past 10 o'clock. The Union prisoners found this small city to be quite unlike the other little towns they had passed through on the Valley Pike. This was, like Winchester, a transportation hub and a supply base for the Confederate Army. It was linked to Richmond and points east and over the mountains to Charlotte in the west by the Virginia Central Railroad. There were factories in Staunton belching smoke into the air; wagons were moving up and down the streets; and people were bustling to and fro in and out of the many stores. This truly was a Southern city, the residents favoring secession and hating the Yankees with a passion. They let that be known.

"Colonel Ely, we will stay here until morning," announced Colonel Murchison. "We have to wait for the enlisted men." The two commanding officers were standing at the edge of a field just east of the town. "We will march to the train depot tomorrow morning at 8. It's not that far from here. Your men can use the rest."

"Thank you, Colonel," came the reply.

"By the way, Colonel, other than that little incident we had the other day, your men have performed admirably on what was a rather grueling journey. I just want you to know that I appreciated that."

"I regret that the incident did happen but understand why they tried it. I am pleased we did not have another."

"Meet with me after *Roll Call* in the morning."

"Yes, Colonel. I will see you then.

Colonel William G. Ely rose at dawn and began pondering what this day would bring. It was Wednesday, June 24, 1863. The men came into formation at 6 o'clock with the *Roll Call* being taken. Everyone was there, all 142 of the captured Federal officers. As soon as it was over, Ely walked over to Colonel Kenneth M. Murchison as directed. They were joined by Colonel Francis H. Board, commander of the 58th Virginia Infantry, who had supervised the journey of the first wave of the enlisted men who had been taken prisoners. Board and his column had arrived about 8 o'clock the previous evening.

"The train will be ready to load in an hour," he informed the other two. "Fifty officers to a car, 80 enlisted men. Officers in the first three, enlisted men in the next twelve. We are due to depart at noon. Another train will be here at 1 o'clock, Colonel Board. You may board the rest of your prisoners on that one."

"What about the rest of the men?" asked Colonel Board. "The ones being led by Captain Paschall and the 54th?

"There will be another train tomorrow morning. They will load then. You will start loading now. Be quick about it.

"Anything else, Colonel?" asked William Ely.

"No, Colonel. Just get your men ready."

Since the men were still standing nearby, he ordered them to Attention and began counting up to fifty.

"This group will be in the first car. The next fifty will be in the second. The rest of you will be in the third. Understood? We march to the depot in an hour."

At 7:30, the parade of captured Union officers started south down Commerce Road, into the city of Staunton to the hoots and hollers of the citizens who had come out to see the spectacle. Marching in a column of two, they arrived at the depot on Middlebrook Avenue about 8 o'clock. Loading of the old cattle cars commenced. Tom Armstrong, Caleb Edwards, and the Reverend Charles McCabe said goodbye to Ben Johnson and climbed into the second car. It was old and smelled of cow dung. The Confederate soldiers who had counted them off climbed into the car, rifles loaded and ready to go in case there was trouble. Four guards with rifles against fifty un-armed officers. It wouldn't have made any difference, even if the Federals had overpowered them. They couldn't get out of the cars. Doors were locked.

There was nothing to sit on, so the prisoners sat on the floor of the car, bunched together tightly. Chins on knees. The only good thing was that cattle cars don't have solid walls. They were slatted, so that cows can breathe on their way to the slaughterhouse or mar-ket. The odor inside the car would have been a lot worse had it been walled. At a little after noon, the train's whistle blew, and it lurched forward.

"Cow manure, no rations, no springs, no seats. This is going to be a bad trip. I can see that," Caleb Edwards mumbled to Tom Arm-strong, opening the bottle and taking a mouthful. "Wow, Johnson wasn't kidding. That stuff is good."

"Charlie, how're you getting along?" Tom Armstrong asked of Charles McCabe.

"Been better, Thomas. Been better."

The train moved along slowly into the mountains. At least there was some scenery. It pulled into the depot at Fishersville, but kept moving. There was really no reason to stop. But, it seemed like the trip was taking forever as the cars swayed back and forth on the mountainous terrain. Waynesboro was next, followed by Afton and Midway. Later in the afternoon, the train pulled into the Char-lottesville depot. It was time for a water stop. Latrine, too.

The men got out of the cars and were able to stretch their legs. They filled their canteens and visited the quartermaster for some hardtack. The poor enlisted men would get nothing. Tom Armstrong glanced up at the clock in the nearby Courthouse tower. It was 5 o'clock, and they had only gone about forty miles. The journey resumed as uncomfortable as it might be.

The train went through a long tunnel, the engineer blowing its whistle in case a bear or a wolf had decided to get out of the sunlight and was resting comfortably on the track. Soon, it was dark, and the sightseeing was over. Sleeping in a sitting position wasn't very restful, especially with pangs of hunger in the stomach. As the train rolled along through the mountains, nobody could tell where they were. But, it passed through Ferncliff, then East Leake about daybreak, chugging toward Richmond. Tuckahoe was next and finally Richmond, a full twenty-two hours after they departed Staunton.

The train was met by Major Thomas P. Turner, the commandant of Libby Prison. The doors to the cars were unlocked, the prisoners being told to get out and form up. They stood at Attention and heard Major Turner... "FORWARD MARCH!"

The column of captured Union officers and enlisted men started marching south on Cary Street. They had gone two blocks when they were ordered to halt. Tom Armstrong looked up and saw the words "LIBBY PRISON" on the wall of the big building, just above the second-floor windows. It was Thursday, June 25, 1863, his 28th birthday.

10 Libby

Lieutenant Thomas S. Armstrong just stared at the big building, there in Richmond, Virginia, the sign upon which had pronounced itself as "Libby Prison." The building was just plain huge. Looked to be some 300 feet long, maybe forty feet high. Probably sixty feet from front to back. Maybe fifty. Inside, it was really three buildings next to each other with doorways that allowed you to go from one to the other. Armstrong counted six chimneys standing tall on the roof that sloped downward and noticed a vacant lot just to the east of the prison. He judged it to be about fifty feet or so to a street, 21st Street.

Armstrong was standing on Cary Street, looking south at the building. Behind it was a canal with some damn big barges that were being pulled by mules on towpaths on both sides. There was a little street between the building and the canal, appropriately named Canal Street. To some, it was known as Dock Street. 20th Street bordered the building on the west. He looked at the building and saw men just like him staring out at the new prisoners. "Fresh Fish" the new ones were called. There were faces in every window. Tom Armstrong was a long way from Zanesville, Ohio.

"Used to be a tobacco warehouse," one of the Confederate guards said to him. "Built about ten years ago. Some fella named Libby bought it. Started selling groceries and marine supplies to the men using the canal and the river." Tom Armstrong looked past the Kanawha Canal and saw the big river, the James, with steamboats going east and west. Factories dotted the south bank with their dockage for the riverboats.

"Looks like the ol' Muskingum," he thought to himself.

"Heard that General Winder gave Libby two days to evacuate the building a couple of years ago. Had no place else to put you Yanks,"

272

said the Rebel officer, prodding Armstrong to move along with the barrel of his rifle. "Had to get all of his wares out fast. Lord knows where he put 'em. Mighta cost 'im 'is business."

"Who's Winder?"

"Runs the place. Provost Marshall for all of Richmond. Brigadier General. Major Dick Turner's the warden here at Libby. Major Thomas Turner's the commandant. Turners ain't related. Those fellas mean business. Hear Dick Turner is a real bastard. Used to be an overseer on a plantation down south of here. Likes to punish people for even the smallest offense. The other one, Major Thomas Turner, is just the opposite, but you won't like him either. He's just following orders, puts him in a bad spot, a lot more of y'all comin' here. Runnin' out of food. Runnin' out of space for y'all. Let's move, Yank."

"Just my luck," Tom Armstrong thought. "Drat. Well, at least I know a little more than I did before. Food shortages. A bad man in charge and a poor soul who has to do what he's told even if he doesn't want to. Darn thing isn't big enough to hold all of us. Wonder what they're gonna do with us." Armstrong didn't like the prospect.

Indeed, the Confederacy was running out of places to put the Union prisoners and, consequently, had started appropriating warehouses throughout Richmond. They would imprison the captured officers at places like Libby with the enlisted men going elsewhere, like Belle Isle which was a favorite for them, sitting out in the middle of the James River. Darn hard to escape from there unless you could swim really well. "Bet that's where Patrick is going," he thought to himself.

As he entered the big Confederate prison, he realized that it might be the last time he would be out-of-doors until he was exchanged, transferred to another facility, or managed to escape. He walked alongside Caleb Edwards and Charles McCabe, who was remarkably calm and at ease with what was going on. One by one, the captives were interrogated by Confederate officers. "NAME…" "RANK…" "REGIMENT…" Caleb Edwards was not happy. He didn't like being yelled at.

Then, it started to get serious. Each man was subjected to a complete search: blankets, canteens, clothing, haversacks, but what the guards really wanted was money. They even took letters from home and diaries. "You bastards took everything I had back in Winchester," protested Caleb Edwards. "Ain't got nuthin' left, you son-of-a-bitch." He never felt the blow of the gun barrel on the back of his head. He crumpled to the floor.

"Get 'im outta here," screamed a Rebel officer. "I'll deal with 'im later."

Armstrong and McCabe picked up the big West Virginian, draping his arms over their shoulders and started dragging him in the direction the others were going. The Confederate guards poked the prisoners with their rifles to keep them moving. It was dark and hot inside Libby Prison. Dirty, too. Armstrong and McCabe struggled to drag Caleb Edwards up the stairs to the second floor with the help of some of the others. He was coming to. "FRESH FISH...FRESH FISH." The inmates were yelling, "FRESH FISH...FRESH FISH."

"Where you boys from? What's your unit? Where you captured? How's the war goin'? How many is there of ya? We kickin' their ass?" Those who had been in Libby for a while were desperate for news. The "Fresh Fish" had plenty of it and would tell the inmates all they knew.

As they finished climbing the stairs, Tom Armstrong figured there were three large rooms there on the second floor with more stairs leading to another floor above where he guessed there were three more rooms. He found out that the hospital, commandant's office, and kitchen/dining room were one floor below. Each room there on the second floor was a little over 100 feet long, just under 50 feet wide, and 8 feet in height. He looked around and saw some pretty sad-looking men. There would be ample time to talk with them who had been there for a time. Libby Prison was already overcrowded, and here were 142 more to squash in.

"There's a privy next door you can use," said the guard, gesturing with his rifle. "You gotta fight the boys from the Middle Room next door to use it. There's also a trough there where you can take a bath. Gotta fight for that, too. You cook downstairs in the kitchen. If you need a doctor, the hospital's down there, too." This coming from the biggest Confederate soldier Tom Armstrong had ever seen. Carrying a big ol' rifle and using it to point where things were. "*Roll Call* in the morning after *Reveille* which is at 6 o'clock and another *Roll Call* at 5 o'clock after supper. If you have any money that we didn't find, you can use it to buy staples from the sutler. We'll buy stuff for you, too. Just give us the money. But, don't try anything funny, boys. Major Dick don't like that. What he does like is whalin' you with his bare hands. Some poor bastard missed the spittoon the other day and spit tobacco juice on the floor. Major Dick saw it and smashed 'im good, right in the head, laughing as he did. Knocked 'im cold."

"I'm not real fun, neither. I like whackin' Yankees around. Like to shoot 'em, too." He was grinning like a Cheshire cat. "Gots lots of free time, boys. Gots lots of free time. Y'all gonna be here for a while."

Caleb Edwards wasn't feeling so good. He had a lump on the back of his head the size of a small tomato, and his head hurt. Well, it should have. He should have known better.

"So," he said, "where do we sleep?" Tom Armstrong could see that Caleb Edwards was clearly annoyed.

"Right here, soldier. Right here."

"On the floor? All of us? Don't look like there's 'nuf room."

"Y'all make room, soldier. Shut up, or I'll shoot you right here, right now," putting the barrel of his Springfield in Caleb Edwards' face." Blow yer damn head right off."

Tom Armstrong noticed there were wooden bars on the windows, but nothing was keeping out the heat and the breeze that June afternoon. He wondered what it would be like in winter. Looking around at the others, not of Milroy's command, the ones that had been at Libby for a while, he saw men just sitting, pale and gaunt, emaciated. Wearing rags, no shoes, dirty unkempt hair and beards. He noticed one man sitting in the near corner talking to himself absently as if he were in some other place. Another was just lying there, dead. Libby Prison smelled of urine, men's sweat, tobacco, and dead animals, most likely rats and other vermin. Ben Johnson had told him about the rats of Libby on the march to Staunton.

He saw a man stand up and take off his clothes, starting to shake them. "Damn, vermin," he swore. "Gotta get the damn lice outta this stuff. Outta my hair and beard. Damn, I gotta take a bath. Mebbe that'll drown 'em." Stark naked and carrying his clothes, he walked through the door to the trough and sat down, water falling on his head from the faucet and rinsing out his clothes. He noticed Armstrong watching him from the doorway. "You'll be doing this soon, sonny. This place ain't been cleaned since I been here. 2nd Bull Run in August '62. What's it now?"

"June '63," answered Tom Armstrong, contemplating everything he had seen, heard, and smelled over the last couple of hours. "Wonder what we get fed. Can't be all that good," he pondered. "This is gonna be ugly." He walked back into the room, through men huddled together, some playing cards, toward the eastern side of the prison. Five windows there. He looked out and saw the James River with its factories on the southern side. There were a couple of churches on the north side, and sentries were walking back and forth on both Cary Street and Canal Street. Peering upstream, he could make out an island, dotted with what he guessed were white tents. "Oh, my God," he thought, "That's Belle Isle. I bet that's where Patrick is. Be with him, Lord, be with him." He realized, suddenly, that when winter arrived, the enlisted men, Patrick Murphy included, would have little or no shelter. Just like the winter of 62 – 63 at Winchester. "I gotta find Caleb. We gotta figure out how we're gonna survive this place. Maybe we can get exchanged."

He walked back to where the captive officers of General Robert Milroy's command were and found the Reverend Charles McCabe, talking to a shorter man, clean shaven, but with a very black mustache that drooped on either side of his mouth. "Thomas, I found an old friend from home in Athens, down near Marietta. We went to school together and attended the same church. He went off to Muskingum College in New Concord while I went to Ohio Wesleyan, as you know. Meet Artemus Stroud. I don't think I have ever talked about Artemus with you."

"No, Charlie, you haven't. Pleased, Artemus. When did they get you?"

"Fredericksburg, last December. My pleasure."

McCabe then explained to Artemus Stroud how he had come to know Tom Armstrong. He continued, "Thomas," said Charles McCabe, "I have been thinking that we will need something to occupy ourselves while we are here. If we don't, we'll probably go crazy like that man over in the corner. Artemus agrees. He's been teaching some of the men history and grammar, and it seems to work. Right, Arty?"

"Yep. I'm using the same lessons I used at Muskingum College when I taught history there for a couple of years before the war. The men seem to like it. Keeps their minds off their troubles. Only thing we don't have that we need is paper and pencils. Have to get them from home."

"You give them work to do?"

"Of course, we must keep their minds busy. When I ran into the Reverend, I started thinking that we could start a school here. He tells me you're a teacher. I'd also like to build a library somewhere in this God-forsaken place. Have to give the men a routine. Seen too many die of boredom. I'm thinking classes in the morning, free time in the afternoon for study or reading, maybe playing cards or other games. After supper, maybe some singing. We should try to get up a little orchestra. We'll need a couple more of the men to teach."

"Arty," said Charles McCabe, "we better talk to Bill Ely about this. He's the ranking officer of our group."

"Let's see him as soon as we can. You right with this, Mr. Armstrong?"

"Sure. Reckon there's a couple hundred of us in here in the West Room. Make the Rebs think we're being good boys. But I want to get outta here."

"T.S.," scolded Charles McCabe. "There'll be no talk of that."

"Okay, Charlie," he said, thinking to himself, "I just won't tell you about it if we get the chance. Wonder where Edwards is. He'd go along. Not sure about Arty Stroud."

Supper that first night consisted of some stale, wormy bread, and some water right out of the James River. The water was more brown than green, cloudy, too. "Wonder what's swimming in it," Armstrong thought. "Maybe the Rebs are really running out of food for us…and themselves. They've fed the army for two years," remembering the desolate fields he had seen on the march to Staunton. Gotta write home and ask them to send food."

His family had no idea how important it was for them to send him food. If they didn't, he would starve to death. In addition, their letters, and any from Francis Porter, were critical to the health of his mind and spirit. That's how depressing Libby Prison was.

At 9 o'clock, the guards ordered "Lights Out." After the Chaplains said their evening prayers, the prisoners lay down on the hard wood floor front to back, sandwiched together with no room to turn over at all. When the man in front of you turned over, you turned over, whether you wanted to or not. No pillows, no blankets, just using your arm to rest your head. Too bad for the man who snored. Missiles of all shapes and sizes would be hurled at him to get him to stop: boots, books, tin cups, you name it, anything the others could find to try to shut the snorer up. First thing in the morning, right after *Reveille*, the scavenger hunt commenced to retrieve whatever you threw at the man the night before.

Reveille was at 6 o'clock. The scavenger hunt followed. Then, it was time to wash up if you could squeeze your way near the trough and the faucet. Four hundred men trying to get to the trough at the same time, elbows flying. The Chaplains' Morning Prayer service followed. Breakfast, if that's what you wanted to call it, came next. It was awful. Taking a cupful of the "soup" from the wooden bucket, Caleb Edwards put his nose near to it and almost puked. "Here's the problem, Sump," he said. "If we don't drink it, we're likely to starve to death. If we do drink it, we may die of whatever has lived in it, lice or maggots or worse."

"Hold your nose, close your eyes, and drink it. We gotta write home for some food."

Guards came into the room for *Roll Call*. Alphabetical order, regardless of regiment. All the sentries cared about was hitting the number. That is, they counted all the prisoners in each room the day they arrived, adjusted it upward if more "Fresh Fish" came in and downward when one of them died or escaped. So, they had a number just before "Lights Out." That was the number they wanted to hit the next morning.

Finally, it was time to exterminate the lice. The Negro fumigators had come in earlier in the morning with tar smoke, but that was not very effective. Really, the only way to kill them was to boil your clothes, but the prisoners at Libby couldn't do that since the only fire was down in the kitchen. So, they had to shake them off their uniforms and drawers and then pick them off their bodies. They could try to drown them, but waiting for the bathing trough to open up would take quite some time, especially for the new prisoners.

Armstrong saw two men, naked, picking lice off each other. The taller one was heard to say, "Damn, I itch all over." It didn't take long to get infected, only a couple of days.

The other responded, "Zeke, only way to get rid of 'em. Wait for the bathing trough or shake 'em off. Can you pick them off my back?"

"Yeah, but I'm not going after the ones on your front."

There they were, a couple hundred naked Union prisoners scratching themselves and each other, picking the lice off and shaking their clothes, just to get them livable. But, the little buggers would be back the next day. A routine was starting.

Artemus Stroud found Charlie McCabe, Tom Armstrong, and Caleb Edwards sitting on the floor in their designated spots, each one six feet by two feet, in the West Room, now affectionately known as the Milroy Room. He said, "Now, here's the chance we have. There's nothing for the men to do until supper at 5 this afternoon. That gives us plenty of time to hold some classes. By the way, I spoke with Bill Ely about our idea. He went to see Abel Streight. Streight's the one everyone thinks of as being in charge of us. Colonel. Commanded the 51st Indiana. Came in here in early May. Big guy, about 6' 2" and, I'm guessing, over 200 lbs. Anyway, he said it was a great idea and that we should get to work. Also, he suggested that we tell the boys to ask their folks at home to send books so we can establish the library."

And so it was to be. Stroud, McCabe, and Armstrong would teach classes. Edwards would become the librarian. The routine in the Milroy Room was getting a little more structure. Colonel Louis N. Beaudry, Chaplain of the 5th New York Cavalry, joined the "faculty" and expanded the "curriculum" to include French, Latin, and

Greek, in addition to McCabe teaching Religion and Philosophy; Stroud, Grammar and History; and Armstrong, Science and Geometry. Colonel Federico Cavada of the 115th Pennsylvania would also join in to teach the Spanish language and military history when he arrived in early July.

A couple of days after they arrived, the Warden, Major Richard "Dick" Turner issued a reminder that each mess had to cook its own meals if they received provisions from home. In the meantime, the prisoners would subsist on the rations that he provided. With twenty men in each mess, that meant that there would be competition down in the kitchen for time to cook. Let's see, with over 1,000 men imprisoned within the walls of Libby, there'd be fifty of them all trying to use the kitchen at the same time. As expected, fights would break out from time to time with the combatants tossed into the dungeon for a few days to keep the rats company.

That placed great importance on boxes from home that contained food, as well other things like books and clothes. Oh, the Confederates provided rations, some beef, bread, rice, and beans, but it didn't happen every day. But, the beef wasn't pink; it was kind of blue, maybe gray. The bread was hard as a brick; probably could have used it to build something. Lord knows there were maggots in the beans and rice. The men would take turns in the kitchen, but, while the food sent from home gave them better sustenance since they could cook it, nobody really liked the job. Not only did you have to cook, you had to clean up as well, washing the pots, pans, plates, and utensils.

It was Independence Day, July 4, 1863. The men of Milroy's Command had been in Libby Prison for ten days. Colonel Abel Streight had told the Room Commanders that there could be celebrations that afternoon after dinner. As the men from the Milroy Room filed into the Streight Room, crowded as it might be, you felt a sense of pride, as they prepared to celebrate the national holiday. Others crowded into the Chickamauga Room and the East Room. None of them knew about the goings on at Gettysburg, there in Pennsylvania, or in Vicksburg, on the cliffs, high above the mighty Mississippi River, but that didn't stop the party. There were patriotic songs being sung speeches being made. In the Streight Room, the celebration was just made for the Reverend Charles C. McCabe. He opened the meeting with prayer, thanking God for the Union and praying that it be reunited once again. Colonel Streight, all 6'2" of him, strode to the front of the room, opened a book and read the Declaration of Independence to the cheers of the officers. And then, not only did Charlie McCabe function as the choir master, but also, he delivered a thirty-minute diatribe against the evils of slavery and how the Union must prevail. He then led the men in a series of patriotic songs; everyone singing and dancing around.

A Confederate sergeant appeared in the room. "Orders from Major Turner," he shouted. "Y'all are to stop all of this and to go back to yer rooms."

"The hell with him," bellowed Abel Streight. "And, the hell with you."

The Rebel soldier leveled his rifle at Streight. "Y'all are to stop this noise. And, stop y'all will." He fired a shot over Abel Streight's head into the wall. It got real quiet real fast.

Streight looked around the room. McCabe said, "Abel, we have celebrated the glorious anniversary of the Union's independence together here for a couple hours. Let us be glad and depart, as the sergeant has ordered."

Streight saw faces that he knew wanted to continue the party, but he did not want to risk anyone getting shot, especially himself. The men needed his leadership. "Very well, sergeant. Very well. You may tell the Major that our celebration is concluded."

There would be a longer, more formal worship service the next morning. There always was on Sundays, but the two Chaplains, McCabe and Beaudry, felt they had been called to remind the men of the importance of a prayer of thanksgiving that Saturday evening, July 4, 1863. Tom Armstrong, and many others, wondered what kind of celebration was happening at home. He was excited and actually forgot where he was for a moment. Suddenly, he missed Francis Porter terribly. He hadn't heard from her in months. Of course, he hadn't had time to write her since they left for Winchester. That seemed like a very long time ago. "Either she is very worried, or she has forgotten me and just doesn't care anymore." The excitement left him.

The men of Charles McCabe's mess, and all the others, were eating their supper two days later, on July 6, 1863, when William Ely burst into the Milroy Room screaming, "Lee's on the run south from Pennsylvania. Meade whipped him two days ago on the 4th of July. Pemberton just surrendered Vicksburg to Grant, too. Whatta day, boys, whatta day." Well, that set off another Independence Day celebration that they would all remember for the rest of their lives.

Charles McCabe stood up and began belting out *Yankee Doodle* at the top of his lungs. Men started dancing with each other to the music, singing as lustily as they could. *Rally Round the Flag* came next; then a bit more somber, *My Country 'Tis of Thee* and *The Star-Spangled Banner*. The men were slapping each other on the back and hollering. *Yankee Doodle* one more time, just for fun. The Rebels just plain hated that song. The men who were too sick and weak could only watch. One man tried to stand, his knees buckled, and he collapsed, dead. His body thrown onto the pile of the others who had died that day.

"We got 'em on the run, boys. Won't be long now till we're home and out of this awful place," Bill Ely screamed. The celebration lasted quite some time and really this 4th of July and the days thereafter were the first time any of them had had any fun. Finally, around 8 o'clock, Charles McCabe and Louis Beaudry wanted quiet. They would hold an impromptu service in the Milroy Room to thank God for the success of the Union Army that day. As the men drew into a circle, some kneeling, some just sitting, McCabe began...

"Father, thank you for the wonderful news about the success of our glorious leaders, Generals Meade and Grant. Thank you for the gallant boys who sacrificed themselves today and for those who were spared. We would pray that you would be with them and with us here in this historic time and give us hope and strength to survive this ordeal. In your name, Lord," and the 200 men in the Milroy Room responded with a very loud,

"AMEN!"

The Reverend Louis Beaudry gave a short sermon of thanksgiving for the Union army and its commanders, and then, the Reverend Charles C. McCabe, in that booming baritone voice, began singing...

Mine eyes have seen the glory
Of the coming of the Lord
He is trampling out the vintage
Where the grapes of wrath are stored
He has loosed the fateful lightning
Of his terrible swift sword
His truth is marching on.

Glory, glory, hallelujah
Glory, glory, hallelujah
Glory, glory hallelujah
His truth is marching on.

The men who knew *The Battle Hymn of the Republic* began to sing with him. It got louder and louder, the guards screaming at them to stop. The Federals ignored their Confederate captors, and Tom Armstrong, Caleb Edwards, and Artemus Stroud were singing as loudly as they could. The crescendo got even louder, not just in the Milroy Room, but all over the prison. Armstrong now knew that the Confederacy was in trouble. He did not know how much trouble, but he knew that the capture of Vicksburg opened the entire length of the Mississippi River to the Union. He also knew that it meant that no food or supplies could come east from Arkansas, Louisiana, and Texas to reinforce the Rebel Army. That had been General Ulysses S. Grant's plan ever since Fort Donelson. "It's working," he thought, "Just like Colonel Leggett told us at Shiloh." But, if food supplies would not be coming, that spelled misery not only for the Confederate Army, but also for the captives in Libby Prison, Belle Isle, and the other facilities where the Federal prisoners were being held.

Tom Armstrong also knew that Lee's defeat at that little town in Pennsylvania, Gettysburg it was called, meant that General Robert E. Lee was retreating back into Virginia. That would create more hardship in the Commonwealth, especially for the civilians who were seeing their food supplies diminish in order to feed the Army. "Now we got 'em trapped. Bet Grant will come east and Meade south. "It's that 'pincer movement' of General Scott," he said to himself. It also meant that there would be more "Fresh Fish" from Gettysburg. Indeed, they arrived on July 10 and were packed into the Upper and Lower East Rooms like sardines in a can. Musta been 250 officers in each one. Shoot, it was crowded in the Milroy Room with the 175 or so who were still alive. How 250 could fit in was anybody's guess.

It was very hot that summer in Richmond, the heat only magnifying the stench of the squalor in Libby Prison. Massive thunderstorms rolled over the city on their way out to sea and drenched the poor souls who were stuck there. Imagine sleeping on a wood floor, so tightly packed in that you couldn't move unless the others did, in a couple inches of water. Might drown, but probably not. Life at Libby went on, and the men of the Milroy Room looked for ways to pass the time. Each day, Charles McCabe, Artemus Stroud, Tom Armstrong, and Caleb Edwards would sit together to think about ways to challenge the men's minds in addition to the classes. Got their minds off their own troubles, especially the pangs of hunger in their bellies and the cries and moans of the sick and starving.

"You know what we oughta do," Tom Armstrong announced one day. He'd been thinking about this since they got to Libby.

"Oh, boy," thought Caleb Edwards. "Here he goes again. This is gonna be good. Wonder what it is this time."

"We oughta have debates on issues of interest to the men. We could think about an issue, maybe related to the war, maybe not, and then choose two men to argue about it. Not mad arguing, but civil dialogue, well thought through, and spoken respectfully to the other side. Can't make it personal. And, we could have judges. Whattya think about that? I'm sure we can think of things to argue about."

Colonels Beaudry and Cavada had joined the group. "I have another idea," said Louis Beaudry. Caleb Edwards just rolled his eyes. "We should have a newspaper."

"One thing at a time, Louis," said Artemus Stroud. "Let's think about what Armstrong said. I kind of like the idea. I'm pretty good at debating. Used to argue with students all the time. Not much difference here."

"Not as good as me," shot back Charles McCabe, with a chuckle, and the game was on.

"Knock it off you two," said Tom Armstrong, trying to look stern. "I'll think of an issue, and then you can tell me what side you're on. I will moderate. Louis and Federico, plus one more, can be the judges. Maybe Bill Ely would like to do it. The rest of the men will listen and, at the appropriate time, can boo or cheer. We're gonna need a Sergeant-at-Arms to keep it civil. We don't need a brawl in here. Good with all of you?"

The newcomer, Federico Cavada, spoke first. "Why not try it? It could provide some entertainment for the men. Are we going to allow anyone to join this Debating Club?"

"I still think we need a newspaper," said Louis Beaudry.

"OK, Louis," said Caleb Edwards, rather sarcastically "how the hell are you going to print a newspaper in here?"

"I'm not. I'll just have the men give me paper on which they have written something or have an announcement. I could call everyone together on Monday or Friday morning, or whatever, and read the papers I have been given. That's how we announce the debates, or if there is to be a lecture or something. Or, if someone finds out the details of what happened at that Gettysburg place. News, fellas, news. I'll call it the *Libby Chronicle*."

"You're on your own for that one, Louis," said Charles McCabe. He continued, "You know what else we need?"

Edwards rolled his eyes again. "What, Charlie?"

"A band. An orchestra. To entertain the men on Saturday night. Give them something to look forward to. We could have dances."

"Shoot," Tom Armstrong offered, "I can have my brother, Jacob, send me a fiddle. Wonder if the Rebs could get us a guitar. I'm sure somebody in here plays the harmonica and the banjo. Could probably fit those in a box from home. How about some drumsticks?"

"We could have concerts," exclaimed Charles McCabe proudly. "I will lead them."

"Of course, you will," thought Caleb Edwards, thinking that these were some damn fine ideas to relieve the boredom of prison life. Maybe a bit ambitious, but damn fine ideas.

"See," said Louis Beaudry, "at the first publication and meeting of the *Libby Chronicle*, I will announce the formation of the band or orchestra, ask men who can play instruments to try to get them from home, and inform them that they can audition in front of Armstrong, here. Maybe a chorus, too."

"Chorus? Now there's another great idea. I will lead that, too," said Charles McCabe.

"Naturally," thought Caleb Edwards. "Naturally."

"I've got it," said Tom Armstrong. "The first debate topic."

"Well?" said Caleb Edwards, thinking that this conversation was going a bit too fast.

"Here it is: The government's right to force men into the military. The draft. There's a lot of anger about it in the North. Paper said that there were riots about it in New York earlier this month."

"That's a good one, Tom," said Artemus Stroud. "Could be real interesting."

"Which side you want, Arty?"

"Whooeee. That's a tough one, Tom. Let me see," rubbing his hand though his thick black hair. "Let me see."

"Well, Arty, don't be taking all day about it," chided Charlie McCabe. "If you don't know what side you're going to be on, I'll choose it for you."

"Just a minute, Charles," said Artemus Stroud, feigning anger toward his friend. "Just a minute. I think I'll take the pro side. I'll advocate."

"Perfect," said Charles McCabe. "I didn't want that side anyway. When are we going to do this?"

"How about a week from Wednesday night, after supper, before Evening Prayer?" said Tom Armstrong.

"I'm game," said Artemus Stroud.

"You're on, Arty," replied Charles McCabe. "See you at 7 o'clock, next Wednesday." That would be August 5, 1863. One of the officers in McCabe's mess had drawn a calendar on the wall by his space. Tom Armstrong looked at it, thinking, "Been here six weeks. Wonder how we can get out."

"Louis," why don't you plan to have the first reading of your newspaper on Friday morning?" asked Charles McCabe. "The debate, the band, or whatever we're going to call it, the choir, and anything else that seems newsworthy. Try to find out how the war is

going. I'll go tell Bill Ely about all of this. He won't have a problem."

"Ask him to judge the debate while you're at it."

Just like that, in the space of about two hours, there on Tuesday,
July 28, 1863, the six new friends had designed some entertainment
for the rest of the imprisoned Yankees in the Milroy Room. They
hoped it would lighten the mood a little. It would, for a while. Tom
Armstrong felt better, but it wouldn't last. He would write to Francis
Porter that very day. It had been a long time since he had.

Libby Prison Richmond, Va.
July 28th A.D. 1863

Dear friend Frank:

Ere this you've been apprised that I'm a Prisoner of
War. On my birthday, I was incarcerated in these walls.
June 25, 1863. I may stay here for years and at present it
looks pretty uncertain. But I hope I shall be let out soon
but all is conjecture. I have very little to hope for.

I'm very well. I've not heard one word from any of my
friends since I came from Winchester & some days before
the Battle. I have not even heard from my Regiment, no,
not one word from anyone. Please write to me. If you expect to get an answer from me you will have to enclose in
your answer to this an envelope, stamps, & 1/2 sheet of
paper. Be brief in your letters. Tell me about your home
& it is all open & inspected.

My love to all of you. Tell Huldah & Johnny that I cut
quite a figure in prison. My wardrobe happens to be not
the most extensive, but I will tell you about that when I
see you. Pray that may be soon. We have prayers night &
morning by the chaplains & two sermons Sundays.

Yours as ever.

Direct to
Lt. T S Armstrong Federal Prisoner

Libby Prison
Richmond, Va
via Fortress Monroe

He wasn't quite truthful with that "I'm very well" line, but he didn't want her to worry any more than she already did. If she was worrying at all. When he finished, he remembered that he hadn't written to the folks at home about his current predicament. Charlie McCabe had told him that there had been a short article in the *Daily Zanesville Courier* about the officers of Milroy's Command being captured and imprisoned, but he didn't know if the family had seen it. He was most concerned about his mother who, at the time the 122nd left Zanesville back in October, was still grieving for his brother, Wilbur. Jane Armstrong had always displayed a tough exterior, but inside, she was a very sensitive woman. She had lost three children after Thomas was born, Wilbur was gone, and now Tom was in prison. She would not know if or when she would ever see him again. Tom Armstrong was very worried about how his mother would cope with this. He was glad Jacob was still at home on the farm.

Addressed to J.G. Armstrong
Norwich, Muskingum Co., Ohio
Libby Prison Richmond Va.
July 31st 1863

Dear Bro Jacob
   How strange my dear Bro is war? Don't you mind how we used to talk of Col. Corcoran and now I am in the same place he was. I am well. Tell mother not to grieve for her son for I am enjoying myself as best I can. She can't send me any more nice boxes & nice socks. I am very comfortable, that is as comfortable as a prisoner is likely to be. I have rather a scanty wardrobe, but enough to keep me warm.

I have an overcoat, blouse, pants, 1 old shirt, & 1 pr socks & an old hat & pair of boots. But as we never leave our room, I don't need any clothes.

So pray for me my dear brother. My love to all. Write to me. Send something to answer your letter, a stamp & envelope. My health is good.

Well I hope to hear from you soon. May God bless you all.

Direct to your affectionate Bro.

Lt. T. S. Armstrong Federal Prisoner

Libby Prison

Richmond, Va.

via Fortress Monroe

He didn't know if that would ease her mind, but knowing that he was alive and that he was "enjoying himself" might be of help. He really wasn't. He would not know if the letter would ease her concern and worry until he received word from home. Next, he needed to get a box of provisions and supplies.

His mother had sent him "nicer" things when he was in Winchester, and now, it would be the only way he and the rest of the men in McCabe's mess, and all the others throughout the prison, could make it. He didn't need "nicer" things, this was survival. What he needed would have to come from Jacob. So, he wrote his brother once again and asked him to build a much larger box, large enough to hold a couple of hams, 10 pounds of butter, a bushel of green beans, salt, pepper, mustard, a gallon of molasses, a gallon of maple syrup, 10 pounds of cheese, a frying pan, a cooking pot, a tin cup, eating utensils, paper, pencil, envelopes, pens, ink, mirror, violin, bow, extra strings, toothbrush, razor, soap, comb, scissors, some thread, dried fruit, dried pork, dried beef, Bible, pipe, tobacco, matches, padlock and key, and books about just about anything. He also asked Jacob to put hinges on the box so that he could use it for storage. He could also use it as a bench to sit on. He wondered, though, if the Johnnies would search the box when it arrived and take out the razor and scissors. He hoped not.

That same day, precisely at 10 o'clock in the morning, the able residents of the Milroy Room had drawn themselves into a circle for the first reading of the *Libby Chronicle*. Those who could not stand just sat or lay in their "spaces." Seemed like there were more of them every day. The Reverend Louis Beaudry stood in the center of the room, holding a pile of scraps of paper upon which he had written notes about the various entertainments that were being planned.

"Any and all of you who would like to sing in a chorus, go see Reverend McCabe. If you play a musical instrument and can get it from home, you can join Armstrong's band or orchestra, whatever you want to call it. We will schedule concerts from time to time. Next, the first meeting of the Libby Debating Society will be held next Wednesday at 7 o'clock after supper, right here. McCabe and Stroud will argue the merits of the government drafting men into the Army. Stroud thinks it should. McCabe thinks it shouldn't."

"I used to like you, Charlie McCabe," came from a voice in the crowd. There was some laughter.

"Oh, shut the hell up, Jethro," called another. "We all volunteered. So, we gotta keep getting others to join us any way we can. If we gotta draft 'em, draft 'em. Just pound salt, Jethro!"

Another voice, "We should ask the Commandant if we can have the folks at home send us some whiskey."

A roar of approval and loud applause greeted the suggestion. Cries of "Talk to him. Talk to him," rang out.

"Where's Bill Ely?" asked Louis Beaudry.

"Over here, Louis."

"Can you talk to Major Turner about this?"

"I can try, but it ain't gonna happen. Whiskey makes a man take more risk than he would ever take when sober. Makes him braver. Clouds his thinking. But, I'll ask Streight to ask him." More cheers from the crowd.

"Settle down," Beaudry instructed. "I have a note here from Colonel Streight. He has challenged us to a boxing match. One of his versus one of ours. A week from tomorrow night. If you have any pugilistic skills, come see me."

"What the hell did you just say?" came a voice in the crowd.

"It means that if you can box, come see me." Beaudry continued, if any of you were teachers before the war, we can use you. We're going to start a school in here, and we want as many of you as possible to consider learning something new. Those of you who want to teach, see Artemus Stroud."

He went on, "We need books. Lots of them. When you write home, ask your families to put as many as they can in your box. When they arrive, give them to Caleb Edwards. Where are you, Caleb?"

Charles Edwards stood up and waved his cap to the men. "We're gonna have a little library here, too, so get me all you can. Commandant said we could have some space downstairs, outside the carpenter shop in the cellar. Likes the idea. Thinks we're behavin'."

Louis Beaudry went on, "I do have one piece of bad news. The two captains from the Chickamauga Room who escaped last week have been captured and thrown in the dungeon. They didn't get very far. Were trying to get to Fortress Monroe. Sentence is two weeks. No food but bread and water. No bath. No light. Rats everywhere. Now, I haven't been down there, but I am told that those who have been put in there call it 'Rat Hell.' Here's the message: If you ever try to escape and don't make it, that's what's gonna happen to you. Or you may get shot or hanged. You all know that a group of eight of ours tried to escape, were caught, and got thrown into the dungeon. The Quartermaster turned them in. Can't trust anyone in here. Not only are there rats running around under foot, but the jail was so crowded that they had to sleep standing up. Tough to do, especially with the vermin squealing all night long. How'd you like to have rats running all over your feet and even climbing up your backside? You can get real sick, and maybe even die, if they bite you. It isn't pleasant, boys."

Later that day, Artemus Stroud, Charles McCabe, Tom Armstrong, Louis Beaudry, Caleb Edwards, and Federico Cavada convened in the corner of the Milroy Room to talk about the college. In hushed tones, so the guards wouldn't hear, Artemus Stroud said, "I forgot to tell you something the other day. Those Negroes, who do the tar smoke every morning, are Union, and they have contact with friends on the outside who are also Union and who feed them information about the war. These folks learn this information from their masters, and then they pass it on to the Negroes in here who tell us in case someone is planning an escape."

"They also give this information to a woman in Richmond named Elizabeth Van Lew, or something like that. "Crazy Bett" they call her. Then, she gets it through the Confederate lines to Union commanders, even as high as Grant. How she does that, nobody knows.

"You might even see her here in the prison. She is a beautiful, cunning, devious, guileful woman, and we must keep her secret. I saw her use her womanly talents on Dick Turner last spring. If she can charm him, she can charm anyone. She's even put up some who have escaped in the attic of her mansion. Now, if any of the letters from home have any code in them, once you translate it, tell the tar smoke boys, and they will get it to their friends and Miss Van Lew. Then, tell Streight. Shoot," he said, thinking out loud. "Here's the problem. The Johnnies have posted spies in here, posing as us, uniforms and all. Be very careful who you talk to. In fact, on second thought, I would suggest that if you get news, you channel it through me. The Rebs think I'm harmless, but I can get to Streight. And, if you hear of anyone planning an escape, I will tell you what I know to help them."

"Arty, you're a damn spy," said Caleb Edwards. "Never would have guessed."

"Let's keep it that way. The classes should help keep up appearances."

The first meeting of the Libby Debating Society began right on time, 7 o'clock PM on Wednesday, August 5, 1863. The combatants were ready. Tom Armstrong sat behind a pine table in the front of the room. Arty Stroud to his left. Charles McCabe to his right. Louis Beaudry, Federico Cavada, and William Ely were seated behind Armstrong. He banged his hand down on the table for order.

"Quiet down!" he yelled.

"Gentlemen, you will each have fifteen minutes to state your case. Does the federal government have the right to conscript men into the armed service? Mr. Stroud, you have the positive response. Reverend McCabe, you have the negative. There will be time for discussion afterward." Addressing the audience, he said, "You may cheer what you agree with, and you may hoot and boo if you disagree."

"Panel of judges, you are to regard the participation of the audience while you judge this debate on the merits of the arguments. We will conclude the debate at 8:30. Evening Prayer will follow so that we can be ready at 9 for "Lights Out.""

The debate went off just as Armstrong had outlined. Arty Stroud's argument was pretty convincing. The Union Army was just plain running out of volunteers. So, if the United States was going to win the war, it would have to coerce men into serving. And, after all, the Confederacy had been drafting men to serve since April of 1862. If that hadn't happened, the war would have been over by now. So, the more men the Union had, the sooner the war would be over. Cheers and boos greeted the teacher from New Concord, Ohio. More cheers than boos, mind you.

Charles McCabe took a more philosophical look at the matter. His argument was that, in America, all white, adult males were free to do as they wished as long as they did not infringe upon the rights of others. Conscription, McCabe believed, was a violation of that right, and the government should not be able to do that. After all, the government was the servant of the people. The Constitution guaranteed that. The people had every right, even the obligation, to overthrow a government that violated their rights, just as the founding fathers had done in 1776. Cheers and boos greeted McCabe as well. Strange, more cheers than boos on this argument as well. "Too much philosophy," thought Tom Armstrong, "but he's right. That's why the United States was formed. To throw off the tyranny of King George III of England. Forget where I learned that."

The discussion ensued. Finally, at 8 o'clock, Tom Armstrong addressed the judges. "Gentlemen, what is your verdict?"

Ely, Beaudry, and Cavada looked at each other. Louis Beaudry spoke. "We find the arguments of both Reverend McCabe and Mister Stroud profoundly relevant and on two different plains. The Reverend has given us a reminder of the role of the people and the government in our country. Our friends in the South have a different view. Many men have given their lives since this all started two and a half years ago. Now, we have Lee on the run and also the complete control of the West. The war will be won and, to Mister Stroud's argument, the government will still need more men to win it. Otherwise, it will be prolonged, and many more men than necessary on both sides will be killed, wounded, die of disease, or rot in a place like this. It is a terrible choice that Mr. Lincoln had to make, but it was the only choice. Therefore, we have concluded that the debate has resulted in a draw." Cheers erupted from the audience. Charles McCabe and Artemus Stroud shook hands. Their logic was stunning.

"Chaplain McCabe, Chaplain Beaudry, will you please conduct Evening Prayer?"

"With pleasure." And then it was "Lights Out."

It was August 5, 1863, and the prisoners of Libby had settled into a routine, although hunger was becoming more and more common. Tom Armstrong wondered when Jacob would send the box, not thinking that the Confederate guards would go through it, taking his food for themselves.

The box arrived unopened on August 26, almost a full month after he had asked for it. He was mighty hungry and thankful that Caleb Edwards had stolen some meat earlier in the week from some of the boys in the Middle Room. "Coulda got my head busted open, but I was starving," he said to Armstrong. "Bloody nose is a bloody nose. No big deal."

Prisoners who received boxes were heroes in their mess, especially if they shared the foodstuffs that had been sent. Jacob Armstrong had done a wonderful job of building the box, four feet long, two feet wide, and three feet high. He found a note from his mother and sisters, telling him they hoped it was everything he wanted. They had packed it full. A jar of grape jelly had broken, but didn't harm anything. The books Armstrong gave to Caleb Edwards who had started the library just outside the Carpenter shop; the clothing, his fiddle, and the food remained locked in the box.

Classes were proceeding, but the teachers were noticing that attendance was starting to dwindle. The sick and the starving weren't going anymore. Someone had organized a chess tournament in which thirty-two of the men competed during the first week of September. The Libby Orchestra was rehearsing under Tom Armstrong's leadership, he, with his violin, and the others with a couple of guitars and banjos, a harmonica, and a "drum," made out of an empty hardtack box. They weren't very good, but nobody seemed to mind. By the time of the Christmas concert, they would be just fine. Tom Armstrong was sure of it.

The chorus was another problem. All that Charles McCabe had were men who just flat out couldn't sing. They were enthusiastic about being in the chorus and sang lustily and with great energy, but they were off key. A few sharp. A few flat. And, to make matters worse, no amount of practice would be of help. McCabe wondered if this was such a good idea, but it was too early to throw in the towel.

By September 1863, things were starting to change at Libby Prison. For starters, Major Dick Turner ordered that all outgoing and incoming mail could only be one page long and could not contain any reference to the war. The mail would be reviewed by censors, and any prisoner found in violation of the rules would get to spend two or three days in the dungeon with the rats.

Then, the prisoners were assured that their families could send them money so they could have the guards buy them food at local markets. The sutler was long gone. Now, in and of itself, this was a nice gesture until you considered the outrageous exchange rate the Confederate guards charged. With the Southern currency losing value quite quickly, "greenbacks" became more and more valuable to the guards, so they basically stole the money from the prisoners.

And, then, the captives realized that their rations from the Confederates had been cut again; hunger was now a real problem. Those boxes from home became even more important. One more thing. Tom Armstrong and his messmates also realized that they didn't have any blankets. The Rebels hadn't thought about that, and winter was coming. The prisoners talked openly about what it would be like to freeze to death.

Disease was rampant. Dysentery was everywhere. Typhoid fever had broken out. The sanitary conditions at Libby were just plain awful; for one thing, the drinking water came straight from the James, and, second, there was no place to wash your hands after using the latrine. Flies and other insects flew in and around it and picked up bacteria that infected the men. The hospital on the first floor of the East Building was full to capacity, including the Chaplain, the Reverend Charles McCabe. When men died, their bodies were simply thrown onto the bed of a wagon on Canal Street. When it was full, the Negroes would hitch up the mules and take the dead to the cemetery for burial. "Used to have coffins for 'em," one of them said. "No more." It was Monday, September 28, 1863.

The final problem was that any hope of being exchanged had flickered out. Only the very sick were taken out of the dreadful prison and put in hospitals. Neither the Northern or Southern officials would compromise on exchange. No hope of exchange began to weigh on the minds of the men. It was tough to keep hope, but some did. Most didn't. Mental illness was widespread. Depression was the most common, but delusions, hallucinations, and suicidal thoughts were not unusual.

"I'd like to see Charlie," Tom Armstrong said to Arty Stroud, "but we aren't allowed. If I go down to the hospital, I might get the fever, too. Don't want that. God, this place is terrible."

"Yes, it is," came the reply. "You ever think about escaping?"

"Yeah, Edwards has mentioned it a couple of times, but Charlie told us to button it on the subject. Said it wasn't worth gettin' shot or tossed in the dungeon for a couple of weeks. I'm beginning to wonder about that."

"Heard that a man who was a tailor before the war promised to make one of the surgeons a nice coat to wear in the hospital. Trouble is, he lied. He made it for himself, and one for a friend, and the two of them just walked out. Don't think they have been caught. Maybe it's not that difficult."

"You gonna try it, Arty?"

"Maybe. If the opportunity presents itself."

"Let me know if it does."

"What about Edwards?"

"He'd go lickety-split."

"OK, so there might be three of us?"

"Yes. And, with the lack of food except what we get for ourselves, things might get desperate," Tom Armstrong replied. "It might be the only answer."

Addressed to Mr. William Armstrong
Norwich, Muskingum Co., Ohio

Libby Prison Richmond Va
Sept 28th 1863

Dear Father. On the 9th of this month, I sent for a box. I've not got it yet. I need it. If you have not sent it, just send me what it calls for also one canvassed ham, 10 lbs. of butter in cans, 1 can of peach butter, a round of dried beef, a can of apple butter also.

I am well and hearty. We have not much hopes of being exchanged and if we are you will know it as soon as I will. The authorities allow us our money now. Any money sent to me will be held and its equivalent in Confederate money given me at rates of exchange. Please send these articles as soon as possible as we need them. I wrote to Mary & Bob last week. I get your letters in about 10 days.

Did you get my letter of the 9th? Lieuts Taylor, Paul, & Anderson are in my mess. They have sent for boxes. I am in good spirits. Chap McCabe is sick with fever in the hospital. Dr Houston is well (our surgeon). Write soon. T.S.A.

Tom Armstrong didn't know if his father would believe that line, "well and hearty," but hoped it might comfort his mother. He didn't know it at the time, but over the next two weeks, the Confederates would cut the prisoners' rations to half a loaf of cornbread, some meat, and vegetable soup, if you could call it that, per day. More and more men were dying every day, their bodies just heaped on the dead pile by the guards and on the wagons by the Negroes.

Now, in and of itself, this ration didn't sound too bad until you looked at, and smelled it. The bread was as hard as a rock; the meat was rancid and could be smelled all the way across the room; and the soup was the home to dead insects that apparently consumed some of it, died, and floated to the surface. But, they had to eat it and hope for the best. Every day, they waited anxiously for the boxes from home.

Armstrong got another jolt on October 15, 1863. Charles McCabe had recovered sufficiently from the fever to rejoin his friends in the mess. He had news.

"Boys, they just told me I'm going home. Being exchanged for a minister from Alabama. I don't know why they chose me, but I am due to leave within the week. I think Beaudry might be going, too. I'll have to go see him."

"What?" exclaimed Armstrong. His good friend, confidant, and mentor was getting out of Libby Prison and would be on his way back to Ohio. Now who would he talk to?

"Here's what I was told," the Chaplain said, looking directly at Tom Armstrong. "I shouldn't have been here in the first place. That was General Early's doing. Apparently, General Butler worked out something with Colonel Ould, the Confederate officer in charge of prisoner exchange. I am to go on one of the 'truce boats' to Fortress Monroe and, from there, by train back to Marietta and then to Zanesville."

"Who's gonna take over Chaplain duties? We need someone to lead our services. And, how about the classes and the chorus?" Tom Armstrong was taking McCabe's departure personally. And badly.

"I don't know Thomas. I will speak with Bill Ely later today. He will find someone, I'm sure."

With that, the Reverend Charles C. McCabe began to make preparations to leave the filth and stench of the notorious Libby Prison. Louis Beaudry, he discovered, was not quite so lucky. McCabe didn't need much time to get ready since he didn't have much to take with him.

On October 22, 1863, Charles C. McCabe had gotten a haversack from the Quartermaster, filled it with some clothes, books, and his Bible and walked out the front door of Libby Prison and into the sunshine of a lovely autumn afternoon and freedom. Tom Armstrong was downright angry, something he hadn't felt in a while.

Being angry in battle was one thing. This was entirely different. Irrationally, he was mad that his friend and mentor was leaving him behind.

"Wonder if I'll ever see him again." Tom Armstrong was sad, very sad.

Add to that, rations were being cut even more. "Haven't had any meat in a week or so," Caleb Edwards complained. It would get worse, fast. The meat ration would be reduced to a couple of ounces every two weeks. It seemed to Edwards and the rest of the mess, including Tom Armstrong, that they were being starved to death. They had two ways around it. The box from home was the key. It could have food, and it could have money. When the food ran out, the only way to survive was to pool the money with that from the others in the mess and ask the guards to buy some for them. They would have to pay that exorbitant exchange rate, but they had little choice. The blessed box from Jacob arrived on October 26, 1863. Food from home, at last.

And, now, as November came and went, it was getting colder, especially at night. Tom Armstrong wrote Jacob asking for a blanket and an overcoat. The prisoners, rightfully, were getting restless. Starving and cold, very cold, there was some talk of a rebellion inside Libby. There were still over 800 Union prisoners and only about 100 guards. Only problem was, the guards had guns and prisoners would die at their hands. The other problem was that many, many of the prisoners were too weak or mentally incapable of fighting.

"Shit, we're gonna die anyway," said Caleb Edwards. "Might as well go down fightin', Tom."

"Might make some sense. Middle of the night, we charge them. Too many of us."

"Fellas," said Artemus Stroud, "I heard that Dick Turner has ordered a ton of black powder to be buried under here. We try that rebellion, the Johnnies will leave this place, and he'll blow us all to kingdom come. Even if he doesn't detonate the powder, what happens when you bust out through the door into fire from Reb infantry and cavalry. Artillery, too. I've been watchin' through the window, and they're everywhere out there. One of 'em tried to shoot me. Bullet whizzed right over my head and stuck in the wall. Better steer clear of the windows, now. A Captain Holmes got killed just the other day. Got too close to the window and took a bullet just in front of the left ear. Died instantly. Another was just sittin' there readin' the paper when a bullet hit him right under the nose. Tore his damn face right off."

And, soon, there would be an order from the Commandant who was quite fearful that the Yankees were communicating somehow with Union sympathizers there in Richmond. So, they were ordered not to go within three feet of a window. Snipers on the street below were to kill them if they got any closer than that. Elizabeth Van Lew was no longer welcome, and Negroes with the "tar smoke" were told to be quite careful about who they talked to. Paranoia was starting to be evident among the Confederates.

They had a couple of other worries. Their high command had decoded telegraphic messages from the Union ranks and understood that General George Meade was following General Robert E. Lee into Virginia. Then, they heard that General Ulysses S. Grant was on the move east from Vicksburg. The Confederate troops in Richmond, including the guards at Libby Prison, now had those threats looming from the outside as well as some very unhappy prisoners on the inside. The Commandant, acting on orders from the Warden, cut the rations even more. The box from Jacob with the blanket and overcoat hadn't arrived.

Artemus Stroud, Caleb Edwards, and Tom Armstrong were huddled in a corner of the Milroy Room. Snow was blowing in through the windows, and it was damn cold. They wished they had blankets.

"Fellas," Edwards began, "you remember when the Johnnies opened up the cellar in the East Building for 'nother kitchen?"

"Yeah," Armstrong responded. "What of it?"

"Just after Chickamauga, last September, if I recall," offered Stroud.

"Well," said Caleb Edwards, "I'm sittin' in the Library sortin' some of the books one day coupla weeks ago, and some officers from Pennsylvania, I think, come in and start askin' about the cellars."

"So?" said Tom Armstrong. "Why are you tellin' us that now?"

"Didn't think it was too interesting then. I tol' them that I didn't think there was anything in the West Cellar, this one was the Carpenter shop, and the East was where the other kitchen was."

"So?"

"Nobody likes to go in the West and the East 'cuz of the rats. Even the guards. I tol' them that, but they wanted to see 'em. So, they did. Didn't come back by me and the library. Guess they went back up the east stairs. Didn't see 'em again for a while."

"They were just seeing where they will cook their meals, that's all," said Artemus Stroud.

"Yeah, that's all they were doing, Caleb," echoed Tom Armstrong.

"I dunno," said Caleb Edwards. He thought, "Something's going on. I better keep my eyes open."

Days passed, and the holidays approached. The men of Milroy's command had been in Libby Prison for almost six months. The classes were starting to see fewer and fewer men attending. There had only been one more debate since the one in early August. Men didn't seem to have much interest. And, Louis Beaudry had been exchanged in mid-November. No more Friday morning announcements. Morale in the Milroy Room was awful. Not as bad in the newly-named Gettysburg Rooms, but it wasn't good. A brawl had broken out in the Lower Gettysburg, just the other day; men fighting and cutting each other with the utensils they had gotten from home. Hospital was full of injured prisoners as well as the sick and starving. No room to treat everyone who needed help. Men just sitting there, waiting to die.

The holidays wouldn't be too joyous a time for the men in the Milroy Room, especially now that Charles McCabe was gone. McCabe, indeed, was back in Zanesville, preaching and lecturing about the horrific treatment of the men in Libby Prison. He thought of the men in his mess often and prayed constantly for their health and safety. He was worried as he now knew what the spring of 1864 would bring, with the advances of the Union Army, just as the Confederates there in Richmond knew. With Lee in retreat and no obstacle in front of Grant over there in Mississippi, the days of the

Confederacy were numbered. But, the terrible fighting would continue until the Rebels surrendered. While McCabe's church in Putnam was decorated with greens, candles burning brightly, and red ribbons to celebrate Christmas, there were no decorations in the Milroy Room or in any other room of Libby Prison.

It sure would be different this year. The little orchestra had added a tambourine and was able to play what sounded like Christmas hymns, heralding the birth of Jesus. Tom Armstrong, fiddle in hand, led the musicians as best he could. The chorus sang along, but was tough to listen to. Neither the orchestra or the chorus did much to improve the sagging spirits of the men. They were lost in thought about what Christmas had meant to them at home with sleigh rides, candlelit church services with lively music and singing, and being with loved ones. And, the food. Roast turkey and chicken, vegetables, yams, potatoes, and the pies. Maybe even some whiskey. Thoughts like this made it even worse. They were cold, especially at night; had to subsist on foul, fetid, vermin-infested rations; were subject to dysentery and typhoid; and had no hope of getting out. This was no way to spend Christmas. New Year's would be little better.

On December 31, 1863, they were allowed to stay up until midnight, but many of the men were too weak or too sick to enjoy the singing."12 o'clock and all is well," the guards called out.

"Like hell it is," said Caleb Edwards. "We're either going to starve or freeze to death or die of some damn disease. I'm for gettin' out of here. Don't know how, don't know when, but I've had it with this place. Wish I had a damn drink."

Looking around, all Tom Armstrong saw was gaunt, frail men with pallid faces, beards not shaven, hair not combed, in rags, no shoes. He had watched them die of disease and starvation every day, with the Negroes coming up to haul their bodies away. Now, there were about 800 men still living in Libby and he wondered, "How will we ever survive? I'm doin' pretty well. So's Caleb. Worry about Arty. He doesn't look so good. But, we ain't got long. God help us if we get sick. Wonder where that box with the blanket and coat is." He was losing hope for the first time.

He didn't know it at the time, but the Confederate Exchange Officer, Colonel Robert Ould, had decided that no more boxes would be delivered to the prisoners in Richmond. They would have to subsist on what the Rebels gave them. Those with money could get food, until the money ran out. That also meant that there would be no paper on which to write to loved ones. Just after the first of the year, the Commandant, Major Thomas P. Turner ordered his men not to purchase anything for the prisoners: food, blankets, clothing...nothing. Period.

And, then the last ray of hope was dashed. There would be no more letters from home. Now, he would never hear from home or from Francis Porter. Depression was setting in. He didn't like it.

11 Escape

"Sump," whispered Caleb Edwards. "I know what those guys are doing."

"What guys?"

"The ones I told you and Arty about. The ones who were asking questions about the East Cellar. You know, 'Rat Hell.'"

"So?"

"They're digging a tunnel. They're gonna try to escape. Heard 'em talking about it. Captain in Pennsylvania Infantry. Major, Kentucky Cavalry. They been workin' in the East Cellar. Think they come down through the kitchen somehow. Don't use stairs. Never seen 'em, 'ceptin' that once. But, I heard 'em. They don't know I know."

"You better tell them, Caleb. Their secret is safe with you."

"Damn Rebels sealed up the East just after Charlie McCabe and the others was exchanged. Look around, there ain't no more chaplains here, none of our doctors neither. I figure the Rebs closed up the East 'cuz they didn't think we needed two kitchens any more. So, they had to go down to the East through the kitchen when nobody's there. At night. Can't go straight down from the hospital. Too many people in there, and they woulda been seen. Wonder how in the hell they done that."

"Good question. Who else knows?"

"Don't know. Maybe I'm the only one. Library's right next to the kitchen. But, yer right, I gotta tell them I know."

It was Saturday, January 2, 1864. Men starving, cold, and sick. No heat, food, or blankets. Just pale, gaunt men huddled together trying to stay warm around the wood burning oven.

"Pennsylvania and Kentucky? We gotta tell Arty," said Tom Armstrong. "He told me that those two were thinking about escaping

304

a month or so ago. Just walkin' out from the carpenter's shop at night past the guards. It would have been easy. But, somehow, everyone knew something was up. They figured too many of us knew about it. The men were talking about it all the time. The spies among us would've alerted the guards. So, the guy from Pennsylvania called it off. Just to shut everyone up. They could have made it though, from what Arty told me."

Armstrong and Edwards got up and walked over the prostrate, freezing Union prisoners to Arty Stroud's "space." Arty was sleeping, sitting up in the icy, liquid filth. His body covered with lice. Artemus Stroud had taken a dramatic turn for the worse since Christmas. Hadn't had anything to eat, was experiencing chills, and his eyes just stared blankly forward. Tom Armstrong's worry about him increased every day.

"Arty, wake up," said Tom Armstrong as quietly as he could. "We have news. Good news."

There was no response from Artemus Stroud.

Armstrong tried again. "Arty, wake up. We have news."

Again, there was no response. Tom Armstrong thought maybe he should shake his friend a little. That should do it. But, when he touched Stroud's shoulder, the man from Athens, Ohio, simply toppled over into the muck, his face contorted in a grimace. Captain Artemus Stroud was dead. Sick and starved to death. Tom Armstrong and Caleb Edwards struggled to fight back the tears.

As the guards came through the Milroy Room to call the roll, they saw the dead man, stripped off his clothing, what was left of it, and heaved his body onto the pile where the other unfortunate, or maybe fortunate, corpses lay.

"Damn, you," shouted Caleb Edwards.

"Shut the hell up and get in line. Don't say nuthin', neither."

"If you didn't have that gun, I'd beat the shit out of you."

"But, I do have it," he said as he belted the West Virginian in the stomach with the butt of his Springfield.

Caleb Edwards' knees buckled. He bent over, trying desperately to breathe. Gasping for air, he rasped, "I'll kill you someday, with my bare hands, you damn son-of-a-bitch."

The butt of the Springfield came down hard across Edwards' shoulders and back of his head, knocking him onto the floor of the Milroy Room. He was out cold. Tom Armstrong put his fingers on Caleb's wrist. "Thank, God," he said to himself, "there's a pulse. Couldn't have handled two in one day."

Armstrong's depression was still there, but, on this day, even with losing Arty Stroud, the news about the possibility of a tunnel, made him feel a little more optimistic. He had not thought it through. Even if the tunneling was successful, and he got out, where would he go in the middle of winter? Where were the Union lines? If "Crazy Bett" was still allowed in the prison, he could find out. But, she wasn't. His main concern right now, however, was Caleb Edwards.

As it turned out, the tunneling had begun a couple of weeks before. Caleb Edwards may have suspected something at that point, but he really didn't know for sure. You see, Colonel Thomas F. Rose of the 77th Pennsylvania Infantry, who had been captured at Chickamauga in September, and Major Andrew G. Hamilton of the 12th Kentucky Cavalry, captured in the Knoxville campaign, had figured out a way to get into the East Cellar, rats and all. Rose had spotted a large sewer that emptied into the Kanawha Canal near Canal Street. The two Union officers thought that maybe they could dig a tunnel to the mouth of the sewer, crawl through it, and then just walk out onto Canal Street. Problem was, how to get to the East Cellar.

Andrew Hamilton had an answer. He had built houses as a civilian before the war, and as he looked around the kitchen, he realized that there was a firewall between it and the hospital to the east. If he could somehow get to the firewall, he could hollow it out and then dig down, breaking through the wall of the East Cellar. But, the question was, how was he going to do that?

Hamilton examined the fireplace on the east side of the kitchen. Nobody was using it anymore, since Major Turner had the ovens brought to some of the rooms. So, using a jack-knife he had borrowed from another man in the Chickamauga Room, as the Middle Room was now being called, he carefully removed the mortar between the bricks of the back wall of the fireplace. Every night for the next two weeks, Thomas Rose watched carefully as his comrade slowly and carefully removed the bricks, one by one. And, every morning at 4A.M., when they heard the guards announce, "4 o'clock, and all is well," Hamilton would stop his work, replace the loosened bricks, refit the mortar, and pile soot on the fireplace, just in case the Confederate guards came down to the kitchen for some reason. There was another reason. Some of the Union prisoners got up at that time, some to use the privy, some to go to the kitchen to try to stay warm. Rose and Hamilton needed complete secrecy.

Finally, on Saturday, December 19, 1863, he had removed somewhere between fifty and seventy-five bricks, creating a hole big enough for a man to get inside the wall. He would only need to dig down four or five feet, below the hospital floor. Major Andrew Hamilton began digging downward and easily broke through the west wall of the East Cellar.

Now, the plan was to tunnel under the east wall of the East Cellar, going south about twenty feet toward the sewer that led to the Kanawha Canal and freedom.

Caleb Edwards came to and hurt all over. "Tom, I gotta go see those guys. Right now." He got up and limped out of the Milroy Room toward the Chickamauga Room to see if he could find the captain of the 77th Pennsylvania.

"Sir, name's Caleb Edwards, 12th West Virginia Battery," he whispered. "Been here since Winchester. Saw you and that other fella, the one from Kentucky, a coupla times down by the Carpenter's Shop, just checking things out. Thought I heard you say somethin' about a tunnel. Here to help if'n you need."

"Damn," whispered Thomas Rose, "Hamilton and I been thinking we do need some assistance. It's going to be more than a two-man job. Can you keep your mouth shut, Edwards?"

"You bet. Been wantin' to bust outta here since the day we got here."

Rose was right, it was more than a two-man job. There was the digger, but there would have to be someone to fan air into the tunnel, so the digger didn't suffocate; somebody would have to figure out what to do with the dirt that was being pried loose; and then there better be a guard in the East Cellar and one in the kitchen. Getting the dirt out of the tunnel was a big problem, but Hamilton came to the rescue again. He had grabbed a spittoon and tied a rope around its neck very tightly. Then, he pulled it along the floor of the East Cellar. It worked very nicely. The digger would fill it, yank on the rope; the man at the open end would slide the spittoon through the tunnel and empty it on the floor of the north end of the East Cellar, where it was black as night. That's where the rats were, for the most part, squealing and scurrying about. Oh, yes, the rats would be another problem. The fanner and the man with the spittoon would have to keep them at bay. Didn't want them in the tunnel but really couldn't keep them out.

When empty, the spittoon would be placed back at the entrance to the tunnel, the rope given a couple of yanks, and it would disappear once again into the darkness.

"I'm going to need thirteen fellas like you. Make three teams of five each. Must be able to work at night. Must swear to secrecy. Must do what I say. Know anybody else?"

"Yes. Good friend of mine from Ohio. Really needs something to take his mind off things here. He's almost lost hope. Name's Armstrong. Lieutenant, 122nd Ohio. You want him to come see you?"

"Yes, Edwards. Have him come by as soon as he can. You can come with him."

When Caleb Edwards returned to the Milroy Room, he found Tom Armstrong lying in his "space," teeth chattering, his body shivering.

"Sump," Edwards whispered. "Come with me. Want you to meet Thomas Rose. You gotta get up and walk around. Get the blood flowin' and warm you up. Rose wants you to help."

"Don't know if I'm strong enough. What's he want me to do?"

"Not sure, he'll tell you."

They walked over to the Chickamauga Room where they found Thomas Rose sitting in his "space." "This here's Armstrong. Says he'll help. Wants to know what you want him to do."

"Empty the spittoon or stand guard in the kitchen or in the cellar."

"Why don't you just tell me?" whispered Tom Armstrong.

"Edwards here is going to be a spittoon emptier. You can do the same, on a different team. Don't want both of you missing at the same time in case there's a surprise inspection. We start tomorrow night. Hamilton and I have been at it for a week or so. Edwards, be in the kitchen as soon as you are sure the men are asleep. Armstrong, cover for him."

It was settled. Caleb Edwards would be on team #1 and Tom Armstrong on #2. Each team would work one night, then have two nights off. It would not be pleasant work, what with the stench in the cellar, the rats squealing constantly and running around underfoot, the absolute silence that had to be kept for six hours, or the darkness. The tunnelers would have to get used to it.

But, it would give them something to do as conditions worsened at Libby Prison during that winter of 1863 – 1864. More and more men were becoming depressed, not only sad and giving up hope. Many believed it would be better to die of starvation, contract some deadly disease, or even freeze to death than to continue to endure the wretched situation in which they found themselves. Some thought it would have been better to get shot and killed in battle. Maybe they were right. They were also beginning to think that the government of the United States had forgotten them, or worse yet, had not forgotten them and was just leaving them here in Richmond to die.

They were cold and hungry, with no hope of a box from home. In fact, they were sure that they heard the rebel guards smashing boxes open out in the vacant lot on the east side of the prison, taking the food and clothing that was intended for them. They had no blankets or fresh clothing and had run out of firewood for the ovens to keep warm. So, they started burning anything they could find, the homemade furniture, shelving, and even the wall of the privy. Who cared about privacy now, anyway?

Those with the will to live started marching every day, even at the double-quick, to try to get blood circulating through their bodies. They would sing patriotic songs while they marched, much to the anger of Major Thomas Turner who promised to punish them. But, the question was, what could he do to them? Put them in the dungeon? Probably wouldn't be any worse than marching around the Milroy Room. Well, maybe the rats would, indeed, make it worse. Caleb Edwards and Tom Armstrong felt all of this misery and were desperate to get out. Thoughts of happy times at home in Norwich with the family and in Hopewell with Francis Porter and her family occupied Armstrong's mind in the cold and dark idleness. He was beginning to think he was losing his mind, but, now, he would have something to do which would keep his brain busy. Edwards thought of home outside Wheeling in the summer. Hot and humid days as a child, but the swimming hole and the picnics his mother provided made for happy memories. Now, there was also his beloved wife, Margaret, and the children, Noah, Susan, and Ezra.

The two friends went down to the library to see if there were books that they could burn to stay warm. The stench coming from the West Cellar made Caleb Edwards vomit. Tom Armstrong wrapped his handkerchief around his face to cover his nose. They looked inside as they heard the dead wagon rumbling closer and closer to the door. Peering out from the Carpenter's shop, they saw the Negro prisoners picking up the distended, blackened, disfigured corpses of the dead and throwing them on the wagon, bound for shallow graves at Oakwood Cemetery. "Poor Arty," said Tom Armstrong. "This is what's going to happen to him. Somehow, I have to tell Charlie McCabe what happened. Poor man starved to death. Lost his will to live. Was a good man."

Caleb Edwards wretched again. Nothing came up. "I gotta get outta here. Grab some books, and let's go," hurrying up the stairs to the Milroy Room.

One of the other tunnelers, Major B.B. McDonald of the 102nd Ohio had found a rope, maybe a hundred feet in length. It had been used to secure a relief package for the enlisted men on Belle Isle that had been delivered to Libby. No one had any idea how McDonald got it. The first thought was to slide down the rope from the kitchen to the cellar and then shinny back up when the night's work was done. But, McDonald had another thought. Having four men climb up the rope at 4 o'clock in the morning was asking a lot, especially of the digger. So, he said to himself, "Why don't I make a ladder out of it? The guard at the top can lower it for us, then pull it back up when we're in the cellar. Then, when he hears the guards yell out, '4 o'clock and all's well,' he can lower it once again. That's our signal to move out, replace the bricks and mortar, and throw soot back on the fireplace."

Thomas Rose let himself down into the East Cellar, followed by A.G. Hamilton, Caleb Edwards, and B.B. McDonald. Edwards didn't know the name of the man left behind as the lookout who would help them out if the Confederates were getting nosy. Rose entered the tunnel and began to dig with the jack-knife, his hands actually worked better. He scraped his way down, hoping to get below the east wall. It was slow going, but digging the tunnel was Rose's passion. When he realized that he had made it under the wall with no problem, he knew he was only twenty feet from the sewer which would empty into the Kanawha Canal. His excitement grew, but the going was tough, and slow. Every few minutes he had to wriggle back to the cellar to breathe. The fanning wasn't working. He would pull the spittoon along until it was full, and as he rested at the entrance to the tunnel, Caleb Edwards would feel his way along the wall to the northeast corner where he would dump it, spreading the dirt with his feet as best he could. The rats apparently didn't like it. Squeals got a little louder every time he emptied it.

When Edwards would return, Thomas Rose would disappear into the black tunnel, knowing that they were close to the freedom that was just a couple of days away. It was the night of January 3, 1864. His hands were bleeding, his fingernails gone, his lungs burning from the lack of air, but he kept going. Freedom was a powerful motivator. Finally, at 4 o'clock in the morning, Caleb Edwards heard the upstairs lookout say softly, "Gotta get 'im outta there. Gotta get back upstairs. A.G. Hamilton pulled on the rope that was around Rose's ankle to let him know that the work for the night was done. He pulled Rose out, and they started climbing the ladder. When they got to the fireplace, Rose took off the dirty, smelly, damp uniform he wore in the tunnel and brought it into the kitchen with hopes it would dry. It was a scene that would be repeated again and again.

By now, Edwards and McDonald were already moving up the stairs, silently. Once out of the cellar, Hamilton replaced the bricks in the fireplace, patched in the mortar, and threw soot all over it. He and Thomas Rose went back up the stairs to the Chickamauga Room to some well-deserved, but frigid, sleep. Nobody cared that they were dirtier than most everyone else.

On the night of the 7th, the team that Tom Armstrong was on climbed down the ladder into the East Cellar, following Thomas Rose. Rose would share the digging duties with Lieutenant David Garbett, also of the 77th Pennsylvania, that night, figuring that rest was important especially with the lack of air. They would relieve each other about every five to ten minutes. Rose was in the tunnel and was pretty sure that he was close to the sewer wall that he would break through to freedom. Water was dripping down on him, slowly at first, but as he dug, the drips became more frequent. Rose ignored it until he heard something that wasn't quite right. The next thing he knew he was under water. He had breached the wall and the force of the water had destroyed it, now filling the tunnel. Rose yanked the rope around his foot violently. Tom Armstrong, standing at the entrance to the tunnel, struggled mightily to pull Rose out. With Rose out of danger, Armstrong and Garbett jammed the old barrel that the spittoon emptiers used to sit on into the entrance of the tunnel to keep the water from flooding the East Cellar.

"Could've drowned in there," said Thomas Rose. "Good work, Armstrong, in getting me out."

"Thanks, Thomas. Least I could do. What now?"

"Don't rightly know. Don't know. But there's gotta be a way out of here. Oh, tell the others what happened here tonight. They are to keep strict silence. I gotta get out of these clothes. Maybe someone else has died, and I can take his. Gotta hide this stuff so nobody finds it."

The conspirators climbed out of the cellar, fixed the fireplace, and returned to their rooms. At dawn on January 8, Thomas Rose of the 77th Pennsylvania Infantry and Andrew Hamilton of the 12th Kentucky Cavalry were peering out of a window on the south side of the Chickamauga Room, hoping that the sentinels below would not see them. Rose had, indeed, stripped the clothing from a man who had just died, burying his own soggy uniform under the four or five that had died that evening whose bodies were piled in the corner.

"See that, Andrew? See that smaller sewer? It's gotta empty into the big one. Maybe if we try to get to that one, that'd work."

"Won't be as direct, Thomas," said Andrew Hamilton.

"I know, but what other choice do we have? Think it'll work?"

"All we can do is try. Tell the teams I want to see them tonight in the kitchen after everyone is asleep."

"Will do."

"Make sure nobody else knows about this. Damned Reb spies might be listening. We gotta keep this quiet."

The three teams met in the kitchen about midnight. January 8 was turning into January 9. Thomas Rose and Andrew Hamilton outlined the plan for the second tunnel escape. They would follow the same procedures since they had seemed to work on the excavation of the first one. They would start a little closer to the east wall toward the small sewer. Problem was, they couldn't see in the tunnel, so they really didn't know if they were going in the right direction. That was Hamilton's job. Keep the tunnel going straight. He would wriggle into it with a broom handle and would ram it straight ahead, so the digger could follow it. Trouble was, he thought, the broom handle was only six feet long. But, really, six feet was long enough since it would take quite some time to dig that far. Hamilton was thankful for that since that meant he didn't have to be in the tunnel all that much, for the stench from the sewage was overpowering. He couldn't fathom how the diggers were handling it. The dead rats in the tunnel didn't help, either.

"It's kind of exciting to be part of the tunneling effort," Tom Armstrong thought to himself. "Takes my mind off everything else in this rat hole." Armstrong was actually feeling a little better, more optimistic. The depression certainly wasn't as bad as it had been, but it was still there, especially during the day and the nights when he wasn't in the cellar. He continued to pray daily for deliverance, thanking God for giving him something to do, instead of just sitting there starving or freezing to death. One advantage of the cellar. It was warmer. No windows. No cold wind.

The work continued for about a week, the teams alternating as planned. On the night of January 13, Rose was alternating with David Garbett, digging toward the small sewer. Rose had just entered the tunnel in relief of his friend when he heard a crashing sound up ahead. He crawled forward and found the tunnel blocked by a piece of iron. Feeling his way around it, he concluded they had unfortunately gone under the place where the old, unused furnace had been thrown, and its weight simply collapsed it into the tunnel.

"Son-of-a-damn bitch," he said. "All that damn work for nothing. Son-of-a-goddam-bitch, Dammit!"

Tom Armstrong was in the cellar with his team that night and heard Rose swearing at the misfortune that had just happened. "Uh, oh, this isn't going to be good," he said to David Garbett.

"Nope. Colonel don't swear like that unless somethin's really wrong."

Thomas Rose emerged from the tunnel. "Well, boys, this one's done, too."

Tom Armstrong could feel the hope and excitement drain from his brain and the depression start to seep back in.

"Now what?" he asked.

"Don't rightly know right now. All I do know is that I'm getting out of this damn place. Son-of-a-goddam-bitch."

Now, you can imagine the disappointment and despair the conspirators felt, but they couldn't tell anyone.

"Caleb, I don't know if I can take any more of this," Tom Armstrong said. "I get my hopes up and then they are dashed, first by a flood, then by some quirk of fate that put the furnace right where we wanted to go. Wonder why Rose and Hamilton didn't see it when they decided to try this."

"Don't know, Sump, but you can't give up. It's our only hope. No boxes, no letters, no nuthin', but you can't give up," the big West Virginian said.

A few of the conspirators were down in the kitchen on January 14 and overheard a squad of rebel soldiers talking about the cave in. All Armstrong heard that gave him a glimmer of hope was that it "musta been the rats." Evidently, the Johnnies had concluded that rats had been in the sewer and had weakened the ground. That was the reason the furnace crashed down. Never even considered there might have been a tunnel.

"Edwards," said Thomas Rose, later that day "come with me tonight. Let's see if Johnny found the tunnel."

Thomas Rose and Caleb Edwards met in the kitchen about 1 o'clock in the morning of January 15, 1864. Opening the fireplace, they let down the rope ladder and climbed down into the East Cellar. They felt their way around and concluded that nothing had changed since they had scrambled up the ladder after the furnace caused the cave-in.

"Looks fine to me, Caleb," said Thomas Rose.

"Nuthin's different. Johnny ain't been here. Woulda thought some of them would have come to see what happened. Said the rats caused it. Them dead ones sure do stink. Whew. Let's get outta here."

"Agreed, but there's got to be a way out of here. We have to get to that small sewer somehow."

"We gonna start again?"

"Yeah. I want to meet with everyone today."

"OK, I'll pass the word."

And, with that, the two men climbed back up the rope ladder, hid it in its usual place in the hole in the wall, replaced the bricks in the fireplace, tucked in the mortar, and threw soot back at it. They climbed the stairs back to their rooms, Rose to the Chickamauga, Edwards to the Milroy.

"We're gonna dig again, Sump," Edwards whispered to Tom Armstrong. "Rose wants to see us this afternoon."

Later that morning, over in the Chickamauga Room, Thomas Rose and Andrew Hamilton were in hushed conversation over a chess board. They had to make it look as normal as possible.

"Andrew, what do you think about digging day and night? Increases the risk of being found out, but it also gets us there twice as fast."

"Whoa, Thomas, have you forgotten about *Roll Call*? That bastard, Erasmus Ross, comes in here with the adjutant and the guards and counts us. You know that."

"Yeah, but he doesn't take us by name. He only wants to hit the number. I think I have a way to help him do that, even if we are in the cellar."

"Huh? We have five of us in the cellar at his morning visit. He comes up five short."

"Not necessarily. What would happen if we have five men counted twice. Five of us near the front of the line, as soon as Ross has passed, sneak around the other side of the line to near the end and blend in. He counts every man in the line, including us two times, and guess what, he hits the number."

"You really think that would work?"

"Let's try it tomorrow morning. Send two of the men into the kitchen just before *Roll Call*. You and I will get counted twice."

The next morning, B.B. McDonald and David Garbett disappeared from the Chickamauga Room at dawn. Precisely at 8 o'clock, on January 16, 1864, little Erasmus Ross, the prison clerk, and Lieutenant John Latouche, the adjutant, appeared in the Chickamauga Room with the usual gang of guards, ordering the prisoners to line up. Andrew Hamilton was about tenth in line with Thomas Ross somewhere around sixty. The clerk and the adjutant walked by, counting. Hamilton waited until they had gone by, slipped out, got on his hands and knees and crawled as quickly as he could to near the end of the line. Thomas Rose followed. They stood up and found a place to stand, where they waited for Ross and Latouche. Came right by them. No funny looks as if to say, "I think I've seen you before today." No nothing. The two Union prisoners just smiled at each other.

None of the other prisoners thought anything of it, two men getting into line late. If nothing else changes, Rose and Hamilton thought "repeating" would work. While Team 1 was in the cellar, Team 2 will cover for them. Team 3 will cover for Team 2. And, Team 1 will cover for Team 3. No problem. Work on the third tunnel would commence that night.

The only problem? The tunnelers were getting weak from lack of food. No meat for two weeks. The Confederate guards were actually asking the prisoners for any scraps they might have. Everyone in Libby Prison was dying of starvation, and it was still damn cold. But, on the other hand, it was warm in the cellar, and somebody had the bright idea of roasting the dead rats. Maybe they could talk the guards into killing a mule or a horse. Could eat that, too. As Tom

Armstrong peered out one of the south windows, he saw a rebel sentinel break open a box that he assumed was meant for one of the prisoners inside the walls of Libby.

Men were dying every day. They plain and simple just lost hope and gave up. Tom Armstrong and Caleb Edwards were lucky. They had something to do in digging the tunnel, and Tom had Francis Porter waiting for him at home, and Caleb had his wife, Margaret, and the children back in Wheeling. That gave them some hope. They were warm on their days and nights in the cellar and when they burned the books, but they were still hungry, even with the fried rats.

At about 11 o'clock that night, the bricks were removed, and the work began on tunnel #3. It would continue day and night toward the small sewer, with the "repeaters" fooling Erasmus Ross at each *Roll Call*. None of the Yankee prisoners knew, though, that Ross was actually a Union sympathizer and would have overlooked the missing men, reporting to Major Turner that he had hit the number every time.

Four days later, on January 20, David Garbett broke through to the sewer. He was elated, for a while. He cracked the casing and found a wooden lining. "Shit," he thought to himself. "Not even Armstrong could get through that as small as he is. I gotta tell Rose and Hamilton."

"Thomas," he said emerging from the tunnel, "damn pipe is lined with wood. Damn, hard wood. Tried to cut my way through it. No way."

"I'll take a look. It's our only hope."

Thomas Rose crawled to the end of the tunnel. It smelled awful, it was hot, there was no light, and the fanning effort to get air in had failed miserably. He hit the wood in front of him as hard as he could with the jack-knife. He felt the wood where he thought he hit it. Not even a scratch. He thought, "Somehow, some way, we have to break this or die trying." He slid back toward the cellar, trying to remember if they had any other tools. "One of these men has a chisel, wonder if that would work."

For the next day or so, the diggers beat on the oak lining inside the small sewer. Armstrong and Edwards even took a turn at it since Thomas Rose was now going to use any one of the men as a digger, just to use all of his resources. The conditions inside the tunnel were so bad that many of the men simply would not go back in. They would come out and throw the chisel down, walking toward the rope ladder. Up they went and with them any hope of escaping from Libby Prison. With no men to work, Rose figured he and Hamilton were on their own. Even though they had met with three failures in the last thirty days since Hamilton opened the fireplace, the two lead conspirators weren't going to quit.

"Thomas," said Andrew Hamilton, "we finally reached the sewer, but we can't break in. What the hell are we gonna do now?"

"There's only one answer, Andrew. None of what we have done so far has worked. So, we have to try from the other side of the cellar. We can tunnel under that vacant lot on the east side of the building. Problem is, I don't know if there's any damn sewers on that side that could flood the tunnel. If there isn't, we dig down seven or eight feet, then we go straight toward Canal Street. Remember that small shed over there, looks like it's on stilts so flood waters don't get in, maybe three feet off the ground. What happens if we tunnel toward it and come up under it? Nobody will see us, not even the sentinels. We time their patrols, and we duck onto Canal Street when their backs are turned."

"You're plum loco, Thomas. How the hell are we gonna do that? Your brain has been scrambled by all the time you spent in the tunnels."

"Crazy? Maybe so, but maybe that's what I have to be right now. You and me, Andrew, and we're getting out of here."

"You're downright nuts. Dammit," Andrew Hamilton said. "Oh, what the hell? Let's dig down tonight. See how easy or hard the dirt is. See if there's any water in it. How far you think we have to go? And, where the hell do we start?"

"Northeast corner of the cellar. No Johnny will look for a tunnel there. Too many goddam rats. As far away from the sewers and canal as possible. Lessens the chance of there being water. Reckon it's about fifty feet, maybe more. Only way it will work if the soil is loose."

"We gonna get help?"

"No, not until we see if this might work. Have to show the men we have a fighting chance to come up out of the tunnel undetected."

"Maybe, I'm crazy, too," said Andrew Hamilton. "What the hell?" Hamilton said again, beginning to doubt his own sanity. "Let's give it a go."

That night, January 23, 1864, Thomas Rose stuck his jack-knife into the flooring of the northeast corner of the East Cellar. It was soft and came up easily. He scooped it up with his hands and threw it on the floor behind him. He was on his own. Andrew Hamilton had remained in the kitchen to stand guard. They had told no one else that they were going to try again. Probably wouldn't have had any takers. So, like they had reasoned, they had to prove to the men, Caleb Edwards and Tom Armstrong among them, that this time it would be different.

Rose was excited. The dirt crumbled in his hands. The clay on the other side had been difficult to dig through, ½ inch with each strike of the jack-knife. This would be a lot easier, he thought. "Better tell Andrew that I'm gonna start down," he thought to himself. Rose climbed the rope ladder back into the kitchen and reported to Andrew Hamilton.

"This will work, Andrew. This will work," he said excitedly. "I will dig tonight. Come down to the cellar in a couple of hours. You can judge for yourself." And, with that, Thomas Rose climbed down the ladder and into the East Cellar.

Using his hands, he dug like a mole until about 2:30 A.M. on Sunday, January 24, 1864. Almost furiously and, with passion, he dug in the dark, with the awful stench and the squealing of the rats. The hole was wide enough to let in the foul air, so he could breathe, but he still felt sick. He heard a voice.

"Thomas, come out and let me see." It was Andrew Hamilton who had descended into the cellar. He wasn't in the hole very long.

"Bravo, Thomas. Might just damn work."

"I figure we have to go down, maybe at a 30-degree angle, about eight feet. Then we level off and dig straight toward that shed. Let's get the men together in the morning to tell them."

"You're both goddam crazy," snarled Caleb Edwards after Hamilton and Rose had explained the new venture to the rest of the tunnelers, their heads nodding in agreement. Edwards had just about had enough. He was tired, sore, starving, and cold. He'd worked hard, sacrificed sleep. Enough was enough.

"Then, come down tonight and see for yourself, Edwards."

"Not worth my time, but what else am I gonna do?"

At 1:00 o'clock on the morning of January 27, Caleb Edwards crawled into the hole that Thomas Rose had dug. He came out backwards, of course, but when he turned to face the two lead conspirators, he was smiling.

"Dirt's soft, easy to dig. We gotta go how far?" Then, thinking to himself, "Damn good thing I lost all that weight. Never coulda got in there. It ain't real big, but it'll do."

Indeed, the tunnel was only 36 inches wide and 30 inches high. Damn good thing the men had all lost weight. They would have to scrunch and wriggle their way some fifty feet, pulling a haversack tied to their shoes, if they had them, to freedom. Well, that was if all went perfectly, as planned. The digging commenced then and there, Caleb Edwards in the lead on Team #1. Thomas Rose sent the rest back upstairs, telling them to post a guard to warn the men in the cellar of guards approaching. Caleb dug for maybe five minutes. He couldn't breathe. That would become the norm. Five minutes, maybe less, in the tunnel, then they had to come out. Next man in. It went like that for the next three hours and stopped when the guard in the kitchen called down to the cellar."4 o'clock, and all's well."

Rose plugged the entrance. David Garbett, Andrew Hamilton, and Caleb Edwards tramped over the squealing rats to the rope ladder and one by one, up they went. They had advanced to the point where the tunnel would level out and could now proceed toward the shed.

"Andrew, make sure you have that broom handle tomorrow morning. We're going night and day until we break through." They found no water in the tunnel.

The enthusiasm of Thomas Rose and Andrew Hamilton was infectious and buoyed the spirits of the other conspirators, but for the rest of the inmates at Libby Prison, it was a continuing hell. By this time, anything that could be burned would be burned. The men of the Milroy Room still had some wood to go, but it would not last long. Rations were getting scarcer and scarcer. Men dying every day from starvation. An awful way to go, especially when you know it's coming. But, by and large, these were men of faith, the majority of whom were convinced that life was soon to get better on the other side, strangers saying prayers over the dying and wishing them God-speed. Most didn't hear. They were too far gone. Some, who could still hear, simply smiled as they took their last breath.

By late January 1864, there was no privacy in Libby Prison. Men huddled together around the oven to try to stay warm. Men jumping up and down or marching in place. That was tough to do because it required energy. Energy requires sustenance. And, food was scarce. What made that worse was that the prisoners could see the rebel guards busting open the boxes that had been sent from Indiana, Michigan, New York, Pennsylvania, Maine, and all the other northern states. Everything you did was out in the open. The tunnelers continued to help Erasmus Moss hit the number, even though he really didn't care. Neither did most of the men. Their dignity had been stripped away. The dashing cavalry officer frying dead rats or whatever else he could find in the kitchen. A colonel washing his own drawers in dirty, awful-smelling water. Using the privy in plain sight of everyone in the room. So, beneath them, so humbling, but the men of Libby Prison had no choice. Some just didn't care. And, some did care and held out hope while the dead pile grew larger and larger every day.

Unbeknownst to all but fifteen of them, the digging in the East Cellar continued day and night. The conditions were awful, but the tunnelers had experienced no problems as they worked their way underground toward the little shed. No water filling the tunnel; no furnaces caving it in. It was smooth sailing. And, over there in the northeast corner of the East Cellar, they didn't have to worry about the rebel guards who just did not inspect that area given the awful stench of the dead rats' decay, the running and squealing of the ones that remained alive, and endless darkness. Couldn't see your hand in front of your face. But somehow, the fifteen became accustomed to it and dug with a purpose, fingernails gone, fingers, elbows, and knees bleeding. They didn't care. This was the ONE!

It was Saturday, February 6, 1864. It was just after *Reveille*. Thomas Rose, Andrew Hamilton, and Captain W.S.B. Randall, of the 2nd Ohio Volunteer Infantry, were standing in a corner of the Milroy Room.

"Today's the day, W.S.," said Thomas Rose. "When it gets dark, go into the tunnel and come up. I think I got us close yesterday. Break the surface and see where we are."

Rose and Hamilton had used the broom handle to measure how far they had gone and were pretty sure that they had made about fifty-three feet, give six inches one way or the other. The object had been to dig under the vacant lot, under the fence that surrounded the prison, and under the shed. Now, fifteen days after they had started tunnel #4, they were going to find out where they were.

Caleb Edwards had wanted to be the one to breach the surface, but Thomas Rose had chosen Randall. Edwards really didn't mind. He would be free that night.

When it was dark, around 9 o'clock that Saturday evening, W.S.B. Randall, who had been on Team 3, wriggled his way into the tunnel and slithered as fast as he could toward the incline to the surface. He figured he might have three or four minutes' worth of oxygen, so he breathed the foul air as long as he could and slid as fast as he could. At last, he found the incline and started digging up. Joyously, and quite suddenly, cool, fresh air was washing all over him. He took several deep breaths to clear out his lungs and wiped the dirt away from his face. Randall inched upward and peered out of the hole in the ground. All seemed well until he got his arms out and pulled himself out to see where he was. In the process, he had kicked a large stone, or so he thought. Turns out it was.

"Dammit, that hurts," he said to himself. And then he looked around. "Son-of-a-goddam-bitch, I can still see the prison. I'm on the wrong side of the goddam fence. Son-of-a-goddam-bitch."

He heard someone coming, and, in his haste to get back to the tunnel, he stumbled over the stone, knocking it loose. He heard it tumbling down a little way and then crash into the fence.

"Dammit," he said to himself. The footsteps were louder and quicker. He might not make it back to the hole. He fell to the ground, face up, now covered with dirt, about five feet short of the entrance to the tunnel. He didn't move a muscle and was a pool of sweat. He did not dare breathe since he figured the sentinel was just looking into the prison yard from the other side of the fence. Finally, he heard footsteps, becoming fainter and fainter. The sentinel was walking away. It was the fifteenth night since they had started tunnel #4.

"The goddam tunnel is short or didn't go the right way," W.S.B. Randall complained to Thomas Rose. "We're screwed, dammit."

Rose listened, then crawled into the tunnel, making it to the hole at the end in just a few minutes. It was lovely, he thought, to have fresh air. So, when Rose came up out of the tunnel, he could see the problem. "Can be fixed," he thought to himself. "Will take some time. Have to move southeast about ten feet." He jammed the broomstick into the earth, pointing it in the direction that he needed to go. When he would start back to the cellar, he knew that he would have to plug the hole.

Randall had told him about the stone, so Thomas Rose crawled toward the fence, felt his way along, and finally located the stone. Getting back to the hole, he plugged it, packed dirt around it, and began the journey back to the cellar, the stench of the air getting stronger as he went. As he crawled along he thought, "Maybe that was a lucky break. Now, we know exactly where we have to go." It was 2 o'clock in the morning on Sunday, February 7, when he came back into the East Cellar. Thomas Rose had made a decision. He would dig alone that day. He would take B.B. McDonald with him to fan the air, but no one else. Andrew Hamilton would stand guard.

There wouldn't be any church this day, and Confederate guards usually took it easy on Sunday, never expecting anything would happen. Around noon, after getting some much-needed rest, Rose and McDonald climbed down into the kitchen, opening the fireplace, and descending into the East Cellar. Rose went into the tunnel, determined not to come out until either he knew the tunnel would work or he died. That day, working by himself, and with a little fresh air coming into the tunnel from where he had removed the dirt around the stone that had plugged the hole the night before, he worked tirelessly into the night. When he was done, he used the dirt he had dislodged to put more patch around the stone that was plugging the hole.

He came out of the tunnel around midnight, totally exhausted. B.B. McDonald was in worse shape since he had had no fresh air to breathe all day. "One more day," said Thomas Rose. "One more day," and they climbed up the ladder into the kitchen.

On Monday, February 8, Rose awoke and hurt all over. There was no way he could finish the tunnel by himself. He rolled over and said to Andrew Hamilton, "I'm going to need help. Go find McDonald and get me one more."

Hamilton crawled over the sick, starving, and dying to B.B. McDonald's "space." "Rose wants you and one more to work with him today," Hamilton whispered.

"Johnston's right here. You know him. 6th Kentucky Volunteers."

"Yes, wake him a little later. Meet us in the kitchen after noon."

"Right." Hamilton crawled back to his space. He told Thomas Rose, "Will meet them just after noon. I'll stand guard, but there's no rumors that Johnny knows anything."

Around 12:30 PM, Captain I.N. Johnston descended, headfirst, into the tunnel. It was the 17th day of work. Rose was manning the cuspidor with McDonald fanning as hard as he could. The three men would trade off, every half hour or so since there was some fresh air in the tunnel. Finally, about 7 o'clock in the evening, Thomas Rose took matter into his own hands. He would finish the damn tunnel himself. He was that close to his dream of freedom.

B.B. McDonald crawled out. Rose told him and I.N. Johnston they could go back upstairs. He would finish it off himself and back down the tunnel he slid. He worked furiously, working up quite a sweat and becoming quite sick from the exertion with little food to fuel him. Around 11 P.M., he ran into a wooden post. "Damn, I'm under the fence." Working his way around the post, he started his ascent, angling up at about thirty degrees. He was on his back now, panting out loud. He wondered if he might suffocate if he worked any harder. He began pounding his clenched fists into the dirt above him. A stream of fresh air found his face. "Damn, I'm there," he thought, becoming more excited with each blow of his fists. Finally, he broke through. He poked his head out and looked around. "Perfect," he thought. He then made the hole large enough to allow his departure from the underground. By God, he was right where he was supposed to be, under what used to be a shed for storing tobacco, behind the fence, sheltered from the eyes of the prison guards. He crawled along, under the shed, southward toward Canal Street. He was free! Actually, he could run if he wanted to, all by himself, to freedom, but he thought better of it. He needed to reconnoiter and needed to see where he was and what the obstacles were. The tunnelers deserved it.

The gas lights in the streets of Richmond allowed him to see quite clearly. Yes, he was free, but he was, at the same time, scared to death. A sentinel approached. Hiding in the shadows, Thomas Rose began counting silently, "one, one thousand, two, one thousand." He counted until the sentinel got to the corner, and when he turned, Rose began counting again. He watched this exercise twice more. The counts were pretty close, close enough to relay them to the men who were so desperate to escape. When the guard turned his back, Thomas Rose came out from under the tobacco shed and went east down Canal Street. Fifteen minutes later, he was back at the shed, having completed a circumnavigation of the big building. He found a board that he dragged back to the entrance to the tunnel, and when he had crawled back in, he slid it over the entrance to conceal it.

Thomas Rose could barely crawl back to the East Cellar, he was that tired. He finally made it, pulling himself up the rope ladder to the kitchen. He repacked the bricks in the fireplace, refitted the mortar, and as customary, threw soot on it. He had to find Andrew Hamilton. Hamilton could not conceal his joy, but they had work to do.

"Andrew, go over to Milroy and wake the boys. Meet us in the kitchen at 3." It was 2:30 o'clock in the morning of Tuesday, February 9, 1864.

"Can't you and me go right now?"

"Dammit, I'm tempted, but the boys have worked so hard. We must let them try to escape as well."

At 3 A.M., the fifteen conspirators were in the kitchen.

"Men, we go tonight. Each of you may take one friend who hasn't worked with us with you. You don't have to, if you don't want to. The tunnel ends under that shed, and there is a fence that shields us from the view of the prison. The guards patrol Canal Street. Imagine Cary Street, too. It takes the guards about thirty seconds to make one pass down the street. When he turns his back, go south toward Cary Street. He will never see you. Then go north on Cary. You can take whatever you can get through the tunnel. Haversack with your belongings. Dress warm since it will be cold out there. I don't know where the Union lines are. Travel at night if you can. Stay hidden during the day. You'll have to find your own food. Hunch is the Negroes will help you. Oh, guard your matches. You will need them for the warmth of a campfire. Just make sure Johnny doesn't see you. Try to stay together, but if you get separated, do not try to find each other, just go. Team 1 will go first. A couple from Team 2 can go with them. I want you to go in batches of 15, no more. Do not travel as a group. Get out of Richmond as fast as you can. They'll find out we're gone at *Roll Call*. Expect bloodhounds. Get in water, I know it's going to be cold, to throw them off."

Tom Armstrong was beyond excited. He would be free in less than 24 hours. Visions of Francis Porter, there in Clinton, Illinois, and his family, back in Norwich, flashed across his brain. It would be dangerous, but he was ready for it. So was Caleb Edwards.

"Caleb, let's just you and me go. If Arty was alive, one of us could've taken him, but he's not. I'll go see Rose to tell him what we want to do."

"Right, Tom. I'll see if I can find a coat and a blanket somewhere. We can worry about food later. Pray for good weather, 'cuz it's gonna be damn cold out there. Ain't looking forward to sleeping with no cover, but it's a helluva lot better than bein' in here." It wouldn't be that simple, but they didn't know it. The Confederate soldiers and most of the people of Richmond would gladly shoot the escaped prisoners.

It had been fifty-three days since Andrew Hamilton had first removed the bricks from the fireplace, and now, freedom beckoned. When Tom Armstrong found Thomas Rose, Rose was talking to an older man. Turns out it was Colonel Harrison Hobart of the 21st Wisconsin Volunteers. He wasn't going into the tunnel that night. Thought he was too old and would slow the others down. But he would contribute in a big way. You see, Rose did not want a stampede down Canal Street or Cary Street. His plan was to permit the prisoners who had not worked on the tunnel to leave the next day. It would take time to get all of them out of Libby Prison, but time was what they had. A few men out at various times during the day after morning *Roll Call*. Not the whole eight hundred. Just those able to travel.

Armstrong overheard Rose. "Harrison, after we're gone, pull the ladder up and seal the fireplace. Wait an hour to make sure all's clear. If it is, open it back up for the next fifteen. Armstrong, good that you're here. You're the first one out in the second group."

"Good, Thomas. Glad to."

"Who's going with you?"

"Edwards. Like our chances together."

"Good pair. Now get out of here and get ready."

Even though Tom Armstrong and Caleb Edwards had a lot to do, the day dragged on and on. They even tried to get some sleep. As they prepared for the most dangerous experience they might ever face in their lives, they said their prayers, made some plans for escape routes, and tried to relax. It was a nice day in Richmond, Virginia that February 9, 1864, relatively warm at just over 45 degrees. Sun streamed through the bars of the windows. The Confederate guards had no idea of what was going to happen that very night.

Getting back to their spaces, Tom Armstrong and Caleb Edwards unlocked the last boxes that they had received from home, the previous November. Armstrong had forgotten about the box and opened it in great anticipation for what he might have not taken out. Indeed, he found a shirt and some socks that he quickly shoved into his haversack along with some hardtack, stale for sure, but better than nothing. Edwards wasn't so lucky. All he found was the compass that his father, Caleb, Sr., had included in the box.

"That'll help a lot," he said to Tom Armstrong.

The rest of the day was spent planning their escape route. This was not going to be easy since the Commonwealth of Virginia was rife with Confederate soldiers. It was even more dangerous for the Federals now since the Battle at Gettysburg which forced Major General Robert E. Lee back into his home state with 50,000 men. Who knows where they were?

"Caleb, I'm smaller than you, and I'm used to being outside. We have to know what's in front of us, so I'll climb a tree every half hour or so to see what's out there. Wish I had some field glasses. Oh, well, we just have to stay away from them. Have to sleep by day and travel by night. I'll reconnoiter from a tree while there's still light, and then we can be off. What's our first move?"

"Getting the hell out of Richmond. Whattya think about going north just like we came south on the Virginia Central? We can walk the tracks at night since we know where they go."

"Darn fine idea, Caleb," and it was settled. They would go northwest along the tracks to Staunton and would figure it out from there.

Night time came slowly. But, by 7 o'clock on the evening of February 9, the first fifteen of the conspirators and their friends, led by Thomas Rose and Andrew Hamilton, moved toward the kitchen. After giving Harrison Hobart the password, the bricks were loosened, and Thomas Rose unlimbered the ladder and disappeared into the darkness. Andrew Hamilton was next. Then came B.B. McDonald and a friend from the 102nd Ohio, followed by I.N. Johnston and a friend of his. The order had been predetermined by Thomas Rose.

Tom Armstrong and Caleb Edwards watched from the windows and saw Rose and Hamilton emerge from the shed onto Canal Street, heading north. Then came McDonald, followed by Johnston. Forty-five minutes later, Tom Armstrong and Caleb Edwards approached Harrison Hobart and gave him the password. Hobart removed the bricks that he had repacked after the first group left.

"Where ya goin,' boys?" Hobart asked.

"North," responded Caleb Edwards. That's all he would say.

"Good luck," Hobart said, as Edwards unfurled the rope and climbed down into the cellar. Tom Armstrong was right behind.

Not fifteen minutes later, Edwards poked his head out of the tunnel and crawled on his belly along the ground under the shed toward Canal Street. When he reached the iron gate in the fence, he slid the latch upward and opened the gate. He waited for his friend.

"Gotta go quick, Sump." They watched the sentinel, and when he turned his back, the two Federal officers silently walked briskly toward the railroad depot from whence they had begun their adventure at Libby Prison. The city of Richmond was lit down there by the depot from the gas lights, and there was light from the moon to let them see their way. While the rest of the tunnelers were coming out under the shed, Edwards and Armstrong really didn't care. They were free, but there was danger everywhere.

While they knew that Rose and Hamilton had gone east, Edwards and Armstrong traveled west to the depot, where they would pick up the tracks of the Virginia Central Railroad. They also knew that they had over a hundred miles to cover and figured they could be near Staunton in a week or so. The rumor had been that there were Union troops in and around Williamsburg, to the northeast of Libby Prison, and the two friends thought that might be a bit too crowded, for if there were Union troops, there would be Confederates as well. The war wasn't over, they knew, and they didn't want to find themselves confronted by pickets or cavalry. They also knew that there were Confederate troops in Richmond that they would have to avoid. Silence was absolutely necessary. But, to them, the least danger was going northwest.

Getting out of Richmond before sunup was imperative since they assumed, properly, that the Confederate troops garrisoning there would be rising then. Not knowing where the Johnnies were was a disadvantage, but even so, they figured that the Rebels certainly would not be expecting to see two Union soldiers in tatters walking along the railroad. But, Tom Armstrong and Caleb Edwards simply could not take the chance and traveled, at first, by night. It seemed to be working. The tracks of the Virginia Central Railroad cut between two hills on the northwest side of the city meaning the path to freedom would be mostly flat. They guessed that the Confederates had forts on the hills and hoped they could sneak by unseen. All they had to do was follow the tracks west at night, avoid the towns during the day, find some cover under which to sleep, and find food. That was all, but enough. Undaunted, they pressed on during the dark of early morning of February 10, 1864. As long as they kept moving, the cold didn't bother them. But, they also remembered that the train that had brought them to Richmond had clattered through the mountains on the way from Staunton. They'd have to climb them, and it would be even colder up there.

They cleared the city limits of Richmond undetected around midnight and decided to push on westward. Five hours later, they saw the first light of the new day and holed up in some dense brush. Tom Armstrong took the stale hardtack from his haversack, broke it with a rock, and gave some to Caleb Edwards.

"What we gotta do is find food. Not sure how we're gonna do that at night. Maybe we'll just have to take a chance during the day. Now, if we get out in the open and see a farmhouse, mebbe we can get some food. Who they gonna tell? And, we can be gone if they do tell someone. Only problem is if they start shooting. Let's try it tomorrow."

"Good, Caleb, I got another idea. What happens if we hear a supply train coming west to pick up stuff for the army back east. Wouldn't be any soldiers on it. Just jump into an empty car. Sure would beat walkin' through the mountains, and we could be in Staunton in a day or so. Could sleep. Avoid the towns. And, if we stole some food, might be a rather pleasant trip."

"Have to get to the next town and wait for one."

"Imagine they come pretty regularly. Lee needs all the food he can get."

"We gotta get a gun, Sump. And some clothes."

"Right." And the two free Federal officers fell to sleep in the underbrush, carefully concealed from the railroad. Later in the day, they realized that a macadam road ran right alongside the tracks and figured that would make the walk easier. But, it also made the movement of Confederate troops easier. They lay perfectly still as the clatter of hoofbeats came and went.

They pressed on, west toward Staunton, Armstrong climbing and searching for Confederate activity. Seeing none, they decided to travel by day.

It was still daylight, around 5 o'clock on Saturday, February 13, as they trudged west on the road beside the tracks of the Virginia Central Railroad. Caleb Edwards had brought a tin cup and scooped up some snow, breathing heavily on it to make it melt. They needed water, and this was the way to get it. Food was becoming a problem, the hardtack was gone, but around 6:30 PM, they smelled something very good.

"Haven't smelled that for a while," Edwards said. "Let's follow it."

The two Union officers left the road and traveled cross country in the direction of the delicious aroma, spotting a cabin with a rather large barn in a clearing some 400 yards away.

"Damn, there's some sheep. Wonder if the folks who live there will feed us."

They walked up to the cabin and knocked on the door. It was opened by a small, older, balding man who asked who the strangers were.

Armstrong and Edwards made up some names and said they were separated from their cavalry unit during a fight with the Yankees a few days before down near Richmond.

"Captain thought we was captured, sir," Edwards stammered.

"Yeah, we was all wearin' Yankee stuff, tryin' to confuse them. Nobody knew who to shoot, so when we was captured by Billy Yank, we told them we was one of them and then that night, we hightailed it outta there," added Tom Armstrong. "We been trying to get back to the unit for a couple days and sure could use some grub."

"We don't get many stragglers out here. Where ya goin'?"

"Staunton, sir," said Caleb Edwards. "We gonna grab a freight when we get to the next town."

They were invited to sit down for a wonderful meal, the likes of which they hadn't seen since they left home.

"You boys get some rest, and I'll take you into East Leake in the morning. Barn's right over there."

"Thank you kindly, sir, much obliged," said Tom Armstrong. "We'll see you then."

"I ain't buyin' it, Tom. Let's get the hell outta here," Caleb Edwards said as they started to retrace their steps back to the road. "This's gotta be a main road to Richmond. Don't trust anyone out here. If there's pickets, they'll know we were here. Footprints in snow, so we gotta get to the road."

Two days later, on February 15, they saw smoke ahead, down in a valley and approached quietly.

"Must be East Leake. Maybe we can hide here until we can steal some clothes and a gun. Could use some food, too." They had successfully traveled 38 miles and were on the verge of freedom.

Tom Armstrong and Caleb Edwards crept into the town as the sun was going down, with hardly anyone on the streets and music coming from a saloon. Torches lit the street, and they saw a livery stable.

"Wonder if we could stay there?" asked Edwards.

"I have a better idea. You know those shacks we saw outside of town. I bet they're Negro. Maybe we can get everything we need from them."

So, they backed away from the little town and found some ramshackle shacks about a mile east.

There was music coming from one of the houses. Tom Armstrong went up to the front door and knocked softly. A large, older Negro woman, with hardly any teeth and her head wrapped in a bandana, appeared. "Madam," he began, "we escaped prison in Richmond a few days ago and are trying to get north. Can you help us?"

"Lawd, have mercy. Sam'l, come here. Gots two boys need hep."

A very large ebony man with white hair and a pipe hanging out of his mouth appeared beside the woman. "Wacha need, boys?" asked Samuel Johnson.

"Place to sleep, some food, better clothes, and a gun," replied Tom Armstrong.

Samuel Johnson, opened the door and waved them in. "Claudee, they needs food," he said, and the woman went to the stove where it looked like some soup was boiling. "Be heppin' as we can."

"Thank you, sir," Tom Armstrong replied. "Much obliged. We are in your service."

Claudia Johnson pointed to a couple of chairs, poured some soup in some rather dirty looking bowls, and gave it to them. "Sleeps 'ere on da flo."

The next morning, all of the Negroes from the shanty neighborhood came 'round to see the escaped Union prisoners who were now on the run. The Negroes told them about the train that comes through East Leake everyday about 2 in the afternoon, gave them some cornbread to stuff in their haversacks, and found some clothes that would replace the tattered Union uniforms. No gun.

After thanking them for everything, Tom Armstrong and Caleb Edwards decided to see if their new disguises would work, strolling into the town of East Leake, Virginia around 1 PM on February 16, 1864, just in time to hear the whistle of a train coming from the east.

"This is looking better and better, Caleb. Could be in Staunton tomorrow."

Caleb Edwards and Tom Armstrong walked into Dooley's Saloon in East Leake, Virginia, threw their haversacks on a table, and walked up to the bar. Edwards had saved some Confederate money and ordered two cups of coffee. They sat down at the table, waited for the girl to bring them, and heard other customers talking about the massive escape from Libby Prison in Richmond. Some 100 got out, apparently. The waitress brought the coffee to the table and walked back to the bar, motioning to the bartender that she wanted to talk. The conversation was quite brief. The bartender immediately took off his apron, put on his hat and coat, and hurried out the back door. Evidently, the waitress had noticed "U.S." stamped on the haversacks. The bartender was "Hell Bent for Saturday" to find the town sheriff. There were two escaped Yankees sitting right there in his bar.

12 Camp Oglethorpe

Aloysius Dooley ran down Main Street, there in East Leake, Virginia, and burst through the door of the livery and found the town blacksmith, Marcus Chambers, hammering away on his anvil.

"Marcus, come quick. Git your gun. There's two Yankees settin' in the bar. Bet they 'scaped Richmond the other day. See if'n you can find some of the other boys. I gotta find Crawford and then tell the mayor."

Marcus Chambers dropped the hammer onto the sawdust on the floor, grabbed his shotgun from its rack, and ran to Hoffman's market across the street. William Hoffman was behind the counter, helping a customer, when Chambers came through the front door.

"Bill, git yer gun. We gonna capture coupla 'scaped Yankees over at Dooley's. Dooley's gonna git Crawford, too. We gotta git the mayor. Let's go."

Bill Hoffman excused himself from the customer, asking his wife, Harriet, to take over. Then, he and Marcus Chambers were out the door in a flash. They met up with Aloysius Dooley who had found Charles Crawford sitting at his desk in the Sheriff's office.

"C'mon, Charlie, git yer gun. Gonna have some fun at my place. Lemme borrow a rifle."

Dooley and Crawford caught up with Marcus Chambers and Bill Hoffman who had alerted Josephus Fergus, the mayor and who owned most of East Leake, that there were Union soldiers at Dooley's. With guns drawn, the five men set off for Dooley's Saloon.

Crawford ordered, "Bill, you 'n Marcus go in the back door. Other two and me go in the front. Wait 'til you see us before you show yourselves."

Crawford, Dooley, and Fergus approached the front of the saloon. Peering through the window, they could see the Yankees, sitting at the table, the smaller one looking at his watch. Suddenly, they got up and started for the door. But, the big sheriff, his sidearm loaded and ready, strode through the double swinging doors, nearly filling the doorway. Dooley and Fergus right behind him, rifles leveled and ready.

"You boys goin' somewhere?"

Tom Armstrong looked at Caleb Edwards. They could run, or they could try to bluff their way out. Neither alternative was particularly attractive. Armstrong nodded toward the back of the saloon and took off, Edwards right behind him. Then, the blacksmith and the grocer appeared, guns drawn. The jig was up. Edwards and Armstrong turned around.

"You boys under arrest," said Charles Crawford, polishing his badge with his left sleeve and brandishing the pistol in his right. He was grinning ear-to-ear. "Over to the jail, fellas." Marcus Chambers picked up the haversacks and threw them over his shoulder. He would accompany Crawford to the town's jail. Two cells, mind you, rifles stacked in a rack. The others went back to work. "Enough excitement for one day," thought the mayor.

The two Yankees heard the door to the cell slam shut behind them and turned around. "Dammit to hell, wonder how they knew," said Caleb Edwards.

"You boys ain't real smart," said Charles Crawford, showing them the haversacks. "Didn't take no genius to figure out who y'all were. Aloysius, here, saw it plain as day. Train to Richmond comin' around 6, so we'll just keep y'all here till then. Aloysius, can you have Virginia bring these boys some food?" It was Tuesday, February 16, 1864, just one week after they had crawled through the tunnel at Libby Prison to freedom.

"Son-of-a-goddam-bitch," Caleb Edwards fumed. "How could we have been so goddam stupid? Threw the sacks down on the table and never thought about the insignia. Son-of-a-goddam-bitch. Now we're going back to Libby. Goddam it."

Tom Armstrong sat down on the cot inside the cell with a forlorn look on his face. It had been easy thus far and hitching a ride on an empty freight later that afternoon would have been perfect. He was as unhappy at that moment as he had ever been in his life.

"Look at it this way, Sump," said Edwards. "At least they didn't shoot us."

"Mighta been better, Caleb," and he lay back and closed his eyes.

They had just finished eating the fried chicken, sweet potatoes, dried apples, and cornbread that Virginia, "Ginny," Dooley had brought them when they heard the whistle of the supply train, pulling into the depot. Coffee was good and hot.

Charles Crawford, pistol drawn, opened the door to the cell. Stopping at the blacksmith's shop, Marcus Chambers placed shackles on the wrists and ankles of the two escaped Yankees and led them out the door. Crawford would accompany them to Richmond and to the prison known as Libby. The train didn't stop that Tuesday evening, pulling into the depot in Richmond about 8:00 P.M. following a two-hour ride. Crawford slid open the freight car door and hopped down onto the platform, with Armstrong and Edwards following. As could be expected, Major Thomas Turner was very happy to see them.

"That makes 54 of the bastards who we caught. Jes' 'bout half of them. We'll git more." He thanked Charles Crawford who would now have to find a room for the night since the next train would not be until the following morning.

The shackles were removed, and guards led Tom Armstrong and Caleb Edwards down the stairs to the dungeon in the back of the Carpenter's Room. It was pitch black, except for a torch at the bottom of the stairs, cold, and damp. The rats just ignored them, squealing loudly as the door to the jail was slammed shut. Corn bread and water for a week. Finally, on Tuesday, February 23, the door was opened, with the guards motioning them to come along. Tom Armstrong was really sick and weak. So was Caleb Edwards. Adjusting to the light, they climbed back up to the Milroy Room, perhaps to die that very day. But, there was food: corn bread, ham, black beans, and coffee. Someone must have received a box from home. Maybe the Rebs were letting them through again. Must be so. Armstrong and Edwards ate voraciously, even though they didn't feel well.

And, then it was sleep. Even on the hardwood floors, it was the best night's rest they'd had in a while except that night spent at the Johnson's place.

There was no activity at all in Libby Prison. Well, compared to what it had been for the fifteen men who had dug the tunnels, it was just damn quiet and just damn cold. The 800 men who were still imprisoned there had lost all energy, many having lost the will to live. There had been over 1,000 just six months before. Death was taking its toll on the men in Libby Prison.

Tom Armstrong and Caleb Edwards reasoned that food was the answer to regaining strength and, since Major Turner had apparently relaxed the policy on the prisoners receiving boxes from home, took pen to paper. Edwards wrote to his beloved wife, Margaret, while Armstrong wrote to Jacob, his older brother. Evidently, the Rebels had relaxed the policy about writing home, as well. They actually seemed nicer now. Maybe they suspected that the days of the Confederate States of America were numbered.

In their letters home, they both requested the same things and lots of them: hams, butter, sugar, coffee, cheese, flour, lard, beans, dried fruit, candles, cans of condensed milk, crackers, soap, you name it, they asked for it. They didn't know whether the boxes would be delivered, but it was worth a shot. They also asked for clothing, some for right now in the cold and then also some for when the weather turned warm.

But, as February passed into March, they continued to avail themselves of others who were still there and who had received a box from home. They ate well and could feel their strength coming back. But, they hated Libby Prison and what it had meant to them since that awful day in Winchester the previous June. But now, there was no way out. Their only hope was to be paroled and exchanged.

Interestingly enough, it was true that the censorship that had marked Major Turner's prison had ended. Men were receiving letters from home that spoke about events in the war, efforts to get the prisoners of war exchanged, political events in Washington, and the Union plans to end the war. And, now, the guards were bringing newspapers into the prison for the men to read. So, the hopelessness of the previous six or seven months was not as dire, but the prisoners' own prospects were ominous if exchange was not possible. And, from what they read, it didn't seem like it was. Once again, the thought came to Tom Armstrong that the United States government, including the War Department and the Army, was content to let prisoners of war in the South just rot in jail.

"Caleb," Armstrong said one day near the end of February, "did we burn all the books?"

"Yeah, why?"

"I was just thinking that we might want to start classes again to relieve the boredom. And, maybe we could have a debate like the one we had with Charlie McCabe and Arty."

"I'm startin' to think you're crazy, too. Just like Rose and his damn fourth tunnel."

"Maybe, but he proved you wrong, didn't he? Wonder if Federico is still here. Wonder if he got exchanged. Let's try to find him and ask him what he thinks. Heard that Rose is here. Got captured up north. Oughta find him, too."

Caleb Edwards thought to himself, "Two weeks ago, Armstrong had given up, just about. Damn sick, too. Now, he's talkin' about classes and debates. Wonder if he is just relivin' the past that allowed him to cope with being in here. Hmmmm. So, we gotta find Cavada and Rose? Shit, Armstrong's the best damn friend I got right now. Better humor him."

It was Monday, February 29, 1864 (yes, it was Leap Year) when more "fresh fish" came into Libby Prison, courtesy of Colonel John Mosby. It seems there had been a cavalry skirmish, now known as the Second Battle of Dranesville, over there in Loudon County, in which Colonel Mosby's Confederate troopers sprung a trap on Captain James Sewell Reed's 2nd Massachusetts Cavalry and 16th New York Cavalry. Twelve Yankees were killed, several wounded, and seventy-one captured who were destined for Libby Prison.

The new prisoners would certainly have some first-hand news of the war and were questioned endlessly by the residents of the big prison. They reported that there was fighting in Virginia between the armies of Union Major General Ulysses S. Grant and Confederate

Lieutenant General Robert E. Lee with Grant pushing Lee farther south.

They also said that Major General William Tecumseh Sherman, who had been active out in the west, was now in northern Georgia with over 90,000 men. Sherman had succeeded in freeing up the Mississippi River, for the United States was now on the move in the deep South. When Tom Armstrong heard all this, he thought to himself, "It's General Scott's Anaconda Plan. The one Colonel Leggett told us about at Shiloh. They're using that pincer movement to surround the Johnnies and cut off their supplies at the same time. Imagine they still got all the ports blockaded, too. It's going to work. Golleee!" His spirits were buoyed by the news. "It will take some time," he reasoned, "but maybe this is the beginning of the end of the Confederacy."

The following afternoon, March 1, Armstrong and Caleb Edwards walked over to the Chickamauga Room to find Federico Cavada if they could. They didn't even know if he was alive, but they had to try to find him.

"Armstrong! Edwards! What the hell are you doing here? Thought you plum made it out." It was Colonel Thomas E. Rose.

"Thomas," said Caleb Edwards, "we almost did, but we were just plain damn stupid." He regaled Thomas Rose with the story; Rose was not amused. "Where'd they get you?"

"About six miles from the lines south of Williamsburg. Thought I had it made, but Rebel cavalry wouldn't buy my story. It was a pretty good one, but they said I didn't talk like them and got suspicious. Next thing I know I'm handcuffed and walking back to this damn place, being dragged along behind some mule. Rebs have filled the tunnel, so at this point there's no way out. At least we're getting food and letters from home, but nobody has any idea of what they're going to do with us."

Tom Armstrong told Thomas Rose about his thinking on Scott's Anaconda Plan. "And, I don't think there's anything the Johnnies can do about it. Not enough men. Not enough guns and other equipment. Not enough food. All we have to do is survive this place, and we will be free." Surviving, in all reality, would take some doing.

"That could take forever, Armstrong. I don't know how long, but most of the men in here don't have the will to live any more. Some of 'em been here over a year, starved, sick, cold. They'd rather be dead. Dead cart getting emptied just about every day." It was snowing in Richmond that afternoon, with some rain mixed in. Tom Armstrong's spirit began to sag once again while he listened to Thomas Rose.

Late in the morning of March 1, the three friends and every other prisoner in Libby heard gunshots. Lots of them. It was almost like there was skirmishing going on right outside their windows. Thomas Rose got up and went to a window, looking south. He couldn't see anything, but he could surely hear the sounds of battle. No infantry. Maybe it was a cavalry engagement. They would find out in the next several days that the Federal cavalry of Brigadier General Judson Kilpatrick had reached the inner defenses of Richmond with 3,500 men.

Kilpatrick's plan had depended on support from Colonel Ulric Dahlgren's force coming in from the north, but Dahlgren was nowhere to be found. Kilpatrick's troopers exchanged gunfire with the Rebel garrison that was seeing to Richmond's defense. The Union general desperately needed Dahlgren's support to fight his way through, and when he realized it wasn't forthcoming, he decided to withdraw to the east. Kilpatrick found out later that Dahlgren's column had been ambushed by Confederate cavalry outside the city. Colonel Ulric Dahlgren was dead, at the age of 21.

It turned out that the Kilpatrick raid was aimed at Libby Prison and Belle Isle. His objective had been to free the prisoners at both and use them to take the city of Richmond, burn it, and then assassinate Confederate States of America President Jefferson Davis and his entire administration. Only a warning issued by the engineer of an incoming train who had seen the Federal cavalry moving eastward toward the capital alerted the Confederate soldiers stationed at Richmond. That prevented the destruction of the city and the deaths of Davis and his staff. Dahlgren's force had suffered serious losses, over 350 killed, wounded, and captured. In his withdrawal, Kilpatrick did make it back to the Union lines safe and sound, ready to fight another day. But, Libby Prison and Belle Isle now had more guests, "fresh fish," who would provide graphic details of the raid and Dahlgren's death. It also turned out that the orders to destroy Richmond and kill Davis and his administration were in the pocket of his tunic. That didn't make the Confederate government very happy and outraged the people of the South when they read the account in their newspapers.

As its population swelled to about 900, life at Libby Prison went on, dreary and drab, as winter lingered over the city. Tom Armstrong and Caleb Edwards had managed to recruit Captain Chuck Riggs of the 123rd Ohio, Lieutenant Oscar Blair of the 12th Kentucky, and Major B.B. McDonald of the 102nd Ohio, who had also been recaptured, to help with setting up classes, but that was made somewhat problematic since there were no books. They also found Federico Cavada whom they asked to take a leadership role in getting the classes started. The curriculum, of course, would be limited, but having these instructional sessions would be good for everyone. Tom Armstrong, for one, would be back in his element, teaching school. He would give the others a week or so to prepare their lectures and to gather up paper and pencils, so the men could take notes. But, most of the prisoners were still suffering mightily in the cold, damp prison, and he wondered how many of them would want to engage in learning. "Not very many, I'm guessing, but we'll try."

The good news was that exchanges seemed to be taking place. Word had it that sometime in the first week of March, there was a huge exchange at City Point, Virginia, where the Union army had established a massive supply depot, some 25 miles south of Richmond. Something like 900 Confederate officers and men were exchanged for about 600 Union prisoners, presumably from Belle Isle, since there were certainly none of Libby's prisoners exchanged. But, that action gave the men hope, once again. And, then, the rumor was that there would be forty men exchanged every week. Now, how they would be chosen was a good question, but, again, it furthered each man's hope that one week, his name would be on the list. Tom Armstrong prayed daily for that relief.

It was true. A week later, on March 14, 1864, forty officers from Libby Prison, identified at random, made their way out the massive front door of the big building, under guard, and headed for the dock on the James River. They were also going to City Point to be exchanged, and then they were going home. Neither Tom Armstrong nor Caleb Edwards, nor any of their tunneling friends, were among them.

"Probly serves us right for escapin' and gettin' caught," groused Edwards. He was right.

Major Thomas Turner knew the men who had escaped and who were captured and brought back. There was no way in hell that he would exchange any of them. They needed to be punished some more, and seeing their comrades walk out the front door was just a subtle punishment, to remind them of their folly. It worked. The morale of the prisoners started to sag even more, if that was possible.

But, the big news that week came from Washington. On March 12, it was announced that General Ulysses S. Grant had been promoted to Lieutenant General of the United States Army by President Abraham Lincoln, giving Grant command of all the Union forces. Only one other man, namely George Washington, had that title conferred on him. In effect, then, Grant was the Union General-in-Chief just like General Robert E. Lee was to the Confederacy. This gave Grant, the master tactician and strategist, complete control of the Union drive to defeat the Confederate Army.

Grant replaced Major General Henry W. Halleck, who was, in Lincoln's mind, a "desk-sitter," holed up in Washington, DC, and who simply relied on telegraphic communication to issue orders to and receive reports from his generals. Grant was completely opposite. He thrived in the field, leading his men in battle, pursuing the enemy, and conferring with his commanders about strategy and resultant tactics. Lincoln had been frustrated by the lack of Federal success thus far in the war and the inaction of many of Halleck's generals, especially Major General George Meade. The President saw in Grant, a man of action. Grant's work at the Siege of Vicksburg in the summer of 1863 proved him to be resourceful, willing to take risks, trying new things when other tactics didn't work, and working closely with his commanders, notably General William Tecumseh Sherman, a fellow Ohioan whom Grant trusted implicitly.

Two other characteristics that stood out to the President were Grant's distrust of the media and his rejection of the limelight. The new commander-in-chief knew that newspaper reporters would somehow find out what the army's plans were, and their papers would print the stories for everyone, including the Davis administration there in Richmond to read. Grant would have to deal with that and would limit, as fast as he could, what his generals told the papers. "Let them just guess" he thought, and that became the Federal operating tactic.

The other thing was that he really didn't like being the center of attention, even though his new role put him there. He wasn't as polished socially as Halleck and some of the other commanders, but he didn't need to be. He was a soldier, reporting directly to President Lincoln, and he would do exactly what Lincoln asked him to do with little debate. That was also one of the things the Lieutenant General liked about Sherman. He would do what Grant asked. Period. And, he really didn't care what anyone thought except Lincoln, Grant, and, of course, his wife, Ellen.

Grant and Sherman had worked well together at Vicksburg and then at Chattanooga in October of 1863, and Sherman was quite pleased to hear that his friend was now the supreme commander of the Union Army. He was also quite sure that things would happen faster, which delighted him. Sherman, you see, lived to be on the march and then to engage the enemy in battle.

On March 17, 1864, Grant and Sherman met in Nashville, Tennessee, at which time the Lieutenant General informed Major General Sherman that he had been promoted to be commanding the Military Department of the Mississippi. In simpler and more pragmatic terms, it meant that he was now in charge of all of the forces in the west and south, from the Mississippi River to the Atlantic Ocean, from the southern borders of Virginia and Kentucky to the Gulf of Mexico. Major General James B. McPherson would replace Sherman as commander of the Army of the Tennessee and report to him.

At the meeting, Grant outlined the strategy. It would be Sherman's job to drive across the Deep South while Major General George Meade would attack Lee's army from the north. That was what General Winfield Scott had termed the "pincer movement" or the "Anaconda Plan." Just like the huge snake strangles its victims, Grant wanted to strangle the Confederacy. And, now, it was his job to accomplish it. And, to his delight, the President would leave him alone to do it. And, to the President's delight, he finally had a soldier in place to do the soldier's job.

While all of this was going on, the Federal prisoners at Libby were languishing in the cold as they had done all winter. Without boxes from home, a food shortage still existed in March 1864, only consisting of corn meal, with the cobs ground up in it, moldy bread, and rice infested with maggots. More men were starving than were dying of disease. If that were not enough, the exchanges were taking place, but none of the prisoners who had escaped and were recaptured had any chance of it. Watching other officers like Federico Cavada walk out the front door was very difficult for Tom Armstrong and Caleb Edwards to watch.

While some things were getting better, like the boxes from home, the mail being delivered, and the exchanges going on, it was still a miserable existence. Yes, these were signs of hope, and when the newspapers came into Libby announcing Grant's promotion, there was great excitement, but there was still a war going on. In fact, one day later in March, Armstrong, Edwards, and a young man named Wilfred Logan were looking out the window as a "truce ship" was coming down the James River when a shot rang out. A Rebel sentinel on the street below had fired his Springfield in the direction of that window, killing Logan instantly. Caught him right in the neck. Tom Armstrong and Caleb Edwards ran from the window, but this was a sobering reminder that yes, indeed, the war was not over, and the Rebels simply did not like them.

The classes were starting, although without Federico Cavada, they wouldn't be nearly as good. And, Tom Armstrong had managed to convince the other prisoners in the Milroy Room that a debate might be entertaining and had scheduled one for Wednesday, March 23, at 7 o'clock in the evening. Boxes had started arriving, not for all of the prisoners, but most of those receiving one were in a sharing mood. So, at least the food shortage was beginning to abate, but the weather was a different story. A major snowstorm had hammered Richmond that week and, with no glass or anything in the windows, there was some six inches of snow in the prison which made life quite unpleasant, especially when the call for "Lights Out!" was made. How in the world could you sleep comfortably in half a foot of snow? You don't. They simply pushed the snow into the corner of the Milroy Room and piled it up.

Colonel Thomas Rose of the 77th Pennsylvania, Colonel Harrison Hobart of the 21st Wisconsin, and Colonel William Ely of the 6th Connecticut had agreed to be judges in the debate. The question of the evening concerned the impact of the media, arguably newspapers, on daily life and was it more significant to people than the sermons they heard every Sunday in the nation's churches. Tom Armstrong and Captain Charles Riggs of the 123rd Ohio took the positive side. That is, they argued that newspapers did, indeed, influence the thoughts and attitudes of the people more than did the lessons of the clergy. Lieutenant Oscar Blair of the 12th Kentucky and Lieutenant Christopher Anderson of the 30th Indiana took the opposite view.

It was a spirited contest that was far from over that Wednesday evening and was scheduled to resume the following night. Tom Armstrong had presented a logical argument, stating that people read the newspapers every day and could not possibly ignore what was printed and that would shape their opinions about the war, politics, and the like.

He said, "The newspapers have a direct political slant. Some Republican, some Democrat. Some support the Copperheads. Some don't. It's just a matter of what newspaper you read and that probably depends on your own political leaning. And, at least in my home town, the *Zanesville Courier* is published every day. If you live in town, you can't help but be influenced by it. It's constant. And, in contrast, we go to church every Sunday, three services, but, at times, people lose interest in what the preacher is saying. And, even if they are listening, they may forget about what was said when they go back to their everyday lives the next day."

There were nods of approval and some vocal support for Armstrong's position on the matter.

Oscar Blair, a fundamental Baptist from Waitsboro, Kentucky, in the southeast corner of the state, had a different view. "What we hear on Sunday, what we pray about every day, and what we read in the Bible guides our lives, morally and philosophically. I don't care about reading the sensational stuff in the paper. We have a weekly at home, but really, there's not much in it that I can do anything about. Can't change the weather. Can't do anything about this damn war. Can't make crops grow faster and bigger. Might be able to do something about the horse race at the county fair or the judging of my momma's pickles. But that's small change, gentlemen. If we want to get to heaven, we better live by God's commandments."

Blair heard several "Amens" when he finished.

The participants looked squarely at the judges. "Well," said Tom Armstrong, "who won?"

Thomas Rose spoke for the panel of judges. "We want to think about this and will render a decision tomorrow after supper. And, if any of you others have an opinion, please come see us."

The matter was concluded until Friday evening, 7 o'clock. Rose addressed the residents of the Milroy Room.

"After giving this matter a great deal of thought today, and listening to several of you who ventured forth an opinion, we find in favor of Mr. Blair and Mr. Anderson, although I will tell you that the vote was not unanimous."

"Who was opposed?" someone yelled out.

"Not going to tell you. Agreed, gentlemen?" Rose asked, looking at Bill Ely and Harrison Hobart.

"Correct, Thomas," said Hobart.

"Absolutely," replied Ely.

"Then the matter is concluded. Congratulations to the participants. Quite thoughtful, educational, thought-provoking. Well done."

Armstrong, Blair, Riggs, and Anderson shook hands. It was nearly time for "Lights Out" and *Taps*.

As March came to an end and April presented itself, Tom Armstrong was becoming more encouraged than he had been in quite some time. Jacob had come through with a box that contained not only fresh clothing but also two hams; some dried beef; coffee and tea; salt, pepper, and sugar; matches; some lard; bacon; some dried fruit; paper, pen, and ink; three letters; and much-needed soap. It was very welcome in the mess since the men were very tired of stale, moldy corn bread and rice that was home to the maggots. Mealtime was now looked forward to, and now there were ovens in every room inside the prison. As usual, the men in their mess would rotate the cooking chores.

Besides learning about events of the war in the paper, Armstrong also learned that there had been an agreement between Union and Confederate officers that the exchange process should be undertaken with greater speed. There was a downside to this, however. Apparently, exchanged Confederate prisoners were now being encouraged to join their former regiments, with some serving as guards in Richmond's prisons. By golly, they looked like they just came out of camp. Sturdy and strong, with clean uniforms, and shoes. Armstrong had read something about that in the *Richmond Sentinel* saying that Union commanders were pretty upset that Northern prisons treated the Confederate prisoners very well while their own boys were treated miserably in places like Libby and Belle Isle. Just didn't seem fair, but he hoped that once the Confederate authorities noticed this discrepancy, they would treat their prisoners more equitably. He forgot, though, that the South was running out of food and clothing since its supply lines to the west had been severed. With that, there really wasn't much more the authorities in Confederate prisons could do.

It was April 12, 1864. Tom Armstrong and Caleb Edwards were looking at the *Richmond Sentinel* from the day before and saw a small article that said that the United States Senate had approved the 13th Amendment to the Constitution that abolished slavery and involuntary servitude.

"Well, I'll be damned," said Edwards. "Can you believe that? Pretty wide margin of vote. Now what happens?"

Armstrong thought for a minute, running his right hand through his filthy hair. "I gotta take a bath," he said, "but to your question. I think anything like this, once passed by the Senate, has to go to the House of Representatives, and if they pass it, then it goes to the states. To become part of the Constitution, the law of the land, some large percentage of the states have to approve it. Two-thirds or three-quarters. I'm not sure about that."

"Wow," said Caleb Edwards. "Southern states get to vote?"

"Naw, they're not part of the Union…yet. Imagine the President wants to get this done before the war ends. Wonder if he told Grant to wait to finish it. Would keep the Southern states from voting."

"He wouldn't do that. Too much blood on his hands. Wants to get it over as fast as he can."

"Maybe, but if the Southern states are back in the Union before the Amendment goes to the states, he won't get it passed."

"Can't do anything about it, Caleb. Let's just see what happens. I hear that Grant told Meade to follow Lee everywhere he goes. That frees up Sherman. Heard Grant told him to reduce the South's capacity to continue the conflict, leaving it up to the General to determine exactly what that meant. Imagine that means marching through Mississippi, Alabama, Tennessee, Arkansas, and Georgia before turning north into South Carolina. It's the Anaconda, Caleb."

"And, we're stuck in this goddam place. Gonna miss all the fun."

"Maybe we'll get exchanged," Tom Armstrong said hopefully.

"Maybe, but I still don't trust the bastards, and I owe that one guy a thrashin'. If we are exchanged, I'll bust him up good on the way out."

But, it wasn't to be. Lieutenant General Ulysses S. Grant formally ended prisoner exchanges on April 17, 1864 based on some pretty darn good logic. It seems that he came to the same realization that Armstrong did. Well-fed and well-clothed Confederate prisoners could rejoin their outfits when they were exchanged, strengthening the Rebel Army. On the other hand, the men who would be released from Southern prisons would be in no condition to fight or even march, with the way they had been treated. So, it made no sense to strengthen the enemy and not do anything for his own forces. Continuing the exchanges simply meant that his troops would be fighting a fresher opponent, and Grant surely saw no advantage in that.

Another event had occurred a few days earlier, but the newspaper reports were slow to cover it. Neither Grant, Sherman, Meade, or the President were very happy about what had happened at Fort Pillow, near Henning, Tennessee, on the far west side of the state, right there on the Mississippi River. It seems that the garrison at the fort was there to keep the river open for Northern commercial and military travel and to keep Memphis safe from a nautical attack. The garrison was only 500 strong, more than half of whom were Negroes who had been recruited to serve in the army after the Emancipation Proclamation was issued on January 1, 1863.

On April 12, 1864, the 3rd anniversary of the attack on Fort Sumter, Confederate Major General Nathan Bedford Forrest, who had been raiding in Tennessee and Kentucky, arrived at Fort Pillow with 3,500 troopers in his 1st Division of the Cavalry Corps. His sharpshooters took the high ground and began shooting, killing and wounding many of the Union soldiers inside the fort. Forrest brought up his batteries and began a savage artillery barrage, complimented by murderous rifle fire from the horse soldiers, now on foot. By mid-afternoon, the general had had enough and demanded a surrender. Major William F. Bradford, commander of his battalion of cavalry defending Fort Pillow, would not surrender. Consequently, Forrest ordered a full assault on the fort, his troopers charging to the front and to the flanks. It was no contest.

Many Union soldiers tried to escape to the Mississippi where a gunboat was moored, hoping that they would be spared. That didn't work. The sharpshooters on the high ground continued their deadly fire, with the flanking companies providing a deadly crossfire. The Union soldiers inside the fort threw their hands up in surrender, thinking that they would be taken prisoner. Instead, the soldiers of Forrest's cavalry began executing the helpless Negro soldiers. Of the 300 Negro soldiers who had begun the day going about their business, only sixty-two survived the massacre.

Forrest didn't think that Negroes should be taken as prisoners, and so he had them killed in systematic executions. The rest of the Union garrison, about 150 men, were marched off under guard to Southern prisons. It was generally agreed in the Lincoln administration that if Forrest was ever captured, he would be tried for the murders at Fort Pillow and hanged. The incident fueled the anger of Lincoln and his generals who determined that they would see the war to its bitterest end.

"Those bastards," said Caleb Edwards after reading the newspaper account of what happened. "I hope Sherman or Meade find the son-of-a-bitch and hang his sorry ass from a tree. Maybe they could torture him first."

"Or, just put him in front of a firing squad. No need for due process here," responded Tom Armstrong, very much saddened by what he had just read. "Defenseless men with their hands in the air just shot dead. God, please rest their souls. Almost feel sorry for what Sherman and Meade are going to do to the Johnnies."

Tom Armstrong thought to himself, "I have seen and experienced enough horror and such uncivilized behavior to last the rest of my life. What men are doing to each other. I knew it would be bad when I came back in, but I didn't know it would be this bad." He wouldn't tell anyone at home or in Clinton, Illinois about any of it. You see, Hopewell, Ohio, had become too crowded for John Porter, so he packed up the family and moved to rural Illinois. Actually, William Armstrong felt the same about Norwich and had just moved his family to Hopewell Township in time to get the crops planted.

> Addressed to Miss F. Porter
> Clinton, Dewitt County, Illinois
> Libby Prison Apr 25, 1964 Richmond, Va
> Frank, Dear friend. Yours of Mar 13 was recd Apr 21. I was very glad to hear from you; did not say whether you was well or not. Your words were kind ones & full of encouragement. I hope all will come out right. I try to be of good cheer. But one can't be blind to the relatives. You know nothing of prison life in Richmond & God grant you never may know the horrors that I could tell you.
> What do you do in your leisure time. I am studying grammar & French here. I should like to know what you are studying. Do you study music. I wish you would. It's so pleasant. But then maybe you would laugh at the idea of one in my position advising you who breathe not the air of a dungeon, but God's free air.
> Frank I often think of you in my duties here if duties they could be called. Well if the government wants us out worse than they want us to stay in prison, why, we would

be out. So, it's our duty to wait patiently & not grumble. I don't grumble. My hopes are bright for the future & for our future especially. May God bless you & preserve you in your trials. Yours as ever. T.

He simply did not want her to worry any more than she probably already did. Caleb Edwards took the same approach when he wrote home to Margaret. The war had been too ugly and so treacherous that they did not want the loves of their lives to know of it. It was their secret, and they would die with it, whether they got home or not.

The good news was that boxes started to arrive with more regularity, the weather was warming, letters were now coming into Libby, and the newspapers contained stories about the war. First, it was reported that on May 4, 1864, Major General William Tecumseh Sherman with his 90,000 men was on the move south from Chattanooga toward Atlanta.

Then, the newspapers reported that, on May 5, 1864, Meade's Army of the Potomac and the IX Corps of the Army of the Ohio under Grant encountered the Army of Northern Virginia of Robert E. Lee at a place called The Wilderness in Spotsylvania County in eastern Virginia. Meade and Grant had upward of 120,000 men as opposed to Lee's roughly 60,000, but in vicious and brutal fighting over two days, the contest proved to be a draw. Over 18,000 Yankees were killed, wounded, or were missing. Just over 11,000 for the Confederates.

But, at The Wilderness, there was a difference this time. In previous battles, regardless of the outcome, Meade and other Union generals would fight and then withdraw. That was what angered President Lincoln. Meade should have pursued Lee aggressively after Gettysburg, but he did not. Lincoln saw that such pursuit was an opportunity to cripple the Confederate Army for good, but it didn't happen. The difference this time? Grant did pursue, pushing his army and Robert E. Lee toward Spotsylvania Court House. He did not want Lee to catch his breath.

So, on May 8, 1864, Grant and Meade, with 100,000 men, met Lee with his 52,000 again right there in Spotsylvania County. It might have surprised the Confederate commander who was used to Union forces withdrawing after battle, but there was no withdraw in the lexicon of Ulysses S. Grant. On May 8, the V and VI Corps of the Army of the Potomac attacked, but the Rebel lines held. Two days later, Grant attacked with elements of three corps but without success. The next day, Major General Winfield Hancock attacked in some of the fiercest fighting of the war. It was bloody hand-to-hand combat with the Confederates forced to withdraw. The battle would rage on for another week with over 18,000 Federals killed, wounded, or missing. The number for the Confederates was just over 12,000, a much larger percentage than that of the Union force. To Abraham Lincoln, this was exactly what he wanted. A general who would not hide behind a desk, rather one who would fight and fight again.

Tom Armstrong and Caleb Edwards were not reading all of this in the Milroy Room at Libby Prison. No, they read it while on a train, headed to Georgia. Grant was getting too close to Richmond, only some 50 miles north of it, and the Confederates believed he was on the march to the capital and Libby Prison.

Thomas Rose had walked into the Milroy Room on May 7, 1864." Armstrong, Edwards, start packin' whatever you have. Just got the word that we're leavin' Libby tomorrow and headin' south. Turner told me they're afraid Grant is pushin' south and will be here in two or three days. So, instead of releasin' us, they're sendin' us to Macon, Georgia."

"Macon, Georgia?" asked Caleb Edwards. "Where the hell is that?"

"80 miles south of Atlanta, from what I am told. Place called Camp Oglethorpe. Maybe 600 miles from here. Goin' to the depot tomorrow morning. Don't know when we leave. Pack up and get ready. Boys from Belle Isle comin' too. Goin' to a place called Andersonville. Not very nice, from what I'm told. Kinda like Libby, only outdoors. Call it Camp Sumter."

"Won't take long to get ready," said Tom Armstrong. "We'll pass the word to the rest of the boys in Milroy." He thought to himself, "Wonder if Patrick will be on the train, going to that Andersonville place."

At 9 o'clock A.M. on May 8, 1864, Tom Armstrong, Caleb Edwards and the rest of the population of Libby Prison, all 800 of them, walked in formation, under guard, to the railroad depot there between Main and Olive Streets. You see, in the two months since Kilpatrick's raid, one hundred more of the prisoners had gone to meet their Maker.

When they arrived at the depot, around 10:00 A.M., they were met by the 3rd Virginia Militia, under the command of Lieutenant Cyrus Gay, and a throng of the saddest looking human beings Tom Armstrong had ever seen: the 500 prisoners from Belle Isle. The men of Libby didn't look too good, but they were certainly better than what they were seeing across the yard. Armstrong looked closely at them, scanning to see if he could spot Patrick Murphy, but they all looked the same. Frail and dirty, many without shirts and shoes. Some unable to stand. He did not see his friend or anyone else he knew. "Drat, wonder if Patrick is still alive," he thought to himself.

It would take some time to process about 1,300 men and assign them to cars, but Lieutenant Gay and his militia of older men and younger boys would get the name, rank, and outfit of every one of them. When they were processed, in groups of 100, they were marched back to Libby Prison where they would have to wait until all of the men were identified. Back in the Milroy for one last time, Caleb Edwards and Tom Armstrong tried to rest. Those who had not been counted and assigned to a car that day were marched east down Olive Street to the Fairgrounds where they would be fed and would spend the night. By the afternoon of May 10, all 1,300 had been accounted for. The loading of the Virginia Central Railroad commenced, officers first in groups of sixty. Then the enlisted men in groups of eighty. Guards from the 3rd Virginia Militia would accompany them on the way to Macon.

While they were waiting, two men assigned to the car Tom Armstrong and Caleb Edwards were in, jumped out to relieve themselves on the side of the depot. Shots rang out, and the others could see the two bodies, slumped on the walk, dead.

"Guess we better ask permission," noted Tom Armstrong. "Probably going to have to sleep in here tonight. Don't think we're going anywhere. Don't hear a locomotive. Break out some bread, Caleb. We got any meat? Fruit?"

The train to Macon, Georgia, pulled out of the depot in Richmond at 9 o'clock the next morning, May 11. The men were packed in the cars like hogs going to the slaughterhouse. Head to foot. And, it was getting hot. The only ventilation came from a small opening in the sliding door to the car. The odor in the car was getting stronger by the hour. The prisoners certainly weren't pleased, and the guards were not happy either. They had better things to do than to transport Yankee prisoners to some place in Georgia. Many of the militia had never been out of Virginia so, in reality, it was kind of an adventure, but they didn't see it that way. They wanted to be back on the farm.

The journey took what seemed like forever, slowing down at every city and town that had a depot to let some of the Federals get out and stretch. The natives would come out to see what a Yankee looked like and were quite surprised to find that they looked just like their sons and husbands who had gone off to fight. But, on almost every interaction, the townsfolk wanted to know why the Yankees had brought the war to the South. Smartly, nearly all of the prisoners ignored the question and simply walked away. Lieutenant Cyrus Gay had permitted them to walk around each depot to exercise their legs, but there was no way on God's green earth that the Lieutenant would let them do anything more. He had a job to do, and, by God, he was going to do it.

The train rumbled south through Virginia to Danville, into North Carolina on the way to Greensboro and then to Charlotte. On the way, it passed through Salisbury, North Carolina, in Rowan County which housed a Confederate prison known as a death-trap. Some of the officers were told to get out of the train. They were staying there. None of them was very happy about it. The reputation of the prison there in Salisbury was already well known. It was, plain and simple, a very nasty place. Nastier, if you could believe it, than Libby. If you went in to Salisbury, you probably weren't coming out alive.

But, at the Salisbury depot, the prisoners and their guards got some relief from the heat and crowded conditions in the cars. Thomas Rose had asked the guards in his car if there was any way to relieve the cramped condition, suggesting that perhaps eight or ten of them could ride on the top of the car. The train didn't go very fast, so they would be safe up there as it rolled along. And, the guards who accompanied them would have their Springfields at the ready in case some fool decided to chance it and leap to the ground below. All it would take would be one. He'd be shot dead before he hit the ground. The attitude of the Rebel guards was "Go ahead, boys, try it. It'll be the last thing you ever do."

Caleb Edwards and Tom Armstrong climbed to the top of the car where there was sunshine and fresh air. They weren't too worried about the smoke from the smokestack as the train lurched forward. Suddenly, they heard, "Shoot the son-of-a-bitch."

It was Lieutenant Cyrus Gay. "Shoot 'im, I say." With that, there was the crack of a rifle. A man who was having difficulty trying to get up on top of the car was shot in the back by one of the guards, his body toppling off the train and onto the bed of the tracks below.

"Judas Priest," said Tom Armstrong. "Those boys aren't playing around. Good Lord! The man was just trying to get up here. Why in blazes didn't they just help him? Instead, they killed him in cold blood. Guess that's who we're dealing with, Caleb."

"Think we've known that for some time, Sump. These bastards are playing for real. Mad that I didn't get to bust up that son-of-a-bitch back at Libby. Oh, well, probly would've gotten shot."

"Probably, and I wouldn't have been real happy with you if you had," Armstrong said. "Maybe I've just seen too much of this to care anymore. Too much death. Too much illness. Maybe I'm just getting hardened to it. Only thing that keeps me sane is thinking about Frank and possibility for our future. Just hope I live long enough."

The train ride was long and arduous and really didn't make sense. It certainly wasn't direct. After Salisbury, it was on to Charlotte, North Carolina, then to Columbia, South Carolina, then to Augusta, Georgia, and finally to Macon. It was only 600 miles as the crow flies, but it took ten days for the train to arrive at Camp Oglethorpe, there in Macon, Georgia. It was Wednesday, May 17, 1864.

Camp Oglethorpe was a lot different than Libby Prison, particularly because it was in rural Georgia. There were about 1,200 officers imprisoned there, but that number would steadily increase as more and more Union men were captured. Unlike Libby, the camp was square, out in the open and encompassing about three or four acres with a twelve-foot-high wooden fence guarding the perimeter. It was located just a mile west of the Ocmulgee River, facing 7th Street on the northwest, between Hawthorne to the southwest and Pine to the northeast. A swamp guarded the southeast.

Sentinels walked the fence at regular intervals with orders to shoot any of the prisoners who tried to escape. Inside the fence was the stockade, about fifteen feet from the outer one, about six feet high, known to the prisoners as the "dead line." They were warned not to go within six feet of it. A creek ran through the southwest corner of the yard, providing ample water for drinking, cooking, and bathing. That's also where the latrines were dug. "Sinks," the Rebels called them.

The men were to be housed in large sheds, some 100 feet long and maybe sixteen feet wide. It would not be cramped like Libby, and it was better than sleeping under the stars, especially when thunderstorms hit. The first task at hand was for the "fresh fish" to construct their own bunks. Until that was completed, it did, indeed, mean sleeping under the stars.

"Just make sure, boys, to give your buddies an ample amount of space," the guard reminded them. "Don't want you too crowded here. Most boys don' use the crick for bathin'. They jus' wait foe a storm to come through. Just stand there naked in the pourin' rain. Don' make no sense to us, but do what you want."

"Well, damn, that's a goddam change," said Caleb Edwards. "They're thinking about our comfort, not like those bastards in Richmond. Look there, Sump, there's men walking around, some are playing base ball, and some are playing tag. Shit, maybe this won't be so bad. Hope the food is good."

Addressed to Miss Frank P. Porter
Clinton, Dewitt County, Illinois
Macon, Georgia May 19/64

Dear Frank,

I am blessed with a reasonable degree of health. I left Richmond on the 7th inst. We are in Camp Oglethorpe at this place. I hope you are well and doing well but I am sorry that I am in such a condition as I am. But there are other & better men than me prisoners. I hope to be exchanged someday. We have good drinking water & a ground to exercise upon. Tis said this place is very healthy. I hope so. I hope to hear from you soon. I have got to stay here until I'm exchanged. Please write to Mary. Well I must close. Direct as usual "By flag of truce." Yours as ever, farewell.

Thos S Armstrong
122 O.V.I.

May angels watch round thy head.
When thou'rt awake as well as asleep

Taps, played at 9 o'clock, meant the end of the day, as usual, but during the summer, the sun was barely set by then so the prisoners just continued their card games, writing letters, and playing chess or checkers.

"Okay, boys" said Thomas Rose to the escaped prisoners who had been returned to Libby, "we gotta go over to that building in the middle for our rations. Have to stuff whatever they give us into our haversacks. They want us in units of 90 men each, don't know why they didn't make it an even hundred. Highest ranking officer in each group to be commander. Then, we divide that up into squads of ten. Don't know that either. Just do it. Just use the same mess you had at Libby if you can."

And Caleb Edwards had been prophetic. The food was plentiful and good. Oh, they had to cook it themselves just like they did at Libby, but they were given bacon, rice, cornmeal, beans, coffee, and salt and pepper. They'd have to get water out of the creek to brew the coffee, so each man in the mess of ten would either cook or go

357

for water every five days. The only hardship was lack of proper cookware, only having a bucket and a skillet, but, even so, it sure beat the hell out of what they had endured in Richmond.

While days in Richmond seemed to last forever in Libby Prison, there was so much to do there at Camp Oglethorpe that time just flew by. *Reveille* at 6, followed by the *Roll Call*, then breakfast, after which the men were free to do whatever they wanted, except try to escape. There were organized games of base ball and cricket, some even tried that new one, football. Cards were broken out early in the morning with all sorts of games including cribbage, euchre, and whist being played. But, by 11 o'clock in the morning, it was time to get out of the sun, go to the newly-formed library or just read the book that you had taken.

Caleb Edwards loved having the library; it gave him something to do every day. Tom Armstrong had suggested that they create a church where they could hold services on Sundays and prayer meetings on Wednesday evenings after supper. They did just that, but, on the other hand, some of the men had created a casino where the men could gamble at cards. Now, how they did that was a mystery since most of them didn't have any money. But, gamble they did, using almost anything of value for their wagers.

Aside from the daily activity, most of the excitement came when the massive gates opened, more Federal prisoners, more "fresh fish," were marched in, just like after the Battle of Spotsylvania when over two thousand Federal soldiers were captured. The inmates would want the news about the war. Where was Grant? Where was Lee? Where was Sherman? But, the problem, for their Confederate captors, was, where to put them? After Spotsylvania, there were another couple hundred officers to house and feed. If this kept up, the good life that the boys from Libby were enjoying would most certainly take a turn for the worse. And, it did.

After the Battle of Cold Harbor, on June 12, 1864, another two hundred officers marched through the gates, making the total at Camp Oglethorpe 1,800 give or take a few. Overcrowding was starting to be a problem, since the ideal capacity for Camp Oglethorpe was 1,200. The additional prisoners found food to be in very short

supply with no prospects for getting better. There was also an out-
break of yellow fever as more and more men visited the latrines,
which weren't being filled in very fast. Adding to the disease problem, the men's excrement and urine began to leak into the creek,
contaminating the water. Dysentery was commonplace, with men
not making it to the latrines, just going wherever they happened to
be.

That afternoon, David Garbett came to see Tom Armstrong and
Caleb Edwards in the "Milroy House." Apparently, Thomas Rose
was getting antsy and thought maybe he had a workable plan to escape. "The Colonel wants to get the hell out of here," said David
Garbett in hushed tones. "He thinks he knows a way. 'Nuther tunnel
or two or three. If Scott's Anaconda Plan works, there'll be more
and more fighting, probly right close by. That means more and more
men coming in here and, just like Libby, food will be in shorter supply, if that's possible. He's also worried about disease, here in this
heat and the open latrines. Men shittin' wherever they are. Latrines
probly breed all kinds of bugs. Lord knows what they might carry.
Nuther case of the fever reported just yesterday. Colonel's 'fraid
there's gonna be more, lots more."

"He's gotta be crazy," whispered Caleb Edwards.

"Proved you wrong at Libby with #4, didn't he?" David Garbett
had a point. It was the second time Edwards had heard that about the
fourth tunnel.

"What's he want us to do?" asked Tom Armstrong.

"He wants all of the tunnelers from Libby who are here to meet
over in the Chickamauga House tonight after *Taps*. You in?"

Armstrong responded, "Yeah, I'm in. Caleb?"

"Agin my better judgment, but I'm game."

The meeting commenced at 10 o'clock in the Chickamauga
House, a shed that was nearest the stockade. Thomas E. Rose had
drawn a picture of what he thought might work, and he sorely missed
Andrew Hamilton who evidently had made it out of Libby to the
Union lines or had been killed trying.

"I spoke to the guys in charge, Bill Nelson, Colonel in the 13th
U.S. Infantry and E.L. Smith, Major in the 19th U.S., and told them
about what we did at Libby. They listened carefully and said they

wanted to organize a mass escape. Sometime in July, a month from now, maybe earlier. They went on to say that they wanted to create the Council of 500. 500 men who would know about the escape plans, sworn to secrecy upon the penalty of death, and who will obey everything their officers tell them to do. We will have five companies, organized as we all were when we left home. They want me to be commander-in-charge since we did it at Libby."

"Why so many?" asked David Garbett. Rose didn't have an answer.

"There's gonna be four tunnels, and we will need as much help as we can get. We did a good job at keeping it quiet at Libby with just a few of us knowing about the tunnel, but these guys see a bigger picture. They see the tunneling activity going on day and night, five men in each shift, rotating every three days. By my count, if each shift works for six hours, we will need thirty men to do the job. Don't know why the Council has to be that large, but they were pretty stern about the 500 number."

"How the hell are we gonna keep it quiet?" asked Caleb Edwards.

"The oath, Edwards. You're gonna have to swear an oath. I already did it."

"You in? If so, I'll give it to you right now. Fact is, I can give it to all of you, right here, right now."

The Libby tunnelers looked at each other. Tom Armstrong said, "Gentlemen, we were committed the last time with no oath. With this many knowing about it, I think it's a good idea. I'm ready to take it. You others?"

They all nodded their heads. Thomas Rose, standing among them, gave them the instructions and began...

"I, (state your full name), do solemnly swear, in the presence of almighty God that, as long as I am a prisoner of war, I will be a true and loyal member of the Council of 500; that I will obey the officers placed over me, and that, if I should be selected by lot to participate in the capital punishment upon a traitor to the organization, I will exert my best endeavors so to do at any and all hazards. So help me God."

He continued, "I want Randall, McDonald, Armstrong, Edwards, and Garbett to be the officers of Company A. They will dig the primary tunnel from right here in Chickamauga. I will show you what you are to do. I will assign the rest of you in the next day or so." It was Wednesday, June 15, 1864.

Thomas Rose dismissed all but the five from Company A and outlined the plan he thought would work.

"You may talk to your friends and recruit anyone who was at Libby whom you trust. We need to start this as soon as we can. I have a feeling we will see more "fresh fish" here shortly, and I really don't want to go hungry again. When we get out we will split up and go north. Heard Sherman is in northwest Georgia, some place called Dalton. We'll try to find his army up there. Won't be easy, but neither was getting out of Libby."

Tom Armstrong and Caleb Edwards just smiled at each other. Rose noticed it and smiled as well.

"Now, this won't be as easy as digging in Virginia," Rose went on. "You will have about 35 feet that you will need to traverse which sounds easier than at Libby. Problem is, the ground is clay, hard as a rock. It will take more time, but that's why I want digging day and night. Any questions?"

There was just one. It was Caleb Edwards. "How we gonna do this?"

Thomas Rose went to the bunk that was closest to the wall facing the stockade and outer fence. "Give me a hand, Edwards."

Accordingly, Rose and Edwards lifted the bunk. "Over here," said Rose. "In this open spot, put it down. Now, once you move the bed, you will dig down about five or six feet. Be sure to preserve the clay that you dig up. You'll have to replace it in the hole when you suspend your work or in case the Johnnies pull a surprise inspection. So, one of you is digging. One will take the dirt not needed to disguise the hole, will fill a couple of haversacks and will hand them off to another of you. Make sure you have a long coat because you will take the haversacks down by the creek and the latrines and empty them there. Then come back by a different route. Probly only one trip per shift. No one should suspect anything since men are going to the latrine all night long, especially the sick ones.

"Another of you will stand guard outside, sentry duty. Be casual. Smoke your pipe, play your harmonica. But, be on the lookout for anything suspicious. If anyone does come by, strike up a conversation with him. Make it loud enough so that you boys inside the shed can hear. The inside guard will signal the digger by pulling on the rope around his ankle, just like at Libby. Pull him out, put these two staves into the hole about two feet down and then replace the clay. Get the bunk and put it back where it was, and everyone lie down. Questions?"

"Seems pretty easy, Thomas," said Tom Armstrong. "First thing, though, we gotta find more men."

"You can do that during the day, Armstrong. I want you digging tomorrow night. Let me know if you have any problems. I trust you men. Randall, you are authorized to deliver the oath, but you have to make sure that the men to whom you give it are trustworthy and will follow our rules."

"Will do, Thomas," said W.S.B. Randall. "Boys, we hafta be vigilant here. There's probly spies among us and probly some who will trade information like this for their freedom. Pretty damn tempting for someone to turn on us."

Rose continued. "Do not tell them about the tunnels until they have sworn themselves to secrecy and to obey orders. If they show any hesitation, don't offer the oath to them. Refusing to give them the oath may cause them to become suspicious and may make them curious. If they do find out what we're up to, they may tell the guards and be freed, perhaps. But, that's a risk we hafta take."

On the night of June 16, Caleb Edwards and David Garbett removed the bunk, and Edwards hit the clay beneath it with his chisel. "Damn, Rose was right. This is gonna take some doing. Clay's hard as a rock. Need a shovel."

"Shovel in here will tip off the guards," admonished David Garbett. "We're gonna have to dig with tools we can hide from them."

"Mebbe clay won't be as hard when I get goin' to the fence." And, Caleb Edwards began working at a furious pace, an hour at a time for each of them, rotating to the other chores. At 4 o'clock in the morning, on June 17, when they heard the guards yell "4 o'clock and All is Well," Caleb Edwards stopped digging, the staves were placed in the shallow hole, the clay was spread around on top of them, and the bunk was put back in place. No one the wiser.

Edwards and Tom Armstrong stole out of the Chickamauga House and headed across the way for Milroy. They had recruiting to do in the morning.

"Caleb," said Tom Armstrong. "We should just switch our bunks from here to Chickamauga or get some guys to change with us. That'd make our work easier."

"Good thought, Sump," came the reply. "Let's get that done today."

"Tell you what. While I'm recruiting, why don't you go over there and see if there is anyone digging closer to here. Would make their lives easier. Talk to Rose."

"Will do." And, Caleb Edwards was out the door toward the Chickamauga House.

The switch was made, and Caleb Edwards took his belongings and those of Tom Armstrong to Chickamauga that very afternoon. Armstrong, on the other hand, was working with W.S.B. Randall on getting recruits for the Council of 500 with great success. None of the prisoners wanted to stay at Camp Oglethorpe although it was much better than it was at Libby or from what they'd heard about the prison at Salisbury, North Carolina.

"God knows, I don't want to go there," Armstrong said to himself. "The death trap. You go there just to die, from what I hear."

"How many do we have, Armstrong?" asked W.S.B. Randall.

"About thirty, W.S. Enough to start the other shifts."

"OK, here's what we'll do," said Randall. "You, Edwards, and Garbett will each take a day. You will need two shifts so make two of the men who were in on the dig at Libby team captain. The three of you can supervise. If work starts after *Roll Call* and breakfast, that's probly around 9 o'clock. They work till 3 in the afternoon. You sleep then, till supper. Be seen throughout the camp until after *Taps* when the next team comes in and goes to work. They're done at 4 in the morning. More sleep for you."

"Got it," said Tom Armstrong.

"By the way, I figured out why they wanted 500," said W.S.B. Randall.

"Why?"

"Overheard Rose talking to Nelson and Smith. They want to take all 500 of us out, armed with clubs or other weapons. When we get out, we are to launch an attack on the guards' quarters, kill them all, get their weapons, then take the camp. Once we do that, we're free to go."

"No kidding. Wow. 500 of us against the guards. Somebody's gonna get hurt, but it might just work."

The work on the four tunnels proceeded without incident. Oh, there was one time when a Rebel guard got a little too close to the Milroy House, but the sentry did as he had been told, warning the men inside of the intruder's presence."

Caleb Edwards broke through about eight feet on the other side of the fence during the night of Monday, June 27. He poked his head up to look around and found that he was just short of 7th Street. Turning around, he saw the outer fence. He knew, then, that it was perfect since the guards were not able to see him. The other three tunnels were open as well. The plan, concocted by Bill Nelson, E.L. Smith, and Thomas Rose, was for everyone to slip out on Thursday morning around 1AM, so the assault on the guards' quarters could be done while most of them were asleep.

Thomas Rose was talking to W.S.B. Randall, B.B. McDonnell, Tom Armstrong, Caleb Edwards, and David Garbett on Tuesday morning, June 28, just after *Roll Call* and breakfast. They never heard the approach. The door to the Chickamauga House burst open, with fifteen armed guards, rifles ready, racing in.

"What's the big idea?" asked Thomas Rose.

"We know you has a tunnel in here," the lead guard said. "Git your ass over there," pointing to the wall farthest from the stockade and outer fence. The Federal prisoners did as they were told while the Confederate guards began picking up bunks, one by one, jamming a spade into the earth below.

"Well, lookee here, boys. Seems we found it. Fill the goddam thing up, right now. What you boys over there know 'bout this?"

"Nuthin," was the response. "Probly done by someone 'fore we got here. Didn't know it was there. Wish we had," said Thomas Rose.

"That's bullshit. You been diggin,' at least that's what the guy from Illinois told me."

"That goddam bastard. I'm gonna find out who it was and kill him with my bare hands. Goddam it. We're screwed agin," sneered Caleb Edwards, watching the guards bring in fill dirt. "All that for nuthin." Agin."

13 Four Prisons, Nine Weeks

"So, they knew about it all along?" asked Tom Armstrong. "How could they? The Council was sworn to secrecy. Nobody would violate the oath."

"You're being naïve, Armstrong. Here's what I know," said Thomas Rose. "Commandant Gibbs told me that one of our Council members sold us out. Name was something like Benson, 16th Illinois Cavalry. Seems he told them about the 500. Went to one of the guards a few days ago and told them what we were up to. He bartered us for his freedom. No escape for him. Nobody's seen him since they busted in on us. Figures, 'cause Gibbs told me that he was paroled the day after we were found out. They don't know where he went, but he's got official papers, so he won't be arrested and brought back here. Don't know who recruited him, but whoever it was got took. Gibbs also told me that Benson had been a spy since we got here, a vital source of information about what we were doing. The tunnels were his ticket out. He just waited for the right moment."

"That goddam son-of-a-bitch," cried Caleb Edwards who was getting madder by the day. "If I ever get out of here, I'm going to Illinois to kill the bastard."

"Illinois is a big place, Caleb," counseled Tom Armstrong. "And, you don't know where in Illinois, and you don't know that he actually went there. He could be in Indiana, Ohio, or Michigan."

That didn't do any good. Caleb Edwards, the big West Virginian, who surely wasn't as big as he was when he first got to Winchester, fumed out of the room.

"At least they didn't torture us," said Rose. "Could've put us on the rack or the spare wheel. Those are just nasty punishments. Being confined to quarters for a month ain't bad, considering."

Lieutenant Colonel George C. Gibbs, commandant at Camp Oglethorpe, had, indeed, issued confinement orders for those he suspected were guilty of digging the tunnels. You see, all four of the escape routes had been discovered at the same time, thanks to Benson, and Gibbs needed to make examples of the prisoners who he supposed had dug them. He could have put them on the rack or the spare wheel, or had them placed in the pillories, but he decided that he could be somewhat lenient. His reason? Gibbs knew something that the prisoners didn't.

The Commandant had been told that Confederate intelligence knew that Major General William Tecumseh Sherman was driving his 90,000 Federals southeast through Georgia toward Atlanta. There had been a serious fight at Rocky Face Ridge, up there in Whitfield County in the northwest corner of Georgia early in May. Although it was technically a draw, Sherman had forced Confederate General Joseph Johnston to withdraw to the southeast toward a little town called Resaca, only sixty miles northwest of Atlanta.

There, it was pretty much the same story. Sherman couldn't break Johnston's lines, but on May 15, 1864, the Union commander flanked Johnston's right and set out to destroy his supply line, namely the Western and Atlantic Railroad. In some of the heaviest fighting in what was becoming known as The Atlanta Campaign, Sherman lost about 5,000 of his 90,000 man force, killed, wounded, or captured. Johnston lost just under 3,000 of his 60,000. When the Confederate commander realized what Sherman was doing, he withdrew once again, going deeper into the center of Georgia and still closer to Atlanta. And, remember, Macon was only 80 miles south of Atlanta.

The fierce fighting had continued at New Hope Church on May 25, Pickett's Mill on the 27th, and Dallas on the 28th. Although there was no clear winner in these battles, Johnston continued withdrawing south, which played right into Sherman's hands. You would think that Johnston would have realized that. Sherman wanted Atlanta with its massive industrial might. The steel mills, blast furnaces, railroad yards, munitions factories, wagon and carriage makers, garment district, and all the people who provided the materiel for the Confederate Army of Major General Robert E. Lee to fight the war. Sherman also wanted to rip up the Western & Atlantic since it really was the last remaining supply line for the South. In essence, Sherman wanted to destroy Atlanta's manufacturing capability and make his assault deeper into Dixie much easier, crippling the army of Joseph E. Johnston.

Based on the intelligence he had received, the Commandant of Camp Oglethorpe reasoned that if Johnston couldn't stop Sherman, Atlanta would fall and then the Union general might just send one of his three armies south to Macon. He really didn't like the prospect of that and telegraphed his superiors in Richmond that perhaps Camp Oglethorpe ought to be abandoned with the prisoners sent north, perhaps into South Carolina, away from the advancing Union Army.

His thinking was supported at that very moment when he received word of the Battle at Kennesaw Mountain, just 25 miles north of Atlanta, that concluded on June 27, the day before he caught the tunnelers. Johnston had been holed up on the mountain, but Sherman, with the size advantage of his army, decided to stretch the Confederate line out as far as he could to make Johnston's force more vulnerable. That worked, to some degree, so on the morning of June 27, Sherman ordered a full-frontal assault up the mountain against the weakened Rebel center that turned into a bloodbath at the "Dead Angle." In another draw, casualties included 3,000 Federals and 1,000 Confederates, but there was one ray of hope in the fight for William Tecumseh Sherman. Major General George Stoneman's Union cavalry had outflanked Johnston's left and was headed for the Chattahoochee River. The Union army was getting closer and closer to Atlanta. Lt. Col. Gibbs was even more apprehensive now.

At the same time, somewhere around 80,000 men of Lieutenant Ulysses S. Grant's army were digging trenches around Petersburg, Virginia. Those trenches would be their homes during the siege that would last until the following spring. Well, actually, it really wasn't a siege in the traditional understanding of what a siege was. This was, and would become, trench warfare conducted over several months, with daily firing at each other, Union soldiers probing the Confederate defenses, and sharpshooters taking aim at anything that moved.

Grant's objective was, like Sherman's, to cut the supply lines to the 50,000 soldiers in Major General Robert E. Lee's Army, and he had to have Petersburg to accomplish it. The Anaconda Plan of General Winfield Scott was working, but, as Tom Armstrong had foretold, it would take some time. However, it was becoming apparent that the death of the Confederate States of America would happen. Nobody knew just when.

"Wonder what happens when Sherman gets here," Armstrong said to Caleb Edwards. "Wonder if we'll be here when he does, assuming, of course, that he is coming here."

"Wouldn't that be somethin'?" Caleb Edwards replied. "That would be the best damn thing that could ever happen. No word on where he's goin,' is there?"

"Naw, Southern papers don't say much. Guess you can't believe what they write anyway. Best source of news is the 'fresh fish,' the ones who've been with Sherman and Grant. They tell it straight. My friend, George Porter, is with Sherman. Just found out. Frank told me. Letter I got at Libby before we came here."

"You got a letter from her? You didn't tell me."

"Yeah, she sent it to my brother, Jacob, who hid it in the bag of flour that was in the last box I got. Two other envelopes, too. One was another letter. Other was a coupla pages from the *Courier* that told where the 78th was. Almost didn't know the envelopes were there. Could have missed them until we baked some bread. George's still with Leggett, Brigadier General now, and the 78th Ohio, she says. In Blair's XVII Corps. Says George is working for Leggett directly. Ridin' at the head of the column."

"Like to meet him someday. Bet he's got some stories to tell."

"Yeah, right in the middle of it at Shiloh and Vicksburg, I'm told. Got shot seven times at Shiloh. Saved by his thick winter overcoat. At the front of the first regiment to march into Vicksburg. Stayed there until recently. Would love to see him. Been a long time since we enlisted back in Zanesville in October, '61. Wonder if John Gillespie is still alive. Bob Hanson? Bet they're wonderin' about me."

On June 28, while the tunnelers were being discovered, the doors of Camp Oglethorpe swung open, and Lt. Col. George Gibbs welcomed twenty-one Union officers, Grant's men, captured two weeks earlier by Confederate troops at the Battle of Lynchburg, almost due west of Richmond in the center of Virginia. This was not an uncommon occurrence since the fighting now was pretty much concentrated in Georgia and Virginia. Oh, there was still some raiding going on in Tennessee by Confederate Major General Nathan Bedford Forrest's cavalry, and there was activity between Major General Philip Sheridan and his Union cavalry and the infantry of Lieutenant General Jubal Early up there in the Shenandoah Valley, but all of this was minor compared to what was going on around Richmond and Atlanta.

When "fresh fish" did arrive at Camp Oglethorpe, they were surprised by the appearance and condition of the men imprisoned there. They weren't as bad as was supposed. Oh, some were worse off than others, primarily due to sickness, but for the most part, the rumors they had heard about starvation and epidemics did not appear to be true. Several of the officers were walking around the camp and visiting with others, some were playing chess or checkers, some were reading, and some were talking with the guards. Yes, they were a rag-tag bunch, a lot of them shoeless, since the Confederates did not supply the prisoners with new clothing, but the men looked healthier than the new prisoners supposed. That disease had not overtaken them was a wonder. They had avoided the scurvy, yellow fever, and dysentery. Lucky for them. Sickness was rampant at places like Andersonville. As they looked around the camp, they were grateful that their comrades in arms actually looked well, comparatively speaking. The new prisoners were quite relieved.

Tom Armstrong and Caleb Edwards knew little of what was going on at Camp Oglethorpe, being confined as they were at the Chickamauga House. The only news they had came from the other men who came in to get out of the brilliant, hot sun during the day and in the evening when the bugler played *Taps*. That's how they found out about the operations of Grant and Sherman which did, indeed, give them some hope. They knew about New Hope Church, Pickett's Mill, and Dallas and would only find out about The Atlanta Campaign by word-of-mouth. They also knew that on June 8, Abraham Lincoln had been nominated by the National Union Party, Republicans and War Democrats joined together, for a second term as President of the United States.

The day before, on June 7, the day when the National Union Party convened its nominating convention in Baltimore, Captain Charles Dixon, Chaplain of the 16th Connecticut Volunteers, and Captain Josiah White, Chaplain of the 5th Rhode Island Heavy Artillery, decided to see how the men felt about the political situation in the country. So, they conducted a survey of their own, asking every man at Camp Oglethorpe who was able and who was not under house arrest, to cast a ballot for their preferred candidate for the office of President of the United States. They went around to all the sheds and gave the men a piece of paper on which they were to choose between Benjamin Butler from Massachusetts, Lowell Rousseau from Kentucky, Hannibal Hamlin of Maine, Andrew Johnson of Tennessee, Abraham Lincoln of Illinois, and Daniel Dickinson from New York. Those were the names that had appeared in the Macon papers as potential candidates. When the ballots were in and counted, Lincoln had tallied 533 out of 625 votes, an amazing 85%. The other 300 or so prisoners were either too sick or were under house arrest to cast a vote. When the vote of the convention was made public on June 9, it seemed, then, to the Chaplains that the soldiers mirrored the sentiment of the convention where the issue had never been in doubt. Abraham Lincoln would run for a second term against a Democratic rival, former Union General George B. McClellan.

Being confined there in the Chickamauga House, without any first-hand information from "fresh fish," getting the complete story about anything was almost impossible. That only added to the boredom of being stuck in their quarters for thirty days under house arrest. The men discovered at the other three tunnels were being confined as well, a message to the rest not to try it. But, the punishment sure could have been much worse.

Unfortunately, being confined, they would miss the celebration that occurred on July 4, 1864. They would hear what was going on, and they could celebrate in their confinement, but they would not be able to participate in the prisoners' joy and happiness of this one day. There were speeches in observance of the work of the founders almost 90 years before, with the men cheering and singing, some crying tears of joy. And, then, Captain William Todd of Company K, 8th New York Infantry, took center stage. Reaching into his trousers, he withdrew a small flag. It was that of the United States of America. The Union prisoners at Camp Oglethorpe went wild, shouting and yelling of their love for the Union, President Lincoln, and the cause.

Then, Captain Todd began singing *The Star-Spangled Banner*, and soon, hundreds of imprisoned Federal officers joined in. Hearing it, Armstrong thought that it wasn't the same without Chaplain Charles McCabe leading them in song, but it would surely do. Then came *Rally 'Round the Flag*. Then, *Yankee Doodle* three or four times, followed by *My Country 'Tis of Thee*. The celebration got very loud and emotional, with some of the older Confederate guards weeping with memories of their lives in the United States before the war. It would, in all likelihood, never be the same for them.

"Three cheers for the Stars and Stripes," yelled William Todd. Cheers rang throughout the yard, even in the Chickamauga Room.

"Three cheers for Lincoln," he bellowed, and the noise got louder.

"Three cheers for our glorious cause." It was louder yet.

Finally, Lt. Col. George C. Gibbs, the commandant, had had enough. He ordered his men to arms with infantry coming into the prison yard. The guards on the walk on the outer fence stood with rifles ready and pointed at the Yankees. Cannoneers manned their guns. All they wanted was for the commandant to say the word, and they would unleash massive fire power that would, if it happened, be a massacre of the greatest proportion. Instead, he sent the chief guard to the center of the celebration who told the prisoners to disperse and stop the singing, cheering, and all, or there would be trouble.

Now, some foolhardy souls in the midst of the celebration thought that they could overwhelm the Confederate guards, but clearer heads prevailed, and the men went back to their quarters. But, something magical had happened that Tuesday afternoon. It was Captain Todd's flag. That was what made them forget how long they had been in prison, how bad the conditions were, and how ragged their clothes were, never mind being shoeless. It reinvigorated their spirits, reminding them of why they had come into the army in the first place, the righteous cause they were fighting for and the promise of final victory that lay ahead, thanks to their own sacrifice and that of those who would continue the fight.

It reminded them of the higher calling, that is, the belief in human rights that was guaranteed in the Declaration of Independence and the Constitution with its Bill of Rights. Young and old, sick and healthy, they all celebrated the basis upon which the country had been founded: life, liberty, and the pursuit of happiness. That gave them hope, both for themselves and their families as well as for future generations to come, as Franklin, Washington, Jefferson, Adams, Monroe, and the others had believed in and stood up for against England and King George III. That was what they were fighting for. Washington's Army had done it, and now it was their turn. The patriotism of the men imprisoned at Camp Oglethorpe ran sky high. The few who were near death felt it, and it was with that spirit that they knew, now, they could die in peace. For the living, it was a day that they would remember for the rest of their lives.

Days passed slowly for the men under house arrest. They had little to do but play cards, checkers, and chess; go to the sinks, accompanied, of course, by Confederate guards; read the newspapers that were brought to them; eat when they could; and sleep a lot. Conversation depended on what was in the paper or what the others told them since they knew nothing else. But, they had to discount what they read since many of the stories about the war were false, written to buoy the spirits of the people of Bibb County, Georgia, of which Macon was the county seat.

The *Macon Daily Telegraph* would report, for example, that in any particular battle, the Confederate forces were victorious. It happened after the Battle of Kennesaw Mountain where, conveniently, the paper had announced that General Joseph Johnston's Army had won, which wasn't true, and then did not report that he had withdrawn farther south, deeper into Georgia, near Atlanta. The paper's readers didn't know any better, so they believed what they read. It kept their spirits up, falsely.

So, on July 18, 1864 when the *Macon Daily Telegraph* printed a story that Johnston had been replaced by Lieutenant General John Bell Hood, none of the prisoners at Camp Oglethorpe knew whether it was true or not. For once. it was the truth. The President of the Confederate States of America, Jefferson Davis, had grown tired of Johnston's continual withdrawals, much like President Abraham Lincoln was tired of General George Meade not pursuing Lee. So, Davis, like Lincoln, chose to elevate a man who was known for action, the native of Owingsville, Kentucky, John Bell Hood.

And, Hood would waste no time in taking that action, for on July 20, just three days after he was promoted, he encountered the Army of the Cumberland, commanded by Union Major General George H. Thomas. You see, Sherman had split his army into three columns. The Army of the Cumberland under Thomas; the Army of the Tennessee, commanded by Major General James B. McPherson; and the Army of the Ohio under Major General John M. Schofield. Sherman ordered Thomas to press on to Atlanta while McPherson and Schofield were told to go to the east to cut supply lines and disrupt any Confederate railroad traffic.

To move on Atlanta, the Army of the Cumberland had to cross Peachtree Creek at several spots, leaving itself open to attack. Hood had ordered the corps of Major General William J. Hardee to advance the Confederate position on the right with Major General Alexander P. Stewart's corps on the left. Hood wanted the attack to occur in the morning, but due to some miscommunication, it did not happen until mid-afternoon. By then, Thomas' forces had not only crossed Peachtree Creek but had also thrown up earthworks of dirt and fallen trees for protection. They had also sharpened some of the trees for abatis, so when the attack came, the Federals were ready for it and repulsed Hardee's charges in some ferocious fighting.

General Alexander Stewart was a little more successful, forcing a large portion of the 33rd New Jersey to retreat, but a counterattack was launched that drove the Confederates back. Now that Thomas had crossed the creek successfully and with the Rebels withdrawing, the Union force had an open road to Atlanta. Both sides had started the day with about 20,000 men. At day's end, they were both down to between 17,500 and 18,000. This campaign was getting costly, but Major General William Tecumseh Sherman had his orders and was inching closer to Atlanta, the second most important industrial center in the South, second only to Richmond. Grant wanted Atlanta crushed and had given the task to Sherman. It would happen, both men knew, they just didn't know when.

The Army of the Cumberland, under George Thomas, approached Atlanta from the west. Major General James McPherson's Army of the Tennessee came in from the east as did Schofield's Army of the Ohio. McPherson's consisted of the XV Corps, commanded by Major General John A. Logan; the XVI Corps, under Major General Greenville M. Dodge; and the XVII Corps under Major General Frank Blair, Jr. and would be engaged early on. As McPherson carefully positioned Logan and Schofield tactically in preparation for a Confederate assault, he realized that his left flank was vulnerable and ordered Dodge to move to its defense. There, he met Lieutenant General William Hardee's Corps and the battle for Atlanta was on. It was Friday, July 22, 1864, and it was hot. So was the fighting.

When McPherson heard the sounds of battle, artillery starting to roar, he rode to the high ground with his aides to see how it was progressing. As they were climbing, seeking the optimal place to view the fight, a squad of skirmishers from Lieutenant General Joseph Wheeler's cavalry surprised them. They were ordered to halt, but Major General James B. McPherson would have none of it. He wheeled his horse to the rear and took off. The Confederates took aim and shot the General, killing him on the spot. He was 36 years old and was considered one of the finest warrior leaders in all of the Union Army. When Sherman and Grant heard this news, they were devastated for they both loved General McPherson. But, war is war. Major General John A. Logan, "Black Jack" as he was known, now commanded the Army of the Tennessee of Sherman's army. Ultimately, that command would be given to Major General Oliver O. Howard.

The battle for Atlanta turned absolutely murderous, being fought mainly on a hill to the east of the city known as Bald Hill. It would last all day, but the Federals held. However, the Confederates still occupied Atlanta, but they had paid for it. Of the 40,000 who had begun the day, somewhere between 5,000 and 6,000 had been killed, wounded, or captured. The Union, under McPherson, then Logan, lost about 10% of its force of 35,000. As things calmed down a little at the end of the day, Major General John A. Logan could see the city down below. It was there for the taking.

Lieutenant General John Bell Hood knew Logan, Dodge, and Schofield were there. He could see them and knew that, at some point, he would be unable to defend the city any further. He telegraphed Major General Robert E. Lee, who, in a return cable, instructed Hood to abandon the city. In a second transmission, Lee also ordered Hood to contact Brigadier General John H. Winder of the Confederate Bureau of Prison Camps, telling him that the men at Camp Oglethorpe and the other Confederate prisons needed to be moved north. Sherman was just too close and appeared to be settling in around Atlanta in siege tactics.

On Wednesday, July 27, 1864, under orders from General Winder, the commandant of Camp Oglethorpe, Lt. Col. George Gibbs, ordered 600 of the men to be ready to be transferred to Charleston, South Carolina the next day. He would leave the decision as to who would be the first 600 to go to the senior Federal officers: Thomas Rose, William Nelson, and William G. Ely. Well, Colonel Ely had been impressed with the escape effort at Libby Prison and with the work of the "500" at Camp Oglethorpe, so naturally, he concluded that the officers of that clandestine group should be the first ones out. That certainly helped the cause of Tom Armstrong and Caleb Edwards. They would be among that initial group to leave Camp Oglethorpe for Charleston, South Carolina. The others would follow, emptying the Camp.

The 600 learned of their fate at *Roll Call* that morning. Ely, Nelson, and Rose had met the night before after Colonel Ely was told that the evacuation of Camp Oglethorpe would take place over the next several days. Thomas Rose told Tom Armstrong and Caleb Edwards that they would be leaving for Charleston that very night.

"Damned if we're not gonna see more of the South," Edwards exclaimed when he heard the news of their selection to leave.

"Sure are," responded Tom Armstrong. "Hope the next place is as good as this one, but I kinda doubt it. Better get ready to go in a hurry. Don't know when we will march out of here. Need to pack everything we have and get some food. Let's see if there's any bread we can take; actually, get anything we can find: meat, dried fruit, just anything, Caleb."

"You bet. Let's get to the commissary before the others."

"Right. There'll be a lot of them scrounging for food to take along. It isn't that far. All we're doing is going northeast to the Atlantic. That's where Charleston is. Let's go," and they were off.

As the preparations to leave were underway, Colonel William Ely, Colonel William Nelson, Colonel Thomas Rose, and Major E.L. Smith were meeting to talk about the journey to Charleston. "Was stationed at Charleston before the war," Nelson began. "My unit, the 13th U.S. Infantry, was garrisoned there. I know this part of the country like the back of my hand."

"Damn," said Thomas Rose. "I forgot you are regular army, career man, right outta West Point. Right?"

"Yeah. While you guys will get out some day, I'm stayin' in. Me and guys like my friend George Custer. Who knows where we're goin' when this is all over, but this is what I was born for. Anyway, here's an idea for you. We're goin' east on the Georgia Southern Railroad. There's a stop for water at Vidalia. Tell the men in charge of the cars that when the train stops, Smith, here, will flash a red lantern out of the lead car where we will be riding. At this signal, the men will overpower the guards, taking their weapons. When they have overpowered them, two or three per car will watch the guards at gunpoint while four or five more will get out and take on the guards on top of the cars. Kill 'em if they have to. Now, two of the men in my regiment were railroaders before the war. They know how to run one of these things. Will need half a dozen men from our car to assault the locomotive, taking out the engineer and the fireman. Tie 'em up, and leave 'em. Maybe just shoot 'em. My men will take over the engine. Then, when we have control of this train, the next thing is to cut the telegraph wires. After that, we start the train back toward Macon. Men can take off any time they want to. Tell them to go north and northwest toward Atlanta. That's where Sherman is. Travel at night, using the north star. One company will stay with us to rip up the track behind the train while we are backing up. Am I clear?"

"Holy shit," said Elwood Smith. "That gonna work?"

"Don't see why not. There's 600 of us and only a handful of them. I'm just damned sick and tired of bein' in prison. It's a gamble, somebody may get hurt, but most of the men will be able to start north. Hood's moving this way, I imagine, toward Augusta, maybe toward Savannah, but it's a risk we have to take. The farther west we can get this thing, the better chance we have. Elwood, make sure that we have a full load of wood and water when we stop."

"Yes, sir, Bill."

"Bill," William Nelson asked, addressing William Ely, "what do you think?"

"Sounds good to me, Bill."

Bill Nelson looked at Thomas Rose. "Tom?"

"I'm game, Bill. Always looking for a chance to escape. Libby, Macon. Why the hell not?"

"OK, it's settled. We go at Vidalia. Everyone out and organize the men for the cars. Make sure there is a chain of command in each one."

During the rest of the day, the first six hundred prisoners were counted into groups of fifty, with the highest-ranking officer placed in charge of his car. Each of them was instructed on the plan. They, in turn, counseled their men, assigning one man to be the lookout for the lantern, six others to take the guards, four more to shoot the Rebels on top of the cars. The rest could scatter in groups of two or three. Trouble was, they hadn't realized that there were spies among the prisoners, namely one of the 154th New York Infantry who was captured at Dug Gap as The Atlanta Campaign was just beginning. No one knew that he was a Confederate sympathizer when he enlisted and had been spying on Union movements from Day One of his service. So, after he was told about his assignment for that evening, he simply sauntered over to Lt. Col. George Gibbs' office and alerted the prison commandant to what was underway.

At 6 o'clock in the evening, Gibbs gave the order for the cars to be loaded for the ride to Charleston. Colonel William Nelson was a bit surprised that ten guards entered the lead car, his car. That would make things more difficult.

Around 8:30 P.M., Nelson nodded at Major Elwood Smith who picked up the red lantern and started for the door. The barrel of a Confederate rifle came down on the Major's head, splitting it open, blood gushing everywhere, all over the senior officers. When Nelson saw this, he also realized that there were five armed Confederate soldiers pointing their Springfields at him, Colonel Thomas Rose, and Colonel William Ely.

"One move an' yer dead," the big rebel guard smirked. "Would love to kill you bastards."

Unbeknownst to anyone in the lead car, the assault on the guards in the other cars had gone smoothly, but the prisoners couldn't figure out why there hadn't been a signal when the train stopped at Vidalia. So, they simply slid open the doors, and peered out into the setting sun. Expecting to see freedom in front of them, instead, they saw a company of Confederate cavalry right there looking back at them, pistols drawn and swords held high.

The commander smiled and said so all could hear, "If you boys want some of this, we'll gladly oblige. So, c'mon down outta there, and we'll slit yer throat. Mebbe jus' put a bullet through your brain. Y'all want that?"

Tom Armstrong looked at Caleb Edwards. "The jig's up on this one, Caleb. That makes three."

"Dammit all to hell. First Libby, then Macon, now this. Son-of-a-goddam-bitch!"

With a fresh supply of water and wood, the train rolled east and pulled into the depot at Savannah, Georgia, 165 miles east of Macon, at about 6 o'clock on the morning of Friday, July 29, 1864. The doors of the cars were slid open, and the prisoners were met by more Confederate cavalry. Under guard, they were led to what looked like a hospital yard, surrounded by a stockade that would prevent any of them from just walking away.

Upon entering their new quarters, Tom Armstrong and Caleb Edwards guessed that it might be around two acres, most of it open, but with some huge oak trees. The stockade consisted of three brick walls with wooden walkways on top for the guards to patrol. The fourth side was made of stone and contained the main gate. Best of all, there was a pump that would give them fresh, clean water from the Savannah River, with the latrine being a trough into which the men could relieve themselves. A hydrant kept water running through the trough, keeping it a little cleaner than what they had experienced in Macon.

They were given Sibley tents, one for six men, and ordered to make a camp of them, lined up in two rows so as to form a street. But, the Rebel guards had heard about the adventurous Yankees who dug tunnel after tunnel to try to escape. So, along with the Sibleys, the prisoners were given wood to build platforms for the tents to sit on, but open on two sides so that the guards could detect any tunneling activity.

Each day, three times a day, the prisoners were marched to the commissary. "My word," said Armstrong to no one in particular on the first day they were there, "dried pork, a little tough to chew; potatoes; salt, and dried green beans." Rations for a week were brought in every Monday. Bacon for breakfast every day but Sunday when the prisoners were given a half a pound of fresh beef. Cords of firewood appeared every morning, but Sunday. Two loads came in every Saturday. *Roll Call* every morning and evening. Everything neat and orderly, the raggedy men standing at attention in front of their tents by company. Church services on Sundays.

The prisoners were given bricks and mortar to build ovens to bake bread, roast potatoes and meat, and boil coffee in the skillets, mess-pans, and kettles that the guards gave them. Newspapers were not allowed, but the Confederate officers enjoyed conversations with their Federal counterparts, engaging them in dialogue about their homes, their loved ones, what was going on in the war, and all sorts of other subjects. It was quite interesting that the Confederates found out that they were just like the Yankees, and the Yankees discovered they were just like the Confederates. Well, almost. There was that matter of slavery in the Southern culture that had caused a difference of opinion.

The prisoners could play cards and other games, walk around the enclosure, watch the various kinds of birds, and form a chorus or two to entertain anyone who would listen. Base ball was becoming a favorite pastime with squads of them squaring off against each other and occasionally against their captors. It was just like life at Camp Zanesville without the drill, of course. And, there was no mail, either going out or coming in. Worst of all, even with the comforts the Confederates gave them, they still didn't know what was to happen to them. They still didn't know if they would be exchanged someday. They just didn't know how long they would be there and if the favorable treatment would continue should they be incarcerated for a long time. And, then, there were some who were just waiting to die.

The Confederates knew that the end would be near if Sherman took Atlanta and Richmond surrendered to Grant. Petersburg, Virginia was under siege by Grant, and Atlanta was surrounded and under siege by Sherman. No one knew how long it would take before the cities fell, but everyone was coming to the conclusion that the days of the Confederacy were numbered.

It was Wednesday, August 18, 1864. While Tom Armstrong and Caleb Edwards were "enjoying" prison life in Savannah, Lieutenant George Porter was sitting in front of his tent at Major General John Logan's camp near Panthersville, Georgia, ten miles east of Atlanta. He was reading a letter from his sister, Francis, at home in Clinton, Illinois. "My God," he said to himself, "Sump is alive. I'll be goddammed. She says he's in prison in Macon. Went there from Libby Prison in Richmond. Son-of-a-bitch. I thought he was dead. Wonder what that prison looks like. Wonder how many Johnnies are guarding it." A plan was starting to hatch in the mind of George Washington Porter, Tom Armstrong's best friend.

"Begging the General's pardon," he said to John Logan, a politician from Illinois before the war, as he knocked on the post at the front of Logan's tent.

"Yes, George. Come in. What's on your mind?" You see, now, George Porter was Aide-de-Camp to General Logan, meaning that he was the General's chief assistant, issuing the General's orders and assisting him in communicating with his subordinates. He had enlisted in the 78th Ohio Volunteer Infantry as First Sergeant under Colonel Mortimer Leggett with Tom Armstrong in October 1861 and had fought valiantly and bravely at Shiloh and Vicksburg before being asked to join the staff of Major General James McPherson in June 1863, during the final days of the siege of Vicksburg. Upon McPherson's death just weeks earlier on July 22, 1864, the new Corps commander, "Black Jack" Logan, asked Porter to fill this critical position for him. Logan knew that Porter had served Leggett and McPherson well, and that he could not refuse such an offer for such a prestigious position on the General's staff, being his top administrative aide, even though he knew George Porter loved a good fight.

"Well, sir, I just received a letter from my sister, Francis, that gave me news about my best friend and who, I am assuming, will someday be my brother-in-law. That is, if he survives Johnnies' captivity. She tells me that he was captured at Second Winchester, sent to Libby Prison in Richmond, and is now in some stockade in Macon. Winchester was over a year ago. I thought he was dead. Nobody can survive those prisons.

George, now that we have that settled," said General John Logan. "What can I do for you?"

"General, with all due respect, under General Sherman's orders, we have Atlanta surrounded almost and are cutting off all supplies of men and materiel to the Rebs."

"I realize that, George, get to the point."

"Yes, sir." He hadn't asked a favor of his new commander, but now was the time. "Sir, I would like to take a detail of my old regiment, the 78th Ohio, and reconnoiter around Macon, to find out how many Johnnies are guarding the prison. When I have that information, I will bring it to you, and perhaps we could send a company or two down there to free the prisoners and send them home. We're just sitting here waiting for something to happen, so why not? Wouldn't take more than a few days. Be back early next week."

"Interesting idea, Lieutenant Porter. However, I am not sure I can do without you for three or four days, but let me talk to General Howard and General Blair about it. Do you want me to talk with General Leggett?" You see, John Logan now reported to Major General Oliver O. Howard. Frank Blair commanded the XVII Corps, including the 78th Ohio under Leggett, and reported to Logan. So, it was important for Logan, as Commander of the XV Corps, part of Howard's Army of the Tennessee, to communicate with his superior and his subordinate about a mission like this. Freeing the federal prisoners would be a psychological defeat for the Southerners, and he did not want to ignore the chain of command.

"That would be fine, sir. I am sure General Leggett will remember Lieutenant Thomas Armstrong. When you talk with General Howard, sir, please give him my compliments and regards."

"Of course, George. Write it up for me. I will telegraph General Howard and General Blair as soon as I have a description of what you want to do. Then, I'll see General Leggett tomorrow. Go tell him I want to see him first thing in the morning, 6 o'clock. You be here, too. We will settle it then."

"Yes, sir." Lieutenant George Porter went next door to his tent, sat down at his desk, and, picking up a pen and dipping it in the inkwell, began to describe his plan for General John Logan. That was part of his duty. When Logan issued orders, it was Porter's job to document them for the General and, when approved, to take them to the Corps Commanders, communicating his wishes. John Logan had watched Porter work in a similar capacity for James McPherson and had been impressed. That was the reason he invited him to be his chief aide. Dependable, smart, respectful, and tough as nails, this George W. Porter. An hour later, Logan signed off on what George Porter had written and called for the telegrapher. At the same time, Porter was off to see his former commander, Brigadier General Mortimer D. Leggett.

The three men met the next morning at exactly 6 o'clock. "So, Mort, this is what George wants to do. Reconnoiter Macon to gauge the Rebel strength, especially around the prison. Then, depending on what he finds, maybe rescue Lieutenant Armstrong and the rest of the prisoners. General Howard says sending this scouting expedition is our decision, but he wants the final say in any rescue operation. Blair's fine with it, too. They applaud your initiative, Lieutenant, but are somewhat concerned that if anything happens here, you won't be here to help me communicate with the Corps Commanders. They do not anticipate anything that would require that, but I just want you to know what they said. That aside now, Mort, what do you think?"

"I like it, General, that is if you can spare Lieutenant Porter. Gives the men something productive to do." Looking at George Porter, he said facetiously, "And, I suppose you want to take Captain Gillespie and some of his men along."

Smiling, knowing that General Mortimer Leggett knew that he and John W.A. Gillespie were the best of friends, said, "Why, of course, General. I wouldn't have it any other way. Wouldn't want to deprive the Captain of such an adventure."

Major General John Logan wasn't in on the Zanesville connection between the two old friends. You see, Mortimer Leggett had moved to Zanesville some fifteen years earlier and knew Tom Armstrong, John Gillespie, and George Porter very well. George Porter would explain the relationship to the General later in the day.

"Very well, then, gentlemen. Lieutenant Porter and Captain Gillespie will lead a scouting expedition to Macon to assess the situation there. Anything else, Mort?"

"No, sir, General. I will have Lieutenant Porter come with me back to camp where we can ask Captain Gillespie to accompany him on this mission. He will be pleased, I am sure."

"Lieutenant Porter, please mark out your route in case I need to send a messenger for you. If I do ask you to return, Captain Gillespie can finish the mission on his own and report directly to me."

"General," said George Porter, sensing some reservation in Logan's words, "would you feel better if the Captain just took command of the whole reconnaissance?"

Logan smiled as he looked at his aide. "In all honesty, George, I would. You are too important to me not to be here. But, please go with General Leggett to talk with Captain Gillespie about it."

When the three friends from Zanesville met in Brigadier General Mortimer Leggett's tent, it was settled. Captain John W.A. Gillespie would lead two squads of his men from Company G of the 78th Ohio to Macon to gauge the strength of the Confederate guards at the prison. They would leave the next day, August 20, 1864 at first light, to return no later than August 27.

Nothing was happening in Panthersville, and George Porter wished he had gone with his friend, John Gillespie. He was studying a map of Georgia when Captain Gillespie and his detail returned from Macon on Friday, August 26, and rode into Major General John Logan's camp. George Porter heard the commotion outside his tent, saw his friend, and motioned for him to come toward the General's tent.

"George," John W.A. Gillespie said, "they're gone. There's nobody there. Macon is pretty much deserted. Lieutenant Joe Miller, here, took one squad south and west around the town. I took mine north and east. We didn't see anything. Only vultures and coyotes tearing at the bodies. The prisoners, including Sump, are gone. One of the townsfolk thought he heard something about Charleston, up in South Carolina."

"Begging the General's pardon," George Porter said as he lifted the flap to John Logan's tent. "Captain Gillespie has returned with news."

John W.A. Gillespie told Major General John A. Logan exactly what he had told George Porter.

"Not surprised. Well done, Captain. I shall salute your men and then you can return to your camp. We are moving out tomorrow. I will tell General Howard about this. Maybe we can find the prisoners as we go. George, stick around. I need you right now. Just received a telegram from the General. We're moving on Atlanta tomorrow. Need to draw up orders. Have to communicate fast."

Yes, Atlanta had been there for the taking for the last month, but Major General William Tecumseh Sherman didn't like the prospect of the cost. A siege, he had concluded, was the answer, to cut off food supplies to the soldiers and the residents. It now appeared to him that the siege strategy had worked.

George Porter and John W.A. Gillespie retired from Major General John Logan's tent. "Just what the hell are you gonna tell Frank, George? She know you were looking for Sump?"

"Ain't gonna tell her anything. She don't know we went looking for him. She finds out that we did and then that we didn't find him, she'll be even more distressed than she already is."

"George, she knows he's down here someplace. Maybe she'll put two and two together. If she doesn't hear that you found him, you could be in deep shit."

"I have to chance it, J.W. Thanks for trying. If she asks, that's what I'll tell her."

Earlier that morning of August 26, 1864, Major General John Logan had received word from Major General Oliver O. Howard that he was to take the XV Corps east once again, to find the high ground around Atlanta to gain a position where he could wreck the Western & Atlantic Railroad. The XVI Corps of Major General Thomas Ransom, who had replaced Greenville Dodge as commander, would connect to the XV and face south. The two corps would form an "L." Frank Blair's XVII would be held in reserve. George Porter raced throughout the camp of the General John Logan's Corps, relaying the orders to the division commanders and answering as many questions as he could. He kind of missed seeing battle as he had done at Shiloh and Vicksburg, but, now, he had more important work to do, serving General Logan. He had no doubt Captain John W.A. Gillespie would be disappointed not being in on the action with the 78th O.V.I. since the XVII Corps would sit this one out.

Preparations were completed by Tuesday, August 30, 1864. All hell would break loose the very next day. Sherman's siege had, indeed, worked, and the Confederate Army was in disarray. It did not look to John Logan that there was any coordination. Thus, when the outmanned Rebels launched an attack north of Jonesborough, it was doomed to fail. They just didn't have the firepower, and their attack was repulsed easily, causing Hood's and Hardee's forces to withdraw back toward Atlanta. The fighting would resume the next day.

After some posturing on Wednesday morning, the Union's XIV Corps, assisted on the right by Logan's XV, finally launched an assault on Lieutenant General William Hardee's corps. In vicious hand-to-hand combat, the Yankees drove the Rebel Army back into Atlanta. In the fight, the Confederate Army lost about 2,300 of its 24,000, while the Federals lost barely 1,000 of its overwhelming force of 70,000.

On the night of September 1, 1864, Lieutenant General John Bell Hood abandoned the city, knowing full well that if he stayed, there would be hell to pay in the morning. His force might be completely destroyed, and he wanted to regroup and fight another day. So, he ordered his troops south to Lovejoy Station, but not before he had them destroy the ammunition magazines and other wartime materiel there in Atlanta. Major General William Tecumseh Sherman had, indeed, finally won the city of Atlanta, but he had not destroyed the Confederate Army of John Bell Hood and William Hardee as he had wanted. Had he done so, the War of the Rebellion likely would have been over. The Union troops marched into Atlanta on September 2, 1864, victorious but with more to do. "Atlanta is ours, and fairly won," was the simple telegram Sherman sent to Secretary William Stanton of the War Department. Stanton, in turn, would tell the President. The Anaconda Plan of General Winfield Scott was working quite nicely.

George Porter was exhausted, having not slept for two days, carrying John Logan's orders to the Corps Commanders and returning with responses and messages for him. It was harrowing work, riding through the hail of rifle and artillery fire, but, in a way, he loved it, every damn minute. He didn't quite know why he did, he just knew he loved being in the thick of the action. Major John A. Logan was lucky to have him, but after the battle, when he had time to think, George Porter was now worried more than ever. Where was his best friend, T.S. Armstrong? Was he alive? He had no way of knowing and would not know that Tom Armstrong and the rest of the prisoners there at Savannah soon would be heading to Charleston.

It was September 12, 1864, and by now, the prisoners knew that Atlanta had fallen to Sherman. They had also heard that Mobile Bay in Alabama had been captured by Admiral David Farragut. That meant the West was completely in Union hands. Tom Armstrong and Caleb Edwards, still in Savannah, had finished their supper and were playing checkers when the order was given that they were heading to Charleston, South Carolina, early the next morning. They were getting used to this moving around and suspected that the Union Army of Major General William Tecumseh Sherman was on the move. They were right.

The two columns of Sherman's Army were, indeed, going to go east once Atlanta was secured with the Army of the Tennessee, commanded by Major General Oliver O. Howard on the right and the Army of Georgia under Major General Henry W. Slocum on the left, north of Howard's column. "Black Jack" Logan had been given permission to return to Illinois to help with the election of 1864, which he did. Once again, George Porter was now Aide-de-Camp to General Mortimer D. Leggett, commander of the 3rd Division of the XVII Corps, heading

At daybreak on September 13, 1864, Tom Armstrong, Caleb Edwards, and the rest of the first batch of 600 prisoners at Savannah marched through the city, under guard, heading for the depot. Another 600 would follow the next day, with the final batch one day later. The Confederate guards looked like they were twelve years old, and probably were, but they did have rifles trained on the prisoners. There were about 100 of them Tom guessed, commanded by an older man, in uniform, white hair and beard, connoting his age. "Probably fought earlier in the war, maybe wounded and sent home to baby-sit these kids. Wonder if they would really shoot us if we tried to take them. Wonder why the Johnnies just don't let us go. Sherman's going to obliterate them."

The train left Savannah about 9 o'clock in the morning, traveling right up the Atlantic coast toward Charleston, where, in Armstrong's mind, all of this trouble had started.

Upon their arrival, the prisoners could see Fort Sumter out in the harbour, which served to heighten their resolve to survive this ordeal or escape. Tom Armstrong was a long way from Zanesville, Ohio. The prisoners were ordered out of the cars around 6 o'clock that evening, and, in formation, the youthful guards marched them down Coming Street to the Charleston City Jail at the corner of Franklin and Magazine Streets, just six blocks from the Atlantic Ocean. They found that it was a horrible place, dirty, with filthy water, latrines that were overflowing, fifty tents for the first 600 officers. 300 of whom would have shelter and 300 would not. Luckily,

Colonel Thomas Rose had assigned Tom Armstrong and Caleb Edwards to his mess in a tent near the gallows in the center of the yard.

Inside that tent, they saw a man praying over the skeletal figure of an enlisted man who was barely breathing, dying of what they supposed was typhoid fever. So, Colonel Rose and the others, just sat down outside the tent and waited for the man to die. He did, a couple hours later, opening the way for them to have some shelter for the night, but that was about all. No planks or bunks, just hard ground to lie on. No blankets or anything to give them cover. "Macon sure wasn't like this," thought Tom Armstrong, thinking of what Patrick Murphy must have gone through at Belle Isle. At least it wasn't cold. Actually, it was just the opposite as they would find out the next day.

At daybreak, Armstrong and Edwards could see that the yard was bounded by a brick wall, about twelve feet high, on two sides. A jail commanded the third, and what looked to be a workhouse of some sort was the fourth. They were shocked at how small the yard really was and quickly realized that the walls and the buildings cut them off from any breeze off the Atlantic. With no breeze, it was going to be fiercely hot in the blazing sun. So, they would retire to their tent around 11 o'clock each day for shelter, but that really didn't do much good.

To state the obvious, the accommodations were pitiful with more men to arrive as the war dragged on. It was just plain awful. The food was likewise terrible: moldy, rancid, and filled with vermin. There wasn't much of it, and it was always the same: cornmeal, rice, beans, and maybe some bacon, all infested by maggots and other unpleasant creatures. Add that to the brackish water, and it was all the men could do just to survive. God help them when they had to use the latrine. Most decided that wasn't a good idea and just found some other place to go. But, that was becoming a problem because of the number of Union officers who were being brought to this place. And, it would get worse as the cases of dysentery increased several fold. Excrement and urine pools everywhere made walking around difficult.

But, perhaps that was an opportunity, an opportunity to be paroled. Sensing the deepening sanitary problem and the threat of more disease, Colonel Rufus Wingate, the commandant of the City Jail, decided that parole was the only answer. If the prisoners would not try to escape or take up arms against the Confederate Army, then comfortable, clean quarters could be made available.

Caleb Edwards was not so sure. "What's the catch?" he asked.

"Doesn't seem to be one," responded Tom Armstrong. "Can't escape this town. Don't have any weapons to fight with. Maybe the commandant has a problem, and this will help him resolve it. I'm taking him up on it."

"Guess I will, too," said Edwards reluctantly, still not sure that it was a good idea.

So, two days later, somewhere around one hundred Federal prisoners left the Charleston City Jail Yard and were marched to a big house on Legare Street, overlooking Charleston Harbor. It would be crowded, for sure, but the men didn't mind, primarily because there were bath houses just across the street that they could use whenever they wanted to. Tom Armstrong and Caleb Edwards hadn't had a bath since a rainstorm in Macon, so when they were told they could use one of the bath houses, they dashed across the street to take advantage of it. Got the lice out of their hair and beards. Soap was rather rough but, quite frankly, they didn't care. They still hoped to be exchanged, but, there at the boarding house, life was tolerable. At least they were clean and had sufficient food to eat, brought to them by the Sisters of Our Lady of Mercy of a convent over there on Queen Street. The nuns ignored the constant shelling of Charleston by the Yankee gunners on Morris Island in order to deliver their mission of mercy daily, not only bringing food, but also tending to the sick and administering to the dying.

On September 22, 1864, word reached the prisoners of Charleston that the cavalry of Major General Philip Sheridan and his forces of about 50,000 Union soldiers had defeated Lieutenant General Jubal Early's Confederate infantry decisively at what has become known as the 3rd Battle of Winchester, up there at the head of the Shenandoah Valley. Yes, the same place where Tom Armstrong and Caleb Edwards had been captured in June of '63. Sheridan, acting under orders from Lieutenant Ulysses S. Grant, was determined to clear the Shenandoah of the Confederate Army and to destroy the fields and pastures that had been feeding it. Needless to say, "Fightin' Phil," another Ohioan like Grant and Sherman, was relentless in pursuit of that goal which would be achieved about a month later, on October 22, 1864, at the Battle of Cedar Creek.

Rumors of exchange were rampant, perhaps the first 600 from Savannah for a like number of Confederates being held at Morris Island. That never happened, and Caleb Edwards, for one, even with the lenient treatment of the guards there in Charleston, was just damn sick and tired of being in prison. On September 25th, word came that some of Sherman's officers who had been captured in the Atlanta Campaign were being exchanged for a like number of Confederates captured in the same fighting. Now, when Caleb Edwards heard that, he was not happy.

"What the hell is going on?" he groused. "Those bastards just got here and now they are back with General Sherman. We've been in captivity for over a year. Maybe they have forgotten about us. Son-of-a-goddam-bitch. I'm getting' outta here as soon as I can. I'm goin' home where they 'preciate me."

"Caleb, let's wait and see just a little longer," responded Tom Armstrong.

"Yer always sayin' stuff like that. Let's jus' figure out a way to get the hell out."

Armstrong began to worry that his friend would do something desperate if he got the chance. He hoped he would see it coming, so he could stop it.

On October 4, they received word that another train ride was in the offing, this time to a prison camp in Columbia, the capital of South Carolina. The following morning, they were loaded onto the cars, arriving at their destination just before midnight. There were only two guards in each car with some sixty Yankee prisoners. Edwards thought they could overtake the Johnnies, even with their Springfields, and get out. But the same questions kept coming back to him. Where would they go? How would they survive?

When they were ordered out of the cars, they were told that the Rebels were really tired of guarding them and wanted the prisoners to swear that they would not take up arms or try to escape, in effect, they were being paroled. Caleb Edwards could not make that promise, so he, Tom Armstrong and the rest of their car, along with all the others, were herded into a field about five acres square. There was a slight problem. No one in Charleston had told the commandant of the camp there in Columbia that 600 sick, hungry, dirty Yankees were coming to pay a visit. So, there were no sleeping accommodations, no food, no water, no latrines, just a big, wide open field.

Help arrived the following day. Again, they were asked if they wanted to be paroled to a grove of peach trees where all of the shortcomings experienced the previous night were to be eliminated. Tom Armstrong and Caleb Edwards thought that was a good idea, and that maybe escape would be possible. They were right. The grove of peach trees was three miles east of where they had been, with just a fence to keep them in. On a cold and rainy afternoon, they were told they could choose a space anywhere in the grove, the latrines had a stream running through them, there was plenty of firewood, blankets were handed out, and rations were issued. It was, once again, like the Confederates knew that the war was coming to an end and were trying to be as humane as possible there at Camp Sorghum, so named because the staple of the diet was cornmeal and molasses. Molasses was otherwise known as sorghum. The first night was, indeed, trying, but at least they had a fire, some hard bread, and a blanket. Armstrong and Edwards spent the night huddled together under a large pine tree in the southwest corner of the grove.

Over the next month or so, the prisoners were free, under guards, to go out into the woods to cut down trees for firewood and to construct houses, complete with fireplaces by which to cook and to keep warm at night. Many of the men who went out to fell the trees were never seen again, just dropped their axes and took off toward the Union lines. Some were recaptured and brought back in and some were shot right then and there, but a lot of them were never seen again. Caleb Edwards had an idea.

"Sump, why don't we do what those others have done? Guards come out with us to watch us cut down trees. What happens if we hit 'em with an axe? Knock 'em silly or take their damn heads off? They go down, we skedaddle. Whattya think?"

"Caleb, I'm tired of trying to escape. The war's going to be over soon. They will have to exchange us. Then we go home. You gonna risk getting killed? Never see Margaret and the children again? Caleb, I'm just trying to make sure you don't make a huge mistake. It isn't worth it. You saw what they did to those guys who disappeared last week. They made it to Augusta, got caught, one guy tried to run and took a bullet in the back, killed him dead in his tracks. You want that? I wouldn't be surprised if Sherman himself came through the front gate one of these days." It was early November 1864, and Tom Armstrong didn't feel very well. The scurvy was back among the men, and he was worried about it. Dysentery, too.

"Dammit, Sump, you always gotta answer. Am I ever gonna win?

"Not if I can help it, Caleb. Just lookin' out for your best interest. Don't want to have to bury you here in Carolina. I will, though, if you make me."

The news continued to be good. The guards were softening, bringing in newspapers. Major General William Tecumseh Sherman was on the march east with 60,000 rested Federal soldiers. No one knew what his destination was... Augusta? Savannah? Charleston? Columbia? All the prisoners knew was that the Federal Army would someday overwhelm the Southerners of Lieutenant General Joseph Johnston, and it wouldn't take very long. They just had to hold on until it happened.

While the guards brought in newspapers for the prisoners to read, they had to discount the stories, even believe that the opposite was true. Just like at Macon. One such account proclaimed that Sherman had lost three-quarters of a million men in The Atlanta Campaign. That would have been about 2% of the entire population of the country. Obviously, that couldn't have happened, so they took the published news with a grain of salt.

Now, new prisoners coming in were a different story. These "fresh fish" were telling the others of what was really going on. The communication network among the Union inmates was strong and lively. When the newspapers declared that the Battle of Franklin (Tennessee) was won by John Bell Hood, the men knew that the opposite was true. Hood's Army was probably devastated, and later they found out that it was.

The "fish" that came in during the second week of November 1864, reported that on November 8, Abraham Lincoln had won his second term as President of the United States convincingly. Apparently, early in the presidential campaign, no one had expected him to win since, even in the North, the people were getting tired of the war and were thinking that maybe, it would continue on and on. Maybe that wasn't worth the cost. But then, two months before the election, William Tecumseh Sherman had taken Atlanta and a surge of patriotism had returned. Lincoln won the Electoral College, 212 to 21, and the Republicans had a ¾ majority in Congress. Lincoln now had the opportunity he had wanted since 1861: to conclude the American Civil War with a Union victory. That would let him bring the United States back together again, ending the massive amount of blood that had been spilled since the Confederate guns bombarded Fort Sumter. And, the President had a plan in mind to do just that.

Tom Armstrong was in a thoughtful mood, even though he felt like shit. A bad case of diarrhea had overtaken him. It was getting cold there in Columbia, South Carolina. Not as cold as Zanesville in early December, but cold enough given that he didn't have an overcoat. Damn good thing Caleb kept the campfire crackling in front of the tent.

"Caleb," he said, "assuming that Hood's Army was completely routed in Tennessee, Sheridan's cleaned up the Shenandoah, Sherman is on the march east, and Meade is chasing Lee wherever he goes, doesn't that say that the Anaconda has worked and that the death of the Confederacy is not far off?"

"When you put it like that, yeah, it does. Wonder how long they can hold out. Like to get home for Christmas."

"Yeah, me, too, but right now, I just want to stay warm. Keep bringing me water, diarrhea isn't so bad when I drink a lot of water. Could use some meat. Haven't had any in I can't remember how long." Armstrong's 165 pounds had shrunk to about 135. A tall drink of water and damn skinny.

"You gotta eat as much as you can, Sump. Don't want you starving to death while we're so close to winnin' this damn thing. Don't want to bury you here in South Carolina. Frank would never forgive me." Caleb Edwards was smiling.

"She doesn't even know you exist. I do imagine she would be pretty upset. I wouldn't know it. I'd be dead. I'm hangin' on, just need warmth, water, and food."

"Can you march?"

"Why?" asked Tom Armstrong.

"Hear that we're moving again.

"Where?"

"Some asylum on the other side of town."

"Guess I'll have to."

On December 10, 1864, with what was left of their belongings loaded onto wagons, 600 Union prisoners were marched through Columbia in the cold and rain to the yard of the local lunatic asylum. And, now the Union inmates were to be housed at the eastern end of the yard; would be given wood, bricks, and clay to build houses; could visit the hospital if need be; had the same rations as they did at Camp Sorghum; and, if they had any money which most, if not all, didn't, might visit the sutler's wagon to buy additional provisions. But, until all of that was done, they had to exist outside in the cold and wet, although they were given Sibley tents for some protection and had enough wood for the campfire. Constructing a house was the first order of business.

Colonel William G. Ely had ordered that the houses be built to resemble camp life, streets and all. Each house would contain thirty-six prisoners, so just under twenty of them would be needed. They would be the same size and shape and would face each other across the street. Colonel Thomas Rose detailed Caleb Edwards as supervisor to oversee the building of three of them with the orders to "Get 'em done damn fast, Edwards."

A week later, with the help of thirty or so men, the first one was complete, fireplace and all. Tom Armstrong thanked the Lord for giving him shelter and saving him from the current ordeal. He was not well physically, but mentally and spiritually, he was in fine shape. He actually felt encouraged that he would survive and get home. Francis Pamela Porter was constantly on his mind.

Caleb Edwards walked into the house on Tuesday, December 20, 1864."Smashed 'em agin, this time at Nashville. Thomas overwhelmed Hood. Gotta be reeling. Heard that from the sutler. Then, and I don't know where it came from, but there's Confederate money everywhere. Men got it, lots of it, buying all sorts of stuff. Meat, potatoes, vegetables. We gotta get you some of that."

"Caleb, however you can do that, do it. Beg, borrow, steal, I don't care. Coffee, too."

Caleb Edwards nodded. He would do whatever he could for his friend. The sutler was bringing in meat and vegetables by the wagon, almost every day. Yes, it was expensive, beef at $4 a pound and cauliflower, 2 for $1, but somehow Caleb Edwards didn't seem to care. He never told Tom Armstrong how he did it, getting all that food. He just had friends, that's all he ever said. Caleb Edwards had become pretty resourceful.

Two days later, on December 22, 1864, the lunatic asylum in Columbia, South Carolina erupted in a joyous celebration. Word had come down early that morning that on the night of December 20, Lieutenant General William Hardee had led his Confederate force out of Savannah and that the mayor of the city, the Honorable Richard D. Arnold and several other dignitaries, had surrendered it to Brigadier General John W. Geary of the XX Corps the next day. Major General William Tecumseh Sherman now controlled the Deep South as well as the West.

With the surrender, he sent a telegraph message to the President of the United States: "I beg to present you as a Christmas gift the City of Savannah, with one hundred and fifty guns and plenty of ammunition, also about twenty-five thousand bales of cotton."

Upon receipt, the President just smiled that smile he was known for. Abraham Lincoln was most grateful for the General's Christmas present. It was the best one he had ever received.

14 Freedom

The racket coming from the South Carolina State Hospital, known to most as the "Lunatic Asylum," there at the corner of Bull Street and Elmwood Avenue in Columbia, was deafening. Twelve hundred Yankee prisoners were celebrating Major General William Tecumseh Sherman's Christmas gift of Savannah to President Lincoln. Cheers and singing of patriotic songs echoed off the massive building that had been constructed in 1827 as a residence for the mentally ill. The "crazies," as they were known at the time, were housed inside with the Union officers in their tents out in the prison yard. The asylum could probably handle up to 5,000 people, if need be, it was that big. The singing and dancing of the Union prisoners annoyed the staff of the Asylum, but there was nothing they could do about it.

Very rarely did Tom Armstrong curse, and he would never take the Lord's name in vain. But, today, December 22, 1864, he allowed himself a simple oath. "Damn," he said to Caleb Edwards. 'Just plain damn. It worked. The Anaconda worked. We're gonna be freed. I can feel it."

"Yeah, think so," came the response, quite calmly." Looks like Thomas destroyed Hood's army at Nashville, so Lee's out there all alone. Grant's gonna crush 'im. Wonder where Sherman's gonna go. Bet he's goin' after Johnston someplace." The big West Virginian, for as angry and frustrated as he was, always seemed comforted by his friend's calm demeanor. Probably saved his life a couple or three times.

"Betcha two bits Sherman's coming north. He's gonna make South Carolina pay for this, I'll wager. Only makes sense. Just trap Lee. Thomas from the west, Meade from the north, Sherman from the south. Ocean's on the east, so Grant has him penned in. Damn!

397

Wonder how long it will take Sherman to get here. Y'know he wants Richmond. Wouldn't want to be a Johnny now. Bet a lot of them look at it and go home. Makes the General's job easier."

"I ain't gonna take that bet. You make it sound too logical, Sump. You always do. Wonder what the Commandant here is gonna do. He'd be smart to see where Sherman goes and then get the hell out of here when our boys get close. They gotta know this thing's over. They just gotta."

"Bet they do. Good thing they're being nice to us. Thank God for the sutler. Say, Caleb, how'd you get all that food? Been wondering about that."

"Never you mind, Thomas, my boy, never you mind." And, that was the end of that.

As they spoke, life at the asylum was looking up. The house was done, including the fireplace; they had plenty of wood for fires to keep warm and cook; the water was bearable; latrines were behind the big building, could go there whenever they wanted; didn't need a guard with that wall of about 12 feet surrounding the yard; and the food was plentiful. Caleb Edwards just kept bringing it in. Add to that, it was warm, compared to Libby Prison. Probably 50 degrees during the day and maybe just 40 at night. Tom Armstrong's world was, indeed, better as he helped Caleb Edwards fashion some chairs while some of the others were working in the tunnel. Armstrong wished he could write letters home and to Francis Porter, but the Rebels weren't permitting that.

Tunnel? What tunnel? You see, Thomas Rose was back at it. In several of the houses, tunnels were being dug, just like at Libby and Macon. Guards didn't appear to be interested, so the work went on smoothly. Dirt was easy to dig, and there were plenty of men in each house to take it outside in the pockets of their jackets to spread around the prison yard where the guards couldn't see them. There was tunneling activity in some of the tents as well. Rose just figured that their captors wouldn't find all twelve of them. Maybe one or two, but not all twelve.

Tom Armstrong and Caleb Edwards took their turns in the hole, digging and watching for any snooping guards. This was a lot easier than at Libby, just about the same as in Macon. Didn't even have to work at night. It really didn't make much sense to Tom Armstrong to be digging tunnels and risking punishment with Sherman on the way, but Thomas Rose had asked him to dig, so he did.

On Christmas, 1864, the celebration was livelier than in previous years, but not as wild as the celebration of the 4th of July or the one just the other day about the fall of Savannah. The men were tired, some sick, and there was nothing exciting like Sherman's conquest. So, the Christmas festivities were somewhat muted. Many of the men were just glad to be alive with the hope of exchange heightened by the news of the military success of the Union Army and gave thanks to God that Christmas night. Then, at precisely eleven o'clock, William Todd and the men of his house, came out into the yard and began to sing...

> Mine eyes have seen the glory
> Of the coming of the Lord
> He is trampling out the vintage
> Where the grapes of wrath are stored
> He has loosed the fateful lightning
> Of his terrible swift sword
> His truth is marching on.
>
> Glory, glory, hallelujah
> Glory, glory, hallelujah
> Glory, glory hallelujah
> His truth is marching on.

And, soon, there were a thousand voices there in Columbia, South Carolina singing *The Battle Hymn of the Republic* with gusto as they gave thanks to God that their ordeal might soon be over. While Tom Armstrong couldn't carry a tune in a bushel basket, he sang along, emotion swelling up in his eyes. Caleb Edwards noticed it, but never said a word about it. He just sang along as well, and pretty well, too.

New Year's Day came and went, and strangely, there was no news about the war. Armstrong reasoned that there wouldn't be any more "fresh fish," so their conduit to the outside world had just dried up. A routine was starting to take over life at the asylum, causing the men to wonder just when would William Tecumseh Sherman arrive. Or, when would the Commandant, Major Elias Griswold, ask his superiors for an order to commence their parole and exchange. But, nothing was happening. Just the tunnels.

While Tom Armstrong was walking back to the house from the latrine one day, he suddenly realized something that had been right in front of his face all along since they came into the Asylum yard three weeks previous. The delivery of wood for their fires was being done by Negroes who came through the main gate every day but Sunday, unloaded their wagons beside the building, and then drove their teams of mules into the middle of the yard to turn around. "They will know something." Armstrong said to himself. "They can tell me what's happening on the outside." He made a mental note to walk by one of the wagons in the next few days to strike up a conversation with one of the drivers.

He did just that on January 20, 1865. One of the wagon drivers had pulled his mules to a halt and had come down to look at the harness and hitch. When Tom Armstrong came strolling by, knowing he was not supposed to talk with anyone from the outside, he stopped to rub his right foot, a ruse of course, within a few feet of the Negro who was inspecting his wagon. "Sherman's cummin," the old man whispered. "Heard dother dey, he's cummin." And with that, he climbed back up into the wagon, turned the mules, and was seen exiting the yard through the main gate. This man would become Armstrong's connection to the outside world.

A week later, the charade was repeated, this time with the man looking at the left rear wheel of the wagon. "Dey stop shootin,' massa. Fite no more." Tom Armstrong was stunned.

"Caleb, it might be over. Negro just told me that they've stopped shooting. An armistice, if you will."

"Naw, that didn't happen. We'd of known about it. Guards would of said something. Don't believe it." But, the rumor was all over the yard. Men gathered, whispering to one another that their freedom was right around the corner. There was room for hope, even if it wasn't true. So, life got back to the routine just as quickly as it had been interrupted. The talk of an armistice quickly vanished.

And, then, the unthinkable happened. At *Roll Call*, on February 3, Major Elias Griswold climbed onto a table to address the prisoners, highly unusual behavior for him. "Must be something big," Tom Armstrong thought to himself. "Wonder what's so important."

"You men have deceived me," the Major began. "I am aware that y'all are attempting to escape. Y'all have tunnels. My men went through one of them while y'all were standing here at *Roll Call* last night. Funniest thing. They crawled all the way from that tent over there under the wall, and ended up on the other side, about six feet from it, right over yonder," he said gesturing to the north. "Now, y'all will stop this today. And, if I find there are any more, we will tear down the houses and burn the tents. I may even restrict the sutler's time inside the wall. We're gonna inspect every house and tent and will fill all the tunnels. Don't do it again. If I find you do, I'll hang your sorry ass or maybe just shoot you!"

"Son-of-a-goddam bitch," groused Caleb Edwards. "I ain't diggin' no more. Tain't worth it. Still mad about those haversacks in East Leake. Shoulda been home by now. Dammit all to hell."

"Now," Griswold continued, "if any of y'all see another one trying to escape, come and tell me. Y'all be protected if y'all do, and God help any of y'all that try to hurt him. Might jus' hang you, too. Understand?"

There was considerable grumbling among the prisoners. Caleb Edwards was just about at the end of his rope. "Some bastard tol' on us, Sump. Wish I knew who it was. Break his goddam neck, the bastard. Same damn thing happened at Macon. Son-of-a-bitch from Illinois sold us out."

Things settled down a bit, but without the tunnels, the routine at the asylum started to get boring. Oh, there were games to be played, and the men could walk about the yard, but that was about it. No newspapers, but the saving grace was plenty of food and plenty of wood. Tom Armstrong, still hungry for news, continued to look out for the old Negro who had told him that Sherman was, indeed, coming and, every day, would make his way to the spot where that conversation took place. If anyone asked, namely a guard, he would simply tell him that he was going to the latrine. Wouldn't arouse any suspicions with that.

So, a week or so later, he strolled out of the house with Caleb Edwards, heading for the latrine when he saw the old Negro turning his wagon around. The two men stopped as they saw the driver climb down off the wagon seat and move to the rear of the wagon to check the hitch. They heard him whisper that Sherman was within about thirty miles of Columbia and was coming fast. The two Yankee prisoners sauntered toward the latrine, hopes flying sky high, and could not wait to tell Thomas Rose and the rest of the men in their house.

When he heard the news, Rose exclaimed, "They'll have to move us again. Wonder where this time." And he was right, for, on the morning of February 14, Valentine's Day, half of the Union officers at the Asylum were marched to the depot three miles east of town in a cold rain which eventually turned to sleet. Marching in bare feet through an icy rain was not much fun for the prisoners, but they had no choice. At around 2 o'clock that afternoon, they boarded freight cars of the Charlotte & South Carolina Railroad. Rumor had it that they were going to Charlotte, North Carolina, about 100 miles due north of Columbia and out of Sherman's reach. But, that meant, as well, that they would be getting closer to Grant and Meade. It sure seemed like the Confederates were fighting a losing battle.

They sat in the cars for eight hours, some getting out to use the latrines that had been dug, but most just sitting in the cold, dark box cars waiting for something to happen. The Confederates had piled provisions in the first car of the train which the guards passed out to the men in the cars that followed. "At least we got somethin' to eat. No meat, though," said Caleb Edwards. "Don't look like the Johnnies are too interested in this. Maybe we could just walk away."

"In this weather?" said Tom Armstrong. "You're crazy, Caleb. Look, I seem to recall that North Carolina was a little reluctant to secede in the first place. Was one of the last ones, I think. A lot of Union sentiment there. My hunch is that we're gonna get exchanged real soon. They got no other place to put us. No reason for us to run now. Besides, my feet are cold. Leather's about gone on these boots. Don't need frostbite if I can help it."

Changing the subject, he asked, "Caleb, whattya gonna do when you get home?"

"We ain't there yet, Sump. But, if I do get home and if they don't shoot us or blow up these cars instead of exchangin' us, I'll go back to the shop. Father's been keepin' it since I been gone. Imagine he's tired of it. Gonna take a long hot bath. Gonna eat a lot of Margaret's cookin' and gonna play with the children. Might snuggle a bit with Margaret. How 'bout you?"

Armstrong smiled. "Think I'll spend a few days at the new home in Gratiot, west of Zanesville about 12 miles. Then, I'm off to Clinton, Illinois, to see Francis. Gotta question for her. Sure hope they don't just open the doors of this thing and start shootin'. I've been through enough. The good Lord has seen us through a lot of bad stuff, Caleb, and I just keep prayin' he sees us through to the end."

"Whattya gonna ask her, Thomas, my boy?" asked Caleb Edwards with a smile on his face and a twinkle in this eye that reminded Tom Armstrong of the big farm boy, Patrick Murphy. Caleb figured he knew the answer but wanted to have a little fun with his friend.

"Oh, nuthin' special," said Tom Armstrong. "Just want to ask her about her brother, George. Find out where he is and when he's gonna be home again."

"I don't believe any of that shit, Sump. I know you too well. We been through too much. Now, yer lyin' to your good friend here. Don't give me that shit." Caleb Edwards feigned anger, but couldn't hold in the laugh. "I know what yer gonna ask her, and I hope she says 'no' to pay you back fer lyin' to me."

"I told you, she doesn't know you exist, and I'm gonna keep it that way. I'll send you a letter, telling you what happens. Just to the shop in Wheeling?"

"Yeah, you lyin' sack of shit."

Now, both men were chuckling. "Darn you, Caleb, I'm gonna ask her to marry me. Satisfied? You happy, now?"

"That's all I wanted to know," said Caleb Edwards, smugly putting the matter to rest. But, Tom Armstrong wouldn't let it.

"Caleb, I had seen the elephant before I came back in. I saw it at Fort Donelson and Shiloh. I didn't fight at either place, but I saw what war can be. I saw it again at Winchester, and now, I have seen another side. The prison life, and I wouldn't wish that on any human being now or in the future. My fear is that future generations will see it, too. God help them. And, Caleb, I hope you never see the elephant again, neither, if we can survive the next few days. God help us if there is a firing squad, or they blow us up. I just want to forget as much as I can about this and spend my life with her."

It was after dark when the cars lurched forward, and the Charlotte & South Carolina started north to North Carolina, carrying over 1,000 Union prisoners, to the depot in Charlotte. The men tried to sleep, but the ride was so rough and the cars so rickety that shuteye was impossible. They arrived about noon the following day and just sat there in the cars, doors slightly open to let fresh air in. Finally, the Confederate guards ordered them out of the cars and to get into formation for the march to their quarters, an immense barn on the outskirts of town. When that was deemed full, those not inside the huge structure were given tents. Tom Armstrong and Caleb Edwards were in the barn and climbed to the loft.

Rumors about imminent parole and exchange abounded through the new prison camp. Most of the men didn't believe it since they had been misled repeatedly throughout their incarceration. Some were so fed up, that, just after sundown, they took off for points north where they thought Grant or Meade might be. Tom Armstrong and Caleb Edwards had settled that question for themselves on the train. They were quite confident that they would be exchanged for Confederate soldiers of the same rank shortly; that was, if the Johnnies didn't form several firing squads to execute them. At supper time, the guards brought bacon, cornbread, dried peaches, and coffee. It was just what the Yankee prisoners needed.

Two days later, on February 17, 1865, all the conversation from the guards concerned the fall of Columbia and that Charleston was being evacuated. Then, the very next day, word came down that the Union force attacked the Rebels who were still at Camp Sorghum. The Yankees were coming to Columbia. There was virtually no resistance.

On the morning of the 18th, the word was that the Confederates now had no choice but to effect the exchange of the prisoners. Cheers erupted when it was learned that Charleston, South Carolina, had surrendered. Hearing that the Commandant there in Charlotte called the senior Union officers together and announced that the exchange would occur immediately, some that evening, some in the morning. That would all depend on the availability of trains to take the Yankees north, farther into North Carolina. He said that he had telegraphed Richmond, telling the high command there that he could not continue to hold the prisoners, and it was now time to exchange them. In response, he had received a wire from Major General Bushrod Johnson that yes, all was lost, and that the prisoners were to be exchanged.

Making the acquaintance of Colonel Thomas E. Rose and helping him dig the tunnels at Libby, Macon, and more recently at Columbia, had definite advantages. Caleb Edwards and Tom Armstrong had impressed the Colonel with their industriousness which he repaid by keeping them close to him whenever he could. This time was no different.

"Armstrong, Edwards, you come with me later today. Ely is coming with us. So's Nelson. They say we're goin' to a place north of here called Greensboro. Not sure why. Not sure what's there. But they're talking parole. Not sure they can handle all of us. That's why we're going today. Ain't gonna wait around. Sooner we get out of here, the better."

"Thank you, Thomas," said Tom Armstrong. "Tired of bein' held captive. It's time to go home."

"Yeah, Tom, you jus' wanna get out to Illinois for that girl" said Caleb Edwards. "Pretty simple if you ask me. Whattya need from us, Thomas?"

Colonel Thomas E. Rose looked at Tom Armstrong with a curious smile on his face. "A girl, Armstrong? You wanna tell me about it?"

"Not especially, Colonel, but I will tell you that she's the sister of the Aide-de-Camp to General Logan. My best friend before the war. She told me he's alive, and he's ridin' with Sherman, under Blair. Known him and her all my life. Gonna ask her to marry me."

"Now, ain't that wonderful. Edwards, you're married. Think Armstrong can handle a woman?"

"Shit, Colonel, after what we been through, he can handle anything. Kept me from gettin' killed a couple times. Dug like hell for you. Knows how to make people feel good. Probly gonna have a raft of children, right Tom?"

Tom Armstrong shot Caleb Edwards a nasty look, then smiled. Edwards was smiling at him. "None of your damn business, Caleb."

Colonel Thomas E. Rose chuckled at the two friends' banter. "Armstrong," he said, "things will take care of themselves. I just want you to get home."

"So, do I, Thomas, so do I. When do we leave?"

"About 5 o'clock. Get everything you own. We're getting' outta here."

Thomas Sumption Armstrong just thought about the Colonel's words. "Freedom…at last."

On February 19, at just about 5 o'clock in the afternoon, just as the sun was going down, Tom Armstrong and Caleb Edwards, with 200 more, boarded a passenger train going northeast to a place called Greensboro, there in North Carolina. It was only 100 miles away, and the train lumbered on through the night. Rumor had it that Sherman had torched Columbia and was rapidly moving north into North Carolina, taking Wilmington, in the southeast corner of the state on the Cape Fear River.

It was chilly in north central North Carolina, but that didn't dampen the spirits of the 200 men who hopped off the train, just after dawn, and set up a camp of sorts right near the railroad depot in Greensboro.

"Don't think we're where we're supposed to be, Caleb," said Tom Armstrong, looking around and not seeing anyone who looked official and who could parole them. "We gotta be going someplace else."

A Confederate officer approached, with four armed men, behind him. "Y'all are going to Wilmington, and you will be paroled there. After parole, you will need to be exchanged for one of us of the same rank. Don't know where that will take place.

"Somebody, someplace, thought we could parole you here, but we ain't got the authority. Ain't got the men to do it. Ain't got no paperwork neither. So, we're sendin' you down south to Wilming-ton. They'll be ready for you."

"How do we get there?" asked Thomas Rose. "Damn Rebels. Damn disorganized," he thought.

"Freight trains comin' through here in next few days. Gonna take y'all to Raleigh, then down through Goldsboro, and finally to Wilmington. Gonna feed you best we can, give you a place to rest 'til the trains start comin' through."

Just then they heard the whistle of a locomotive, coming in from the south. It slowed to switch tracks to the east, and, without stop-ping, continued on its way. Another freight train was on the siding at the depot.

"Y'all can get inside those cars," the Confederate officer said. "Only place we got shelter for you. Looks to me like it's gonna rain. My men will bring you rations 'fore it does." So, Armstrong, Ed-wards, and Rose climbed into an old cattle car. It was cover from the rain that had just started to fall, but it was damn cold in there. Winter does come to North Carolina. Thankfully, there was no snow. The only thing to do after the rations of cornbread, dried peaches, potatoes, and water were consumed was to sleep until they left for Raleigh.

When the sun was coming up on Tuesday, February 21, 1865, they heard the whistle of the steam engine, signaling that it was time to go. It was only about 75 miles to Raleigh and took just over six hours for the train to get there. The depot was jumping with Union soldiers, tired, dirty, and ragged, but joyous nevertheless. Enlisted men and officers, it didn't make any difference any more. They were all Americans who had endured a civil war and the torturous condi-tions of Confederate prisons. Rose, Armstrong, and Edwards climbed down from the cattle car, ran down the platform, and jumped up on the train for points east.

When they arrived at Raleigh, they climbed down from the car into the midst of Union soldiers, some sitting down, some milling around. "Whattya all doin' here?" asked Caleb Edwards.

"They wasn't ready for us in Wilmington. Lotsa folk down there. Too many, I gather," came the response from the first Union officer they saw. "Sent us back here to wait."

"Got any news 'bout Sherman?"

"Yeah. Fort Fisher fell to General Terry and Admiral Porter, a month ago. So, Johnny couldn't come up the river any more. Meant last rebel port was closed up tight. No Southern ships in or out. Kills their trade. Made Wilmington the next target. Schofield came up the river on Porter's fleet to clean house along the way at Sugar Loaf, Fort Anderson, and Town Creek. Now, he's movin' on Wilmington itself. That's why they weren't ready for us. Probly won't be until it is secure."

On Wednesday, February 22, 1865, the Confederates began to parole the Union soldiers. It was havoc, everyone trying to be the first in line, pushing and shoving, with punches being thrown. Maybe bedlam is a better way to describe it. It was almost a riot, but soon, some officers took charge of the melee and brought the men back into some semblance of order. They were told that they would be paroled in order of the length of time they had been in prison. Now, everyone understood that the men might not be truthful about it, but the Confederates had kept a record of where the prisoners had come from and when they were imprisoned.

Nevertheless, it was still mass confusion when someone, and nobody knows who, decided that some of the men could go to Goldsboro, some 50 miles southeast of Raleigh to be paroled there. Half the men would take the cars in a couple of days. That would certainly ease the situation. So, on February 25, some of the prisoners were loaded onto wagons and taken out to a vast open area in Raleigh that had once been Camp Crabtree, the home of thousands of Confederate soldiers for training prior to deployment to the war. Housing was still there, a creek ran through it, there was a mess hall, and, of course, the walls were high enough that no one would be able to climb them. The cold rain kept everyone inside with the ground turning to mud, but no one seemed to care. There were some delays, but most of the Yankees believed that they were to be paroled and then exchanged, Tom Armstrong and Caleb Edwards among them, Armstrong more convinced than Edwards.

Three days later, on February 28, 1865, in the pouring rain, and after another train ride, the Yankees were marched, under guard, into the center of Goldsboro and were told to form a line, by twos, in front of what appeared to be the City Hall. Tom Armstrong and Caleb Edwards dutifully lined up, and when they entered the building, the officer at the door handed each of them a piece of paper.

> I, the undersigned, _____
> Prisoner of War, Captured near_____, by
> _____
> Command, hereby give my Parole of Honor, not to bear arms against the Confederate States, or to perform any military or garrison duty whatever, until regularly exchanged; and further, that I will not divulge anything relative to the position or condition of any of the forces of the Confederate States.
>
> This _____ day_____, 1865.
> _____
>
> Witness, _____

"Fill it out and give it to the Major when your turn comes," was the order.

"Who captured us, Tom? I forget who it was," said Caleb Edwards.

"General Johnson, I think. Called him 'Allegheny.'" It was now their turn, and they handed the Confederate officer who was seated behind a table, the forms they had filled out.

"What now, sir?" Tom Armstrong asked.

"Fall in with the others. You will go to the depot. Train will take you to Wilmington where the exchange will take place."

"Thank you, sir," Armstrong said, and with that, he and Caleb Edwards walked out the back door of the City Hall into an open area where there must have been two hundred men just like themselves, dirty and ragged, a bit skeptical about what the Rebels were really going to do, but guardedly happy that freedom might just be around the corner.

It was mid-afternoon when the doors to the cars opened, and the guards told them to get in. Tom Armstrong was wondering if the Confederates had told them the truth that, in fact, they were going to Wilmington. He sat there, with the others, for quite some time, wondering about that and deciding that, if it was not the truth, he had been through a lot worse. Firing squad not too appealing. That would be the worst. But, what the Rebels had said was true. The train started slowly down the track just about sundown and, after three or four hours, it stopped again. The doors were opened so the men could use the latrine and grab some rations which they did, but, in the process, they learned that this outpost was the last one the Confederates held on the way to Wilmington. Their spirits rising, they had to wait until morning for the train to get up steam again.

Early on March 1, 1865, it started south once again, but soon stopped, 10 miles short of Wilmington at North East Bridge. The doors were opened, and the men could not believe their eyes, for there were Union officers, in their blue uniforms milling around outside the train. A cheer erupted inside the cars. Told to get down, the men did and had to walk single file through a gauntlet of Confederate guards, stopping at the end of the line in front of a Confederate officer and one from the Union. Each man was accounted for by both officers who agreed that each prisoner was now free. Then, each one was told to walk toward a rather large building about 100 yards away. They passed through another line of Rebel soldiers toward the building. When they passed the last one, it dawned on them that they were, indeed, FREE, for the first time in months, or even years. No Rebel guards, only Union soldiers, excitedly asking them about their experience, their regiments, and their homes. It took a while for their freedom to sink in. When it finally did, there were cheers and shouts of joy, men hugging each other, and some crying, never thinking this day would come.

In groups of twenty-five, Union officers led the newly-freed Yankees toward the Federal picket line which, when they arrived, snapped to attention and saluted them. Most of the men were just too damn tired to return the salutes, happy as they were. They had been paroled from prison and now had noncombat status, waiting to be exchanged. In the distance was a hill that they would have to climb, but it was such a welcome sight that nobody thought much about it. You see, at the top of the hill they could see Union soldiers waiting for them, one of whom was waving the Stars and Stripes.

As they neared the top, a brass band commenced playing *Yankee Doodle* quite loudly and with great spirit. Soldiers were lined up on both sides of the road, applauding the former prisoners and waving their regimental battle flags.

The procession moved on. It was glorious. It came to a halt at the headquarters of the commanding officer, the men crowding around to hear his words of welcome. Caleb Edwards wasn't paying too much attention. He smelled coffee, and looking past the commandant, he saw tables piled with food. When the commandant finished speaking, he invited the men to partake of the fixins', and quite a rush ensued.

"Take as long as you want and eat as much as you can," was the order. Caleb Edwards, Tom Armstrong, and the rest of the men dug in like they had never eaten before. Well, it had been quite some time since they had been given piping hot, boiled pork; warm cornbread with butter, fresh corn and turnips, and hot coffee. There was even some cheese.

It was just about 1 o'clock in the afternoon of March 1 when they were done. Armstrong wasn't sure he could walk he had eaten so much, but they were told they had a ten mile march to Wilmington in front of them. When they arrived, an officer at the Registration Desk enrolled Armstrong and Edwards, so the exchange process could begin.

"Lieutenant Armstrong, it must have been a long time in those joints, wasn't it?"

"Yes, sir, it was. How long will I be here?"

"Beats the devil out of me. I gotta find a Rebel lieutenant 'fore you can be exchanged."

"How long's that going to take?"

"No one knows. Best thing you can do is go to Camp Parole up in Maryland. That's the place where Federal troops on parole from prison await their exchange before returning to their regiments. They will work on the exchange and will tell you how to find yours."

"Well, I'll be darned. It's true. I'm free. Going to Maryland. Thank, God." Leaving the Registration Desk, he went outside, found a quiet place, knelt, and prayed a prayer of thanksgiving. "Lord, when all this started back in Zanesville, I put my faith and trust in you which has been rewarded. It is only through your will being done that I am here, and I am free. Charles McCabe was right. Many times while I was in captivity, I promised you, Lord, that I would serve you for the rest of my life if I got out of this thing. I will do it gladly when I get home."

He felt a hand on his shoulder. Looking up, he saw Caleb Edwards grinning at him. "Been exchanged, Sump. Some fella from Alabama. A gunner like me. Even up trade."

Even though it didn't seem quite fair that Caleb was headed home, and he wasn't, Tom Armstrong stood up and looked Caleb Edwards right in the eyes, "Caleb, I don't know what to say. You will be my friend forever. God bless you and keep you. You have seen the elephant, and I hope you never see him again. Good luck getting home. I will write you about that question I have to ask Frank. Maybe we'll come to Wheeling someday."

"That would be good, Thomas. You're the best friend any man could ask for. I will never forget you and what we have been through. Elephant was damn bigger than I thought he would be. Thank you. You got me through it." The big West Virginian threw his arms around Armstrong, giving him a bear hug. Releasing his friend, he looked at him and said, "So long, Sump. See ya sometime." With that, he turned, wiping his eyes with his handkerchief, and ran back into the registration tent to arrange immediate train travel to Wheeling. Caleb Edwards was going home, never to return to the horrors of war. Suddenly, Lieutenant Thomas S. Armstrong felt alone. Very alone. But, at least he knew he wasn't going back to prison. That did give him hope.

The next morning, March 2, 1865, the paroled Union officers received a great surprise. After breakfast, they were told to go out into the parade ground of the camp where they saw clothes: blue uniforms. Weren't quite new, but it was better than they had had for quite some time. Almost in unison, they tore off the rags they had been wearing and rummaged through the pile for trousers, shirts, drawers, socks, jackets, kepis, and shoes. They hardly recognized each other when they put the new stuff on, laughing as they looked at each other.

At 10 o'clock, orders came down for half of them, including Tom Armstrong, to report to the docks where a steamship, the *General Sedgwick*, would take the parolees up the coast of the Atlantic Ocean to Annapolis, Maryland, where Camp Parole was, a distance of some 400 miles. Now, most of the soldiers had never been on a ship in the ocean before, so the trip was eye-opening to say the least. They were glad they had buckets in the hold and on deck since seasickness reached epidemic proportions with the ship's constant rolling. It was the worst passing through Cape Hatteras; the seas were heavy; a "strong breeze" coming hard out of the northeast, causing waves to crash against the hull of the ship and cold spray to come over the gunwales. Tom Armstrong just sat down there in the hold, praying to God that he would stop puking and that the rolling ship would not sink and take him with it. He had been through too much to have his life end that way. "Never thought about drowning," he thought to himself in the middle of his prayer.

Two days later, he heard cannon booming from the ships in Chesapeake Bay. The Stars and Stripes fluttered proudly from their masts. When a tugboat approached the *General Sedgwick*, an officer, so it seemed, came on board with news. You see, the day before, Abraham Lincoln had been inaugurated for a second term as President of the United States. The officer said that the success of William Tecumseh Sherman in taking Atlanta, and then Savannah, had turned the tide of public sentiment in Lincoln's favor in the election. Now, the President, with the help of Ulysses S. Grant and William Tecumseh Sherman, would get to finish the American Civil War. The news spread like wildfire through the ship, the men cheering in celebration.

The next day, Monday, March 6, Armstrong had climbed out of the hold and was standing by the rail on the foredeck when he heard, "Land, Ho." Looking up, he saw the outlines of a fortress there on the western shore. "Where are we?" he asked no one in particular.

"The Chesapeake Bay, mate," one of the sailors said. "That's Fortress Monroe. Going north for a coupla more days. Annapolis by Wednesday, the Cap'n says."

An hour later, the *General Sedgwick* was anchored in the Chesapeake Bay, just east of the Fortress, rocking gently back and forth.

413

Provisions of bread, ham, and cheese were brought on board with kegs of fresh water for the men to consume. About 5 PM, Tom Armstrong heard the rumble of the engines and then the call "Weigh Anchor." It was a pleasant day, there in southern Virginia, with warming temperatures, very little wind, and what-looked-to-be calm seas. The next thing he knew, the *Sedgwick* was chugging north, not very fast, maybe at eight knots or so, but nobody seemed to care. He could see sailboats, dotting the bay and going about their business but mostly heading into port at Fortress Monroe before it got dark. "Hope I never see that place again," he thought to himself.

The *Sedgwick* plugged away as night time fell on the calm waters with the moon shining brightly in the sky. For once in a great while, Thomas S. Armstrong felt content. Sure, he missed the companionship of Caleb Edwards and hoped he would see him again someday, but there was a calming effect of the steamer gently rolling north to Annapolis and freedom. The big ship entered the port of Annapolis late in the afternoon the next day and, after the sailors had it moored to the pier, the soldiers walked down the gangplank to the cheers of others who had arrived earlier in the day.

As he was trying to figure out what to do, good fortune smiled on him as he recognized another officer of the 122nd Ohio Volunteers, Lieutenant Judson Paul, whom he had known somewhat back in Zanesville. Father was a meat-packer and mother was a seamstress. Had three or four brothers and sisters. "Armstrong," he hollered, "That you? Good to see you again." Judson Paul had escaped the battlefield at Winchester on June 15, 1863, had been captured on the way to Harper's Ferry, and then was sent to prison in Danville, Virginia. He had languished there for several months before being sent to other prisons in Georgia and South Carolina. The two men found a bench there on the wharf and were exchanging stories when Judson Paul said, "You look pretty good in that uniform, Tom, but we got something better." He pointed down the street, they were off.

After a few minutes in the store, Armstrong asked, "You mean he's going to let me have a brand new uniform on credit?"

"Yep, that's the first surprise. I got another one fer ya. Paymaster wants to see you tomorrow morning. Ain't gonna give you all yer owed, but he's gonna give you something you ain't seen in awhile. Then, you come back and pay the man."

"I'll be darned. Isn't that just the finest thing?" said Tom Armstrong. And, then, "where's this Camp Parole?"

"I'll take you Tom and get you registered. Then, we'll have supper in the Mess Hall."

Wearing their new uniforms, shoulder boards and all, the two men walked back up the street, turned left, and walked some more, until Tom Armstrong saw something he hadn't seen since the summer of '62. There was Camp Parole with Federal soldiers walking about freely just like at Camp Zanesville. No wall. No guards. Just three or four rows of fifteen buildings to house the men, a wide main street, another set of buildings or two across the street, more open space, and what looked to be the camp headquarters with a huge United States flag flying overhead. And, there were more buildings to the north. It was one damn big place.

"We go over there," said Judson Paul. "Over to the Colonel's headquarters to get you signed in."

Saluting the major behind the desk, he said, "Armstrong, Thomas S., Lieutenant, 122nd Ohio. Captured June 15, 1863 at Winchester, sir."

"Welcome, Lieutenant," said the major, scanning the roll for Tom's name and scratching it off when he found it. "You may go with Lieutenant Paul, here. He will show you around. I trust you will find everything you need. If not, just ask."

Saluting once again, Armstrong replied, "Yes, sir, thank you, sir," turned on his heel like he had been trained, and walked out the front door. He did not think that freedom could feel any better.

Lieutenant Judson Paul led him to his bunkhouse where he found bedding, his bunk, and a place to hang his clothes. "Jud," he said, "later today after we get things done, I want to write a couple of letters. We have a place to do that?"

"Right over here, Tom. Paper and ink all set. Take as much time as you want."

Annapolis Md
March 8th 1865

415

My Dear Frank

I am in "God's Country" again. I was paroled for exchange at North East Bridge near Wilmington, N.C. I am pretty well only a cold caught on board the ship off Cape Hatteras on the way hither. I hope to see you before long. I suppose I shall get a leave of absence before 2 weeks have elapsed. I shall know more in the future. I hope you still remember me as of the former times when you told me I had won your heart. Then my dear you was 22 & blooming as a rose. But now you have grown older as I have also. But shall that separate whom God has joined together. Frank I've always been true to you. You have my affections which I have sometimes thought you doubted. Tho I always knew you loved me, that is I mean when your mother used to laugh at you and tell you I was jilting you.

You remember there was a long time when I did not come to see you. Don't you? Well. that's the time, I mean, that I believe you thought I at least was treating you ill. Is that not so? Tell me now, do you love me or not for if there is any misunderstanding between us and we should get married, we, at least, would be guilty of perjury & sin against our God.

Have you kept in good health? Are you ready to marry? If so, please tell me in your letter to me. Write to me at Zanesville for I presume I will not be here when your letter comes here. I am ready to marry as soon as I see you & arrange my military affairs. I ask you if you are ready, that is, have you an outfit. If you need money, send me word in your next.

Frank, burn this immediately will you not? It would look so simple to anyone else, but to me it is my true sentiments to you. I love you as well as one man can love the woman of his choice among others.
Fare well
From your lover & well wisher

416

Obviously, Francis Porter didn't burn the letter. She treasured it, but there it was. The proposal. "Are you ready to marry?" Tom Armstrong had thought about writing that line for quite a while, and since he had not heard from Francis Porter in a long, long time, just about seven months, wondered how she would respond. "Maybe she thinks I'm dead. Or, maybe she found some nice young farmer at church. Thoughts of dread clouded his mind. Maybe she will say 'No.'"

In the days that followed, Jud Paul introduced Tom Armstrong to the other men in their bunkhouse who were waiting to be exchanged. They spent time swapping stories about their experiences during the war, none more harrowing than the one he told about Libby Prison. Paul looked a little embarrassed when Armstrong told them about Company I being left behind at Winchester while the others escaped to Harper's Ferry, but he qualified that by saying that "Orders are orders."

During those conversations, he learned that he would have to apply for a Leave of Absence which he did the next day, March 9, 1865. Jud Paul had told him it would take some time to wind its way through the army's red tape. Finally, he was called to headquarters where he was told that he could leave for ten days the following Tuesday, March 14. In the meantime, there were games to be played and books to be enjoyed, but Tom Armstrong could not wait to get on that train for home.

Annapolis, MD
March 10, 1865

Dear Brother Jacob

I am in "God's Country" again. I was paroled for change at North East Bridge near Wilmington, N.C. I am pretty well only a cold caught on board the ship off Cape Hatteras on the way hither. I applied for a Leave of Absence from this place which was granted, and I shall be leaving here on Tuesday, the 14th inst. I have been told I will arrive in Columbus on the night of the

15th, so can you come get me at Zanesville on the morning of the 16th. Ohio and West Virginia Railroad.

I will tell you all about my time in the south and please tell mother and father their prayers have been answered for I am coming home. I can't stay long as I have to be back by the 22nd inst.

My love to all.

Your loving bro, T.S.

Jacob Armstrong's hands were shaking when he saw the letter dated March 10, 1865 from Annapolis, Maryland. It was Thomas's handwriting all right. "Damn! He's alive," he thought to himself. Gingerly opening the envelope, he read the letter. He read it again. "He is alive. I'll be damned. I gotta get home, fast. Hadn't heard from him in a year or so." Making sure the supplies were secure in the wagon, he started waving his hat excitedly and yelled at Maude and Sampson, "Be gone, Maude. Be gone, Sampson. I have news!" With that, Jacob Armstrong started westward toward the Armstrong farm in Gratiot. He would be there before supper.

Four hundred miles to the west, her hands were trembling when John Porter, Jr. gave her the envelope. "It's from Thomas, Johnny. He is alive! Oh, God, my Thomas is alive!" John Porter steadied his sister whose knees had suddenly weakened, helping her to a chair by the big dining table. "Praise the Lord, he is alive," and she started to weep tears of joy.

Reading the letter, her heart jumped at the question of being ready to marry. "It is finally coming true. He did not think it fair of him to marry before he went off to war, and I could not do anything but agree with him," she thought to herself. "Now, it will happen. I must tell Mother. She will, of course, tell Father, but I am sure Thomas will want to talk to him himself." More tears were streaming down her face. She did not know what she had done to deserve this joyous news, first, that he was alive, and second, he wanted to marry her. "The Lord be praised," she whispered softly. She took paper and pen out of the drawer in the desk and began to write to him as he had wanted, to Zanesville. "He is coming home. I do hope he comes here."

Back in Gratiot, Ohio, Jane Armstrong also burst into tears while she read the letter that Tom had sent to Jacob. He hadn't said much except that he was coming home and would be there in a few days. She didn't care how long he stayed. He was alive. She ran to the front porch and rang the big bell that would ordinarily mean that it was time for dinner. But, it wasn't. She just wanted the family to come together to give thanks to God that Thomas was alive. Jacob was to go to Zanesville on Tuesday to get him.

William Armstrong came galloping in from the field in the southwest corner of the property, there in Hopewell Township, just across the county line into Muskingum County. When he reined in Cricket, his second son's new horse, he could see that his wife had been crying, but, now, she was wildly excited. "Children, Thomas is alive! He is coming home. Father, Jacob just received this letter. He is alive. He doesn't say how he is, but he will be here on the noon train on Thursday." Her husband sank to his knees, the others followed, and William Armstrong led his family in *The Lord's Prayer*, the 23rd Psalm, and John 3:16. He then made his own supplication of thanks to God for the blessing they had all just received, noted by one small piece of paper that his wife was clutching tightly to her breast.

In the meantime, Captain Judson Paul had taken Tom Armstrong to see the Paymaster who had given him two month's wages. Armstrong looked at the money, counted it, thought for a moment, and just said, "Thank you, sir." He hadn't had any money of his own in a long, long time, especially over two hundred dollars.

From there, it was down to the haberdashery to pay the man for his new uniform, and then it was to see the Quartermaster to get the supplies he would need for the journey home, namely a new haversack with "U.S." embossed on it, canteen, and gun belt with a brand new Colt. He would stuff as much food as he could into the haversack.

With the paper authorizing his ten days' Leave of Absence tucked inside his jacket, around 1 o'clock on the afternoon of March 14, 1865, Tom Armstrong set off for the Annapolis railroad depot, looking to catch the 4:00 train of the Pennsylvania Railroad Company north. He bought a "through" ticket to Zanesville which would be a long, but relatively easy, journey.

There were other soldiers on leave going home so striking up a conversation was easy. All of them had stories to tell. Arriving at Harrisburg, Pennsylvania around midnight, a group of Ohio boys, including Armstrong, ran down the platform for a different train. The conductor had told them it would be on track #6. They hopped on the train for Columbus, Ohio, found seats, and it was then that Tom Armstrong ate some cornbread, drank some water, and decided it was time for some shuteye.

The next evening, the train pulled into the depot in Columbus and Armstrong knew that his brother, Jacob, would be meeting him in Zanesville the next morning. He was really hungry, so he took out some cornbread and dried pork and ate right there in the station, washing it down with water from his canteen. The bench didn't look too comfortable for sleeping purposes, but he had not slept well on the ride from Harrisburg with the climbs, curves, and whistles blowing in the tunnels, through Pittsburgh and, changing trains, on to Ohio on the Ohio & West Virginia Railroad. So, using the haversack for a pillow, he stretched out and tried to sleep. He woke at daybreak, startled by the whistle of a train preparing to depart for points east, and went outside where he found a pump that would provide the water for him to wash up. As the Central Ohio was leaving, he jumped up onto the platform between two of the cars, found a seat in one of them and handed his ticket to the conductor.

Two hours later on the morning of March 16, 1865, the train pulled into the depot in Zanesville, Ohio, there on Linden Avenue. As the locomotive came to a stop, steam spewing from the pistons, he saw his brother, sitting on the seat in the buckboard. The past two and a half years seemed to melt away. The two brothers shared a long embrace. Jacob Armstrong threw the haversack into the back of the buckboard, and gently poking

Sampson with the whip, they started west, down the National Road, for Gratiot.

"Thomas, I don't know where to begin. So much has happened here, but I imagine more happened to you."

"Yeah, it was a bad experience, but I am here, thankfully. God brought me through it. I will tell all of you about it when we get home."

"I do have something to tell you, T.S. We are no longer living with Mother and Father."

"What?"

"Yes, Matilda O'Leary and I got married a year or so ago, and we bought the spread just south of theirs. We see them all the time, and she will be there when we get home. When you meet her, call her Mattie."

"Who's Mattie? You're married? Shoot, Jacob, where'd that come from?"

"Met her at church, in Gratiot. Teaches at the school. Folks been in Ohio for quite a while. Came here from Mahoning County up north, just after you left. Family's from someplace in Ireland, County Donegal, I'm told. Up in the northern part. Grow potatoes here like they did there. Raise sheep, too, just like us. Loved her the minute I saw her. Whatta 'bout you?"

"Not sure. Sent Frank a letter asking her about that. Haven't heard. She did say in an earlier one that George and Grace are engaged. Getting married this summer out there in Clinton. I gotta get out there, but it won't be for a while. Gotta get back to the camp in a week."

"Papers say Sherman is coming up the coast. Took Fayetteville. Sheridan's coming south through the Shenandoah. Siege still on at Petersburg."

"It's over, Jacob. Believe me, I saw it. Lee's got no place to go. He's trapped. No food, no ammo, men desertin.' It's over. That's why I am here. A free man."

It didn't take long to travel the 12 miles or so to Gratiot. Halfway through town, Jacob Armstrong urged Sampson to go left off the National Road onto Center Street, crossing South

Street and continuing about three miles until they came to a road going off to the west.

"This is it, Tom. My place is just south of here. Father's fields and mine run together down there. We'll go see it while you're here."

The house looked much like the one in Norwich with the big front porch where the entire family was sitting. Frank and Gus, now 14 and 10, ran to greet him with the dogs. Frank had grown to at least 5 ½ feet with Gus not far behind. The collies, Duke and Holly, raced down the path. They hadn't seen him since the summer of '62, but they knew. The master was home. The four Armstrong boys and their dogs walked up toward the house, Mary, Fla, William and Jane standing there to meet them. His sister, Matilda, her husband, Abram Hull, and their children from just over the rise in Claylick, were also there. William Armstrong had his arm around his wife in case she might faint at the sight of her second son.

When Tom Armstrong walked onto the large porch, he shook hands with his brother-in-law, and kissed his sisters on the cheek and told them how glad he was to see them. Matilda seemed to have aged, but, yes, she was, indeed, the oldest. Mary was 26 now, a good 5 ½ feet tall just like her younger brother, her raven hair pulled into a bun, and the ever- present apron tied about her waist. She looked just about the same as when he left. But, it was Fla who was the surprise. Flavilla Armstrong had blossomed into a beautiful young woman at the age of 21, not as tall as either of her sisters and slimmer, too. Her dark brown hair hung down to her shoulders. Tears were running down her face as she saw her brother for the first time in three years. She was sure he had been killed or had died in prison and was over-whelmed with joy as he dropped the haversack on the porch floor, unstrapped the gun belt from his waist, hung it on the back of a chair, and turned to see his mother. He would never wear the Colt again.

"Mother, it is very good to see you. I thought of you often," he said as he leaned over and kissed his mother on the right cheek. "You don't know how glad I am to be home."

"Thomas, I never thought I would see you again. The Lord has been good to me. He has brought you home. My prayers have been answered. Praise God! Are you well?"

"Yes, Mother, reasonably well. Need to put on a little weight though. Had a hard time of it ever since I got captured and went to prison. I will tell you all about it in the next few days since I don't have to go back until next Tuesday." He said that he would tell them, but that there were parts that he would, or could, not.

"Yeah, Tom," said Frank excitedly, "I wanna hear about all the shootin' and killin' and chasin' Rebs."

"Me, too," cried Gus.

"We'll have time for that, boys," said William Armstrong. "It is very good that you are here, safely, son," shaking hands, then hugging Tom. "I have prayed for you every day."

"Thank you, father. I am sure that God listened to all of you, and maybe me, to deliver me from the troubles I have been through. Charles McCabe was right. Put my faith and trust in God, and here I am. Jacob, how's Aspen? I want to go see Charlie and Beccie in Zanesville."

"Tom, that can wait. Before I get to that, I want you to meet Mattie, and this is Thomas. We named him that in case you didn't come home." Tom Armstrong said hello to the young woman standing before him, cradling a baby in her arms. "A baby," he thought to himself, quite surprised. "Jacob? Thought he was too busy helping father with the sheep."

"It's nice to meet you, Mattie. Jacob has told me a little about you. Hello, Thomas," he said looking at the child. Mattie Armstrong just looked at him in his uniform. She'd never seen a real soldier before and wasn't sure what to think, even though Jacob had told her what to expect.

"My pleasure, Thomas," she said, smiling and feeling more comfortable. "The baby thinks so, too."

All Tom Armstrong could do was return the smile. "She's very pretty," he thought to himself. "How'd Jacob deserve that?"

Mattie Armstrong was a little smaller than Fla, with flowing reddish blonde hair. "I hear you are a teacher. So was I. We will get to know each other much better, Mattie, in the coming days and weeks. Now, Jacob, tell me about Aspen."

"Well, I just have to tell you that Father and I had to put her down a year or so ago. Buried her up in your favorite field. She got bit in the leg by somethin', skunk, racoon, somethin' and got confused, agitated, and was bouncin' off the walls of her stall. Runnin' a high fever, burning up. Doc Russell said it was rabies. No cure, so it was best to put her down."

With the emotion of being home and now hearing this, Tom Armstrong started to weep. "Poor, poor, Aspen. I hope she didn't suffer long," he said, wiping his face with his handkerchief.

"No, Thomas," said his father, "it was quite quick. We bought another mare for you, in case you came home. She's a buttermilk Morgan, about 15 hands. Named her Cricket. Tomorrow, we can ride over to Jacob's if you like."

"That would be fine, Father." Looking at Matilda, Mary, and Fla, with a regained composure, Tom Armstrong smiled and said, "When's dinner?"

"Thought we shouldn't interrupt," said Matilda Hull, the oldest of the Armstrong sisters. "Give us a few minutes." And, the three women ducked into the house.

It was warm, that March 16, there in central Ohio, maybe about 60 degrees. Nice for March. Still some traces of snow piles from the winter, but not much. Matilda Hull called the others inside for a traditional "farmer's dinner," with fried chicken; redskin potatoes; warm beans and corn in a succotash; plenty of bread; cold milk; hot coffee; and, of course, apple pie, served with a slice of cheddar cheese. Tom Armstrong began to tell them the story of the last thirty months.

"I think I told you that Colonel Ball and Major Granger relied on me to help them get the regiment organized since I had seen the elephant with the 78th. Well, I had a lot of help. Father, do you remember when you told me to see if Patrick Murphy would serve as sergeant?" William Armstrong nodded through the smoke from his cigar. "Well, Patrick did everything I could've asked and more, 'specially after Eddie Bristow got killed."

"Eddie's dead?" asked Jacob Armstrong.

"'Fraid so, died in a skirmish at Winchester. "I'll get to that fiasco in a bit. So, we trained at Camp Zanesville. Tom Black and me as lieutenants reportin' to Dan Gary, part of Company I. "Bout a thousand of us in the 122nd, but Bill Ball wanted me to help the other company commanders with drill. Had to rely on Tom and Dan to help with that. Oh, Dan got shot at Winchester, too. Mighta lost a leg."

"You know his wife, Mary, was killed when the roof of the market collapsed some time ago while you were gone," said William Armstrong.

"Yeah, heard that. He came back to Zanesville for the funeral. Was never the same."

"Imagine so."

Tom Armstrong continued, "At camp, I had great help from Chesley Simpson and Thaddeus Brennan as well as Murphy and Bristow. Taught them how to shoot the Enfield, so they could train their men. Simpson and Brennan reported to Tom Black. Bristow and Murphy were mine. Couldn't have served the Colonel and the Major without them. Fought right beside Murphy at Winchester after Eddie was killed. Became a good friend. Would trust him with my life. No idea where he is now. Or, Simpson. Or, Brennan.

"If you remember, we left in late October '62 and took a roundabout way to get to Winchester, Virginia, at the head of the Shenandoah Valley. Awful pretty country up there in the mountains and knew that we would spend the winter there. We got there around New Year's, '63, thinking we were just going to guard the B&O Railroad and set up camp overlooking the town when some good fortune befell us. Seems a young man we called "Hitch," from up near New Philadelphia, wanted to scout for us so we said, 'Why not?' He comes back one day sometime later and says a mess of Rebs were coming north.

Rode with a big trapper named Lindsay who lived in the mountains and who could watch Rebel movements and never be seen. Well, Hitch and Lindsay report that there's thousands of 'em comin' north, so I tell Gary, Granger, and Ball. There was only about eight thousand of us, and if thousands of Johnnies were coming, I didn't like our prospects. Bill tells General Elliott who goes to tell General Milroy who dismisses the information and said that we were wrong and that we were staying.

"Orders are orders, so we dug in and prepared for what we knew could be the worst. So, one day, to kill some time, I was wandering around the artillery units, you know, the big cannon, just to see what kind of protection we had. Those things can shoot over a mile away. So, I meet this big lieutenant from West Virginia, Caleb Edwards, whose men would be called on to fire the guns, and we strike up a conversation. From Wheeling. More about him later. You following this?" he asked.

"If you don't mind, Thomas, let's let the girls clean up the table, and I would like to rest," said Jane Armstrong. Can we talk more after supper?"

"Certainly, Mother. Enjoy your rest. Jacob, can we go meet that new horse? Cricket, I think you called her."

"Sure. Be good to catch up with you in a little more detail. Want to come along, Father?"

"No," said William Armstrong, "you boys go ahead."

"Can we come?" asked Gus, fervently hoping to ride with his older brothers.

"Not this time, Gus," replied Jacob Armstrong. "You and Frank can come with us tomorrow when we go down to see Mattie and the baby."

Gus Armstrong was disappointed. So was his brother, Frank, but they knew that what Jacob said was it. Period. They would ride with their brothers in the morning, thinking, "Maybe Tom'll tell us 'bout the shootin' and killin.'"

The Armstrong brothers started walking toward the barn. "Jacob, just where do I sleep? Wash up? By the way, where's my Springfield?"

426

"Sleep up in the loft back of the house, or you can come to my place."

"Naw, better stay close to Mother and Father. Stream running through?"

"Yeah, big one, bigger and better than Norwich. We'll go to it now. Gun's in the house. I'll go back and get it."

Tom Armstrong wandered about the barn, seeing where things were put, when Jacob came in carrying the Springfield. Handing his brother his rifle, he said, "She's over here, T.S." Tom walked over to Cricket's stall and fell in love with the horse right away. Butternut in color, fifteen hands, and looked like she had gotten her exercise.

"Just been keepin' her ready for you," said his older brother, smiling. God, he was glad his brother was home.

Saddled and bridled, with the Springfield snug in its holster, Armstrong planted his left foot in the stirrup and swung up onto the horse. She didn't protest at all, her tail whisking the horseflies away. He walked the big mare out into the corral. You see, he hadn't been on a horse since they left for Winchester, and he was going to take it easy at the start.

It came back quite easily, so when Jacob opened the gate to the corral, Tom guided Cricket out at a trot, but he could feel that she wanted to lope. "Well, girl," he said, "if that's what you want to do, that's what we will do." And they were off, with Jacob right beside, riding due south toward Jacob's farm. They found the stream that ran through the Armstrong farm. Tom marveled at the rippling, sparkling water that ran over the rocks. Hadn't seen anything like that in some time. Stopping to rest, he let the horse drink as much as she wanted.

When they crossed the road on the southern edge of William Armstrong's property, they were now on Jacob's land with its wide open fields and tall trees off in the distance. The stream continued to run southward. The two Armstrong brothers walked their horses south in the warm sunlight, talking about how Jacob had come to own the farm. "Profits from the sheep sale, last coupla years. Father lent it to me. Payin' it back as I can. Show you all of it when you come down tomorrow. We better get back, don't you think?"

"Yeah, I'm tired, so maybe after supper we can play some music and sing a little. I have a few days to tell you the story."

"Good idea, Tom. When're you going to Clinton?"

"Don't know. Will apply for Leave when I get back. Wait'll she hears about you and Mattie, with a baby, no less. Just wish I would hear from her."

"You gotta get straight to Clinton, brother. Women want to be asked in person. Might get on your knees, flowers, too. You gotta talk to John. Gotta ask him. Don't even think about stoppin' your ass here when you get leave. Train straight to Clinton. Got it?"

"Got it. Never thought about it that way. Been in prison too long. Thanks, Jacob."

"Don't mention it." The Armstrong brothers were just getting back when the sun was setting. It was time for supper.

After breakfast the following morning, Tom Armstrong continued the story. Jacob had come back, but he left Mattie and the baby at home. "We knew the Rebels were coming. Hitch and Lindsay said so, and we sent a scout party to check. When we got back, General Elliott went to General Milroy again. He wouldn't listen. When Johnny arrived, fighting broke out, we call it a skirmish, and that's when Eddie got it. Reb ran him through with his bayonet."

"Oh, how awful," said Flavilla Armstrong.

"Yeah, it wasn't pretty. Buried him right there in Winchester. So, we were getting shellacked, so we hunkered down inside one of the forts. Word came down that we were going to try to escape to Harper's Ferry, middle of the night. Now, we're sneakin' out of Winchester, mind you, we been there a coupla months or so, with as much as we could carry. Thought we were going to make it past the Rebs, but that's when their artillery opened up. We were ordered into the fight, but a lot of the other regiments had orders to turn northeast and to hightail it toward Harper's Ferry, leaving us and the 110th alone to fight them. Patrick Murphy right by my side. That's when Dan Gary got shot. Simpson and Brennan took him to the back lines. Never saw them again. Ran out of ammo, and then we saw the white flag. Next thing you know, I have to surrender my sword, we get herded into a corral, and some officer says we're going to Richmond."

"Tom," said his brother, "Mattie would like you to come to the house for dinner. Can we go now, with the little ones, and hear more about what happened later today or tomorrow?" "Sure, Jacob, I'm not sure I can go into much detail about prison life. The tunnel stories might be interesting, but you don't want to hear how they treated us. Not sure I want to talk about it, either."

On the way, the two younger Armstrong brothers decided to race. Tom and Jacob were content to lope along. "Jacob," Tom said, I have been doing a lot of thinking about how I want to spend the rest of my life with Frank. God delivered me home and will take me to Clinton where I pray she will agree to be my wife. If she does, I am thinking about repaying the Lord and becoming a minister in His church. What do you think about that?"

15 Frank... Appomattox... Lincoln

"You wanna do what?" asked Jacob Armstrong, staring incredulously at his younger brother, who was sitting in the saddle atop Cricket. It was a good thing that Gus and Frank had raced ahead to the house since the elder Armstrong was sure he didn't want his younger brothers to hear what was coming next. But, what he heard was not what he expected.

"Jacob, the Lord got me through some horrible situations. I put my faith and trust in Him and was rewarded. Coulda been wounded or killed at Winchester like Eddie; coulda tried to escape on the way to Richmond and got shot by a firing squad or hung; coulda died from dysentery or the fever at Libby; coulda lost my mind at the futility of it all; coulda been shot when we got caught escaping from there; coulda starved to death like my friend, Arty Stroud; coulda been shot at Macon for trying to escape. It was awful, Jacob, just awful. Twenty-one months of it. And, now I'm sittin' here with you on this nice March day at home, goin' to see your wife and son. There had to be a reason, Jacob. Serving God for the rest of my life is the only answer I have for you. Just like when I left. Maybe not rational, but it's what I'm supposed to do."

"Well," responded Jacob Armstrong. "Just who's gonna help father with the farm? I got my own crops and stock to worry about. Who's gonna help him?"

"I don't know. Maybe he can hire a coupla hands. Maybe somebody out here. You know I'm not cut out for that life. You are. I'm a teacher, and now I want to teach in the service of God."

"You talked to Francis about this?"

"Nope. Gonna do that when I get out there, maybe later this month. Gonna give her time to think about it. But, I'm going to go see Charlie McCabe tomorrow to see what he thinks."

The brothers rode on in silence, the hoofbeats of the horses beating a regular rhythm. When they arrived, the big border collies, Digger and J.J. came racing down the wagon path to meet their master. Jacob and Tom dismounted, tousled the heads of the two dogs and started for the house where they found Mattie Armstrong and her nephews sitting on a big swing, baby Thomas asleep in her arms. Jacob drew some water from the well, the boys all washed up, and then pitched in to put dinner on the table. Mattie put Thomas in his cradle, still very much asleep; Jacob said grace; and then it was time to eat. Yes, the typical farmer's mid-day meal. Tom Armstrong thought to himself, "Jacob's got a good one here, already gave him a son, shares his beliefs, cooks darn well, and knows farming. Can't do much better than that, but I will," he mused, smiling at the thought.

"Jacob, can you take me to the train on Tuesday? I have to get back to Annapolis."

"Sure thing, T.S."

They talked about her teaching, but now, with the baby, Mattie couldn't do that anymore unless someone came in to look after him. She wondered if her mother-in-law could do that. Maybe she could drop Thomas off at the house and then go off to teach at the school there in Gratiot. She made a mental note to talk with her husband about it and to have him ask his mother. The afternoon passed quickly with the brothers sitting on the big swing and Jacob telling Tom about what had happened at the two farms during the previous thirty months. Frank and Gus were shooting marbles at the bottom of the porch stairs. But, soon it was time to get back, so Tom bid Jacob and Mattie a good day, told his younger brothers to mount up, climbed aboard Cricket, and started north back to the family farm.

That evening, after supper, he told the family a little about the march to Staunton and the train ride to Richmond, but he found it very difficult to relate the horrors of the battle and what he had done there. He just left it that he had been captured and sent to Libby Prison in Richmond, but he also found it really hard to talk about prison with his family, even about the tunnels and the escapes. He just couldn't do it and wasn't really sure why. Oh, he told them about Caleb Edwards getting whacked upside the head by the Rebel guard, but he didn't know if, by not telling them, he was protecting them, especially his mother, from knowing the terrible things that happened to him there or if he just didn't want to remember. He decided that it was a little of both. He was sure not to tell them about his conversation with Jacob earlier in the day. He had to talk with Charlie McCabe first.

Bright and early the next morning, March 18, 1865, after he had finished breakfast, he saddled Cricket and started down the path for Putnam, hoping, of course, that the Rev. Charles C. McCabe was at the Methodist church. When he got to town, his first stop was to see Gretchen Palmer at her boarding house to tell her that he was home, safe and sound, and to visit a little about the goings-on in Zanesville and Putnam. She was very glad to see him, asked him to sit a spell and have some coffee, with their talk lasting until about 10:30 that March morning.

"Thank you, Mrs. Palmer," he said, "but I must be going. I want to catch up with Reverend McCabe. He's still at the Methodist church, isn't he?"

"Yes, Thomas, he is. He will be quite surprised to see you. He thought you were a casualty at Libby Prison. Prayed for your soul in church."

"Well, then, I might just have a little fun with him. Thank you again. I am sure I will see you around town when I get back for good." With that, he unhitched Cricket from the railing and slowly walked her down Main Street to the Methodist church. Opening the door, he crept silently toward the Reverend's office, and when he got there, he let out an eerie, "McCaaabe, it's meee," followed by a hearty belly laugh that echoed throughout the church.

Now, Charles McCabe had seen the elephant, too, and wasn't frightened of much, but this was a bit unsettling. It came again, "McCaaabe, it's meee." McCabe picked up a broom to use as a weapon, if need be, and cautiously stepped out of the office door, the broom raised high ready to be swung at whatever it was. He gingerly walked around the corner, his fear increasing with each step, and then he saw Tom Armstrong just sitting on the stairs. "Yes, McCaaabe, its meee," followed by a peal of laughter. "Thought I was dead, did you? Would've come back to haunt you, Charlie. That would've been fun."

"Thomas," Charles McCabe stammered, "How? When?...I mean it's good to see you."

"Couple of days ago. It's a long story. I will tell you when I am back for good. I hafta get back to Annapolis on Tuesday, but there's something I hafta talk to you about. Maybe Beccie, too, as this will involve her, as well."

"Come to the house. She will make us dinner. We can talk then. What's going on?"

Sitting around the dining room table at the parsonage, Tom Armstrong told Charles and Rebecca McCabe about his idea of joining the Methodist ministry. Rebecca had gotten out some ham, hard boiled eggs, some carrots and celery, warm bread, and tea for their dinner, a might different than at home. They were sipping their tea, with just the right amount of milk and sugar, after finishing their meal, with Beccie McCabe clearing the table of the dishes. As she did, she listened to the two friends' conversation.

"Thomas," began Charles McCabe, "do you know what this means? Really know? You will have to do things that others won't, like minister to the sick and dying, giving hope to their families; being at your church every day; preaching the gospel every Sunday; and generally being with your congregants all the time. You will be asked to look at life differently, from a moral and spiritual perspective, and will have to take sides in debates, following your interpretation of the Bible."

"Charlie, when I come back this summer, I want to know everything, the good and the bad, the easy and the difficult, what it will mean for Francis to be a preacher's wife, what it will mean for the children, what I have to do to be ordained. All of it."

Rebecca McCabe re-joined them in the sitting room. "Does Francis know anything about this?" You see, she and the Reverend were quite aware of Tom's love for Francis Porter.

"No, Beccie, I haven't talked to her since I last saw her in the summer of '62. I don't even know if she will have me."

"Well, Thomas," Beccie McCabe continued, "if she agrees to be your wife, can you have her come to Zanesville, so I can tell her what to expect? She deserves to know everything that a minister's wife is asked, no, required, to do. I would like to meet her anyway, if she is going to become a part of the Armstrong family."

"I will surely do that, Beccie. I am going to Clinton when I get my next Leave of Absence to ask her. It all depends on what she says."

The conversation lasted well into the afternoon with Tom Armstrong telling the McCabes how and why he came to this decision. It was not the battle, no, it was Libby Prison where he had felt sadness and compassion for the men who were dying alone. Actually, it was the death of Artemus Stroud that convinced him that he should join the ministry. Comforting his friend, Arty, in his last days, Armstrong felt outrage at the way his body had been simply thrown onto the dead pile, left to rot. But, he kept it to himself, not even telling Caleb Edwards. He just wanted to make sure that it was the right thing for him to do, praying every day for God's guidance and that Francis Porter would understand and be glad.

"T.S.," Charles McCabe said, "I have to review for tomorrow's services. Will you please excuse me?"

"Certainly, Charlie, I must be on my way home. Time has just flown by. Thank you for your counsel. I will come back and see both of you after my trip to Clinton." With that, he shook Charles McCabe's hand, kissed Rebecca's cheek gently, turned and headed for the door, and soon was riding down the National Road, west, toward Gratiot.

"How was everything in Putnam?" Flavilla Armstrong asked.

"Oh, just saw Charlie and Beccie McCabe. I just wanted to tell him what happened to me after he was sent home a couple years ago. And, I wanted to hear about the goings on around here. It was a good visit."

"I'm glad. Haven't seen Beccie since we moved here. Maybe we should have them out the next time you get home," said Fla, noticing that her brother was pretty deep in thought.

"What? Oh, yes, Fla, that would be good. I will mention it to him when I see him next."

"How's Francis, brother?" she said, taking a little risk.

"Don't know. Hope to go out there later this month if I can get Leave. Got some things to talk to her about."

"I'm sure you do, I'm sure you do," the young woman said, smiling at her big brother.

The next day was Sunday, March 19, 1865, and it was time for church. The Armstrongs attended services every Sunday at the Gratiot Methodist Church, right there on South Street in Gratiot, just like they had gone to church back in Norwich. It was a small sanctuary, but everything in Gratiot, Ohio was small. Only about forty people lived in the town, most of whom just operated their stores to serve the farmers from the surrounding area. And, just like at Norwich, the parishioners would take turns leading the services, William Armstrong was no exception.

Tom Armstrong had not been in a real church in two and a half years and enjoyed the service and the message from Elder Scott and Elder Williams about the immorality of slavery, even over two years since President Lincoln had issued the Emancipation Proclamation. There were no more than twenty people in the room, but they were certainly engaged in singing the hymns, no organ, mind you, and the prayers and the weekly message. These people of Gratiot were pretty well informed for being such a small town, since they did see the *Daily Courier* every now and again at Wescott's Emporium and knew a little about the war and the freedom of the Negroes. Echoing the sentiment of most Northerners, they held the belief that no man should be the property of any other man. Some, including Tom Armstrong, even knew that President Abraham Lincoln shared that belief.

The day proceeded as Sundays always had back in Norwich, and Tom Armstrong kept recalling that day in what seemed like a long time ago when he had received his father's blessing to re-enlist in the United States Army. What had happened since then had been a horrible experience, but his faith had been strengthened, and now he was home. He still worried, that Sunday, about what Francis Porter might be feeling about him and what she would say about him becoming a minister.

He spent the day on Monday working with his father around the house and barn, wanting to make sure that everything was secure from a money standpoint. The flock of sheep was twice as large as it had been in '62, and sales of them at the Licking County Fair had been brisk. The folks over at Richard Peterson's bank in Newark were agreeable to lending on the basis of the future sale of sheep and the season's crops. Repayment had been made with the proceeds which had always been more than the loan, so it seemed like all was well moneywise. Tom Armstrong just wanted to make sure that his family was all right. He concluded that after a ride out to see the size of the flock of sheep. But, he still had to have that conversation with his father about joining the ministry. He hoped that would be easier than the one they had when he was going to re-enlist.

All of that could wait since he had to get back to Camp Parole. At the crack of dawn on Tuesday, March 21, he said goodbye to the family, climbed up onto the seat of the buckboard where Jacob was waiting, and started the journey back to Annapolis, Maryland where he hoped he would be exchanged in short order. When he arrived the next day, the first order of business was to obtain another Leave of Absence as soon as possible. In the meantime, his second order of business was to get his financial affairs in order since he had not been paid since April 30, 1863. Armstrong had figured that he was owed $2,321, minus the $210 he had been paid when he got there. $2,111 was a lot of money. He would have to find out how to get it and how to protect it until he got home again. He had reasoned that a request to the Paymaster General's Office in Washington was a good way to start and had sent a request for his back pay the day before he left for home.

When he walked back into the bunkhouse, Lieutenant Judson Paul handed Tom Armstrong an envelope. It was from the Paymaster General's Office. Inside was a short communique stating that he had calculated correctly and that he could visit the Paymaster right there at Camp Parole. Fearing foul play, Armstrong decided to make that visit when nobody was around and then to stuff the money in his mattress until he left for home. But, the Paymaster had a better idea: just come to the office the day he was leaving and collect the back pay then. Nobody would be the wiser. Just hide the money in the bottom of the haversack and be gone. That simple. With that settled, getting Leave was next.

What Tom Armstrong and the rest of Camp Parole didn't know was that the day before, on March 21, 1865, President Abraham Lincoln had left Washington for City Point, Virginia, 15 miles southeast of Richmond, there on the James River, aboard his steamer, *River Queen*. The President just wanted to get away from the capital for a while and to meet with Lieutenant General Ulysses S. Grant and the Union leadership about ways to end the war. While he was there, the President also had the chance to visit in the camps with the soldiers who had served so well and who cheered him at every turn. Lincoln was tired of the war, and Grant knew it. The General would have to end it as soon as he could.

A week later, the President met with Grant, Major General William Tecumseh Sherman, and Admiral David Porter for the final time. Lincoln, quite anxious to end the fighting and the bloodshed, made his wishes known to the others; that was to end the conflict quickly without another major battle. Grant and Sherman were not sure that could be accomplished, but they were sure that the end of the Civil War was in sight. The President retired with Admiral Porter to the *Malvern*, Porter's flagship, to return to City Point and the comfort of the *River Queen*. He hadn't felt this relaxed for a long, long time, probably since his initial campaign for the presidency five years earlier. Prosecuting the war had been difficult, until he found Ulysses S. Grant and made him the supreme commander of the Union Army. That had resulted in more bloodshed than he ever dreamed of, but, now, he knew, based on the conversation with his generals, the end was, indeed, near.

Further, nobody at Camp Parole knew that Sherman was coming north, and coming fast. He and his 60,000 Federals were now in Goldsboro, North Carolina, only 53 miles southeast of Raleigh and just 165 miles south of Richmond. Now, the general's plan was to join forces with Major General John Schofield's Army of the Ohio of 30,000 men for a joint action on the Confederate capital. Lieutenant General Ulysses S. Grant, with Major General George Meade commanding the Army of the Potomac and Major General Benjamin Butler with his Army of the James, already had a total of 125,000 effectives finishing off the siege of Petersburg that had begun some nine months earlier. Together, then, with about 215,000 seasoned fighters, Confederate General-in-Chief Robert E. Lee, with perhaps one-quarter the number of troops, just over 50,000 men, didn't stand a chance. The Confederate capital of Richmond was in serious jeopardy. Grant had the power now, but Lee wasn't quite done yet.

The Confederate commander had realized that if he could thin out the Union lines at Petersburg, his army might be able to break through them and hightail it south to meet up with General Joseph E. Johnston who was campaigning in North Carolina. On the night of March 24 – 25, Lee sent Major General John B. Gordon to lead a surprise attack on Grant's far right flank, east of Petersburg. Bloody fighting broke out just after 4:00 A.M. with the Rebel force securing about a half a mile of trenches and a number of batteries. It was looking good for the Confederates until several companies of Major General John Parke's IX Corps mounted a counterattack and drove the Confederates back even farther than where they had started that morning. The surprise attack, earlier considered a success, was a dismal failure. There would be no Confederate breakout. To make matters worse, Gordon lost about 5,000 men which he really couldn't afford to do since the Rebel army was quickly running out of able bodied fighters. You see, desertion, exhaustion, and starvation had become a plague on Lee's forces.

With that, Petersburg, Virginia fell to Grant on March 25, 1865. But the Confederate Commander-in-Chief had saved what was left of his Army. Richmond was doomed, but Robert E. Lee still thought he had a chance to prolong the war. It wouldn't last long since on March 31, the Federals drove Lee's lines back toward central Virginia, southwest of Petersburg, at the Battle of White Oak Road. Later that day, "Fightin' Phil" Sheridan engaged the forces of Major General George Pickett, of Gettysburg notoriety, at the Battle of Dinwiddie Court House which would lead to one of the bloodiest battles of the war: The Battle of Five Forks.

That fight commenced about 1:00 P.M. on April 1, with the Federals holding a 2 to 1 advantage in manpower, 22,000 to just about 11,000. The rout was on. For the rest of the afternoon, Sheridan's troopers, now on foot, pummeled the front and right flank of

the Rebel position with Major General Gouverneur Warren and his
V Corps attacking the left. It was over before dark with the Union
forces now holding the South Side Railroad, Lee's last supply line.
The Confederates also suffered here, losing about 3,000 men while
Sheridan lost maybe 800. General Robert E. Lee's worst fears were
now recognized. Grant had just too much firepower to overcome.
The Civil War should have ended that day. But, it didn't.

The road to Richmond was now wide open. The Confederate
army simply had no answer for the overwhelming force now coming
toward Richmond. "Sam" Grant, as his friends called him, had his
army placed right between Johnston and Robert E. Lee, and it was
Lee that Grant cared most about. Instead of joining him, Grant decided Sherman should take care of Johnston. And, Lee knew that
Richmond was destined to fall; it did so on April 3. His only hope
was to combine his forces with those of Joe Johnston, but he would
have to go through or around the Union army to make that happen.
Depression was quietly overtaking the Confederate commander-in-
chief, but he would not give up. Not just yet.

With all these goings-on, life at Camp Parole was pretty boring,
until Tom Armstrong received notice that his application for a two
week Leave of Absence had been approved on March 24. He could
start for Clinton, Illinois on March 29 and sent Francis Porter a note
saying that he would be taking the train from Annapolis to Harrisburg, then through Pittsburgh, Columbus, Indianapolis, and Terre
Haute to a place called Pana, Illinois. There, he would transfer to the
Belleville and Southern Illinois Railroad for the short journey to
Clinton. He guessed that he would arrive later in the day, April 1,
1865 and hoped that she and her father could meet him at the depot.
But, before he would leave, he would stop by the Paymaster's Office.

Early that morning, Wednesday, March 29, 1865, Tom Armstrong jotted a note to his father telling him that he would be in Zanesville on April 5, coming in from the west, asking Jacob to come
pick him up. His brother would have to figure out what time. Then,
after his visit to the Paymaster, he put the bills in a small box,
wrapped it in brown paper, and stuffed it in his haversack. Assured

that his money was safe, it was time for the journey to Clinton, Illinois, there in DeWitt County in the center of the state, 780 miles west of Annapolis, Maryland. He had packed the haversack with as much food as he could, packed his pistol in it, too, and started for the depot where he would catch the 11:00 A.M. Pennsylvania Railroad train for Harrisburg. Upon arrival, he would catch the B&O west, repeating his steps from just two weeks previous, but, this time, riding right through Columbus and Indianapolis to Illinois. This trip would take almost twice as long. It seemed longer as the train rolled through the hills of Pennsylvania and then into the flatland of Ohio, Indiana, and Illinois, finally pulling into the station at Pana, Illinois around 6:00 A.M. on Saturday, April 1. He would have to wait until 9:00 A.M. for the Belleville and Southern which would take him to Clinton.

When he boarded and sat down, he took off his gloves and hat and placed them on the seat beside him. The train was pretty empty. Seemed like nobody was going to Clinton this day. Next thing he knew, his palms were sweaty. "For cryin' out loud," he thought to himself, "all you're going to do is ask the woman you love to marry you. You never get nervous. Not even seeing the elephant. What's the matter with you?"

The steam engine chugged along north toward Clinton, passing through Assumption, Moweaqua, Macon, Decatur, Forsyth, and Maroa. "Nice little towns," he thought, "Decatur is bigger." It was after noon when the train pulled into the depot in Clinton, Illinois, steam escaping from the locomotive's pistons. Peering out the window, there she was, with her father, sitting in a buggy a few steps from the platform. "Now, whatta I do? Kiss her? Give her a hug? She's really pretty. Oh, my." It wasn't that warm that late March day, but he could feel the sweat running down the small of his back. "Stop it, calm down." The conductor called for all the passengers getting off there in Clinton, so he scrunched the hat on his head, picked up the haversack, and made his way to the door, climbing down onto the platform.

The worries that Tom Armstrong had soon vanished when Francis Porter ran up to him and threw her arms around him. "Thomas, I thought I would never see you again. Then I got your letter, and I knew you were alive and were coming for me. I have missed you so," she blubbered through her tears of joy.

Stroking her hair, his calming influence took over. "Yes, my love, I am here. I am well. I have missed you terribly, but now we are here. Together. There is much to talk about, and I have a lot of time to spend with you." He kissed the top of her head and smiled, she returning it. Slowly, they walked down the platform arm-in-arm to the stairs leading to where John Porter had parked the buggy.

"Hello, John," said Tom Armstrong, putting out his right hand for Frank's father to shake. "It is very good to see you, and I hope you and Amanda are well."

"Thomas, you just bein' here has made us very happy," shaking his hand vigorously. "You must tell us about what happened to you. It is so good to see you and to have you here. We should be off. I think Amanda has dinner waiting for us. "Francis has worried so, and now that worry is gone. Praise the Lord."

"Yes. Praise the Lord, indeed, John. Let's be off. I want to see the new farm." He thought to himself, "This is going to be easier than I thought it would. Whew!"

John Porter put the haversack on the seat next to him, allowing his daughter and her young man to sit in the back where they could talk. It was about twelve miles to the farm, northeast of the town of Clinton, in DeWitt Township near the small village of Parnell. The ride through the countryside that spring day in the middle of Illinois was most pleasant with Frank Porter telling him what everything was and who lived on what farm. He had never seen her quite so excited before. Yes, it was going to be much easier.

When John Porter pulled the buggy down the lane, crossing the railroad tracks of the Illinois Central, Tom Armstrong could see a farmhouse in the distance, maybe a quarter of a mile away. The lane was somewhat dusty with the horse clip-clopping along. He thought it would be good to get out and walk, but the horse and buggy carried on. When they were closer to the farmhouse, here came the Sheepdogs, Boomer and Rascal, racing down the path to where Porter had parked the buggy. The dogs knew, just like his father's did, barking and jumping up. Tom Armstrong wrestled a bit with them and told them to calm down which, of course, they didn't.

"Tom," a familiar voice called out." 'Bout damn time you got here." It was John, Jr., bigger than Armstrong remembered but just as handsome, blonde hair and beard, hat pushed back on his head.

"Good to see you, Johnny. How've you been?" he replied, shaking his hand.

"Never better, now that the damn war is almost over. Read 'bout it in the *Daily Public* when I was in town last week. Good damn news, Tom. Good damn news. You gotta go back?"

"Yeah, got ten days. Then I gotta go get exchanged. I'll tell you about it. Where are the others?"

Amanda Porter was standing on the large front porch, ringing the dinner bell. Billy and Joe Porter came running out of the barn while Huldah, Mary, and Amanda came in from the garden they were planting.

"Thomas, I am very glad to see you. We all thought we had lost you," said Amanda Porter, Frank clinging to his side. "We prayed for you every day and every night, and God has seen you home."

"Thank you, Amanda. Yes, He has. It was terrible, but I never lost faith. It is wonderful to be here with all of you," he said, looking at Frank Porter.

Her sisters all gave Armstrong a hug, tears streaming down Mary's face. The younger boys came up and just wanted to play.

"Billy, Joe, leave Thomas alone," scolded their mother. "He has had a long trip and needs some refreshment. Come inside, Thomas. There is food waiting for you all. Might not be hot, but it will do."

Actually, Tom Armstrong could not have been happier than he was right then. He just wanted to propose right then, but knew he had to talk with John Porter. He would do that that very afternoon.

After he had washed up and eaten, Francis Porter took him out to the barn where he would sleep. When they were alone, they shared a long kiss, holding each other very tight. "I have to talk with your father, Frank, right now."

"I know, and he knows what you're going to talk to him about. Remember that letter you sent. Don't worry, silly, it will be just fine."

"Silly." He hadn't heard that since August '62. Sure as the devil, no one would have called him silly since then. But, she could.

They heard John Porter bringing the buggy toward the corral outside of the barn. "You go talk to him," said Frank Porter. "I'll be waiting."

Tom Armstrong walked out the large sliding door in the front of the barn, to find John Porter unhitching the horse from the buggy and taking him into the corral. The two men then pushed the buggy back to its place on the side of the barn and walked slowly back toward the house. They talked a little about the sheep and the crops that were about to be put in, and when they reached the porch, they sat down in two big, wooden chairs on the south end.

"So, Thomas," smiled John Porter, "why'd you come all the way out here to Illinois? You coulda stayed where you were or just gone home."

Tom Armstrong couldn't tell if Porter was joshing him or not and presumed he was. "You know why I'm here, John," getting straight to the point. "I would like Francis' hand in marriage, if that is all right with you and if she will have me."

John Porter just stuck out his hand, shaking that of Tom Armstrong. "Welcome to the family. We couldn't be happier. Where will you live? Here or in Ohio? What will you do for a living?"

"Don't rightly know. Haven't talked with her about any of that, but thank you, John. I will." The two men talked for a few more minutes.

"You better go talk to her, son."

"Yessir. I think I shall." Tom Armstrong got up, walked down the steps, back to the barn where he knew Frank Porter was waiting. "Francis Porter?"

"Yes?"

"I have just spoken with your father," with a false formality, "and he has given me permission to ask of you a favor."

"Oh?" thinking, "Why doesn't he get on with it? We've talked about it in our letters, so let's go. He's enjoying making me wait, I can tell."

Taking her hands in his, "Would you consent to be my wife?"

Frank Porter threw her arms around his neck and squealed, "I thought you would never ask, silly. Of course, I will marry you."

And, that was that. They walked back to the house, hand-in-hand, to tell the others, but they wanted to tell Frank's mother first.

"I already know, Thomas. John just told me that you talked to him. You have made all of us, especially Francis, very happy. You may call me 'Mother' from now on."

The other Porter children were thrilled. "Who's gonna tell George? asked Huldah.

"I want to do that," replied Frank Porter. "Tom, did you mention this to him?"

"No, not directly, but it won't come as a big surprise. We can write him together if you want. Gee, you and Grace will be sisters-in-law."

Tom Armstrong and Frank Porter spent the next day, Sunday, at church, but they did not let on to anyone in the gathering about what had happened the previous day. They didn't even sit together, Tom, John Porter, and his sons on the right side; Amanda, Frank, and girls on the left. However, everyone in the small congregation knew. But, sitting there in church gave him time to think about his decision to enter the ministry. He would wait to tell Frank until he had talked further with Charlie McCabe and was absolutely certain that was what he wanted to do.

Meanwhile, on the night of April 2, Confederate General-in-Chief Robert E. Lee was sensing defeat which was magnified at about 4 o'clock in the morning of April 3 when the Union guns unloaded a most serious and heavy bombardment on the Rebel position. Lee had already started sending his troops south through Petersburg, but when the infantry attack came shortly after the artillery assault, he knew that he could not defend his position any longer. The Federals met his troops at Petersburg with some damn awful hand-to-hand fighting, some of the worst of the entire war. As the sun was setting, Grant ordered the fighting stopped, planning to resume it in the morning, but Lee and his men managed to escape under the cover of darkness.

With somewhere around 35,000 men, they took off out of Richmond that night, hoping to get to Danville or Lynchburg, due west of Richmond and then, on the Danville Railroad, to head south to meet up with the troops of Joseph Johnston. Lee had been advised that there was a trainload of provisions at Amelia Courthouse, some 35 miles west of Richmond, and he desperately wanted to feed his starving army. He figured he could regroup there while the men were being fed, before going south, but there were two problems that he didn't know about just yet.

First, Lieutenant General Ulysses S. Grant had the Confederates out in the open, not firmly ensconced in their trenches at Petersburg, which was right where he wanted them. Basically, the Rebels would be no match now since Grant had more men, more guns, more food, and the smell of victory. And, second, he had "Fightin' Phil" Sheridan and his cavalry who had cleaned out the Shenandoah Valley and now were ready to help end it all. As an aside, Grant did find it interesting that his two best generals, Sherman and Sheridan, were from the state of Ohio, just like himself. Coincidence, sure, nonetheless, but those were the two who were going to help him finish it off, and soon.

On Monday, April 3, Francis Porter and Tom Armstrong rode around the Porter farm with Armstrong seeing where everything was. They sat for a while near the creek that ran through the property and only made one decision. They would get married on Sunday, October 1, 1865 right there in Clinton, Illinois, presuming, of course, that he would be exchanged and mustered out. Armstrong said he would try to get Charlie McCabe to perform the service. There was no doubt that the Reverend would. But, in late afternoon, it was time for him to head back to Gratiot, 400 miles to the east. Before they stepped into the buggy, they shared another long kiss and held each other very close, expressing their love for each other. He promised to come back as soon as he could, and then they were off to the depot in Clinton, both happier than they had ever been in their lives.

Riding on the train back to Pana, Tom Armstrong was lonely once again, just as he had been when Caleb Edwards went home. But, this time, there was more hope. He had the rest of his life to spend with Francis Pamela Porter. The nightmares, however, still haunted his sleep. And, the memories of prison would trouble him during the day, if he let them. He would have to tell Frank about all of this the next time he would see her. He would also tell her about his plan to enter the ministry of the Methodist Church. When he would do that, he didn't know. But, he had to make sure she was prepared for that life.

The trip to Zanesville was pretty uneventful, but things did get interesting when he got home. The train arrived at about 1:00 A.M. on Wednesday, April 5, so he lay down on a bench at the station, using the haversack for a pillow, and tried to get some sleep. Jacob woke him just after 8 o'clock, and they headed for Gratiot with one stop before they left town.

"Jacob," Tom Armstrong began. "I did it. I asked her to marry me, and she said 'yes.' Really didn't think she would say 'no.' She had expected it, but let me play it out."

"When?" asked his brother.

"October 1, there in Clinton. I gotta ask Charlie if he will conduct the ceremony. Can we stop by the church? I want to tell him. This is all dependent on when I get out. Hopefully, this summer."

"Good for you, Tom. Congratulations." Jacob Armstrong wanted more details, but his brother seemed quite relaxed, just intent on seeing the Rev. Charles C. McCabe. All Tom wanted now was news about the war. Maybe they could stop at Wescott's store and get a copy of the most recent *Courier* on the way home.

Fortunately, they found Charles McCabe in his office at the church. Tom Armstrong gave him the good news to which his friend shook his hand and gave him a big embrace.

"Beccie will be thrilled when I tell her. Is Frank coming here before the wedding? Beccie wants to talk to her about becoming a preacher's wife. October 1? In Clinton? I wouldn't miss it, T.S. Might even sing *The Battle Hymn*."

"You better, Charlie, even if it is a wedding. I will see you before I go back in a week. Want to hear more about the ministry. And, yes, I will have Frank come here sometime this summer. I may just go and get her, so I can tell her about what I want to do. She mentioned something about me taking a school out there, and we need to talk about that, too. Where we live, too. More to this marriage business than I reckoned." And, with that, the Armstrong brothers shook hands with Charles McCabe and walked out of the church. It was time to go see the folks at home with the good news and, incidentally, give his father the money to save for him.

When they arrived at the farm out there south of Gratiot, they found their mother sitting at her spinning wheel, pumping the treadle with her right foot and humming a hymn that was familiar to both of them, *Oh, For a Thousand Tongues to Sing*. With Thomas home and Easter right around the corner in a few days, the song just seemed right that day. Jane Armstrong was very happy and was about to become even happier.

"Mother, where's Father? I have something to tell you."

"He's out in the barn. Jacob, can you go fetch him?"

William Armstrong entered the large farmhouse, a bit dirty from his work in the stalls, so, after he got cleaned up, Tom Armstrong told them that he had been out to Clinton to see the Porters and that, as of a couple of days ago, he was engaged to be married to Francis this coming fall. Charlie McCabe would do the honors.

"I've been wonderin' 'bout that for some time, Thomas," said his father. "We both have, right, Mother?"

"Oh, Thomas, you have made me so happy. First, you're here, then you're getting married. Wait'll we tell the children." And, yes, she was also thinking about grandchildren.

"Mother, Father, there's more. I already told Jacob, but you need to know, too. I haven't told Frank about this but will the next time I see her. At some point in the next few years, I want to go to divinity school and become a minister of the Methodist Church. I spoke with Charlie about it, and he has agreed to counsel me as to what all is involved. Beccie will talk with Frank, since this will be a different life than the one I think she is planning, me being a school teacher and principal."

"Why, son?" asked William Armstrong.

"Pretty simple, Father. The Lord spared me from the horrors of war, the battle where Eddie got killed and the awful prisons like Libby that took Artemus. God brought me through it, and I just want to serve Him for His graciousness."

"Thomas," said Jane Armstrong. "I am very proud of you. You are a fine teacher, and now you will make a fine minister as well as a fine husband. Let us celebrate tonight."

447

And, celebrate they did with good food, more stories, (but not about the war), singing of familiar songs and hymns, and plenty of laughter. Mary and Flavilla were certainly enjoying the notion that Francis Porter would now be in the family, but the boys, Frank and Gus just weren't quite sure of what to make of it. There they all were, William Armstrong's family, but without Wilbur, and even Jane Armstrong seemed to be getting over that. She was just glad that Thomas was back with them and didn't have to go back to the Army for a few days. Those days in early April 1865, however, would change the United States for good.

So, with Lee abandoning Richmond, early in the morning on Monday, April 3, 1865, the capital of the Confederate States of America fell into Union hands. The night before, the administration of President Jefferson Davis escaped and any and all citizens, who could find any kind of conveyance, left as well. Then, mobs of people roamed the streets, setting fire to anything and everything, especially facilities used to prosecute the war and many of the government buildings. When the Union soldiers arrived that Monday, their first chore was to put out the fires and then to see what was left of this once proud Southern city.

The next morning, President Abraham Lincoln, aboard the *River Queen*, accompanied by Admiral David Porter on the *Malvern*, set off for Richmond up the James River. The river was filled with various obstructions, so a change had to be made from the princely steamboats to a barge with a dozen of Porter's sailors on the oars but without any cavalry or infantry protection. Just them. That was agreeable to the President. But, on the other hand, Admiral Porter was concerned about an assassination attempt on the President what with Richmond being a Southern city. The President didn't seem to be bothered by such talk. Actually, he was used to it, having heard rumors about assassination possibilities since he was first elected President in 1860. While he was revered in the North, he was hated in the South. On this day, however, all he wanted to see was what was left of the Confederate capital, the barge landing behind a big, old tobacco warehouse. As Abraham Lincoln and his party walked up 20th Street and turned right on Cary Street, he noticed the name on the building: "LIBBY PRISON."

At the same time, General Robert E. Lee didn't know it, but Ulysses S. Grant had ordered his army to pursue the weakened Confederate army west and south to block any movement there. Lee had been on the road for three days and now had but half the men he had started with due to exhaustion, hunger, desertion, and death. To make matters worse, "Fightin' Phil" Sheridan, riding hard with his cavalry unit and three corps of infantry, was moving faster than Lee was and actually got to Danville before the Confederate commander could. On April 5, Sheridan's force destroyed the Danville Railroad, so as a result, Lee had no place to go except further west to try to flank Sheridan, hoping to cross the Appomattox River and head south.

The other thing that Lee didn't know was that the trainload of provisions that was supposed to be at Amelia Court House was really a trainload of ammunition. So, when the first Confederates arrived, they stormed the train, thinking that there was food to be had, but when they broke open the cars, all they found was 200 crates of ammunition and 96 carts to carry it. They really couldn't use any of it because they were so hungry and exhausted. Many of the soldiers just sat down, there in their rags, and just waited to be captured.

Sheridan maintained a route south of the main force of the Confederate Army, effectively preventing it from moving toward North Carolina. On April 6, Sheridan caught the Rebels at Sailor's Creek, a small tributary of the Appomattox River. In another bloody encounter, Sheridan's infantry isolated about one-quarter of Lee's army, captured some 6,000 of them, and wiped out its supply train. Fatigued and starving men and no rations. It was a pretty bleak situation for the Confederates.

"Fightin' Phil," wasn't done. His forces kept moving west with the intent of destroying the Confederate supply lines. When they arrived at Appomattox Station, they found three unguarded supply trains. His men, with some railroad experience, fired up the trains and steamed east about five miles to the camp of the Union Army of the James, effectively commandeering the supplies. When the Confederates realized what had happened, they opened up with a heavy artillery barrage, aimed at the Federals there at the station. The Union commander, Brevet Major General George Armstrong Custer, ordered an attack on the artillery some two miles away from the station out on the Lynchburg stage road. The fight that developed was quite disorganized, and it took until 9 o'clock that evening for the Union soldiers to break the Confederate lines, with the Rebels retreating to Lynchburg and Appomattox Court House. Some say the desperation of the Confederate troops made this one of the most vicious fights of the entire war. The Union lost about 1,500 men, the Confederates, about 7,500. But, even though his corps was almost destroyed, Lee continued to look for an escape route.

Word had come from the Confederate commissary that 80,000 rations had been sent to a village called Farmville which was only twenty miles from where Lee now stood. He could be there in one day, could fill the bellies of his starving army, and continue the escape south over the High Bridge crossing the Appomattox River. It was not to be, for while they were gobbling down the much anticipated food, the Federals attacked again.

The situation for the Confederates was hopeless, but some of the survivors of Sailor's Creek still headed west. Fightin' Phil" and his cavalry raced to get ahead of them which they did at the quiet, little village of Appomattox Court House, about 100 miles west of the fallen Confederate capital. But now, General Robert E. Lee was trapped. His 8,000 men were now cornered by Grant's 60,000, including the 122nd Ohio Volunteer Infantry. But, Lee would not even think of surrendering his army.

In the afternoon of April 7, under a flag of truce, Grant sent Lee a message suggesting that the Confederate General do just that, surrender. That evening, about 10 o'clock, Lee read the note, not agreeing with Grant's assessment that the Confederate situation was hopeless, but he did wish that no more blood be spilled. In his response, he indicated his disagreement, but then informed Grant of his desire to know the terms of such an action. Grant replied that the only condition would be for the men of the Confederate Army to pledge that they would not take up arms against the government of the United States. He also offered to meet the Confederate commander the next day to discuss the details of the terms of surrender.

Robert E. Lee had another idea, that being to discuss with Grant, not the detailed terms of surrender, but rather the manner in which peace would be restored in the aftermath of the war. In his reply, he offered to meet with the Union commander only to discuss that and not the terms of surrender. Now, restoration of peace was a political issue that Grant knew was outside of his authority, and he began to think that the only way Lee would surrender was by force. He would send another note in the morning of April 9, 1865, Palm Sunday.

On the morning of April 9, 1865, Lee tried one last breakout, but it was of no use. The Yankee force was simply too big and too mobile for any chance of escape, but the Rebels still tried before realizing that they were, indeed, surrounded with no place to go. Robert E. Lee read the latest missive from Ulysses S. Grant in which the Union Commander basically told his counterpart that he, Grant, had no authority to negotiate a complete peace settlement to bring the Southern states back into the Union. He also told Lee that by surrendering, he would help that to get under way sooner and more easily than if the fighting continued.

Now that the breakout had failed, the General-in-Chief of the Army of the Confederate States of America simply had no choice, but he continued to try to get Grant to do something that the Union commander was not authorized to do. He sent Grant another note, offering to meet that day. When Grant read it, he was losing his patience with the Confederate general. He dictated another note, saying once again, that he could not negotiate a peace, but that the only way to end the fighting was for the Southerners to stack their arms. Enough was enough. This time, Grant was being true to the nickname given to him after the successful siege at Vicksburg. The surrender would have to be unconditional.

Lee, now, agreed, but it pained him terribly on this day, after four years of constant fighting, to have to go see Lieutenant General Ulysses S. Grant. When they did meet at the home of Wilmer McLean, the two men could not have been more different in their appearance, Lee in a full dress uniform, complete with sword and sash, while Grant arrived in his customary private's shirt with his trousers tucked into boots that were covered with mud. After some pleasant small talk about their experiences in the Mexican War, the Union Commander repeated his terms of the previous day, adding that all supplies, ammunition, and other stores would become the property of his army. Lee agreed but asked that since the members of his cavalry and artillery units had supplied their own horses, might they be allowed to return to their farms with them. He also asked if the officers could take their side arms, horses, and personal belongings back to their homes. Grant agreed with both and set to writing the terms of surrender.

Robert E. Lee then added that all of the Federal prisoners he had taken on this latest march would be released, since he didn't have enough food for them. Grant, sensing the hunger which the Confederates had endured, offered to feed Lee's men and ordered rations to be provided. It was as amiable a surrender as could be imagined. Grant finished writing, an aide copied it, the two men read it, after which Lee dictated his reply to one of his own aides. It was dated 4:00 P.M., April 9, 1865. Grant then ordered "Fightin' Phil" Sheridan and George Meade to insure that there was no celebration among the Federal troops. They were to provide the defeated Confederates with as much dignity as they could. Meade then asked if his officers could go to the Confederate camp to renew friendships that had become so strained over the past four years. Lee consented gladly. Then, the two commanders shook hands and departed the McLean house. For the most part, then, the American Civil War was over. Well, for the army it was over, but there were many Southerners who did not feel that way. One in particular, a Virginia actor named John Wilkes Booth.

On Monday, April 10, Tom and Jacob Armstrong took the wagon to Putnam to get supplies at Chauncey Wescott's store and found the town jumping with excitement. Church bells pealed; a brass band was playing; the streets mobbed with people, some cheering, some crying; the saloons full, even though it was only 1 o'clock in the afternoon. When they pulled up at Wescott's, Tom saw William Ball, talking in an animated fashion with someone Tom didn't know. Turns out it was the new banker in town, a fellow by the name of Ralph Cunningham. Ball recognized Tom and trotted over to the wagon, waving the *Courier*.

TELEGRAPHIC
LAST NIGHT'S DISPATCHES

GLORIOUS NEWS!

LEE SURRENDERS!
HIS ARMY, ARMS, & STORES
GRAND DICTATES TERMS!
Official Dispatches
War Department

Washington, April 9 – 9 P.M.

Maj. Gen. Dix

This Department has received the official report of the surrender this day of Gen. Lee and his army to Lieut. General Grant.

[*Signed*]   EDWIN M. STANTON

Secretary of War

HEADQUARTERS, ARMY OF THE UNITED STATES, April 9 – 4:40 P.M.

E.M. Stanton, Sec of War

Gen. Lee surrendered the Army of Northern Virginia this afternoon upon terms proposed by myself. The accompanying additional correspondence will show the conditions fully.

[*Signed*]   U.S. GRANT

Lieutenant General

April 9, 1865,

General – I received your note of this morning on the picket line, whither I had come to meet you and ascertain definitely what terms were embraced in your proposal of yesterday with reference to the surrender of this army. I now request an interview, in accordance with the offer contained in your letter of yesterday for that purpose.

Very respectfully
Your obedient servant
R.E. LEE, General

"Jacob, it's over. The war's over. I knew it would happen. I just knew it." Tom Armstrong could not contain his excitement.

"Well, I'll be damned," replied his brother. "No more fightin'. No more killin'."

"Yeah, and I bet I get exchanged pretty soon. There's gonna be a whole lot of Reb officers looking to go home. Bet Grant paroled them first, then will exchange them just like Johnny did to us. Bet I'll find out when I get back to Camp Parole. Gotta be on the train on Thursday."

"Then, what?"

"Don't know, but I think I have to report to the 122nd again and get mustered out. Gave some thought to making it a career, but that didn't last long. Then I gotta get back to Clinton to talk with Frank about our future."

It was tough getting the wagon loaded and headed back to Gratiot what with all the people celebrating in the streets. But, they managed and soon were on the way home.

When they arrived at the farm, the Armstrong brothers ran to the house yelling, "The war is over! Lee surrendered yesterday! It is over!" Jane Armstrong just fell to her knees, praising God for the peace that was to come and the safety of her second born son. Fla and Mary danced around the big great room with Frank and Gus just staring, not quite sure of what was going on.

"Where's Father, Mother?" asked Jacob Armstrong.

"Out with the flock, northwest, I think."

"Sump, you go tell him. I gotta go tell Mattie. The war's finally over."

Tom Armstrong ran to the barn, saddled Cricket, and took off northwest into the sun. He found his father, tending the sheep with Duke, the big collie helping out.

"It's over, Father!" he screamed. "The Rebels have surrendered! Yesterday! Saw it in the paper in town today! Party going on there right now!

"Praise the Lord," offered William Armstrong. "No more killin'. No more boys dyin,'" he said quietly. "And, you're coming home. For good"

"Yes, Father, but I don't know when. I have to be back at Camp Parole by Saturday. Who knows how long it will take to get exchanged and mustered out."

They heard the sound of the bell, indicating that supper was ready, and, with Duke leading the way, the two men rode back to the farmhouse, talking about the war, Tom's upcoming marriage, and his future plans.

"I really want to go to divinity school and study to be a minister, Father, and I think I will go talk with Charlie about it tomorrow. Francis asked me to think about becoming principal of a school out there in Clinton, so maybe I'll have to do that first. But, I really want to talk with her about the ministry. She also needs to talk with Beccie McCabe. Problem is, I don't know when I can get back out there to see her. Wonder if I should have her just come here."

"That's up to you, son. But, always make sure that you communicate honestly with her and she with you. No secrets."

"Wouldn't have it any other way, Father." They rode on as the sun was setting in the west. Yes, he would go see Charlie McCabe in the morning.

The family Armstrong ate their supper with excited, animated conversation about what it meant for the war to be over and for Thomas to be engaged to be married. After the meal, the little boys started playing checkers on the floor; Tom, his father and sisters just talking, wondering what would happen to the South. But, sheer gladness that Tom was home. It was just like old times before the war broke out. Talking, laughing and carrying on. Jane Armstrong just stood by the fireplace, smiling. Her family was back together, and she didn't have to worry any more.

When Tom Armstrong shook hands with his brother, Jacob, at the train depot in Zanesville, the following Friday morning, he had no way of knowing that this would be a dark day in the annals of American history. His life was very good at the time. The war over, out of the army, engaged to be married, a job waiting for him in Clinton, Illinois. He hoped he would never see the elephant again, riding back to Columbus, then aboard the B&O for Harrisburg before transferring to the Pennsylvania RR that would take him back to Annapolis.

It was Good Friday. He had almost forgotten that. Should have been in church. But he was on a train, back to Camp Parole. It seemed that the ride took longer than when he had come the other way. And, when he arrived at the Relay House at Annapolis Junction, 25 miles northwest of Annapolis, to be processed that Saturday afternoon, it was buzzing with activity.

"WHAT'S GOING ON?" Tom Armstrong shouted over the din to the sentry at the door.

"PRESIDENT LINCOLN WAS SHOT LAST NIGHT!" the sentry yelled.

"HOW? WHERE?"

"DON'T KNOW. IMAGIN' THE COMMANDANT IS TRYING TO FIND OUT."

"OH, MY GOD! THAT'S AWFUL! HE'S OUR LEADER. I BELIEVE SO MUCH IN HIM AND NOW THIS. IS HE ALIVE? DEAD? WHAT NOW?"

"N0 ANSWERS THERE. MEBBE WE'LL FIND OUT MORE TODAY OR TOMORROW."

Later that day, he left in a wagon for Camp Parole, sharing his grief with other soldiers who had just returned from Leave.

The next morning, Easter services on Sunday, April 16, at St. Anne's Episcopal Church, right there on Church Circle, facing the State House, were somber. Flags flew at half-staff. Black bunting clothed the inside of the church. Instead of the joy that was normally felt on Easter morning, celebrating the resurrection of Christ, the parishioners spoke in hushed tones. The music was somber, at best. The rector, Ernest Lennon, wearing black, and not white, walked slowly down the aisle, followed by lay ministers. When they reached the pulpit, the rector stepped to the lectern, dabbing his eyes.

"My friends," Lennon said, not in his usual boisterous voice, "I have terrible news that I must share with you. On the evening of Good Friday last, a man shot the President as he and Mrs. Lincoln and their guests were watching a performance at Ford's Theater in Washington. He was attended to immediately for a gunshot wound to the head and was carried to a boarding house across the street for comfort. I was informed last evening that President Abraham Lincoln died yesterday morning just after 7 o'clock."

Gasps and cries came from the pews when the people heard the news. Many people just burst into tears. Tom Armstrong and Jud Paul sat there stunned. They had figured something was terribly wrong when they saw the flag at the Statehouse fluttering at half-staff and then the black bunting at the church. But, they could not come to terms with it. Armstrong kept thinking, "The President is dead! The President is dead! After all he's been through. He's dead!" Jud Paul was weeping, wiping his eyes with his handkerchief. The service continued according to "The Great Vigil of Easter" in *The Book of Common Prayer*, but the people were not in a celebratory mood. It was a sad, sad day in Annapolis, Maryland and in all of the North. Not so in the South.

The rest of the day was spent almost in complete silence. Oh, there was definitely anger at the man who pulled the trigger, someone said his name was John Wilkes Booth, a Southern sympathizer and accomplished actor. But the details were sketchy at best.

While they were at the Relay House, the men who had returned from Leave on Saturday had been told to report to Camp headquarters on Monday, the 17th. Tom Armstrong went over there around 1 o'clock that afternoon. Standing in line with the others, the man in front of him showed him a newspaper he had picked up that morning at the train station in Philadelphia.

THE LATEST NEWS
BY TELEGRAPH

THE MURDER OF THE PRESIDENT,

ESCAPE OF BOOTH, THE ASSASSIN

**Inauguration of Andrew Johnson
as President**

CONDITION OF SECRETARY SEWARD

EXCITEMENT THROUGHOUT THE
COUNTRY

The President's Last Hours

WASHINGTON, April 15, — 11 A.M. —*The Star Extra* says: At twenty minutes past seven o'clock, the President breathed his last, closing his eyes as if falling asleep, and his countenance assuming an expression of perfect serenity. There were no indications of pain, and it was not known that he was dead until the gradually decreasing respiration ceased altogether.

The Rev. D. A. Gurley of the New York Avenue Presbyterian church, immediately on its being ascertained that life was extinct knelt at his bedside and offered an impressive prayer, which was responded to by all present.

Dr. Gurley then proceeded to the front parlor, where Mrs. Lincoln, Captain Robert Lincoln, Mr. John Hay, the Private Secretary, and others were waiting where he again offered prayer for the consolation of the family.

That afternoon, still saddened and stunned by the news, Tom Armstrong took pen to paper...

Annapolis Md. April 17th 1865

Dear Father

I am here at Annapolis. I am halting between two options, whether it would be best for me to stay in the service or resign & take that school in Clinton. If I stay, I will have the unpleasant feeling of being in the regiment where the men have formed an attachment to other officers. I have been so long separated from them that I will be as if among strangers. I will be a junior to many an old Sergeant and Corporal. My knowledge of military affairs is nearly forgotten or perhaps was never known. Then I look again at the good feeling I will have if I can go out of the service & can say proudly I served as a soldier in the Army of the glorious Republic for 3 years and can return with the proud satisfaction of feeling I've done my duty.

You have all the news by the papers about the sad fate of Abraham Lincoln. I have felt sad and gloomy ever since but maybe Providence removed him at this crisis for a good and wise purpose. We cannot see it but God knows best. His leniency to traitors has killed him. We could ill spare the good, kind hearted Abraham Lincoln, but time will tell us the sequel. We are stronger & more united & Andrew Johnson will deal roughly with traitors.

I shall write to you as often as convenient & I have anything to write. The war is virtually at a close. Jeff Davis issued a grand proclamation at Danville which you have read no doubt. But that was before Lee's surrender. I wonder if he thinks Lee's surrender was a strategic move to draw (up) Grant's forces into a snare & for the capture and dispersion of his army. I wonder if the Confederacy won't turn up in Mexico next. Some think Jeff Davis' movements are designed only to cover up designs of escape.

Farewell.

Write to me soon

From your aff son   Thomas. S. Armstrong

Annapolis, Md.

Rather than stay in the army, Tom Armstrong was leaning toward becoming the principal of the school out there in Clinton, postponing thoughts of the ministry. He figured that he and Frank could live north of town, nearer to her school than his, but that wouldn't happen. And, really, he had served his country proudly and well and, in all reality, had had enough. And, as he thought about it, perhaps the death of President Abraham Lincoln was God's will, part of His Holy Plan. That, Tom Armstrong would never know.

The next day, still feeling lonely and sad, he wrote to Francis Porter...

Annapolis Maryland, April 18, 1865
Clinton, DeWitt County, Illinois

Mon Amie

I received no word from you yet though I wrote immediately upon my arrival home. I still expect to hear from you though perhaps the fault is in the mails.

I am in excellent health and able for the duties that may come upon me. I cannot tell you what disposition will be made for me, for I know not as of yet. Nearly all of the paroled prisoners have arrived here. I reported on the 16th inst. though my leave of absence expired on the 14th. I was declared at the Relay House, also at Annapolis Junction west of here. At the former, I heard the sad news of the horrible murder of that great and good man Abraham Lincoln. How sad! Our nation weeps. The cities are clothed in the shroud of mourning, the flags are draped in black & suspended at half-mast.

Tomorrow the officers go in a body to Washington to attend the funeral of the greatest man in the world. May God pity us! for indeed we are stricken with sorrow that moves the soul. Gen Grant has given us leave to go and I shall avail myself of the opportunity.

My father has no wish to move West at present. He thinks it would be much more beneficial to us to remain where we are at present. But I differ with him, having, as you know, more evidence that there is more of the world than that which lies around and adjacent to either Gratiot or Hopewell, than he has, for you know, "I've traveled."

Well I'll close, hoping to hear from you as soon as convenient.

My kind regards to your father's family, also to Jos. J. Kelly & family, also to others whom you please. Wishing you a kind farewell, I subscribe myself.

Very respectfully,
Your obedient servant   T.S. Armstrong

Annapolis, Md.

Wednesday, April 19, 1865, dawned bright and warm, the nicest one of the new spring. The officers of Camp Parole piled into coaches of the train for the ride to Washington, D.C., a distance of about thirty-five miles. As they passed through Bowie, Springdale, and Glenarden, they could see flags flying at half-staff, buildings shrouded in black, people just milling around. Everyone knew that this was the day they would say "Goodbye" to Abraham Lincoln.

When the train approached the city, the men could see throngs of people, all anticipating the funeral procession that would start at the White House and would end at the Capitol. They were situated on the top of buildings, hiding in trees, and generally trying to find any view. Lieutenant General Ulysses S. Grant had authorized the officers' trip to march in the funeral procession with the Commandant of Camp Parole, Colonel John Power, just having to show his orders to the guards on Pennsylvania Avenue. He and the other officers left the train, formed up, and under Power's command, began their march to the White House there at 1600 Pennsylvania Avenue. When they arrived, about noon, they found the Executive Mansion to be draped in black, mourning the death of Abraham Lincoln. Power's order was "At Ease."

The crowd was quite impressive, and the officers from Camp Parole took their place in the line of soldiers assembled to pass by the coffin of the late President. A little after 2:00 P.M., the procession would begin to move now that the services in the East Room had been concluded. The column of soldiers came to "Attention." Members of the Veterans Reserve Corps carried the coffin out into the sunlight and placed it on the horse-drawn hearse at the Main Gate of the White House, there on Pennsylvania Avenue. Power, said to the men of Camp Parole, including Thomas S. Armstrong, "Forward March," and they began to walk slowly toward the coffin. As they approached it, they removed their caps, and when they passed by it, saluted the fallen President.

Shortly thereafter, they heard the commander of the Veterans Reserve Corps issue the order to move out. The hearse driver snapped the reins, telling his horses to begin the mile-long journey to the Capitol building. Tom Armstrong fought back the tears as he watched it slowly start down Pennsylvania Avenue. The command came from Colonel Power, "Forward, March." The column of Union soldiers in lines of eight, followed the hearse down Pennsylvania Avenue to the Capitol. Then, after watching the Veterans Reserve Corps carry the coffin into the Capitol Building, the men of Camp Parole were ordered back to the station for the ride back to Annapolis.

Armstrong was too shaken by all of it to do much but sit in the shade that April afternoon. He didn't want to talk to anyone. He didn't want to eat. He just wanted to be left alone.

The next morning, bright and early, he was feeling a little better. After breakfast, he decided he needed to "talk" with Francis...

Annapolis Maryland April 20, 1865

My "own" dear

Early yesterday morning nearly all the officers left Annapolis, in a body, for Washington City to attend the funeral obsequies of our late, lamented president, Abraham Lincoln. We arrived there, marched to the White House. The assembly was immense and the funeral procession said to be the most impressive demonstration which ever occurred at the Capital. After the religious services at the Executive Mansion were over the procession moved. The funeral car draped in black upon which the splendid coffin that contained all that remained of Abraham Lincoln stood in the avenue in front of the mansion. Reverently we lifted out hats as we marched passed. Tears fell as we thought of the good and great man who has fallen. "We mourn a martyred father" was our leading thought. We marched to the Capitol, halted and formed. The car arrived and the body was born up the steps to the Capitol and deposited in the Rotunda from whence it will be taken to Illinois.

The city was crowded with persons, thousands of them from distant cities, nearly the whole population were out. Every prominent point on Pennsylvania Avenue the line of procession was occupied by those who wished to obtain the best view. You will see a description of the whole affair. It was the most extensive affair I ever saw. I was at the funeral of Abraham Lincoln. But one thing I regret is I never saw him. We returned on the train last evening. The bells were ringing in Annapolis when we got here. I attended the Catholic Church. The funeral services were said there with an appropriate address by the priest was made.

Frank I should like you to attend school this summer -- that is if you wish to. Let me hear from you. I am well. As soon as I can get out of the army I will come and see you -- and more.

Don't forget to write soon as I am anxious to hear from you. Believing you as ever my own true dear, I bid you an affectionate farewell from your true lover.

Thos. S. Armstrong

He stopped and stared at what he had just written, shaking his head. It was very difficult to believe, but it was true.

"I was at the funeral of Abraham Lincoln."

16 Civilian Life

The sadness of the President's death lingered with Tom Armstrong and would for quite a while, but he did receive some good news. On Friday, April 21, 1865, he had been summoned by Colonel John Power, the Commandant of Camp Parole, to be in his office the next day at 2:00 P.M.

"Good afternoon, sir," Armstrong offered, having taken off his hat and saluted.

"Good afternoon, Lieutenant. I have news. I think you will be pleased. I am advised that you are going to be exchanged next Tuesday, the 26th, for an infantry lieutenant from Mississippi. You are ordered to report to your regiment, the 122nd Ohio Volunteers, presently stationed at Danville, south of here in Virginia, on Monday, May 8. You and Lieutenant Paul may go together. Make your own arrangements. Railroad's torn up, I hear, so you better requisition horses and plan for a long ride. It's 250 miles southwest of here. Almost to North Carolina. Probably take three or four days. Good luck, Armstrong, and God Speed. You have been a very valuable member of this man's Army." He shook Tom Armstrong by the hand and showed him out.

"Yes, sir, thank you, sir. I have been waiting for this day for quite some time, as you know. I appreciate everything that you have done for me here and would like to thank you for the opportunity to attend the President's funeral. I shall never forget that day."

"You are very welcome. Goodbye."

"Goodbye, Colonel." With that, Tom Armstrong ran back to his quarters to find Judson Paul.

"Jud, we're going back to the regiment, in a week or so. Paperwork being filed for us to be exchanged. Whoooooeee!"

464

"Well, damn, how about that?" said Judson Paul. "I already knew. Talked to Power this morning. Didn't want to spoil the surprise for you. We better find the Quartermaster and get all the things we're gonna need. What in blazes is the regiment in Danville for? Spent too much time there. Wasn't pretty. This time it'll be better. Damn!"

The two friends spent the next day in Annapolis, just walking around, enjoying the weather there on the shore of Chesapeake Bay. Camp Parole was only a little over three miles west of the town, so it was a relatively easy walk, even though they had been pretty inactive when they were cooped up in prison. The sun was out, it was about 64 degrees, and people were getting out to do their shopping. They found a saloon for lunch, O'Bryan's, on Duke of Gloucester Street near Church Circle and not too far from the hospital that once was the United States Naval Academy. The conversation centered on the 122nd.

"Wonder where they've been since we got captured," said Tom Armstrong. "Wonder if all the men survived. Kinda doubt it. Wonder how many in prison. Saw Colonel Ball back in Zanesville."

"Heard Captain of my company, Hering, got discharged. Sick or something, right after Winchester," said Judson Paul. "Bill Wilson got promoted in his place. Damn, that woulda been me, and I get stuck in some horseshit jail in Danville. Oh, well."

What neither man knew was that there had been wholesale changes in the leadership of the 122nd Ohio Volunteer Infantry.

After lunch, they walked back to Camp Parole, to the Quartermaster's Office and told the clerk what they needed including horses with saddles, bridles, holsters for their weapons, the works. They also needed guns, Enfields preferably, and ammunition. Since they would be traveling overland from Annapolis to Danville, through Culpeper, Charlottesville, and Lynchburg, they figured it could be quite hazardous. Lots of little towns on the route, too. Who knew who or what they would find in them. Yes, the war was over, but word was that Joe Johnston was still operating in North Carolina, trying to outwit William Tecumseh Sherman. Could be coming into southern Virginia. And, there were rabid Southern sympathizers running around in Maryland and Virginia. Without weapons, the two Yankees would be sitting ducks. Oh, yes, they would also need food, canteens, bedrolls, coffee, a pot or two, matches, and a map.

The following Tuesday, April 25, 1865, Lieutenant Thomas S. Armstrong and Lieutenant Judson Paul were exchanged for lieutenants, one from Mississippi who had been captured at the Battle of Sailor's Creek and one from Georgia, who had simply quit, and had just been waiting to be captured by "Fightin' Phil" Sheridan's men on their way to Appomattox. The exchange, done there at Camp Parole, was affected by the War Department of the United States, and they were ordered to report back to the 122nd Ohio Volunteer Infantry that was currently stationed in Danville, Virginia.

The next week dragged on for Armstrong and Paul. They did hear that Federal troops had tracked down John Wilkes Booth to a farm on the road to Bowling Green, Virginia, near the town of Port Royal. There they had surrounded his hiding place and shot him. It was something like 2 o'clock in the morning on the 26th when the troopers arrived in Port Royal and discovered that Booth was hiding in a barn. Apparently, the Federals gave him a chance to surrender, but he did not come out, so one of the Yankees torched the barn to force him out into the open. He never made it. Approaching the barn door, rifle in hand, a sergeant, from all reports, fired his pistol through a small opening, hitting John Wilkes Booth in the neck. The shot didn't kill the actor right away, but his strength slowly ebbed, and he died just about sunup. His body would be taken north and was buried anonymously in Green Mount Cemetery in Baltimore.

"Damn, they got the son-of-a-bitch," said Judson Paul. "Shoulda let the barn burn. Fry his sorry ass. Shootin' him, too easy. Make the bastard suffer."

"You're in a good mood," Armstrong replied sarcastically. "But, I agree with that, Jud. Killin' the President. You oughta get the worst."

There was more news. On the day that Booth was killed, Lieutenant Joseph E. Johnston surrendered to Major General William Tecumseh Sherman down near Durham, North Carolina. Sherman, you see, had established headquarters in Raleigh, two weeks earlier and was planning to continue taking the towns through North Carolina and Virginia, all the way to Washington. On April 17, 1865,

Sherman had received a communication from Johnston proposing to temporarily suspend hostilities so that the politicians could come to some sort of agreement on how to establish the peace. Sherman rode to the meeting with Major General Judson Kilpatrick's cavalry for protection with Johnston riding with General Wade Hampton's mounted troops.

After initial conversations between the two, they put the whole thing about establishing the peace in the hands of Confederate President Jefferson Davis and Union Secretary of War, William Stanton. William Tecumseh Sherman graciously accepted Johnston's surrender on April 26.

Other than staying up with the news, there wasn't much to do except make sure that they had everything they needed, not just for the trip to Danville but also for when they re-joined the 122nd. In preparation, they spent a lot of time poring over the map to determine the best and safest route.

"Tom, we better stay out of those towns," said Judson Paul. "Folks there might not take too kindly to two Federal soldiers on horseback. Could get shot. Might get thrown in jail again. Don't want either of those to happen."

"Darn right, Jud," replied Tom Armstrong. "Not sure I want to travel at night either, but that might be the best way to get there."

"Let's just see what happens and decide then."

Finally, it was time to go, but he thought he better tell Francis Porter what was going on. So, in the morning of Wednesday, May 3, 1865, once again he took pen to paper...

Annapolis Md. May 3/65
Dearest Frank

Tomorrow I go to my Regt. I was going on the 6 o'clock train in the morning via Washington but not now. I am in good health. Hope you have improved since your last. Was exchanged Apl 26. The War Department take no heed scarcely of resignations sent in by mail. But the officers who have done so, in part, are ordered to join their Commands. My order is dated May 2. I've not sent in any resignation yet & shall not now.

Ain't you glad to hear the war is over? Are not we a happy people? Today, Lincoln reaches his last home. At Home! But Dead. How the American people love that man. Great and good man, may he rest in peace.

Well I hope you are well & in good spirits. I will close hoping you may be happy in this world -- enjoy life -- life be long -- that you may be etc., etc.

From your amant   T.S.A.

He rose early the next morning, as usual, met Lieutenant Judson Paul, and headed to the stables where they saddled the horses, stowed their gear, holstered their rifles; Springfields, not Enfields; and were off to Danville, heading west toward Bowie, in Maryland, then to Washington, DC, and turning south toward Culpeper, Virginia. It was a nice day for a ride. They figured it would take them about twenty hours give or take, give or take a few, depending on what they found or what found them. The first night, they would camp somewhere between Culpeper and Charlottesville. If they could find a creek or stream, that would be all the better.

While they rode along, they were amazed at the carnage in the fields, horses and mules, hundreds of them, bloated and black in color. The stench was overpowering. There were also the carcasses of men who had not made it, lying there, eyes wide open and ghastly looks on their faces, just rotting away. It was almost too much to see. At one point, Jud Paul reined in his horse, turned to the side, and vomited. Who knows who the dead men were and who they reported to. Of course, that didn't make any difference now except to their families back home.

Late in the day, they found a stream, a tributary of the Robinson River, so the map said, and made their camp for the night in a small clearing in the woods, hoping, of course, that no one would see them. They let the horses drink from the stream, lit a small campfire, and proceeded to warm some beef, bread, potatoes, green beans, and coffee. As night fell, they decided to take turns on the watch, each sleeping a couple of hours and then trading off. Tom Armstrong had the first watch.

"Damn, wish I had some whiskey," said Judson Paul. "Would taste right fine right 'bout now."

"Shoulda brought some, Jud."

"Nice time for you to think of that," came the reply. Tom Armstrong was reminded of Caleb Edwards and his sharp retorts. Caleb also liked to imbibe from time to time. "Wish I could find a still."

"That isn't going to happen. Maybe get some hooch in one of those towns we go through. Maybe Lynchburg or Charlottesville. Armstrong's mind traveled back to East Leake after the escape from Libby Prison and didn't want that to happen again.

The two lieutenants guessed that they had about 180 miles to go, maybe a little less, which meant at least two more days in the saddle, going deeper into the South. Probably a lot more dangerous the farther south they went. Tom Armstrong looked at the map.

"Maybe we can make it to Lynchburg tomorrow. Looks about half way. Looks like the James River flows along there. Maybe we can find a hiding place near it. That gets us into Danville on Saturday afternoon if nothing goes wrong."

"I'm game, Tom. Let me get some shuteye. Wake me in a couple hours."

The moon had come up. Tom Armstrong sat with his back up against a big ol' oak tree and thought of Francis Porter and what life would be like as a married couple. Listening for any strange sound, it was pretty quiet there in the woods of central Virginia. It was about 9 o'clock on May 4, 1865. Two hours later, he woke Judson Paul who took over the watch, lay down next to the big oak, pulled his hat down over his eyes, and fell fast asleep.

Armstrong was on watch when the sun came up just after 6 that Friday morning. It was still pretty quiet. He got some water out of the stream and started some coffee brewing, waking Judson Paul just as it boiled.

"Time to go, Jud," he said, sipping on the hot brew. "Think I know the best way south."

That same ritual was practiced that Friday and Saturday, reaching Danville about 5 o'clock in the afternoon, May 6, 1865. When they arrived, Judson Paul took the lead since he had been there before. They found the town swarming with both Union and Confederate parolees, anxiously looking for ways to get home or back to their units. Paul and Armstrong were a bit anxious themselves until they found the building that had once been a prison that was serving as the headquarters of the Union Army. The 122nd, it turns out, had been ordered to Danville, after serving at the Battle of Appomattox Court House and being present at the surrender. It was there to help preserve law and order during this tumultuous time. They learned where the 122nd was and went off to find it, looking for Major Moses Granger whom they supposed was now commanding it, seeing that Colonel William H. Ball was home in Zanesville.

They got quite a surprise. First of all, when they found the regimental headquarters and walked inside to present their orders, they didn't recognize a soul in the place. An officer, who identified himself as Captain William Shaw, Acting Assistant Adjutant General, ushered them into a waiting room outside what they presumed was Moses Granger's office. Presently, the door opened, and an officer in a new blue, Union uniform stepped out. He was average in height, slender, with closely cropped brownish hair, and a reddish beard that stuck out from his chin. He identified himself as Brevet Colonel Charles Cornyn, commanding officer of the 122nd Ohio Volunteer Infantry. Returning their salutes, he invited the two lieutenants into his office. Armstrong and Paul just looked at each other as if to say, "Who the hell is this?"

"Gentlemen, welcome back to the 122nd Ohio. It is good to see you hale and hearty. Just so you know, I have been in command of the regiment for little over a month. Colonel Ball resigned his commission on February 3 of this year. Major Granger on December 10 of last. Resigned after regiment's involvement at the Battle of Opequon, Third Battle of Winchester. Sure you heard about it."

"Our compliments, Colonel. No, really haven't heard much about it," said Judson Paul. 'Nuther fight at Winchester, huh?"

"Yes, Lieutenant. Part of Sheridan's Army of the Shenandoah. Defeated Jubal Early's brigade. Oh, yes, I should tell you that Joe Peach of Company A and John Ross of Company K have been promoted to Major and are helping me with the command. Still have about 500 in the regiment. Since you left Zanesville, have had 7 officers killed, 86 enlisted men mortally wounded, and about 140 die of typhoid, dysentery, smallpox, etc. Have no idea about those, like you, who were captured. Assume they're dead."

"Pretty good assumption, Colonel," said Tom Armstrong. "You got any news on Company I, my old outfit?"

"Talk to Captain Shaw, our Adjutant. He can tell you. Boys, we're moving out in a week or so. Going to Richmond, then Washington. There's going to be a Grand Review of the U.S. Army later this month. Parades of all the troops in front of President Johnson, General Grant, and other important people. We're scheduled to march on the 23rd with Sheridan. Make sure that all the bayonets are polished, the men clean, and close order drill followed."

"Yes, sir. May we be dismissed?" said Tom Armstrong, saluting Colonel Charles Cornyn.

Returning the salute, he replied, "Yes, you are dismissed. Welcome back."

In the outer office, they found Captain William Shaw, the Acting Assistant Adjutant General. Tom Armstrong asked about the command of Company I. The Adjutant responded that Dan Gary may have lost his leg after the wound he received at Second Winchester. Shaw really didn't know. He had been excused from service for obvious reasons. Discharged on December 7, 1863 and was home in Zanesville. Armstrong then asked about Tom Black. Once again, the Adjutant responded. Black, he said, was wounded at the Battle of Cold Harbor on June 3, 1864 and had received a medical discharge on December 19, 1864. Home in Fultonham running the family store, he thought. A fellow by the name of Captain John M. Williams now commanded Company I, with the lieutenant positions not filled.

"Captain Williams will be glad to have you back, Lieutenant Armstrong."

"Yes, sir, looking forward to it."

Tom Armstrong thought that there had to be some men he had served with still in the company and wondered how he would discover the whereabouts of the Kearney brothers; their uncle, Thaddeus Brennan; Chesley Simpson; and Patrick Murphy. Again, the

Adjutant had an answer, not a complete one, mind you, but an answer. Thaddeus Brennan had been promoted to 2nd Lieutenant in Company B on June 30, 1864 and was still serving in that capacity. His nephews were also there.

Chesley Simpson had been wounded at the Battle of Monocacy a week or so later, on July 9, receiving a medical discharge on November 6, 1864. Word was, Armstrong would find out later from Thaddeus Brennan, that Simpson had recovered and was working on the family farm back in Muskingum County. He had taken a Minie ball in the right shoulder but had gotten patched up and was sent home. Doctors worried that he would never be able to use his right arm ever again, but that turned out not to be the case. That left the whereabouts of Patrick Murphy a mystery. And, the Adjutant did not have an answer for that, since the last time Murphy had appeared on the Roll was June 15, 1863. Armstrong worried that he was dead, not having survived Belle Isle. It wouldn't have surprised him if Patrick had met his Maker there since the survival rate in prison, especially Libby, Andersonville, and Belle Isle was pretty low.

Captain Shaw then said that Armstrong and Paul could report back to their Company Commanders, Armstrong to John Williams and Paul to Benjamin Power, since there was still work to be done. He also told them that after the surrender, they came to Danville on the march, arriving on April 27. Further, he said that after 2nd Winchester, the 122nd had fought valiantly and courageously as part of the 3rd Division, 6th Corps, of Major George Meade's Army of the Potomac. It had been mainly in Virginia and had been engaged in serious fighting at The Wilderness, Spotsylvania, Cold Harbor, Petersburg, and Monocacy before being ordered to join Major General Philip Sheridan's Army of the Shenandoah.

In mid-July 1864, that order was given because of the knowledge of the Shenandoah Valley that the men of the 122nd had. Then, the regiment had fought the Rebels at Snicker's Creek, Charleston, Halltown and Smithfield, and, of course, Opequon, as they cleared the Valley of the Confederate presence. Under orders, then, from Lieutenant General Ulysses S. Grant, Sheridan chased the Confederates down through the Valley and joined Major General

George Meade's Army in the taking of Petersburg. Once Petersburg fell, Major General Robert E. Lee's Army of Northern Virginia, what was left of it, had escaped to the west. Sheridan followed him and his Army west to Sailor's Creek and then to Appomattox to participate in the surrender. The Adjutant was sorry that Bill Ball, Moses Granger, Dan Gary, and Tom Black, as well as Armstrong and Paul, were not there to see the war end. So were Jud Paul and Tom Armstrong.

"Gentlemen," Tom Armstrong hollered, "we will be reviewed by President Andrew Johnson and other high-ranking officials next week in Washington, DC, as part of the Grand Review. I want your bayonets polished, shoes shined, uniforms cleaned, and you marching in order, straight back, in step, according to *Hardee's Tactics*. I want this company and this regiment to be the best of Sheridan's Army. Am I clear?"

"Yes, sir," came the response. The men of Company I remembered that Armstrong knew what he was doing and how he helped them get ready for the war that was waiting for them. Armstrong's advantage? The men trusted him.

"We will drill every day until we leave," he added, and the grumbling started just as it had at Camp Zanesville in August 1862.

On May 16, 1865, the 122nd O.V.I. boarded the cars of the Richmond and Danville Railroad, arriving in the former capital of the Confederacy the next day. Sitting in the train, Tom Armstrong wondered why Colonel Power had told them to go to Danville on horseback when the Richmond and Danville was running. Didn't make any sense, but that was the army for you. They were ordered to Richmond to keep law and order since there were still some Southern sympathizers hell bent on causing trouble. That sentiment would remain in many people's minds for months, even years, or lifetimes.

The regiment stayed in Richmond for about a week before moving on to Washington on May 22 for what the men thought would be participation in the Grand Review of the Union Army the next day. Meade's Army would march on May 23, with Sherman's on the 24th, both being reviewed by President Andrew Johnson, Lieutenant General Ulysses S. Grant, and many other dignitaries.

"Whattya mean we're not marching, Captain?" asked Tom Armstrong. "The men are ready. They worked really hard to get prepared. What do I tell them?"

"Lieutenant Armstrong," answered Captain John Williams. "I am told by Colonel Cornyn that Lieutenant General Grant heard of a Confederate uprising in Louisiana or east Texas and sent General Sheridan and a brigade there to put it down. Seems Kirby Smith is causing trouble. Refuses to surrender. President Johnson, General Grant, General Sherman, General Meade, and General Sheridan will hold a special review for us when Sheridan gets back. We will stay here, at Bailey's Crossroads, until then."

"Very well, Captain, but the men will be disappointed not to march with the others. Imagine there will be quite a crowd." Then, he thought to himself. "Damn, I bet George will be there, marching with Sherman's Army. Wonder if I can get a pass to go see him."

"Lieutenant, just how in the hell would you ever find him? asked John Williams. There will be 150,000 men marching those days. Meade on Tuesday, Sherman on Wednesday. Might be twice that many watchin' it. You'll never find him."

"Even if I write him and tell him where I will be?"

"Doubt it." And that was that.

Tom Armstrong and the rest of the men of the 122nd were disappointed when they were told that Sheridan's corps would not get to march with the others. Actually, Armstrong was more disappointed that he would not be able to see George Porter. Word came back that Lieutenant General Kirby Smith finally surrendered on June 2, 1865 at Galveston, Texas before Sheridan could get there. That was a major disappointment for the General since he was looking forward to being the one to finish the war. Upon his return, though, the VI Corps would be properly reviewed on June 7.

Baileys Cross Roads near
Washington, D.C. June 4 1865

Dearest

I am well, have not heard from you since I wrote to you last. I got a letter from your Bro. George at the Relay House Maryland. He wrote me a short pencil letter. I have not heard anything of him since. I suppose he was in the Grand Review of the 23rd or 24th of last month.

I'll relate you my experience since I last saw you last. I reported at Annapolis Md April 16. Left there for my Regt went by Washington, Fortress Monroe, Richmond, to Danville Va. where I found it. The Corps (6th) started for Richmond. We stayed there about a week. Marched through from there passed Fredericksburg to this place. Our Corps will be reviewed next Tues. or Wednesday. I am in for 3 years or life I guess. What would it be best for me to do, resign if I can?

If I find I have to stay in the service, I'll send you word. Maybe I'll not get out as I am mustered in since the order of April.

I am still in hopes of being with you soon. I am sorry your health is not good this summer. Tell me all the news. Our Regt goes out of the service soon. I saw the 14th, 17th, 15th and 20th Army Corps march through Richmond. The 2nd Corps of the Army of the Potomac told me Sherman's men took the prize in the Grand Review, but just wait 'till the 6th Army Corps, Gen Phil Sheridan's old favorite Corps, is reviewed.

Mr. Isaac Hull died of smallpox lately. I was told so by a letter from Mary.

Well hoping to hear from you soon, I close my letter to you.

Farewell, my dear friend & kind well wisher

From your own,
Tom
Address
Co. I 122 O.V.I.
2d Brig. 3 Div 6th A.C.
Washington, D.C.

A week later, he got a surprise. He and the rest of the 122nd would be mustered out in two weeks. No more thoughts about staying in.

OH.

Thomas S. Armstrong

2nd LT__, Co. I__, 122 Reg't Ohio Inf.

Age 30 years.

Appears on an
Individual Muster-out Roll
of the organization named above. Roll dated

Washington, DC,   June 25, 1865.

Muster-out date   June 25, 1865.

Last paid to   March 29, 1865.

Clothing account:

Last settled: N/A 186__;   Drawn since $ 0

Due soldier $_____/100;   Due   U.S.

$_____/100

Am't for cloth'g in kind or money adv'd $0/100

Due U.S. for arms, equipments, &c $0/100

Bounty paid $_____;   Due U.S. $_____/100

Remarks: Mustered in, October 8, 1862, 2nd Lt;
Captured June 15, 1863; Paroled February
28, 1865
Presents no evidence of debt to the Gov't as on
Roll

Charles M. Cornyn
Col.
Commanding the Reg't

On June 25, on Tom Armstrong's 30th birthday, the 122nd Ohio Volunteer Infantry, along with the rest of the 6th Corps of Sheridan's Army of the Shenandoah, was mustered out of the service of the United States in a brief ceremony just outside Washington. The ceremony itself was short and sweet, with Brevet Major General J.C. Robertson of the 3rd Division of the VI Corps presiding, thanking the men for their loyal service to the President and to the United States.

Five days later, Tom Armstrong and the rest of the 122nd were discharged. They were now free men. He would make the same trip back to Gratiot that he had two months before, riding the B&O Railroad for the last time. That is, until he went to Clinton, Illinois. The Colonel gave each man a copy of his Discharge papers to show anyone who asked that he was, in fact, no longer in the service of the United States Government.

> To all whom it may Concern
> Know ye, That Thomas S. Armstrong, a Lieutenant of Captain J. M. Williams Company (I,) 122nd Regiment of Ohio VOLUNTEERS who was enrolled on the 16th day of August ore thousand eight hundred and Sixty-Two to serve three years during the war is hereby Discharged from the service of the United States, this 30th day of June at Washington, D.C. by reason of End of Hostilities.
> Said Thomas S. Armstrong was born on June 25, 1835 in the State of Ohio, is thirty years of age, five feet ten inches high, fair complexion, blue eyes, brown hair, and by occupation, when enrolled, a Teacher.
> Given at Washington, D.C. this thirtieth day of June 1865.
>
> Charles M. Cornyn
> Col.
> Commanding the Reg't

"Well, Captain, I guess that's it," said Tom Armstrong, sticking out his hand to Captain John Williams. "I'm going to go and find Lieutenant Paul to see if he wants go to back to Zanesville with me."

"Mr. Armstrong, I hear tell that you were of vital importance to this regiment when it was formed, having seen the elephant and all, and teaching the men, working with the Colonel, Major, Captain Ross, and Dan Gary. We are in debt for your service, sir. Thank you."

"Thank you, Captain. It's a long story, and someday when you would like to get a glass of lemonade or two at Wescott's Saloon back in Putnam, I will tell it to you. When we do that, be sure to tell Mrs. Williams that you will be tied up all afternoon."

"I would like that, Tom, or should I call you Sump. I hear that's what your friends call you."

"Tom, Sump, T.S. Anything, but Lieutenant," Armstrong said smiling. "Anything, but Lieutenant." And he was off to find Judson Paul for the trip back home. He had survived it all, and was going home in one piece, none the worse for wear. Well, psychologically a bit worse. Walking along to find his friend, he said a prayer of thanksgiving for deliverance from the elephant, both from the battle and from the prisons. But, he was getting a tad angry.

Addressed to Miss Frank P. Porter
Clinton, DeWitt County, Illinois
At home, Gratiot, O.

July 9, 1865

Dear Frank

I am a citizen once more. I am living under my own vine and fig tree. I only need one thing to complete my household furniture and that is a wife -- Do you think I can succeed in getting one? Write to me without Reserve & tell me when you can be ready for me or whether you can't. Tomorrow is your birthday, I believe. I wish I could have been in a condition to come out to see you at that time. Well if I can't get ready as soon as I want you to tell me when you want me to come.

I was mustered out on my birthday at Washington D.C. Was discharged the 30 day of June & was paid off the next day. I came immediately home. Attended Mr. Isaac Hull's funeral on last Sunday. On my way home, found Father, Mother Bro Jacob, Sisters Mary & Fla there. We had a grand 4 of July in Gratiot. The youth & chivalry of the band met there. The glee club from Brownsville sang well. Hon T.J. McGinnis spoke. Mr. T. Dick Student at Law read the Dec of Independence.

We adjourned for Dinner. Took mine with Father, Mother, Mary & Fla. Each family took their dinner with them.

I want to hear from you soon.

Farewell from your free friend

He had begun to wonder if she had changed her mind. After all, Francis Porter had eagerly, and excitedly, accepted his proposal of marriage in April. Now, it was early July and he hadn't heard from her in quite some time. He thought to himself, "Wonder how she is going to react to that line about being successful in getting a wife. Maybe I should change it. Nah, I have to tell her what I am feeling. Hope the wedding is still on."

When he had finished writing to Francis Porter, Tom Armstrong thought "I said I would write Caleb and tell him what Frank's answer was. Better do that right now." So, he wrote to Caleb Edwards at his blacksmith shop in Wheeling, West Virginia, telling him that, yes, Francis Porter had consented to become his wife and that the wedding would be in the Methodist Church in Clinton, Illinois in the afternoon of Sunday, October 1. He invited Edwards and then made sure to mention that he and Frank would like Margaret to be there, too. He said that the Rev. Charles C. McCabe would perform the service and that Rebecca "Beccie" McCabe would also be there. Armstrong then told Edwards that he had also invited Thomas Rose, Andrew Hamilton, Chesley Simpson, Thaddeus Brennan, Tom Black, Dan Gary, Moses Granger, and Bill Ball. Now, Caleb didn't know all of these men very well, if at all, but Armstrong wanted to make sure that Caleb wasn't the only veteran of the Civil War who was at the wedding beside George Porter and himself. Oh, and Caleb would have the chance to meet George of whom Armstrong had spoken so much.

Armstrong's mind wandered back to Winchester and being taken prisoner, having to say "Goodbye" to Patrick Murphy. He thought to himself, "I wonder if Patrick is alive. If he is, bet he's wonderin' if I am. Maybe I should just write him a letter, over there in Norwich. If he didn't survive Belle Isle, maybe his folks will write and tell me."

So, taking out another sheet of paper, he penned a letter to Patrick Murphy, in Norwich, over on the east side of Zanesville. He told Murphy that he was living on the farm in Gratiot, anyone there could tell him where the farm was, that he was engaged to be married, that he would probably be moving to Clinton, Illinois to take a position as principal of a school in the fall, and that he would like to see him sometime that summer. He also mentioned that he was thinking about going into the ministry one day and that he would be meeting with Charles McCabe about it the following Saturday morning.

Well, it turned out that, indeed, Patrick Murphy had survived the horror of Belle Isle, as Tom Armstrong had at Libby Prison, trusting in God to see him through. Yes, it had been freezing, food was scarce, men were shot trying to escape swimming across the James River. Some who tried just drowned. Patrick Murphy had lost about 50 pounds and weighed about 140 now, but other than that, his health was remarkably good. As could be expected, he had made a lot of friends there on Belle Isle but also lost some due to starvation and freezing to death. Murphy was an inventive sort, and conjured up all sort of ways to stay alive, most likely the same ones that Armstrong used at Libby. He had come home at the end of February.

In mid-February, 1864, Patrick Murphy and some of the other captives had been transferred from Belle Isle to the prison in Salisbury, North Carolina. A year later, he was paroled. Then, two weeks later, on February 25, 1865, all the able-bodied former prisoners at Salisbury were sent to Goldsboro, North Carolina to be exchanged under Lieutenant General Ulysses S. Grant's new exchange program. Murphy was one of the lucky ones. He came back home to Norwich, wondering whatever happened to his friend, Tom Armstrong, and working on the family farm with his father and brothers. He was puzzled, though, that he hadn't seen the Armstrongs in church since he got home.

Needless to say, he was quite surprised when he was walking by the Post Office there on Main Street, in Norwich, toward the feed store, when the postmaster told him there was a letter for him from somebody named Armstrong from over there in Gratiot, town other side of Zanesville in Hopewell Township. Reading the letter, a plan was starting to hatch. He would surprise Tom Armstrong the following Saturday at Charles McCabe's church, guessing that his friend would get there bright and early like he always did. Yes, Tom Armstrong had been among the earliest risers in the 122nd Ohio Volunteer Infantry which Patrick Murphy could not understand. It was one thing to get up at 5:00 A.M. to milk the cows on the farm, but quite another to get up before *Reveille*. But, that was who Tom Armstrong was.

On Saturday, July 15, 1865, Patrick Murphy rose early, washed up, ate a hearty breakfast, saddled his horse, and was off to Putnam. His wife, Abigail, whom he had married in May, was none the wiser, still being sound asleep.

When he walked into the Reverend's study, seeing the back of Tom's head, he exclaimed...

"Darn glad to see someone else beside the Chaplain who survived prison after being captured at Winchester."

Tom Armstrong knew immediately who it was, turned and saw Patrick Murphy, with the ever-present twinkle in his eye.

"Patrick, you're alive. It's wonderful to see you. How have you been?

"Been home since the end of February. Recuperated from something I caught at Salisbury, started to gain weight. How you been?"

"Just got home a week or so ago. It's a long story. Let's go over to Wescott's after we talk here, and I will tell you all about it. I will say, now, that it wasn't pretty."

"Mine, neither. So, whattya doin' here?"

It was Charles McCabe's turn. "T.S. told me that he would like to become a minister in the Methodist Church, just like you did. So, we're going to talk about that this morning. I want him to have a very clear idea of what he's getting himself and Francis into, as Beccie and I did with you and Abigail."

The three men enjoyed a lively conversation that morning Rev. McCabe really getting into what the life of a minster was like. He said that he had talked with Patrick about it after he came home, Beccie had talked with Abigail about it, and all had agreed it was something that he, Patrick, wanted to do. Divinity school, perhaps right there in Ohio, was next. Tom Armstrong listened intently to what his two friends had to say, nothing of which really surprised him.

They adjourned to Wescott's for lunch and a glass of lemonade. Tom Armstrong and Patrick Murphy exchanged some of the particulars about their captivity. Murphy was fascinated when Armstrong told him about the escape from Libby Prison and getting caught at East Leake.

"Not real smart, Sump."

"Actually, pretty damn dumb, Patrick."

Parting ways, Murphy promised that he and Abigail would be at the wedding in October. Tom Armstrong was very pleased. As he was leaving the saloon, he was completely caught off guard. His friend, John W.A. Gillespie, with whom he, George Porter, brother Wilbur, and Bob Hanson had enlisted in the 78th O.V.I. was tethering his horse at Wescott's hitching rail. It was odd, not seeing his friend in uniform.

"John Gillespie, that you?"

"Sump! I thought you were dead. George told me you were in prison, Richmond. Thought you died."

"Almost, J.W. Almost. When'd you get home?"

"Mustered out last December and discharged in January. Missed all the fun. Been out at the farm since. Had a helluva run with McPherson, Logan, and Sherman. I'll tell you all about it, but I want to get back home with the stuff Henrietta told me to get. Got married two years ago. Baby girl, Rachel, born a year ago. Sump, it is very good to see you."

"You, too, John. I'm out at the farm in Gratiot. C'mon out sometime. Getting married in October. You and Henrietta gotta come. George's sister."

"You sly dog, you," said John W.A. Gillespie.

"Before you go, how's Bob Hanson? Heard he was losing his vision."

"He got transferred to Company E. Hear he was captured at Chattanooga last November. Have no idea where he is."

The two friends said their "Goodbyes," Gillespie saying he would come out to visit on Wednesday, the 19th, but he really wanted to get home.

A couple of weeks later, Tom Armstrong received a letter from Francis Porter in which she scolded him for the remark about "getting a wife," but, in the next sentence, she said she loved him more than anything and asked him to come to Clinton in early August. Tom Armstrong was relieved and wrote her back saying he would be there on Monday, the 7th, and telling her that he would like to stay a week since he had some business to attend to in town with the Clinton School Board. That conversation, he said, would be about his accepting the position that he had been offered by mail. He needed the particulars of the arrangement that the Board had in mind, especially about his salary. He was keenly aware that he would need to save some of it so he could afford to go to seminary at some point.

On Saturday, August 5, Jacob Armstrong took him to the depot in Zanesville to catch the 3 o'clock P.M. train for Columbus and points west.

"Jacob, I'm going to talk to her about me becoming a minister. I just hope she understands."

"So do I, Sump. I've come to the conclusion that this is the right thing for you to do. You will help many, many people with their faith. The stories you can tell will be an inspiration for them. I know Mother and Father are pleased. I am, too."

"Thank you, Jacob. It was important to me that you were fine with it. I know you wanted me to come back home and work on the farm, but, as I told you, that work isn't for me. This is what I have been called to do."

At 2:30 P.M, he boarded the B&O at the station there in Zanesville for the trip to Clinton, Illinois. In his letter, he had told her he would be arriving on the 9 o'clock train on the morning of Monday, August 7, asking if she and her father could meet him at the depot.

When he jumped down on the platform there at the station in Clinton, Francis Porter ran to him and threw her arms around him.

"I am sorry that I didn't write more often," she said with tears in her eyes. His anger was completely gone, he loved her so.

"That's OK, my love. I was just worried, that's all." They walked to the buggy arm-in-arm.

On the way to the farm, Frank and Tom talked about the wedding and everything that had to be done. He also asked her if they could take a ride that afternoon. Of course, she said, they could.

When they arrived at the house, they stepped out of the buggy, John Porter taking it over to the barn. Walking up the porch steps, he said "Hello, Amanda. Beautiful day, isn't it?"

"Thomas, you may call me 'Mother' from now on," she reminded him. "Yes, it is beautiful. How was your trip?"

"The usual, Mother. No excitement." Francis Porter was beaming at him, calling Amanda "Mother."

"Come in, get cleaned up, it's time for dinner." Calling to her husband, "Father, you can do that later. Come in for dinner."

The conversation was mainly about his plans to accept the School Board's offer, if it met his expectations. He would go see Colonel John Kelly, the Chairman, in the morning at his store to talk about it. Francis was sure that the Colonel would be fair. He told them that the Board had offered him the position of Principal at The Select School there in Clinton, but he wanted to understand the details of that arrangement. John and Amanda Porter were quite impressed. Their son-in-law would be the Principal of the best school in town.

That afternoon, I am told, Armstrong and Francis Porter rode out to a secluded spot out on the northeast corner of the farm, over near the village of DeWitt, where, holding her hands in his, they talked a little more about the wedding. Then, it was time.

"Frank, I have determined what I am supposed to do for the rest of my life in addition to loving you. I will not tell you of all the horrible things that happened to me or those awful things I saw, but I am sure that my faith and trust in God brought me back to you."

"I am sure of that, too, Thomas. Our prayers were answered, and I couldn't be happier."

"Well, I gave this a lot of thought while I was in prison."

"What?"

"Frank, I want to go to Theological Seminary and become a minister in the Methodist Church."

"Oh, Thomas," she said sweetly, smiling at him.

"If it is all right with you, I will teach until I have saved up enough money so that I can go to the seminary to study and you can live on while I am gone. Reverend McCabe tells me I can complete everything in a year and a half, then get ordained and see what church I can serve."

"I will teach, too. That would give us more money. Maybe I can stay here with Mother and Father while you are away. But, I think that is a wonderful thing. I am proud of you for taking this step. I know we won't ever have a lot of money, but that's not important. I will have to learn what it means to be a preacher's wife. But, you are a wonderful teacher, and you will make a wonderful minister. Wait 'till we tell them. They will be very pleased."

"When the McCabes are here for the wedding, Beccie will tell you all about what this means for you. It's a different life, but Rebecca McCabe loves it. I hope you will, too."

"Thomas, if this is what the Good Lord has called you to do, then I am blessed to be with you on this journey."

"Thank you, my love," he whispered and kissed her gently. She returned it. Now, this wasn't exactly how she had seen her life playing out, but how could she disagree? A preacher's wife would be what she would become. For him. As for Tom Armstrong, he loved her even more, if that was possible.

Now, going to seminary would not happen for some time, but Tom Armstrong just wanted to be completely honest with Francis Porter about his plans for their lives together. She listened intently to him as he went on, asking questions now and then, smiling with pride that her husband would see the ministry as his lifelong vocation. Methodism ran strong in the Porter family and had for years. She was very pleased to support his wish to do this and hoped it would happen.

"Do you want to go to town tomorrow? I was thinking that while I am talking with Colonel Kelly, maybe you could see if we can still have the wedding at the church. Should also tell the people at the inn that we are having out-of-town guests."

"That's a very good idea, Tom. I can tell Reverend Hall that Rev. McCabe will perform the ceremony, and we can lock up the church when we are done. I am sure he will not mind."

The next morning, they rode into Clinton, hitching their horses right in front of Colonel John Kelly's feed store. Tom Armstrong went in while Francis Porter walked down Main Street, crossing Madison Street, to the Methodist Church, about half a block down.

"Colonel Kelly, I presume. My compliments. I am Thomas Armstrong. I have enjoyed our correspondence and would like to know details of the position you have offered me."

"Welcome, Mr. Armstrong. And, congratulations. That is a very fine young lady who will become your bride."

"Yes, sir, thank you sir," lapsing back into his respect for superior officers.

The Colonel continued, "As I wrote to you, we would like you to become the Principal of The Select School on the northern end of town. We were impressed by your letter where you talked about your teaching back in Ohio. So, that you know about. Also, we would like you to teach Grammar and Mathematics, Algebra, in particular. There will be about sixty scholars. Now, for this, we will pay you $100 per month on the 15th."

Tom Armstrong looked at Colonel Kelly, calculating in his head."$100 a month? That's less than I got in the army. But, it would still be more than enough to cover living expenses, assuming I can find a house here to rent. Might even have some money left over to put in the bank. And, if Frank teaches, we can put her wage in the bank as well."

"Colonel, that is very generous, and I am glad to accept. When do we start?"

"School opens on September 18, but be aware that, as the time of the harvest nears, you will close it, so that the scholars can help their families bring in the crops. We will pay you for that time, don't worry. School year is six months. Done in March so the scholars can help with the planting."

"Yes, sir, thank you sir. I'm glad I came by. Oh, do you know of any houses here in town that we might rent? Or, is there a boarding house where we might stay?"

"Certainly, Mrs. McClure has a boarding house over on East Street. She lost her husband, Elmer, at Antietam back in September, '62, and has opened her house to folks like you and Miss Porter. Mrs. Kelly and I know her well. Goes to our church. We will speak to her about it. When are you going home?"

"Probably on Friday."

"Can you come to town on Thursday? I am sure it will be acceptable to Mrs. McClure, and I would like to introduce the two of you to her."

Tom Armstrong said that they would and stood up, put out his hand to shake that of Colonel John Kelly, saying "Yes, sir, thank you sir. I must go and find Miss Porter."

"You are very welcome. See you on Thursday morning."

With all of that swimming around in his head, he walked briskly toward the church, and there was Francis Porter walking toward him. It was all set, as she had told him in a letter, 2 o'clock in the afternoon of Sunday, October 1. Reverend Arthur Hall thought it a bit unusual to have a wedding on Sunday, but he went along with it, offering to assist the Reverend Charles McCabe, if he so desired. Also, the proprietor of the Clinton Inn, Jonas Watkins, had told her that all she had to do was tell him the number of people to expect and he would make room for them.

"They're going to pay you what?" Frank Porter asked, somewhat stunned.

"$100 a month. $50 to teach and $50 to be Principal.

"But, that's a lot. They only pay me $20 a month."

"Yes, dear. I was quite surprised myself. So, I took it before the Colonel could change his mind. He's going to find us a boarding house as well. Can we talk to Mother and Father about it? Whew, this has been some morning."

"Yes, it has, yes, it has."

They walked back down Main Street toward Col. Kelly's store, passing by William Gibson's General Store which was right next door to Kelsey's, a favorite watering hole frequented by cattlemen, sheepherders, farmers, and the townspeople. Now, this, apparently, from what Frank told him, made it convenient for shoppers to get what they needed from Mr. Gibson and to wet their whistle at Kelsey's before going back home. It was almost custom, there in Clinton, for the men to do their shopping, load their wagons, and then slip into Kelsey's for a nip or a brew and, perhaps, a game of cards. "Regulars" they were called. Might even see the mayor or Colonel Kelly bellied up to the bar from time to time.

"I think Caleb would like that place," he said somewhat absently.

"Who's Caleb? You never mentioned him," she said.

"Caleb Edwards. Oh, he and I spent a lot of time together in prison, escaped together, and got caught. Big fella, from West Virginia. I've invited him and Margaret to come to the wedding. Told him you wanted to meet them."

"Who else have you invited that I don't know about?"

"Some of the boys I served with. About six or seven of them. Don't expect all of them to be here. I will let you know so you can tell Mr. Watkins."

He was thinking, "We might just want to have a party at that saloon when the boys get here. George and J.W.A. would like it, I'm sure. So would Caleb." He made a note to talk with her about it. She just might want a little party of her own.

When they got back to the house, there were two unfamiliar horses tied to the hitching rail.

"Oh, my," said Francis Porter with excitement in her voice. "George and Grace are here. I told them you would be here, and he can't wait to see you and have you meet Grace."

"George is here? Wow, I haven't seen him since they sent me home from Shiloh."

Just then, George Porter emerged from the house. "Sump, it's you," he said, bounding down the stairs and giving Tom Armstrong a bear hug.

"George, it's so good to see you. You must tell me everything."

"And, likewise, brother. I knew you were in prison, J.W. tried to find you at Macon, but the place was deserted."

"Moved us to Savannah. Thought Sherman was getting too close. Tell me about him. Pretty intense, from what I hear."

"Yeah. Was in meetings with him, General Grant, Howard, and Logan. Man definitely knows what he wants and how to get it. Grant just let him talk. Logan took our orders from him. My job was to get the orders to the brigade commanders once Jack signed off on them. No one talked back to Sherman. He did listen, though, to Logan, Howard, Schofield, and the others. But, that march through Georgia and South Carolina was something. Hey, I got an idea. Let's you and me go hunting tomorrow, just like the old days in Hopewell. We can talk more then."

"Sounds good to me. I'll tell Frank, and she and Grace can work on the details of the wedding. Yeah, and I have an idea for you. Friend of mine wants to come out here and settle. Wants to talk with you."

"Sure, 'enough. Is he comin' out to the wedding?"

"Yeah, I'll tell you more about it later.

Grace and George Porter, Francis Porter, and Tom Armstrong sat on the big front porch for much of the rest of the afternoon, that Tuesday, August 8, talking about the war, mostly from George's experiences since Tom couldn't talk about it, and about life in Clinton. The Porters had purchased a home in town on West Jefferson Street, two blocks south of the center of town, and George was trying to buy William Gibson's grocery store up there on Main Street, not far from Kelsey's Saloon and Colonel Kelly's feed store. Gibson had agreed to sell. So most of the time, Grace minded the store while her husband was out at the farm helping his father with the sheep. However, George Porter made sure he was in the store on Saturdays when many of his customers came in to do their shopping and to drop by the barroom in the back of the store for a snort. You see, that was how he got the latest news and gossip. And, he said, there was a whole lot of that about the upcoming marriage of Francis Porter to that man from Ohio. Tom Armstrong just laughed at the thought.

Amanda Porter looked around the house that afternoon and smiled to herself. "They are all here," she thought to herself. "I wonder what the chances were that both George and Thomas would survive that awful war. I would imagine not very good. God be praised for bringing them both home."

George and Grace Porter took off for home around 5 o'clock, promising to be back in the morning. That evening. Tom Armstrong told John and Amanda Porter and the rest of the family about his plans to enter the ministry. They were all quite delighted. No, he didn't know when he would go to seminary, but he was going to go.

George and Grace Porter arrived the next morning, bright and early. Tom Armstrong had asked Johnny Porter if he could take one of the horses in the barn for the hunt that morning and was busily saddling Ruby, a beautiful reddish-brown Morgan mare when George walked into the barn, ready to go. They spent the day, looking for deer, fox, pheasant, almost anything that moved and did bring home a couple of birds which they promptly gave to Amanda Porter, thinking they had brought home tomorrow's dinner. While they were out in the fields, they talked about the war, and Tom found that he could tell George about Libby Prison and how bad it was. He couldn't do that with anyone else. He also told him about Caleb Edwards and his wish to settle there in central Illinois.

Then, he asked, "George, could you see if we could have a party at Kelsey's the day before the wedding? I have some friends from the war coming, as well as family, and thought we might celebrate a little. I also spoke with Frank about the ladies having a little tea party at Lacey's on Monroe Street, around the corner from Main. Maybe we could do that while we're in town on Thursday talking to Mrs. McClure."

"Sure thing, Sump. Sounds like a good time. I'll have Grace talk to Mrs. Lacey tomorrow."

The parties were set; so was Mrs. McClure's boarding house. His position at the school was finalized. Tom had talked to Frank about seminary and the ministry. Everything he had set out to do that week had been done. It was time to go home.

In the evening of Thursday, August 10, Tom Armstrong and Francis Porter had gone for a walk just to be alone.

"Thomas, I shall miss you. Can you come back before the wedding?"

"Yes, dear," he said smiling at her and holding her hand. "I will need to work with Colonel Kelly about the school, so yes, I will be back, probably in about three weeks. May just stay. School starts two weeks later. But, I will miss you, too." He caressed her face and held her tight, giving her a big kiss. "I love you, Francis Porter, and I can't wait to be married to you."

"I love you, too, Thomas, and I can't wait either."

She rode in the back of the buggy with him the next day to the train station in Clinton. They exchanged one more kiss. He shook hands with John Porter, and it was time to go.

When Tom got home on Saturday night, August 12, he told his brother, Jacob, about all of this. He told him about the party at Kelsey's which was right across the street from the Clinton Inn. There could be a poker game or two and plenty of whiskey and beer. No guns. The belts of the guests would have to be hung on the pegboard beside the bar with Seamus Kelsey, the owner and barkeep, making sure they stayed there. Jacob had to make sure that the party didn't get out of hand since the wedding would take place at 2 o'clock P.M. the next day, and he needed those who attended to be somewhat sober when it began. That was, indeed, a worry, but Jacob Armstrong figured that George Porter, his brother, Johnny, and he could keep things under control.

The next step for Tom Armstrong was to inform those men he had invited of the arrangements, to plan on arriving on Thursday, September 28, on the 9 o'clock train from Pana. From the station, then, they could walk to the Clinton Inn where he and Jacob would meet them. He was a little disappointed that only about half wrote back and said they would be there, but he couldn't worry about it. He was glad that Caleb Edwards and Margaret could make it as could Patrick and Abigail Murphy, John W.A. and Henrietta Gillespie, Chesley Simpson, Thaddeus Brennan, and Tom and Cornelia Black. Some of the Porter's neighbors and friends would also be there as would the entire Armstrong family, including Matilda and A.T. Hull. It promised to be a wonderful weekend, highlighted by the wedding of Francis P. Porter and Thomas S. Armstrong.

He also told Jacob that on Saturday, September 30, the women would have their own gathering at Lacey's Tea Room, around the corner on Monroe Street. That one would be tame compared to what might happen at Kelsey's. Amanda Porter and Jane Armstrong with their daughters and some of Amanda's friends would be there, and it would give Francis Porter a chance to visit with Beccie McCabe and to meet Margaret Edwards, Cornelia Black, Henrietta Gillespie, Abigail Murphy, and Mattie Armstrong, along with her son, Thomas. She didn't know if any of the others were bringing their wives, but, if they did, it would be fine with her.

Everything went according to plan the week of September 25 there in Clinton, Illinois. There weren't many weddings there, especially in October. The weather turned out to be perfect, not too hot, not too cold. No rain. The McCabes arrived on Wednesday, the 27th and were invited to stay at the Porter farm, an invitation they accepted graciously. The same invitation was extended to John W.A. and Henrietta Gillespie, but this one came from George and Grace Porter. Patrick and Abigail Murphy could stay with the Porters' next-door neighbors. Tom and Cornelia Black and the Edwardses could stay at Mrs. McClure's for the weekend. The others could stay at the Inn.

The Armstrong clan arrived on September 28 as well and would stay in town with other Porter friends, close enough to walk to the church. George had arranged for a couple of wagons to be available after the service to take the guests out to the farm for the party, so it appeared to Tom Armstrong that everything was in place. Nothing could go wrong, and nothing did. Well, almost nothing.

Even before the gathering at Lacey's, being out at the Porter farm gave Beccie McCabe the chance to speak seriously with Francis about what it meant to be the wife of a preacher. She had already had that conversation with Abigail Murphy in April when Patrick had told her he was thinking about it.

"Francis, please understand that if Thomas is called by a large congregation as Charles was, in Putnam, that is one thing. Life is more secure and predictable being in one place for a longer period of time. But, on the other hand, if he is called by a smaller congregation, he could be serving two or three churches at the same time and that would mean he would be traveling a lot. In turn, that would mean that you might be living in a little town like Hopewell, raising the children by yourself, a lot of the time. You also have to hope that the churches could provide Thomas with enough money to live on."

"I don't mind living in a small town, Beccie. That's really all I know. Not having Thomas at home with me and the children, well, that bothers me. I will speak with him about it, although I did tell him that I would support whatever he decided to do. He better talk to me about it before he does," Francis Porter said, smiling.

"The other thing," said Beccie McCabe, "is that he will be doing church business at all hours, attending meetings, doing hospital visits, preparing sermons, presiding at weddings and funerals, just all the things that ministers have to do, while usually trying to raise a family. I just want you to know that it is just a different life than that of a farmer's wife."

"It sounds like it Beccie. I know what it is to live on the farm, and I have watched Mother all these years. When I talk with Thomas, I will share this with him so that he is aware it is something that I will not be used to. Hopefully, I can grow into it."

"You will do just fine, Francis."

This visit brought the two women close together, and they would remain dear friends for the rest of their lives.

"Thank you, Beccie. I never thought about all of this. I was just happy for Thomas and the life we will have together. I hope I can become a very good preacher's wife."

"I'm sure you will, Frank, I'm sure you will."

The gathering for the wedding also gave Caleb Edwards the chance to explore an idea. He wanted to forget about the war; was tired of blacksmithing; saw the wide, open spaces of the east and now saw even bigger ones here in the west; was intrigued by the prosperity of Clinton and De Witt County; and decided that, if Margaret would go along, he would do something there, leaving Wheeling, West Virginia, behind. He was standing by the bar at Kelsey's with an empty shot glass in front of him when Tom Armstrong came up with a man a man a little taller than Tom Armstrong, thick black hair and mustache.

"Caleb, meet George Porter. George, Caleb Edwards."

"Good to meet you, Porter. Heard a lot about you. All good."

"Heard the same about you, Edwards. Two of you had a helluva time in prison."

"Yeah, should have made it home when we 'scaped Libby. Just was stupid."

"So, I'm told," said George Porter smiling. "Sump, here, tells me you have an idea. Let me get you a drink, and let's go into the back room where we can talk. Too damn noisy in here. Gonna have to calm things down in a bit. Sure hope nobody's cheatin' at cards. Tom, tell that jackass playin' the piano to tone it down. This thing just might be gettin' out of hand."

Seamus Kelsey put a bottle of whiskey on the bar. George Porter took it and led Caleb Edwards through a door in the back. He filled a glass and chugged it down. Caleb did the same. "Thanks. Here goes. I'm tired of being a blacksmith. I'm tired of the city. Seeing all the open spaces during the war made me think I want to be out here. Maybe open up a place like this. Kinda like saloons like this. Don't mind a shot every now and again. Don't mind a little poker game, neither."

George Porter smiled. He hadn't exactly expected this from Caleb Edwards, but, fortunately for the big West Virginian, Porter had an answer.

"Caleb," said George Porter, "Seamus has been telling Father for the last year that he wants to go to California. Can't until he sells this place. You want to buy it?"

"Don't know if I have enough money. You know a banker in town who might help?"

"Sure, James Ferguson, president over at Farmers and Merchants. Right up his alley."

"If Margaret and I stay here till Monday, can we go see him?"

"You bet, I'll go with you. I'll even help you out myself. They heard a commotion from the bar. "Shit, fight just broke out. I gotta stop it."

"I'll help you, George," and the two men ran into the bar to see two other fellows engaged in a real donnybrook, everyone else cheering them on. George Porter grabbed a rifle from Seamus Kelsey and fired a shot out over the swinging doors. The fighting stopped. The next shot might be at them. Order and some decorum were quickly restored. You just didn't mess with George Porter, especially when he had a rifle in his hand.

That night, Caleb Edwards mentioned the idea to his wife, Margaret, who was, quite honestly, apprehensive about it. The plan was that, with a little financial assistance from George Porter and the support of James Ferguson's bank, Caleb Edwards would become the proprietor of Kelsey's, of course, leaving the name on the sign above the swinging doors. He and Margaret would talk more about it on the way home.

On Sunday, October 1, 1865, the folks who could found their way to the Methodist Church for the 10:30 service, but all would forego the afternoon and evening services. There was something more important to do.

After hearing the church bell ring three times, at 2 o'clock that afternoon, Tom and Jacob Armstrong walked out in front of the people sitting there in the church, right by the altar, waiting for Huldah, Mary, and Amanda, Jr. to process down the aisle before John Porter and Francis did. Repeating their vows for Reverend Charles McCabe, Tom slipped the gold band onto Francis Porter's third finger of her left hand. He had had it engraved at Bonnet's Jewelry Store in Zanesville, "TSA to FPA." That was all.

When Rev. McCabe announced that they were man and wife, they shared a tasteful kiss in front of their friends and family, turned, and walked down the aisle of the Methodist Church, not looking at anyone, just straight ahead, since that was the custom back then. Tom Armstrong did cast a quick glance as he approached Patrick Murphy, sitting there in the pew right on the aisle. He didn't change his expression, but he saw something that made him smile, inside. Patrick smiling back at him, with, yes, that twinkle in his eye.

The party at the Porter farm lasted most of the rest of the day with music and singing; lots of food; games of horseshoes; good talk among old friends and new; speeches from John Porter, William Armstrong, Mr. and Mrs. Thomas Armstrong, and, of course, Charles McCabe, who, on cue, began singing…

Mine eyes have seen the glory
Of the coming of the Lord
He is trampling out the vintage
Where the grapes of wrath are stored

He has loosed the fateful lightning
Of his terrible swift sword
His truth is marching on.

Glory, glory, hallelujah
Glory, glory, hallelujah
Glory, glory hallelujah
His truth is marching on.

...with everyone joining in for all six verses which was followed by cheers and well wishes for the newly-married Armstrongs.

"My friends," said Charles McCabe, "this has been a great day that the Lord has made. As we close it, I pray for His blessing on Francis and Thomas Armstrong. May they have a long and healthy life together. I also offer the Lord our thanks for the successful conclusion of the war and bringing us all home safely. I also pray for the soul of Eddie Bristow who we lost at Winchester. He was a very fine soldier and a very fine man. And, Lord please be with us all as we travel to our homes, wherever they may be." He concluded...

"The Lord bless you and keep you. The Lord make his face to shine upon you. The Lord lift up His countenance upon you, and give you peace. Amen."

"Amen," echoed from everyone there at the Porter farm. It had been a glorious day, perfect, in fact.

So, everything that Thomas and Francis Armstrong had wanted, back in August, 1862, had come true, especially that he had survived the horrors of war, the battles, the sickness, and the prisons. They sat in the swing on the big porch while night began to fall, holding hands, with her head on his shoulder, wondering why the Good Lord had brought them together. They would spend a lifetime trying to figure that out, not coming up with anything other than it was just supposed to be. They were just grateful that it was.

Epilogue

Two weeks before the wedding, Tom Armstrong assumed his duties as Principal and instructor at The Select School in Clinton, Illinois. Francis Porter resumed her teaching at the Main Street elementary school in Wapella, Illinois, five miles north of Clinton. Right after the wedding, they had moved into Mrs. Blanche McClure's boarding house.

In the summer of 1866, Caleb and Margaret Edwards packed up their children and belongings and moved to Clinton, Illinois, where he became the owner of Kelsey's Saloon. They made fast friends of Grace and George Porter and would remain so for the rest of their lives.

That same summer, Patrick Murphy entered the theological seminary of Bexley Hall at Kenyon College in Gambier, Ohio, a little over 50 miles northwest of his hometown of Norwich to study to become an Episcopal priest. He had some friends who introduced him to the Episcopal church and liked the liturgy better than the Methodist. So, after talking with Charles McCabe, he had taken this step.

Francis and Tom Armstrong moved back to Zanesville, Ohio in the summer of 1866 where he took a position as the Principal of Putnam High School. In 1867, their first son, Edgar, was born, followed by Frederick in 1873, their daughters, Olive in 1875, and May in 1879. Son, Ford, born in 1874, died a few days after his birth.

In the fall of 1871, Armstrong enrolled in the Boston University Theological Seminary. Two years later he was ordained as a minister in the Ohio Conference of the Methodist Episcopal Church.

During his ministry, The Reverend Thomas S. Armstrong served several churches in southern Ohio including stops at Johnstown, Hebron, Asbury, Racine, New England, Coolville, White Cottage, Commercial Park, Richmond Dale, and Lucasville.

Francis P. Armstrong assumed her role as a preacher's wife with great enthusiasm and held the family together while the Reverend Armstrong was away. Just like Rebecca McCabe, she learned to love the life she had chosen as his wife.

498

In May, 1882, an epidemic of typhoid fever hit the town of Racine, Ohio, where the Armstrongs were living at the time. Edgar Armstrong was one of the unfortunate ones who contracted it, and, on May 10, he passed away. To make matters worse, Francis Armstrong also was infected with the virus and died nine days later, on May 19. Edgar was just 14 years old, his mother, 41. Both were interred at Woodlawn Cemetery in Putnam.

The Reverend Thomas W. Armstrong retired from the ministry in 1897. Frederick was 24 years of age and had moved to Chicago. Olive was 22, married and living in Newark with her husband, R.E. Beard. May Armstrong enrolled at Ohio Wesleyan University that same year, so father and daughter moved to Delaware, Ohio. Armstrong taught religion at the university and helped out at the Methodist Church on William Street. May Armstrong completed her studies in 1901 and became a teacher at the high school in Zanesville. She and her father took up residence on Main Street just down the street from the Methodist church where he had enlisted in the 122nd Ohio Volunteer Infantry forty years before.

The Reverend Charles C. McCabe was elected a Bishop of the Ohio Conference of the Methodist Church with his final assignment being Chancellor of American University from December 1902 until his death in December 1906.

A year before, in 1905, May Armstrong moved to Rock Creek, Ohio, to become the Principal of the high school there. The Reverend Thomas Armstrong moved in with the Beards at their home in Newark. Three years later, Olive, too, became ill, and died on July 8, 1908. Armstrong moved back to Zanesville to live with his youngest daughter who had returned from Rock Creek that summer.

A year later, he contracted some form of cancer, presumably, fought it, and finally succumbed to it on September 16, 1909. At the time of his death, he was 74 years of age. On Sunday, September 19, 1909, the Rev. A.M. Courtenay presided at the funeral service at the Grace Methodist Church in Zanesville, praising Reverend Armstrong throughout his homily, concluding with...

Yes, Reverend Armstrong saw the elephant twice as a young man in our nation's Civil War, serving his country honorably, nobly, with courage and faith, enduring the horrible life of Libby Prison. Through the grace of God, in whom the Reverend had placed his faith and trust, he survived only to serve the people of this region in the Methodist Episcopal Church.

A race well run, Thomas Sumption Armstrong, a race well run. May you rest in peace. Amen.

The Reverend Thomas S. Armstrong would be buried alongside Frank at Woodlawn Cemetery in Putnam.

And, then it was over. The life of Thomas S. Armstrong, filled with the love of his family, and especially his beloved wife, Francis, the children, his country, his friends, his ideals, his ministry. He never spoke of the Civil War to anyone. He had placed his faith and trust in the Lord and that prayer had been answered. Yes, he had, indeed, seen the elephant as the Rev. Courtenay had proclaimed, and through the grace of God, he had survived.

Good thing, for you see, Thomas Sumption Armstrong was my great grandfather.

Author's Note

It has been a special pleasure for me to tell this story about my great-grandfather about whom I knew so little before this project began. I truly hope you found it to be good reading and that you learned from it as well. It is a true story based on 180 handwritten letters that he wrote to Francis, Jacob, and others in his family about his experiences in the Civil War. Primary and secondary research supplemented the letters to complete the story that you have just read. I am grateful to Francis Porter Armstrong, my great-grand-mother, for saving all of the letters that Tom wrote; May Armstrong Harvey, my grandmother and Mary Harriet Harvey, my mother for preserving the letters until we found them almost 25 years ago; my wife, Paula Bodwell Harvey, who encouraged me to write this story, proof-read every sentence, and helped me get the letters ready for the archives at Ohio Wesleyan University where they have been digitized for the world to see. I am grateful to my great-grandfather, Thomas Sumption Armstrong, for giving us these documents that tell this incredible story. The life he led was exemplary in the service of so many others. Thank you, Granddad, or should I just call you Sump?

TWH
Cleveland Heights, Ohio
June, 2018

Partial List of Works Consulted

Biographical History of Northeast Ohio. Chicago: The Lewis Publishing Co., 1893.

Cavada, Federico F. *Libby Life: Experiences of a Prisoner of War.* Philadelphia: J.B. Lippincott & Co., 1865.

Dew, Charles B. *Apostles of Disunion: Southern Secession Commissioners and the Causes of the Civil War.* Charlottesville, VA: University of Virginia Press, 2001.

Downer, Edward T. *Ohio Troops in the Field.* Ohio State University Press for The Ohio Historical Society. 1961.

Fehrenbacher, Don E. "Why the War Came." *The Civil War.* New York: Alfred A. Knopf, 1992.

Foote, Shelby. *Civil War a Narrative: Fort Sumter to Perryville.* New York: Random House, Inc., 1986.

Foote, Shelby. *Civil War a Narrative: Fredericksburg to Meridian.* New York: Random House, Inc., 1986.

Foote, Shelby. *Civil War a Narrative: Red River to Appomattox.* New York: Random House, 1986.

Granger, Moses M. *The Official War Record of the 122nd Regiment of Ohio Volunteer Infantry.* Zanesville, OH: George Lilienthal, Printer, 1912.

Hamilton, Andrew G., *Story of the Famous Tunnel Escape from Libby Prison.* Chicago: S.S. Boggs, 1893(?)

Harper. Robert S. *Ohio Handbook of the Civil War.* Ohio Historical Society for the Ohio Civil War Centennial Commission, 1961.

Howe, Henry, LLD. *Historical Collection of Ohio: An Encyclopedia of the State.* Cincinnati, OH: C.J. Krehbiel & Co., 1888. http://www.civilwarindex.com/armyoh/rosters/122nd_oh_infantry_roster.pdf

https://search/ancestrylibrary.com.search

McPherson, James. *Battle Cry of Freedom.* New York: Oxford University Press, 1988.

Milroy, Robert H. *Report of Maj. Gen. Robert H. Milroy, U.S. Army Commanding Second Division, of Operations, June 1 – 15.* Baltimore, MD, June 30, 1863.

Newsome, Edmund. *Experience in the War of Great Rebellion.* Carbondale, IL: E Newsome, 1879.

Reid, Whitelaw. "Ohio in the War." *Her Statesmen, Her Generals, and Soldiers.* Volume II: The History of Her Regiments and Other Military Organizations. New York: Moore, Wilstach, & Baldwin, 1868.

The Official Roster of the Soldiers of the State of Ohio in the War of the Rebellion, 1861 – 1865, Vol. VIII, 110th – 140th Regiments – Infantry. Published by the Authority of the General Assembly, Cincinnati: The Ohio Valley Press, 1888.

Wittenberg, Eric J. and Scott L. Mingus, Sr. *The Second Battle of Winchester: The Confederate Victory that Opened the Door to Gettysburg.* El Dorado Hills, CA: Savas Beatie, LLC, 2016.

About the Author

Dr. T. W. Harvey is a retired Associate Professor of Finance at Ashland (O.) University. He has published two books, *Quality Value Banking: Effective Management Systems that Increase Earnings, Lower Costs, and Provide Competitive Customer Service*, with Janet L. Gray, and *The Banking Revolution: Positioning Your Bank In The New Financial Services Marketplace*. He was born and raised in Cleveland Heights, Ohio. He graduated from Hillsdale College with a BA in English; from Case Western Reserve University with an MBA in Finance; from Cleveland State University with a doctorate in Management and Strategy. He and his wife, Paula, reside in Cleveland Heights, Ohio.

Made in the USA
Monee, IL
13 December 2022

20426804R00292